Quest Academy:

SILVERS

Book 1

BRIAN J. NORDON

TABLE OF CONTENTS

CHAPTER 1:
FIRST CLASS

Sal smiled at the uniformed attendant who had lifted the velvet rope on their arrival. His parents walked in front of him, stopping at the door of the luxury carriage while they waited for the guests ahead of them to go inside and find their compartment.

Turning on his heels, Sal glanced down the platform at the vast crowds of people packing onto the train. There were no velvet ropes or attendants in those sections, but rather a host of security professionals who weren't afraid to shove passengers back if there was a moment of uncertainty.

Sal examined the mounted turrets atop the train carriages. Each of them was primed and ready, rotating in intervals to ensure full coverage and protection. A quick glance forward caused Sal to meet his father's gaze, who looked at him expectantly.

"You waiting for an invitation there, Sal?" He made a sweeping gesture at the area outside the train carriage. "It'll still be here when you graduate, don't worry." With a nod toward the carriage interior, Petro started forward, but paused abruptly. "Soph, can you bring that small case? Yes! That's the one!"

Sal stepped onto the carriage, following his parents along the narrow corridor. His mother stopped abruptly in front of him, her shoulders tense. "What is it now? You'd swear these people have never been on a train before." Her sentence finished with gritted teeth.

Petro turned around, a weary grin on his face. "This might actually be their first time. Be nice. Sal might end up becoming friends with their kid."

Sophia gave her son a pointed look, as if to say, *Don't you dare.*

Chuckling to himself, Sal leaned against the wall and looked out of the window opposite, showcasing the bustling metro station.

There was only one track, and it operated a single service. The train consisted of over thirty carriages and with mounted turrets adorning each one, it was by far the safest mode of transport between reclaimed zones. Sal leaned closer to the window and looked to his left, wanting to see the crackling red barrier in the distance.

Their train was going to pierce through it after gaining speed and blitz through to the next safe zone, before the demons would have a chance to react. Any that were unlucky enough to be in proximity to the train would find out just how powerful the turrets were.

To prepare for departure, a shimmering reflective shield slid down the exterior of the train, covering Sal's view. He barely had time to turn away from his reflection before the headache began.

His father gave him a reassuring smile from farther ahead as he looked back at Sal. "You shouldn't avoid it. It's good training for them." He pointed at his own silver irises that brimmed with magical energy.

Sal's eyes were practically identical to those of his father, but only in appearance. Their capabilities were miles apart.

Attention, passengers.

We will shortly depart Silver Sanctuary.

Please secure yourselves appropriately. We estimate a Red Zone time of just under five minutes, so please do not move from your assigned areas until we've safely entered the next safe zone. This service will stop at the Sage Community Hospital, Memorial Square, Cemetery Gardens, Guild Towers Upper, Mercantile Quarter, Guild Towers Lower, Quest Academy…

Sal perked up at the announcement of his destination. Both his parents looked at him, but their emotions were wildly different. Petro's face was a mask of pride, while Sophia's was filled with barely concealed apprehension. A huge sigh of relief brought Sal out of his reverie as Sophia finally moved forward with Petro's small case still in hand.

The offending family who held them up was nowhere to be seen and Sal knew they were lucky to have escaped his mother's wrath.

The luxury private cabin was very much worth the wait, with a plush interior and its own private bar. Without so much as missing a beat, Petro practically shouted his order to the waiting bar attendant as he turned on the television. He manually changed the channel from a nearby interface, looking for something on the list of channels. "Ah, Hunter Network!"

Before Sophia or Sal had even sat down, the sound of breaking news filled the cabin. Sal sighed inwardly. Everything was breaking news these days, and people from his father's generation were addicted to listening to it.

Initial outbreak on Fifth Street.

Grade 2 Demons sighted. Leecher and Prowler. Response team dispatched from the reclamation guild, Paradox. Residents are advised to stay in their homes until evacuation teams arrive.

Our in-house analysts have determined that if this outbreak escalates and we lose Fifth Street, our quarterly territory loss will be four percent higher than last reported.

Reports of classist bullying on the refugee cruise liner, Darwin, have resulted in calls for reform. Over sixty percent of surveyed refugees have stated that they'd prefer to take their chances on the mainland rather than suffer within the guaranteed protection of the mobile, floating fortresses. We have yet to receive a comment from government officials regarding the report.

Quest Academy is about to welcome a new cohort of cadets this week.

Thousands of students will travel from the neighboring districts, aspiring to earn an official place in the academy. The introduction of a formalized education system for Heroes has long been called for by the United Guilds Association.

They hope to discover new talent for the guilds, while reducing the training time of new recruits.

Without a word, Petro spun in his chair and pointed at Sal, grinning. He turned his head and craned it closer to the television as though he were trying to hear it more clearly. "My son, off to join the academy!"

His lighthearted banter was rewarded with a small gasp from across their room. All three of the Argento family turned to glance at the girl who was serving drinks. Her eyes were wide as she looked at Sal, as though seeing him for the first time. A half second later, she gave him a wide smile before getting back to the drink preparation.

Sal laughed at that, raising an eyebrow as he met his father's gaze. "If it wasn't a mandatory enrollment, I'd have guessed you were trying to get rid of me…"

Petro's smile didn't leave his face as he waved his hand in the air, as though suggesting that there might be some truth to the statement. His eyes didn't leave the screen as he listened to the ongoing news report.

A recent artifact expedition returned with great results!

It marks the eighth consecutive delving mission, with specialist guild, the Delvers, breaching the demonic portals and recovering high-value weaponry and equipment.

We've been informed that the Argento Auction has yet to reveal details of these new artifact acquisitions, but a statement has been made by the Guildmaster of the Delvers Guild, Shade. "We're confident that it's our best haul yet."

When asked for details regarding casualties suffered during the expedition, Shade refused to comment.

There has been a rising negative sentiment toward the Delvers Guild, with the public criticizing the reckless endangerment of Heroes, as well as the guild's continued refusal to push the front lines with the Reclamation Guilds.

Petro's smile faded into a grimace as he got to his feet and took the small case from Sophia. "Can't even take a day off to see Sal enter the academy? We're charging them extra for this." He looked at Sophia, who gave him a humoring nod. Just as he was about to open the case, he glanced up at the attendant, who was slowly making their drinks and smiling at Sal.

"Best haul yet, my ass," Petro spat. A few clicks later, it was open for Sal and Sophia to see. "What do you see, son?" Petro turned the case around to face Sal.

Without thinking, Sal activated his ability. His silver irises glowed as they started the Appraisal process, picking apart every detail of the item.

Name	[*Unknown*] Glove
Origin	Portal Artifact
Age	[*Unknown*]
Grade	Uncommon (Upper)
Dimensions	Circumference 8.5 inches
Materials	Prowler Hide	[*Unknown*]	Dreadcloth
Attributes	[*Unknown*]

Abilities	Phase Shift	Steal
Power Source	External Essence	
Evolution	No	
Quality	Terrible	
Condition	8%	
Value	Est. $14,000.00 – $35,000.00	

"Let's see…it's a torn piece of cloth armor? Probably in the last few uses before being completely destroyed. I can see runes, and they seem powerful…but they're incomplete because of the damage. My best guess would be that it was a Rare or Epic piece, but now it's barely at the rank of an Uncommon piece. Can you Restore it, Mom?"

Sal turned to his mother, who looked at it apprehensively.

Before she could say a word, Petro closed the case. "Great analysis, but we shouldn't waste your mother's essence on this. If it really is at Rare grade or above, we'd be picking her up off the floor. It'll take someone with a higher version of the Restore ability to bring it back to perfect condition. Shade has only paid me for an Appraisal, and that's all we're going to give him."

He put the case to one side and accepted the offered drink from the attendant with a smile.

Attention, passengers.

We are now entering the Red Zone.

Please adhere to all safety precautions until the next announcement. Any signs of passengers disregarding these procedures will be dealt with. Any anti-social behavior will not be tolerated on this service. Your safety is our primary concern.

Sal could sense the urgency in the announcement and wondered what constituted anti-social behavior. The entire carriage lurched violently to one side as a series of loud screeching noises were heard from outside. Sal gripped the chair armrests and looked over at his father wordlessly as they heard a rhythmic interval of mechanical thumps. They both looked at the ceiling of the carriage at the same time. "Are the turrets firing?"

Petro nodded and gestured for Sal to put on his seat belt. Both he and Sophia did the same as the attendant secured herself in a seat by the bar. Even with all the shields and attempts at soundproofing, Sal could hear the inhuman screams from outside.

Closing his eyes, he calmed his breathing and tried to focus on the repeated blasts from the turrets above. Rattling glass from the bar area broke his concentration and Sal opened his eyes and turned around to meet the very calm gaze of the attendant.

It was reassuring to see her so composed and when she smiled in his direction, Sal felt himself calming down. If the employee wasn't worried about their current situation, then maybe he didn't need to worry either.

A whirring noise from above echoed down into their compartment and Sal felt the vibrations coming from his seat. When the next volley of attacks sounded out, Sal could hear the change of direction to the other side of the train. A few minutes of consecutive blasts continued, until the turrets fell silent.

Sal hoped that it was because all the demons had been defeated. He didn't even know if the turrets were a deterrent or devices designed to kill them. *Was their technology evolving as quickly as the demons? Was this a normal event for people that used the train regularly?*

His thoughts were interrupted by the sound of applause and cheering that echoed out from the surrounding carriages. Everyone was celebrating their survival and it was a stark contrast to the sheltered life he had lived until now.

Petro took off his seat belt before the sign gave him permission and suffered a glare from Sophia.

Attention, passengers.

We have cleared the Red Zone.

Thank you for your patience. Our next stop will be Sage Community Hospital.

Sal's breath caught in his throat as the shields moved away from the windows. They were now in a safe territory, guarded by the barriers. Sal jumped out of his seat and pressed his face to the window, looking back at the Red Zone, hoping to see something of note.

He was rewarded with the sight of the following carriages covered in green blood. The wall of the barrier that kept the Red Zone at bay shimmered constantly at different points, indicating demons repeatedly trying to break through.

Petro stood beside Sal and tapped the glass window. He followed Sal's line of sight to the barrier before he sighed. "It's nice to know that our insanely high tax bracket actually goes to some use." He smiled at Sal before gripping his shoulder. "Are you nervous?"

Sal looked away from the carriages and met his father's eyes. "A little. It kinda feels like I'm running away from reality." He looked back out to where the barrier was getting smaller and smaller in the distance.

Petro sighed as his grip tightened slightly on Sal's shoulder. "It's only for a few months. You go in, keep your head down, flunk out after the first semester…and then you can come home and work with us."

Sophia appeared on the other side of her son and gave her thoughts on the conversation they'd been having for years. "Worst-case scenario, you stop hating your power and you pass the first semester? Maybe get into a cool class, make some friends…Who knows?"

Sal wanted to shake his head and smile, but his father's grip felt different this time.

Petro looked at him earnestly and chided him gently. "There's no point in worrying over something that hasn't happened yet. Just go in there, see how you feel…and remember that you have our full support."

Sophia nodded in agreement.

After a moment of silence, Petro turned back to his son with a grin. "But if you'd like to go on and graduate…we could really do with that Hero tax break you'd get for the family."

With that said, Petro laughed and took a seat on the lounger. Sophia rolled her eyes and joined him, leaving Sal to stand at the window alone. Despite it always causing headaches, Sal looked at his reflection in the glass and inspected himself.

Almost instantly, his appearance faded and he saw threads of power coursing around his body like a circuit board. Sal used his power to weave the threads into different shapes…knowing that the right combination would unlock an entirely new ability.

Next stop, Quest Academy!

Sal disengaged his power and whirled around. His parents stood at the center of the room, with all his luggage.

Sophia just shook her head with a smile. "You always look so tranquil and free of worry when you use your power. I didn't want to interrupt you!" Her hands raised defensively, as if preempting Sal's complaint.

Petro placed an empty glass on the bar and pointed to the corridor they had entered from. Before he moved to leave, though, he seemed to remember something and reached into his coat pocket.

He slid an envelope across the surface to the attendant. "Thanks for looking after us." Her shocked expression was a sign that she wasn't used to getting tips, but Petro had no intention of waiting for her thanks. He picked up a suitcase and moved to the corridor.

Just as Sal went to follow his parents, the attendant spoke to him in a warm but excited voice. "I'll be cheering for you! Consider me your first official fan."

Sal gave her a smile as he left the carriage. But he wondered why a Hero was pretending to be a train attendant.

CHAPTER 2:
QUEST ACADEMY

SAL SHIELDED HIS EYES AS HE GOT OFF THE TRAIN. SUNLIGHT REFLECTED FROM practically every angle, with each skyscraper completely sheathed in reflective glass. It was hard to fathom that this was a university campus, especially when he considered the huge artillery guns atop each of the buildings.

Blinking a few times, he tried to acclimatize to the lighting.

"They're a technical wonder," his father said, his awe obvious. "Are you seeing this, Sal? Those buildings right there." Petro pointed at the five skyscrapers around them. "They absorb the magical essence from the atmosphere and somehow convert it into power. I've no idea how many cores it must take to power those guns, but they can apparently keep firing for hours in the event of an outbreak! And there's at least half a dozen of them."

"Yes, thank you…all of these." Sophia gestured to Sal's luggage and moved out of the way of a porter who had come to assist them. "Do you need a name or identification? So he knows where to find them later?" She finished with a smile aimed at Sal.

The porter shook his head and handed a black metal card to Sophia. "This is the room assigned for Salvatore Argento. I was sent to pick up his luggage specifically. You'll be told everything about your room arrangements and class schedule at the induction meeting taking place in the plaza." He pointed through the skyscrapers, gesturing toward their destination.

Petro moved his small case away from the porter. "Not this one, thank you."

With a few more nods and smiles, the porter was gone, with all of Sal's belongings stacked on a trolley.

"Guess there's no turning back now," Petro muttered as he gave Sal a playful dig in the ribs.

Sophia shot her husband a withering look before linking her arm with Sal's. "Come on, let's not be late. We want to make sure we've got a good spot."

Sal followed her gaze to the train carriages that were still spewing out students. Many of them must have been the first in their family to unlock an ability, with the Quest Academy being the first stop in their journey to riches and fame. Some of them were unsteady on their feet and looked shaken.

Some of the mounted turrets had been ripped off the top of the carriages and there were huge gashes in the metal shields of one that had failed to retract. He wondered how they repaired it before it took off for the next stops.

Before he could think on it too much, he followed his mother's lead and walked toward the plaza. A few other families had taken the luxury compartments of the train, but most of the affluent people had used their own forms of personal travel.

"Little excessive, don't you think?" Petro laughed as a luxurious private aircraft touched the ground. There were a series of them hovering above, waiting for landing space. Most of them sported the same design, but there were a few that looked custom-built.

Sal agreed with his father's stance on excessive wealth. It was nice to be able to afford comforts in life, but wasting money that could be used to help people was completely out of touch. Their family business, the Argento Auction did it's best to help those in need, with a good chunk of profits being donated to rehousing refugees in the reclaimed zones.

Petro started to complain about it as they walked toward the Plaza. "A single one of those aircraft could re-home a few dozen families in a safe sector. Not to think of the essence they're using, or the cores they need to operate it? We should ask people what they think. Would they like reassurance that the barriers protecting them from demons are being sufficiently powered…or should we allow the mega-wealthy to take some of those cores for their own personal use?"

Sophia scoffed and shook her head. "And just where do we get those cores, hmm? Who carves the cores out of the demons after killing them? They're mega-wealthy for a reason. So what if they take a couple for themselves? We need them to keep doing their job."

As if it were an afterthought, Sophia raised her hand and pointed at Petro. "And yes, I know…the same core that powers a private aircraft can power an entire train and help hundreds of people."

Sophia's tone became exasperated as she finished both sides of the argument without letting Petro speak. "But how many more people could take the train if we were to take away the first four luxury carriages? Where is the line between us and them? What side are we on? Are we poor compared to them?" Sophia gestured roughly at the aircraft. "Or are we obscenely rich to them?" Her hand waved at the clusters of people getting off the end of the train.

Petro paused before turning to Sal and completely changing the topic. "So…what classes are you thinking of taking?"

Sal laughed as they made their way toward the plaza.

The area surrounding the train station was incredible. The platform was man-made and attached to the various skyscrapers. It was like a floating stadium constructed between the surrounding towers.

Above them, several other constructs stretched out, containing private gardens, sparring areas, and landing zones. Sal could have sworn a private aircraft landed on one of the topmost platforms near the tops of the skyscrapers. As impressive as they were, they couldn't rival the view of the city.

The only other prominent buildings that could hope to dwarf Quest Academy were the guild towers in the distance. Each of them pierced the sky in their own distinctive architectural shapes, but all of them stood proudly in a circle, protecting the academy within.

"Whoa…" Petro breathed as he laid eyes on the academy plaza.

It was an amphitheater, with thousands of seats circled around an enormous stage. Rather than being built up, it dipped down into a curve, with the stage being at its lowest point. Sal led the way down a series of steps to get to their seats. The winds were stopped by the protective barriers, and small orbs of orange light emanated from between the seats, offering a comforting warmth.

Many of the seats were already occupied, and Sophia waved at a few people she recognized. Petro shook his head as he turned around constantly, trying to take everything in.

Sal eyes were practically in overdrive at the sight of so many powerful people. He couldn't tell what skills they had, or what their abilities were…but their internal threads of light were on a level he hadn't witnessed before. One practically dominated his vision with how bright the light was.

With a concerted effort, he broke eye contact with the threads and tried to quell the growing unrest in his chest. It was one of the many downsides of his power, but he was used to calming it. When he got himself under wraps, Sal nudged his father and asked about the identity of the person he had just inspected.

Petro only needed to take half a glance before his face broke into a smile. "Oh, I'd say he was as bright as a sun? Yeah?"

Sal nodded as he took a steadying breath, and Petro continued, including Sophia this time as he gestured at their pained son.

"He just used his eyes on Neuro. Guess how that went?"

Sophia gave Sal a comforting smile and rubbed his shoulder. "He's the most powerful telepath in the world, but there's a rumor that his daughter is even stronger. Mind Control, apparently!"

She glanced around the stands. A frown crossed her face as she reached into her bag, withdrawing a small black case. "Put these on."

Sal groaned inwardly as she pressed the pair of sunglasses into his hand. "I'm fine. I can control it…I just won't look at people."

Sophia closed her bag and placed it at her feet, leaving the sunglasses case in Sal's hands. Petro gave him a gentle nudge and gestured for him to put the glasses on.

Maybe it was for his own benefit or an act of solidarity, but Petro withdrew his own pair of glasses from the pocket of his blazer and put them on. Sal felt like less of an idiot and had to admit that he felt a lot better the moment he put them on.

"Thanks, Mom," he muttered in defeat and noticed a small smile appear on her face.

Ladies, Gentlemen, Heroes, and Aspirants!

Welcome to Quest Academy!

Please take your seats. We will be starting our induction event shortly! Note that our staff wear white uniforms and will be around shortly to offer refreshments. We would ask all guests to kindly refrain from recording the event as we will be discussing topics of a sensitive nature.

Thank you.

A series of drones circled overhead, emitting a faint light as they scanned the rows of guests. As if confirming their attendance, a compartment under the seat slid open smoothly to reveal a handheld device.

Petro was fastest out of the three and quickly scanned through the documentation. "It's a non-disclosure agreement. Fairly standard, so don't worry."

Sophia and Sal didn't need any further reassurance and accepted it immediately. Their screens flickered to reveal new information, with a full itinerary of what was to be covered in the induction. Each of the options was interactive, and Sal started to investigate the different classes that would be available to him.

Looking down at his own device, Sal scrolled slowly and was surprised at how different the curriculum was from previous years. He had researched the classes in the past, but it looked like everything had changed. Sal clicked into one of the Masterclasses that had an impressive looking Hero on the icon. A list of prerequisite classes and grades appeared at the top, and no matter which option he selected, he was met with another wall of requirements.

Petro looked at Sal's device with a raised eyebrow. "Isn't this a bit overkill?"

With no context, an enormous screen flickered to light above the center stage. It was shaped like a giant circle that would allow each person in the amphitheater to clearly read it. After a few moments, names started to populate the screen, allocated into place based on their seating.

Sal's name appeared, but it didn't register his parents. The nearest name to him was someone called "Christopher Gage," who sat two seats away. Leaning around his father, Sal looked back to see Christopher staring right back at him. Sal gave him an awkward smile and a nod, but Chris returned a quizzical look that reminded Sal he was wearing sunglasses in a shaded space.

Glancing back at the board, Sal could see hundreds of names now listed there.

Sophia, on the other hand, was still going through the device as she investigated each of the classes. "It's absolutely overkill." She looked over at Petro. "This reads more like a military camp than a university curriculum."

"As it should! We're at war with demons, in case you hadn't noticed."

The voice came from directly behind Sophia. Sal turned to look and saw a heavily scarred older man clutching at his son's shoulder. Even with the sunglasses on, Sal could tell that there wasn't an ounce of magical essence in the haggard man, but his son definitely had a spark of power.

Sophia nodded slowly and gave Sal a solemn look. "I'd hoped our kids wouldn't need to suffer through the pain we did. I didn't mean to cause offense." She gave the man a sympathetic nod and turned back toward the screens. A few moments passed, with more than a few people waving at Petro and Sophia.

Sal was eager for things to start, and just like that, it did. A chorus of classical music sounded out, drowning all the chatter from the stands. It sounded like an anthem of sorts, and it gave their host plenty of time to get onto the stage. A slender, middle-aged man with fading blond hair stepped into view and gave everyone a warm smile.

I'd like to thank you all for your patience. I wanted to give you time to get settled and read through the curriculum. You can probably tell that we're not pulling any punches this year.

But to explain why that is, I need to explain a little bit more about myself.

I know many of you here, but I'm incredibly excited to see a lot of new faces in the crowd. The rate of awakenings is growing, and the potency of the next generation is unparalleled. Thank you for entrusting the next generation to the Quest Academy.

My name is…well, you can call me Quest.

Quest's tone was friendly and judging from the number of smiles in the audience, he was a well-known figure among the previous generation.

When I first discovered my power, I thought it was useless. Recognizing essence signatures? What does it even mean? Well…in my head, it was like…law. I could pinpoint how strong a demon was, just from looking at its essence composition. I could even see how strong my peers were because they were using essence too.

As I worked on my ability, it branched out, and I could see skills and how they develop. I decided to create a structure of my own, that anyone could understand, which I called the System. It was just rules for all the things I saw, and terminology that people could follow and understand. If I told you that a demon—let's say a Prowler—what if I told you that its essence signature had this shape? It would probably mean absolutely nothing to you.

Everyone in the crowd looked up to see an intricate weave of pulsating threads. Sal was speechless as he took off his sunglasses for a better look. It was the first time he had encountered a replication of what he, himself, saw in people. The headmaster wasn't done, though, as he turned around with a flourish, only for the picture to be replaced with a scale containing different threat levels.

But what if I told you, it was a Level 6? Oh yes, now we understand exactly what we're dealing with, and we have a point of reference. Now, what if I can pinpoint an essence signature of an impending portal? Could we calculate its expiration date?

These were the concepts that I spent years working on and adapting into the System. My nickname became Quest because I embarked on an endless pursuit of knowledge. My mission is to create an accessible system that could be understood by the masses, that would give us an advantage against the demonic hordes. Powerful people joined my cause, and we founded this institution. The guilds all follow the System, and we're all on the same side in this war.

Quest paused, as though considering his next words carefully. He looked up at the screen, which had reverted to the list of names. With a click of his fingers, the screen changed to reveal an empty leaderboard. Silence washed over the crowd, with everyone hanging on his words.

We developed a new technology that could potentially change the world as we know it. It requires an incredible amount of investment and resources that we, frankly, don't have. Even if we did, we need to be very careful in how we use this opportunity. In my research of essence signatures, we've discovered a method of imprinting those signatures into internal cores.

The excitement on his face was infectious, but the audience seemed split at those words. A few cheers ripped through the crowd, followed by ecstatic applause, which was adopted by the confused attendees too, until the whole amphitheater shook in unanimous celebration.

Thank you. But as I said, I want to make things accessible, so let me explain. This new technology allows us to artificially implant abilities into students who hold an affinity for it.

The halfhearted applause was replaced with a thunderous roar of approval. It was the most incredible news that they had heard in such a long time, and many of the attendees were openly weeping, smiles on their faces.

Sal understood the impact very clearly. The greatest limitation they had against the demons was the random nature of which ability would be assigned at birth. Removing that limitation would allow them to grant powerful abilities to the best suited students.

So, why is our curriculum closer to a regimen? Because we're going to create those affinities in your children. We'll build up their knowledge and capabilities to such a level that we'll be able to enable them with the skills they'll need to really make a difference in this war.

Better yet, this technology has been tried, tested, and proven. Our implanted skills are at the level of inherent, so the students will feel as though they've had it their whole lives. It's a level of mastery that we've strived for over the years, and now, we've achieved it.

Unfortunately, as I mentioned…this opportunity comes with a heavy cost. We don't have the resources to help every student. With this in mind, we created a new system for our incoming students. The first semester at Quest Academy will be grueling. Everything you do will be by your own efforts.

There are ways to earn advantages in Quest Academy, but all of them require your capability and determination. Your status right now means nothing within these towers. Your family connections mean nothing. Your wealth is useless here.

Your progress will be watched closely by our staff, and at the end of the semester, we will finalize your rank and assign you a class. Heroes are more than the people fighting on the frontline. They're the Defenders who hold our territories, the Controllers who dominate the battlefield, the Supports who keep our people safe. When you get your class, and you're ranked…the top ten percent of you will be given a new ability that will be yours forever.

Welcome…to Quest Academy.

CHAPTER 3:
FIRST ASSIGNMENT

SAL'S HANDS SHOOK THROUGHOUT THE ENTIRE PRESENTATION AS HE LISTENED in absolute wonder to the headmaster. Before he realized it, the presentation was over and he stood with his parents, cheering, and clapping as though his life depended on it. He couldn't put it into words, but just looking at his parents, he could see that they were experiencing the same revelation as him.

As the noise died down from the rapturous applause, Sal found his voice and spoke excitedly to his parents. "The symbol? Did you see it, the one he put up for the Level 6 demon? That's what it looks like when I look at people. Do you think we have the same ability?"

Sal listed off question after question, but neither of his parents were able to answer him. Sophia shook her head in surprise, but the smile never left her lips.

"This really does sound like it could turn the tide," Sophia said to Petro as they made eye contact.

Petro laughed. "Why only students? Wouldn't it make way more sense to give the powers to established Heroes?"

Sophia snorted, which seemed to confuse Petro. She quickly clarified with an apologetic wave of the hand. "Sorry, I thought of you trying to get a front-line ability to go and join the war."

Petro shot her a look of mock indignation, but his act broke almost immediately when he laughed. They weren't alone in their joy, as all the surrounding families spoke enthusiastically about Quest's announcement. The only exceptions were a few students who looked up at the empty leaderboard in worry. Sal noticed several of them in the crowd and felt conflicted. Even if they said that there was no advantage to being from a wealthy status or whatever, it would still exist.

All guardians and parents are invited to attend the Quest Academy mixer that will take place shortly in the Sky Lounge. Please follow our members of staff, indicated by their white uniforms.

All prospective students are required to report to their dorms. You will find a gray uniform that indicates your status as a classless first-year. We ask that all of you wear your uniforms and report to the nearest person wearing a white uniform, who will give you further instructions. Official induction starts tomorrow, but your conduct shall be monitored from this moment onward. Good luck.

Sophia's jaw dropped as she looked at Petro with wide eyes. Sal glanced at his father in confusion, wondering whether he heard it wrong. But Petro barked a laugh to cement the fact that it was real.

"Give me a hug before you go." Sophia's words might have sounded like a request, but it really wasn't.

Sal bent slightly to embrace his smaller mother, but his attention was on where the other students were going. He didn't know where the location was.

"Are you listening to me?" Sophia's voice cut through his momentary panic.

"Yeah, what is it?" Sal bluffed as he disengaged from the hug. His mother held out a black card for him to take.

"You're not going to get very far without this." She fussed slightly as she put it in his jacket pocket. "Now hurry on and see if you can find us before we go. I want to see what you look like in the uniform."

Sal saw a group of students congregating in one space, but all of them looked confused and out of their depth. It didn't fill Sal with any confidence in their ability to find the dorms. He paused for a moment and realized that it was probably a test, to see who could find them. *Was that what they meant by monitoring them?*

A white uniformed member of staff approached and tapped him on the shoulder. "Excuse me, but please make your way to the dorms." He gestured to one of the towers. "Over there."

Sal's heart sank a little. "Thank you," he muttered and inwardly cursed himself for overthinking it.

He was maybe only a few steps into his journey when he saw a black-haired woman with green eyes biting her lip as she looked at the different groups of people. Sal put her out of her misery.

"It's not a test. The dorms are straight over there." With a single point of his finger, Sal walked straight past her and led the way. He could have sworn that he heard her cursing under her breath.

After a few more footsteps of walking ahead of her, Sal felt weird and slowed down. When she caught up, she gave him a sideways glance that was filled with suspicion. Neither said a word for a few moments until the girl shouted out a name with a relieved smile.

Before Sal could react, the black-haired girl muttered a halfhearted thanks before jogging forward to walk with her friend. He wondered whether the sunglasses made him look like a creep. Sal took them off and slid them into his pocket.

After a couple more minutes of walking, Sal realized just how big the platform was. Although he could see the hulking skyscraper in front of him, it was a long trek to the platform entrance. Another annoying realization was the sharp pain in his chest when he sprinted for a segment of the journey.

It was a stark reminder that he was incredibly unfit compared to the people around him. That realization was in the form of some students, especially those with physical-based abilities. One leapt about thirty feet ahead of him from somewhere behind, while another zipped past him in a burst of super speed. It was at that moment that Sal had tried to jog, with zero success. Despite looking relatively fit, Sal felt anything but. An entire life of walking around an auction house hadn't done much for his fitness.

When he finally made it to the entrance, there was a bit of a backlog as students inspected a single map that held their destination. Sal spotted the speedster and the jumper a couple of places in front of him, and it made him happy to know they didn't get that far ahead.

A couple of students, already in gray uniforms, rushed out of the lobby at breakneck speed and ran off in the direction of another tower. Another moment passed before another gray-garbed student burst out of the corridor and ran out of the building.

Sal cursed himself for being complacent. There was definitely a test component here, but it wasn't finding the dorms—it was getting to wherever they were going. Turning back toward the map, his gaze met the black-haired girl, who seemed to have reached the same conclusion.

She hesitated for only a second before speaking in a quiet but controlled voice. "What's your name?"

"Salvatore Argento."

Before he could ask for hers, she disappeared from sight. A few of the people in the queue exclaimed in surprise as they were shoved out of the way by an unseen force. Sal resisted the urge to activate his eyes, because he knew it would likely be a horrible idea, especially if he needed to run soon.

Sal grit his teeth as he looked at the crowd. There were at least two hundred people in front of him, all clumped into a narrow space. There was no way it wasn't an intentional design flaw, especially with how well laid out everything else was.

Just as Sal contemplated pushing forward, an ethereal hand materialized on his arm. Wincing slightly, the black-haired girl with green eyes reappeared beside him, grinning.

"Salvatore Argento, Floor 51, Room 6. We're even."

With that, she turned on her heel and ran toward the stairs. Sal didn't hesitate and followed to see which stairwell or elevator he needed. It took him all of twenty seconds to realize that he was fucked. The elevator had an insane queue, and he was thirty floors away from his room. He had to descend from floor eighty, and it would require a trek all the way back up to this platform. A total of sixty floors, not including finding the room and changing…while racing against other students for some unknown reason.

Sal gritted his teeth and wondered whether it was worth going at a leisurely pace. He didn't want to come last, especially if this was a test. Taking a steadying breath, he turned around and looked at the speedster he had seen before. Activating his ability, Sal looked at the glowing threads that converged in a pattern at the center of the speedster's chest.

He had replicated his parents' abilities several times, but never a physical-based one. The speedster's ability looked easy to copy, and if he tied a few knots in the pattern, it would lower the potency down to a manageable level. Despite that knowledge, every part of his brain screamed at him not to do it, because of the risks involved with using a foreign power his body had never acclimatized to.

Just as he was about to discard the idea, another student ran out of the stairwell and burst past Sal. It was all he needed to make his decision, "Fuck it."

Sal activated his ability. His silver eyes glowed as countless threads of congealed light appeared before him as the students mashed together in the hopes of getting closer to the map.

He searched through them until he found the one he was looking for. The speedster's threads were weaved in a basic shape that looked quite simple. There were a few knots in the thread, and as much as Sal wanted to correct them in his own replication, he resisted the urge. With the image firmly planted in his head, Sal started to weave his own threads in a perfect imitation of the speedster's, knots and all. Then, just like he had assembled a circuit, Sal tested it by sending his power through the new weave.

Everything stopped.

Sal's heart beat ridiculously fast, but he ignored the sensation, taking it easy. His body wasn't made for this power, and had never trained for it, or built up any resistance. He was literally taking someone else's ability, which meant there was a lot of opportunity for things to go wrong. But Sal wasn't going to stand there and agonize over it. He had a room to find.

He set off on a light jog, sighing as he went down set after set of stairs. It was nothing like what he was hoping for. It was like time around him slowing down while he moved normally…which was kinda shit. A journey that would normally take him about twenty minutes or so was now possible in less than one. A few times, he slowed to a walk when his heart rate increased too much, but he didn't let go of the power.

As it was a physical-based ability, he would probably be in serious muscle pain tomorrow morning…but there'd be no issue in terms of essence exhaustion. The speed ability wasn't even testing his internal essence at this rate.

Since he had a lot of time to think to himself during the journey, he wondered if he'd be able to ever control an ability like that black-haired girl. Floating like a ghost all the way to the room would have made things so much easier. In his current state, it felt like there was zero chance of that happening, as it was a huge limitation of his power. He needed to understand exactly how an ability worked; otherwise, it could end up killing him. Speed was a risk, but he already knew how to run, so it was intuitive by comparison.

Finally, he found the door to his apartment and activated the key. He realized he had to keep it against the sensor for an age before the door would recognize it. Opening the door at an unprecedented speed nearly shattered the hinges, but Sal ignored that as he quickly saw the gray uniform that lay on the bed.

Deactivating his power for fear of tearing the uniform to shreds, Sal quickly undressed as he looked around the room. It was much more generous than he imagined, with an entire wall made of glass looking out onto the city. There was a workbench in a separate room, accompanied by what looked like a specialist training area. The bed was more than big enough and the bathroom had a rainfall shower. There was a mounted screen on the wall, which held a message on it.

Welcome to Quest Academy.

Your first assignment is already underway. Your preliminary ranking will be determined by the order in which you reach your destination.

With a thousand students to focus on and assess, our staff are going to have to make some choices on who to watch closely. Faculty are always looking for exceptional talent to join their Masterclasses, so make sure you're showing how exceptional you are from the beginning.

It's harder to climb from the bottom than it is to stay at the top. Good luck.

Below the message was a map marker showing the location of the mixer. Sal finished dressing and thought about activating the speedster power again. His body was starting to ache, and he was sweating profusely. He had made good time to be in the top half, but another thought niggled in the back of his head. His parents were going to be at that mixer, surrounded by their peers and clients.

Sal knew he was okay with being in the middle of the pack, and his parents would want him to be careful…but it would look good for business if he did well in front of everyone. Gritting his teeth and ignoring the flaring pain in his legs, Sal left the room and closed the door before setting off on a jog again. He activated the ability and pushed himself with the promise that it would all be over soon.

The upstairs battle was much harder than he thought it would be, but he was resolute. He had set his mind on the goal and no matter how much he wanted to talk himself out of it, he imagined the surprise on his parents' faces when he arrived in the top few hundreds of people. That thought alone fueled him to pick up the pace and get up the stairs faster.

He took a few steps at a time, and noticed that when he leapt upward, he nearly floated due to the momentum. The next few sets of stairs involved an initial jump at the base, floating upward, turning on the stairwell and aiming the momentum before repeating the process. It was a lot less demanding on his limbs, and Sal arrived back in the lobby with energy to spare. He burst forward into a run, using the new momentum method to launch out of the lobby and toward the mixer.

Sal's heart rate had started to slow, and his stride became more natural as he took lunging steps forward, and he enjoyed short rest moments as he glided through the air. He couldn't figure out if the ability was acclimatizing to his system, or if he was just delirious from exhaustion.

Before he could give it anymore thought, he arrived at his destination, signaled by all the expectant parents and guardians, cheering for their kids. Sal deactivated his power but had done nothing to counteract the momentum of his approach, which resulted in him sliding across the floor feet first…until he slowly came to a stop in the center of the room. Sal was mortified but tried his best to keep his composure as he looked for his parents. He hoped he wasn't too late.

"—vatore Argento," the headmaster's voice shouted as he gestured up to the leaderboard that now held Sal's name.

Sal couldn't see his parents, but an enormous group of students dressed in black uniforms with colorful shoulder patterns cheered for him. It was the second and third years of the academy, and their applause deafened the best efforts from the adults.

He could barely move his body, so elected to stay where he was until the feeling came back to his legs. He glanced up at the leaderboard to see how he did.

For the second time that day…it felt like time had stopped.

Rank 42: Salvatore Argento

CHAPTER 4:
TOKEN OF INTENT

COUNTLESS PEOPLE SAL HAD NEVER SEEN BEFORE CONGRATULATED HIM AS HE walked between the tables. He was at the disadvantage that his name was literally announced and written on a gigantic leaderboard, but there was no way to identify any of the people in the room who had decided to wish him well. Sal could see from the corner of his eye that a whole group of others in gray uniforms were getting similar praise. He wasn't sure whether he was supposed to go and stand with them, but decided to wait until he was told to go somewhere.

The area for the mixer was a huge hall, not unlike a gymnasium that was repurposed for an event. Two walls were dedicated to stands that held the current academy students, who all looked to be engrossed in conversation. It was still disconcerting to have so many people paying attention and watching.

Sal clapped whenever a new name appeared. They were somewhere after the first hundred now, and it looked as though a lot of the audience had lost their enthusiasm for cheering on every new arrival. Apparently, it had dulled around the thirty mark, but Sal's power-slide had fixed that.

As he made his way through the groups of people, he returned pleasant smiles, but kept looking out for his parents. It irritated him that the few people who stopped to speak to him urged him to join the Offensive class rather than Support.

Turned out that the Argento name was synonymous with Support class, and too many people felt at ease telling Sal how much of a mistake it would be for him to follow in their footsteps. A few more comments were enough for Sal to get sick of it. *Were they that strapped for Offensive front-liners, or were Support just seen as useless?* Either way, Sal found it very easy to be offended on behalf of his parents.

The Argento Auction was a necessity in the current landscape. Not a single front-liner would know what their weapon did without a proper Appraisal. *Who repairs their gear? Support. Who maintains the barriers? Support.* Sal was reeling off all the reasons in his head and inwardly seething when Petro finally found him.

"Sal!" Before Sal could get in a single word, his father embraced him in a bear hug with the widest smile on his face. "Come on, we need to get back to your mother before she arranges your marriage. One of her childhood friends has a daughter starting here, so hurry up."

Sal couldn't tell whether it was a joke or a threat, but he forced his aching legs to comply as he followed his grinning father across the room. The wide grin never once left Petro as he responded to a few lighthearted quips. It warmed Sal's heart to know that he had made the right decision in rushing to the finish line.

The Argento family weren't really a part of the social elite. They were necessary outsiders who were brought into the fold when their talents in Appraising were needed. They'd be invited to functions but would be seated on the outside tables. It was never a snub, but it was never anything more than keeping up with appearances.

Maybe that was why Sal found it so hard to stomach the fake praise and platitudes from the people around him. His parents knew how to play the game, and to an extent, so did he. It didn't mean that he had to like it.

"And here we are. Cynthia, this is Sal. Told you I'd find him, Soph," Petro exclaimed as he gestured for Sal to introduce himself to the older woman.

Cynthia looked like the exact opposite of his mother. Where Sophia was small but elegant, Cynthia was…not. Sal took her hand and gave her a warm smile. "A pleasure to meet you, Cynthia."

Rather than answering, the middle-aged woman smacked Sophia on the arm. "Fuck, he has those same eyes as Petro. Are you sure he's yours?"

A shrill laugh followed, and Sal understood why they needed to rush back to find Sophia. She needed saving.

Cynthia wasn't done, though, and continued to grasp onto Sal's hand. "My little Tabitha is on her way, and I'd love you to meet her. She's not arrived yet…but she was never the fastest. Smart girl, though."

Sal couldn't tell whether Cynthia was criticizing her own daughter or trying to sing her praises. Either way, he wasn't overly enthused about an awkward encounter with a mini-Cynthia, so he excused himself to go to the bathroom. Petro gave him a knowing look, while Sophia's expression pleaded with him to return soon.

Despite being a good dozen steps away, Sal still heard Cynthia's voice cawing away. "Only twenty years younger, I'd go for him myself."

Sal ignored the pain as he moved his legs faster in the opposite direction. In his haste, he accidentally bumped into a tall man with blond hair. Sal caught himself from stumbling but the man, staggered and Sal reached out to catch his opposite shoulder before he fell over, apologizing in a panic.

The man looked around warily and made eye contact. Sal's power flinched in a familiar way, as if a power was being used on him. Then the man burst into laughter, catching Sal off guard.

He placed a hand on Sal's shoulder as he wiped away a tear with his free hand. "Apology accepted…I wanted to see if it was genuine, but I wasn't expecting to see how Cynthia just traumatized you." He laughed as he spoke, and Sal finally recognized him as Neuro, the telepath.

Sal laughed. "Don't suppose you could just erase the last twenty minutes of my life? I'd rather forget the power-slide as well as…Cynthia's suggestiveness."

Much to Sal's astonishment, Neuro stopped laughing and gave him a surprised look. "You're the Argento boy?"

Not sure how to proceed, Sal offered his hand. "Salvatore Argento, but everyone calls me Sal."

Neuro's smile returned as he accepted the handshake. "Neil. But everyone calls me Neuro."

After shaking the hand of one of the most powerful people in the world, Sal realized that he was not living in the private gated community of Silver Sanctuary anymore. He couldn't tell whether his legs were like jelly because of the interaction, the speed, or the crippling desire to go to the bathroom.

The atmosphere had really lightened and the happy chattering, with the occasional spatter of applause for arrivals, felt very chilly in comparison to when Sal had arrived. It was hard to look at the crestfallen faces of the late arrivals, but Sal wondered whether this early ranking was also a psychological test for the students.

Were they maybe testing resolve? He cursed and told his brain to shut up until he went to the toilet. The most gratifying moment was finding an empty stall and just sitting down for a few moments.

"I'm telling you, it's fucking bullshit! She clearly cheated, but they still put her fucking name up on the leader board," an annoyed voice sounded out from near the sinks.

Sal frowned at how stupid this person was to start bad-mouthing someone, in a public space, when they had no idea who was listening.

"You know who she is, though," another voice answered. "What could they do?"

An aggravated sigh was the only response, and Sal wondered whether that was going to be the end of it. But it turned out that the annoyed voice still had more hate in the tanks.

"Imagine what would happen if a man used that ability? Yeah? Mind controlling a bunch of students? Make them move out of the way, or stop them from taking first place? What would people say then?"

Despite his best intentions at being subtle and just listening, Sal snorted in laughter at the student's reasoning.

A deathly silence enveloped the entire restroom, followed by a resounding smack against Sal's cubicle door. "Find something funny, asshole?"

Sal finished up and flushed the toilet behind him. With a flick of the latch, he opened the door and stared at the short and burly-looking student who stood in front of the door with his chest puffed up. His face contorted in anger, and Sal had absolutely no intention of putting him at ease.

"What rank did you finish?"

"Sixty-seven," he barked before pointing out in the direction of the mixer. "But it would have been much higher if it wasn't for that bitch."

Sal shook his head and walked past the student and started washing his hands. "I came in at rank forty-two. I didn't see any mind controller or a queue of people. Sounds like you're just looking for someone to blame. But if you ask me?" Sal turned and looked directly at the man with an earnest expression. "I would not fuck with someone who can control your mind. What happens if they make you jump out of a window?"

The student hit the cubicle door again. "I wouldn't fall for it again. I'd resist it."

Sal rolled his eyes as he turned to leave. A fist connected with the side of his face, the punch more of a shock than painful, probably because the boy had to launch it upward and at a weird angle. Sal activated the power of the speedster. It was fading from memory, but the remnants were more than enough for what he needed. It didn't need to be super speed; he just needed more time to think.

As the movements of the two men slowed, Sal took the time to see what he was dealing with. He wasn't a fighter by any stretch, but he understood how basic physics and biology worked. His assailant was full of openings and weak points. His stance was horrible, and all Sal needed to do was exert a little pressure in the right spots to neutralize the threat. Sal slowly disengaged the power and made his move.

Sal's lifted his right foot slightly and swept it to the left, causing his attacker to lose balance completely.

As his eyes widened in surprise, Sal's right hand appeared at the side of his face. The second guy watched as his friend's head bounced against the ground and lay there in an unconscious heap. Sal's fist and legs ached in pain, but he just gave the second guy a level stare before leaving the bathroom. He was relieved to find that he wasn't followed out.

Taking his fingers away from his face, Sal wanted to know whether the punch had left any sort of bruise. He cursed himself for being an idiot on the first day at the academy. His mother would be worried sick if she thought he was making enemies on his first day. There wasn't going to be much visitation over the next few months, so she wouldn't sleep knowing that he might be in danger.

Sal picked up an empty glass from a nearby table and raised it to see whether he could spot any sort of reflection, but it was useless.

"It's definitely empty. I can try to find you a full one if you'd like?" a nearby voice exclaimed.

Sal glanced up and saw a strikingly beautiful woman with dark-red hair raising her own glass.

"I'm getting one for me, so what's one more? Wait…" Her blue eyes narrowed as she stared at Sal. "Are you allowed to drink?" Before Sal could even muster an answer, her face broke into a wide grin. "Doesn't matter. I was going to get you one anyway. It'll be our little secret."

Sal wanted to protest, but she disappeared into the crowd. He stood there for a moment, wondering who she was when he felt a light tap on his shoulder. Turning around, Sal saw a staff member dressed in a white uniform.

"I didn't want a drink. I don't know her," he said quickly. "I was just holding the glass up." Sal raised the glass and pointed at the terrible reflection. "See? Just to see if there was a mark on my face."

The man in white held up his hands and smiled gently. "Please, no. That's not why I'm here. You can drink whatever you want. Also, there's no evidence of a bruise on your face. It must have been a pretty weak punch." His smile remained, and Sal relaxed as he put down the glass before his mind caught up with the situation.

Sal let out a humorless chuckle. "Yeah, I didn't mention anything to do with a punch." He looked at the white uniform and wondered whether he was going to be expelled before he even started. "I may have been a little excessive, but I can assure you that it was self-defense." He waved his hands as he spoke, until something heavy was placed in his right.

The woman with dark-red hair was back, and her eyes practically sparkled. "You hit someone?" She looked at the staff member, who bowed deep with respect.

Alarm bells rang in Sal's mind as he looked at the drink in his hand even as she draped her arm over his shoulder. He might be expelled, he did knock someone unconscious, and now this strange woman who people bowed to had given him a drink.

As he tried to process everything going through his head, the mysterious woman laughed and took a long drink. "Never figured an Argento would be able to throw a punch. How did he do?" Her question was aimed at the man in white, who nodded respectfully and gave Sal an appraising look.

"He exploited his opponent's weakness and knocked him unconscious in less than a second. He didn't throw any punches."

Taking another sip of her drink, the woman turned her full attention on Sal and waved the man in white away. Much to Sal's surprise, he nodded deferentially and departed, leaving Sal alone with her. His heart raced and he couldn't help but feel like he was being stared down by a predator.

The air around him suddenly felt very heavy. It was like an unseen force was pushing him from all angles as he was overcome with a severe sense of dread. Sal's legs were on the verge of buckling, when suddenly all the pressure disappeared, and he was once again on the receiving end of a smile.

"Those skills of yours are interesting, little Argento, but you're still just a cub."

Her eyes finally left Sal's face, and he felt as if he were just released from the jaws of a tiger. The woman placed her drink on a nearby table and withdrew a stack of metal cards from a pouch strapped to her bare thigh. She glanced back over at Sal as if estimating something before her attention went back to the cards. Her right hand flicked up, and Sal staggered back when a dagger materialized out of nowhere and landed in her palm. Twirling it around between her fingers, she glanced up at the leaderboard and muttered, "Why is your name so fucking hard to spell?"

Sal watched her engrave his full name into a bronze card, but curiosity overcame him, and he activated his eyes. He was mentally exhausted, but he wanted to Appraise that dagger. Much to his surprise, it was harder than usual, which could only mean that it was of a much higher grade than he was used to.

He poured more power into his eyes and gasped when he saw the results. It was an Epic ethos blade. His father had Appraised one of them years ago, and he still bragged about how long it took to crack that Appraisal. The client had been the Reavers Guild.

Her hand paused at Sal's gasp and she looked at him curiously. "What?"

Name	Ethos Blade
Origin	Portal Artifact
Age	[*Unknown*]
Grade	Epic (Upper)
Dimensions	12.75 inches | Blade 8", Shank 4.75"
Materials	Gloomhusk Fang | Voider Heart | Hellfire Titanium
Attributes	**Unstoppable**: Can bypass any defense other than the hide of a Gloomhusk. **Apparition**: Weapon can be concealed and revealed by its wielder. **Recall**: Weapon can teleport to the wielder within line of sight.
Abilities	Unstoppable | Apparition | Recall
Power Source	External Essence
Evolution	No
Quality	Excellent
Condition	93%
Value	Est. $85,000.00 – $145,000.00

Sal kept his mouth shut for fear of saying something stupid and shook his head as though it were nothing.

The woman tilted her head and twirled the knife in her hand. "I sensed a significant surge of power from you, and you gasped. Why?" Her tone was friendly, but her face was anything but.

Sal winced and pointed at the knife. "Epic ethos blade. It can cut through anything. Except the scales of a gloomhusk, apparently." When the woman continued to stare, he shifted uncomfortably and swallowed hard. "The Reavers Guild commissioned the Appraisal of the only known ethos blade, which makes me suspect you're Villa, the vice-captain of the Reavers Guild." Sal tried his absolute best to break her gaze, but it felt impossible.

The woman continued to stare at Sal before she lifted the metal card and shattered it in her fist. More than a few people looked over at the commotion, and Sal wondered how great it would be to go back to the moment when his biggest problems were Cynthia and a fucking power-slide.

Finally, the smile returned to the woman's face, and she shook her head wistfully. Reaching back, her hand didn't falter as she pulled out a silver card. The engraving this time was done in seconds, and Villa lifted the card to inspect it. Turning back to Sal, she gave him an ominous smile.

"Consider this our letter of intent." She handed him the metal card and paused with a thoughtful expression. "A potential partnership that's mutually beneficial." Villa winked at him before moving on to a different area of the crowd, her card pouch completely concealed by her dress and her knife nowhere to be seen.

Sal stood in stunned silence until he felt a familiar presence at his side.

Petro whistled lightly. "For your first negotiation with a guild, you did pretty good…but I have some notes." His voice was gentle and reassuring as he gestured at the silver card. "Let's get some fresh air."

Sal nodded numbly as he followed his father out of the tower, the metal card clutched tightly in his hand.

CHAPTER 5:
SAGE ADVICE

SAL TOOK A DEEP BREATH BEFORE HE LOOKED AT HIS FATHER. HE HAD SPENT the last five minutes telling him about everything that had happened since he went to find the dorms. Petro wasn't given a moment of reprieve throughout the rant, so when Sal finished, he offered an inquisitive gesture to see whether he could finally provide some input. Sal nodded as he continued to pace around the small greenery area outside the lobby.

Petro smiled as he got to his feet. He placed his hands on Sal's shoulders and ushered him to a seat. "I'm talking now, so I get to do the frantic pacing. You do the listening, okay?" His tone was light but his expression was somewhat conflicted

Sal looked at him and waited.

"First of all, if you tell this story again, you need to lie to your mother. Either you tell her that you discussed it with the kid and learned how to use his power, or you lie and say that you just ran really fast. She might not believe either of those excuses, but both of them are better than the reality of you telling her that you copied a power that you knew *nothing* about. I'm not criticizing you. It was a creative solution to a difficult problem, which is praiseworthy…but not when it could potentially be a risk to your life." Petro's tone was reassuring and Sal knew that it was for his own benefit, so he wouldn't feel like he was being judged.

"I'm sorry, Dad."

Petro chuckled at that and gave Sal a reassuring smile. "You're lucky your mother didn't see your entrance, but she did hear it was pretty dramatic from Cynthia. Oh, and we met Tabitha, by the way. Seems like a nice girl. Definitely not your type, though." Petro raised a hand and waved his fingertips toward his neck in a dismissive gesture. "The fight in the bathroom doesn't need to be a big deal, we'll tell her you hit yourself in the face when you were changing to make it to the mixer on time."

Sal nodded appreciatively and smiled. He loved that he was able to rely on his father like this. Even though they were coming up with countermeasures against his mother's anxiety, it felt good to have someone on his side.

His father didn't even bat an eyelid at Sal putting another guy down in the bathroom, and that, alone, meant so much. There was no disbelief in his capabilities or questioning of motives; it was just facts, and Petro was happy to deal with the facts.

With a click of his fingers, Petro brought Sal's attention right back to him. "Don't go zoning out on me. We're almost done. I know you're waiting for the good part, but to wrap up the situation for your mother, tell her that you shook hands with Neuro, and he said you can call him Neil. She'll love that." Petro finally pointed at the silver card that Sal was still gripping tightly in his hand.

"First of all, don't worry about Villa. Despite her fiery disposition, she's one of the good ones. I've dealt with her on multiple occasions, and I'd happily do so again. She used one of her skills on you tonight…her aura skill…which is designed to weaken or terrify demons. She used a part of that to see how you'd react. I have my own feelings about the topic, but Quest Academy is different than the world I know. Maybe those kinds of horrible, barbaric tests are necessary to evaluate your mental state? I don't know. What I do know is that you passed her test…and you surprised her."

He sat down beside Sal and tapped the metal card. "This might be hard for you to understand right now, but this token is a huge compliment."

Sal's eyes widened, and Petro nodded.

"You were probably thinking that she wanted to recruit you for the Reavers? Maybe join them out on a hunt or two during your studies?" Petro laughed as he shook his head. "No, it's nothing like that. It's more like a work order. Villa has essentially expressed an intent to work with you in the future. Now, if she was to give you a Bronze token, you'd be one of their contractors. They could come to you with an Appraisal request, or something like that."

Petro tapped the token again. "Silver is a preferred supplier. It means Villa wants her people to go to you first. Any new items that come in, that they want Appraised…they'll request you. Now, why is that a huge compliment? Well, you've never worked as an Appraiser in an official capacity, so it's a huge show of faith in your capability. But…since you're at the academy, the partnership with the Reavers will allow you to complete work orders and earn their custom currency. Quest was telling us about it while you were off running around the dorms. They have their own economy here, and it rewards hard work."

Petro hugged his son with one arm as he tapped the card again. "Don't feel defensive about the Support class. That's what your mother and I do, but it doesn't define you. You could use this token to earn money with your natural gifts, and maybe specialize in something you're passionate about. You're unique in the fact that you could walk into that room and replicate any skill you see. But we both know that's not the full extent of your power. Is being number one important to you? Do you want to win the war? Reclaim territories? Do you want to save lives?"

Petro got to his feet and brushed his trousers with his hands. "Just know that whatever you decide to do, your mother and I will support you."

Sal exhaled slowly as he also got to his feet. "Thank you for that. I think the aura thing messed with my head a bit." Looking down at the card in his hand, Sal appreciated it a lot more, but a question popped into his head. "Wait, if silver is preferred supplier, does that mean they have exclusivity on my services?"

Petro laughed. "That's my boy. Absolutely not, but let me explain why." With that said, Petro led them back into the lobby. The corners of his eyes wrinkled as a proud smile crossed his face.

***

The leaderboard flashed a few times to indicate that all students had been accounted for. Many of the audience seemed to have forgotten that they were waiting on people, so the final applause, with everyone knowing their hands wouldn't be subjected to it anymore, was thunderous and carried an air of relief.

Countless white uniformed staff came out holding platters of champagne in celebration as Headmaster Quest took to the stage.

Congratulations to all students.

The preliminary rankings are complete.

I would like to now reveal a few things that we may have forgotten to mention. In the interest of keeping things fair, we gave you all the same assignment, to ensure that your motivations in arriving were pure. In truth, there was more at stake than we initially let on.

Many of your guardians may have informed you that Quest Academy has its own currency. None of your wealth or status will help you within these towers. Instead, we use Q-Credit. You'll be given accommodations, meals, educational materials, and everything you'd expect from a university.

Q-Credit applies for extra-curricular activities like hunts, and field excursions…buying Crafting materials, using certain equipment, purchasing better gear. But most importantly, Q-Credit is vital at the start of your semester, because you can buy your spot in classes with limited spaces. For example, if we had Fury come in to do a guest lecture from the Inferno Guild, we'd limit that to a few hundred spaces.

Sal saw the crestfallen faces of the lower-ranked students. Whatever justification they had made to themselves that stopped them from trying to get there faster, it was meaningless in the face of not meeting Fury from the Inferno Guild. Sal grew up with Fury being one of the coolest Heroes in the war against the demons. That said, Sal thanked his brain for persevering through the pain of using that speedster skill.

That's just an example of a class.

If you have enough Q-Credits, you'll be able to enroll in specialist courses that will develop you toward unlocking an Advanced class. We've already told you about the skill implanting…so now, we should tell you about skill imprinting. It costs a lot of Q-Credit, but we're able to take a skill you already possess and make it inherent. For those of you with abilities you need to wrestle to control? Imprinting will make that ability feel like it's second nature to you, as easy as breathing and blinking.

More than a few people staggered at that statement. Sal understood their reaction more than anyone because it'd been something he'd battled with for as long as he could remember. Headaches from seeing too many people's abilities, having to wear sunglasses so he didn't accidentally activate his powers. But worst of all, the constant reminder that he could potentially kill himself by accidentally replicating a destructive power. His mind raced at the possibilities that this would open for him. He needed to know how much it cost and what he needed to do to get there.

You will find full pricing guides in your dorm rooms, as well as a rundown of everything I've discussed this evening.

What I want to speak about now is how we've shifted to a more competitive landscape at Quest Academy. We've already informed you that we can't provide skill imprints or implants to everyone who just shows up. We need to ensure that the best of the best are getting the resources they need to give us the best chances of taking control of this war.

So, how do we ensure we're getting the best?

Well, as we've confirmed tonight…not everyone is motivated by the same thing. Recognition and attention from staff wasn't a golden ticket for close to five hundred of you.

For the first time in Quest Academy history, we're introducing an Elite class, called the Saviors. We've taken the name from the first generation of Heroes who made the ultimate sacrifice to ensure our survival.

We hope to create the next generation of Saviors.

Thirty of you will be in the Elite class.

We will select you at the end of your first semester.

If you're selected, you will receive a free imprint and training toward an implant of your choice. Saviors are not bound by the progression paths we've set out for our other classes. They will be eligible to take all classes that further their development, in addition to specialist classes designed just for them.

Right now, __all__ of you have an equal chance to become a part of the Savior class.

Discussions broke out left, right, and center. Everyone wanted to know more about this new Savior class. Sal noticed a few sour expressions from the stands that held the older students. It would make sense that they'd be bitter about not getting the same opportunity. It was as though Quest had read his mind, or maybe he read the room, as his next words addressed exactly that.

Our aim is to give as many resources as possible to the next generation of Heroes, but that's not to say that we're abandoning our current roster of students. First-years, as I've said, will have thirty places. Second-years, we will select fifteen people…but for third-years? There will only be five.

At the end of each calendar year, families will be invited to the Quest Academy Showcase. It will highlight the progress of our students and allow them the opportunity to challenge someone ahead of them in the rankings. This will also apply for the Saviors, but will be limited to those within the top one hundred rankings.

You'll be able to find more details regarding duels in your dorm rooms.

Lastly, before we wrap up the announcements for the evening, please be mindful that we have a code of conduct, and violations of it will not be accepted.

Quest looked up at the leaderboard, which highlighted a single name at rank sixty-seven. Sal's breath caught in his throat as he recognized the number of the guy who had punched him in the bathrooms. His place flew through the ranks until it landed at the very end, pushing everyone else up a single space. Quest smiled warmly as he looked back to the crowd.

I told you that this was just the preliminary rankings.

We wanted to watch you carefully…and watch you, we did.

The entire leaderboard shifted and changed with names leapfrogging over others, while some plummeted down the ranks. It was an effort to keep track of the movements, so Sal looked around the room instead. Of all the eyes that were facing upward, one set looked straight at him. Sal waved awkwardly at Villa, who merely gestured at the board with a wide smile.

We invited some special guests to check out the new talent.

Some of you made quite the impression on them. While others failed to meet the mark. There will be other opportunities, but as it stands, these are the new preliminary ranks. Well done, to all of you. Your place on the leaderboard will determine the number of Q-Credits you'll be granted, which you'll find in your academy account back in the dorm.

Guardians, thank you so much for coming to support our new students.

It's time for you to say your goodbyes, because in a few hours, each and every one of these kids will be starting their journey to become a Hero.

Sal didn't even notice his mother's embrace, or when Quest left the stage. His eyes were glued to the leaderboard, and to the position Villa had gestured at only a moment ago. His ranking had changed.

"Well done on breaking into the top twenty, Sal. I had to put your name forward." Neuro leaned forward out of nowhere and grasped Sal's elbow, a wide smile on his face.

Sal broke out of his reverie and returned the smile, but Neuro wasn't done.

"They'd have called it favoritism if I voted for my own kid, but even without it, she got number one. Promise me you two won't kill each other."

Sal shook his head as he tried to glance over Neuro's shoulder to see his daughter, but it was no use; he was too tall. Instead, he just thanked him earnestly. "Thanks so much, Neil."

Neuro disappeared, and quite a few others made their way outdoors to say their goodbyes.

Sophia turned and looked at Sal as though he had two heads. "I spoke to Cynthia for an hour, and in that time, you managed to get a gig with the Reavers and you're calling Neuro by his first name? I feel like one of us got the short straw here." Her face was a picture of shock and happiness, which put Sal at ease.

When Petro joined them, he was shaking his head in surprise. "Who are you and what have you done with my son?" He pointed up at the leaderboard to clarify what he was talking about, but Sal was right there with him in absolute disbelief. Looking back up at the numbers, there was no denying it.

Rank 19: Salvatore Argento

CHAPTER 6:
MORNING AFTER

The first thing Sal noticed when he got to his room was that his door had been damaged from his earlier entrance. It could still open and close, but it just needed a little encouragement from his shoulder to do either of those things. In the greater scheme of things, it was a minor inconvenience and nowhere near enough to wipe the stupid smile off his face.

The evening had been an absolute whirlwind of emotions, and Sal was both exhausted and elated. He kept picturing the smiles on his parents' faces. He was never one to throw himself into danger, or actively compete with others, so it was a definite surprise for them to see him go all out. Sal leaned his back against the door and shoved it into a closed position before he exhaled loudly. His mind was a flurry of activity and he wanted to do a thousand things all at once.

Q-Credit balance? Check the prices of the skill imprints? Find out what classes he'd have tomorrow and where they were? All of those things were at the top of Sal's mind, but none of them got in the way of him and the bed. With the last ounce of power that existed within his muscles, Sal leapt triumphantly onto the bed, which welcomed his body with a soft embrace. Before he could so much as change out of his uniform, he was asleep.

Rise and shine.

Introduction will take place in the amphitheater in one hour.

Welcome to Day One of Quest Academy!

Sal's eyes opened as the announcement echoed throughout the building. He didn't see where the speakers were situated in the room but was grateful for the wake-up call. He hadn't set any alarms and likely would have remained unconscious if left to his own devices. He knew himself well enough to know that he needed to get out of bed instantly, or there was a very high risk that he'd go back to sleep. The only problem with that scenario was that he could barely move from all the muscle pain he had accumulated the night before.

He cursed and winced all the way to the bathroom, where he turned on the shower. His clothes were creased and covered in what he hoped was his own drool, and getting out of them was absolutely torturous. He kicked them away and almost cried in relief as the hot water distracted him from the pain.

Opening his eyes, he realized he didn't know if there were any towels. He hadn't looked around much and was practically in autopilot mode as he tried to wake himself up. By some miracle, his arms were fine, and he was able to wash his coarse black hair and his face. He felt stubble on his chin but would be able to get away with it for a day or two before it needed attention. Turning off the shower was always a trial, so Sal turned the dial to its coldest setting. It had the miraculous effect of making him leap out of the shower, fully awake.

"Ugh." Sal groaned as he shivered.

He flung open every drawer in the bathroom until he found a large gray towel. His body still ached, but the shower had definitely helped. Sal poked his head out of the bathroom and looked to the screen on his bedroom wall. He had fifty minutes to get to the amphitheater, so there was no need to really rush.

When the steam cleared from the mirror, Sal rethought his shaving strategy the moment he saw his face. Minutes later, his toiletries kit was unpacked as well as a few other essentials that he'd need. He'd wait until he had time in the evening to unpack properly. With a toothbrush in his mouth, Sal returned to the screen and tapped at the console below it. It wasn't a TV and didn't come with channels, but it was connected to the academy intranet.

Sal was met with a list of options he could choose from, and he glanced over the different titles in alphabetical order: Class Modules, Directory (Students), Directory (Faculty), Facilities and Maps, Rankings, Workshop, etc. He navigated down the list until he saw the option for Q-Credit.

Name	Salvatore Argento
Alias	*[Unknown]*
Profession	Student
Starting Role	Support
Rank (Student)	First-Years - 19th Silver Cohort - 2nd
Ability	*[Not Registered]*
Essence	*[Not Registered]*
Academic Reports	Core Modules: (M = Mandatory) • (M) Skills: No Grade • (M) Survival: No Grade • (M) Combat: No Grade Elective Modules: • None Selected
Reputation	**Quest Academy**: *[Unknown]* **Guild Association**: *[Unknown]* **Hunter Bureau**: *[Unknown]*
Affiliations	**Argento Auction** (Sponsorship: Tier 3) **Reavers Guild** (Silver Token Holder)
Scout Status	N/A
Accreditations	N/A
Threat Level	*[Unknown]*
Wealth	600 Q-Credit
System Notes	*[Unknown]*

Sal had no idea whether or not that was good, but he assumed that it was on the higher end considering that he landed in the top twenty out of a thousand students. It was a competitive advantage to start with and might open him up to resources that the others couldn't access yet. He'd need to look through the price list to understand his own position.

He tapped the console to bring up his schedule for the semester, but it looked as though the timetable wasn't populated yet. His eyes flicked across to the different color codes and saw the names of the compulsory modules that he'd be undertaking.

Introduction to Quest Academy
Introduction to (Dungeons, Towers, Breaks, Portals)
Introduction to (Classes, Roles, Grading, Evolution)
Introduction to (R&D, Battle Equipment, Crafting)
Introduction to (Guilds, Factions, Societies, Sects)
Introduction to (Survival, Encounters, Conquest)
Introduction to (Trade, Bounties, Wagers, Commission)

Sal raised an eyebrow. A small part of him had expected a huge focus on combat, but there was a lot more theory involved and tactics. He didn't want to get ahead of himself, but he started to consider that Quest Academy wouldn't be so bad after all, and he might even retain his high rank. Sal dismissed that thought and shook his head. He didn't have the perseverance or mindset to push forward and become a Savior. But that didn't mean he was going to give up either.

Sal glanced at the creased gray uniform that he had slept in. His mother would laugh at him if she saw what he was going to use her power for. Restoration was an incredible ability for the Argento Auction, allowing treasured artifacts and relics to be brought back to their former glory.

He activated his power and replicated the weave he had done a thousand times. He had memorized his mother's gift when he was a child and used it constantly to fix things he had broken. Sal smiled as he aimed the Restoration ability on the uniform. The added bonus was that it brought items back to their best appearance, which, in Sal's case, was last night. His power smoothed out the creases and removed the stains. Despite it starting as a gray uniform, it looked practically regal by the time Sal was finished with it. He wasted no time in getting changed and checked the screen for how much time he had left. Sal sighed upon seeing that he still had twenty minutes.

He did one last check of the room to see whether he was forgetting anything, then checked himself one last time in the mirror, making sure to avoid eye-contact with himself. When he was satisfied with the result, he left the room. The door took a lot more effort to move than he remembered the night before, but he pulled and shoved it to get it open enough for him to slide through. Closing it was much easier but drew the attention of a few other students walking along the corridor to the elevator. Since Sal was in Room 6, he was practically beside it. The familiar ding indicated that one had just arrived, so Sal shoved the door closed and made the mistake of running to the elevator.

"Hold it for me, please."

His muscles screamed, but he gritted his teeth and forced a smile when he saw that someone was holding the door open for him. The arm belonged to a sandy-haired boy who was shooting a glare at a girl with blonde hair who repeatedly tapped the Close Doors button, ignoring Sal's presence completely.

When Sal finally entered the elevator, another voice called out from farther down the corridor. The sandy-haired boy was unwavering in keeping the doors open, and Sal understood the blonde girl's frustration. The three other people in the elevator shared guilty looks, as if to confirm that they had held up the elevator a few times already.

Sal turned to the door and looked at the sign above the floor options. "Looks like one more person is probably our weight capacity, so we're good to go after this one."

With their new addition, who thanked them immediately, the sandy-haired boy removed his arm and let the doors close, much to the relief of the blonde, who finally stopped hitting the button.

She turned to the group. "We're going to have to stop at the next thirty floors, and if you're holding it for every single person, we're never going to get there!"

Rather than answering, the sandy-haired boy turned red.

"We're at weight capacity," Sal said, putting the boy out of his misery. "It'll go straight to our destination."

The blonde was about to retort when she suddenly closed her mouth. The elevator wasn't stopping. Rather than looking embarrassed, her face broke into a relieved smile.

"Thank fuck for that. I can't be late again…I think my parents disowned me after my result last night."

The sandy-haired boy turned to look at them. "Worse than eight hundredth?"

Sal grimaced and clapped him on the back. "It's day one, there's plenty of time to catch up. I'm Sal, by the way. I live in Room 6 on Floor 51."

"Hannah, Room 3." Her answer was confident as she stood up straight and looked squarely at Sal. "Why are you asking for room numbers instead of rank?"

Sal shrugged and gestured vaguely. "Just thought it would be nice to know who my neighbors are. You can check everyone's rank on the leaderboard, so it's not a big secret or anything."

Hannah paused before shaking her head with a sigh. "Sorry, I'm so on edge and thinking everything is a test. The way you spoke when you got in the elevator…and your uniform looks almost white, I thought you might have been a member of staff coming in to check on us."

"Kane, Room 10." The sandy-haired guy gave them both a respectful nod. His eyes lingered on Sal's uniform for a moment.

Sal made a mental note to hold himself back from Restoring the uniform too much in the future. The other students hadn't fared much better in the wardrobe department, with many of them wearing creased or stained uniforms. His uniform definitely stood out for its immaculate appearance, and he wondered if that would end up being a bad thing.

The other students in the elevator didn't pipe up with their own room numbers. They had turned their backs the moment Kane and Hannah mentioned their low ranks. Sal couldn't believe they were segregating based on a number that hadn't existed twelve hours ago.

Hannah ignored the group and turned to Sal with a knowing look. "Let the cliques commence."

The elevator doors opened, and Sal was met with the sight of hundreds of students slowly making their way toward the amphitheater between the huge towers. Some of them were holding coffee cups, and Sal swore an oath to whatever deity was listening that he'd be awake earlier tomorrow to get his fix.

"I'm getting a chai latte, you want one?" Hannah asked as they stepped into the lobby.

Sal followed her gesture to see a series of pop-up vendors littered around the sides. There were breakfast options, lunches, coffees, pastries…everything. They still had time, so Sal wandered over with Hannah, and Kane wasn't too far behind.

When the prices came into view, Hannah stopped abruptly with a grimace. She glanced around and pointed toward a large queue of students huddled around a few metal dispensers. "The free coffee is over there."

Sal carried on walking to the vendor, unfazed. "An Americano, chai latte…and Kane? What do you want?" He turned around to look at the two of them. "It's my treat for holding the elevator for me."

Kane shook his head.

"If you don't tell me, I'll get you a chai latte, and it sounds horrible."

Kane bit his lip before finally conceding. "Flat white, please."

Hannah stared at Sal as though he had two heads. "There's free coffee over there."

The vendor smiled as he took the order. "That'll be six Q-Credit in total. Please use your dorm card to complete the purchase."

Sal tapped his card against a payment device on the countertop and stood to one side to wait for their order.

Hannah almost exploded in exasperation as she moved closer to Sal to speak in a hushed whisper. "You don't have to play it cool, you know? Six Q-Credits is a lot."

Sal raised an eyebrow and wondered whether he had underestimated the value of the academy currency. He raised the drink to his lips and pondered how different a premium coffee could really be.

With just a single sip, the fatigue throughout his body completely disappeared. Sal stared at the cup in shock and heard both Hannah and Kane curse audibly as they came to the same realization.

It was Kane, though, who finally said what everyone was thinking. "I think my coffee just healed me?"

CHAPTER 7:
COLORFUL COHORTS

BY THE TIME SAL HAD GOTTEN HALFWAY THROUGH HIS COFFEE, HE WAS ALREADY at the amphitheater, with time to spare. Students were still arriving and picking their seats. More than a few clusters of people had already formed, and it looked from their back-and-forth that they were already very familiar with one another. Not that he was bitter, but it was something Sal had never really experienced growing up.

A part of him was curious what it would be like to have a large group of friends, but another part of him rationalized that considering he made it this far with few close contacts, he could probably keep going with that approach. His former friendships didn't deteriorate because of his personality; it was always because of his power. Even when he tried to hide it, people would look down on him or pity him, and when he used it, they'd hate or resent him. Being able to reproduce anyone's ability in its ultimate form didn't really earn him too many friends. It was just easier to act like an Appraiser and keep a low profile. The only people in Sal's life who treated him well were his family and their close friends. Sal wondered whether Villa and Neuro would have treated him the same way if they knew the full extent of his abilities.

"I don't think I've ever felt this alert. It's insane!" Hannah exclaimed abruptly from the seat beside him, causing Sal to jump ever so slightly. She laughed before apologizing to him earnestly. "I'm sorry. I didn't mean to startle you. It's just, I feel ready for anything! That coffee was amazing." She looked past Sal to where Kane sat quietly, as though urging him to share his own experiences, but Kane kept his attention on the leaderboard. "You said your name was Sal, right?"

Sal glanced up at the leaderboard with a grim smile, waiting for the other shoe to drop. He wondered whether they'd turn their backs on him like the others had in the elevator, or if they'd try to cling to him because of his higher status. He didn't like the part of himself that naturally assumed the worst-case scenario, but he also didn't like that his instincts were usually correct.

Kane nearly choked on his coffee when he found Sal on the board. "You're in the top twenty! Why didn't you say so?"

Shrugging, Sal decided not to answer. He didn't want to make excuses or try to win them over. If they felt uncomfortable sitting with him because of a number he was given a day ago, that was a pretty clear indicator of their personalities.

Hannah came to his rescue. "You heard him. He wanted to get to know his neighbors, not see each other as numbers. Thank you for the coffee, Mr. Argento." Her voice had a playful tone as she pretended to sound dignified.

Kane stared at them for a few more moments, then back to his own dismal place on the leaderboard. If he had pride, it certainly wasn't getting in the way of his ambition. "Any advice for how I can move up the board? You must know what you're doing if you're that high."

Hannah turned in her seat and made it clear that she wanted to know the answer too, but Sal didn't have any sage advice for them. Instead, he condensed a lot of the information he heard from the night before and rehashed it for them.

"Don't be stupid. Take risks and challenge yourself. That should probably work well in your favor. As long as they know you're trying, and you're playing by the rules, you'll likely move up the board."

Kane and Hannah nodded and smiled.

Welcome to Day One.

This will be an introductory course to Quest Academy.

We'll be calling out names and assigning them to different groups. This will be your cohort for the entire semester. Each cohort will be on a different module rotation to ensure that our lecturers have manageable group sizes. As some of you may already be aware, your schedule only contains mandatory courses. It is up to you to enlist in optional courses that will help you reach your goals. Some of those optional modules are already available for enrollment, but as you've heard, spaces will be limited.

As Quest spoke to the gathered students, the leaderboard above changed to show the optional courses that were available for selection. They appeared beside the mandatory core subjects and had a thicker font to indicate their importance. As much as Sal wanted to pay attention to all the students being sorted into different cohorts, his focus turned to the different classes he'd be able to select. If his theory was correct, his current wealth put him at a competitive advantage against most of the students. Although that sounded great in theory, Sal had no idea what he wanted to do, or whether he wanted to specialize. His main goal was graduating and making his parents proud, and hopefully being able to use his gifts for good.

Module Selection Categories:
Skill - Foundation (Mandatory)
Field - Foundation (370/500 seats remaining)
Combat - Foundation (Mandatory)
Survival - Foundation (Mandatory)
Crafting - Practice (43/200 seats remaining)
Analysis - Foundation (181/200 seats remaining)
Administration - Foundation (98/100 seats remaining)

Combat, Survival, and Skill modules are an absolute necessity for new students.

You'll learn the basics of how to scavenge in a Red Zone, defending yourself against demons and treating wounds. You'll learn how to hunt and how to evade demons.

Most importantly, you'll also learn how to harness and best utilize your abilities. These modules are not exhaustive and are instead designed as a foundational introduction to each category. By completing the module, you'll become eligible to take the next grade.

Completing more modules now is an investment in your later years at the academy. We will have eligibility criteria for certain events, such as Field Raids or Boss Battles. If you want to be a part of those teams, you'll need to have the qualifications.

Additionally, there are modules that cover Crafting, Administration, and Analysis. Each of these modules are picked from specialist tracks that will allow students to take on contract work to earn Q-Credits and recognition.

There will be more specialist modules introduced in the coming weeks, but these are the ones on offer now. If you cannot afford to reserve a seat on your chosen module, you will have another chance to enroll at some point in the future.

We typically recommend that students complete the introductory classes provided, as well as three core modules and one additional elective. The choice of what you undertake is completely up to you.

Introductory Courses:
Introduction to Quest Academy (You're Here)
Introduction to (Dungeons, Towers, Breaks, Portals)
Introduction to (Classes, Roles, Grading, Evolution)
Introduction to (R&D, Battle Equipment, Crafting)
Introduction to (Guilds, Factions, Societies, Sects)
Introduction to (Survival, Encounters, Conquest)
Introduction to (Trade, Bounties, Wagers, Commission)

Once you have completed the introductory courses, you will be eligible to select from a list of Advanced courses.

These will deal with specialist topics and successful completion will greatly enhance your overall module grade. There will be eligibility criteria as well as a considerable fee, but these courses are essential for those wishing to become specialists and enroll in the Savior class.

Planned Courses:
Skill Foundation (Discovery)
Skill Growth (Develop)
Skill Mastery (Advanced Techniques)
Heroism as a Business (Mercenary, Guild, Support)
Combat (General, Advanced, Specialist)
R&D (Appraisal, Repair, Creation, Upgrade, Blueprint)
Survival (Exploration, Foraging, First Aid, Signals)
Field Practice (Beginner, Intermediate, Advanced)
Field Encounter (Scout, Hunt, Secure, Defend)
Field Conquest (Reclamation, Subjugation, Boss Fight)

This afternoon will be dedicated to giving you all a tour of the campus and introducing you to the different facilities we have on offer.

You will be able to enroll at any Administrative terminal, or you can wait until you've seen what they have to offer before committing to their module. In your assigned groups, you'll visit the Analysis department to register your existing skills and receive your Q-Card. It will act as a single source of truth for your time at the academy, containing a rundown of your progress through different modules, your level of skill, and a few other details that will be relevant in the future.

Research & Development will have special trackers available for purchase, and Administration will have your interface tablets containing all relevant course material.

Sal could barely conceal his shock, so much so that Hannah asked him if everything was okay. He only then realized that it probably wasn't common knowledge to the other students, but the trackers they were selling from the R&D department were likely the same trackers that were purpose-built for the lead scout guild, Source. Sal didn't want to miss any information, so he gave Hannah a quick rundown of what they were.

"My family runs an auction house, and those trackers were pitched to the guilds as an alternative method of Appraisal. They can do a lot of the basics, but also work on low-level skills, weak demon analysis, targeting, and all sorts of data. They're insanely difficult to produce and they're just selling them to students?" Sal shook his head as he turned back to look at the headmaster. There was no way they were actually affordable.

We're planning some team-building and group activities for lunch in the afternoon, which will be followed by a visit to our workshop.

For top-ranked students who have already received their Q-Credits, there will be a few items up for sale by our second and third-years. Be sure to check them out as those same students have gone through a lot of what you'll experience. They might have some equipment or gear that will make your life easier.

For those of you who know what you want, and you have the Q-Credit, you can commission someone in the workshop to make your product. For those with no Q-Credit, don't despair…there are a number of students who will work for raw materials instead.

Lastly, you will meet your lecturers at the end of the day, and it will be an opportunity for you to learn more about the different courses and modules available. Seats will likely fill fast, so please don't delay in your decision-making.

Now, how are we coming along with the sorting?

Quest looked up at the leaderboard and clicked his fingers. The information about the modules melted away and was replaced with ten rows of numbers. It wasn't in descending order, but instead went from left to right, with an inverse for the second line, but then returning to normal from the third onward.

Was it their way of trying to even out the power level of the top twenty? Sal felt he should have been in the Black team, but he was in Silver, because of that inverse.

To best determine progression, we thought it was unfair for each of you to be competing constantly as a group of a thousand, so we developed a new system.

Remember your color. That will be your family for the first semester.

There are one hundred students in each color family, and we've tried to distribute the power levels as fairly as possible.

For the vast majority of you, your peers are either ten places above or below you. We realized that for team-based activities, following this pattern would give an unfair advantage to certain teams based on the top twenty students in the rankings.

For that reason, instead of Rank #1 being with Rank #11, we've reversed the order for the second line to balance out the power level. Rank #1 is now followed by Rank #20. Which means Rank #2 is followed by Rank #19.

With this in mind, we believe that any of the color families should be able to compete with each other fairly.

Gold	Silver	Bronze	Red	Orange
Rank #1	Rank #2	Rank #3	Rank #4	Rank #5
Rank #20	Rank #19	Rank #18	Rank #17	Rank #16
Rank #30	Rank #29	Rank #28	Rank #27	Rank #26
Yellow	**Green**	**Blue**	**Black**	**Purple**
Rank #6	Rank #7	Rank #8	Rank #9	Rank #10
Rank #15	Rank #14	Rank #13	Rank #12	Rank #11
Rank #25	Rank #24	Rank #23	Rank #22	Rank #21

Our intent was to create a competitive landscape. You will each try to reach the top of your respective family, with special rewards and incentives in place for those of you who reach the top ranks. There will also be relegation tournaments for the bottom-ranked students, giving them an opportunity to show their capability and jump up the list.

By the end of the first semester, if you're in the bottom quarter of your class, you'll be invited to my office to determine whether Quest Academy is the right fit for you.

Your ranking will be updated every month.

Our introductory semester lasts half a year, so you will have five opportunities from this moment to show us that you belong here.

Thank you for your time. I'll now hand it over to our staff members who will be starting your tours. You'll see that each of them has a particular color uniform, matching your family.

Best of luck. I'll be popping into your classes from time to time to check on your progress, so do your best.

Sal blinked, trying to comprehend what was happening, but it was Kane who put things into perspective.

"Did you just become Rank #2 in your group?" Not knowing how to respond, Sal turned to the smiling Kane, who shrugged nonchalantly. "Have to say though, Orange #86th sounds so much better than my last one. Better get going—thanks for the coffee. If I don't get kicked out, I'll make it up to you sometime." With that said, Kane got to his feet and made his way down the steps to where the groups were forming.

"You too?" Sal asked as Hannah got to her feet.

She turned and gestured toward a group forming to the left of the stage. "Looks like I have to go that way. You said you're Room 6, yeah? If we've got time later, let's hang out. We'll drag Kane along too."

Before Sal could say a word, she was gone. He followed her movements and saw that she was in the Purple family, but he had no idea what rank she was. He wondered what their abilities were and whether it would be rude to ask them about it later. Getting to his feet, he made his way toward the Silver group.

At least the color was going to be easy to remember.

CHAPTER 8:
WHITE EYES

WALKING IN A GROUP OF A HUNDRED PEOPLE, ALL MOVING IN THE SAME DIRECTION, towards a neighboring skyscraper, and trying to listen to one person…was an absolute nightmare. The chattering of awkward introductions and people shouting across one another to catch the attention of those they recognized made the entire experience that much more tiresome. Sal lost count of the number of people who had pushed past him to get to their friends. He didn't recognize a single person from the night before and wondered whether he was going to end up being a social pariah.

He glanced over the different faces as he tried to read their expressions. Some of them looked nervous, while others looked completely jaded or checked out. *Were they from the lower ranks and didn't feel too good about their place?* Since the sequence of rank for the Silver family followed his rank of #19, it meant that there was someone in their list at Rank #999. Sal couldn't imagine what they were feeling, but at least they were now Rank #100 in the Silver group. *Maybe that would feel better?*

"Are you fucking kidding me?"

A familiar voice sounded from somewhere behind Sal. He didn't even need to turn around because he had only heard that same annoying tone the night before. The sound of people being shoved out of the way was Sal's indicator that his would-be attacker from the night before was closing in on his position.

Sal couldn't believe that in a group of a hundred people, this guy still didn't have the tact to read the situation. *Was he really going to pick a fight here, in the middle of everything, in front of a staff member?* Sal balled his fists and activated his eyes, when the guy stormed straight past him and onto his real target…his friend from the bathroom.

"What the hell, man? You ratted us out?"

It wasn't so much a question as a statement as he shoved his accomplice without warning. More than a few people in the group turned to look out of curiosity, but nobody made any effort to step in and stop it. Sal didn't hang around to see what the outcome was. He didn't want anything to do with those guys, and if he appeared in front of them, there was a high chance of something kicking off. A small knot tightened in his stomach. He was off to a shitty start with this group. That said, they only accounted for two percent of the group. There were bound to be some good ones in here too.

Years of working in the auction house and talking to customers had made Sal competent at communicating and keeping conversations going. His icebreakers were good, but that confidence stemmed from familiarity and confidence in his ability to Appraise literally anything a customer put in front of him. Being surrounded by kids his own age, with their own special abilities…he was way out of his depth.

The staff member leading the group called everyone to an abrupt halt and waded through the crowd to a commotion at the back. Sal turned to see that a fight had broken out between the two of them, and a voice burst out from behind him in alarm.

"He's going to fall over the edge! On the right side."

Sal whirled around to see who was speaking. A set of ethereal white eyes stared through him as though he wasn't there. *Was she blind?* His first thought was ridiculously unhelpful as a despairing wail ripped out of one of the students. Whipping his head back to see what happened, Sal gasped as the aggressive kid was knocked a full twenty feet into the air at a sharp angle. He couldn't even think in the split second it took for the guy to sail over the edge of the platform.

The staff member leaped in the air and grabbed the student's foot, stopping his momentum completely. He looked irritated rather than worried, and Sal realized that this small action was nothing to him. When he landed, he kept hold of the student's leg and held him aloft, upside down.

"Did you learn absolutely nothing from last night?"

Sal did a double take. *It wasn't the same person from the night before, so how did he know about the incident? Was there something else the guy did, or did all the staff talk to one another about what happened?*

"I'll repeat myself for the people in the back. I doubt you were able to hear me over this racket." He still held the student upside down as he spoke. "Fighting outside of designated combat zones is strictly forbidden. Even then, you need the explicit consent of your opponent. It should go without saying that we don't fight people on a floating platform, eighty floors high. As I was telling the rest of the group, the use of powers is perfectly acceptable. You're here to learn how to refine them. What is not acceptable is using those powers against others. We'll be registering your skills today, and you'll be informed if yours is allowed to be used on a day-to-day basis."

He finally let go of the student's leg, who crumpled to the ground with an agonized groan. "Spoiler alert." The staff member stared at the student who launched the bully into the air. "Yours will definitely not be allowed."

Sal's breathing returned to normal, and his heart stopped racing. He turned back to look at the girl with the ethereal white eyes, only to find blue eyes looking back at him.

"Yes?" she asked, and Sal couldn't think of a single word to say.

"Oh, eh…sorry."

He turned back to the crowd and cursed himself for just standing there like an idiot. Maybe it was an olive branch or genuine curiosity, but the girl tapped him on the shoulder to get his attention. Sal turned back, expecting her to grill him for staring, but she was smiling.

"I know it's super rude to ask, but you've an eye-related ability too, don't you? Can I ask what it is?"

Here it was. The moment Sal always felt conflicted about. He could tell her the truth, or he could lie and tell her what he usually told people. A part of him screamed that he should just lie.

Another part of him warned him that this girl literally predicted future events with her eyes. Lastly, his brain kicked in to remind him that they were on their way to get their skills registered.

There would be no hiding from that, and it would be on his record when they found out. Maybe it was because he took so long in answering, or maybe it was from her own guarded nature, but the girl raised her hands apologetically and leaned back slightly.

"Sorry, it was rude to ask."

Sal smiled back as he resigned himself to the backlash that would undoubtedly follow. "Skill Steal. My eyes are silver because I took my father's Appraise skill when I was a kid. It helps me navigate my own power. I can re-create any ability my eyes can see."

He took a breath at the look of awe on her face. Normally he stopped the explanation there, but something in him decided to tell her the full extent of his ability. Maybe it was the desire to be honest, or maybe he was looking for the validation that he was right about people. Sal had yet to meet a single person who didn't resent him after seeing his power.

"I could look at your ability right now, see how your threads of power are woven…re-create it, but without any of the limitations. But I've no idea how to control the power, which is a huge limitation. And if I try to take multiple skills or hold a powerful one for too long, I end up unconscious for a few days." Sal explained the downsides in the hopes that she wouldn't think it was the perfect ability.

She didn't even blink.

He primed himself for the typical demand for him to prove it, but she surprised him with a different question.

"Can I use my power on you? It's like a Foresight ability, that gives me glimpses of potential futures. I've gotten to the point that I can harness it and narrow my sight to certain people, but like you said, it's a bitch to control. It's exhausting for the first part, and it always feels like it's seconds away from slipping through your fingers." Her smile was disarming as she shook her head guiltily. "I was going to be one of those people I absolutely hate and be like, prove it."

Sal was completely dumbfounded and he didn't even know her name. He offered his hand. "Salvatore Argento, but my friends call me Sal."

She took his hand and shook it with a grin. "Divinity. Before you ask, my mother had a series of visions of the future when she was pregnant with me. It was between Divinity and Destiny, so I think I got lucky."

Sal's shoulders dropped as he relaxed into the conversation. "Sure, you can use your ability…but I want to know what you see." Just as a precaution, he turned around to see whether the staff member was still talking to the crowd, and Divinity caught on to his apprehension.

"Actually, let me check." Before Sal could inquire what she was talking about, her eyes had turned white. A second or so later, a surprised smile appeared on her face. "Looks like you've got good instincts. That guy catches me using my power on you, and he gets even more annoyed."

She laughed and looked past Sal. The staff member was just a few steps away. "He would have told us that he expected this sort of stuff from the bottom-ranked people, but not of the Rank #2 and Rank #19."

Sal's eyes widened slightly. *Divinity was the second-most powerful person in the rankings?*

As if to confirm her words, the staff member gave them a glance as he passed. "I hope you two will be good role models for the rest of the Silver group."

Maybe it was just a passing comment, but Sal nodded. In the space of twenty four hours, he had been acknowledged by a series of strong people and even his cynical brain had to accept that maybe they could see something in him. The commotion settled down after a few moments and the tour resumed. There were a few stifled laughs emanating around the back of the group, likely at the expense of the now-humbled bully and his target. The front of the group was much calmer, throwing occasional looks of disdain behind them as they spoke. Sal couldn't help but wonder whether their group would ever become a cohesive unit, or if the cliques would win out.

"If I explain how my ability works, and how I control it…would that help? I mean, if you copied it?"

Divinity's voice sounded hopeful as she continued to walk beside him. She was still looking straight forward but his power was clearly on her mind. "But if you're able to use the power without any limitations, my method of control probably wouldn't be effective, would it?" She answered her own question with a frown, but Sal was already hooked.

"Yes! That's exactly it! It's like someone telling you how they fill a cup full of water at a faucet and how their method works really well for them and when they turn off the faucet. My power is more like…standing under a waterfall and holding that cup. It doesn't always translate, but knowing there's going to be water is still a big help."

Divinity's smile grew wider. "We could always use the trial-and-error method? I can look a few moments into your future as you use the power and give you advice on what your future self says? I've always thought it would be a cool training method, and it helps me calibrate to looking up an individual's future."

Sal was stunned by the thought, but more surprised by Divinity's friendly and open attitude. Why was she so accepting and friendly toward him?

As her eyes caught his, her smile faltered. "Sorry, I was getting ahead of myself there. I didn't mean to spook you. This is my first time meeting someone with a cool eye power, and I'm gushing a bit, sorry."

Sal shook his head and raised his hands. "No, not at all. I'm just really…not used to this reaction. Usually, people don't believe me. Then I use the power…and they resent me, because they see me use their personal power at its highest form. Likely better than they'll ever achieve themselves. It's typically devastating to them, and a part of me really doesn't want to show you."

Sal's expression became bitter as he spoke, but he pushed that aside and gave Divinity a gentle smile. "It's really nice to talk about powers like this."

Divinity's smile reappeared. "Trust me, I understand completely. When you can tell the future, people treat you like a horoscope. I can only see certain outcomes, and if things don't go the way people want…who do you think they blame? It's super hard to know if people actually want to get to know me, or if they want their own personal Magic 8 Ball that will tell them what they want to hear." She shook her head and gestured at the students around them.

"I don't deserve Rank #2. There are countless people who are more capable, but I was able to foresee the competition and went to the dorms early. I could see who to talk to at the party last night, and tailored my approach to what impressed them the most. What do you think will happen when we get to the Combat test later today? I'm sure as shit not going to be much of a Rank #2, that's for sure."

"Wait." Sal stopped abruptly. "What Combat test?"

CHAPTER 9:
PURPLE PUNCH

SAL AND DIVINITY CONTINUED TO SPEAK THROUGHOUT THE TOUR. SHE TOLD HIM that there was a Combat test later in the day, and the knot in Sal's stomach tightened. It wasn't an area he was confident with, and despite the wondrous effects of the coffee, he didn't think his muscles would be fit to take the speedster's ability again. It kept playing on his mind, and judging from Divinity's expression, she noticed that he was feeling conflicted. They both did their best to talk around the topic, rather than worry openly in front of each other.

"A scholarship? How did you manage that?" Sal asked as he was drawn back into the conversation.

Divinity pointed at her eyes, as if it were a default answer. "Predicting a demonic outbreak a few days ahead of schedule was enough to get them to notice me. When they saw that our…means weren't particularly high, they stepped in to help. There are a couple of caveats, though. They've picked a few modules for me that I need to attend, like Analysis, Field, and Survival." Divinity listed off the three with her fingers. "They said that my visions would go from useful to invaluable when I know what I'm seeing."

Sal exhaled as he shook his head. "That's incredible. You're already pretty much a Hero, but they're going to make you an even better one. I've got no idea how I'm going to be able to help people. Do I become a copy-cat of the strongest person here? Is there an ultimate power that would save the world that only I can use? Would my fragile willpower and body be able to withstand it?" Sal chuckled as he listed off his fears.

"You even have direction in which classes to take. I don't know what to pick, and the number of available seats is going down already." He gestured at the screen that showed the available modules.

Before Divinity could offer him any sort of reassurance, their attention was pulled by the staff member at the front of the pack.

"The Gold group has just finished breakfast, so we'll be entering the canteen now. Please be advised that although we offer a complimentary buffet, there are premium options available to those of you who can afford them." With that said, he turned and led the way into the dining area.

Divinity practically snorted as she turned to Sal. "Have you seen the prices of those premium options? It has to be a trick to siphon off Q-Credits from the gullible rankers."

Sal's expression brightened as he realized he knew something that Divinity didn't. "I bought a premium coffee earlier today, and they were something like two credits each. It completely restored my fatigue. I was like a corpse this morning because I used a physical skill yesterday, but now…I feel completely fine."

Divinity's expression went from disbelief to curiosity as she separated from the crowd going toward the buffet and veered off toward the premium options.

Sal followed her and was surprised to see her eyes turn white as she walked. He didn't want to interrupt her, but he also felt the need to warn her to be careful. Her eyes widened as she turned to each vendor. *Was she asking each of the vendors what their options were?* Before he knew it, her blue eyes were back, and wide open in shock.

"Come with me."

Sal followed her out of curiosity. They passed a coffee place, a pastry stall, a grill, and a few others…only to arrive at a smoothie bar. Sal was about to protest that he wasn't the biggest fan of them, but Divinity raised a hand.

"Trust me."

Those two words put Sal completely at ease, and his curiosity grew even stronger. He took his card out of his pocket to pay, but Divinity waved him away.

"My treat. You can get me one next time."

Sal didn't protest and actually warmed on the inside, knowing that they'd be meeting again in the future. It was a different experience from Hannah and Kane. An ingrained cynicism had made him take baby steps with those two, but Divinity was different. She was a higher rank than him and knew about his powers. Sal tried to grasp at the doubts in his head, looking for a reason to be wary of her…but his mind came up blank. He resigned himself to going with the flow and seeing what happened.

Divinity handed him a large container of purple liquid with a straw. Sal refused to believe it was the normal serving amount but accepted it gratefully. Before he took a drink, he looked her squarely in the eyes. "Can you glance into the future and see if this ends up giving me the shits?"

The laugh that exploded out of Divinity was enough to make heads turn. Sal panicked and tried to shush her, but it was no use. All solidarity was gone as he jokingly abandoned her. He found a seat far away from her and made a show of covering his face, as though he didn't know her. Divinity wiped a tear from her eye as she joined him.

Her blue eyes practically sparkled as she looked at him. "Can I try my power on you now? Before you take a drink."

Sal was about to lift it to his lips when he paused. "Go for it." He placed the container back on the table and folded his arms in anticipation. It was his first time seeing her eyes go through the change, and he had to admit that it looked awesome. The irises became an icy blue, which grew in intensity before it blossomed out and flooded the rest of the eyeball. When they were fully white, it looked as if she saw right through him. Sal thought of activating his own eyes to see how her power presented itself but stopped himself. She had gone to the effort of asking his permission, so he'd give her the same courtesy.

"Okay, now take a drink."

Divinity's face didn't reveal a single tell. Sal had been trained by his father in reading facial expressions, which was useful in all parts of life…but was useless to him now. Divinity waited patiently as Sal took a long drink of the purple liquid. He was so caught up in his head that he hadn't anticipated the suddenly cold sensation hitting his mouth. He let out an almost panicked noise, which elicited a chuckle out of Divinity. The taste was a blend of black currant and apple, and he wasn't sure how he felt about it.

The coldness of the drink was refreshing, but it didn't pack as much of a punch as the coffee did. Sal frowned as he tried to pick up on any sort of feeling from it…but there was nothing. Divinity's voice broke him out of his reverie.

"Okay, that should be enough."

He glanced up to see she was still using her powers, and he glanced around while he waited. The canteen was large enough to fit a few hundred people, which allowed space for the different groups to sit together. A few people sat by themselves, while the largest groups didn't number more than five or six people. Sal turned back to Divinity and unconsciously checked her out, which lasted less than a second and caused him to sigh. Quest Academy clearly designed uniforms to hide anything remotely interesting.

"And we're back," Divinity exclaimed with a laugh as she raised her own drink excitedly. It was the exact same color as Sal's, and he suddenly felt like a test subject.

"So, what did you see?"

There were a few moments of silence as she took a drink, and she looked at him innocently before answering. "You definitely get the shits."

Sal chuckled as he felt the last of his reservations about Divinity evaporate. She was on the same wavelength as him, had a great sense of humor and he found himself enjoying her company quite a bit. Rather than asking her for her findings, Sal just sat patiently and waited for her to continue.

"None of the effects are listed, so they're trying to enforce a trial-and-error approach, I think," Divinity said as she gestured at the different vendors. "The coffee did exactly what you told me. The effects will run out after about three hours, though, so be prepared for your muscle fatigue to return."

Sal nodded appreciatively as Divinity continued.

"Some of the drinks and meals had no immediate effect with taste alone, so I looked a bit further throughout the day to see if there was any change." She smiled widely as she turned to the smoothie bar. "And this one here was the most dramatic shift in results. I saw it happen for me already, but I wanted to see if it would work for you."

Sal waited for her to finish the sentence, but she just smiled and took another long drink, leaving him in a state of pained anticipation.

Rather than begging, Sal played the waiting game.

Divinity broke almost instantly, as if she were excited to tell him. "There's very little we can do to prepare for the Combat assignment, because there are some absolute monsters in our cohort. Some of the foods from the grill vendor help you, but your best results come from one of those energy drinks over there." Divinity pointed at one of the vendors in the middle.

Sal questioned where she was going with this, because that sounded like the best option for him. Her smile didn't disappear, so Sal wondered if the purple drink was going to be even better.

"But before that is the Skill Registration," she said. "I think they've put us in this room with all the vendors for a reason, and that's why this drink is so damn expensive." Divinity gestured at their cups. "Drinks and food don't go above five Q-Credits. But these were twenty each."

Her voice was energized, and Sal could only stare at her, dumbfounded.

"It boosts our aptitude for a short time." When Sal didn't react, Divinity tried explaining it in a different way. "Without the drink, you went into the registration, and it gave you Appraisal, Skill Steal, and Mend. Okay?"

Sal nodded slowly, wondering why his mother's skill was in there too, but Divinity continued.

"With the drink, you got All Sight, Skill Master, Restore, and Quick Step. You essentially get a whole new power registered because of that drink, and an upgrade. You'll tell me that it feels different, and that it's not slipping away like the other powers. I don't know how it's possible, but this drink somehow reacts to the Skill Registration and gives you that Quick Step ability."

Sal sat in absolute disbelief. There was no way it was a lie. He didn't even know the name of the speedster ability he took, but in his future, it was down as Quick Step. He stared at the drink in front of him and shook his head. An idea popped into his head, but he hesitated.

Divinity caught the look and grinned. "You want to change the future and check, don't you?"

Sal's eyebrows shot up. She saw straight through him.

She laughed. "In the future, you immediately regret that you registered a physical-based ability. You'll tell me that you wish you had tried something more compatible, that didn't leave you in agony after use."

"I didn't know that there were different power levels for abilities. Like, Appraisal is what I thought I had from my father, but it's apparently All Sight? And Mend is a weaker variant of Restoration? I used that speed ability yesterday, but I used a weak Restoration skill this morning to clean my uniform."

Sal sighed as he leaned back in his chair. "What does the Skill Registration even do? Isn't it just a few words on our Q-Card to say we can do something?"

Divinity shook her head. "I'm pretty sure it's a minor imprint. A lot of people talk about feeling more at ease with their powers after the registration, so I don't think it's a complete process to turn your ability inherent, but enough to make you comfortable with it. So maybe, it'll give you some control over a new skill?"

Sal was confused, but he was grateful for everything Divinity was telling him. He probably would have been happy to have another skill, but he was very much the type of person who would feel regret over not making the optimal choice. "How far into my future are you able to see?"

Divinity placed her elbow on the table and rested her chin on her palm. Her face was a picture of curiosity. "Days, weeks, months…depending on where I need to look. It's easier if I know what I'm looking for."

"Let's say here. Every week at this break time?" Sal suggested and paused. Divinity nodded, which was Sal's sign to continue. "Every time we meet, I'll tell you the ability of a person that I think is the best. That I wish I had myself…would that work?"

He had no idea whether he was being an idiot, which made the stare Divinity gave him even more unnerving. He didn't know the limits of her power, so he might have been asking for something unrealistic or unfairly demanding. Just when he was about to apologize, she leaned forward and spoke in a serious tone. "We can do that, but it's going to cost you."

Sal leaned forward in his seat too and took another drink. He could practically hear his father's voice in his head, repeating the absolute rule of any negotiation: *Never accept the first offer.*

Divinity extended her hand. "If you want this help and we're going to be meeting every week, you're going to have to be my friend." Her smile widened as she made her offer. "That means we don't worry about rank, and we help each other going forward. Deal?"

Laughing, Sal quietly apologized to his father as he immediately accepted. "Deal."

Divinity glanced over at the other students, who were starting to clear away their plates. "Guess we don't have much time left…Let's see."

Sal waited apprehensively as he finished the rest of his drink. Divinity was going to take a bit of time, and he didn't want to sit there just staring at her, so he decided to make himself useful. He got up from the table and went over to the vendor with his empty container in hand.

"Excuse me, but what was the name of this drink?"

Rather than answering immediately, the vendor scratched their chin. "It's called Purple Punch on the menu…"

Sal caught his drift and took a step closer, raising his payment card in expectation.

The vendor laughed and waved the card away. "Good instincts, but I'm not that miserable. I'll tell you this one for free. It may be called Purple Punch on the menu, but we call it Sleeping Tiger."

Sal thanked the vendor and started to walk back to their table.

"Good luck in your Skill Registration," the vendor called out with a knowing smile.

CHAPTER 10:
PERFECT SKILL

DIVINITY LOOKED ABSOLUTELY EXHAUSTED, AND SAL FELT TERRIBLE FOR asking her to use her power so much. He was tempted to buy her a coffee before they left the canteen, but she refused in fear of negating the effects of the Sleeping Tiger. She was still smiling, albeit tiredly, and was already a few months into the future, with a few promising answers, apparently.

Each time she took a small break on their journey, she filled him in. Sal was at the point where he wanted her to stop and would just settle for whatever the most recent answer was, but Divinity was having none of that. She wanted to find a skill that Sal was excited about, and apparently his demeanor in each vision was one of indifference rather than genuine anticipation.

The biggest struggle was going to be in finding someone he could interact with and acquire their power before the Skill Registration. A heavy exhalation from beside him told Sal that Divinity was back. They stood near a water dispenser in one of the corridors while the group of students meandered forward toward their next destination. It only took Divinity a few minutes to get a vision, so all that happened was that they fell behind a bit in the crowd.

"Okay, we've finally got an excited Salvatore," Divinity exclaimed with a relieved grin. "Only took us about three fucking months. You're a picky bastard."

Sal made a mental note that Divinity's irritation scaled with exhaustion. He gestured at the water, but Divinity shook her head.

"Let's catch up with the group first."

A few students at the back of the group hung back to allow Sal and Divinity to go ahead of them. Sal guessed they didn't like people walking behind them, so he didn't think much of it.

Divinity gave them a tentative look and gestured for Sal to move farther up the pack.

Most people let them through without so much as a glance, while others gave questioning looks. Eventually they were near the front, and Divinity finally relaxed. Her voice was heavy, but Sal realized after a moment that she was whispering intentionally.

"Those ones at the back just now, I'm pretty sure I saw them in a vision. I can't be sure if it'll happen or not, but I think they're going to bully people for Q-Credit. Strong people with low ranks are being blocked from progression because of the Q-Credit system…so people like us would be a perfect target in their eyes."

Sal was more than aware of the difference between Support classes and Offensive classes. He remembered as a child when his father had been strong-armed into certain deals and agreements just on the basis of his customer being stronger than him. That changed after he negotiated protection from the United Guilds Association, but Sal and his family remembered the time before that vividly.

Maybe that was one of the reasons he was so cynical? He didn't know or care. The idea of bullies targeting the weak was incredibly frustrating, and he wanted to hang back to see whether they tried it.

Divinity's hand caught his sleeve before he could move. "You need to be up here for the next part. Trust me."

Before Sal could respond, the staff member turned and clapped loudly. "Group Silver." The shout was unpleasant for those at the front but effective for those at the back. "We're going to be entering the workshop now. Please form an orderly line in groups of four. We're going to limit it to five groups at a time, and your arrangement is only for touring purposes. Don't try to find an optimal group; it'll only waste time. Be mindful of how long you spend on each area as it will limit the time of the people behind you."

His warnings fell mostly on deaf ears as students scrambled to find their friends. A few people moved from the front to the back to group up with people they liked. Divinity and Sal moved a little closer to the staff member, who noticed them immediately.

"You two, and you two. Form up and head in. Stick to the left and go clockwise. I'll hold the rest off for a few minutes so don't feel like you have to rush." With that, he winked, and they were off with their new group.

A stifled giggle from their left introduced Sal to a strikingly beautiful girl. He wasn't sure he had ever seen someone so enchanting, and he felt an incredible urge to make her happy.

"Could you knock it off, Victoria? He's with me." Divinity sighed, causing Victoria to jump in surprise.

"Oh, Divinity. Shit, yeah, sorry."

With a wave of her hand, Victoria deactivated the ability, releasing Sal from its power. His senses returned in full force, and he couldn't understand why he had just acted like that.

Divinity guided him to their first destination. "You've just met Rank #69, Victoria."

Sal turned and gave her a polite nod. There was a lingering sensation in his mind, but it was fading. She was a pretty girl, yes…but not intoxicatingly so.

Victoria gave Sal an apologetic smile. "Sorry about that. I was milking the staff guy for information, and I think you got caught in the crossfire." Beside Victoria was a male student with a simple smile on his face. Victoria took notice of Sal's glance and shook her head. "Yeah, don't worry about him. He's a plus one in case of emergency. Isn't that right, boo?"

The smiling student nodded gratefully, and Sal could have sworn he saw traces of drool around his mouth.

Sal shuddered and was once again incredibly grateful for Divinity's support. A pinch on his shoulder caused him to reflexively reach for it. He turned to see Divinity with a relieved expression.

"Okay, that's better. This whole plan goes to shit if you're under her charm ability, because…" Divinity's smile was wide as she pointed toward a woman standing between two sets of machinery, looking skeptical. "That person right there has the perfect skill for you."

Divinity didn't have time to explain, but Sal trusted her. They moved as a group to the first desk, where an aproned man with a bushy beard started to explain how commissions and work orders operated. Sal was going to ask him about getting his door repaired, but Divinity gave him a dig with her elbow.

"I'll stall us here, while you go on ahead and talk to her. I don't know what the skill is, but the future you is absolutely dreamy about it. Go on, hurry."

Sal nodded as he moved over to the second table that held the bored woman. She looked positively regal in comparison to the aproned man. Rather than the uniform he was accustomed to seeing the staff wear, she wore jeans and a flannel shirt with rolled-up sleeves over a tight black vest underneath. It was hard to guess her age, but Sal would have guessed that she was in her mid-twenties. She was leaning against the table like it was the only thing keeping her upright.

Sal had no idea how he was going to break the ice, but luckily, she did it for him. "Welcome to the workshop. If you stayed long enough at the first table, my colleague would have told you what we do here and how we operate. Are you interested in being a Support class, or enrolling in one of our courses?"

The boredom in her voice was so blatant that Sal almost laughed. She sounded so rehearsed that he doubted she'd hear his answer if it wasn't a stock reply. Before he could say anything, she slid a tablet in front of him. "Please register your interest by signing your name and then move on to the next stage of the tour. Thank you." Her eyes glanced over to the hordes of students waiting for their turn to get in, and Sal witnessed the last shreds of her soul dying on the spot.

"I was given this by a guild." Sal placed the Silver token on the table. Since he was in the workshop, he guessed that the Crafting department would recognize the token. Services for guilds typically fell into the Support category.

Her eyes flicked across the token and widened ever so slightly. She picked it up and lifted it into the air. "Forge! Look!"

Sal turned to see a more senior worker squinting at the raised token. If the bored woman was in her mid-twenties, then this man had about thirty years on her. His face finally broke into a grin as he pointed at Sal, as if to say, *This guy?* Sal had no idea whether he should be offended or if the smiles were mocking in some way.

Forge called over one of the younger workers and gestured for them to take over the woman's table. "What are you waiting for? Show him around."

Sal turned back to the woman, only to find her grinning at him. "What's your name, kid?"

He was not expecting the *kid* word to sting as much as it did. Swallowing his pride, Sal offered his hand to her. "Salvatore Argento, but my friends call me Sal."

Rather than shaking his hand, she placed the token back in his. "Hope you don't mind, but these things are precious." She wiggled her fingers at him, and Sal noticed she was wearing an interesting set of gloves.

Before he could stop himself, he slipped into the habit of just activating his ability. The gloves weren't artifacts but were constructed. His brain caught up with his eyes a moment later, and he started to apologize.

But she was watching him intently. "No, don't stop. What do you see?"

This was his chance. Rather than inspecting her gloves, Sal looked at her with his power. He couldn't tell what her power was, but he could see her threads. There were some knots, but much fewer than he was used to seeing.

The power distribution was controlled, which was really good to see. It meant that whatever ability she used, it had an output that she could control. The threads led to her eyes and fingers…Sal smiled; that wouldn't be invasive at all.

Overall, it didn't look like anything extraordinary, so Sal started to replicate the threads in his own body. He wasn't going to activate it or power it up, but would instead keep it for before the Skill Registration event. When he came to the point of adding the knots, Sal hesitated. The registration had apparently recognized the difference between power levels from Mend to Restore, which led Sal to believe that the strongest version of a skill would likely result in the best outcome.

With that in mind, he didn't add any of her knots to his replicated threads and instead created a perfect version of the weave. It had been years since he had done this, but he wasn't worried. If he was just holding the skill in place for a few moments, nothing bad would happen. Sal finished up his recon, and then focused on her gloves. He didn't want to resurface empty-handed.

"Whoa, that was fast," the woman exclaimed as Sal's eyes returned to normal. "I thought Appraisers took forever." She lowered her gloves and inspected them before glancing up at him. "So, what's the verdict? Are they good?"

Her expression was a little guarded this time, and for some reason, Sal felt he should be honest with her. "It's my first time seeing anything like this, to be honest. I'm more used to antique gauntlets or power gloves, but those are custom-made for Crafting. They were normal gloves at one point, made with infused cotton. Good for added resistance against electricity, but great for negating the conductive metals that were added. From a quality perspective, I'd put them at Uncommon grade, but for a craftsman who needs their precision buff, they'd be closer to a Rare. You'd easily get around $4,500.00 for it."

Sal couldn't pinpoint the moment he had slipped back into auction mode, but the shock on her face sobered him up. He didn't even have time to apologize before she raised a finger.

"What about now?"

Sal's eyes widened as he saw her power activate. The gloves on her hands glowed momentarily as they took on an entirely new form. Not just her hands, but her entire body began to pulsate with a surge of internal essence. Sal's eyes shot to her neck and saw that a crystal pendant was fueling the transformation. When the process was complete, Sal was absolutely speechless.

The gasps and cheers from the body of students reached his ears, and an amused smile appeared on the woman's face. Her jeans and overalls had transformed into a tight armored suit that fully covered her from the neck down. Each of her hands had turned into mechanical claws, with each finger equipped with a different precision tool.

To everyone else, it probably looked like a completely new set of equipment, but Sal's eyes didn't lie. He looked at her in complete shock. "How did you make the equipment evolve?"

Her laugh was musical as she deactivated her ability. She took off her gloves and threw them onto a nearby bench. Turning back to Sal, she finally offered her hand. "I'm the resident Crafting lecturer…"

Sal shook her hand, still struggling to understand what he had seen. It made absolutely no sense.

He could still hear the cheers from the students outside. She raised her free hand and gave them a wave.

"My fans call me Upgrade."

CHAPTER 11:
RESTORATION

Upgrade walked ahead of Sal as she gestured at all the different tables in the workshop. She had already told him that she'd give him the personal tour considering it was likely that he'd be spending a lot of his time with them in that workshop. As she walked ahead of him, Sal tried to keep his eyes on the back of her head, or look at the benches she gestured toward. It was increasingly hard to focus after seeing her in the tight armor. Sal finally understood the university's policy on not giving students form-fitting uniforms.

He had no idea that she was the Hero, Upgrade. She was one of the few Support-class Heroes who managed to get a name, and clearly it was well deserved. One of the biggest distractions on his mind was the weave of power he was holding onto. He had the flawless version of her Upgrade ability and not only that, he'd seen it in use. He needed to understand more about the necklace she was wearing…*Was it a conduit? A storage device for materials?* He couldn't figure it out at all.

Upgrade turned around, then laughed. "Hey, do I need to give you something to assess to get your attention?"

"Huh?" Sal's attention snapped back to her, wondering what he missed.

She put a hand on her hip and gave him a sympathetic look. "I'm going to guess you're not used to talking to girls?"

Her tone was almost condescending, and Sal felt the need to defend himself.

"That's not fair. You're not like normal girls."

Upgrade tilted her head and gave him a thoughtful look. "Oh, normal? So, what does that make me?"

In his internal struggle to find the right words, Sal gesturing vaguely up and down at Upgrade and blurted the first thing that came to mind. "You look…better."

Biting her lip, Upgrade brought her hand to her chest and looked away. She tried to stifle the impending laughter but failed. Sal ended up receiving the most sympathetic look she could muster.

"If this is what you're like with zero teasing…" She took a step forward and cupped her hand around Sal's chin. "Then what would you be like when I go all out?" Her face was suddenly close to his and a playful grin took shape. "Hmm?"

Sal staggered back and his heart raced. He bumped into a workbench and apologized to it as he turned. Any composure he had remaining evaporated into an air of awkwardness and embarrassment.

Upgrade's laughter was once again musical as she covered her mouth. Tears formed at the edges of her eyes, and she gracefully swept them away with her fingertips. Her face was a picture of disbelief as she regarded Sal. "Wow. I guessed a little innocent…but, wow."

A few other workers looked up from their tables, and Sal noticed that more than half of them were women.

Upgrade turned to them and provided context in a conspiratorial whisper. "Our newest Appraiser here is weak to flirtation. So don't use that against him, okay?"

Everyone in the room stared at him and his cheeks flushed red.

"Don't mind Upgrade. If you give her an inch, she'll take a mile..." A slender guy appeared with a friendly grin. He wiped what looked like green demon blood from his hands before offering one of them to Sal.

"You're an Appraiser, yeah?" When Sal shook his hand and nodded, the man fished out a small stone and held it aloft between two fingers. "Fancy giving this a go? If you do, I'll teach you the best way to make Upgrade lose interest in you."

Sal turned his head to where Upgrade was laughing with another woman while looking over in his direction.

"Deal," Sal muttered as he activated his eyes. "I'm Sal, by the way."

The stone was a core. They came in a lot of different shapes and sizes, but neither of those factors mattered when assessing its value. It was about how much magical essence was stored inside it, and how refined it was. Sal only knew the basics about essence, and would never claim to have any expertise regarding the refining process, but he knew values inside and out. The stone had a series of carvings that were obscured by the guy's fingers.

"May I?" Sal reached for the stone.

With no hesitation, the guy let him take it. "What do you see, Sal?" he inquired quietly while using his free hand to usher the other workers closer.

Taking a steadying breath, Sal rotated the stone in his fingers. His eyes were picking up details that he'd never have noticed by sight alone and cross-referenced them with troves of stored information in his brain.

"It's a core, at least Rare in quality but lacking in essence storage. Smooth detail shows me that it was refined by a novice who didn't know its value, which resulted in essence leak from these ridges here. That reduces the value of the core to about a fifth of what it should be. But then there's the attempt at making it self-replenishing. I say attempt, because instead of a self-replenishing rune, the etching is an absorption rune. The result is a useless item that can only absorb a person's attention, like an unwitting Appraiser, perhaps?"

Sal glanced up at the man. "So would you like to take it back, or would you like more details on how much you've fucked it up?"

Silence fell across the room and Sal turned to look at the assembled workers. He should have controlled his temper. These people were Heroes, staff and seniors at the university. Upgrade's face was absolutely priceless, though.

Sal gripped the core in his hand. He had everyone's attention now, so why not use it? If he was going to work with these people, he wanted their respect. Reluctantly, he relinquished Upgrade's power as he pulled up the familiar threading of his mother's ability. The only change that he made was the removal of his mother's knots. He was going to use the ultimate version of Restore, which was overkill. Was he being petty? *Maybe.* Did he care? *No.*

He turned back to the guy who had handed him the core. "Actually, let me fix it for you."

Sal threw all his power through the thread and focused on the item in his hand. The core glowed white as it pulled on the magic in his fingers. Each of the grooves reformed into its original state, but Sal kept the etchings intact, refining them with essence that he guided with his eyes.

Gritting his teeth, Sal checked his work with his Appraisal and made a final adjustment before releasing the power. The core was no longer small enough to hold between his fingers, and he cupped it in his hand. Maybe it was the exhaustion of using the Restoration ability at full power, but Sal was in no mood to keep a jovial tone to his voice.

"Rune etching and refining are supposed to add value to an item. This core would be classified as Rare in its original state, but with the addition of a correct self-replenishing rune and no leakages…it's closer to Epic grade."

Upgrade was over in a flash and took the item out of Sal's hands. With a single touch to her pendant, she transformed one hand into a precision claw and inspected the core with a variety of different tools. "Francis, I need eyes on this now. Gosia, check the leaks!"

Sal glared at her. *Did they not believe him? Had they brought him into the workshop to tease and humiliate him?* If his Appraisal skill wasn't so high, he likely would have been caught in a trance, with his attention being absorbed. *Would they have just laughed at him?*

He looked at Upgrade one last time, making sure that he had her skill memorized completely. The weave came to him much more fluidly as it was his second time preparing it. Everyone was engrossed with the newly restored core, and Sal had had enough of the workshop and its workers. He'd register the Upgrade skill and he wouldn't need to rely on any of them…he had his own personal workbench back in the dorm room.

He didn't know whether it was the exhaustion talking or his insecurity, but he had no desire to stay there and wait for them to critique his work. He steadied himself against a workbench for a moment then walked back to his cohort. He needed to find his group.

***

"It's actually a fucking Epic." Upgrade breathed heavily as she triple-checked the item. "Gosia, how are we looking?" With a single thumbs-up from the other side of the core, Upgrade got the confirmation she was looking for. "Really? No leaks? Amazing…What about you, Francis?" Upgrade turned and saw her rune expert staring at it in disbelief.

"It's…perfect."

Upgrade nearly danced on the spot as she canceled her ability. There was no way in hell she could afford this with her salary, but she had to find a way to have it. It far surpassed the core she wore around her neck. Her ability started to prompt her with blueprints of all the different ways the core could be utilized in her designs, but she pushed them away and tried to concentrate.

She couldn't believe she had witnessed a student—a *new* student—break through the Broken Core of Attention Deficit while Appraising its flaws perfectly. That alone was enough for a mic drop, but he fucking Restored it with pinpoint precision, *and* corrected the attempted runes? Upgrade thought back to the moment that his eyes glowed and his hands became instruments of light. It was the most incredible thing she had ever seen.

"Okay, I'll admit, this is completely your win. I'm still going to tease you for discounts from time to time." Upgrade turned around, but Sal was nowhere to be seen. She looked at the others, but they looked equally confused at his disappearance.

With a few tentative steps, Upgrade walked back the way they came. Maybe he had got lost somewhere. She scanned the rows of benches. When she got back to the main area, there was a huge group of students moving from table to table, asking stupid questions. When she finally caught sight of the workshop owner, she made her way over to him.

"Forge, have you seen that kid I was with? The one with the Silver token?"

Forge snorted. "That was two groups ago. These ones are in the Black cohort, and they'll be finishing up soon." He started to walk away.

Upgrade could barely focus. She knew that it had taken some time to verify the work, but did it really take that long?

"Oh, and I think you're losing your touch," Forge said. "That kid, with the silver eyes?"

Upgrade nodded slowly, wondering where he was going with this.

"Yeah, I asked him if he was signing up for the Crafting module you're teaching. Never seen a kid respond so fast in my life. Flat out refused. I pushed him on it…and he said that you lot weren't his type of people. Who knew a kid could be that fucking classist, to snub a Hero of all people?" Forge chuckled as he made his way across the workshop floor, stopping to answer questions for anyone who asked.

Upgrade gritted her teeth, recounting everything that had happened and thought about it from Sal's perspective. Cursing herself, she let out an aggravated yell and pinched the bridge of her nose.

"Whoa there. Kinda scaring the kids, Upgrade…You okay?" Forge walked back to her, and he looked concerned.

More than a few of the students looked over at her in confusion. Some had lingering stares, but it likely had little to do with her outburst. Forge urged her to walk with him.

"I fucked up, Forge. Really fucked up…He probably hates us."

Forge's expression was a clear indicator that he was going to tell her to calm down and that it probably wasn't that bad. Upgrade skipped that part and filled him in on the situation.

"Kid walks up to me, doesn't have his group. Cool, that's fine. I give him the spiel…usual drill. He shows me the token, and who is it fucking from? Villa! The Reavers have made a contract with this kid, so I'm sure as shit thinking that he's gonna be tough as nails to have got their attention. He's an Appraiser too, so I ask him to check out my gloves…see how good he is?"

Forge raised his arms and tried to back away slowly, but Upgrade moved with him.

"He's really fucking good, saw through the gloves immediately, so I revealed my Hero suit. Kid looked like he just fell in love, so I teased him a bit…He's going to be working with us, so might as well get a discount because he's crushing on me, right?"

"Upgrade, slow—"

"So the teasing is maybe a little one-sided…It was cute having an innocent kid fawning like that. I was about to stop when fucking Dickwad Five Thousand rocks up with that damn core."

"Marcus," Forge corrected quietly, but Upgrade was having none of it.

"Dickwad Marcus pulls out that stone after hearing that the kid is an Appraiser, wants to play a trick on him, and I go to stop it from happening. The guys slow me down because they want to see what happens…"

"You humiliated him."

The disappointment in Forge's tone really drove it home. No matter how much she tried to justify their actions to herself, they were the bad guys.

Forge patted her on the shoulder and gave her a reassuring smile. "I'll speak to Marcus. I can get him to apologize to the kid, and maybe he'll reconsider the class. But I don't think Marcus is the only one who owes him an apology."

Upgrade took a steadying breath as she gave Forge a meaningful look. "The core didn't dupe the kid. He Appraised it in seconds, and talked through everything that was wrong with it. That was enough for us to lose our shit…Absolute baller move, not going to lie. It was fucking awesome. I was about to hug the damn kid, but he goes one better. Turns out he has another skill—Restoration! His eyes start glowing and that broken core transformed into something completely new. No leaks, perfect etchings, stable core, and it works perfectly. It's over there right now, replenishing itself! We're Craft people—we were on that item from the moment he was done to just now."

Forge's frown deepened. "He can Restore, Appraise, and has silver eyes? I think you just alienated the heir to the Argento Auction."

Upgrade closed her eyes as she finally made the connection. He had told her his name, but she had been too preoccupied with that damn token.

Forge clapped his hands. "Let's work on a solution here. We can shortlist him and give him a place in the course for free? Throw in some materials, his own bench and maybe some mentoring from our top Hero?" Forge gestured at Upgrade, who nodded as she took off her flannel shirt and tied it around her waist. Forge looked at her apprehensively for a moment before guessing her intent. "You're going to look for him now, aren't you?"

Upgrade glanced at the doors at the other side of the room. "He should be at the Skill Registration about now. I'll be back in a bit."

CHAPTER 12:
REGISTRATION

"I'VE GOT A CONFESSION TO MAKE." DIVINITY'S VOICE WAS HEAVY AS SHE looked at Sal. "I'm incredibly relieved to know you're just as exhausted as me." Turning around and walking backward in front of Sal, she placed her hand over her heart. "It makes me warm and fuzzy on the inside to know that the top two students in the Silver cohort…are probably going to fall asleep on the mats during the Combat exercise."

Sal broke into a wry grin, and Divinity raised her hands in celebration. "I did it! We've cracked the grump." Her blue eyes sparkled as she danced in a circle.

Sal waved her away but kept smiling. He was incredibly grateful to have Divinity's support. After he had told her everything that had happened with Upgrade, he was content to brood for a while and overthink each part of the encounter. Divinity was having absolutely none of that, though, and took it upon herself to lighten the mood and bring him back to the light.

They were both nervous as they entered the Skill Registration area. Despite the towers being incredibly tall, they weren't the widest…which had resulted in the tour being across multiple floors. If there was a logic to their movements, none of the students had figured it out yet. Instead, it felt more like they were constantly going back on where they already visited.

Divinity had suggested that it might be a form of cardio exercise, but it was highly unlikely. That said, a few hours later, they were at their destination near the top of a tower. The views out the windows were stunning, and Sal could almost see the port on the far side of the city. Towering grids of light were visible in the distance, showing the safe territories that had been reclaimed to date. Guild towers stood imposingly high into the sky, offering reassurance to any that saw them.

The interior was really impressive too. Fantastical machines were littered across the room and made the place look more like a production facility than the workshop they had visited earlier.

"Whoa, look at that one." Divinity pointed at a giant tube filled with a clear liquid.

Sal's eyes informed him that it was some form of liquified essence. He had never heard of anything like that, and he was curious to know what it was doing in a Skill Registration area.

He turned his head and pointed at another one. "What about that one?"

When Divinity followed his gesture, her eyes went wide. "It looks like an electric chair."

Welcome again.

You're probably sick of my voice at this point, but this part of the induction is incredibly important, so make sure to pay attention. As we learn, develop, and grow, we like to remind ourselves where we came from. The last generation of skill refinement is all around you.

As you get closer to our assessment area, you'll see the evolution of our technological capabilities.

When the war first started, and the outbreaks began, we, as a country, put all our resources into offense and fighting the demons. Funding was thrown to anyone who could hit them hard.

And hit hard we did, but they kept coming and more portals appeared, followed by towers and then even dungeons. Our methods of hitting hard didn't solve the problem.

Quest's voice was automated this time and came from the speakers around them. It was like a guided tour, with different segments of audio playing when they reached a new area.

Sal had learned a lot of the history from his parents, who had grown up during the wars, but not the worst part of them. He had been sheltered from a lot of the harsh realities other people had faced. His parents had powers, so were looked after. People who didn't have powers didn't have the means to pay for protection, or the exorbitant prices of living in safe zones. Their role in society was to wait for the Heroes to reclaim enough territory for them to return to their homes.

Magical essence was already leaking into our atmosphere, and we knew it was going to change us…but not in time for us to survive as a species. When our tactics of hitting hard stopped being effective, we switched our strategy. Research and development was something we did exceptionally well as a people throughout history, utilizing the learnings of our ancestors as we unlocked new technological breakthroughs.

We had never started from scratch before, and there was no right or wrong approach. Everything we learned was a result of trial and error. There exist schools of thought in other safe zones around the world…that don't believe in us getting skills to fight the demons.

They believe our abilities are afflictions and see all of this as some form of divine retribution. Acts of God and all that.

Divinity's eyes widened as they reached an area filled with artifacts. Crude shapes and carvings stood on display in protective transparent cases all around them. Tablets in a foreign language, feathered and colored totems. They were all from the other side of the portals. Sal didn't give them anything more than a passing glance for fear of exhausting himself further, but he thought they all looked outlandish but interesting.

Speaking of gods. The demons have their own faiths…with all of these relics hinting at a greater power on the other side of the portals. We've made great strides in breaking down their languages, but we're nowhere near full translations just yet.

Who knows, maybe one of you will have the power that we need to unlock the secrets of the war. Maybe your skill will help us grow crops. Heal wounds.

Maybe your skill will be strong enough to push the demons back to where they came from. Maybe you'll take back our lost territory. Who knows…

Sal had to give it to Quest. He certainly knew how to inspire a crowd. All of the students were smiling at the prospect of using their powers for good. Most of them resonated with the concept of being strong enough to fight demons, but the lower-ranked people with Support classes looked to be just as inspired.

These are the reasons we need to register your skills.

You may have the answer we need to a problem that might not yet exist. Some of you have extraordinary abilities already, more potent than any generation that came before you. You grew up in an environment with incredibly dense magical essence, which has unlocked some truly amazing gifts. Some of them you'll be very familiar with…but there are others that might be hiding within.

Our Skill Registration might open up doors that you didn't realize existed.

Good luck.

The tour area ended, and Sal turned around to see the full cohort at different stages of the tour, with some only beginning it. Divinity dragged him to the top of the queue with a wink. He didn't question her decisions anymore. It was hard to argue with someone who had an impeccable record and could see into the future.

The doors in front of them opened into an even more magnificent room. A golden staircase the width of a highway wound upward in a huge open-plan area. The windows bathed the entire area in light, and the gold shone beautifully. Collective gasps rippled through the students, and Sal couldn't help but marvel at it all. A series of uniformed staff stood at the base of the staircase, smiling.

"Gold cohort has finished with their registration and are enjoying refreshments in the Sky Lounge. When you finish your registration, please make your way to the top of the tower, where you'll see your assigned seating." One of the staff members gestured upward, and Sal gaped at the sight.

The staircase was like a stretched-out spring that hugged the sides of the glass walls. At the top, they could see a platform with a completely transparent floor. In the center, between the staircase, was a series of transparent tubes that looked to be the width of a car. Before he could figure out what they were, a large capsule shot up from the unseen floors below, through the tubes and all the way up to the platform above.

The staff member turned and gestured at the tubes. "Don't worry about going back down all those steps. We have rapid transport tubes to take you to the lobby. They're like elevators but use essence instead of cables."

Divinity tugged at Sal's sleeve, and he realized he must have been staring in awe for a bit too long. Shaking his head, he followed her up the stairs. They were very much at the front of the crowd. The staircase leveled out after maybe thirty steps and created a wide floor area, then resumed its ascent farther off in the distance.

As for the makeshift floor they were on, there was a series of loungers and cubicles that faced the glass walls of the tower. Divinity kept them moving, but Sal wondered what their purpose was.

"They're study areas. Probably a premium area, though," Divinity remarked as she gestured at a small terminal that stood to the side of the cubicles. Sal guessed it was a payment station, and wondered how much it would cost to study there.

When they reached the next set of stairs, Sal wanted to give up, but Divinity urged him onward. He wasn't really serious, but felt an overwhelming need to complain about everything. He was tired, both physically and mentally. His internal essence was probably depleted, too, and he was genuinely worried that he might have screwed up his chances of getting a good result at the Skill Registration. He had been internally battling with his actions in the workshop, and he couldn't help but feel that everything he did was unnecessary and foolish. Activating a full-potential skill in front of others as a "fuck you" was the height of petty behavior, and his parents wouldn't have approved. Well, his father might, if he knew the context, but that wasn't the point.

"Are you finished feeling sorry for yourself?" Divinity laughed as they reached the next floor. "Because we're here."

Divinity rolled up her right sleeve and approached one of the attendants.

There were about ten machines, all looking practically identical in their craftsmanship. Out of curiosity, Sal activated his eyes and pushed through the fatigue to inspect each of the machines. He didn't understand a lot of the information, but he was able to grade and assess them against each other.

"Divinity!" Sal called out quickly to catch her attention before she committed to using the wrong one. She looked back at him curiously and saw that he was pointing to one of the machines farther down the line. "Use that one. I'll wait until you're done."

Divinity hesitated before she moved away from the first machine.

The attendant raised an eyebrow. "Smart friend you have there."

Divinity shot Sal a questioning look as she was ushered to the other bench but he just shook his head and continued to point at it.

"I'll explain later. Use that one." Rather than queuing at another machine, Sal waited behind Divinity for his chance to use the same one.

The uniformed staff noticed that her sleeve was already rolled up and raised an eyebrow. If they were curious about something, they didn't say anything.

Sal's eyes were locked onto the machine. The build quality was slightly better than the others, but the main difference was the power source. It looked like the core that powered the machine had just been replaced. It was practically brimming with magical essence in comparison to the ones that looked like half-spent batteries.

Unlike the barbaric machinery they had seen during the tour, these ones looked modern and sleek. Just the action of the staff member sliding the arm chamber up to accommodate Divinity's height was a sign of how far advanced this equipment was. If they had time to design for comfort, they must have been confident in its performance.

Divinity inserted her right arm into the chamber. She smiled as the attendant walked her through the process. Nodding, Divinity's eyes clouded over as she activated her power. Sal's eyes snapped back to the core as a huge ripple of power coursed through the machine and melded with Divinity's essence. It looked like the two powers fought for a moment, before calming and becoming one. Divinity's eyes widened as she stared at the machine with a sense of wonder. Sal didn't want to presume, but he didn't think she had expected this outcome.

As the attendant helped her remove her arm, the power split into segments, but still swirled on a small plate near the surface of the machine. A few inputs were confirmed, and the power stabilized and became static. He watched in awe as the plate popped out and was handed to Divinity. *Was it really that simple?*

Divinity's grin was practically goofy as she sauntered past him. Her exhaustion was at its peak, but she didn't seem to care in the slightest. "You pick good machines."

A staff member guided Divinity toward a lounge area where she could rest for a few moments. Sal waited patiently as the machine attendant reset everything.

After a couple of minutes, the attendant glanced over their shoulder and suggested that Sal could try another machine rather than wait, but Sal shook his head.

"Nope. This is the one for me."

As he waited for his turn, the rest of the cohort queued up behind people who had taken the other machines. One or two people stood behind Sal, and he couldn't help but feel a surge of anxiety. To calm himself, he went through the Upgrade ability weave one more time, strengthening his hold on it and making sure that he could activate it without any hesitation, like a normal skill. The attendant sidestepped and gestured for Sal to approach. Breathing quickly to psych himself up, Sal nodded and moved toward him with his arm outstretched.

"Calm your nerves. It doesn't hurt. Can I have your name?" His smile was friendly and professional.

Sal's mind eased a little. "Salvatore Argento."

The attendant gestured at the fresh plate that had been inserted into the machine. "Just relax, Salvatore. See that plate? You're going to need to activate your ability with as much power as you can…and don't worry about essence exhaustion. We have a core here that will act as your battery. Go all out, and we'll register the best result of your skill, okay?"

Sal stared at the attendant as though he had two heads. "You want me to go all out?"

CHAPTER 13:
CONSEQUENCES

SAL COULDN'T BELIEVE HIS EARS. *HE WAS ABLE TO USE A CORE INSTEAD OF HIS OWN power?* It was essentially removing the only limiting factor of his ability, and he didn't even need to worry about holding back. When the attendant nodded again, Sal realized he was holding his breath. "Sorry, that sounds amazing."

"That's the spirit." The attendant laughed as he started using the inputs. "Give it your best shot, on my mark."

A few moments passed, and Sal felt sponge-like grips encasing his arm within the chamber. It wasn't an unpleasant feeling, but unfamiliar. He resisted the instinct to pull his arm back and tried to concentrate.

The attendant raised three fingers and started counting him down. Sal looked past the hand and spotted a familiar figure watching from afar.

Only two fingers were raised now, and Sal gritted his teeth in preparation. Upgrade appearing wasn't important right now.

One finger remained, and Sal wondered whether he should apologize to her. He glanced at her and was surprised by her expression. It wasn't curiosity, but apprehension. Sal's eyes snapped back to see the last finger curl down, and it was as though time stopped. It wasn't like the speed ability he had used in the past, but rather like nobody around him existed at that moment. The only thing Sal could see was the reservoir of power. He knew that he could pull it all into himself and use it, but there was simply too much.

Sal subconsciously wondered how much he could use before his time was up. His internal threads were begging to use the power, and for the first time in his life…Sal didn't hold back. His eyes flared as he first used his father's skill. The power shot straight from the core and into his eyes, but the sensation wasn't painful. He felt the core testing him; his eyes told him that it was about to end the procedure, but Sal couldn't let that happen. There was so much more to use.

Sal pushed his mother's skill into the fray. The Restoration ability caught the core by surprise and it hesitated before flooding more power into it. The threads that Sal intricately weaved had grown into ropes of absolute power. He was so used to managing them that there wasn't a single knot, even at its ultimate stage.

The core was getting complacent again, so he threw the newly memorized Upgrade skill at it. The weaves grew thicker, and Sal's eyes reacted immediately to the skill. He unconsciously knew that it was compatible with his eyes, but that could wait. He had a much bigger problem.

Each of the abilities he produced at the ultimate stage had taken up nearly all the available space in his body. He could sense the core fluctuating, as though it was deciding to end the process there. Sal needed to make more room in his body, but he didn't know how.

Instinctively, he looked at the weaves and saw how inefficient they were sitting beside each other. Sal couldn't explain his desperation to keep experiencing this foreign power. It felt as if his entire life he had been scraping water from a puddle, only to now experience a fall into an ocean, and he wasn't prepared to let it go.

Sal started to rearrange the weaves of power. They weren't tangled, and they weren't knotted...but his eyes told him that they could overlap and intertwine harmoniously. Excitement surged within Sal as his new creation took hold. It left room for more weaves, but Sal didn't care about that. This new weave incorporated everything, and it still left plenty of room for him to weave other abilities in the future.

Sal pulled on the power of the core, and it flowed like a river for a few moments, before the current died down. Sal felt a sudden resistance, but the weave needed more power. Sal pulled more from the core and could tell that it was scraping at its reserves. Sal didn't care...he was so close to being done. He was practically begging the core to just give him just a little more, but it looked as though it were about to break at any moment.

A rush of power appeared from a whole new source, flowing with an even greater intensity than the one before. Sal rejoiced internally as the weave completed itself perfectly. The overwhelming desire for power finally shifted, and the weave rotated healthily in his body. Sal had no idea what he had just created, but it felt absolutely right. The new power source retreated, but Sal didn't fight it this time. He let it happen. There was nothing more he could do.

A jolt passed through Sal's body as he awoke in a daze. His legs were sprawled out in front of him, and an attendant was holding up his torso, with their head hooked under his left shoulder. Sal blearily looked at his arm, only to see trails of blood dripping from it. Sounds started to come back to him but he still couldn't focus properly.

His cohort stared at him in a mixture of horror and awe. Sal tried to focus on the area where Upgrade had been watching him, but she was nowhere to be seen. A few more blinks cleared things up, and Sal saw Divinity at the front of the crowd, being held back by an attendant.

"Sal, can you hear me? Are you okay?" a voice called out.

Sal furrowed his brow in confusion. *Didn't he introduce himself as Salvatore?* He turned to face the voice and saw Upgrade only a few feet from him, in her suit of armor. Her arm was in its mechanical form and was jammed into the side of the machine. Sal took a breath as he tried to focus, but everything was spinning. Concern marred her face, and he swallowed hard.

"Sorry...for leaving."

And with that, everything spun into darkness.

***

Sal's eyes flickered open. He was back in his room with his head resting on a pillow. His bags still needed to be unpacked and he wondered why he had gone to bed again without doing that.

"Oh, it looks like he's waking up. We'll have our answers soon enough." Quest laughed as he poured himself a fresh cup of tea. The headmaster glanced to the other side of the bed and raised the pot with an unspoken question, and Sal heard Upgrade refuse the offer of a refill.

Quest tilted his head and looked Sal straight in the eye. "How are you feeling, Mr. Argento?"

Sal blinked as he fully woke up. He expected to be wracked with pain, but to his surprise…he felt great. He opened his mouth to answer but caught sight of what looked like a new door on the far end of the room. His eyes flared up instinctively but instead of the usual appraisal information, he was bombarded with a slew of suggestions on how to improve the door.

Sal took slow and steady breaths as he tried to calm his thundering heart, but something was wrong. He was used to his eyes picking up details and giving him information, but now it was so much more detailed.

"You might need to walk him through this part," Quest advised gently as he brought the cup to his lips.

Sal turned in his bed to see Upgrade in a chair next to him. Her face was unreadable as she stared at him with crossed arms.

"You're seeing blueprints everywhere, aren't you? Plans to improve things or convert them into something more efficient?"

Sal nodded as he took a deep breath. His mind whirled. *How did she know that he could see those things? Was this a part of the Upgrade ability?*

As if answering his own question, Sal shook his head and spoke aloud. "It can't be my power…I'm not using it."

Quest lowered his cup and smiled. "Actually, I can answer that one." He leaned closer to Sal and gestured at his right arm. "Your Skill Registration was an absolute success. So many factors came together to create the perfect registration. We just didn't have a powerful enough core to sustain your needs."

Reaching into his coat pocket, Quest rooted around until he produced a metal plate. "This is your completed Q-Card, with all of your abilities mapped out. I'll admit that there were a few surprises, and one entry I'm going to need your help identifying." His laugh was warm and genuine as he placed the plate on the bedsheets so Sal could reach it. "I told Upgrade that you probably swiped her ability in the workshop. Was I right?"

Sal looked between them and wasn't sure whether he should have felt ashamed or not. He never wanted to deceive others and didn't want to lie, so he nodded.

The unreadable expression on Upgrade's face turned into confusion. "Of all the skills you could take, why would you pick mine?"

Maybe it was because he had just woken up, or the fact that Quest and Upgrade knew so much already, but Sal decided to tell them the truth. "My future self picked it out of all the skills he had seen in the university. I trust his opinion."

Upgrade's eyes narrowed before she glanced over at the headmaster. "Are you sure he's okay?"

Quest waved her question away as he looked intently at Sal. "I'm going to need you to explain that part in a little more detail."

Sal shrugged. "I met a girl called Divinity and she can glimpse into the future. I told her about the premium vendors, and we found a drink called Sleeping Tiger. Sorry, eh…Purple Punch. We both drank it, and she told me that my registration would be great because of it."

Sal glanced at the two of them and saw that they were apparently keeping up with him, so he continued. "I was going to have a physical-based skill added because I used one for the first assignment, but I didn't want that, so we came up with a plan to get a skill I'd be excited about." He paused to see whether they had questions. When none came, Sal finished up. "I said I'd tell her my favorite skill every week going forward, so she checked the future until she found one that I was really excited with."

Sal turned and pointed at Upgrade. "Yours."

Upgrade shook her head. "It has downsides! Material costs, power consumption…there are so many other abilities that are better!"

The headmaster looked at the plate on the bed. "I heard about your performance in the workshop. Your father's Appraisal ability is nowhere near your level, nor is your mother's version of Restore. That means, that this one here…" Quest pointed at a single line on the plate and looked up at Sal. "It's called Skill Master, and I believe it's the reason you're able to bypass the normal limit of these abilities."

His finger moved down the plate and his finger broke into a smile. "Which brings us to the elephant in the room. In all my years of working at this academy, I have never seen *this* skill before. It hasn't been documented in any of the guild registries either." Quest paused as he glanced over at Upgrade with an excited grin. "My hypothesis might be wrong…but, I think you may have just created a new ability."

Upgrade's stoic expression broke as she gaped at Quest. "But he's seeing the blueprints! He has Upgrade!"

Quest picked up the plate and showed it to her. "It's not written on his card, but I agree. I think he has the Upgrade ability, but it's a part of something much more interesting."

As Quest and Upgrade spoke to each other, Sal had a sudden flashback of the registration, when he started to weave the different threads to make more room. In a panic, he brought up his power…and was rendered speechless at the beautiful pattern that flowed inside him. It was practically flawless and brimming with promise.

His Appraisal, Restore, and Upgrade skills were all woven into the thread. More incredible was the fact that it was active without him being conscious of it. Sal fed a small amount of power into it and saw it fire around the threads at a speed he didn't know was possible. His eyes started to acclimatize to the room and everything around him practically brimmed with potential. Fantastical designs materialized out of nothing, and he wanted nothing more than to bring them to life.

Upgrade's eyes locked onto Sal, but her question was to Quest. "Can you tell if it's a good one?"

The headmaster chuckled. "What are the different grades of Crafters?"

Upgrade's expression was a clear indicator that she wasn't in the mood for guessing games, but she forced a smile onto her face. Raising her thumb and fingers on her left hand, she put them down one by one in a monotonous tone. "Comcraft, Uncomcraft, Rarecraft, Epicraft, and Legendcraft."

Quest grinned at her while pointing at Sal. "And now I'd like you to meet our first documented *Mythcrafter*."

CHAPTER 14:
VISITOR

SSAL LEARNED THAT HE HAD BEEN TREATED IN THEIR IN-HOUSE MEDICAL facility before being brought back to his room, and that Upgrade had fixed his door while he was unconscious. After a short interrogation, Quest and Upgrade left, allowing him to get some rest.

It was already evening, but he was wide awake. He couldn't get Upgrade's expression out of his head. Her face literally broke into a look of horror and awe. To get a reaction like that from her, he wondered whether his new ability was that amazing.

Sal couldn't help but grin as he got out of bed. Because he had missed a chunk of the day and he had a whole bunch of Q-Credit, they were holding open a single seat on all the modules so Sal could pick whichever classes he was interested in. They didn't want the incident at the Skill Registration to prevent him from getting a place in his chosen class. Sal almost missed the glance that Quest gave Upgrade when he listed their conditions.

Sal would be under the direct supervision of Upgrade when he went to the workshop. She chose that time to apologize for the behavior of the team, including herself. Sal accepted gratefully and apologized for overreacting and fixing the core.

Other conditions included a few special contracts that might appear every now and again. Upgrade reassured him that his performance on those projects would greatly influence his standing with the university. Quest hinted that successful completion of the projects could be a great avenue into becoming a part of the Savior program.

Sal walked from the bed and turned on the screen to check his schedule for the following day. He clicked on his profile as it showed a small notification bubble beside the icon.

Name	Salvatore Argento
Alias	[*Unknown*]
Profession	Student
Starting Role	Support
Rank (Student)	First-Years - 19th Silver Cohort - 2nd
Ability	**Skill Master** (Rating: Advanced) (Category: Replication) **Mythcrafter** (Rating: Master) (Category: Invention)
Essence	Essence Control - 77% Essence Refinement - 2% Essence Calibration - 21%

Academic Reports	<u>Core Modules</u>: (M = Mandatory) • (M) Skills: No Grade • (M) Survival: No Grade • (M) Combat: No Grade • (M) Crafting: No Grade <u>Elective Modules</u>: • None Selected
Reputation	**Quest Academy**: [*Unknown*] **Guild Association**: [*Unknown*] **Hunter Bureau**: [*Unknown*]
Affiliations	**Argento Auction** (Sponsorship: Tier 3) **Reavers Guild** (Silver Token Holder)
Scout Status	N/A
Accreditations	N/A
Threat Level	[*Unknown*]
Wealth	594 Q-Credit
System Notes	[*Unknown*]

Sal raised an eyebrow at his essence and ability. He didn't know what the different percentages represented or what the different categories meant, and despite his curiosity, he pulled his attention back to the module selection. He needed to make sure he made the right choice. Quest had put Crafting down as a mandatory module for him. He assumed that was the workshop with Upgrade and her team, but he couldn't be sure.

Either way, it was a relief to have some direction. He still had another module to pick, and he wanted nothing to do with Field practice. Analysis seemed like easy grades with his eyes, so Sal marked himself down for that. It looked like it wasn't scheduled to start for another month or so, which would give him enough time to focus on the others.

Administration was the last module available…and it looked to be pretty unpopular from the number of seats remaining for the class. Sal didn't want to put himself under pressure by taking on too much, but a small voice in the back of his head told him to take it. *Maybe the lecturer would give out extra credits because there were so few of them?* He glanced at his choices and nodded.

Academic Reports	<u>Core Modules:</u> (M = Mandatory) • (M) Skills: No Grade • (M) Survival: No Grade • (M) Combat: No Grade • (M) Crafting: No Grade <u>Elective Modules:</u> • Analysis: No Grade • Administration: No Grade

It would have been ideal if he could have switched out Survival with something else, but there was nothing he could do about it considering it was mandatory. He shrugged, and was about to close out of it, when he caught sight of the abilities list. Skill Master and Mythcrafter both sounded incredible, and he smiled at the sight of them. Even if he was kicked out of the university and went home to his parents with just that ability, he'd see it as a complete success. It would be useful to their auction house, even if he didn't know how to use it, yet, or how good it was, but he was confident.

Taking a step back, Sal almost tripped over one of his suitcases. It was now coming into day two, and he still hadn't unpacked.

"Might as well get it over with…" Sal muttered as he started going through each of the cases.

It was a mini adventure in itself as he managed to find a whole set of things he didn't know were in the apartment, including a washer and dryer. Packing the shelves of his closet took a bit longer than it should have, as Sal kept switching things around to see what felt right. Just when he was about to reach for the T-shirts again, his eyes ignited and displayed the most optimal arrangement that could be completed. The small sensation made Sal pause.

"That's new…" He spoke quietly as he turned to the rest of his luggage.

Using his eyes again, the same thing occurred, and Sal even knew how to pack and stack the cases to minimize their floorspace. With his eyes in constant use, Sal followed their instructions and was amazed to have it done in absolutely no time. It was like each task became a checklist item for him.

Just when he was about to finish up, there was a faint knocking on the door. Quest and Upgrade had put him to bed in his uniform, so he didn't need to throw anything on. Sal walked around the bed and went to the door, only to pause in surprise. What had previously been a door that operated on a hinge…was now a sliding door that opened with a touch of a button. Upgrade had said she'd fixed the door. But her ability wasn't Restoration or Repair; it was Upgrading, and that's exactly what she had done.

Sal tapped the button and the door glided into an unseen recess in the wall. He watched it go in astonishment, as did Hannah from the hallway. She pointed at the door, her face a picture of confusion.

"Ah, I completely forgot!" They had agreed to meet up in the evening, but that seemed like a lifetime ago.

Hannah hiked her thumb over her shoulder. "Want me to leave?"

Sal shook his head. "Do you want to come in, or go somewhere else? Where's Kane?"

Hannah raised an eyebrow. "Yeah, he's definitely not going to want to talk to people after that Combat encounter." Before Sal could reply, Hannah looked over his shoulder and into his room. "Hey, is yours bigger than mine?"

Without so much as another word, she walked straight past him and into the room. Sal followed her in, only to find her counting her steps toward the glass wall. When she reached her destination, she frowned.

"Only looks bigger—it's the same as mine. What did you put in your workroom?" Hannah poked her head into the room with the bench, and looked disappointed to see the default options. "Didn't you pick a specialist package from the Administration office?"

"Just…wait a second." Sal raised his hands to stop her talking. "I'm a bit behind with everything. I was knocked unconscious during the registration event. Woke up here a while ago, so I missed whatever the Administration package thing is, and I've no idea what happened to Kane."

Hannah's eyes widened. "You're the one who fried the machine? They said a core was faulty, but nobody believed them."

Sal shrugged. "I don't know…maybe?"

Hannah made a contented noise as she sat on his bed and put her feet up. "You better get comfy, Sal, there's a lot to catch up on."

Sal smiled as he wheeled out a chair from the workstation and sat down.

Hannah turned and gave him a level look. "Basically, we're in a university filled with monsters. That Combat encounter was just…horrific! Kane had his leg shattered by this little girl. She builds momentum by running and took him out immediately. Everyone laughed when she tried to help him up, but she wasn't strong enough. He's probably going to hide in his room until he gets kicked out."

Sal felt horrible for Kane, but Hannah was only getting started.

"There's a guy who throws lightning. It looked really cool, and he pretty much teleports or moves at super speed. It took like, four or five rounds before he was taken out. Oh, sorry, the Combat encounter was kinda like a survival thing? One person would be challenged, and the winner stayed on. The longer the person stayed, the higher their result. After five wins, they would retire and someone else would start. Only way out of it was winning five times or being beaten. That whittled down everyone real fast, but then they started pitting the winners against each other. That Momentum Girl was one of the first to go, slide tackle from Lightning Guy. There was a girl who literally made every guy surrender, but she got her ass kicked by a girl who could alter her size."

Hannah made a gesture of picking something off the floor and then throwing it down at the ground. "It was awesome! Apparently, her charm ability didn't work on the same sex. Thought Giant Girl was going to take the prize, but…get this. There's a guy with super strength who can jump ridiculously high. Literally head-butted Giant Girl under the chin, and she was down.

Pretty sure she fell on some people, which was pretty funny. He was the front-runner, but then there was a guy with fire and yeah, strength guy is weak to fire."

Sal didn't even bother to stop her. He was amazed at hearing about all these abilities.

Hannah paused for a moment. Her mumbles were complemented by her fingers, which counted the different competitors at different stages. Suddenly, her eyes lit up.

"Ooooh! Have you seen the Rank #1 yet? First of all, she's gorgeous, and I kinda hate her. She can control minds. Remember I said that Charm Girl made people surrender? Not this one—she made them fight themselves. Full on punching themselves in the face, or making them choke until they fell unconscious…It was, really dark. Ah! There's a guy who can make ghosts. They're super weak and were destroyed almost immediately, but it was a really odd skill and I thought it was cool."

Sal gave Hannah a tentative look but didn't say anything in case she wasn't done, but she folded her hands on her lap and took a breath before shaking her head. "You really should have seen them, man. These people are strong."

"What about you? How did you fare with the combat?"

Hannah's face broke into a smile. "Are you trying to find out my power?"

Sal laughed. "I'd be lying if I said I wasn't curious."

Hannah sat up properly and pointed the two fingers of her right hand like a gun. She closed one eye and aimed at a location over the edge of the bed. Her thumb came down on the pretend gun and a floating orb of blue light left her fingers and suspended in mid-air where Hannah had aimed. She did this on all four corners of the bed, until there were four floating orbs above her. Raising her two fingers to her lips, she blew on them with a laugh, causing the orbs to shoot lasers into each other and then down at the ground. By the time Hannah had holstered her gun hand, she was surrounded by an impenetrable barrier.

Sal tentatively touched the wall. It was rock solid. He pressed his full body weight against it, but it didn't even flicker.

She raised her hand. "I'm able to keep people out."

The resistance disappeared, and Sal face-planted into the mattress.

Hannah's laugh was explosive. "I'm sorry, but that was hilarious." She lifted her feet closer to her torso to give Sal room to recover. "As you've probably figured out, I can also let people in. It's very much a defensive ability, and I managed to win three rounds by forcing opponents into a stalemate. Ran out of energy and couldn't continue, so I had to surrender." Hannah shrugged as she dispelled the prison and looked at Sal expectantly. "Okay, you're next. What's your power?"

Sal rolled to his back on the mattress and told Hannah everything that had happened throughout the day. He even told her about the awkward encounter in the workshop. Hannah's face was priceless when he told her how he had found out about the skill from conversations in the future with Divinity, but Sal kept going, happy to have her undivided attention. He explained how his power worked, and how energy was usually the limiting factor…

"The core! That's why it shattered. Holy shit, how much power did you take?"

Sal laughed and raised a hand. "I'm getting to that part."

He explained how the registration went, and how he had wanted to have the best outcome, and had maxed out all the skills he had on hand.

"But I didn't have enough room in my body, so I integrated them…which apparently created a whole new skill." Sal finished with a clap, startling Hannah.

He groaned momentarily as he got to his feet, went over to the screen, and activated the terminal. He pointed to his registered abilities and smiled back at Hannah. "Here's the proof. I've got two skills. Skill Master, which lets me use weaves and create skills. Also, Mythcrafter! Which is a combination of Upgrade, Restoration, and Appraisal. I don't know much about it yet, but the headmaster was pretty excited about it."

Hannah stared at the screen and then back at Sal in absolute disbelief. "You're able to Craft Mythic-grade items!"

Sal just stared blankly at Hannah. "Oh, yeah…that's probably why the headmaster was so excited."

CHAPTER 15:
FIRST TIME

The sound of Hannah running back from her room made Sal laugh. He couldn't believe what was happening. Only a few seconds after telling her about his ability, and then making the excuse that he didn't have any materials to work with…she was off the bed and racing to her room.

Sal was certain the other students could hear her shouting for him to wait for a minute. True to her word, she came back with the widest smile ever and a hastily stuffed backpack in her hands. Without any prompt or ceremony, she flipped the bag and allowed the contents to fall onto the bed. In between breaths, she gestured at the different items on display.

"This…from the…administration…Use whatever you can!"

Sal reached for a bottle of water to hand to Hannah, but she waved it away. "No, no—this first. Come on!"

Her excitement was probably clouding her judgment, but Sal relented as he took a knee beside the bed. Activating his power, he was studying the components she had brought when he heard a stifled gasp from beside him. Looking up, he saw Hannah staring at him with her hand covering her mouth.

"Dude, your eyes are fucking awesome!"

Sal shot her a relieved smile. "Ah, I thought it was something bad. Thank you."

"I mean the silver was super cool, in a cold and intense way…but the purple looks magical!"

Sal paused. "Purple?"

Hannah tilted her head. "You should probably check yourself out in the mirror…"

Without another word, Sal jumped up and rushed past her to get to the bathroom. *She was obviously winding him up. There was no way his eyes had changed color.*

He gripped the sink and looked down at his hands, psyching himself up before looking at the mirror.

His irises pulsated with violet, and he was fascinated by the vibrancy reacting to the amount of power he pushed through it. For the first time in his life, he was looking at his eyes without getting an immediate headache. Sal continued to just stare wordlessly at his own reflection, not believing it was real. A smile crept onto his face as inspected his eyes closely for the first time.

He wanted to see what they looked like when he activated the power fully, so without any sort of preparation or testing, he channeled his internal energy into the weave and gasped when everything in the room suddenly changed.

His eyes emitted an ethereal glow as countless blueprints flooded his mind. His brain unconsciously discounted many of them but held on to some that had potential. Sal could see a customization path for nearly every item in the room.

Looking back into the mirror, his eyes caught sight of his uniform and the reaction was much more prominent.

Sal couldn't explain why, but he instinctively knew how to improve it. It took a lot of willpower to resist the urge to customize his uniform. He couldn't help but wonder whether he'd be able to make a cool armor like the one Upgrade had. As he left the bathroom, an image of Upgrade's suit appeared in his mind. A second later, Sal froze on the spot as he stared off into the distance.

Hannah looked up from where she had been sorting through the different materials. "Oooooh, they're super bright now! Are you using them at maximum?" When she didn't get an answer, a hint of concern crept into her voice as she got to her feet. "Hey, you okay in there?"

She waved her hand in front of his face, causing him to blink and stagger back.

He focused on Hannah, lost for words. With a great amount of difficulty, he closed his eyes and deactivated his power. The rush of adrenaline that coursed through his body was unlike anything he had experienced before. He reached for the bottle of water that he had offered to Hannah and took a long drink before looking back at her.

"Welcome back?" Hannah asked cautiously. "You kinda spaced out there. You okay?"

Sal had no idea how to phrase what he'd seen, but he decided to try. "I thought of a suit of armor, and it literally appeared in my head!"

Hannah just laughed. "Yeah…that's normal."

Waving his hand at her and shaking his head, he laughed. "No, I mean…the blueprint appeared, from something I had only seen in passing, without this ability! I've somehow managed to break down a memory of an item and I know how to re-create it!" Sal was excited as he explained. "But the version that I saw was incomplete. I can see everything that was wrong with it. Well, not everything, but a lot. But then something cool happened."

Turning suddenly, he pointed at Hannah, which startled her. "You waved your hand in front of me, and the armor changed. It morphed and suddenly had a protective barrier as a feature. *Your* protective barrier!"

Hannah's eyes narrowed. "Are you trying to tell me that your eyes want to turn me into armor?" She folded her arms and tilted her head with a smile. "I'll be honest, it's not the worst chat-up line I've received." She made a show of flicking her hair and gave him a mock satisfied smile.

Sal continued to think about the blueprint he'd just seen. It had only been a passing thought, but his body was practically itching to start on the armor. He didn't even need it. He wasn't going to be heading into battle any time soon. His mind shifted to the gloves Upgrade wore. They looked so basic, but transformed into something incredible. A rustling noise caught his attention, and he turned to see Hannah holding up some of the raw materials that she had sorted on the bed.

"They probably aren't good enough to make anything cool, but they should cover the cost of a premium coffee."

"Let's see if we can make something,"

Sal activated his ability again, looking at all the components with an open mind. His instincts were to Upgrade each component, but he resisted that prompt. He wanted to build something useful, but his eyes dismissed the materials in front of him. It was going to take some getting used to, but there was a layer of resistance that he couldn't explain. It was like the ability didn't want to use low-grade material.

As if to test the theory, Sal picked up a small ingot of discolored metal. Hannah visibly perked up, but Sal put it down and picked up another. Hannah's shoulders sagged as Sal did this with every piece of material on the bed. Folding his arms, he looked at them for a few more minutes and when Hannah seemed on the verge of snapping at him, he let out a relieved sigh.

"Okay! Let's go!" Sal grinned at her, but she had absolutely no context about what was happening.

Getting to his feet, Sal groaned. The leg he had been sitting on had fallen asleep. With an awkward stagger, he managed to get to his closet and withdrew a set of gloves. He was going to try to make Crafting equipment like Upgrade.

Sal sat back down. "This might take a little while, but hopefully it's not too painful to watch!" His eyes glowed even more vibrantly as his fingers started to compress the solid metal into a new shape.

Hannah moved around on the bed as she stared at the process intently. When Sal started making adjustments to the now pliable metal, her eyes widened ever so slightly. When Sal's hands smeared the metal against the fabric of the gloves, Hannah almost interrupted. She had probably guessed what he was doing by now and realized that there wasn't enough metal to cover all of the fingers, but Sal just smiled at her.

After a few moments, he glanced up. "Hannah, can you put one of your blue orbs here, please?" He gestured at an area beside the glove.

Her expression went from excitement to trepidation. She stared at him, as though weighing up the pros and cons before she eventually gave him a nod. With the same gesture as before, Hannah shot an orb of blue essence to the location he specified.

He smiled as he continued to shape the metal in his hands. "Thank you!"

Hannah looked like she desperately wanted to ask what he was doing, but she didn't utter a word. She leaned forward and watched him pinch the blue orb and trace an invisible line to the gloves. The result was instantaneous; the blue orb disappeared, causing Hannah to gasp and jump up.

"Now for the fun part," Sal joked as he studied the crudely designed gauntlets.

He didn't need to use an Appraisal skill to know they were absolutely trash. With no tools or experience, he'd tried to shape the idea he had in his mind. The skill fought against him the entire time, but Sal persisted and tried to Craft something new, rather than follow the steps that the ability prompted him with. The results of that process was not pretty.

Worn leather gloves, with plating around some of the fingers on both sets, were infused with high-quality essence and Hannah's power signature. Sal just hoped it would be enough for the next part. He let the prompts take over, and they did exactly what he had hoped for. His eyes locked onto the rough design, and he was almost giddy to see that there were upgrade suggestions that brought the item closer to what he intended. Sal flooded the design with his energy and let it do most of the hard work.

It was quicker than Sal thought, but it packed a much heavier punch than he expected, too. If he was to estimate…bringing them from Common to Uncommon had taken about a quarter of his energy reserves. Well, maybe that wasn't completely accurate because he had been using his power constantly in the prototyping stage. He had around three-quarters of his power left, so risked going a step further and aimed for Rare grade.

The gloves themselves were still glowing, preventing Hannah from getting a proper look at them. A trickle of black gunk seeped out of the construct that looked like it would never come out of the sheets.

Sal grit his teeth as sweat poured from his forehead. He had underestimated how much power it would take to refine and Upgrade the gloves to the Rare grade. He had already cleansed the material impurities, but shaping the metal and reinforcing the leather was proving to be one hell of an exercise.

Something more concerning was sticking in the back of his mind…he needed to add something more to the gloves to truly bring them to Rare grade. The materials and power weren't enough, and he had clearly overlooked that factor. At this stage, it was just going to be a high-quality Uncommon, and Sal didn't want to waste all his power for that. He wasn't a snob when it came to quality but having grown up in an auction house, he knew how much of a gap there was between the two grades…and in their values.

Sal thought of anything he could use and a solution came to mind from the day before. He bit his lip in concentration as he tried to engrave an etching onto the metal. It was faster using his power and more efficient than using a tool, but it siphoned from him at a ridiculous rate. He wanted to close his eyes and go to sleep, to stop what he was doing, but his mind was on fire with anticipation. He was creating something that didn't exist before, and he was close to finishing it.

Never, in all his life, did he feel such a sense of ownership and pride. He wasn't taking something from someone else…he was using his own power, that only he possessed. With that thought alone, a surge of power washed through him and into the gauntlet, completing the upgrade.

Sal sighed as he closed his eyes and fell flat onto the bed, not caring that he was lying in a puddle of material sludge. His first creation was complete, and he was happy to watch it cool down.

Hannah pulled at Sal's arm as she pointed at the gloves. "What the actual fuck, Sal? Are you fucking with me? How did you make this?"

The gloves were black leather, with a silver metal casing for the thumbs and first two fingers. The joints looked to be expertly crafted and the etching engraved into the casing. A faint hint of blue energy darted around the engraving, giving the impression that the gauntlets were breathing with power.

Rolling onto his side, Sal propped his head up and smiled. "Why haven't you tried them on?" He gave her a look of mock confusion.

Hannah's face went pale as she looked between Sal and the gloves. "You…didn't." Her voice cracked as she looked at them in absolute shock.

Sal's smile never left his face. "I made the casing to mimic your gesture." He held up his hand like it was a gun, and Hannah's eyes widened. "But I needed you to share your power to really make them yours."

Sal reluctantly sat up and groaned at the pain coursing through his body. He wouldn't be able to stay awake for much longer, and wondered whether he was ever going to give himself a break and get a good night's sleep. Glancing back at the stupefied Hannah, he picked up the gloves and threw them at her, which she caught in a panic. His eyes locked onto them in mid-air and his Appraisal flared up.

Name	Barrier Gauntlets
Origin	Crafted
Age	New
Grade	Rare (Lower)
Dimensions	Circumference 6 inches
Materials	Faux Bovine Leather | Iron | [*Unknown*] Essence
Attributes	**Prism**: Can create a customizable prism by directing essence with the gloves. **Barrier**: Creates a protective shield in front of the wearer. **Repel**: Barrier and Prism have a pushback effect and chance to reflect damage.
Abilities	Prism | Barrier | Repel
Power Source	External Essence
Evolution	No
Quality	Good
Condition	100%
Value	Est. $9,500.00 – $15,000.00

"Don't throw them!"

With shaking hands, Hannah put on the gloves and gasped as they shrank to fit her hands. Her expression was conflicted, as though she wanted to find words that just wouldn't come. When she opened her mouth to speak, a sudden realization crossed her face and she stared at the gauntlets in shock.

Sal guessed that it was her first time equipping a piece of equipment that had been made specifically for her. He wondered if the essence would blend well with her own and there was only one way to find out. He raised his hand and mimicked her gesture from before.

Tears rolled down her face as she marveled at the gauntlets that were brimming with her power, but she seemed to understand what he wanted her to do.

Hannah laughed happily as she pointed her finger at the wall in front of her. With her fingers outstretched and her thumb cocked, she practically whispered the word. "Bang."

Sal grinned as the entire room was coated in a protective layer of icy-blue energy. He marveled at the sudden change in her power and couldn't help but be proud of what he had achieved. He got up from the bed to inspect the barrier, "Not bad for a first tr—"

Sal didn't have time to finish his sentence as Hannah's lips found his.

Her gauntlets grasped at his shirt as she pulled him down a few inches to her level, her heels finally resting on the ground as she kissed him passionately. When Hannah broke the kiss, she breathed heavily and looked at the open door that led out to the corridor. With a moment of hesitation, she let go of Sal and walked to the door.

Sal's heart thundered as she closed the door and turned back to him with a suggestive smile.

"So, let's set some boundaries first…" Her fingers deactivated the protective shield around the room and placed it around Sal instead.

He tentatively put a hand against the wall and realized that it was solid. He was about to check behind him to see whether it was back there too, but his eyes locked on Hannah as she slipped out of her gray uniform. She was inches away from him as she turned and shimmied the waistband over her impressive curves to fall at her feet below. It was a private show, just for him, and he could look but not touch. His heart thundered in his chest as he watched her throw the covers off the side of the bed.

She sauntered past his temporary prison, swaying her hips as she did so…before getting comfy on his bed. Her skimpy lace underwear strained against her large breasts. Without so much as another word, she snapped her fingers, and the barrier was gone.

Sal practically ripped the uniform off his body, his eyes never once leaving Hannah for fear she'd disappear. Shoes were kicked off in every direction as he climbed the bed to kiss her again. Their lips locked for a moment, and the noise of satisfaction she made sent shivers through Sal's body.

She took his hand and slid it down her toned stomach. Hannah's voice turned sultry as she whispered into his ear. "Just so you know…" Her lips pulled at his earlobe as her warm breath washed over his skin. "The gauntlets are staying on."

CHAPTER 16: WORKSHOP

SAL LAY IN HIS BED AND WATCHED AS HANNAH GOT DRESSED. THERE WAS NO seductive teasing this time, but she shot him a smile when she caught him looking. When she zipped up her pants, she stretched her back and ran her gauntlet-covered hands through the wild mane of blonde hair. Sal's eyes were once again drawn to her perfect chest before it was cruelly covered by their horrible uniform.

She laughed at his visible dismay, giving Sal a sidelong glance. "Just so there aren't any misunderstandings…this was just a bit of fun. Let's not make it weird, or the next three years are going to be pretty fucking awkward. What do you say?"

Exhaling slowly, Sal finally regained the ability to think with his actual brain. A large part of that recovery was aided by the ugly uniform she now flaunted.

"Absolutely." Sal smiled dreamily as he sat up properly on the bed. He pulled a sheet over himself to regain a little bit of modesty. "Happy to do whatever you want." He gestured vaguely, as though it made perfect sense.

Hannah laughed as she picked up her shoes. "Oh, I know you are." And with a final wink, she was gone.

A few moments after his door closed and when he was sure that she was back in her room, he raised his hands over his head and celebrated silently. He didn't want to overstep the mark with her and be labeled a creep, so he'd keep everything respectful. Sal would have been happy just to have a friend at the university, but when she brought over materials for him because of the coffee he bought her, he was struck by a sense of gratitude. The gauntlets were something he thought she might like. But for her to lay in bed beside him…and tell him how powerful they made her feel…

Sal took a steadying breath as he pulled the blankets up from the floor and wrapped himself into a blanket burrito. He didn't want to get his hopes up for something more, but he really hoped that they'd get to spend a few more nights together like that. Turning his head, he could smell her perfume on the pillow beside him. Sal smiled as he finally let exhaustion take him off to sleep.

***

Classes for the day had a much later start than usual, which Sal guessed had to do with the grueling Combat exercise that everyone was subjected to the day before. He wasn't going to waste the day lying in bed and decided to use the few extra hours to catch up on things.

To say he was in high spirits was an understatement because Sal couldn't remember a time when he was happier. His whole life, he felt like he was taking skills from others and that nothing was ever truly his. Channeling the power of other people and doing it well was really impressive to some, but it never felt enough for Sal. But now? He had Crafted a Rare-grade artifact on just his first attempt.

Sal had his premium coffee in one hand as he walked to the workshop. He justified the cost because of the effects it gave him, but he resolved to find a way to earn more Q-Credit. The task of the day was to discover how he could sell items in the university. Sal had his Silver token that Villa gave him, and he was curious whether he could start doing Appraisal work immediately.

Another thing he wanted to figure out was the dress code, because a few of the high-ranked students were proudly wearing pieces of armor instead of the ugly uniform. Sal already assumed that there was a grade cap on the items that could be worn because nothing he had seen was beyond the Uncommon rank, and even seeing them was somewhat rare. Thinking back to the days before, when he saw the second and third-years, he tried to remember what they had worn. They had looked like uniforms, but sleeker. Anything was better than the gray garb the first-years received.

When Sal finally arrived at the workshop, he saw a completely different setup from the day before. Rather than having a huge open space for the students to navigate between tables, the workstations were spaced out generously, leaving only narrow paths between them. He hadn't noticed yesterday, but a series of glass doors led into private booths. There were a few individuals in them already, either studying or doing precision work that needed peace and quiet.

"Mr. Argento!" Forge's booming voice filled the room, causing more than a few people to glance up from their desks. Not one of them looked annoyed at the interruption, which Sal found odd.

"Upgrade isn't here yet. She's more of a night owl than an early bird!" Forge gripped Sal's hand and gave him a powerful handshake. He gestured at the various workbenches around the room. "Would you like a proper tour this time?"

"I'd like that, thank you…but I was hoping to ask a few questions, if that's okay?" Sal queried as he followed Forge.

Forge waved his hand. "Of course, that's the only way to learn. What do you want to know?"

Sal withdrew the Silver token and showed it to Forge. "How can I start using this and earning Q-Credit?"

Forge grinned as he clicked his fingers. "That's an excellent place to start the tour. Follow me!"

Sal fell into step behind the large, aproned man as they walked past all the benches.

Forge looked over his shoulder as he gestured at the people around them. "Everyone you see here is either a third-year or in the GPP. Sorry, Guild Partnership Program. We're the only accredited specialist training facility in the city, so if the guilds want to have a licensed Crafter…they can only get that stamp of approval here."

As if to identify themselves as part of the partnership program, some of them glanced up and offered a friendly wave.

Forge gestured to a row of elevators in the distance. "We're going up to the Credit floor. Do you want to stop for a refill?" His eyes landed on Sal's coffee cup and a slight smile tugged at his lips. "It's not the fancy vendor stuff, though. If you're looking for something that'll keep you working through the night, you need to talk to Alex. He's one of our guys and does Alchemy as a side gig. His coffee will have you doing marathon sprints in this place!"

Sal followed Forge's gesture to see a grinning man holding a coffee cup aloft in greeting.

The elevator was much wider than any of the ones Sal had entered so far, and Forge once again proved himself to be a trove of knowledge. "We had a custom order for a Naginata blade just the other day, and the casing for it alone is taller than all our other elevators. These ones were custom-built for our larger orders, and you can even go all the way down to the ground floor where there's easy access to the loading bay. Same up top if you're getting something air delivered."

Forge pointed in the different directions as he explained, but for now he tapped a button for a floor only a couple of stops away. When they cleared the first one, Sal could see through the glass doors to an industrial-looking floor filled with machines.

"Ah, we'll get to that part later." Forge laughed. "We'll get the Credit floor sorted first, and then we can take the stairs down to manufacturing."

Sal was grateful to have a guide and enjoyed the larger man's company. After a few moments, the elevator pinged, and the transparent doors opened to reveal the trade floor. Unlike the workshop where everyone was curious and friendly, the faces in this location were anything but. The luxurious surroundings filled him with a sudden pang of familiarity, which was only reinforced by the looks of contempt from the well-presented staff members standing around the room. Their uniforms were elegant and refined, and Sal almost snorted.

"Is this an auction house?"

Forge blinked as he turned to Sal. "How did you know?"

"My father took me to public auctions all the time to show me how the competition operated...sorry, my family runs an independent auction house." Sal realized that Forge likely had no idea who his family was, so he provided context. To his surprise, the larger man nodded with a smile.

"Argento Auction, yes? Petro is one of the good ones. We've worked with each other in the past."

Sal laughed as he looked around at all the vultures staring at him. He could practically read their minds. They would be seeing a first-year in a gray uniform being shown around by one of the "workers" from the workshop floor. Even though Forge was a prominent figure in the Crafting scene, he wouldn't be making these people any money, so he was useless to them.

Forge gave Sal an apologetic look. "Em, maybe let me do the talking...they can be a bit..."

"Prickly?" Sal nodded in understanding.

Forge grinned.

The man behind the counter had the decency not to sigh at their approach. "Welcome."

That was all he said, no introduction to services or a follow-up to ask how he could help. He simply acknowledged their existence, and Sal could sense that Forge was keeping himself in check as he spoke.

"I'm giving this kid a tour and showing him around, but while I'm here, I had a question for you."

"Yes?" This time the sigh was set free as the suited man gave Sal a dubious glance.

Forge ignored the contempt in the man's voice. "What credit facilities can you offer a token holder?"

Sal was about to reach into his pocket to retrieve it, but Forge signaled him to hold off on. Behind the counter, the man frowned.

"Credit is only granted in exceptional circumstances. If the nature of the work is long and arduous, we offer a basic stipend to cover missed income. There is an overdraft facility if they need to make emergency purchases…or, we can provide discounted rates on material acquisition. They would need to be at least a Bronze token holder for any of that to be a possibility."

Sal had to admit that even though his demeanor was shit, he knew his stuff.

Forge nodded appreciatively. "What if it was a Silver token holder? To give you some context, we've got two guys who are going to be joining us. First is an absolute hotshot Appraiser, managed to identify an Epic grade in less than a minute. A guild backed him and gave him a Silver token, and I told him we could get him some good rates here."

Forge's tone was almost conspiratorial as he leaned closer to the desk. It was as if someone had slapped the man in the face. The look of shock was replaced by a wide smile after a moment, and he, too, leaned forward.

"I'm pretty sure we could work something out…" He started to type at a console behind the counter and equipped a tracker over his left eye to work out the details. "So, an Appraiser who has been verified up to Epic grade? Should I put you down as the assessor to that claim?"

Forge shook his head and smiled. "Upgrade has personally vouched for the capability of this individual, as well as Villa of the Reavers Guild."

The man faltered for only a moment, then resumed his questions. "We would be interested in conducting a negotiation with the individual."

Forge's hand appeared below the countertop and gestured for Sal to hand him the token discreetly.

Sal could see where this was going and happily did so.

Forge's smile was plastered on his face as he lifted the token and slid it across the counter. "He has given me full authority to negotiate on his behalf. He was hoping for discretion because he's a part of an established auction family…doesn't want to be seen competing with his father, Petro Argento."

Forge turned the token over to reveal Salvatore's name etched into the metal.

Rather than answering immediately, the man exhaled slowly before smiling. "Are there any other factors that could help us close this deal?"

Forge nodded with a grin. "He's looking to get into Crafting, of all things, so I could make up a shopping list that I think would sway him. Just send me your proposed budget, and I'll take care of the rest."

Sal was sure the man would be offended, but he looked relieved at the suggestion. Apparently, this auction was happy to pay for problems to go away.

His smile was still fixed as he almost reluctantly offered his hand to Forge. "Those terms work for us. We'll have a proposal drafted this morning and sent down to your workshop. If they're not acceptable, please let us know so we can recalibrate and find a solution that works for both sides."

Forge took back the silver tablet and pocketed it with a smile. "The second person I wanted to talk to you about is right here."

Sal had the composure to not act surprised, but he had absolutely no idea what angle Forge was using. The man cocked an eyebrow, but after the negotiation he'd just had with Forge, it was clear that he wasn't going to make any wild assumptions.

Forge gestured at Sal and practically whispered to the auctioneer, "Did you hear about the kid who broke the Skill Registration machine?"

With a slight frown, the auctioneer raised his hand and gave them an apologetic smile.

Forge faltered at the sudden interruption. He shot Sal an apologetic look and waved his hand to suggest that it would be fine. A gorgeous woman in a black suit appeared behind the desk as their original helper moved away to another area.

"Sincere apologies, but my colleague needs to attend a meeting with our management board as per your last request. The acquisition of key talent is something that we're always very interested in, but we're not in a position to sponsor first-years without any form of track record or guild backing."

Her apologetic smile was in no way sincere, but it was nicer to look at than the other guy's attempt. Sal merely shrugged as if to say, it is what it is.

She leaned forward over the table and spoke directly to Sal. "Since you've come all this way, why don't we take your details, and we can schedule in an exploratory chat for when you get your ranking at the end of the semester?"

Forge nodded. "Well, he's not been given the name officially yet…but he's probably going to be Myth when he graduates. He's a Mythcrafter, which is the stage after Legendcraft and Epicraft. The headmaster verified it himself and told me that Myth here is the only person in the world with this ability. He hasn't signed terms with any of the guilds yet, but, you know what? Policy is in place for a reason, so we'll respect your decision and have him chat to you next semester. Sound good, Myth?"

Forge was a terrible actor, but he was better at keeping his cool than the woman. Her eyes widened and her face went deathly pale.

Sal couldn't help but laugh at the ridiculousness of the situation. "Sounds good, Forge."

CHAPTER 17:
CONTRACTS

"MYTH, WAS IT?" THE WOMAN ASKED TENTATIVELY AS SHE PUT ON HER WARMEST smile. "I hope I didn't offend you just now. You have to appreciate that there are a thousand students coming in a year, with hundreds of them having Support skills that could be commercialized. With how the rankings go, not everyone gets to stay on at Quest Academy. When we sign a contract with a person, we invest all our resources into ensuring their success."

Her sweet talk activated almost instantly, and Sal was happy to oblige. He wasn't going to agree to anything today as the best approach was to leave them wanting. All of the leverage was in his court, so he didn't need to rush into any sort of agreement.

"I'm Vanessa, by the way…I'm not sure if you mentioned it or not, but could I ask for the name you used when joining the academy?" Her smile had evolved into charming as she attempted to worm information out of him.

Sal shook his head slightly and Vanessa moved straight onto the next topic, for fear of offending him.

"How about we talk about some hypotheticals then?" Her eyebrows raised as she looked at Forge too. "Since you brought Myth here to contract with us, there might be facilities or services that you wished to avail of?"

Forge's grin widened as he gestured at Sal to continue.

"Well, I'm a first-year with zero resources. I need a way to start earning, as well as a method to improve my skills. Mythcrafter allows me to Restore and Upgrade items, as well as Craft new inventions…up to the Mythic grade." Sal had no idea how to do that yet, but Vanessa didn't need to know that.

"My own internal power isn't sufficient for the bigger projects, and right now, I probably couldn't Craft, Restore, or Upgrade anything beyond Epic grade because of that limitation. If I had cores of energy that I could work with, then I'd be capable of much more."

Vanessa just stared at Sal. "You say that with so much conviction. Have you Crafted much before?"

He heard the challenge in her voice, and happily took it.

"I created a set of Rare-grade gauntlets with just a few chunks of metal and black gloves. They were imbued with an individual's power to bind it to them, and I put in a self-replenishing rune to make them self-sufficient. Oh, and yesterday I fixed a shoddily modified core, and Restored it to an Epic grade."

Even Forge looked shocked at the news of the gauntlets.

A sudden thought occurred to Sal. "I won't sign exclusivity over to anyone. I want the option to sell my items to the other students."

Vanessa smiled and gestured at Forge. "Luckily for you, we might just have a new Appraiser joining us. If you get a certification from an Appraiser that the item is fit for use and does what it's supposed to, you can sell your items to others. Before you go down that route, though, I would suggest you hear out the offers of exclusivity as they can be incredibly lucrative."

Noting both of their expressions, Vanessa refrained from pushing the issue. "Since you're still a first-year, there may be buyers who try to undercut you in price. If you wish, we could facilitate your commercial needs, and act as your broker for contracts?"

Sal nodded. He liked the sound of that…but was committed to not negotiating today. He'd let them sweat while he built up some accomplishments, and then he'd see what offer they came back to him with. He was incredibly appreciative of Forge's help with all of this. Sal could read people and sell items but had no idea how to sell individuals and their abilities, so Forge's input was invaluable.

Vanessa presented Sal with a personalized gift bag, filled with luxury goodies and practical items. She made a show of writing down her contact information and handed it directly to Sal. "If you need absolutely anything, or you'd like to talk about our services…or just get to know what we do up here, I'm your girl."

Sal held his breath until the elevator descended to the previous level. When the doors opened, he let out an explosive sigh.

Forge laughed. "Pretty stressful, wasn't it?" He scratched his bushy beard as he gestured for them to explore the industrial area.

"Why did you pretend I'm two different people? Won't they find out immediately?"

Forge shook his head as he held up his finger. "Appraisal is vital to our business. We need them more than anything else, and we're usually at the behest of those bastards up there. Any single item that is Crafted or improved or repaired…nobody knows if it's any good until an Appraiser tells them. You get an Appraiser seal of approval? You're in for a good time. Maybe I was being selfish, but I wanted them to pay your wages, while you worked down here with us."

Forge grinned, as though the plan were ingenious. "You get preferential rates from them, and you get to side gig with your coworkers. You Appraise something for them, they give you some materials you need. Down here, that would take a few seconds. Up there? It would take hours' worth of administration and statements."

That part made sense to Sal, and he was happy that he'd get to spend more time in the workshop.

Forge turned back to him and held up a second finger. "You saw how they reacted when they judged you without listening. I find it bizarre that they're responsible for finding the values of things, yet are so blatantly blind to talent. Even though Mythcrafter sounds incredible, it's going to take you a long time to make items for people, and it has a high overhead cost of materials without any guarantee of success. Appraisal only costs energy and takes a lot less time, so it's likely going to be your primary earner. We just needed to drive up the price of Salvatore, so that Salvatore can charge Myth for all his work…Why work twice as hard for a single job, when you can get paid twice for a single job?" Forge raised his hands as though the answer were completely obvious.

Sal smiled, but his cynicism was back. "That does sound amazing, but they're going to see through me. All they have to do is check with the headmaster, and they'll find out there's only one of me."

Forge wagged his finger. "I wouldn't be so sure. The headmaster suggested we use a different persona for you, so we could protect your identity. He'll confirm the existence of Myth, as will both Upgrade and I. I would suggest that you don't spread information about the ability so it doesn't bring us unwarranted attention. Anyway, let's get on with this tour. You're going to have classes, and I've got plenty of work that I need to get back to."

Sal followed Forge through the industrial area of the workshop. Some of the machines were using lasers to cut into delicate metals, while others were printing small components for assembly.

Forge gestured at one of the printers. "We always need the same things, so rather than buying it in bulk, we manufacture it and factor it into the price. These machines can work off any blueprint you input, and they can be bought from other students or bartered. Some will be better than others, and you can try creating your own from scratch when you take that module. Upgrade is fantastic at them, so talk to her if you're interested in knowing more."

Sal nodded as he continued to follow.

"This beautiful bastard is likely going to make me redundant! A portable blacksmith with operational forge. Excellent for purifying metals, but even better for creating blades! If you've any interest in that area, let me know." Forge looked like a proud parent as he stood with his hands on his hips.

The device was rustic in appearance with a blazing furnace that caused Sal to shield his eyes.

Forge glanced in the opposite direction as he led Sal away from the fires. "Over here are the precision tools for laser engraving." Forge reached into a drawer beneath the device and pulled it out to reveal mounds of dust. "Always empty the trays. That's rule number one."

Sal's eyes lit up at the sight of the multicolored dust…not because it was beautiful, but because his ability recognized it as a viable material. "Where does the dust go?" Sal asked as Forge slid the tray back in.

"Sometimes the Alchemy guys want it, but most of the time we stabilize it and dispose of it."

After another few minutes, Forge reached a transparent door that had a faint glow behind it. "These guys are technically a part of the Crafting team, but we all see them much more in the Research & Development category. It's a blend of technology and magic, but they run a lot of our infrastructure around the academy. If you poke your head in there in the future, you might learn a thing or two about magic programming…otherwise, you'll have to wait until you get to the advanced stages of your R&D courses."

With that, Forge concluded the tour and took Sal back down to the floor where he had met Upgrade for the first time.

"Hope that was informative and fun! When your contract comes down for the Appraisal gigs, we'll put it on your desk." Forge moved to one side and gestured at the new desk that had been erected in the time they were gone. "I needed to stall you for time, and they wanted to do something nice for you after that mess yesterday."

Sal looked around at all the Crafters who were pretending to be engrossed in their work, but their smiles sold them out. He was genuinely touched by the gesture and was pleasantly surprised to see Upgrade in the chair beside his station.

Forge cleared his throat. "Upgrade insisted that you sit beside her…"

"So I can keep an eye on you, and tease you relentlessly."

Forge chuckled and shook his head as he left them to it.

Sal stepped closer to his desk. There was a large package waiting for him on the surface. When he opened it up, his breath caught in his throat. He didn't know what all the components were, but it was a complete toolset, with everything being at least Rare grade in quality. His eyes didn't react to the tools in the way he thought they would, but he was still overjoyed to have received them.

Upgrade pulled her stool closer and leaned her elbows on the side of his bench. "You like 'em?" She cupped her chin with her palms as she smiled.

Sal was speechless as his auction house brain started to calculate how much those tools should have cost. He stopped his brain from adding up the numbers and just appreciated them for what they were.

"I love them, thank you."

Upgrade grinned as she clapped him on the shoulder. "Everyone pitched in to apologize for yesterday, and to welcome you to the team." She gestured at the crafters who were still burying their heads in their work.

Sal looked up. "Thank you!" Then he remembered what Forge had told him about the Crafters looking out for each other. "I don't have class for another hour…so if anyone would like anything Appraised for free, just bring it over!"

Sal sat at his desk and was about to start going through his new tools when nearly everyone shifted over to him with items in their hands. He laughed and closed the tool set before gesturing for the first person to approach.

"Only conditions I have…" Sal could see the man tense up as he was about to hand over an item, a slight look of apprehension flashing over his features. "Is that you need to tell me your name, what you do…and an embarrassing story about Upgrade." The crafters laughed, and even Upgrade herself cracked a smile from her bench.

"Come on, loud enough so she can hear it."

CHAPTER 18:
REALITY

"I WAS TASKED BY THE HEADMASTER TO TEACH YOU LOT ABOUT DUNGEONS, BUT it's hard to make kids like you understand the dangers of the world out there." Sinclair gestured off the platform behind him, revealing the city behind him.

"You're alive. Which tells me that you grew up in safety. That's a weakness you're going to have to overcome during your time here. Your survival instinct will be absolute muck and you'll die an early and painful death." His voice was calm and steady as he spoke. "How many people here think they could win in a fight against a demon?"

Sal turned around and was surprised to see more than a dozen hands raised into the air.

Sinclair didn't look surprised in the slightest and just shook his head in disappointment. "I didn't even tell you what type of fucking demon it was, and you lot already think you can take it down? Okay, out to the front here, all of you with the hands up."

Sinclair shot his hand forward and pointed to a student in the crowd. "Nice try. Your hand was up—get out here now before I pull you out."

Some of the students shuffled awkwardly, but there were still those who walked forward proudly.

Sinclair looked deflated as he regarded them all. "Do any of you know what a Prowler is?" As some of them nodded, Sinclair took a knee and grunted from the exertion. He whipped open one of his equipment boxes and retrieved a skull that he slipped onto his hand. It was long and pointed with two rows of vicious-looking teeth.

As Sinclair got back to his feet, he lifted the skull to show everyone. "This is a Prowler skull. They're one of the most common demons you'll encounter on the streets, after Leechers. Their main characteristic is that they're quiet, or at least, that's what the manuals will tell you. Let me rephrase it in a way that's a bit more enlightening. These fuckers are faster than you, stronger than you, and their bite will take off a limb…but the worst thing about them? They're predators that hunt in packs, and you lot are all prey. So, who here still thinks they could take on one of these?"

Sinclair raised the skull again and looked at the students who had raised their hands. Eight of them bowed their heads or smiled awkwardly, but four continued to hold their hands aloft.

He sighed as he started to take off his shirt. "For legal reasons, I would like to clarify that I have told these students they would die in front of a Prowler, but they have insisted that they would succeed. If it takes four deaths to save ninety-six, I'll take those odds every day of the week."

Gesturing at the staff who stood off to the side of the arena, Sinclair motioned for them to move closer. "Medical teams are here to save you after you start bleeding out, so make sure to thank them properly when you wake up in the infirmary, okay?"

Sal glanced at Divinity to see whether she had any idea what was going on, but the look of absolute horror on her face made him second-guess his need to know. After finishing up in the workshop, he had rushed over to the main amphitheater for their introduction to dungeons. But all that had happened so far was their new professor, a Hero called Sinclair, listing off all the horrible things that could happen to them out in the Red Zones. Sal didn't recognize any of the people who had raised their hands, but he couldn't help but wonder how Sinclair was going to change their minds.

"Lastly, to everyone watching this…pay close attention. You're going to see a Prowler that has revealed itself, is isolated from its pack, and it *will* attack. All these factors are rare when you're in a Red Zone. You never know when you're moments from death, regardless of how strong or amazing your power is. You, as an individual, are not prepared for the harsh reality of demons."

With that said, Sinclair threw his shirt to one side and leapt forward at a terrifying pace. In the flash of an eye, his white skin vanished, replaced by sleek black fur.

Collective screams of panic pierced through the students as nearly half the group fell back in terror, with some already crying. Sal barely retained his footing, but wasn't so sure he'd last when he saw the razor-sharp teeth clamping on the shoulder of the first student. The momentum of the Prowler's body carried it over the student's shoulder until it landed on the ground. With the student still clamped in its maw, it viciously flung the injured body toward the medical staff.

It had only been a second, and one of them was down. Not a single one of the confident kids activated a power, and just like that, the second one was down with an enormous gash along his chest and leg. The Prowler's paws ripped through skin and bone, and a resounding snap before the victim's howl echoed out.

Of the two remaining, one fell to the ground in complete defeat while the other ran away. The Prowler pawed at the defeated student's head, knocking him unconscious before slowly padding after the fleeing student. The entire Silver cohort watched in a terrified silence, hearing the frantic panting and pleading wails, until the Prowler sprung. To call it a charge was a disservice. It was like a black blur teleporting and slamming into the back of the student, claws ripping into his back and dispatching him with ease.

Sal fell to his knees as he watched Sinclair, back in his human form, walking back toward them while whistling cheerfully. In his hand was the ankle of the last student he took down, dragging him unceremoniously closer to the medical team, who glared at the professor. Without so much as an apology, Sinclair chucked the weeping student over to them, and turned back to the class before verifying they caught him.

"So, let me ask you again. How many people here think they could win a fight against a demon?"

The students looked utterly defeated. The ones capable of returning his gaze had a haunted, faraway look. Picking up his shirt and putting it back on, he chuckled humorlessly.

"You lot need a bit of a reality check. You might be sitting up here in these luxury towers…but it's only training. Your real job, and your future? It's out there, fighting these fuckers and taking back what we've lost. How many of you do you think we'd have lost if that was a real pack of Prowlers?" He paused for a moment and shook his head. "Doubt any information is going to be sinking into those fragile heads of yours…so let's wrap it up for today. Next lesson, you're—" Sinclair grinned as he clapped. "Ah, where's the fun in telling you? You'll find out tomorrow."

***

"Come on, you couldn't have missed us that much." Upgrade sounded genuinely curious as Sal walked toward his bench. Her smile faded when he got closer, then broke into a grin. "Looks like someone met Sinclair!"

A smattering of laughter came from the other benches, but with more than a few looks of sympathy for good measure. Sal didn't respond to anything as he took a seat and looked at the bench in front of him. The whole experience went through his mind again and again. He understood that there were risks in the Red Zone, and he knew that they were a real force…but the stark reality of having one of them attacking in such a ferocious manner? It was too surreal for him to process.

Sal glanced around the room, not focusing on anything in particular, and realized that he had been living in a bit of a fairy tale. Yes, he could make really cool stuff, or Upgrade things…but how was him Appraising items or Crafting gloves going to win against a force that powerful?

Sinclair was going easy on them, but it was still enough to shock him to his core. All of the students shared the same look, and it was bewildering to see some of the other cohorts laughing and smiling, being so carefree with their time. Their joy was a clear indicator that they had yet to meet with Sinclair, and Sal barely managed to suppress a shudder of anxiety.

"Snap out of it." Upgrade clicked her fingers in front of his face.

He blinked as he looked up at her and saw her frown.

"Stop overthinking it. You got a taste of the real world just now, but don't let it drown you in worry or anxiety. All the students go through it, and Sinclair is by far the most successful professor in this academy. He has saved so many lives, by making them drop out. Don't be one of those people." She placed her hands on both sides of the toolbox he had been gifted that morning and slid it forward so that it rested directly in front of him. "Rather than sitting here worrying, use your gifts. That's how you turn the tide."

Sal nodded slowly, but he still felt emotionally drained.

Upgrade smiled. "Well, if you're feeling that bad…you're probably in no mind to review this contract proposal from upstairs." She lifted the toolbox to reveal an official-looking envelope addressed to him. There was even a wax stamp securing it in place.

Turning the letter around in his hands, Sal wondered what sort of verdict they had come up with.

Upgrade's fingers tapped against his workbench, and she leaned closer to him. "I swear to fuck, if you don't open it right now and tell me what it says…"

Her impatience made Sal want to draw it out for longer, but he was curious himself. He opened his tool kit and saw a fine engraving knife with a sharp edge. Using it as a letter opener, he slid the envelope open without disturbing the wax seal. Upgrade looked at him as if he were crazy, Sal waved like it was obvious.

"I can Restore the envelope and pretend I never opened it, put them under pressure to send more stuff."

As he opened the letter, Upgrade stepped in behind him and started to read the contents over his shoulder. "Rights to work in the workshop, that's good." She mumbled her thoughts aloud as she went through it. "Non-exclusive? Well done on wrangling that. Ooooooh, you're getting access to their materials! Looks like you're going to get a delivery every few weeks with new materials for your own personal use, but this is the cool part!"

Sal was a much slower reader than her and looked at where she was pointing. Her voice was excited for him, and Sal decided to listen to her rather than reading. He could have a proper read of it when she was done.

"Bonuses are really rare for contract workers. If you hit your targets, which look to be pretty easy for you…you'll get some significant Q-Credit. But I like this part more. You can build up purchasing power with them by forfeiting Q-Credit rewards."

Upgrade leaned in closer. "Lucky son of a bitch. This is a great contract! You can earn some credit, buy shit from them without paying commission or brokerage fees, and they're feeding you materials…all without exclusivity, which lets you Appraise for the other guilds, too, if they give you their tokens."

Shaking her head, Upgrade sighed and went back to her own bench. "You should totally accept!" She swiveled on her stool, but instead of stopping at her desk, she continued in a full rotation until she faced Sal again. "Out of curiosity, with those materials…what are you going to make?"

Sal didn't even need to think about the answer. He had been practically planning it all from the moment Sinclair had torn into those students.

"Prowler-proof armor."

Upgrade's laugh echoed throughout the workshop, and only got louder once she saw that Sal was being serious.

He sat in silence, waiting for her to stop, and when she did, she made a suggestion that chilled him to the bone.

"Well, if you want to test it out…I can ask Sinclair to help you out? He'd be more than happy to assist."

CHAPTER 19:
AMBITIONS

The food hall was bustling. It was one of the few locations where all the different cohorts could mingle at the same time. Their schedules were different throughout the day to add variety to the classes and rotate individual professors, but the lunch hour and evening meals were on a set rotation.

Sal knew the catering facilities were open almost around the clock, but there were key hours for the best set menus that nobody wanted to miss. It was the difference between sandwiches and steak. When it finally came to his turn, Sal went through the motions of saying yes and no until his meal was fully customized to his tastes and handed to him. He grabbed a bottle of orange juice and made his way over to an empty table, not even bothering to look around to see whether he knew anybody.

"Hey," Divinity called out as she approached from the opposite direction with what looked like a pile of vegetables on her plate. It couldn't have been more different from the steak and mashed potato combination that Sal had going on. She walked with him to the table and sat with a sigh.

"I'm still shaken up after that class. How are you faring?" Her voice was tired.

Sal sighed as he looked at his tray and realized he hadn't grabbed any cutlery. He stared numbly at his meal before a steak knife and fork were slid across the table to where he sat.

He smiled as he took them from Divinity. "You have the absolute best power."

After a few minutes of eating in silence, Sal shook his head. "I feel so out of place." He glanced over at a table where some students were laughing and joking, he just couldn't understand how they were so carefree.

"I can't think of anyone who could possibly fight someone…no, something like that!" Sal shuddered before taking a drink.

Divinity, on the other hand, seemed to finally realize something. "It's because you weren't at the Combat encounter." Her face broke into a relieved sigh. "You haven't seen what these classes are capable of. Silver cohort is mostly Support-class people, so we don't have that many stars…like, did you know someone managed to protect themselves from Sinclair?"

Sal's fork clattered against the plate as he stared at Divinity.

She nodded. "Oh yeah, there were a few of them! You wouldn't have seen it, but there's a guy who can move like lightning, and he evaded every single attack. He didn't take down the Prowler, but he didn't get killed either. Another girl shot a shield at him, which trapped him and protected the other students, but there was a guy who apparently punched the Prowler out of the air during that first attack."

Divinity's voice grew with excitement. "There are people here who are doing their roles really well! We just need to do ours too."

Her words finally started to resonate with him, and he gave her a slight smile, but she wasn't done.

"Sal, I can see glimpses of the future, and I have seen some absolutely incredible things happen! Many of them aren't possible without you." Divinity popped a cherry tomato into her mouth and gave him a smile. "Stop overthinking it and play to your strengths. We're not all made to fight on the frontlines."

With that said, Divinity gave him a wink and got back to eating.

Sal smiled. "Thank you, I needed that."

Divinity rolled her eyes. "I know you did. Future? Remember? Without me, you'd be moping for the next week and getting nothing done!" She gestured vaguely at the room as she laughed. "There are lots of changes we need to make if you've any chance of getting into the Savior class."

Sal's eyebrow cocked. "Is that what we're aiming for all of a sudden?" Divinity was the Rank #2 in the entire year, and it made sense for her to be ambitious…but he didn't anticipate her trying to take him along with her.

Divinity nodded as she tapped the side of her head. "I've made out a good chunk of the roster already, but you're not on it…well, I don't think you are."

Sal had never seen her uncertain before about a vision. "Why aren't you sure?"

Divinity sighed and shook her head. "I've pinpointed the announcement ceremony but can't see any of the faces. All I have so far are the code names! Guess who gets landed with Oracle, by the way?"

Although she pretended to be upset, Sal could tell she was happy at the prospect of being in the Savior class.

"Now, everything could change, as this is only one course of events…but there's nothing about you or any code name that I would ever see you owning. I've a good idea of who is who, but it can still change. Like earlier, remember what I said about the girl with the shields? She was never a contender for the Saviors, but now suddenly she has a shot. You never know what changes people, and maybe there will be events like the Prowler attack that changes our trajectory through the future."

Sal started to wonder whether she was talking about Hannah. *Was the fact that she had a Rare item creating enough of an impact to get her noticed?* Leaning back in his chair, Sal started to think about it more clearly. *He had the capability of changing who would enter the Savior class with equipment he made…but for some reason, he himself wasn't successful?* It made him completely rethink the theory, and Sal couldn't help but laugh at his own ego.

Divinity listed off the names she was having issues with, and one of them caught Sal's attention.

"Wait, that last one…they're in your vision?"

Divinity nodded. "Myth? Yes, but I can't see anything to do with them. They're like a ghost!" Her voice carried a tone of annoyance which melted away when Sal's face brightened with a laugh.

***

Sal nudged the door button with his elbow, causing it to automatically close behind him. Both of his hands were full of materials and the toolset the Crafters had gifted to him. He had debated leaving it in the workshop, but when he received a whole new set of tools from the Auctioneers on the Credit floor, he decided to bring the best ones back to his room. He wouldn't be too devastated if he ended up losing one or two tools from the Uncommon-grade set that they got for him, but he'd be distraught if he lost any of the Rare-grade set.

After his meal, he called his father for advice on the contract, and Petro had a few suggestions to sweeten the deal. Sal relayed the suggestions to Forge and within the hour, the contract was amended, and he was walking back to his room with his spoils.

In the back of his head, he kept thinking about what Divinity had said about Hannah moving up through the ranks because of her equipment. She had even said it to him in bed about how powerful they made her feel, and he wondered if he could help others like that. Sal resisted the urge to lock himself in the room with the workbench. He needed to come up with a strategy. He was currently being too reactive for his own liking.

"Okay, so what do we know?" Sal placed the tools and materials onto the workbench before returning to his bedroom. "Mythcrafter is the skill. I can Craft all grades from Common to Mythic…apparently."

As he spoke, he wrote down everything he knew onto his tablet. "Can also Upgrade and Restore as part of the ability." He gauged how much energy he had spent on the different actions, remembering clearly all the different phases of the gauntlet refining. "Without any Crafting expertise and just raw power, I can create a Rare-grade item of small to moderate size." Each note gave him a clearer picture of where his weaknesses were. "Components can be upgraded with power, but it's exhausting and creates sludge stains." Sal gave his bedsheets a side glance and made a mental note to clean them before going to bed.

On a separate tab, Sal wrote down all the ideas that he had for Crafting. His armor concept was completely driven by fear, but that didn't necessarily make it a stupid idea. If he was to think about his Crafting as a commercial business, he would have a huge market interest from anyone who had met Sinclair and wanted protection.

"But how do you even stop a Prowler attack?" Sal muttered as he opened another tab and started to take notes, or rather a shopping list. "Either we learn how to make runes, or we take powers from students and imbue them into the equipment?"

He didn't want to relegate himself into being a one-trick pony and decided that he needed to learn other rune patterns instead of just the self-replenishing one. He had seen many of them over the years, but had never studied them in detail. His eyes had saved the self-replenishing rune like a template in his mind that he just needed to place onto a surface. Sal hoped that he could eventually get to that point with other, more powerful runes.

After about an hour or so, Sal looked down to see at least a dozen tabs on his tablet with various amounts of considerations he needed to make. With a sigh, he turned and activated the console to see the different options available to him. One of them was the internal store where he could use Q-Credit.

A premium coffee cost two credit, a Sleeping Tiger drink cost twenty, and a module early-enrollment cost a hundred.

Thankfully, Sal had been picked for the Crafting class, so he wasn't charged, and nobody wanted to do Administration, so he didn't need to compete for seats on that course…but Analysis had cost him. Of his original six hundred Q-Credit, he was down to four hundred and ninety…and that was only after a few days at the university. Sal navigated through the store and found a list of categories. He scrolled down to find stuff for his room when another option caught his eye.

"Weaponry and Equipment?"

Sal turned around properly so he could study the screen in more detail. The listings were…extensive, and Sal, for the first time, was at a bit of a loss. He could see the pictures of the items, but his eyes didn't tell him anything more than that. He was stuck reading the inventory listings that were woefully vague about details, and Sal wondered whether he just had high standards when it came to the qualities and details of a product.

"Let's sort by…Crafted!" With his selection in place, Sal barely saw a dent in the list, revealing that most of the items for sale had been Crafted.

"Rare?" he asked as he ticked on the item quality, only to see a few dozen items on display. Some had set prices, which looked to be exorbitant, while others opted for the bidding war model. Sal saw a gray chest-plate that looked similar to their uniform. Sal clicked on it and was surprised to see that it was Crafted by a third-year.

> **Gray Guard!**
>
> **Scale armor handmade by Rank #34 – Fabi Maccles**
>
> Each scale was carefully shaped by hand, with a total build time of two months. Made with refined cobalt-infused steel to give the gray a bluish hue upon activation. Gray Guard is impervious to direct blunt attacks, and is Prowler claw-resistant.
>
> **Starting Price:** 300 Q-Credit.

Sal shook his head at the woeful Appraisal. If it was even a true Rare-grade item, then it would likely have more effects than what was listed. He had to re-read the cobalt-infused part, because it made zero sense to him. "Is it a real thing, or marketing bullshit?"

Sal was about to open another tab when he remembered why he had gone to the store in the first place. Sighing to himself, he navigated back to the main page and moved down to the dorm improvements section. He wanted to get a corkboard or something so he could write down his to-do lists, but the university once again surprised him.

"Complete renovation?" Sal looked at the price and shook his head. "Who the fuck would pay five thousand Q-Credit for this?"

He had sorted the list from high to low but accidentally double-clicked the console, showing him the most expensive option on offer. Sal clicked it and ended up staring at the screen: a luxurious penthouse apartment, with multiple rooms.

Sal's fingers nearly trembled as he clicked on each of the rooms, only to find a workshop equipped with the same machinery he had seen on the industrial floor. There were even Alchemy stations and rune benches. Another room contained various rolls of cloth and a cluster of mannequins. Most impressively, other than the hot tub, was what looked like a combat training room.

"Five thousand Q-Credit." Sal breathed as he looked at the description. "A month!"

Clicking the price filter again, Sal was rewarded with a list of items that could be purchased for as little as five Q-Credit, and he felt much more at ease. He couldn't help but wonder, though, if it really was possible to earn that kind of money. *If that guy was selling Rare equipment at three hundred...why couldn't he?*

And with that, Sal started to make his shopping list. In the back of his head, the makings of his own little commercial empire started to take root.

CHAPTER 20:
PRACTICALITIES

SAL GLANCED AT THE TIMER BESIDE HIM AND GRIMACED. HE HAD BEEN WORKING straight for close to five hours, and he needed to go to sleep soon if he was going to have any chance of surviving the next day.

"Or we could just buy premium coffee?" Sal muttered as he turned the timer to one side so it was out of view.

He turned back to his current project that was laid out in front of him. His lackluster gray uniform had transformed into something entirely new, but Sal was nowhere near done with it yet. With a resigned sigh, Sal tapped his tablet again to bring up a picture of the rune he wanted to engrave into the material. His eyes weren't able to pick up anything from the static image, so he had to sketch it out by hand and hope that his eyes would understand what he was hoping to achieve.

"Come on…" Sal groaned as he finished the most recent arrangement. His eyes activated again and tried to send a portion of his power through the rune he had just Crafted, but it wasn't responsive to his attempts. It had been like this for most of the night, and Sal was reaching his breaking point.

On the screen beside him, almost tauntingly, was a crash course in runes that cost fifty Q-Credit. It had been made by one of the third-years, and was a breakdown of class notes and helpful tips. Sal had read through the description a few times and knew that it was for panicking students coming close to exam periods, and not for students in their first week at the academy. *Was he really desperate enough to throw credits at something he was going to learn eventually?*

Gritting his teeth, Sal tried to push power through the engraving again, but nothing happened. His pitiful attempt at a crafted rune was so bad that his eyes couldn't find a single way to Upgrade it or refine it. As far as his ability was concerned, Sal had just drawn a terrible picture and there was nothing that could be done to improve it.

"Fuck it." Sal finally justified the purchase to himself and bought the crash course. The download was unexpectedly long, and Sal checked the files to see what was going on. He was surprised to see that the student had created daily diaries, weekly summaries, project breakdowns, and step-by-step tutorials. It was a lot more intensive than he had expected, and Sal sighed in relief as he navigated to a video that seemed to deal with the problem he was facing.

…and in between lines, make sure that your needle is always imbued with essence, otherwise the rune will be incomplete. As you know, I like to keep a straight and steady line for the entire thing, but others like to dip back into the essence to strengthen certain areas of the rune. Strengthening is only really important if you're using multiple runes on a single piece of equipment. They'll start competing for the same amount of energy, so strengthening is a great method to balance a weaker rune with a stronger one.

Sal paused the video and rooted through his box of tools until he found what looked like the needle from the video. It was like an old-school fountain pen with a triangular blade that narrowed into a fine needle-like point. He realized that he was skipping ahead and instead searched for videos that would explain how to imbue the needle. Sal was rewarded a half second later with another video that showed a pair of hands holding a less impressive version of the tool he held in his.

…contains a little fragment of a core. Common models run out of charge after a few days, and can be recharged for a fee, but the Uncommon and Rare sets have self-replenishing runes that allow the Crafter to use them around the clock! If you're serious about becoming an engraver, you'll want to invest in getting an Uncommon etcher as fast as possible. They are an absolute game-changer! Even though the etcher is fully charged, it's not yet imbued with a magical signature, which is unique to you.

There are two ways to do this, and the first one requires a high degree of skill control, where you channel the power straight into the etcher. For those of you who can't navigate power like that, don't worry. The other solution is to prick your finger with the needle until it draws blood. It'll be a little painful, but essence courses through your blood and it will create a signature for you. Until you can control your energy, this is a quick trick to make sure you don't fall behind your classmates.

Over the next couple of hours, Sal watched at least a dozen videos from the alumni and learned a ridiculous amount that he didn't know. Before he even realized it, the sun started to rise in the distance, and he knew he'd need to fall back onto his premium coffee plan to get through the day. Even though his body was tired, his brain was still firing on all cylinders and wanted to jump straight into Crafting to apply the tips and tricks he had been learning.

"Let's start with this…" Sal muttered as he raised the etcher in his hand. With a flicker of his power, he brought forth one of his own tendrils of essence and imagined it connecting to the core shard in the pen. Not only did it work immediately, Sal could have sworn that the needle started to glow.

"And now, let's see if you work." Sal straightened his back and looked at the countless sketches of runes sprawled around the desk, all of them in shards of fabric. He didn't want to try it on the gray uniform straight away and fuck it up. Even though he could Restore it, it was a silly waste of power.

"Please work," Sal breathed as he started to draw the rune again, this time with the etcher fully powered and tied to his essence. He had stupidly been using one of the carving blades, because it had made sense to him at the time. The etcher left clear lines of pulsating energy, and Sal was amazed to feel no difference in his power levels. When he had placed the rune on the gauntlets, it was by bludgeoning it onto the metal with his power. Even though he knew he could make mistakes, Sal didn't want to rely on his powers to fix everything. He wanted to be good at something in his own right.

"Come on…just a little more…" Sal said as he gently brought the line to completion by closing off the pattern. Much to his surprise, the pulsating energy that followed the needle continued through the line after the etcher left the surface.

It shot around the lines as though it were a racetrack. There were areas where the power slowed down or seemed to struggle, so without thinking, he smoothed out those lines. The pace picked up and it got faster and faster until the entire drawing started to glow.

"Whoa." Sal's eyes widened as the rune activated. *He had done it!* His eyes were telling him that the rune in front of him was a minor protection rune, and he could already see new patterns emerging and upgrade routes to make it more advanced. Without wasting any time, Sal placed the completed rune to one side and brought his gray uniform front and center. He knew what he was doing now.

With a quick turn of the timer, Sal reset it and looked out the window to the rising sun. "Ah, slow down. We're just getting started."

He grinned as he brought up a series of runes that he wanted to engrave on his uniform. They were all basic ones, but they would act as the foundation for upgrades. The idea had come to him when he had sorted through the assortment of materials he had been given. He didn't want to waste them on items that he'd sell to others, and instead wanted to find a way to use his skills efficiently and cheaply.

Sal couldn't think of anything cheaper than applying runes to existing uniforms and then using his power to Upgrade them into stronger variants. Sure, there'd be some material and energy cost, but nothing in comparison to creating an entirely new piece from scratch.

He bit his lip and furrowed his brow as he concentrated on etching the different patterns. His eyes started to resonate with the drawings and offer suggestions on how they might complement each other. They weren't really suggestions, but rather patterns that made sense to Sal.

Sal took a step back from the bench with a satisfied smile. Little beads of light were finally flowing through the pattern, but it was going to take a while before they navigated the course. The first rune that Sal had created was about the size of his palm, but this one combined five different runes that were connected by a sprawling labyrinth of lines. Each of them were drawn in a way that would best carry their respective magical charges. Sal didn't know how, but he instinctively understood how to best place the runes alongside each other and how to connect them perfectly.

"What the…" Sal blinked as the sound of the timer registered for him. He turned it off and looked out the window to see the sun much higher in the sky. "Guess it's a shower and then class?" He groaned audibly as he turned toward the bathroom. He couldn't help but give the uniform a proud glance before he made his way to the bathroom, and he wondered whether he'd have time to Upgrade it before class started.

After his shower, he decided that he needed to try the upgrade. He wouldn't be able to concentrate on anything else throughout the day, so Upgrading the uniform now…was kinda like an investment in his learning? His justifications were weak, but it didn't matter because his mind was made up.

Taking a few silver ingots from his pile of materials, he wondered whether they'd integrate well with the gray color. He started the upgrade and poured his powers into the uniform. Unlike the gauntlets, which had exhausted him by pulling out buckets of his power, this experience was completely different. It was like he was slowly pouring water into a mold, filling each of the tiny grooves with both power and intent.He could have rushed the process or pushed his power at it, but that felt wrong, so he went at the pace set by the runes. There was no rush to complete the runes, and instead, Sal felt opportunities occurring naturally, where he could refine it in ways he hadn't imagined.

When the gentle glow finally subsided, Sal was rooted to the spot. He still had most of his energy remaining, and he had only used a single ingot of silver…but somehow, he had managed to create a Rare-grade piece of equipment.

Name	Protective Shirt
Origin	Crafted
Age	New
Grade	Rare (Lower)
Dimensions	Chest 42 inches | Neck 17.5 inches
Materials	Cotton | Refined Mythcrafter Essence | Reinforced Wool
Attributes	**Defiant**: Shirt negates piercing and blunt damage. Chance to reflect damage. **Untouchable**: Attempts by others to remove the shirt will cause Repel to activate. **Adrenaline**: Shirt abilities are always active.
Abilities	Defiant | Untouchable | Adrenaline
Power Source	External Essence
Evolution	No
Quality	Good
Condition	100%
Value	Est. $12,000.00 – $16,000.00

What had once been a dull gray shirt was now completely silver and adorned with beautifully crafted runes made of metal. The pattern meshed all over the shirt and although it retained the flexibility of fabric, it offered the same protection as plate armor. Sal slipped it on and was surprised to feel it constrict around his form and improve his posture. He finished getting dressed and gave his bed an apologetic look before leaving the room. He had a full day ahead of him, but his mind focused on the coffee he would find just a few floors away.

Maybe it was because of how tired he was, but Sal didn't register the reactions of the people around him until he had taken his first few sips of the premium coffee. He had essentially made his way to the lobby like a zombie and hadn't interacted with a single person. He didn't even know what class he had today or where it was going to be.

Clarity surged through him as the coffee worked its magic, and Sal suddenly realized that people were staring at him. He looked down at his chest with a smile and stopped when he saw the silver runes glowing against the gray material. His eyes traveled farther down, and he saw how much of a contrast the shirt was to his normal gray pants.

"Close enough." Sal shrugged as he made his way to his next class.

CHAPTER 21:
VERITAS

SINCLAIR SAT IN THE LECTURE ROOM WITH HIS FEET UP ON THE TABLE. HIS fingers were linked behind his head, and he watched as the last of the group hurried in to take their seats. When the doors closed and the lights dimmed, he clicked a device in his hand, which started a presentation. It was a series of slides with questions written on them. With a groan, Sinclair turned in his seat, put his feet on the ground, and placed his elbows on the table. He looked weary, as though he were exhausted.

Sal related to the man at that moment.

Sinclair sighed as he gestured up at the screen. "I'm supposed to talk to you about our history. How many people used to be alive before the portals opened up, how much territory we lost that are now referred to as Red Zones…all the facts." His expression was grim as he let the device in his hand drop to the table with a clatter. "Instead of going through numbers that don't matter to you, I'll tell you about the things that should."

His eyes locked onto the group as he folded his arms and leaned forward. "Who here has heard of the Bastion?"

Although the tone was neutral, Sal could see the anger in his eyes.

More than a few hands went up, and Sinclair nodded.

"When everything started going to shit and it looked like we were going to be overrun completely, the Bastion program was announced. An exclusive get out-of-jail-free card for the ultra-wealthy." Sinclair pointed his finger directly up. "Shot themselves into space where they'd be safe."

His hand slammed back on the table. "We typically joke about Bastion trying to pull the strings from orbit, since they don't have any magical essence in their bodies. Their relevance and influence is all but gone since the majority of you haven't heard of half of them…but, they're still a threat to us. Who can tell me why?"

A single hand was raised in the crowd, and Sinclair indicated for her to answer.

"Because there are people still loyal to them here?"

Sinclair smiled and shook his flat palm from side to side. "Almost there. Bastion is a threat to us because they control a lot of our media signals and are responsible for pushing their propaganda on the general public. Worse than that? Reclamation guilds are being privately bankrolled by Bastion. Who can tell me why that might be a bad thing?"

Another hand raised, and Sinclair indicated for them to answer.

"Because they're reclaiming rich territory instead of areas that would benefit refugees."

Sinclair turned and shot the student a smile. "Correct in one. You don't want to know how much money is spent on keeping those mansions safe from demons, for whenever the Bastion returns…and who knows when that will be?"

Sinclair shook his head as he finished the rhetorical question. "That Prowler attack yesterday was a necessary lesson. Your whole lives, you've been exposed to media curated by assholes who don't even live here. Indoctrination through hope of salvation and a brighter tomorrow. Who here was a fan of Valor? Leader of the Veritas Guild?"

Sal raised his hand and saw that he wasn't alone in his fandom, as practically all the group had their hands raised. Valor and the Veritas Guild had been a staple in their childhood; they'd heard about how he retook key territory from the enemies, and how he used his powers to protect the weak.

Sinclair didn't share any of their smiles. "And how many of you realized that Valor doesn't exist?"

A handful of people raised their hands, and Sal was shocked to see Divinity's among them.

Sinclair gestured for her to elaborate, and she obliged.

"None of the landmarks on the broadcasts were from the listed safe zones, and the Veritas Guild wasn't registered with the United Guilds Association."

Sinclair nodded as he gestured to another student to give their reasoning.

"Valor claimed to have fought a horde of demons in my district, but it never happened. The footage showed really old versions of the area that was destroyed decades ago."

"And the demons you saw in those broadcasts? Complete fabrications." Sinclair shook his head in disgust. "To teach you about portals, demons, dungeons, and towers…I need you all to forget everything you think you know about them."

Sinclair walked around to the front of the desk and leaned against it. "So let's start from the beginning. What is a portal? It's a giant, fuck-off opening, usually in the sky that can appear anywhere. Where does it lead? That depends, but the answer is usually to another world." Sinclair's tone was both dramatic and exasperated.

"So now we know what a portal is—what is a dungeon? It's the domain of a powerful demon, usually filled with traps and various forms of loot. Sometimes, the demon is the dungeon, but that's a conversation for another time. You'll sometimes hear people talk about dungeon portals? Well, those are portals that have special conditions to be met before they can be closed. Usually, killing demons." Sinclair's explanation was to the point, and he flew through the different categories.

"What's left?" he muttered before glancing up. "Ah, yes. Towers! Imagine a series of dungeons stacked on top of each other. Every floor will have a demon that needs to be defeated before combatants can move up to the next floor. There are rules with towers that make them more popular for Heroes and Adventurers, but they're not to be underestimated." Sinclair's voice started to trail off as he leaned back against the desk.

"This introductory course is going to be straightforward. I'll teach you about the different demons you'll encounter in each location, and you will learn to combat those demons in teams. At the end of the semester…"

Sinclair's smile grew predatory, and Sal was immediately transported back to the previous day when he had ravaged the students.

"You're going to clear a tower floor together, without my help."

***

If Sal could have gone back in time, he would have gone to the night before and made himself go to bed. The coffee may have had magical effects, but it wasn't nearly enough to keep up in Sinclair's classroom. After dropping the bombshell of their final exam before the end of the semester, Sinclair went on to explain about twenty of the most common types of demons and all their characteristics and traits.

Sal wasn't the only person shocked and horrified, which was a slight relief. Sinclair had told them the highest grades of demon were referred to as lords. They were able to take on humanoid shapes and communicate and were labeled as highly dangerous and manipulative.

There was just something that didn't sit well with Sal, and it was the fact that the Prowler was the second weakest of all the demons. No matter how strong he got, he wasn't sure he'd be able to deal with even seeing a Prowler, let alone a lord.

Sal shook his head as he left the classroom with the group. They had a break before the next class, and Sal wondered how much sleep he'd be able to get if he rushed back to his room.

Unfortunately, Divinity intercepted him. Her eyes were glued to his new shirt, and Sal just knew there were a thousand questions incoming. With an internal groan, he almost asked Divinity to get his answers from the future so he could go and sleep, but when he saw how excited she was, he thought better of it.

"Did you make that!" Divinity gasped as she ran her finger across the silver mesh. Her eyes darted up at Sal questioningly. "Whoa, you look like shit! What happened?"

As though he were an old man who needed assistance, Divinity looped her arm with his and guided him to a nearby area with seats and loungers. "Tell me everything. I want to know what it does…are they runes? How long did it take you?"

She asked question after question, all at once, and Sal barely managed to keep track of her words. The effects of the coffee were wearing off, and he wasn't sure how much longer he could stay awake.

"Was up all night making it. Haven't come up with a name, though," Sal answered as he made his way through her questions. "Learned how to etch and make runes, so I used my eyes to map out the different ways they could work together…and complement each other."

Divinity's eyes narrowed when his words slurred, which he interpreted as confusion on her part.

"This one is for protection…but when it's combined with the blunt resistance, it creates a knock-back effect." Sal smiled as he tried to focus on the runes.

It was taking more and more effort to remember what the others did, and he started to feel like something was wrong. It wasn't just exhaustion. He looked up and was about to ask Divinity for help, but her eyes were already white. He could have sworn that she grimaced, and it sent a pang of anxiety through him.

After what felt like an age, Divinity blinked and gave Sal a sympathetic look. "We need to get you to the workshop. I'll take notes for you in the next class, so don't worry…okay?" Before she moved, she glanced at the shirt again, then shook her head. "Come on, I'll walk with you."

Sal nodded as he got to his feet. He didn't even have the energy to ask what she saw. The best he could manage was just to follow her.

****

A wolf whistle echoed throughout the workshop when Sal made his way through the row of benches. Upgrade was standing in the distance with her fingers at her lips, ready to send another whistle. She was clearly the first to notice his newly redesigned shirt, and it didn't take long for the other regulars to get up from their desks to have a closer look. Divinity had already left and rushed off to their next class, but Sal couldn't remember what she had told him.

He almost walked past his own desk, and Upgrade caught him by the shoulders. "Looks like someone did their first all-nighter! Maybe we should—"

Her words caught in her throat as she stared at his improved uniform. Her hands traced along the silver mesh as she inspected each of the runes. After a few moments of her pawing at his shirt and turning him around to look at all of the different runes, her eyes widened. "Are you fucking serious? Francis!"

Their resident rune expert rushed over, excitement on his face. "Another Restoration?"

Upgrade took a step back and gestured vaguely at Sal's uniform. "I can't make sense of them. It looks like they're working together?" Her eyes snapped back to Sal's face, who was about ready to fall asleep at any moment. With a frown, she shook her head. "Wait a second, Francis." She raised her hand to stop him from inspecting the shirt. "Sal, take off your shirt."

Sal tried, but his arms refused to work. He wearily looked at them, confused, he couldn't recall a single time he'd felt this foggy from staying awake all night.

Upgrade cursed and moved in to assist him. When she grabbed the shirt, one of the patterns flashed.

Sal stared numbly as Upgrade was thrown backward into one of the benches. The look of anger on her face was terrifying, and Sal was actually relieved that his body chose that moment to pass out.

CHAPTER 22:
LIMITATIONS

"DREGS." UPGRADE REPEATED THE WORD.

Sal clutched at the blanket covering his torso.

Upgrade pointed at the crystal pendant around her neck. "I wear this as a source of power, because my internal essence isn't enough to fuel my suit. If I tried it without the core, it would work for a while, but then I'd get the dregs. You should never run yourself down to that point!"

Upgrade managed to stress her point without raising her voice. She took a breath as she paced around the room, seeming to choose her words carefully. "You had five interlinked runes. Did you even consider the power consumption to wear it? No, you didn't…because you haven't been taught that yet!"

Sal watched as she paced around the workshop's canteen. He sat on an incredibly comfortable couch, and in front of him was a special brew of coffee made by their in-house Alchemist barista. Each sip dispelled another wave of brain fog, with every sip making him see how much of an idiot he had been. He kept replaying the moment Upgrade had been thrown across the room and felt horrible for causing that. Closing his eyes, he berated himself before Upgrade's voice cut through his thoughts.

"Didn't you hear what I said?"

Upgrade's voice was still stern, but there was more behind it. Sal looked up and saw her holding the shirt he had made.

"You haven't been taught the main principles of Crafting yet. You're still going through induction week and shouldn't be working on personal projects for at least another month!" Upgrade turned the fabric around in her hands.

"Francis isn't half the Appraiser you are, but even he could see that this is a Rare-grade piece of equipment. To make that in one night is incredible, especially with your first attempt…but please don't test your creations yourself, okay?"

Sal finally understood the other emotion in Upgrade's voice—concern. He nodded and tried to apologize to her again, but she raised a hand to stop him.

"You're a Crafter, Sal. Never apologize for that. Just don't let those skills kill you, okay? We need a few Mythic-grade items out of you before you croak!" And with that sentence, Upgrade broke into a smile as she handed back the shirt. "You could probably sell this to someone in the senior classes who have internal essence to spare. Heck, there are a few guilds that would probably take it off your hands. You could send it up to the Credit floor?"

Upgrade gestured at the mug of coffee on the table. "You can take that with you, and give me that blanket for a second."

The blanket was the only thing stopping Upgrade seeing him topless, and he felt very self-conscious all of a sudden.

She didn't bat an eyelid as she activated her suit. "Who do you think peeled your shirt off?"

Without so much as another word, Upgrade took the blanket from him and her now-mechanical arms started to work on it earnestly. "I'm no Tailor, but this should do for the rest of the day!"

Sal watched in awe as her hands cut and mended the fabric, shaping it while rotating it. In a few heartbeats, she was done and threw the result at him. Sal's eyes noted that it was a Common-grade item, but it had increased durability because of Upgrade's craftsmanship. By the time he had put it over his head, Upgrade was moving out the door.

"Come on, and don't forget the coffee. I don't want to have to explain things a thousand times, so drink up."

Sal was surprised at how well the blanket-shirt fit him. There were no traces that it had been a blanket, so he wasn't worried about people staring at him for the time being. He wondered whether he'd be able to dye it gray but pushed that thought out of his head as he grabbed his Rare shirt and the coffee cup.

When he followed Upgrade through the doors, he was happy to see a group of relieved faces staring back at him from the workbenches. Francis was the only one who still looked anxious.

Upgrade shook her head at him. "Nope, not today, Francis. You can ask him about the runes another day. Need to show him the core-shed."

A resigned slump was the only answer from Francis as Upgrade led Sal toward one of the closed-off spaces that Sal had assumed were private offices.

Upgrade tapped her hand against one of the sensors, which was enough to open the large sliding doors.

A wave of cold air hit Sal, and he was grateful for his new shirt.

"We keep them cold so they don't leak any essence, but this is our core-shed. It costs Q-Credit to get them on loan, because we don't flat out allow people to buy them. They're usually more valuable by themselves than whatever the Crafter used them for. Here's your one." Upgrade moved to the side to show Sal the core that he had Restored a few days before.

"It's Epic grade, and it spent a day at the top of the tower, getting essence from the atmosphere. It can hold a large amount of essence when it's full…maybe as much as the cores from your Skill Registration?"

Upgrade laughed as she gestured at cores at the other end of the room. Rather than being circular and on display in small, carved-out pockets of metal like most, the cores for Skill Registration were locked in a frame with a series of wires wrapped around them.

"They're prepared like this so we can just slot them into the machines. The one you fried might take a bit more repair work. The headmaster suggested that we leave it for a while, until you're qualified to repair it."

Although Upgrade laughed, Sal wasn't sure if she was joking or not. He was nowhere near able to work on machinery yet, especially if he was fucking up on fabrics and etchings. Sal sighed inwardly as he drank more of his coffee. It brought him warmth and, apparently, bursts of clarity. Glancing at Upgrade, he chose his words carefully.

"If you had my ability, what would you use it for?" He was worried that he might offend her by comparing their capability, but it seemed he was overthinking it.

Upgrade smiled. "How would I use it? Being able to Mythcraft? Hmm…If you asked me when I was a first-year, I would have said a weapon. Definitely." Her grin grew wide as she thought about it a little more. "Honestly, all the way through university, I would have made things that made my life easier…but now that I'm a bit older, I would probably make something that helps other people. I've Upgraded our essence catchers, barrier devices, train turrets…you name it, and I've tried to Upgrade it!"

Upgrade's excited expression was one he hadn't seen on her before. "Imagine what a Mythic-grade train turret would look like! What sort of essence gathering could we get if you were the one Upgrading the catchers? Maybe you'd be able to make an unbreakable barrier?" She shook her and laughed. "As amazing as those things sound, the material costs and effort required…they'd be impossible to justify. Especially when you're going to be capable of making weapons that every guild would bite your arm off for."

Sal's mind whirled with possibilities that he hadn't even considered before. He had been thinking about himself and how this power would make his own life easier, but it had the potential to save so many lives. He paused when his thoughts reached a stumbling block.

Sal touched the core in front of him, and he could see with his eyes that it was brimming with essence. It was useless a few days ago but it had been transformed into a vital resource. He had done that to prove a point, and yet he felt as though he were the one missing the point. The silver shirt that he held in his hands suddenly felt like a waste, and he realized that he had been approaching his ability from the wrong direction.

Looking back at Upgrade, Sal offered her the shirt. "Let's sell this and use the Q-Credit to build something useful."

Upgrade raised an eyebrow as she took the shirt from him. "A noble spirit in one so young? It's a fine idea, but it's going to take a lot more than a shirt to make a difference…are you prepared for that?" She smiled, but her eyes challenged him as she waited for his answer.

Sal didn't even need to consider it; this was what he wanted to do. "Please teach me."

With a laugh, Upgrade left the core-shed and beckoned for Sal to follow her. When it was securely locked, she moved to another room farther down the row. Glancing back, she turned and took the coffee cup from Sal's hand and placed it on a nearby bench. "No liquids in here."

That was the only context he got as he followed her into the room. It was cold, like the last one, but the interior was completely different. His eyes practically cooed at the sight of blueprints everywhere, and he didn't know where to look or rest his eyes. He finally landed on the smiling face of Upgrade, who extended her arms and gestured at the countless displays around them.

"This is our design lab, where we draw up proposals. Your eyes might be able to create blueprints, but you're going to learn to draw them here. Every invention of note from the last few decades…has a blueprint in here!"

Upgrade was in her element as she made a beeline toward a particular shelf. Her hand traced along a row of cylinders before she found the one she was looking for. In a graceful sweep, she withdrew a cylinder from the shelf and removed its cap.

Sal watched her roll out the physical blueprint on one of the many tables in the room.

Upgrade spoke to him excitedly as she pointed at various features, but Sal couldn't hear her. His eyes lit up. Until this moment, his ability tried to create solutions based on minimal information. Sal's breath caught in his throat as he saw thousands of tiny details that were wrong on the blueprint. He instinctively knew how to correct them, but forcefully tore his eyes away from it to look at Upgrade, who grinned at him.

"First thing we need to teach you is how to create blueprints! You can sell them back to the university if they're of high quality, and you can also take commissions. But this one here..." Upgrade pointed at the blueprint that had caught his attention. "...is a blueprint I created a few years ago, and it's probably the first thing I'd make if I had your ability. Material cost was insane and like ninety percent of it would have to be commissioned out to other Crafters with specialist skills...but if it worked? How many lives would it save? I come back to look at it every few months to see if I can improve it or make it more realistic."

Sal's eyes returned to the blueprint, and his heartbeat quickened. Every part of him wanted to start correcting and refining the blueprint, but he didn't know how. He didn't want to delude himself by thinking that his ability would solve every issue or magically make the best version of everything. The shirt that knocked him unconscious should have been lesson enough that his ability wasn't infallible.

He deactivated his eyes, allowing him to see the blueprint in its basic form. He smiled at Upgrade, deciding he should take things one step at a time. "Can you teach me how to make one of these?"

Upgrade laughed as she walked around the table to stand beside him. Reaching under the desk, she picked up a single role of graph paper and laid it out over the existing blueprint. As Sal smoothed it out over her drawing, Upgrade handed him a pencil. "It's an archaic method, but it's good practice."

Before Sal could say a word, Upgrade touched a button at the side of the desk, illuminating the surface and making the original blueprint much more visible. After a few moments, a chime filled the air, and Upgrade slid out the original blueprint from underneath the new page. Sal's eyes widened at the sight of the drawings still being displayed on the table, despite Upgrade rolling up the original and placing it back on the wall. He lifted his blank page and saw that the drawings were coming from the surface of the table.

She stifled a laugh and gestured at the light table. "Well...maybe not that archaic. But this way, you get to try out those ideas without fucking up my design."

Sal chuckled to himself as he reactivated his eyes and saw the same issues popping up that he had seen on the original design.

Rather than leaving him to his work, Upgrade pulled over a stool and sat beside him.

"Theory is great, but learning by doing is better. I'll help you as we go...but the first part of every blueprint is the title." Her finger tapped the top of the page, and Sal leaned across and wrote the proposal blueprint title in his own handwriting, followed by his own name.

Self-Sustaining Combat Drone – Salvatore Argento

CHAPTER 23:
ACCUSATION

Divinity sat quietly with her hands laid flat on the table. She bit her lip as she alternated between looking down at her hands and looking back up at Sal. She had asked to speak with him before they got food as she wanted to clear the air between them.

Sal was happy to have the opportunity to apologize to her for what happened with the shirt, but another part of him was watching all the happy faces with their food streaming around the canteen.

"Sal, I know that the shirt wasn't your fault...and that it could have happened to anyone. The Skill Registration incident was a freak accident too, and you missing the Combat session was unavoidable." Divinity took a steadying breath between sentences.

Sal frowned at the mention of the Combat session. He wasn't sure why she was bringing that up all of a sudden, but he didn't interrupt her.

"I appreciate that you don't know what is around the corner like I do, so it's unfair of me to get annoyed by things that haven't even happened yet." Divinity winced ever so slightly, and Sal anticipated the next word perfectly.

"But..." He started for her and opened his hands as if to give her space to speak.

Divinity nodded solemnly. "But yes...your recent actions and...your actions to come, don't really help the Silver cohort. After induction, we start getting assessed more harshly as both individuals and as teams. You're Rank #2 in our group, and you need to start stepping up if we're going to be on the same team."

Sal wanted to laugh at the ridiculousness of the conversation. They were still in their first week, and she was annoyed with him for how he wasn't performing in a future that had yet to happen? He wanted tell her that she was overreacting, but she hadn't done a single thing to make him distrust her.

She'd helped him get the Purple Punch and pick out the Upgrade ability, which led to him getting the Mythcrafter ability. She guided him to the workshop to get the shirt off when, without her, he might have collapsed in a heap somewhere or been locked away in the infirmary. With those considerations in mind, Sal decided to accept whatever blame she was throwing in his direction.

Her voice was strained as she quickly explained what was going to happen in the future. Her panicked voice was only made worse by Sal's continued silence. "You eventually stop going to classes. You don't make any effort to get to know other people in our cohort, which makes them unwilling to group up with you for the team-based exercises. When we have to go into the field, you get exemptions from Upgrade or the headmaster...which results in everyone resenting you for special treatment."

Divinity's voice got higher in pitch with each reason, and Sal could see the start of tears at the edges of her eyes.

"Even though you don't turn up to classes, don't do assignments, they still keep you here. So many people are sent home, but you're still here, without even trying." Her voice finally ran out of energy, and her shoulders slumped in defeat. "Eventually, I come to hate you too."

Sal exhaled slowly. Any lingering resentment evaporated at Divinity's last words. She didn't look hopeful in the slightest, and Sal wondered if he was destined to disappoint her and ruin their friendship regardless of the choices he made. Yes, a part of him would jump at the opportunity to skip out of Combat or Survival classes. He didn't feel any attachment to anyone else in the cohort, nor was he supposed to. They were just temporary classes until they were ranked at the end of the semester.

"I'm sorry…okay? You've been a great friend to me since I've gotten here, and helped me every step of the way. Whatever I can do to make it right, let me know and I'll do my best." Sal said in an earnest voice as he thought through his next sentence. The headmaster and Upgrade had cautioned him about revealing too much about the Mythcrafter ability, but Divinity had to have put the pieces together.

"When I registered the Upgrade skill, it didn't turn into a super Upgrade ability like I told you." Judging by the surprised expression on her face, she definitely hadn't put the pieces together. "It combined with the Restoration and Appraisal abilities that I already had and became Mythcrafter. It's an ability that allows me to create Mythic-grade items."

"You're Myth?!"

Sal nodded and was happy to see a delighted smile cross her face. "I guess that in the future you saw, I was spending a lot of time with Upgrade and the headmaster to work on secret projects. Right now, I'm working on a really cool project with Upgrade, and I would happily skip the next month of classes if it meant I could work on it! But," he said quickly, realizing what he just said, "I'll do my best to not miss classes, so I can help with the upcoming challenges. Thanks for letting me know!"

He glanced eagerly at the canteen behind Divinity, and she laughed and waved him off.

"You're free to go, but you better come back!"

***

"Don't you ever get tired of steak?" Divinity asked with a raised eyebrow. "Like, it's not even real. Are you sure that you want something artificially processed like that?" She averted her eyes from Sal's plate as he happily cut into it.

He chuckled as he gestured at the plate. "I will never get tired of steak. Also, I've no idea what the real thing is supposed to taste like, but this one does just great." As if to emphasize that point, he groaned as he shoveled more of it into his mouth, eliciting a shudder of disgust from Divinity.

She had pretty much finished her salad and was patiently waiting on Sal to finish. It took a few more minutes of silent judging before his cutlery hit the plate.

He wiped his mouth with a napkin and gestured with his hands. "Are we able to talk about stuff now?"

Divinity nodded and leaned forward. She had cut him off when he came back with his plate and told him that she wouldn't be able to concentrate on him explaining and eating at the same time, and that she'd listen to him when he was done.

"Okay. I was thinking about what you said…that I wasn't there for our other classmates and how I pretty much let the cohort down," Sal began as he straightened his back in the chair.

Divinity shifted uncomfortably in her seat. She looked like she wanted to interject and apologize for how she had spoken to him before, but Sal raised a hand and smiled.

"Oh, I'm not bitter about it or anything, don't worry. I was just thinking about your visions and how we might be missing something."

Divinity cocked an eyebrow but didn't interrupt.

Sal smiled as he raised his hands defensively. "I've no doubt that what you've seen will happen, and I'm not trying to weasel out of any blame my future self might deserve. It's just that you saw Hannah as one of the top graduates. The girl who was able to make those shields? Well, I made equipment for her, and suddenly she appears more prominently in your visions?"

Realization washed over Divinity's face as the mystery behind the new vision was solved. "Wait, so you made that happen?"

"Yes, I made her some gauntlets and infused them with her own power…allowing her to access more essence and giving her a method of recharging faster. It's likely a game-changer right now based on our current abilities and trajectories, but how will it be in six months? That's what I want to know," Sal explained excitedly. "What if there are people we could promote to the top ranks who wouldn't get there normally? I could create custom equipment that would showcase their abilities."

Divinity didn't interrupt him, probably because she already knew how the future would play out. If he was Myth, he was going to make things for people anyway.

"What if we were able to prevent people from getting expelled prematurely? You said that so many good people went home? We can jump-start their potential with knowledge of the future and the best equipment!" Sal grinned at her shocked expression. It meant that he had caught her off guard, which was always exciting. "There are a hundred people in our cohort, which means that there has to be a group composition that suits us perfectly. Something that will help us sail through assignments and allows us to use our abilities to their fullest. What do you think?"

Divinity stared at him as though he had two heads. "So instead of trying to team up with the best people, you'd enlist those at the bottom of the rankings?"

Sal nodded, as though it were obvious. "We were essentially judged on a race and then a popularity contest. Why should a thousand people be judged on their physical capability? Hannah's shield could save countless lives, but she was in the low hundreds. I'd rather create a group of people with useful abilities than align with high-ranked people like me who got lucky."

Divinity listened to Sal as he spoke through his ideas, and put forward a few of her own, then they discussed the best course of action. His suggestion for her to use her power on each student was immediately quashed as it would lead to her exhausting herself or passing out. She suggested that she try to look into alternative timelines of the students she saw getting expelled, but there was no guarantee that it would give them what they needed.

They left the canteen and wandered around the amphitheater outside the towers, spending nearly an hour discussing the different ideas, but each of them became more and more challenging because of the sheer number of students they would need to assess. When Divinity half-joked that they should just break into the registration office, Sal stopped walking abruptly.

A wide grin cross his face. "Could you teach me how to control your power?"

CHAPTER 24:
DIVINITY

SAL SAT WITH HIS LEGS CROSSED, HIS EXHAUSTION THROUGHOUT THE DAY WAS long forgotten. His entire focus was on Divinity as she explained the principles of her power. He had dismissed the idea as soon as he said it, because he couldn't imagine a person being comfortable in revealing the limitations of their powers, yet Divinity was practically giddy at the prospect of explaining it to him. Apparently, she had wanted to try this out, too, when she first found out about his ability. Her logic was heartbreakingly earnest, though, and Sal was left speechless when she requested that he use his ability to prevent outbreaks. That had been her only condition in teaching him how to use the ability.

She believed he would be able to see much farther into the future than she could, which meant that he'd be able to save more lives if something she couldn't see was on the horizon. Although she had referenced her abilities before, he had no idea how regularly she sent in reports of pending portal breaks to the academy. Sal felt humbled when he heard what she was already doing for society and knew that she was already a hero.

Divinity framed her power in a much more understandable way than Sal had expected. Most people used their powers instinctively, almost like breathing, but Divinity was able to break it down piece by piece and explain how it worked.

"So, if you think of a large event as a focus point, use that as a reference or anchor. It works best if it's a strong memory, especially to start with, then you can move around it from moment to moment. Visualize it like a web being constructed, with you never straying too far from the focus point, but building out a net that expands in every direction." Her fingers traced the outline of a net as she spoke, watching Sal's reaction intently as she did so.

"Remember I told you about the ceremony that happens in a few months? When the Saviors are picked? That could be your focal point in the future. You can build a net around it and explore…but you'll need to use a different approach to get there in the first place."

Sal nodded in understanding. It was vital that he grasped how the power worked for him to be able to use it properly, especially the methods that would prevent him getting lost within the power. Although he was a little confident in the fact that both of them had eye-based skills, he knew that control would likely be harder when dealing with visions. The other factor that he needed to be conscious of was that he would be channeling the best version of her power. He tried not to think about what he would see and instead listened to Divinity's instructions.

"Rather than a web, I want you to imagine a tree." Divinity's voice was calm as she moved her hand and wiggled her fingers downward. "Imagine that the past is a set of roots, deep in the earth. They are facts and events that have already happened. The trunk of the tree, at least in this example, is brimming with potential…and branches are ready to shoot off in every direction.

"You can continue to grow upward and experience things as they happen…that will show you the future as it is, wherever your tree is planted. You want to see what will happen in a certain place in the future? Plant a tree there in your mind and watch it grow tall." Her hand gestures mimicked what she was saying, and Sal nodded.

Divinity moved her hands back to the imaginary tree between them. "The energy that allows you to grow your tree can be pushed outward to create branches. It will be harder, and you'll need a clear understanding of what it is you're hoping to find or see. Follow that branch and see where it goes. But know that the farther you go from the trunk of your tree, the weaker your branches will become. You'll break out of those visions faster than others, so be careful."

Her smile returned as she gestured back to her other hand. "Which brings us back to the web! When you find a point in a branch that you want to explore, imagine there are twigs and leaves around your branch. These are events that you can latch onto, and you can build your web around them. Find out all the information and build a picture to see all the possibilities around them. That's how I use my power. It's grown with me over the years, and I can go farther up the tree and wider with the branches…but who knows what it will be like for you?" The excitement in her voice was clear as she clapped, surprising Sal, who was almost in a trance-like state.

"You're up! Do you want to maybe try to replicate my power with the knots? Is that what you call them?" Divinity suggested gently. It was clear that she didn't want to overwhelm him with the power and mess up their opportunity to see more of the future.

"If we're at the same level, I can guide you through the basics while you're using your power. It might be easier for you to look at the future right here! Since we're beside the amphitheater, it should be easy for you to see a preview of tomorrow's lessons?" Catching what she just said, Divinity quickly corrected herself. "Sorry, I don't mean easy! I just think it could be a good exercise to start with."

With a nod, Sal activated his eyes and slowly exhaled as he looked at Divinity's power. As the strands of light became visible, Sal voiced his concerns in a distracted voice. "Just remember, that what you see in the next few moments is your power…not mine."

He had intentionally waited until he couldn't see her reaction before speaking. The strands of light brightened, and he thought for a moment that Divinity ignored his statement, but a half a second later, her voice reached his ears, and it sounded amused.

"I want to see how incredible you can make it, so if you're going to go all out, please don't hold back to make me feel better!"

Sal's vacant expression was adorned with a slight smile. His eyes glowed intently. Striking and intense, staring straight through her.

He shifted suddenly, and got to his feet, idly tracing his fingers in the empty air in front of him.

Sal inwardly cursed at the multitude of knots in her thread, more than in any person he had scanned with his eyes. Her ability was choked at literally every turn, and the fact that she could see anything at all in the future was a miracle, in his opinion. He started to unravel the threads in his own replication, but it was a lot more complex than he had anticipated.

Lifting his hands like a reflex, Sal was surprised to see that his fingers were accelerating the process of the threads. He began to wonder if he had tried using his hands with his power before, but couldn't recall any time that it had been necessary. With his eyes, he placed the two sets of threads together: his own and Divinity's. He was so caught up in the process of unraveling and using his fingers that he didn't notice the moment his hands touched Divinity's threads.

The moment that his hand contacted her thread, Divinity gasped. Her eyes widened in shock as she looked at her own body, her hand quickly going to her chest as her breathing elevated. Just as she opened her mouth to speak, Sal's fingers stopped in mid-air, and he sighed in relief.

"I think that should do it?" Sal breathed as he activated Divinity's power.

The silver thread that he had painstakingly weaved took up pretty much all the space around his Mythcrafter ability. It was floating in his body and the threads were reinforced perfectly, but he double and triple-checked them just to be on the safe side. He wasn't sure exactly what to expect from going all out with it, but he felt that he had the basics down from Divinity.

His power surged through the thread of light and pulsated excitedly. Faster than Sal had ever seen it, the thread sped around the weave until it practically vibrated. What was once silver turned into a white glow, and Sal finally felt as if he had primed the power like an engine, and now just needed to turn the key.

Divinity's response died in her throat as Sal activated the power. His eyes burst into an ethereal white, and two ethereal wings sprung out from his back. They flared in the evening air before curving quietly and wrapping around Sal's glowing torso. Lines of light shot through his body near the surface of his skin, like his veins were pulsating with angelic essence. Divinity collapsed to the ground, tears flowing down her face as she stared at him.

Sal's right hand moved forward and pointed at Divinity. Shapes materialized from nowhere, taking the form of students from the academy. Premonitions of the future playing out in front of him, all at an incredible speed.

He cried as he watched countless fates of pain and destruction. The overwhelming majority of futures were in ruin. Everything in the distant future was doomed to die, with only a handful of branches making it into the skyline. Even though he was confused at what he was seeing, and he lacked the context or anchors that Divinity had recommended for him…he was able to zoom in on the highest branches.

A part of his brain told him that those were the best chances of survival, and for victory. The only problem was that he had no idea who the people in those visions were…when it was, or where. A lurching sensation told him that he didn't have much time left; the forest around him started to unravel.

Using instincts rather than logic, Sal counted back from the tallest branch he could find. The root was at the academy, and the highest branch had contained a vision he couldn't understand. He went to the base of it and in his haste, felt more and more of the forest tearing away.

Sal grasped the branch with his mind. It was much earlier in its development, and it was closer to the trunk. It was more familiar this time, with some faces that looked vaguely familiar. He tried to remember them, but the destruction of the forest caught up with him. In a last-ditch effort, Sal tried to glimpse the main deviation from the trunk. It was the beginning of that branch and was the catalyst for making it through the countless destructive outcomes.

Sal's eyes widened as another event flashed before his eyes.

CHAPTER 25:
HEALING

 in a panic as the visions faded into darkness, blending back into the current timeline. His heart thundered as he twisted and turned to see the surrounding amphitheater. A few chuckles carried across from passing students, but nobody paid too much attention to them.

When he looked around for Divinity, he saw her kneeling on the ground beside him. Her eyes were still white, telling him that she was still looking into the future. From where he was lying, and her posture, he realized that she had been cradling his head while he was out for the count.

He now keenly knew what it was like to be torn away from a vision, so he didn't try to alert her. Instead, he tried to make sense of the visions he had seen. So many of them were dependent on factors he knew nothing about. The concept of having facts as anchors in those visions became much clearer, and Sal cursed himself for straying too high up the branches. The jumbled images were fading from his mind, and Sal did his best to sort them all out before they slipped away like a dream. Only one of them was burned into his mind, and it was the last one that he saw—the catalyst to bring them onto the optimal branch.

"You're back! What did you see—" Divinity's excited voice cut through the noise but faltered when she saw the ghastly expression on Sal's face. She reached forward and grasped his arm.

Sal jerked at the sudden movement and had to calm himself before answering. He had never felt so jittery in all his life, and his internal energy felt like it was running off fumes.

"How long was I—" He put a hand on the ground to steady himself as he tried to sit up. Everything around spun, like he was drunk. Each word was painful to muster and left him breathless. Blinking rapidly, he abandoned any attempt at a conversation and focused on his breathing. Divinity's voice echoed out, much louder than he was expecting, and Sal's torso swayed, trying to hold onto his mind and not slip back into unconsciousness.

The theme of his entire day was apparently to curse his poor decisions and he berated himself for being so useless. First the shirt had managed to drain all his energy; then, after a few hours of drawing blueprints, he figured he had recharged enough to attempt Divinity's ability?

Shaking his head in annoyance, he gritted his teeth against the swarm of vertigo that rocked his senses. When he turned to look at Divinity, her gasp sent a wave of alarm through him and that was what finally broke him. Sal cursed the darkness that enveloped him as he slipped unconscious for what seemed like the thousandth time that day.

***

"What the hell was he Appraising for him to go off the edge like that?"

A musical voice laughed as Sal started to rouse. He felt a gentle stream of foreign energy washing through his mind, eroding the darkness as his senses started to return.

"You can keep your credits, though. I much prefer the idea of an Oracle owing me one."

The voice continued in that singsong cadence as Sal finally found the strength to open his eyes. Whatever he had expected, his current situation wasn't it. Instead of the infirmary or his own room…he was still in the amphitheater, surrounded by a handful of students. He didn't recognize any of them, except for Divinity, who was by his side. Her eyes were locked onto his face, and relief blossomed across her features when they made eye contact.

"You're back!" She sighed as her shoulders finally loosened.

When Sal turned his head to the other side, he saw another girl grinning at him. Her mane of red hair was floating upward as a side effect of her power, and her eyes glowed a vibrant green. Sal felt more energy rushing through him, relieving him of any remaining aches or pains. With a quick glance to his chest, her palms resting on it, with a faint green glow emanating from them.

"You're a Healer?" Sal blurted, without feeling an ounce of pain.

That same musical voice sounded out as she turned her head toward Divinity. "Yep, he's definitely an Appraiser. How did you figure it out?" Her attention turned back to Sal with a mocking smile as she slid her hand up to cup his chin.

Divinity was about to interject but Sal's eyes rolled back as a wave of unfamiliar energy flooded his head.

"You know you need to give these bad boys some time to heal, right? You don't want to go blind, do you?"

Her musical voice held an edge this time as Sal felt his eyes burning. It wasn't an unpleasant feeling at all. He tried to activate his eyes to see what was happening, but the wave of energy overpowered his attempts.

"Ah ah, none of that," the girl chided with a laugh as she looked back at Divinity. "Your price just went up. Rank #2 must have gotten a lot of credits during the opening ceremony? I'd say you could afford to treat your friend here." The voice was still musical, but her tone had become predatory. "I'm sure he'll pay it back, won't you, Mr. Appraiser?"

To emphasize her point, the energy Sal had been gifted dislodged in an instant…as though it was about to vanish and leave him with fragments of his own recovered essence.

"What do we say? Do we have a deal?" The Healer practically cooed, which was followed by a few laughs from the students who surrounded them.

Divinity looked like she was about to fold. Sal was furious with himself for constantly putting pressure on Divinity and knocking himself unconscious through his own ineptitude. As the Healer held her power away from him, there was nothing blocking his eyes from activating.

His eyes blazed a vibrant silver as he looked through the Healer, who wasn't even paying attention to him. The weave was one of the fastest he'd ever replicated, and he didn't give a shit whether it went out of control.

He wasn't going to let Divinity get strong-armed by someone who would try to capitalize on the vulnerable. It wasn't a sense of justice so much as it was an act of fighting against his own uselessness.

With the weave in place, Sal activated the Healing ability and saw what was happening around him. There were seven people bathed in light, all connected by bonds of light that were anchored to the Healer beside him. Feeling the essence he had been temporarily gifted, Sal traced it to her arms, where she was holding it ransom. He sensed that it wasn't her own, but a mixture of essence that she was gradually siphoning off the three students who stood around her.

Judging by their triumphant grins, they were expecting this sort of outcome and were very likely in on the plan. All those thoughts lanced through his mind in the split second he made his decision. He pulled on the essence through the bonds first, to get a feel for how it moved and traveled through the connections. Luckily, the Healer didn't notice, but the goons definitely felt it. By the time Sal had amassed enough energy to replace what had been gathered in front of him, the Healer turned to look at him.

"Hey, what the fuck are you—"

Before she could finish her sentence, Sal pulled all the energy he had gathered from her group and used her as the vessel to administer it into his own body. With a yelp of shock, she tried to remove her palms, but it was too late. It rushed through her arms and passed through the bond she had established with him.

The result was instantaneous. Sal felt invigorated beyond anything he had ever experienced. All the aches and pains he had accrued over the last few days vanished. Better than that, the healing energy darted around his body, looking for things to do. Remembering what she had said about his eyes, Sal navigated the energy to his head and was more than a little panicked to find the essence had found injuries that needed healing.

"How did you—" The girl stared at her arms as if they alone had seemingly betrayed her. "You're not an Appraiser at all!"

Sal shrugged as he got to his feet. "And you're not a good Samaritan. It probably goes without saying, but we won't be paying your price." He dusted himself off and offered his hand to Divinity, who was still kneeling and staring at him in bewilderment.

The Healer, on the other hand, turned her head to her group, her musical voice long lost, only to be replaced by a venomous snarl. "Looks like they're not paying. You know what to do!"

Her intent was clear, and Sal finally appreciated that the other students were indeed her goons and essence resource. A part of him admired how she had single-handedly created such an enterprise within the first week of the semester, but most of him pitied her poor judgment.

When the group made no attempt to move, the Healer whirled on them, only to find them hunched over and breathing heavily.

"I can't believe you leeched all their power just to save yourself...," he said, loud enough for the rest of her group to hear. "What a shitty thing to do!" Only Sal and the Healer knew he was lying, evidenced by the growls of anger coming from her group.

Sal decided to add one more layer to ensure this group was disbanded for good. "Divinity, could you check to see if these guys end up losing their powers completely by hanging around with this one?" He pointed at the Healer, who was panic-stricken at seeing what Sal was doing.

Divinity shook her head and hid a small smile as she pretended to look into the future. "Only one loses his power, but another one dies…I think?" Her feigned shock and terrible acting still managed to resonate with their audience, with each of the goons gaping at her in horror. "Please make better friends," Divinity requested, giving them a gentle smile.

Maybe it was her pleading tone, but one of them actually nodded as he painstakingly got to his feet. The Healer hadn't said a single word throughout the charade. Her green eyes were still glowing as she stared intently at Sal.

"You can stop trying to establish that bond again. It's severed now, so you won't be getting any of that power back." He pointed at his eyes for added effect, and the Healer stiffened when his silver irises turned green, imitating her own power perfectly.

The disgruntled group of students looked like they were ready to have a few strong words with the Healer, so Sal and Divinity left them to it. As they walked away, they heard the panicked reasonings of the Healer turn into threats of violence. Divinity glanced back and grimaced at the sight of the students once again on the ground, clutching at their chests; the Healer returned the stare with unfiltered rage.

"Sal, I think we just made an enemy," she whispered.

Sal barely registered the words as he guided them toward the Administrative offices. "We have bigger problems than that, I'm afraid." He sighed as he shook his head. "We need to go and see the headmaster to tell him about the visions I saw with your power."

Divinity looked like she still had a thousand questions for him, but the expression on Sal's face made her pause.

"Are they bad?" She watched his face intently for any indication that she was right.

Sal stopped abruptly and pointed past the gigantic towers around them. Through the gaps, the faint bluish hue of the protective barrier could be seen in the distance. It was the city limit that protected them from the Red Zones.

"That one breaks first." Sal turned around and then pointed at the other barriers in the distance, all at different angles. "Then that one, and then that one…"

Sal's voice hitched as he recalled the events in his vision. "Until the city is overrun, and the academy and guilds are destroyed."

CHAPTER 26:
CALAMITY

WHATEVER RECEPTION SAL HAD EXPECTED IN THE HEADMASTER'S OFFICE, THE reality was far from it. The receptionist took one look at Divinity's Q-Card and fast-tracked them into Quest's office, where they only had to wait a couple of minutes before his arrival. Sal and Divinity sat in ornate wooden chairs that were situated in front of an imposing mahogany desk. Its polished surface was almost reflective and incredibly eye-catching. There was another seat to their left that was currently unoccupied, and Sal wondered whether they were expecting another person to join. With a nudge of his elbow, Sal got Divinity's attention and tilted his head toward the other chair.

Divinity didn't miss a beat. Her eyes clouded over as she looked into the future.

"There's no need for that!" Quest's voice echoed out from behind them as he entered the office and closed the door behind him. "Neuro is on his way over, so we can get to the bottom of this." He strode purposefully toward his desk and withdrew a remote from the pocket of his vest. With a single click, an audio clip sounded out and featured an unfamiliar voice.

Tower Security Report:

Pillar of light appeared at the amphitheater.

**Students identified as Salvatore Argento, Rank #19
and Divinity Khan, Rank #2.**

**Atmospheric essence spiked to record levels which coincided with the
"Angel" appearance, as reported by eyewitnesses. Power signature
identified as Divinity Khan.**

Essence signature identified as Salvatore Argento.

Rather than seating himself at his desk, Quest walked in front of it and leaned against it so he was only a few feet away from Sal and Divinity. "So, we have the Skill Master, Salvatore Argento…who we've established can replicate any skill and push it to its maximum potential." His left hand gestured at Sal while his right hand unfurled and gestured to Divinity. "And Divinity Khan, who can glimpse into the future. With the report I've received from security, and the knowledge we have of the two of you, I hope you can appreciate why I got in contact with Neuro immediately. Whatever you saw in the future, we want to see it too…and Neuro is the best person to translate those visions for us."

With a glance at the closed door, Quest sighed. "Was there a big fuck-off dragon in your vision?" The sudden cursing from the headmaster caused Sal's eyes to widen. Before Sal could say a word, Quest raised his hand and closed his eyes. "No, actually…don't tell me. We'll wait for Neuro." When an uncomfortable silence carried its way through the room, Quest shook his head in annoyance.

"Forget I mentioned the dragon…we have a few people who can see into the future. They've got conflicting ideas of what's to come, and some are much more convincing than others." Quest waved his hand wildly in rotations as he tried to downplay his own concerns. "Neuro is part of a team we assembled called the Doom Society. Horrible name, not a fan of it myself…but they get the job done. We move our resources around and avoid disaster. Your vision might be something that is already being prevented by our team, so there might be no reason to worry."

Despite his encouraging words, there was still an awkward tension in the air, and Sal guessed that the dragon he was referring to was one of those unavoidable or unpreventable scenarios.

Just as Sal was about to ask more about it, the door behind them opened to reveal an out of breath Neuro. His eyes lit up at the sight of Sal, and he pointed in recognition. "Are you the man responsible for making me rush across districts?" An easygoing smile crept across his face.

Sal felt more at ease in those few seconds with Neuro than he had in the few minutes they had spoken with Quest.

With only a nod in greeting to Quest, Neuro took a seat and turned his attention to Sal. "Mind if I take a poke around in there for a bit? See what you saw and all that?"

The fact that he was asking permission made Sal like him even more, and he nodded in response.

Neuro grinned as he put his hands on the arms of his chair and half lifted, half dragged it around so he faced Sal. "Just think of everything you saw and bring it to the front of your mind. If you start thinking silly thoughts, or anything like that, don't worry, I can sidestep them like a pro."

Neuro closed his eyes as he activated his power. When they opened, there was no discernible change in his appearance. Nothing about his eyes indicated that he was using his ability. Sal wondered whether there was a way for him to do that without his eyes changing color, and Neuro smiled.

"Like I said, Sal, I'll be able to sidestep some thoughts…but I need you to give me my destination. Think about the visions you saw."

Shaking his head a little, Sal cleared his mind and reluctantly recalled all the images he had seen. He tried to go through them slowly, but they came to him out of order and in flashes. He wasn't sure how to do them in order and couldn't actually remember which ones he saw first.

He took a steadying breath, conscious that he needed to give Neuro as much to work with as possible and tried once again to catalogue the visions he had seen. Few of them made sense to him, outside of the places he recognized. When his heart stopped thundering, Sal calmly went through the instructions that Divinity had given him, and he recalled the forest that was filled with branches. He tried to retrace his footsteps through those visions and attribute certain scenes to the branches he was navigating.

"Excellent work, Sal. Keep it up."

Neuro continued to encourage him as he went through scene after scene in his mind. There was one that he felt was important to share, but it wasn't going to come up until much later. Sal went down the branch of events, eager to move away from the death and destruction at the top…but an unfamiliar force kept bringing him back to that horrific scene, exploring it from different angles and attempting to identify locations and people.

Sal gritted his teeth as they went through it again and again until the force finally relented and let him return to another place on the branch. It was such a relief his shoulders relaxed and he let out a sigh.

"Fantastic job, Sal. What came before those events? Let's go down the branch..."

Sal barely registered the fact that Neuro knew about their branch concept but didn't let it distract him. He wanted to be as useful to them as possible and showed them everything he could recall. It went on for what felt like hours, but was, in actuality, only a few minutes. Lastly, at the point of deviation, Sal brought forward the moment he had identified as a catalyst. What surprised him most was that Neuro was able to read his intent with ease. He didn't know how to describe it, but it felt as if he could sense Neuro's approval.

"Incredible. Just...incredible." Neuro patted Sal on the knee and leaned back in his chair, a wide grin on his face. "You can open your eyes now, Sal. You did an incredible job of showing me what you saw."

With a glance at Quest, Neuro snorted dismissively. "It's not the dragon—could you stop worrying so damn loudly for a few minutes?" Neuro picked up his chair and moved it so it once again faced Quest's desk. He looked back to Sal and gave him a reassuring wink before turning his attention back to Quest.

"I'll need to make my report to the group and disseminate the information we've got from Sal, but I can tell you the basics for now. He managed to identify four calamities in his vision, but with a level of clarity I never thought possible. As I said, none of them were anything to do with Chronos, so we don't need to worry about a dragon apocalypse any time soon." Neuro spoke matter-of-factly as he raised a hand into the air with four raised fingers.

"We knew about the Lunar Tower. Sal saw an outcome where we didn't kill the tower lord, which resulted in an invasion and the destruction of the north-most barrier." Neuro glanced at Sal and Divinity, who gaped in horror, but he shook his head. "We've known about that tower for a while now and we're sending our best guilds to take it down while it's weak. Don't worry about that one."

Quest tapped his desk and gave Neuro a pointed look, which the Hero didn't miss. His next finger curled downward as he resumed speaking.

"Downtown portal break, happens near the hospital district. Lots of injured Heroes got wiped out and enraged guilds ran to their deaths...but we know the date and time of that one and will pre-emptively evacuate the hospital and ensure the portal is taken care of before it escalates to a break."

Sal watched as the third finger moved.

Neuro's voice was still calm as he continued, but there was a hint of curiosity behind his words this time.

"We knew there was a dungeon break, and all our information about it has been after the break...but would you believe that Sal here has seen where it is? We assumed it was on one of the islands off the coast because of the victims on the *Darwin* cruise, but it's actually underwater at the port. We'll need to research that one in more detail, and I'd love to invite Sal to the group to see if we can learn more about it. Maybe take Divinity, too, show her the ropes before she joins us full-time?" Neuro suggested, his eyes never leaving Quest's face.

It seemed to dawn on the headmaster that they had new information about one of the upcoming calamities, and he wasn't going to step in the way of saving more lives. He smiled and shook his head weakly. "Yes, of course you can bring them over…but make sure that it doesn't interfere with their classes too much. What was the fourth?"

Neuro turned and gave Sal a smile.

"A student of the academy is expelled before they get an opportunity to enter a Red Zone. Their power absolutely thrives in that environment and without the guidance of the academy, they end up losing their mind. Our fourth calamity has the highest destructive potential based on their ability, which grows stronger when surrounded by death. It would appear that Sal has already come up with an effective countermeasure for us."

Quest's face was white. Despite him staring at Sal, his question was very much aimed at Neuro. "You'd trust a child with countering a calamity?"

Sal glanced at Neuro, who merely nodded for him to speak. The vision was hard to describe to the headmaster, who hadn't seen the pain on her face, but Sal had seen flashes of her time at the academy and saw how tortured she was. Before he spoke, he looked at Divinity and smiled.

"We're going to become her friend." Sal turned his attention to Quest. "And help her join the Savior class."

Quest's face finally broke into a smile as he turned in his chair. He shot a knowing look at Neuro, who grinned and held up his hands in defeat.

"What makes you think you'll be able to get into the Savior class yourselves? Thirty students out of a thousand puts you at a three percent chance. I hope your current ranks aren't making you complacent!"

Sal opened his mouth to retort, but Divinity got there first.

"So, you're saying that we're not going to be compensated or acknowledged for both identifying and preventing a calamity?" she asked, a hint of confusion in her voice. "Can't say it's a huge motivator for us to look into the future again for this Doom Squad thingy you're running."

The headmaster folded his arms and looked at Neuro with a shake of his head. "You knew they were going to say that, didn't you?"

Neuro didn't answer and instead cupped his chin with a smile, as if waiting for something to happen. As if to emphasize his point, he looked past Sal's chair to where Divinity was seated. "Isn't there something else you'd like to share with the group? Normally, I wouldn't pry…but it's practically screaming out of you."

Divinity coughed uncomfortably as she glanced first at Sal and then at Quest. "When Sal was replicating my power, I think he unblocked a part of mine…somehow. I can't explain it, but I feel more powerful. Like I can see the future more clearly and for longer."

Neuro whistled loudly as he turned his cupped chin to look at the headmaster. "Students who can Craft Mythic-grade equipment, see into the future, and help others reach their full potential?" He laughed as he looked at both Sal and Quest's shocked expressions. "Yeah, that three percent seems like a pretty shitty estimate to me, too."

CHAPTER 27:
OVERWHELM

DIVINITY WAS A FOUNTAIN OF APOLOGIES AS BOTH SAL AND SHE MADE THEIR WAY to the elevators. Sal's mind was racing, and his attempts at calming down Divinity had failed miserably. As soon as he opened his mouth to speak, she resumed her tirade.

"Seriously, though, I wasn't going to say anything about it until I spoke with you, but Neuro was right there, and he knew about it, and I was dying to find out if it was true or not, so it just kinda came out! I'm so sorry!"

Sal wondered when she took breaths as she jumped from one fear to the next.

"I mean, it's exciting that they're going to test it and find out! I'm sorry, I mean that I find it exciting, but it's probably stressful for you to have to go in there and try to re-create something you didn't even know about! Ugh, I should have just shut up and said nothing. I'm so sorry!"

Divinity bit her lip and scrunched her face in a grimace as she agonized about her actions. "Maybe it won't be so bad? Can you imagine if your ability actually worked that way? Whoa! Would that mean I could get angel wings like you had?"

"Angel wings?" Sal asked, confused, but Divinity was still going.

"If that girl wasn't such a raging bitch, imagine her being able to heal entire groups of people on the battlefield! We'd have no casualties. There are so many amazing powers you could upgrade! But the headmaster is right…the change might only be temporary. We need to wait for a day or two to see. It's exciting, though, isn't it?"

Divinity's grin seemed to finally win through the war of guilt and excitement, and Sal was grateful for the outcome. He scratched the back of his neck as he tapped the button to summon the elevator.

"I guess it's pretty exciting. I'm just relieved that they already knew about those other calamities. It sounds like we helped them discover more about that third one, and hopefully us joining their team will help us get closer to the Savior class?"

As the doors of the elevator opened, Sal took a step through them and turned on the spot. He was still thinking about everything he had seen in those visions. His respect for the academy and the guilds had grown because of it.

"How many disasters do you think they've already countered?" he mused out loud, before looking at Divinity for an answer.

"Well, I know I diverted at least three of them before enrolling. Four, if we can befriend our mystery calamity. There were dozens of others that I glimpsed in the past, but they already knew about them." She shrugged but still smiled. "It's nice, though, knowing that even if I miss something…someone else has the ability to catch it and prevent a disaster."

Sal hadn't thought about it that way and found it to be quite a relief too. The visions and events had been horrible, and he was genuinely worried that they were all going to die. He was grateful for people like Divinity who looked into the future daily to keep them safe. She truly was an incredible Hero already, and it put his own efforts into perspective. He wasn't sure how much he was contributing to society like Divinity was. The conversation he had with Upgrade was still on his mind, too.

Would he be able to build something that would help society? Was there a better use for his powers than squirreling away in a workshop, creating pieces of equipment? Up until a few weeks ago, he had imagined a future where he either worked in an Administrative function for one of the bigger guilds or moved home to work in the family auction house. Now, he was predicting future calamities and apparently able to Craft Mythic-grade equipment. If what Divinity had said in that meeting was true, he might even be able to un-knot the weaves in other people.

"You okay, Sal?"

Divinity's voice caught him off guard, and he realized that the elevator door was open. Divinity stood with one foot in the lobby and the other blocking the door from closing. With a shake of his head, Sal apologized as he stepped past her and exited the lift.

"Just a lot of stuff to think about…kinda just feeling a bit lost." He gave her a sheepish smile, but Divinity's frown didn't budge in the slightest.

She gripped his shirt sleeve to stop him from walking away and looked him straight in the eye. "Trust me, I know."

Divinity gestured to her eyes and then at Sal's. "I can see the future. The events that everyone is terrified of or hopeful for, I have the answers…and this power thrust me into some serious conversations from an early age. Things no little girl should see. Countless tests and verifications…I had to use my power again and again, but it helped me realize how many lives we were saving. It made the lack of a fun childhood more bearable. Every day since my powers manifested, I've been told how special I am and how vital my success is for the future of humanity." Divinity's voice softened as she tugged at his sleeve.

"I've been conditioned for years, and I still get overwhelmed from time to time. You, on the other hand…have been working with your family, and nobody—not even you—knew the extent of your abilities. I'm not sure if anyone has told you yet, Sal, but you're special too. Probably the most special of us all. And I think you're going to be an absolutely incredible Hero."

And with that, Divinity released her hold on his sleeve and slipped ahead of him in the lobby. "If you quote me on that, I'll deny it. So enjoy the flash of sentimentality while it lasts, okay?"

Her laugh filled the air, and Sal couldn't help but smile. Her words resonated with him, and the feelings of helplessness and being overwhelmed felt that much more bearable with the knowledge that he wasn't alone.

"Thank you, Divinity. I needed that." Sal admitted with a shake of his head as they made their way back to the dorms.

***

Exhaustion hit Sal hard, and he needed to really focus to make sure he got off on the right floor for his dorm. It was only when he was walking back alone that he admonished himself for how he was treating his own body. He had pulled an all-nighter Crafting that shirt, been knocked unconscious twice from lack of energy and using an ultimate version of an ability, and then he had his essence ripped away and restored by a crazy Healer looking to swindle them. The emotional weight of seeing numerous calamities, followed by having his mind read—by Neuro, of all people…and in front of the headmaster—had been a lot for him to handle. Despite all of Divinity's reassurances, there was still a massive feeling of pressure and expectation on him that he wasn't comfortable with. All of it was finally catching up with him.

As the doors opened on his floor, Sal forced himself out onto the corridor and turned right. Hannah was leaning against the wall, and pressed heavily against her, was a male student. Even in Sal's tired state, he could read their body language. The guy stopped caressing Hannah's waist and locked his eyes onto Sal's.

Hannah looked conflicted about what to say to him, but Sal made it really easy for her and walked past with a friendly smile.

"Have fun."

He hadn't made it three paces before she called out to him.

"Are you going to the party tomorrow night? They're calling it Survive, because…you know, we made it through week one!" She laughed as she said it, and Sal turned to answer.

The first thing he noticed was the dark expression on the guy's face, but he ignored it and instead looked at Hannah.

"No idea. All I can think about is bed right now. I'll let you know tomorrow, okay?"

Before Sal moved away, he saw that she still wore the gauntlets he had made for her. Maybe it was his tired brain, but he raised two fingers to his mouth and blew against them, much like her signature move. It resulted in a hearty laugh from Hannah and elicited an aggravated reaction from her current suitor.

Pushing himself away from Hannah, he moved toward Sal purposefully. "We have a problem, pal?"

Before Sal could so much as blink, the guy crumpled to the ground, holding his broken nose with his hands. A solid blue wall stood proudly between Sal and his would-be attacker. Sal glanced past the fallen student to see Hannah performing the same gesture he had just mimicked.

She shook her head and opened her own door. "Think about that party, yeah?"

Hannah didn't spare her guest another glance before slinking into her room and closing the door behind her.

Sal stood in the corridor awkwardly before backing away slowly to find his own door, leaving the wounded student to flounder around, clutching at his face.

A few moments later, he was in the safety of his own room, but locked the door for good measure. He clumsily disrobed, taking off his trousers and haphazardly throwing his makeshift blanket-shirt to the ground. When his eyes caught the open door that led to the workbench, Sal grimaced and made his way across the room to close it.

"Not tonight, Sal."

He looked at the bed and whispered under his breath that he'd be falling into it soon, but first he needed a shower. In just a few steps, he reached the bathroom door, which was when he noticed a package on the ground beside his main door. It was tucked flush against the wall and he hadn't seen it coming in. With a glance at the label, he saw that it was the organizer he had ordered from the Credit Store the night before. It honestly felt like a week ago at this point, and Sal promised himself that he wouldn't go near it until the following morning.

An hour later, Sal had managed to shower…but had also broken his own promise and was setting up the new board in his room. He moved his workbench around to sit in front of the glass window, while the wall was now adorned with the large board that was slowly filling up with handwritten notes. He deleted countless tabs one by one as he populated his board with a series of objectives and observations. He had learned from an early age that the only way to declutter his mind was to get it all written down somewhere.

In the next hour, he had all his visions documented, as well as a full list of everyone in the Silver cohort. He knew less than ten percent of the class and wasn't sure how he and Divinity were going to determine which ones were worth saving from expulsion. When he finally stepped away from the board, he smiled proudly at it. Sure, it needed some more refining and organizing, but it listed everything that had been floating around in his head. It wasn't even midnight yet, but Sal was near the point of collapse. His eyes narrowed in on a single name on the board, and he vowed that he wouldn't allow the fourth calamity to occur.

Rank #986, Melanie Delahunt.

The Necromancer

CHAPTER 28:
PERSPECTIVE

SAL'S HEART BEAT RAPIDLY AS A LOOMING SENSE OF DREAD OVERTOOK HIS senses. He stood in front of a locker with his own name hovering over it. To call it a locker was a disservice. Maybe it was to promote fairness or allow students to create countermeasures, but the locker was more like a display case of armor and equipment. The default equipment was a glorified tracksuit with some protective materials added for good measure. Sal wasn't so much confused by the locker or the equipment; it was more the fact that he had unwittingly walked straight to his next class without speaking once to Divinity. They were separated into two queues, and only when he got to his place did he realize what was about to happen.

Introduction to Combat. Class 2.

"No women around to protect you today, pal," someone sneered from behind him, and Sal didn't even need to turn his head to see who it was.

The nasally tone was the dead giveaway. Hannah's suitor had apparently been a part of the Silver cohort, and his black eyes had locked on to Sal from the moment they entered the gym. With a slight turn to the left, Sal also caught sight of the lowest rank in the Silver cohort, #999. The glare that Sal had received from him showed that he, too, remembered the altercation in the bathrooms from their first day. Gritting his teeth, Sal resolved himself to the fact that he was likely going to get his ass kicked today. With that thought firmly in place, he gradually changed. He needed to think of a way to come out of this Combat lesson without too much punishment.

"Ears not working? Or are you too good to speak to us lowly mid-rankers?"

The voice was closer now. Sal tensed in anticipation of a shove that never came. His heart still thundered. Maybe it was the adrenaline, but he clenched his fists. A shadow appeared in Sal's peripheral vision, and the bruised eyes of his would-be assailant from last night came into view.

"Ooooh, maybe there's a little bit of fight in you after all? Here I thought you were just a Support Simp! Hmm?" He glanced down at Sal's fists, and gave him a toothy smile. "What are you gonna do? Sucker punch me again like a little bitch?"

Sal blinked as he turned to look at him. "You know that was Hannah's power, right? You ran into the shield she put up?"

Sal fully expected him to double down on his suspicions and continue to antagonize, but the guy frowned, before turning and leaning his back against the locker.

"You serious?" His voice was devoid of any menace, replaced with curiosity.

Sal nodded slowly and pointed at his eyes. "Yeah. I'm an Appraiser…I can't make shields."

The guy with the busted nose stared at him for a moment. "Fuck!" He slammed his fist against the locker behind him, shook his head and continued to curse at himself, then smiled at Sal. "Sorry, man. I saw red last night. I thought you'd suckered me. Can't believe it was her…Fucking bitch!"

Slipping on his gym gear, Sal offered his hand awkwardly. "No worries, mate. I'm Sal, by the way."

The guy didn't hesitate in the slightest as he shook it. "Dave…Rank #669." His toothy grin returned but he looked past Sal. "Hey, Fuck-Face, you staring at something?"

Sal turned to see Rank #999 turn away quickly. "Ah, he and his friend jumped me in the bathroom on the first day. He got relegated to second-last place."

Dave looked at Sal suspiciously. "And what did you do? Report it?"

Sal could hear the challenge in his words, and he knew there was a test here. Shrugging, he looked Dave square in the eye and answered, "I put his friend out cold."

The bark of laughter told Sal a lot about Dave. Apparently, strength and honesty were the main avenues to becoming friends.

"Hear that, Fuck-Face? An Appraiser put your mate on his arse!" Dave laughed as he returned to his own locker. He smiled at Sal. "Can't believe you're actually a Support, man. Are you fucking with me, or is that really your power?"

Sal tapped the side of his nose as he left the changing area, causing Dave to laugh once more, and carried on taunting the lower rank boy in the background as Sal made his way to the main testing area. Class wasn't scheduled to start for another few minutes, so Sal looked around for Divinity. It would be great to have her insight before he had to fight someone. Without knowing what he was up against, he was likely doomed to a world of pain.

The students around him seemed to know exactly where they were going. They filtered out and stood at terminals that surrounded a large square with cushioned flooring. Barriers similar to those that repelled the demons were erected around the square, creating a form of cage that reached impossibly high into the air.

Sal estimated that it must have been at least ten floors' worth of empty space reaching upward. Natural light streamed through the windows, illuminating the gym area. He followed a set of students around the terminals in the hopes of finding one that was free. He wasn't sure what he was supposed to do because he had missed his first Combat class due to the Skill Registration incident.

He finally found one, but it wouldn't turn on when he tapped it with his finger. He placed a palm on the screen, but nothing happened.

"First time?"

A sultry voice appeared to his right, and Sal recognized it as belonging to the girl who could weaponize her pheromones. He raised his arm to cover his nose and mouth, which elicited a burst of laughter from her.

"You're safe, trust me. You need to swipe your Q-Card for it to work." She gestured at her own terminal and slid her Q-Card down the side of it, activating it. With a pointed look, she gestured to Sal to try it on his own. "When students are fighting, you're prompted with questions about their performance and stuff. It's pretty chill, so don't worry about it."

A red light appeared over the entrance they had just walked through, and the girl made a tutting noise of mock disapproval. "Slowpokes get punished." She glanced back at Sal and pointed at the red light. "If you come in after the light goes red, you get detention." Her tone became a little quieter as she leaned closer. "Apparently, they make you run Combat drills until you collapse!"

Sal grimaced at the prospect and inwardly congratulated himself for not dawdling around the locker area. He wanted to thank her for the advice about the terminal when he realized he had forgotten her name.

"I'm Sal, by the way."

The girl smiled at him. "I know."

It wasn't the answer he expected and he floundered a bit, with curiosity winning out.

"Can I ask how you know my name?" He was a little flattered up until she pointed at her terminal with a sweet smile. She looked like she was holding back laughter as she stared pointedly at his terminal that he had yet to activate. With a frown and more than a little foreboding, Sal swiped his Q-Card and was met with a screen displaying two faces.

First Combatants: Salvatore Argento, Rank #19
vs.
Dominic Walters, Rank #29

Sal's stomach lurched as a mixture of anxiety and adrenaline surged through him. He looked through the crowd and saw a huge majority of them staring back at him expectantly. A large student was already making his way into the center of the square, flexing his arms as he did so.

Sal's eyes couldn't pierce through the barrier to find any information on the guy, which only made it worse. The guy looked to be far more superior at fighting, and he had no information to go off of. Sal couldn't think or recall a single weave in his addled state. Not the speedster, or the Healer, or anything remotely useful. All he had was his eyes, and they weren't going to magically take this guy down.

"Ah! Mr. Argento. Glad to finally meet you! Welcome to Combat class."

A voice boomed from the now-closed doorway. A tall man with a slender build reclined against the doorframe. It took only half a second for him to recognize the Hero, and Sal couldn't help but thank the heavens for such a boon to land in his lap. As Sal opened his mouth to reply, he activated his eyes and looked straight into the lecturer.

"I've been a huge fan of yours since I was a kid," Sal admitted honestly as he looked at the composition of the power.

Professor Rust laughed good-naturedly as he gestured toward the entrance of the ring. "The rest of your cohort can tell you that buttering me up doesn't change the lineup! So, let's see what you can do, Mr. Argento. Who knows? Maybe I'll become a huge fan of yours after this!"

Sal blinked and smiled back at Professor Rust. "I'll try my best."

With a clench of his fist, Sal's heart settled as excitement started to form within. Professor Rust was known as one of the most popular combatants across all the guilds. He never lost a fight because his ability always gave him the last laugh.

Absolute Counter.

It didn't matter how big or strong his opponent was. Sal would be able to counter absolutely any attack that was thrown at him. He had the weave already in place and it was set. Even though he had never used it before, he imagined that it would instinctively react to any attack. Sal was prepared to deal with the muscle pains that would follow, but it would be a small price to pay to avoid humiliating himself and being a glorified punching bag to one of the Offense classes.

"Ah, did anyone tell him?"

Professor Rust's voice sounded concerned as Sal stepped straight into the cage. He had half a second to wonder what he was referring to, when the answer hit him like a bolt of lightning. All his essence disappeared upon entry into the square, leaving Sal without an ounce of power. It took all his effort not to fall to one knee, and Professor Rust's voice echoed in the back of his head as the students burst into laughter.

"I'll take that as a no, then. Mr. Argento…as you're likely feeling right now, this is an essence-free zone. You're not always going to have your powers or a ready supply of essence, so you need to learn how to defend yourself when you're at your absolute lowest. I gave the rest of the cohort this lecture earlier in the week, but I'll condense it down for you now."

Professor Rust listed all the reasons it was beneficial for students to learn their limitations.

Sal barely heard a word he said as he fought to refocus on everything in front of him. The sudden loss of his powers was incredibly disconcerting. Sal felt his hands becoming slick with sweat as his vision started to blur around the edges. He fought off the incoming panic attack and tried to slow his breathing so he could come up with some sort of plan.

"You've another minute or two to get your shit together, and then you're up. You can surrender if you wish, but just know that everyone here is compiling a report on your performance. The longer you fight, the more valuable information it will yield. Good luck."

A laugh escaped Sal's lips as he realized he had been completely outmaneuvered. He had been fearing this moment since arriving at the academy. His plan of asking Divinity for tips so he could trick his way past difficult situations was one thing, but to try to use someone else's capability to fight his own battles…it was essentially a form of running away. He didn't have any special abilities in this room, and he had no formal training in any type of martial arts growing up. Sal was confronted with the cold reality that his privileged life was catching up with him, and it was likely going to punish him for his complacency.

Still, he looked around the room at all the faces of the Silver cohort and realized why his future self had abandoned these people and avoided classes. It was a cage match of taunts and insults, and he wanted to be anywhere but here. He finally caught sight of Divinity, and she looked absolutely terrified for him. He hoped that terror hadn't come from a vision.

Sal stood up straight and looked directly at his opponent. The siren that indicated the start of the fight rang out, and despite everything he expected of himself, Sal launched forward faster than he thought was possible.

CHAPTER 29:
ADRENALINE

THE LOOK OF SHOCK ON DOMINIC'S FACE WAS FUEL FOR SAL AS HIS FIST CONNECTED with the other guy's chiseled chin. To Sal, it felt as though his hand bounced off the surface rather than following through, but adrenaline coursed through Sal, and he let his panic captain the ship. It resulted in an erratic flurry of attempted punches, all of which glanced off Dominic's upper body and face.

The larger man lifted his arm to shield his face, and Sal moved closer. Strength was sapping from his arms and the adrenaline was waning. It was likely that Sal didn't have much left in him, but the arms were shielding Dominic's face and not allowing him to get any punches through. As the crossed arms moved higher to protect his face, Sal saw an opening and did his absolute best impression of an uppercut. His wrist met the boulder that was Dominic's chin, and both students staggered backward.

Dominic shook his head repeatedly and held out an arm in the air to try to maintain balance while Sal clutched at his wrist, which ached painfully. Sal knew that his element of surprise was gone to shit, and that he was likely to get flattened the moment his opponent got his bearings.

With a single twist of his head, Sal saw Divinity gaping at him in absolute shock. It suddenly dawned on him that she wasn't terrified anymore. *Did that mean that his defeat wasn't guaranteed?* Dominic's staggering became more controlled, and Sal knew he had only a second or two to make his decision. His wrist was fucked up, and his breathing was labored. He likely couldn't punch anything with his left hand, and he didn't have much faith in a kick.

Crouching low to the ground, Sal bit his lip as he rushed forward again, hoping to use the low center of gravity against his opponent. Dominic was still shielding his head with one arm, and not clearly looking at Sal, but that was no reason to be complacent. He had the advantage of muscle and endurance.

As Sal's steps came within earshot, Dominic whirled around with his arm fully outstretched and fist clenched. The attack swept straight over Sal's head, and he realized that Dominic was terrifyingly fast, too. When the attack didn't connect, Dominic glanced down to see Sal's shoulder collide with his stomach. Dominic didn't have time to tense for the impact and ended up winded. Sal hadn't anticipated the attack being successful and ended up rolling to the side in a heap.

With an agonized grunt, Sal forced himself to his feet and raised his useless wrist in front of him in preparation for the counterattack. Dominic lay on the ground, clutching at his stomach, trying to breathe, but Sal dismissed all the thoughts that tried to celebrate prematurely. He was convinced that this was a trap of some sort, but he couldn't figure out what. Sal twitched as he stared at Dominic. The adrenaline and panicked racing of his heart pushed him to finish it quickly, to either surrender and get it over with, or launch forward into an attack to find out if it were a trap.

What felt like an age was over in a split second as Sal rushed forward again. Dominic curled into a ball, and Sal changed his attack at the last moment to avoid breaking his foot against Dominic's elbows. He tried to jump over him, but clearly misremembered how far he could leap. Maybe it was down to having used the speedster ability earlier in the week, and now, he was just regular Sal…and regular Sal fell short, and landed heavily on Dominic, his elbows unintentionally slamming down into his exposed sides. Dominic's wail of agony echoed throughout the entire gym, and Sal rolled away from him in a panicked daze.

Sal flinched as Professor Rust grasped his hand, and he couldn't hear a word the lecturer was saying to him. The shaking in his body continued until the professor guided him out of the cage, where his essence was no longer blocked. It rushed around his body like a warm embrace, and clarity finally returned to Sal as he turned back to look at Dominic.

An attendant in a white uniform knelt at his side with a single palm resting on his rib cage. Everything seemed silent until Sal's ears finally started to register sound from all around him. His eyes widened as he saw many of the Silver cohort giving him a round of applause. Professor Rust was also clapping, and it took Sal a few moments to realize that it was for him.

"Well, Mr. Argento. It looks as though you've made a few new fans today. You can count me as one of them."

***

It took about an hour for Sal to calm down from the adrenaline high of fighting without his power for the first time in his life. He had numbly gone through the motions of watching the next six fights. Some lasted only a few minutes like his had, which he was initially shocked to hear as it had felt like an age to him. But others took much longer when there were pairings that were either cautious or cowardly. There had only been one fight that took a while and that was filled with action, and Sal gripped the terminal as he watched the ferocious display of punches and kicks. Combat class was scheduled for the entire day, so they were likely going to see everyone in the Silver cohort duking it out against each other.

"Victoria, by the way."

The girl beside him introduced herself out of the blue when the tenth fight finally concluded. Sal was busy inputting his analysis of the fight and didn't register what she had said for a moment. He glanced up and saw her giving him a warm smile.

As if to justify her reasoning, she gestured at his face. "You didn't look like you were with it the first four times I introduced myself. Happy to see that fifth time was the charm."

Sal apologized, but she raised her hand to stop him. "Don't. It was refreshing to be ignored by a guy for once. Was half-tempted to charm you into answering after the third attempt." She spoke as she inputted her own results, shooting him a smile between sections. "I have to say, though, your fight was not what I was expecting…or anyone, really."

Wincing a little, Sal scratched the back of his head. The fight felt like a dream at this stage, and he was happy to put it in the past and forget it. Victoria, on the other hand, seemed eager to discuss it.

"Like, Dominic is a strong guy. He's a pretty sure bet for the Savior class, but you beat him?" She shook her head as though it made absolutely no sense, but her attempt at getting a clue out of Sal wasn't getting her anything either.

The best he could do was shrug, which only caused her to laugh more.

"Aren't you going to brag or boast a little? You took down someone from the Defense class."

Sal paused at those words. He had spent the whole time thinking of Dominic as an Offense class fighter and hadn't considered that he might have been from one of the different disciplines. *Was it because he was strong and fast?* Sal made a mental note to research the people in his cohort more. It wouldn't serve him well to constantly think of people in only Offense or Support roles.

"You're aiming for Controller class, aren't you?" he asked Victoria.

Victoria's smile turned wide. "Bingo. There are a few strong Controllers in our year, though, but I'm the best out of the Silver cohort."

Despite her words, Sal didn't think for a moment that she was boasting or bluffing about her capability. It felt more like she was explaining a simple fact.

Victoria tilted her head as she looked back at Sal. "And what about you? Can you really call yourself a Support after that? They might end up putting you in the Offense class if you keep that up."

Sal shook his head as he looked back at his terminal. "Definitely a Support class. That fight was just years of adrenaline being let loose. I don't think I could do it again. I'd lose in a heartbeat," Sal answered honestly as he watched the next combatants enter the ring.

Victoria didn't press the subject, and they continued to monitor the fights in silence for the next while. Another five or six fights passed before Victoria finally spoke again.

"Did you really fuck Hannah?"

Sal whirled around in shock and saw a wide smile on Victoria's face, despite the fact that she wasn't even looking at him.

"Oh, I'm one hundred percent taking that as a yes."

Sal tried to find words to explain. He didn't know whether he should deny or acknowledge it. *The only way she could have known was through Hannah herself, but how did Victoria even know Hannah?* Sal's mind was a torrent of conflicting thoughts, but Victoria didn't let him stew in them for too long.

"We're planning a party for tonight…which you're invited to, by the way. Mixer for the different cohorts and stuff. Met a few girls at the canteen from the different cohorts and got talking to Hannah…admired her new equipment." Victoria wriggled her fingers in reference to the gauntlets. "And would you believe that she was dying to tell someone about how amazing her new Crafting friend is?"

Victoria's voice turned conspiratorial as she grinned at Sal. "Apparently, he's super attentive to the little details. Really understands how to handle equipment and doesn't finish until the job is done. Sounds like a very reliable Crafter to me." Victoria's eyebrow cocked as her grin curled around her words. "So, tell me, Sal…how do I get myself a set of gauntlets?"

Sal looked between Victoria and the cage, and considered going for another round with Dominic to escape this conversation. He had no idea whether she was just teasing him or actually flirting, so he decided to play it safe with what he did know.

"Bring me materials and what you want made, and I'll give you a quote." He was proud of himself for keeping his composure. Even if she was teasing him, he wasn't going to let her completely disarm him.

Victoria looked a little disappointed but shrugged in defeat. "You're no fun."

Sal did his best to focus on the matches still taking place. It was great research on one hand, as he was able to see the combat capabilities of his cohort, but on the other hand, it left him none the wiser about what their actual powers were. Their rankings didn't mean much to him, either, as he didn't feel that the race was a fair indicator of everyone's potential as a Hero. His eyes still couldn't pierce through the barrier, despite him trying more than a handful of times.

The only reward he got for his efforts was a blueprint on how to Upgrade the terminal in front of him, which was a funny surprise when it happened. Victoria, on the other terminal, hadn't engaged in any more conversation, which put Sal more at ease. He couldn't help but wonder what Hannah had told her, but he knew he'd need to set things straight with her at that party later.

"Attention, everyone! We're going to take a pause here between the sparring matches," Professor Rust called out as he stood in the center of the ring. "We've seen some great scraps, and I want to reiterate why this is so vital for your own development. In our first class, you got to use your abilities against each other, and you were ranked accordingly…but are you only as powerful as the abilities you were born with?" He paused as he looked around at each of the faces at the terminals.

"What happens when you run out of essence on the battlefield? Do you just give up? The essence that grants us our power is seeping into our atmosphere through dungeons, portals, and towers. When demons die, they release their accumulated essence. Every generation that came before you…was weaker than you are now. They didn't have flashy powers or custom weapons…they had their wits and their bodies. You are all here because your families survived through limited means."

Professor Rust raised his arm and pointed at a group of students before slowly rotating, gesturing at each person. "Each and every one of you came here to learn how to be a Hero. Who are you without your powers? Do you feel crushing defeat and weakness? Because if you do, you have a lot of work to do. If you feel strong and capable? Well, you have even more work to do, and I'm sure Sinclair will manage to beat that hubris out of you." Rust smiled as his hand fell back to his side.

"To truly learn from the ground up, you need to understand your weaknesses. I've looked at some of the reports, and halfhearted is being kind. Treat this assignment seriously and help your classmates. You're able to help them see their faults that they don't even know exist! We'll resume shortly. And if you need even more incentive to help your fellow classmates…I'll award Q-Credit for the best Combat analysis reports at the end of the day. Understood?"

A chorus of affirmation swept across the room as a hundred students answered at once.

Rust nodded and left the cage. "Right, let's get this show on the road!" And with a clap, the next participants entered the stage.

CHAPTER 30:
RESPITE

"YOU'RE SERIOUS?" SAL ASKED IN SHOCK, BUT DIVINITY WAS STILL LAUGHING as she tried to explain it properly.

"Yes! You got knocked unconscious almost immediately in my vision! I don't know what changed, or what the catalyst was…but something happened at the start of the fight, and I could suddenly see you leaping!" Divinity's laugh interrupted her explanation as she raised her hands to mimic the action. "Into the air to do that elbow slam thing!" Shaking her head, she looked back at Sal in disbelief. "You were like a man possessed!"

Divinity's spar had been pretty one-sided, but Sal had to do a double take when he watched it play out. His new friend had kept a few secrets of her own. She had launched into a full spinning kick, knocking her opponent out cold. The fight had barely lasted a few seconds, then Divinity was back at her terminal, grinning at Sal's dumbfounded expression across the gym.

"Are we going to talk about those martial arts skills?" Sal asked after she stopped laughing, but Divinity shrugged off the question and switched the topic back to Sal.

"Will I meet you at Survival class after the break? I'm skipping lunch to get a shower. It feels like that gym is all over my skin." She shuddered for added effect, but Sal shook his head in confusion.

"I have Administration class next. I didn't think there was a split of classes in induction week?"

"Oh, well…I'll see you later at the party? Victoria invited me. She said you were coming along, so I said yes." Divinity paused. "You okay?"

Sal shook his head with a reassuring smile and gestured that it was fine. "Yeah, Victoria is a hard one to figure out. She was teasing me earlier about some stuff and I've no idea how to talk to her."

Divinity's eyes lit up and she grinned. "Ah, I finally understand that vision…See you later!"

Before Sal could say another word, Divinity was on the way to her dorm with another laugh, and Sal couldn't help but feel that it was at his expense.

Sal stood in the lobby outside the gym and wondered whether he should go and get food, or get to the classroom early for the next lecture. He eventually decided with his stomach and walked toward the canteen near the dorms. Apparently, the Combat reports would be sent to each student after being vetted by Professor Rust.

He wasn't too hopeful about what they might say as his entire fight was the result of panic and fear. He started to go through all the different fights in his mind and was surprised to see that most students had some form of formal martial arts training. There were different styles that got in super close and took opponents to the ground, and there were flashier ones like Divinity's kick. Victoria's fight had been one of the most confusing as her opponent tapped the ground and surrendered immediately. Sal wondered whether she had threatened the student beforehand, or if there was more to Victoria than he understood.

Stopping abruptly, Sal shook his head and cursed inwardly. *Why was he still thinking about her?* Maybe going to the party tonight was a bad idea. He didn't want any drama, and having Hannah, Divinity, and Victoria all in one space? It felt like it was going to create some form of melodrama that he wanted nothing to do with. Putting those thoughts out of his head, he decided that steak would cure all his current woes.

***

Sal was relieved by the simple fact that there was no cage in the classroom. Obviously, it would make no sense for there to be one in an Administrative class, but he was still grateful that his body wasn't going to be taking any more punishment for the day. As the other students streamed in, Sal was surprised to see that many of them were completely unfamiliar to him. *Was he in the wrong area?* He walked along the connected aisles that made up the lecture hall. At its base was a huge screen, accompanied by a desk and an empty chair.

As the area where the students gathered, they didn't have spaced-out desks like the workshop or the terminals. Instead, this room had screens embedded into the surface of the curved wooden structure. Sal guessed it was wrong to call it a desk as it resembled more of a carved semi-circle that elevated up in tiers toward the ceiling. He climbed the stairs and shuffled through an empty aisle of seats, and his anxiety spiked when he saw that it was assigned seating.

Off to one side was a cluster of staff members wearing white uniforms. But rather than helping the students, they seemed to be engrossed in conversation with one another. A few of them shooed and dismissed the students who asked for help. Eventually, one of the slightly more helpful staff members gestured to a place at the wall, and Sal's eyes followed the direction to where a clump of students stood. It looked like a notice was placed on the wall to indicate the seating arrangements.

Even with his incredible eyes, there was a limit on how far he could read writing, so Sal sighed and resigned himself to trudging back down the stairs to find his seat. Before he managed two steps down, a light whistle pierced out from behind him, low enough to only be heard by a few people, but enough to catch his attention. Kane sat on one of the chairs and gestured to a seat on the aisle in front of him, two seats into the section. Sal turned back and moved into the aisle and saw his name written on the screen portion of the desk. When he turned to thank Kane, he paused at the sight of crutches propped up beside his desk.

"I heard you got hurt, are you feeling any better?" Sal asked, but rather than answering, Kane moved the crutches so they sat underneath the desk.

Sal didn't miss the wince of pain that crossed his features. When it became apparent that Kane had no intention of answering, Sal thanked him for spotting his seat. He didn't know Kane well enough to pry, and it was obvious that he didn't want to talk about it. Sal wondered whether he'd be able to recall the weave the Healer had used so he could replicate it and maybe help, but he dismissed the idea almost immediately as he had no idea how to control that power outside of healing himself.

When Sal looked down at the desk at the front of the room, an imposing figure leaned against what looked like a bladed staff. His smile was a mixture of friendly and menacing as he watched the students hurry to their seats. Sal couldn't help but feel that he was quietly telling everyone to hurry the fuck up.

He waited for a few moments before barking at people to sit anywhere for the moment. "Right, so…let's use this." The figure placed a device around his ear. "Is this better? Can you all hear me now?" With the last few words, his voice sounded out from unseen speakers around the room.

"Don't just sit and stare at me. If you can hear me, tell me!"

Sal and the rest of the class answered at different times that they could hear him, which seemed to be enough to sate their new professor. Clearing his throat, he placed the bladed staff on the desk and moved closer to the nearest aisle of students. Dark-brown eyes inspected each of them as he shook his head in apparent disappointment.

"How many of you picked the Administration class because you want to make money? Hands up!"

Most of the students looked at one another in confusion, while Sal's hand shot into the air immediately. He was only one of maybe a dozen who hadn't hesitated.

"Oh, thank fuck we have a few honest ones! Then let me ask you this. When people think of Administration, what do you think comes to mind? It's menial clerical work, isn't it? Do they think we're the people who file reports and pile up stacks of paper every time there's an accident or an outbreak? That's not what the Administrators do. Not even close.

"We're the titans of industry, because we know how this new world works, and we provide a structure for others to follow. Throughout your time in this class, I'm going to teach you how to treat your Heroism as a business. You're going to learn how to manage yourself within a guild so you rise to the top, and how to negotiate your contracts like a pro.

"Some of you will come out of this class with little more than a whiff of commercial capability, but that taste of knowledge will put you miles ahead of your peers. But if you pay attention, and you learn what I have to teach? Then you could very likely be the next generation of guild masters.

"My name is Jez, and I'm the leader of the once-prominent Bastards Guild. Judging from some of the haunted looks, you've likely met Sinclair and maybe even Lars? We were one of the finest front-liner squads in the city, and the Reavers are still trying to beat the records we've set. Why is this relevant? Because we were the most profitable Guild in operation, with no government funding and no investment partners. Everything I've learned over the years is going to be presented to you over the next few months. Our Bastards Guild hung up the Hero gloves to come here and teach you lot how to be better than us. And may I just say, it's going to take a lot of fucking work on your part to even come close.

"In front of you is your new best friend. It's a folio that contains an idiot-proof guide to progressing in this class. Just by opening it, you will have achieved your first rank within this course. As you complete tasks and assignments, your rank will increase. Ah, a hand up already? Likely wondering what ranks have to do with Administration? It's a good question."

The student who raised their hand faltered and a few other hands shot up, until Jez finally slowed his talk and looked at them all in confusion. A girl from the front row gestured at the desk in front of her.

"What folio?"

Jez was terrible at hiding his anger, but thanked the student. He whirled around to the Administrators who stood off to one side, extending his arms and giving them an expectant look.

"Why are you lot still clucking around like hens? You had one fucking job. Come on, then. I'll help you. No, no, don't bother. We can hardly fucking start the class when they don't have the materials."

Jez stormed across to the side of the room and lifted a huge stack of gray binders that looked to be made of a leather-like material. He waved off the mortified Administrators and their attempts to placate him.

"Personally, I think it's a hilarious first impression for our new students. They come in to learn the wonders of the Administration world, and their first experience is that we can't follow simple instructions? No, let's put a positive angle on it."

Jez walked up the aisle with a stack of folios. He threw them in the air, causing them to rotate rapidly and arc downward in the distance. The pack landed precisely on the desk across the room, in front of a shocked student who just stared at it. Jez was in no way or form paying attention as he continued to complain to the Administrators. Sal watched in fascination as each throw started off with a huge arc in the air before touching down perfectly in front of the students.

"Positive angle! By the end of this one class, you'll have more career prospects than this lot."

With that, Jez picked up the last stack of folios and marched up the stairs to where Sal sat. Rather than throwing the next batch of them, Jez reached into the pile and placed one directly in front of Sal, who stared at it in shock. The leather case had his name carved into it. Looking around the room, Sal realized that Jez knew who each of them were already.

Jez offered him a wink before his thunderous voice insulted the staff again.

CHAPTER 31:
DRIVE

SAL DIDN'T HAVE HIGH HOPES FOR THE ADMINISTRATION CLASS WHEN HE'D signed up for it. In the back of his head, he thought he was going to be rehashing a lot of the things he had learned from his father. After only a few minutes of Jez speaking, Sal had to admit that he was wrong in his assumptions. Sure, he was going through the basics, but it was by no means a beginner's guide to everything. The only advantage Sal had over the others in the class was that he didn't need to take as many notes, but there was still a lot for him to learn, even on day one.

"One of the most valuable resources you can have in this academy is information. Sure, you can go and chase the Q-Cred like everyone else, but in those instances, you're competing against your whole cohort. Now, what if you had something that nobody else did? It could be a unique ability of yours, a training method, something you've discovered around the academy? You can trade that with other students multiple times, rather than just once.

"You'll see Crafters squirreled away in that workshop trying to create a magnum opus, but they'll only ever be able to sell that once! But…what if they sold the design? That could be sold to multiple Crafters, bringing in a much higher yield. The process, expertise, the secrets…that's where the true value lies. You need to become information brokers, knowing what to look for so you can seize opportunities as they appear!"

Sal smiled as he took notes. He could picture the guys in the workshop with their backs hunched, working tirelessly on something they hoped would be extraordinary. Jez's perspective was a wild one, but it made complete and total sense. His eyes widened as he thought of Fabi Maccles, the girl who had created the series of tutorial videos that he had bought for fifty credits. He wondered how many people purchased that same pack from her, and how much it likely yielded in comparison to her doing the actual engraving or crafting work for someone. Sal added a whole new column of ideas for his own instructional videos. *Maybe he could just sell blueprints for Q-Cred?*

"Administration is different from the other classes, and some of you might have enrolled in the hopes of having an easy semester. Well, I'm here to tell you that you're half-right. This will be very easy for you if you're hard-working and have an ounce of talent. It's going to be your worst nightmare if you can't cut it. The best information is going to be available in the later classes, but you need to earn your place in those classes. Starting from today, you all have two weeks to earn your place in the next phase of the course. I know many of you will drop out, thinking that it's unfair or modeled to cater to the high-ranking kids with some Q-Cred.

"I'm a fair man, and I know how much Q-Cred each of you have. None of it counts toward the assignment. All of you start from the same point, but you'll need to use your own wits and abilities to get ahead. If you break the rules of conduct, your accumulated Q-Cred will be forfeited to those who follow the rules. You'll also have to answer to me. I want to see a breakdown of how you earned every credit.

"So, now we're going to talk about the different ways you can make Q-Cred, even if your power is useless. Has anyone here heard of the Credit floor above the workshop? If you have commercial skills that are useful to them, they'll employ you on a contract basis. You can sell crafted or bartered items that have value, such as used cores, weapons, equipment, and armor. That's for the high-tier stuff. But for your level, you could barter with other students. There's an entire book in that folio on negotiation techniques, establishing needs versus wants, but that's something we'll delve into properly in another class.

"Creating a service is by far one of the most lucrative things you can do in the academy. We already have a few Appraisers in our midst, and a couple of Restorers. Those skills can make bank to begin with, but don't get complacent, because your peers will overtake you quite quickly. Same goes for Crafters. You need to rise with the tide, rather than sticking to the one thing that works for you. What do I mean by that? Well, how much Q-Cred would you earn from making a sword? Let's say a hundred. How many swords can you make in a week? Probably three. If you push yourself, that could be four. How do you grow from four hundred Q-Cred a week?"

Jez didn't answer, so it wasn't a rhetorical question this time. Sal thought about the answer, but a few people beat him to it.

"Make more expensive weapons?"

Jez shook his head and pointed to another raised hand.

"The Crafter would improve over time, so raise the price of the sword?"

With a shake of his hand, Jez frowned playfully and told him that it was a good effort, but no. Answer after answer was rejected, and a thought suddenly struck Sal. He raised his hand, and Jez pointed for him to continue.

"Outsource production for a fee?"

Jez clapped and pointed straight at Sal. "That's what I'm talking about. Let's say that the Crafter makes good swords, and they're in high demand. What if he outsourced the production, but put his name on them? Clients are getting their swords and paying a hundred Q-Cred for them, and our Crafter is making a healthy margin on each sale after paying their outsourcer. That is the power of a good brand! I can tell you all right now that I would happily leave my favorite weapon at the Argento Auction."

Jez gestured with one hand to the bladed staff on the desk, and then up at Sal, who sat awkwardly in his seat. He then pointed at another student and explained how he'd always fly in their family's brand of car. Another student was praised for their family's restaurant and so on. Sal wasn't the only shocked face in the group as Jez listed more than a dozen families and their specialty.

"That's the power of a good brand! In Quest Academy, you're going to need to create your own brand among your peers. Some of you might be content to exist within the shadows of your established family businesses...you can probably guess my opinion on that stance. Others, and I hope there are a few, will go on to make their own mark on society. But that's us getting ahead of ourselves, isn't it? Money, information, and brand...all those factors are incredibly important for your continued success.

"I told you at the start of this class that I was the leader of a guild, and I also told you that I didn't get government funding or sponsorship. Let's talk about those two credit facilities and how they're relevant to you. As we start this class, I'm going to be talking about a lot of concepts from a generalist perspective, because one size definitely does not fit all. I have you for the next few hours, and I could tell you more and more about how to pass the assignment in two weeks, but a lot of that will come down to your natural capability and your ingenuity. What I'd prefer to use the rest of this time for is to inspire you.

"While I've been standing here talking to you, I've generated close to five thousand Q-Cred. I've invested in a few guilds that are currently out in the Red Zones, delving into dungeons and portals. With the agreement I put in place, I'll be getting a substantial chunk of their take until they reach a point that they can buy me out. Typically, that takes about four years. My sponsorship to them had an emotional weight tied to it. They were failing Quest Academy and they needed Q-Cred to buy their way into their final year. Funnily enough, I have a ridiculous amount of Q-Cred. Do you see where I'm going with this?

"By having Q-Cred, I was able to stop students from getting expelled by paying their way into their next semester.

"By having Q-Cred, I was able to buy a minority stake in more than five graduate guilds. Two of which have progressed to Initiate status.

"By having Q-Cred, I can stand at the top of any of these towers and piss down on the world below.

"Because if you have Q-Cred, the rules change for you."

***

The next few hours flew by for Sal, and he knew in his heart that he had found his favorite class. Jez had sat at the edge of the table and did exactly what he set out to do. Every single student who left that classroom was inspired and brainstorming how they were going to pass the next assignment.

Sal's imagination was on fire as he considered the position he was in. He had Appraisal, Restoration, and Crafting all in one, which would be great to get some start-up funds for the next class. He would be able to make some blueprints that he'd hopefully sell repeatedly, and there was so much to think about from a brand perspective too. It was probably the first day that he had felt excited after a class, and it had nothing to do with Crafting or the workshop. Sal wanted to call his father to find out more about Jez, because he clearly knew the family.

After only a few steps he overheard some students talking about a party later in the evening. Sal's stomach sunk. He was so excited to get started on the Administration assignment that he'd forgotten about the party. It didn't take much mental gymnastics for Sal to justify his actions, and he headed to the workshop, telling himself that he had time to do both. The Q-Cred that would be counted was set to zero at the moment, and Sal wanted to impress Jez as much as possible. After hearing about how powerful Q-Cred was in the academy, and even beyond the institution…Sal looked at it through a completely different lens. He didn't regret any of the purchases he'd made or what he used them for, but he did acknowledge that he needed to start earning Q-Cred rather than just spending it.

Jez had given them insight into how they could take their first steps into financial independence in the academy, and Sal had more resources than most people in that class. For that reason alone, he wanted to prove that he wasn't one of the complacent ones. Jez knew exactly what Sal could do, so Sal wanted to go beyond those expectations.

The workshop was busy as always, but there were a lot of fresh faces around that looked like first-years. Forge moved between groups, explaining how things worked. Sal realized that he was probably ahead of schedule in learning the ropes of the workshop, since his Silver cohort hadn't had the Introduction to Crafting yet. Upgrade was nowhere to be seen, but a few of the other regulars were at their seats, and Sal gave them a nod when they glanced up. He didn't wait around, though, as he moved straight to the elevator that would bring him up to the Credit floor. As the door opened, a few of the regulars shouted good luck to him, and Sal smiled as the doors closed and the huge space moved upward, revealing the beautiful auction area two floors up.

Vanessa was nowhere to be seen, which was absolutely perfect for Sal. She and the attendant both knew him as the Mythcrafter. The stalls were on the shop floor area, but according to the map he had been given before, the work order area was a set of private booths to the left. A uniformed woman gave him a quizzical look, but he handed her the Silver token he had gained from Villa.

"I'm only available for a few hours, so I thought I'd work through some Appraisals. Do you have anything that I can work on?" Sal spoke with a confidence he actually felt.

This was his domain, and he knew it well. He had been dealing with these kinds of people all his life.

The uniformed woman inspected the token and her face broke into a wide smile. "Ah, yes. We have you on file as wanting complete anonymity…so I hope you won't feel offended for me not using your name?" She spoke softly as she gestured for Sal to follow her deeper down the corridor. "I can set you up in one of our private booths. Are you comfortable with meeting the Reavers Guild face-to-face? A group of them arrived a short time ago and have just finished their preliminary checks."

Sal nodded, and the woman took it as a sign to continue.

"Normally, we'll have a backlog of items at the ready, but we outsourced several of them to different Appraisers. Would you like to verify those Appraisals yourself?"

Sal laughed at that and shook his head. "Not for free. If you're happy to foot the bill for handing it to your in-house Appraisers rather than waiting for me, that's up to you."

Her smile tightened as she opened the door to the booth. "I'll let the Reavers know you've arrived. Please fill out all Appraisal documentation on completion so we can process them for payment."

And with that, she was gone, and Sal was left in a well-lit room filled with plush couches, an area for refreshments, and, most importantly, a large table adorned with Appraisal tools. Sal grinned as he activated his power. He had everything he needed with him.

CHAPTER 32:
APPRAISAL

SAL INSPECTED THE ROOM AND WAS IMPRESSED WITH THE FACILITIES THEY HAD available. He wondered whether the uniformed woman knew that he was able to fill out the Appraisal documentation, or whether she had hoped he'd have to humble himself in front of her by asking for help. Either way, the less interaction he had with the staff of the Credit floor, the better.

He didn't have long to wait before there was a knock at the door on the other side of the room. Sal called out that they could enter, and was surprised to see a uniformed man step through first. His face lit up at the sight of Sal then he moved to one side and allowed their guests to walk through.

In all the dealings of the Argento Auction, Sal was used to business types. Agents, managers, sponsors…they were the ones who were picking up pieces or getting Appraisals done for their teams. A lot of them were vanity purchases, rather than being for purpose. Spotting those people was a talent in itself, because money was of no object to them, and they loved to hear how incredible the piece of equipment was. Petro had always told him to embellish stories with those types of customers, and make it sound much better than it actually was.

Sal's gaze flickered over the entrants coming into the room and he knew that none of those stories were going to help him in this instance. He was dealing with a much more straightforward type of customer. The actual end user, rather than salespeople.

"Are you fucking serious? He's a kid." The first man turned to the uniformed man.

Sal was curious who he would side with in this instance. If the attendant asked to see the Silver token, it would undermine Sal's professional reputation. If he pushed back on the guild member, then Sal would know they had his back.

In the briefest of moments, the attendant hesitated before nodding and approaching Sal. "Could I please verify your token?"

Sal raised an eyebrow. "No, you can't. That was done before I entered this room." Sal gestured to the door. "You can go and tell Villa that she made a mistake by asking me to do this job. Would you like to verify with her?"

The attendant froze on the spot. He turned to the guild member and apologized for the apparent confusion but insisted that Sal had been vetted already.

With a wide grin, the guild member looked at Sal and then back at the attendant. "You heard him. Go check with Villa that he's the real deal." Their playful torment of the staff member continued for a few moments before they waved him off.

Sal used that time to look the first guy over. He was carrying a long item wrapped in a thick blanket. He was tall and well built, with an impressive chest piece of plate armor that looked custom-made. His arms were covered in some form of leather, and Sal guessed that he needed flexibility for whatever his role was. A helmet with a built-in visor was cradled under his other arm, and Sal saw a targeting array on it. With just those bits of information, Sal wondered whether this guy was a long-range fighter.

"You've met Villa, and you're still alive? That's pretty telling." The guild member chuckled as he placed the blanketed item onto the table.

He consciously took a step back, and Sal was happy to see that despite their terrifying presence, they still adhered to etiquette. In the background, the woman dressed completely in black leathers stared at him intently. Two belts crossed her torso, each holding a set of knives that looked to be designed for throwing. Sal tore his eyes away as she unzipped the fabric covering her chest, revealing some cleavage.

Another guild member snorted at her. "Trying to get a discount?"

She shot him a grin. "Maybe it's just hot in here?"

Sal walked around the table and turned his back to the rest of the Reavers. He was there to do a job. He didn't want to get distracted, and that woman was definitely a distraction. With a sigh, he carefully unraveled the blanket to reveal the piece of equipment within. It took three rotations to unfold the blanket, and Sal stared at the item in confusion. Whatever he had been expecting, a sniper rifle had not been it.

"Guessing this didn't fall out of a portal." Sal chuckled as he moved around it slowly. "Am I looking for anything in particular?" He turned around and looked at the sniper, but the Reaver wasn't going to give him any clues.

"You tell me, pal."

Activating his eyes, Sal looked at the sniper rifle properly and was surprised by a few things all at once. Throughout his life, he had Appraised all kinds of items…but with the added ability of Mythcrafter, he was now in the unique position of seeing how all those items were made. The components of the sniper rifle became distinct. He could see a few fundamental flaws in places, but excellent craftsmanship in others. What was also unexpected was that Sal could visualize the blueprint to make the weapon…and also how to improve upon its design. He thought back to Jez's class and realized that this could be his route to making some good money! He could create blueprints of the weapons he Appraised and sell them to other Crafters. Sal smiled as he did another rotation of the rifle.

Name	Maslow's Sniper Rifle
Origin	Crafted
Age	28 years
Grade	Rare (Upper)
Dimensions	58 inches | 24 lbs.
Materials	Gunmetal Alloy | Doom Pearl | Infused Steel | Infused Iron

Attributes	**Lock:** Medium chance to track locked targets. **Headshot:** Headshots will have a small chance to apply critical damage. **Grounded**: Rifle negates some distance penalties and gives a small boost to range. **Lucky Shot**: One in three rounds will be infused with essence for critical damage.
Abilities	Lock | Headshot | Grounded | Lucky Shot
Power Source	External Essence
Evolution	No
Quality	Poor
Condition	43%
Value	Est. $65,000.00 – $110,000.00

"Are you Maslow?" he asked finally, causing the sniper to straighten.

"Yeah, how did you know?"

Sal ignored him and continued to look at the gun before speaking again. "This weapon has been refitted at least three times. The barrel comes from what I would imagine was an Epic-grade weapon. It infuses every third bullet with a protective shield that will pierce pretty much anything it hits. Your problem is that the barrel should be doing that with every shot. You have a scope that is Uncommon, but your visor is likely compensating for it."

Sal gestured at the helmet under his arm, and the Reaver cocked an eyebrow. Just as he was about to speak, Sal cut across him. "Your pistol grip and trigger are Uncommon too, so I'd say there are shots that don't even register when you pull it. None of this is in harmony, so I'd be surprised if you're actually hitting the mark. Stock is Rare grade, so I'd say that when you're aiming, it feels like a dream from your shoulder all the way to the muzzle. Fuck all kickback, but unresponsive on the trigger?"

He did another rotation and sighed again. "If you want this to sell, you'd be better off dismantling it and doing it piece by piece. If you want it to shoot, you need to get a new pistol grip, trigger, and firing mechanism. Barrel and stock are good, but this thing needs a much better scope if you're going to use it seriously. As I said, Upper Rare at best."

Sal glanced up to see a conflicted expression on the Reaver's face. This was usually the point that they'd try to drive up the price or argue about authenticity of parts, but to Sal's surprise, neither of those things happened.

"It only shields one in two shots, so how do you make three?"

Sal pointed at the Reaver. "You're the only variable. Are you infusing the bullets before you load them?"

The Reaver grinned. "Yeah, something like that." He turned back to the other Reavers and gave them a nod and a satisfied smile.

Sal waited for the next item, but the sniper wasn't done yet. He leaned both of his palms against the table and looked between the sniper rifle and Sal.

"I've brought this in to three workshops, including this one. All of them have done their refits. The barrel and stock are from my dad's old gun…but the scope, firing mechanism, and grip are the three new additions. Are you telling me that they've fucked it?"

Sal nodded. "If this was an Epic-grade weapon, then yes. They've absolutely fucked it. It might not seem like a huge downgrade to go from Epic to Upper Rare…but this thing is nowhere near as good as it should be. I'd say even Myth would have a hard time bringing it back to its former glory." Sal gave the Reaver a solemn look before ushering for the next person to approach the table.

The sniper raised his hand to stall his friend. "Wait, Myth? Who's that?"

Sal gave him a look as though he were crazy. "Really? You haven't heard of him yet? The Credit floor signed terms with him earlier in the week. Restored an Epic-grade item on the spot with his bare hands." Sal saw their eyebrows raise and pushed a step further. "They have me Appraising some of his stuff, and its pretty damn fun. Thought he was just a Restorer, but he's able to Craft Epic-grade items too!"

The sniper nodded to the girl on the couch, who seemingly understood what he wanted. She vanished from the couch with only a slight wisp of black smoke indicating that she had been there at all. Sal's words caught in his throat as the Reaver turned back to him.

"Myth. I'll remember that name. Thanks for that. What about you? Who are you?"

Sal extended his hand and reached into his pocket to reveal the Silver token that Villa had gifted him. "Salvatore Argento."

A spark of recognition crossed the Reaver's face. "You're Petro's son? Argento Auction House?"

Sal nodded and gave him a smile. "Hoping to get by on my own merits, though, so if you've got other items you'd like Appraised and you've money to spend, I've another few hours to kill."

The Reaver grasped Sal's hand and shook it. "You probably saw Maslow on the engraving, but they call me Watcher. I've been called a lot worse."

Then, in the burst of distortion and black smoke, the leathered rogue was back and holding onto the attendant from earlier. He looked positively terrified and very uncomfortable as the rogue-like Reaver untangled herself from him and gestured to Watcher. "He's all yours."

Sal took a tentative step backward, wondering if the rogue had a Teleport ability.

Watcher nodded and jutted his hand over his shoulder. "Blink, this is Sal. He's one of the good ones."

Blink tilted her head and gave Sal a look as though he were the one being Appraised. Her black lipstick eventually widened into a smile. "Nice to meet you, kid. How would you Appraise this?"

Before Sal could react, Blink stood in front of him with an ornate dagger in her hands, held just above her chest and dangerously close to Sal's neck. She was obviously going for the shock factor, but Sal was transfixed by the blade.

Blink glanced back at Watcher with a laugh. "Can't tell if the kid is checking out my rack or looking at the blade."

Watcher shrugged. "Either way, he has good taste!"

The attendant looked back and forth and seemed to have gotten his bearings. He apparently wasn't used to being teleported to and from rooms by a Reaver. Clearly Blink had briefed him before teleporting back and the Administrator had started talking about due diligence and procedure, but Watcher silenced him with a raised hand.

"I don't care what you all need to do. I want this Myth guy to fix up this gun. Okay? Villa will handle the payment."

The Administrator nodded repeatedly as he gratefully took his exit.

Sal, on the other hand, took the blade from Blink and turned it over in his hand.

Name	Siphon Blade
Origin	Portal Artifact
Age	[*Unknown*]
Grade	Epic (Upper)
Dimensions	14 inches | Blade 9.25", Shank 4.75"
Materials	Leecher Blood | Fey Ether | Hellfire Titanium
Attributes	**Siphon:** Blade will absorb all available essence from target and wielder. **Vital Thrust:** Blade will target vital areas of the opponent. **Jagged**: When embedded into a target, removal of the blade will cause drastic damage. **Cleave:** When used in a slashing manner, the blade will cut through most defenses.
Abilities	Siphon | Vital Thrust | Jagged | Cleave
Power Source	Target Essence
Evolution	Yes | 58% to Legendary
Quality	Excellent
Condition	85%
Value	Est. $180,000.00 – $240,000.00

"This is a really good Epic grade! It gets stronger the more essence it gathers." Sal looked up with excitement and surprised Blink with a smile. "There's an evolutionary trait in this blade. See this line here, that travels along the edge? It's absorbing essence from those you cut with it. How are you not exhausted from holding it all day?" Sal shook his head as he handed it back to Blink, who held it awkwardly.

She was clearly confused by his Appraisal. "I do feel tired between fights, but…you're saying that this knife is the cause?"

Sal nodded. He had been just as naive with the shirt he had Crafted. "That thing is an essence sponge. Normally, I'd suggest you get a replenishing rune engraved onto it, but that would ruin it completely. Give that thing enough essence and you could be holding onto a Legendary grade! My best estimate is that it'll take another few months of constant fighting and absorption before it's ready for transition. I'm really excited for you, and hope you'll show me when it changes."

Blink's surprised face broke into a wide grin as she looked Sal up and down. "How old are you, kid?"

Watcher spun around and pointed at Blink. "No fucking the Appraiser!"

CHAPTER 33:
BLUEPRINT

Sal couldn't help but laugh with the Reavers. Maybe it was their name, or Villa's reputation, but he had always been a little nervous about them in the past. But watching how they laughed and joked with each other, it was hard to see them as terrifying. He had absolutely no doubt that they were more than capable of switching off the charm and being a terrifying force of nature. Sal just needed to be professional and that would be enough to get him his Q-Cred and build up his reputation with them.

From the idle chitchat, he had been able to piece together that Watcher was one of the team leads in the guild, with Blink and Trench being two of his seniors. They had already gotten most of their spoils Appraised, but after hearing about him being a Silver token, they wanted to show him their top equipment. Trench was one of their Defense class people, and he wanted his boots Appraised. It had been a pretty straightforward one where he wasn't using high-quality laces, which resulted in the boots nearly falling apart whenever he tried to use them. Sal wasn't sure whether he was naturally closed off or whether he was a bit of an asshole, but from how he spoke and interacted, Sal didn't want to spend too much time getting to know him. Maybe he just wasn't a fan of the back-and-forth like Blink and Watcher.

All in all, it seemed like the Reavers were satisfied with Sal's performance, and he chatted to them for a while. He told them that if they were requesting him specifically, that they should ask for him during the evenings after classes. If they wanted face-to-face meetings, they'd need to be in the workshop downstairs going forward, and the Reavers had no issue with that at all. After they left him, Sal filled out all the paperwork and marked down the time it took for each Appraisal. He rounded it up to the closest hour before signing them with his name. Rather than following the Reavers out to their VIP area, he went back through the door that led to the corridor and walked back the way he came.

That same uniformed woman met him with the practiced smile, and he handed her the completed forms. She raised her eyebrows at seeing the grades of the various pieces of equipment but didn't say anything about it. With a nod, she processed his requests and asked for his Q-Card for verification. He instead presented the token and asked for them to send it to his student account. Sal didn't want to take the risk of her seeing Mythcrafter on his Q-Card. All it caused was a moment of hesitation as she went around standard procedure.

When everything was processed, she slid a piece of paper in front of him that explained the cut taken by the Credit floor. It was standard stuff for renting the room from them and using their equipment. The charge was clearly inflated, and he was glad he had informed the Reavers to meet him on the workshop floor in future.

Sal pointed to the charge on the document. "I'll meet them down in the workshop going forward. I'll leave the luxury accommodations to your more experienced Appraisers. Are you able to process the payment, or do I need to go to a different desk?"

Her smile tightened at the loss of the rental income, but she maintained her professionalism. "Your clients have already processed the payment on their end. You've received an additional tip from Watcher and Blink, with a note that you should buy yourself some new threads for your party tonight."

She reached across the table with a receipt that was folded. It was customary to wait until you left the auction before you looked at the figures, but Sal didn't want to get fucked on his first rodeo, so he opened the slip of paper and glanced at the statement.

Client: Watcher (Reavers)

- Service: Appraisal (Silver Token)

- Contractor: Salvatore Argento

- Fee: Upper Rare Grade (87 Q-Cred)

- Additional Bonus: Tip (50 Q-Cred)

Client: Blink (Reavers)

- Service: Appraisal (Silver Token)

- Contractor: Salvatore Argento

- Fee: Epic Grade (137 Q-Cred)

- Additional Bonus: Tip (50 Q-Cred)

Client: Trench (Reavers)

- Service: Appraisal (Silver Token)

- Contractor: Salvatore Argento

- Fee: Rare Grade (87 Q-Cred)

Credit Floor Costings:

- Appraisal Transaction Fee: 13 Q-Cred (Auto Deduct)

- Private Booth Rental: 25 Q-Cred (To Be Paid)

- Rare Grade Appraisal Tools: 10 Q-Cred (To Be Paid)

Sal glanced at the final number and saw that he was walking away with three hundred and seventy-six additional credits for two hours' work. The significance of those figures wasn't lost on him, especially considering Jez had used an example of a blacksmith earning a good four hundred credits in a given week. To the class, those numbers seemed aspirational, so it was definitely impressive.

Sal wasn't going to be complacent, though. He folded the paper, thanked the attendant for her help, and gave her a genuine smile and a fake promise that he looked forward to seeing her again. She remained at her station as he moved through the corridor toward the elevator when Vanessa appeared out of the shadows. The relief on her face made Sal feel as if he had just saved her from certain death.

"Ah, you got our message! So quickly too!" Vanessa breathed as she stood in front of him with her hands clasped in front of her.

Maybe it was because it was close to the end of the day, but her blazer had been discarded at some point, which left her in a form-fitting blouse that did everything to retain Sal's attention.

"We just got a custom order in for Myth! I know we haven't gone through all our due diligence yet, nor have we really introduced you to the team…but I was wondering if you'd be willing to help us out on this one and take on a commission early?"

Her smile was hopeful, and a spark of compassion ignited in Sal's chest. A part of him wished that it had been the guy who had found him, because it would be so much easier to negotiate with someone he didn't find so damn attractive. Sal frowned apologetically as he gestured toward the elevator.

"I'm really sorry. I was just meeting with an Appraiser. I'm planning on going to a party with the other students tonight, and my week is blocked with induction stuff. If I was to take a commission this early, it'd literally be at the expense of making any friends! I'd love to help you, but…"

Sal extended his hands as though it were completely out of his control. The best stance to have in a negotiation was not having to make the first offer. By presenting Vanessa with his constraints, it was on her to find the sweet spot.

In fairness to her, she was good. Sliding her hair behind one ear, Vanessa gave Sal a thoughtful smile. "Hmm, that does sound like a tricky one. You really would be helping me out with this, and I'd definitely owe you big time."

Her posture had changed ever so slightly, using the sensual card first.

"We actually got in a batch of cores yesterday, and we had you earmarked for the delivery coming in two weeks. I suppose if you were to start early, it would make sense to get you those cores early too."

Sal had to admit, that was a pretty enticing offer, but he wanted to see what else she'd put on the table before he accepted it.

Vanessa leaned in close and whispered in his ear. "If you do this gig, you'll be able to get an in with the Reavers Guild…and they pay pretty damn well for people with talent. Just ask your new Appraiser." Without missing a step, her voice was practically melting his ear. "You do this for me, and I'll sing your praises to every single guild that comes through those doors. You get some cores and…" Vanessa moved her head until she faced Sal, her eyes gleaming in anticipation. "I'll owe you one. Sound good?"

Sal nodded. He had set it up for himself to work on the gun, but all of this was an added bonus of cores, guild introductions, and sexual frustration. "You've got yourself a deal. And don't worry about owing me anything! I'm looking forward to working with you in the future." Sal gave his best apologetic reassurance.

He needed a good working relationship with her, so he wasn't going to screw it up by having her think he was a lovesick puppy. For that, he was happy to play the part of a naive Crafter who had yet to discover his worth.

Vanessa seemed pleasantly surprised. "Thank you so much!"

Her hug caught him off guard, and he needed to disengage before his body absolutely betrayed him and his negotiation. With a grateful wave, he excused himself to the elevator, but saw her through the transparent walls. As he was moving down, Vanessa smiled and waved as she intentionally moved closer to the door. As the elevator went down, Sal glanced up to see that Vanessa was still very much ensuring she had him wrapped around her finger. Her legs were slightly parted, as though inviting him to look. Sal very nearly hated himself for obliging.

***

With a tap of his Q-Card, Sal gained access to the Blueprint room. Upgrade had granted him access, but only after spending hours going through the rules with him. He wasn't allowed to alter any of the existing blueprints and needed her permission to copy or iterate on any high-level concepts. She wanted to encourage him to try his best but didn't want him to reinvent the wheel. There would be plenty of opportunities for him to work on long-term projects that would benefit society, for now, she wanted him to learn his craft through practice and iteration.

Sal took an empty sheet and sketching tools from the stationery kit by the door. He propped himself up on one of the workbenches and switched it to his profile. The first sight he was met with was the drone, but he saved that for another time and opened a fresh file, which turned the surface of the table blank. With his new sketch paper in place, Sal brought the memory of Blink's knife to the forefront of his mind and started to draw.

He had no idea how it had happened, but his eyes were able to see how the essence weaved throughout the knife. Unlike other objects where he could see how to make them better, or to Upgrade them…the knife showed him a story of when it was Common grade, Uncommon, Rare, and now Epic. He was able to see it transition and evolve gradually as it moved through those stages.

Sal took note of all the measurements, the materials, and all the runes and etchings on the blade. His eyes had somehow picked up the ability to recall every detail of the item, and Sal was able to replicate it on the sheet in front of him. There were certain things that he didn't recognize or understand on an individual basis, like some of the runes…but his eyes told him that when those runes had been interweaved and put together, they created an evolutionary trait in the item. The prospect of being able to create evolution-based equipment was exciting to Sal, but they would need a strong core to sustain that growth.

He wondered what would happen if he left Blink's knife in the core storage space. Would it evolve by absorbing the essence from the cores around it? Or would it just sit there and wait to be picked up? Sal looked at the calculations he had written down for the energy consumption of the blade and realized that making the weapon any bigger would cost a dramatic amount of essence and require an enormous core. Which meant that the knife was likely the most suitable contender for the evolutionary trait.

Despite how distracted Sal got when thinking of all the different permutations of the knife, his hands never stopped with their sketches. His blueprint was already at the level that a craftsman would interpret and work off of, but it wasn't enough for Sal as he made tweaks and changes based on the images of the knife that were in his mind. He fought off the Mythcrafter ability that tried to make suggestions along the way. Sal wanted to replicate the knife perfectly before making any alterations with his abilities.

In the next few minutes, Sal moved into a state of deep concentration as he refined the blueprint. He made sure that every nick and flaw on the Epic item was represented until he was positive that he had the perfect blueprint to re-create Blink's knife exactly. Sal took a deep breath as he smiled and activated his Mythcrafter ability. The blueprint changed in front of his eyes, and Sal consciously saved his perfect version before starting on his enhanced version.

The logic that he had was that if an Epic-grade knife was an existing evolution, then why couldn't he create the previous iterations at the other grades? What if he was able to create a better starting point for the knife with his new skill? Instead of spending a ridiculous amount of time and resources trying to create a Mythic-grade item, why not just create a perfect base weapon that had the evolutionary capability of becoming a Mythic-grade weapon? Sal smiled as he followed the instructions of his eyes, improving each part of the blueprint as he went.

His thoughts of the party had long since dissipated, but he knew he had time.

CHAPTER 34:

LATE

Sal gasped for breath as he finally made it back to his dorm. He had spent way too long working on the blueprint, to the point that Upgrade poked her head into the room and asked whether he was intending on being a social pariah. He wanted to run off at that moment, but Upgrade held him back to talk through the designs he was drawing. It resulted in him losing another chunk of time but getting a lot of incredible feedback from Upgrade. He could tell from her expression that she was excited by his project, and he wished he had more time to talk to her. When he left, she mockingly called after him that she would have loved an invite…but that she'd stay in the workshop and wither away with all the other oldies.

What had made his late arrival that much more apparent was the fact that he passed the amphitheater, which was in full swing with a huge group of first-years already gathering. Now that he was in his room, he darted to the closet and tried to find something that would make him look presentable. It was an opportunity to see people without them looking like gray blobs, and he wasn't going to ruin his first impression by looking like a blue blob. Sal dropped the blue shirt as he went through some of the other options. Black slacks made him look like he was going for an interview, so he instead tried white…which made him anxious about spilling anything on them. He shook his head and looked at his wardrobe in disbelief. Most of his stuff was gray because it matched his irises, but now, that color was his worst enemy as it was synonymous with their uniforms.

"Ugh, fuck it. Start with the top. White shirt, can't go wrong." Sal was about to put on the shirt when he caught his own scent. The shirt fell to the ground as Sal cursed his way to the bathroom to have a quick shower.

Sal was delighted by the fact that he didn't cut himself once while shaving. He was in danger of growing a five o'clock shadow after a few days of not shaving, which was nowhere near as bad as when it had first started growing in tufts and patches. He had wanted to grow it out, but it was too itchy, so he went with clean-shaven most of the time. With a glance in the mirror, he realized that his hair was getting a bit rebellious, and he made a mental note to get a cut soon.

As the aftershave was in his hand, Sal wondered whether it would look like he was trying too hard. With a shrug, he put it on anyway. In a moment of curiosity, he activated his Mythcrafter ability and his gray irises burst into a vibrant purple. It was little to no effort to keep it active, and Sal wondered whether it was worth holding it for the duration of the party. With a shake of his head, he relinquished the power and went back to his wardrobe.

"White shirt, gray V-neck sweater…rolled sleeves? Yes…open collar? Yes." Sal spoke to himself as he got ready, his eyes lighting up when the obvious solution came into view. "And jeans!"

After triple-checking himself in the mirror, Sal opened the door and stepped out into the corridor. He was already late, but at least he wasn't going to arrive in his gray uniform. It had been awhile since he'd felt good about his appearance, and he was curious to know what everyone else looked like in their normal clothes. Closing the door behind him, he checked that he had his Q-Card with him before making his way to the elevator.

"Sal! Come quick before someone else nabs him!"

Hannah laughed as she motioned for Sal to come over to her. He had barely stepped onto the steps leading down into the amphitheater when he was spotted by Hannah. Beside her was a guy with a serious expression on his face who was pinching a variety of plastic cups. Before he made it two steps, Divinity called out from his left.

"Sal, I want you to meet someone!"

He was caught completely off guard by the sight of Divinity in regular clothing. It was official—the uniforms were evil. Dressed in jeans and a cut-off top that exposed her midriff, she completed the outfit with knee-high boots and a leather bomber jacket. It took him a moment to realize that she was standing next to someone he didn't recognize. Black hair, cold blue eyes, and the mother of all resting bitch faces. The mystery girl was wearing a black skirt that went down to the ankles; her torso was a mixture of a corset and white shirt, which made her look oddly like a pirate undertaker.

Divinity's smile grew a little wider as she motioned for him to come and meet the new person. As Sal got closer, the pirate undertaker girl gave them both a withering look.

"Hey, look…it's weird that you're talking to me, but I'm not interested in your friend. Can you leave me alone?"

If exasperation was personified, it was this girl.

Divinity tried to placate her as she turned to Sal with a pleading expression. "Eh, Melanie, this is Sal…Sal, this is Melanie!"

Everything suddenly clicked with Sal, and he moved forward, about to offer his hand when he caught Melanie's expression. She looked incredibly uncomfortable with the situation and ready to snap at any moment. With that in mind, Sal decided to switch gears.

"Divinity, did you tell her about the vision?"

He looked between the now startled Divinity and the suddenly curious Melanie. "Ah, I'm really sorry, Melanie. We weren't actually sure if we should tell you or not…but if Divinity met you here tonight, then perhaps it's fate?" Sal tried to amp up her curiosity while dampening her suspicions. By the way she shifted and moved, he could tell she wanted to know more.

She unfolded her arms as she tilted her head to one side and frowned. "What sort of vision?"

Sal grimaced, as though he were reluctant to tell her. After a few more moments of building suspense, he sighed and pretended to resign himself to telling her.

Divinity had the beginnings of a smile on her face. Sal gestured for Melanie to take a seat on one of the stands as he also took a seat. Rather than sitting between them, Divinity went down to the lower level and knelt on one of the seats there, looking up at them.

Sal maintained eye contact with Melanie as he turned, choosing his words carefully. "There were a few visions, but a lot of them start the same way. You start hearing voices, thinking that you're going insane. Your concentration is all over the place and you can't focus on your work."

Melanie's eyes widened, and Sal played off a few of his suspicions as facts from the visions. "You're worried that you don't belong in the academy, or that your power isn't matched to be a Hero?"

Her shoulders straightened, and she looked positively panicked. Her eyes darted between Sal and Divinity, and her voice turned into almost a whisper. "I hurt someone in the future, don't I?"

Her fear was clear as day, and Sal could see that her mind was racing at all the horrible things that were likely to happen in the future. If this was what she was like with just a single sentence, he could absolutely understand why she had self-destructed in the future. He shook his head slowly and smiled reassuringly.

"There is a future where everything goes wrong. You get expelled and listen to the voices, let them overwhelm you. That future results in a lot of casualties…demon and human. You end up becoming one of the most powerful people in the city." He paused to gauge her reaction, which showed absolute disbelief. Sal wondered which part was the stumbling block but pressed on.

"In another future, everything goes right. You get into the Savior class, and you learn how to control your powers. That future ends up saving thousands of people, and you become one of the greatest Heroes in existence."

Divinity jutted her chin at Sal. "He's Rank #19 and I'm Rank #2. We've seen what happens in the next few months and years. This semester is the absolute worst way to assess *your* abilities, which is why you get expelled at the end of it. If you work with us, we can get you into the top of your class and hopefully into a Red Zone before the semester ends."

Sal winced slightly, and Melanie stared at Divinity in horror. "Going into a Red Zone? Are you crazy?"

Reassurances weren't going to talk her off this ledge, so Sal went with curiosity again. "Melanie, would you like to know what your power is?"

Whatever tirade Melanie was about to go off on muted. She looked at Sal with wide eyes and couldn't keep the hope out of her words. "You know what my power is?"

Sal nodded and turned a little more in his seat. "I don't know what it said on your Q-Card, but it's likely a weak version of your real talent."

Melanie nodded as she withdrew her Q-Card and held it out for Sal to have a look at. "It said I'm a Spirit Channeler, but that they don't have anything like that on record."

Sal noticed that Melanie was also in the Analysis class. Her module selection avoided anything in the field, which was a definite mistake.

He handed the Q-Card back to her. "Spirit Channeler makes sense in a way. The voices you're hearing aren't coming from your own head—they're remnants of the deceased. And as you grow more powerful…you'll be able to enlist those voices to help you. Your power is Necromancy, which is controlling the dead."

Sal paused and looked at Melanie carefully, hoping that she wouldn't freak out. Instead, to the surprise of both him and Divinity, a wide smile appeared on her face.

"You're saying I can control the dead? And that the voices in my head aren't me going crazy?" When both Sal and Divinity nodded, Melanie let out an explosive sigh of relief. "I genuinely thought I was going crazy! So, like…what do I need to do to make sure I don't follow the first vision?"

Sal could tell that she didn't completely believe them, but the fact that she was talking openly to them and willing to humor them was enough for him. He spread his hands as he answered.

"The first vision happened because you didn't make any friends or get ahead in your classes. We're not asking you to be besties with us, or try to force anything, but we'd like to help you as much as we can. If you stick with us, there's a much higher chance you'll succeed and become a Hero." He waited a few moments for her reaction, and it didn't disappoint.

Melanie snorted with a shake of her head. "I thought you were some creepy couple trying to enlist me or something. Legit, until a few minutes ago, I thought this was the most elaborate chat-up line of my life. Have to admit, it's pretty flattering being told you're going to be an unstoppable killer in the future."

Divinity's musical laugh was back as she gestured at Sal. "Be honest, though…is it worse being told that you're potentially going to become a calamity, or being hit on at a party?"

Melanie pretended to think about it before wincing apologetically at Sal. "Being hit on has to be worse."

Sal was completely dumbfounded by this turn of events. "Whoa now, I didn't do a thing! You called me over, remember?" Laughing defensively, he raised his hands and got to his feet. "Want a drink or anything?" Both girls reached down to pick up their plastic cups, indicating that they were fine. Sal gave them a mock bow. "I'll see you later." Before he managed to make it down the steps, Divinity called after him.

"Say hi to Victoria from me." Her eyes sparkled mischievously as she shooed him away.

Shaking his head, Sal took in the sights of the amphitheater. The evening air was cool, but the atmosphere was exciting and warm. There was at least a few hundred people in the stands, spread out into groups, laughing and joking. In the center stage, there was music and lights moving around, and Sal could see Hannah dancing with a few others. On one side, a guy handed out cups while students held their Q-Cards at the ready.

Out of curiosity, Sal walked closer to see what was going on. One of the huddled groups in the stands went quiet at his appearance, which Sal found to be a bit odd. With just a glance, he saw the culprit with crossed arms in the center. Sal didn't actually know her name, but wasn't likely to forget her. A small part of him wondered whether he'd be able to pay her to heal Kane. It was unlikely, though; he had most definitely soured that particular well. Rather than pretending he didn't know her, Sal gave her a nod and a smile as he made his way down the stairs.

CHAPTER 35:
PARTY

"Better late than never!" Hannah called out from the stage, and Sal slowed his walk to take in the sight of her.

She wore a form-fitting blue dress and was currently dancing with a plastic cup raised in her right hand. Her blonde hair was styled to one side, which obscured half of her face, but he was still able to see her wide smile. Even though the music had a quick enough tempo, she managed to move her body in a sensual fashion, so much to the point that Sal started getting some flashbacks of their night together.

With an awkward cough, he broke eye contact and made his way to the queue that had amassed around an unfamiliar face. The chattering of students was oddly comforting to him, and he wasn't sure whether it was because everyone was dressed normally, or whether everyone was happy…it just felt like a nice moment, and he was glad to be a part of it. He moved closer in the queue and saw that the guy at the top was pouring water into a plastic cup. With a surge of essence, the water changed color and was passed to the awaiting student, who held out his card for payment.

Sal blinked. *They were making alcohol with their power?* If they were charging by the glass, for hundreds of students…they were likely making a killing, especially considering the minimum transaction was one Q-Cred. Sal couldn't help but marvel at the ingenuity of it. If he had converted a large container, it would have saved him energy, but likely cost him a huge amount of sales. He wondered whether he used an excuse to keep it to single conversions.

As he got closer in the queue, he decided that he didn't actually want to drink anything. He hadn't eaten all that much through the day and didn't want to risk getting drunk and spending a stupid number of credits. With a glance around, he saw that more than a few guys had done the opposite and drank their fill. There was a lot of crude thrusting happening on the dance floor, which was spurring a lot of the sober dancers to leave the platform.

"What can I get you? Q-Cred up front, one per drink."

The line was practiced and smooth, complimented with a reassuring smile as he gestured toward a sign that had all the possible drink combinations. Sal gave it a cursory glance and decided to just take a water, causing the guy to frown ever so slightly.

Rather than insult him, Sal held up his Q-Card and smiled. "Guessing you're in Jez's Administration class? This is a great idea!" The transaction went through, and the impromptu barman gave Sal a grin.

"I'm a second-year! You're going to be in for a rough ride if you manage to stay in his class, but fuck me, is it worth it!"

Sal stepped away from the queue with his water in hand and wandered around for a bit. Hannah was still dancing her heart out, but the stage was very much invaded by a lot of inebriated men. Sal wasn't going to give them more than a passing glance, but they were practically shouting over the music in slurred voices. It became a challenge not to hear them. By the time Sal had walked around the stage, he had heard three or four of their attempted chat-up lines. Hannah had managed to get one about how well-connected the guy was with the guilds and that he'd be able to look out for her when she graduated. Another girl had been invited to the second-years' showcase, where he'd dedicate his victory to her.

Sal drank his water and watched as they continued to gush and promise the girls everything. Hannah gave Sal a look and rolled her eyes, which caused him to smile as he walked around. He looked up the rows of steps to where people were gathered, and it was just a very chilled evening. He rarely went out like this. There had been some friends who were into the social scene, but that was never really Sal's vibe. Clubs with music weren't really his thing.

From a young age, he had been to charity balls and gala fundraisers with his parents. Any big ceremony that happened that was even closely adjacent to the auction house resulted in them getting invited to something fancy. They were events that no self-respecting Hero would find themselves caught dead in. Being surrounded by rich and opinionated people was exhausting, and Sal would happily never go to one again.

As he became lost in his own thoughts, he didn't immediately notice the music changing to something with an even higher tempo. What did finally get his attention was the hands that covered his eyes from behind. They were warm to the touch and caught him by surprise. He was about to turn when he was chastised.

"Ah, ah, ah! You need to guess who!"

Sal smiled. "Sinclair?" he guessed with a mock tone of terror, causing Hannah to laugh as she released him.

"Any chance you're up for saving me?"

The dance floor was clustered with second-years dancing with one another. What made it sad was that it was entirely made up of men, who kept trying to subtly steal glances over at Hannah. The party was supposed to be exclusively for first years, so their presence and behavior told him pretty much everything he needed to know about them. Sal wanted nothing to do with them and gave Hannah a light shake of the head.

But she was insistent and pulled him toward the stage. "Come on, I picked this song. I know you're able to dance!" Her eyes lit up as she yanked at his arm.

Sal tried to excuse himself when one of the more daring second-years came up and put his hand on Sal's shoulder.

"I'll dance with you, love. You don't need to try to make me jealous."

Hannah looked at the guy as though seeing him for the first time. "No thank you, I made my choice. Let's go, Sal."

She strode purposefully toward the center of the dance floor, which managed to pierce the collective of tipsy testosterone. With a turn on her heel, Hannah pulled Sal's arm to the point that it cradled her waist. Her shoulder was tucked under his as she grinned up at him. "I told you that you'd regret telling me."

Sal sighed with a smile as he took her hand and twirled her out from under his arm. "I thought pillow-talk was sacred, yet here you are using it against me."

His feet glided across the floor to keep pace with her, and their bodies entwined and moved like one. Hannah's dress flourished with each abrupt turn. Sal's hips moved in time with Hannah's, and he gave her a withering look.

"Is this really what you wanted?"

Her laugh was infectious as her body twirled and moved in time with the music. Her eyes kept snapping back to his, and he laughed as he jokingly tried to throw her away, before pulling her back dramatically, all the while she spun around his arm. As Sal turned, he noted that the floor was slowly being reclaimed as each of the guys drew back for fear of getting caught up in one of the spins. It probably looked as though Sal threw Hannah like a weapon, before coiling her back to throw again. His rapid foot movements probably didn't put the drunk men at ease either.

He guided Hannah to the center of the stage and weaved around her, his legs darting left and right against hers in perfect harmony. Hannah's breathless smile was beautiful, and she matched his movements, her eyes flitting between strides, measuring and adjusting her stance as she let Sal move her body around the floor.

Sal, on the other hand, was pushing Hannah to see how far she'd go. In his eyes, she had opened Pandora's box, and there was no closing it now. If she wanted to dance, he was going to make it so that she never asked him again. Salsa, tango, foxtrot…he had done them all over the years at those galas, so a bit of a swing on a stage surrounded by drunks was an absolute cinch.

Yet, despite his best efforts, Hannah kept pace with him. What she may have lacked in technique, she made up for in tenacity. When the song finally came to an end, Hannah's fingers gripped Sal's sweater as she looked excitedly into his eyes. "You went easy on me, didn't you?"

Sal realized that his plan had backfired as she looked at him, ready to demand another shot. Just as Sal was about to answer, applause rippled throughout the amphitheater. Sal glanced around in shock. A number of students in the stands whistled in their direction while clapping. He gave them an awkward wave of thanks as he moved toward the steps leading off the stage. Hannah moved in step with him and linked her arm with his as they walked.

"Fucking cock-tease!"

Sal looked at the second-year who had spoken and was surprised to see that a couple of guys stepped up behind him, backing him up.

"What did you say?" Sal gave him an opportunity to retract the statement, but with liquid courage and a group behind him, the drunk doubled down.

"I called her a cock-tease…but now that I'm looking at her." He gestured at the linked arms. "Maybe she's a whore too?" And with that, he reached into his pocket and withdrew his Q-Card. "How much, love? You're just a first-year, so how about ten Q-Cred? Hmm? Buy yourself something nice." His cackles of laughter came out like a hyena, spurred on by his friends, who snorted at his remarks.

Hannah's grip tightened on Sal's arm, but he barely felt it. He took a step forward. "Are you serious? She doesn't want to dance with you, so you call her a whore?"

Hannah let go of his arm and waited at the steps. "Sal, leave it."

Her voice wasn't as strong as usual, which made Sal's protective instinct flare up. Taking on three second-years wasn't a smart move. He wasn't feeling particularly smart, though; he was angry. They were here to have a get-together after a tough week. It was supposed to be a safe place for them to unwind. But the second-years apparently thought otherwise. Sal steadied himself as he looked directly at the mouthy student and weighed his options.

"You're supposed to be training to be a Hero…" Sal shook his head in disbelief as he turned back to Hannah with an apologetic smile. Fighting them was exactly what they wanted, and it wasn't worth it. Hannah's relieved expression told him that he had made the right choice…in her eyes, at least.

"What the fuck did you just say to me?" the second-year shouted as he rushed forward with his right fist bursting into flame.

There was an almost feral energy in him as he moved, and Sal flinched as his fist bounced roughly off a glimmering blue shield. Hannah's hands shook as she tried to reinforce it, and Sal could see how much she was struggling without her gauntlets. The ringleader shouted taunts as he increased the intensity of the flame.

"Still feeling brave, huh?" He jutted his head forward and pulled his shoulders back in a threatening flex. As if to add to the menacing energy, his two friends moved to stand on either side of Sal and Hannah, to ensure that there was nowhere for them to run, their stupid grins signaling their intent to fight.

"Boys, boys…boys! What on earth are you doing?" Victoria's voice cooed from the other side of the stage. Sal turned to see her looking intently at the second-years as she spoke. "Hannah and I went to all this trouble to create a party for everyone to enjoy! And you're ruining that. All that effort, being thrown away. You're only here because one of your friends is useful for making drinks."

She sounded frustrated and annoyed, and Sal genuinely wondered whether she was capable of reading a room. As Sal glanced back at the group of guys, he was surprised to see them all looking at Victoria with…remorse?

Victoria continued to speak to them, her anger coming through in her words. "Since I've thrown so much away, I think it's your turn, don't you? Let's get those clothes off. You're giving us a show, aren't you?" There was venom in her tone, and Sal realized she *had* heard everything that had happened. "Come on, aren't you going to be little teases for us? Smile for the camera, boys!"

Sal gaped in horror as each of the students stopped what they were doing and started to strip naked on the stage. Each of them followed Victoria's instructions to the letter, trying to please her in any way they could. Victoria was relentless in torturing them, making them pose for photos and getting them to declare their names, ranks, and dorm numbers so she could report them.

When Sal didn't think she could go any further, she instructed their ringleader to set fire to all their clothing, which he did with ease. She chose that exact moment to release them from her ability. Each of them experienced a very different point of realization, where one saw his belongings on fire, another that he was naked, and the last one realized that everyone in the amphitheater was laughing at them.

Victoria put a hand to her mouth and stared at the one who insulted Hannah. "Indecent exposure on campus? In front of so many impressionable young women! How could you?"

The student tried to cover his privates as he leapt off the stage and ran toward the dorms. His friends weren't far behind him, to the tune of roaring applause echoing out from the amphitheater. When they were gone, Victoria turned to the crowd and raised her hand, holding three Q-Cards.

"Drinks are on them!"

CHAPTER 36:
FRIENDS

As Sal turned around, he saw Divinity looking at him with relief on her face. He was still linking arms with Hannah, which didn't seem to escape Divinity's notice. Sal expected a sly smile or some teasing from her, but he got none of that as she turned back to Melanie. At some point throughout the altercation with the second-years, many of the first-years had moved down from the stands and came closer to the stage.

Through the cheers for free drinks, Sal could barely hear what Hannah was saying to him. Wincing ever so slightly at the continued roars from the crowd, Sal gestured to one of the stands, and Hannah moved in step with him. Glancing back over at Divinity, Sal gestured to where they were headed, and she nodded in understanding.

Before he managed to make it two steps, a hand grasped at his elbow. It wasn't aggressive, but it also wasn't something he could ignore. With a turn, Sal was surprised to see Dave looking at them.

"Were you two a thing? Man, why didn't you say so!" He scratched the back of his head awkwardly, as Hannah looked at him in astonishment. She gave Sal a confused look, but Sal couldn't give her anything more than a shrug and a smile.

Dave hiked his thumb over his shoulder at the stage.

"I saw all of that! Surprised you didn't put him straight down, man, like in the Combat class!" Dave shook his head wistfully as he gestured to another place in the crowd. "Dominic is over there, by the way. Was chatting to him earlier, and he wants to meet you in a less hectic environment…said he never got to shake your hand after the match."

Dave shrugged as though it were no big deal, but Sal was pleasantly surprised. He made a mental note to track down Dominic, quashing the little voice in his head that told him it was a trap and that Dominic wanted revenge for beating him in the ring.

Hannah looked at Sal incredulously. "Dominic 'Earth Shield' Walters? You put him down?"

Before Sal could even ask about his nickname, Dave leapt in to fill in the gaps, happy that he knew something that Hannah didn't. Where Sal would have been glad to keep to the facts, Dave had no such restraint and did a full play-by-play of everything that happened.

Sal had to admit that Dave's rendition was a lot more flattering than the reality he remembered. It reached a point where Hannah looked like she was about to scoff and call bullshit, when Victoria appeared behind them with a laugh.

"It's all true. You should have seen him. He was like a man possessed! Who knows what would have happened if I hadn't stepped in and spoiled all the fun?"

Victoria's eyes narrowed on Hannah's arm clutching at Sal's.

But rather than Divinity, who didn't react, Victoria continued with a few choice words. "Are you two official now? I was telling Sal here that I might want to get my own pair of custom gauntlets made, but if you're exclusive…guess I'll have to inquire elsewhere?"

She pouted playfully, but there was a serious edge in her voice.

Hannah looked at Victoria as she slowly took her hand away from Sal's arm. She shot him an apologetic glance. "We're not exclusive. We're just friends!" Hannah nodded and then tilted her head slightly before adding a minor caveat. "With benefits."

Dave's eyes whipped straight to Sal, and his hand shot straight up. What Sal thought was going to be an attack turned out to be an awaiting high five. The grin on Dave's face didn't falter in the slightest when Sal gave him an imperceptible shake of the head. He wasn't going to gloat in front of people, and Dave seemingly realized that as he turned the awaiting hand into a clap against Sal's shoulder, completing his congratulations.

Hannah just looked at Dave in confusion. "How the hell did you two become so friendly?"

Victoria interjected. "So, you won't get pissy if I ask him to make me something?" Her eyes bored into Hannah, who looked to be quite uncomfortable.

Sal moved into her line of sight and gave Victoria a gentle wave. "I can make this easier. Orders are closed for the moment. I've got a few personal projects I want to work on and I'm not looking for any new clients." Sal gestured at the stage behind them. "Really appreciate you helping, even if your methods are…terrifying." Victoria smiled at what she thought was a compliment, but her overall demeanor was tense.

In a flash of light, another guy appeared beside them. Sal stumbled back at the sudden appearance, and the new arrival had the good graces to apologize.

"Sorry, I'm Seth. People call me Bolt." He turned to Victoria with an anxious expression. "Drinks guy is cutting us off. Those naked guys were his friends!"

Gritting her teeth for only a moment, Victoria sighed as she waved the group away. "We'll talk another time. Apparently, I've a party to attend to!" With that, she gave Hannah a pointed look and left them.

Sal felt the tension wash out of him. He had no idea how she had such an effect on him. He wondered whether it was just a fear that she was going to use her powers on him and that he wouldn't be able to stop her. He turned to Hannah, wanting to have a conversation about the gauntlets, but her expression was conflicted.

When she met his eyes, she gave him an apologetic look and squeezed his hand with hers. "Sorry, Sal. I should go and help Victoria. We arranged this thing together, and I won't hear the end of it if I leave her high and dry."

He blinked and nodded. "Sure, but can we talk later?"

Hannah gave him a sly smirk as she squeezed his hand a little tighter. "I'll drop by your room."

Just like that, Sal was standing awkwardly with Dave. He glanced up at Divinity, who was sitting in the seats he had previously gestured to. She must have known not to interrupt their conversation, and Sal was glad for less drama.

As Sal started to walk up the steps, Dave's voice came in a whisper behind him. "Dude, are you friends with the hottie in the leather jacket? Introduce me!"

Sal smiled and shrugged. "No problem, man. But she probably already knows everything about you." He glanced at Dave, but he was staring at Divinity with a curious expression on his face.

"Is she from our cohort? I've never seen the goth before."

Melanie was still sitting beside Divinity, and they both seemed to be in animated conversation. He was happy that they had managed to connect, as it made it much likelier that they were going to avoid that fourth calamity. As they reached the girls, and before Sal could get a word out, Dave jutted out his hand to Divinity.

"Dave Delgado! Rank #669." He winked at her and smiled, which Sal found oddly funny.

Divinity gave Dave a slight nod. "I hope you don't mind, Dave, but I'm not going to encourage you in any way or form because you'll read into every little action as a sign that I'm into you. Which I'm not. We can happily talk and you're welcome to join us, but just know that I have absolutely no interest in you."

Sal blinked as he looked at Divinity, but Dave just laughed.

"We'll see. You'll eventually succumb to the Delgado charm!"

Divinity shook her head. "I won't. What finally makes you stop is when you realize I'm the Rank #2, Divinity Khan, and that I'm the girl with the spinning kick." Her voice was matter-of-fact, as though she were explaining something incredibly obvious to a child.

Dave's expression matched that of a child being told something incredibly obvious, and both Sal and Melanie got to watch in real time as her identity dawned on him. His eyes widened, and he pointed at her as everything clicked into place. "Fuck! You're her! Future Girl."

Dave looked in wonder at Sal, and Sal finally appreciated that there were two very different definitions of the term *late to the party*.

"Melanie." With a dismissive shrug and wave, Melanie gestured to herself as if to ask whether Dave wanted to introduce himself to her too. In true Dave fashion, he gave her a passing glance and went back to Divinity.

Sal whistled and leaned closer to Dave. "Know the way you respect strength and competency?" His whisper was loud enough for the girls to hear, and Divinity smiled knowingly.

Dave grinned as he pressed his finger against Sal's chest, emphasizing his point. "Qualities of a real Hero!"

Sal glanced at the finger before gesturing at Divinity. "Em, Future Girl had a vision that Melanie…becomes the most powerful Hero out of this whole academy."

The sour look that he got from using Divinity's impromptu nickname was worth it when Dave finally acknowledged Melanie.

She did a seated theatrical bow before laughing heartily. Raising her plastic cup, she took a drink and made light of the awkward situation.

"There was another vision where I apparently kill everyone because nobody wants to be my friend." Her eyes locked on to Dave, and Sal wanted to burst out laughing. Divinity didn't have the same restraint and let the giggles free.

Dave, in a moment of self-awareness, moved forward and took the seat beside Melanie. "Dave Delgado. Pleasure to meet you!"

Sal laughed as he moved into the space beside Divinity. "Having fun?" He reclined into the seat, not realizing how tense he had been feeling.

Divinity's smile faded. "It's not always fun seeing into the future, because I see things that don't always happen…" Her tone was reluctant, and she looked down. "There was a future where you fought those boys, and you disabled their powers."

Sal's eyes widened. He had no idea what the extent of his powers were, but if he was able to disable them, that would be huge. He wanted to ask Divinity more about it, but the expression on her face stopped him. Divinity actually looked hurt.

"When I jumped on the stage to help, one of them hit me and you took away their powers. You looked terrifying…and after we saw the stuff with the calamities, I started to wonder if you might end up turning into one too."

Divinity's face grew red, and she whirled around in a panic. Sal got the impression she hadn't meant to say that last bit aloud.

He looked down at the stage. "I was thinking that it didn't sound very much like me, but when you mentioned they hit you…yeah, that's a whole different situation."

Divinity gestured to where Hannah was bickering with Victoria. "Isn't it the same as what just happened, though?"

Sal shook his head. "Completely different. I've no idea where I stand with Hannah, and there's stuff we definitely need to talk about…but you're pretty much my best friend." He turned back to look her in the eyes. "If I'm honest, I'm surprised that I stopped at taking their powers."

A few moments of silence passed between them before Divinity finally leaned her head against Sal's shoulder. "You're pretty much my best friend, too."

CHAPTER 37:
PRIORITIES

A FEW HOURS LATER, THINGS HAD STARTED TO WIND DOWN WITH THE PARTY. There were going to be classes the following day, and more than a few people realized that they couldn't show up drunk to them. Bolt, the lightning-quick guy, was zipping around the place, picking up plastic cups, and Sal had no idea whether he was being helpful or under Victoria's charm.

She sat on the edge of the stage as various people came up to her with questions. She was a natural leader by the looks of it, and many of the students seemed to depend on her. Interest in the stage seemed to fizzle out after the naked guys ran off, and the drinks only lasted another hour after that before the second-year called it a night and stopped mixing drinks. Victoria had somehow managed to convince him to stay for the extra hour and he was happy to get extra Q-Cred. They continued with music and the drinks that were left, but when that ended, it devolved into clusters of students chatting to one another.

Dave had eventually gotten tired of Melanie's monosyllabic answers, or finally got the hint that she wasn't interested in him. Either way, he wished them all well and went off to find someone else to talk to before the end of the party. Melanie called it a night soon after, and Divinity had to stifle more than a couple of yawns in the hour that followed. Sal offered to walk her to the dorms, but she shook her head and yawned again.

"Nah, I'll be fine."

When she got to her feet, she stretched her arms over her head, and Sal couldn't help but admire her figure.

Divinity's voice was strained as she reached the peak of her stretch. "Back to gray blobs tomorrow. I swear, they do absolutely nothing for me." With that, she turned around and posed in front of Sal as though asking for his opinion on her outfit. When she saw how uncomfortable he was in responding, she laughed. "Oh, come on, you can say I look good."

Sal nodded immediately. "Very good. You look very good."

Divinity laughed and shook her head. "It's no fun when you're forced to say it. Like this…Sal, you're looking handsome tonight." She put a hand on her hip as she checked him out slowly.

Sal sighed as he got to his feet and imitated her posture perfectly; he tried to do her voice as best he could and repeated her words back to her. Divinity rolled her eyes with a smile as she walked up the steps to the edge of the amphitheater.

Sal followed behind her and couldn't help but admire how well her jeans fit. "Love your jeans?" he ventured, which got him a laugh from up ahead.

"Okay, that's better. Thank you for noticing."

Divinity sashayed back and forth with a laugh, and Sal certainly wasn't complaining. Unlike with Hannah, Sal felt completely at ease around Divinity, and he could be his regular joking self. He just didn't want to risk his friendship by attempting anything with her. It was only their first week in what could be three years of working together, and a surefire way of making this awkward was to make a mistake in a heated moment.

At the top of the stairs, Divinity turned and smiled. "You've a wide smile on your face in the morning when I see you, so I don't think you need to be told to have fun."

Just as she was about to turn off for the dorms, Sal stopped her and asked a question that he was curious about. "Have you ever looked into your own future? To see who you end up with?"

Sal had no idea whether it was rude to ask, but judging by the sad smile on Divinity's face, he regretted asking.

She just shrugged. "In all the futures I've seen, I end up alone. I don't know if it's because of my work, or because I push people away…" Divinity exhaled as she gestured at her eyes. "I can't see the emotions behind the actions, so I don't know why the future me is like that. I kinda have you to thank for giving me that realization. I need to understand the circumstances around the scenes rather than what they're showing me."

Sal just stared at her quietly, and Divinity tried to make light of the situation.

"Sorry, didn't mean to be such a downer with that one. Let's just say, who knows? Not every outcome happens, right?"

Her attempts at humor were forced, and Sal returned her smile. As Divinity turned back toward her dorm, she called back over her shoulder, "Besides, we're Heroes! We're supposed to be saving lives, not living happily ever after!"

"Goodnight!" Sal called after her, which she acknowledged with a wave before disappearing into her tower.

Turning back, Sal looked down at the remains of the party and didn't see any sign of Hannah. Victoria was still orchestrating the clean-up, and Sal was surprised at how conscientious she was. Rather than going down to help them all, Sal decided that it was time for bed. He thought about what Divinity said. Sure, a part of him was excited about whatever was going to put a smile on his face…but he was also troubled by the expression on Divinity's face.

He couldn't imagine someone like her ending up completely alone. If it happened, it had to be down to choice. She was smart, funny, strong…incredibly powerful and beautiful. Sal shook his head as he tried to understand it. She was essentially the perfect woman. With that thought, Sal faltered as he started to question whether he liked her in that way.

Pinching the bridge of his nose, Sal shook his head and wished he could blame his thoughts on alcohol, but he was as sober as the moment he arrived. After a few moments of deliberation, he realized that he was overthinking everything and that it didn't matter. He was friends with Divinity, and everything was fine between them. Victoria was just trying to get under Hannah's skin, but it didn't work.

He wasn't going to complicate his life further, and he was happy to have a little fun with Hannah on the side. Sal nodded. There was nothing else to think about. He needed to focus on his classes, projects, and his own future. Everything else could take a back seat.

When he finally made it to the lobby, he was almost at the elevator when he saw Hannah in a nearby chair, a bottle of water in front of her. Sal walked over to her, and her expression was suddenly crestfallen. Before he could say anything, she bit her lip.

"Sal, I'm so sorry…but can we have that chat another night? I promise I'll make it up to you." Hannah gave Sal a hopeful look, and he nodded.

"Of course. Are you okay?"

Hannah sighed in what was probably relief and frustration as she just gestured to the amphitheater outside. "It's just…Victoria. She decided to report those guys, and now I have to give a statement." She gestured at the water bottle in front of her. "Just need to make sure I'm sober enough for it! I can't believe she did this to us now. This could have waited until tomorrow!" Hannah closed her eyes with an aggravated sigh before she took Sal's hand and squeezed it. "I promise I'll make it up to you." And with that, she picked up her water bottle and left the lobby, leaving Sal with zero plans for the rest of the night.

***

"Okay, I'm seriously starting to think you hate fun," Upgrade mocked as Sal walked into the workshop. She pointed at the clock on the wall above the elevator. "You were gone like five hours! Get drunk, go to bed, make stupid decisions!" Her voice was exasperated as she looked around at a few of the smiling faces around her. "Do all the fun shit before you become like us! Don't skip all the good parts!"

Sal waved the comments away as he approached his bench, but Upgrade stood up from her own and held up a hand.

"Hold up! Who are you and what did you do with Sal?" Her eyes shamelessly looked him up and down, and Sal felt a small swell of pride as she gave him an approving nod. "You scrub up well! Might be worth Upgrading your uniform so you don't have to wear that damn blanket-shirt."

Sal laughed as he got to his desk. "I'll have you know that I fully intended to get an early night, but then I remembered that Vanessa was going to be leaving a few cores for me to work on! Early present in exchange for Myth's services. Did they arrive yet?" He was hopeful as he looked at Upgrade expectantly.

With a hand on her hip, she sighed. "If I tell you that they're here, you're going to start working, aren't you?"

Rather than answering, Sal just gave her a wide smile.

Upgrade groaned. "Everything is set up in Room 17. Just don't stay up all night, okay?"

"Yes, ma'am!" Sal saluted as he practically jogged toward the room.

Sal's Q-Card opened the door smoothly. The cold temperature inside made him shudder in excitement. He was finally going to work with cores, and he knew exactly where he wanted to start.

The room itself was quite ordinary, with an illuminated design board filled with schematics on one side of the room, a large workspace with a streak of light at its center, and an intricate multitool mechanism directly above it. Other than those, the only thing that caught Sal's attention was a long couch that rested on the other side of the table. The air conditioning was on and pumping the room with cool air, which he quite liked.

Sal pulled an engraver down from the multitool and was pleasantly surprised to see that there was practically no resistance from its tether.

There was a laser cutter, a fabrication printer, and even a small industrial forge. Saving the best for last, Sal turned around and regarded the ornate chest that waited for him on the floor. It had his name etched onto the surface, giving it an incredibly premium feel.

Myth.

Sal grinned as he opened the chest, feeling a rush of excitement as he saw several trays holding individual cores. Each one came adorned with an Appraisal tag. There were multiple bolts of fabric, stacks of metal ingots, vials of colored liquid, and even more than Sal could have ever expected. He carefully unpacked the case and had to stop himself from checking out and inspecting everything. He didn't have a huge amount of time and didn't want to repeat the instance of staying awake all night.

Regretfully, Sal repacked the case with all the cool items, leaving him with what he needed. Every part of him wanted to start making the knife that could evolve. His creativity was practically begging him, but he reminded himself of the promise he made. On the other side of the table sat Watcher's sniper rifle. He hadn't ever manufactured parts before, but he figured that he'd need to start somewhere.

Instead of going straight into the improvements like he was so accustomed to, Sal applied the lessons that Upgrade had taught him. He brought out a fresh sheet of sketch paper and started to inspect the sniper rifle from all angles. Just like he had done with the knife, he drew all the measurements of the existing weapon, all the components, how it fit, and anything that could be useful. It was much faster than he had expected, which brought a smile to Sal's face. His practice was paying off.

Upgrade entered the room and lay down on the couch. "So, spill…why are you back here and not out there getting wasted?"

Sal continued to draw the precise lines, looking between the drawing and the rifle. "Party was ending. Guy serving alcohol called it quits and people were getting tired."

Upgrade twisted her head toward Sal. "Did you at least make any friends? Come on, I'm here all day. Give me some drama!"

Sal shrugged as he worked. "I've a good friend. You already met her. Divinity?"

With a groan, Upgrade sat up so she could see Sal better. "So, you've got nothing juicy?" Shaking her head, she got to her feet and was moving toward the door when Sal decided that the company was preferable to silence.

"There was almost a fight."

"Finally!" Upgrade turned on her heel and skipped back to the couch with a grin on her face. "Tell me everything!"

Sal paused from his drawing as he told her about the party, what had happened with the second-years, and how Victoria had intervened, but Upgrade put up her hand to interrupt.

"Who is this Hannah girl? You were dancing? You can dance?!"

The onslaught of questions caused Sal to laugh until Upgrade stood in front of him with her hands outstretched.

"Sorry, Sal, but it's the only way I'll know if you're telling the truth. You're going to have to show me these dance moves!"

Sal stared at her in disbelief before he burst out laughing.

Upgrade shook her head. "I can lock you out of this room and make it so you can only use the workshop during core hours. But it's your choice!"

She held out her arms expectantly, and Sal finally conceded as he put down his pen. With a resigned groan, he took her offered hands and moved around her, turning her body with the momentum into a twirl.

"Ta-da!" he exclaimed in a deadpan voice before tapping his feet against the tiled surface. "Can I get back to drawing now?"

Upgrade looked thoughtful and kept a hold of his hands. "I think we need a few more opinions." With that, Upgrade danced out the door, dragging Sal with her as she spun herself of her own accord. "Did you all know that we have a dancer in our midst?"

A few tired faces were their audience, and Upgrade raised her hand in the air with a flourish.

"I'd like it to be known that Sal wants to dance with me and is in no way under duress! I definitely didn't say that I'd lock him out of the workshop if he refused. He just really wants to share in all of this creative energy." Her laughs between sentences were accentuated with dramatic dance moves that threatened literally every workbench around her.

"If he's not going to go to parties, we might as well bring the party to him!"

Sal managed one last glance at the chest of materials and his incomplete blueprint before Upgrade grasped his shoulders.

"So, Mr. Argento…show us how the Auctioneers dance!"

A few whistles and cheers came from the benches, and Sal laughed along with them. With a glance at the grinning Upgrade, he decided that he might as well just give in.

"Try to keep up."

CHAPTER 38:
UPGRADE

"I'M TELLING YOU, HE HAS ROBOTIC LEGS. IT'S THE ONLY LOGICAL EXPLANATION!" Upgrade groaned as she clutched at her calves.

She and a few of the others were sprawled out on the couch in Room 17 as Sal was walked through the steps of using the industrial forge and the fabricator. Upgrade seemed to be under the impression that she was going to drag him around the workshop in an elaborate dance, but the roles quickly reversed, and Sal had very much had the last laugh. As a reward for the show, a few of the Crafters offered to help him out with the sniper rifle restoration. Martin was currently walking him through using the fabricator.

Sal watched in awe as the firing mechanism was printed in front of him. Each of the tiny components was being replicated as he fed the machine his essence. He did as he was instructed and applied the layers of energy within the lines of the printer, and small lasers solidified that essence with the material. It was creating an essence-infused component.

He was delighted when his eyes immediately calibrated to the task and offered him a more precise measurement than the guidelines set out by Martin. He couldn't explain how he knew, but Sal was sure that this machine was going to help him create components at Epic grade.

"Sal, lift your jeans! Are your legs real?" Upgrade insisted as she put down her wine glass.

Gosia, beside her, snorted in laughter, and Sal had to do his best not to laugh.

"Yes, they're real."

He was much more at ease talking to them now that he had made a few small pieces with the fabricator. He was really getting the hang of it, and his eyes had taken over a lot of the difficult things to keep track of. Sal didn't need to worry about how much essence he was using or making any mistakes because his Mythcrafter ability highlighted any issue, and it also allowed him to fix any minor mistakes with his raw essence. Right now, Sal was sure that the component he was making was going to be Upper Rare grade at minimum, and that was without any finishing touches or upgrades.

"Now don't forget the lenses!" Martin gestured over at the industrial forge, where the glass from the dismantled scope was being heated.

Sal nodded and focused on finishing the firing mechanism first. He knew that he would have overthought every single part of this process had he tried it by himself, but with the steady hand and guidance of Martin, he was moving through the stages like it was second nature.

"Upgrade, are you sure Martin isn't the lecturer? I'm learning loads from him up here," Sal teased as he finished the mechanism and placed it onto the table.

Upgrade didn't move from her seat, but her eyes narrowed onto Sal. "Funny guy. Wait until your first class with me. I'm going to take the piss out of you in front of all your friends!"

Sal shrugged. "Assuming you can ever use your legs again, right?" He shot her a grin.

Upgrade turned to Gosia. "I'm actually going to kill him. I don't care if he's half robot. I'm going to kill him."

Martin gestured for them to be quiet as he motioned for Sal to listen to the forge. "Your eyes can probably see it better than any of us here, but you can hear the change in the material when it reaches the peak temperature."

Sal couldn't hear any sort of difference, but his eyes could see the changes in the lens as it absorbed the liquified essence. One of the bottles that Vanessa had gifted him was apparently perfect for enhancing the sights. The casing was easy to replicate with better materials, but the key differentiator was going to be the lens, and his eyes could already tell that it had come out much better than expected.

Sal's heartbeat quickened as he started to engrave the lens with the rune that Francis had picked out for him. It took multiple assurances from the Crafters that the engraving would be transparent, but Sal still couldn't understand it. He was drawing on what was essentially glass, and it was absolutely going to obscure the vision of whoever looked through it. Despite those concerns, he followed their advice and channeled his energy throughout the process. With all the components now complete, Sal assembled them as the lens cooled.

Upgrade winced a few times as she watched Sal, criticizing his lack of technique, which deteriorated into her barking corrections at him.

Rather than getting defensive or ignoring her, Sal did his best to change his approach and follow her instructions. He knew that with the cores, he'd probably be able to use all the raw materials and force the upgrades like he had done with the gauntlets. With the quality of the materials, combined with the energy from the cores, they'd likely be Epic grade.

His weakness wasn't his power; it was his technique. It was incredibly wasteful to throw all that essence and materials at a weapon when he could do it for a fraction of the cost. That said, Sal was going to cut some corners by Upgrading small pieces at a time. Sal glanced at the sketches on the table and had to move one of them to the side. At some point during the evening, Upgrade had gone into the blueprint room to get his evolving dagger sketch to show to the other Crafters, then had left it on the table.

As the page slid over the other drawing, Sal stopped abruptly. In those few heartbeats, Sal couldn't hear Martin or Upgrade or anyone else in the room. All he could see was the evolution rune overlapping the sniper rifle. His eyes couldn't distinguish the difference between the two schematics and rather than seeing them as two different blueprints, they instead tried to solve the problem they thought they were being presented with.

The Mythcrafter ability created a solution that Sal had thought impossible—a path to creating an evolutionary sniper rifle. Sal's eyes didn't move as he started to redraw and correct everything he was seeing.

Upgrade groaned as she got to her feet. She looked like she was about to say something snarky when she caught his expression. His eyes were glowing in their vibrant purple. She glanced at Martin, who shrugged.

Sal didn't respond to their attempts at conversation and instead started to sketch and draw.

"Bit late for corrections when you've already made the parts...What did you mess up?" When she moved closer to have a look at what he was drawing, she froze. Shaking her head, she looked at Martin and pointed at the drawing. "Are you fucking seeing this?"

Sal barely heard a word they were saying as he went through each of the designs. He couldn't believe it made sense. It looked like the stupidest idea of all time, but his eyes said it could work, and they hadn't been wrong yet.

His previous desire to do everything the slow and steady way had been thrown out the window because the new design demanded stupid amounts of ingenuity and power that only his ability could provide. It would require a team of master craftsmen to make it and a lot more than the materials they had.

Martin looked at the design and then glanced at Upgrade. "An evolutionary sniper? Bullets tethering to targets over that distance? There's no way that would work! The dagger makes sense because it's literally embedding, but a sniper? It sounds more like a fishing rod in this schematic." His laugh was filled with total disbelief.

Upgrade didn't share his mirth, sobering up as the design took shape. "Sal, it's a nice concept and all, but it's not what the client asked for." Her tone was level throughout all of the excitement, but it needed to be stated. "You have your brief, and you've got your components. You just need to finish the assembly and send it home, okay?"

Sal's eyes flickered back to silver as he took a step back from the table. Gosia, Martin, and Upgrade looked back at him with various stages of concern and disbelief. He could tell they wanted the best for him and that they were trying to guide him in the right way.

The problem was that they didn't see what he saw and were going by a few strokes of a pen. Sal frowned. He knew he'd be able to finish the Epic sniper, which was the actual brief, as Upgrade had said. There was no way that he'd be able to brute-force his way to making the schematic he'd just designed because the material cost would be extraordinary, let alone the core consumption. Even if he had all the techniques that he needed, it would take forever.

Sal wondered whether he could outsource certain components to them and then just Upgrade them. It was a sound theory, but their capability was too low. It would be perfect if they'd be able to work on Epic-grade items rather than just Rare.

Sal faltered as he came to a realization. He hadn't asked Divinity about the power change when he unknotted her ability. *Surely, she would have said something if there was a negative outcome?*

With nothing left to lose, Sal brought his hands together and spoke tentatively. "Hypothetically...if I was able to enhance your abilities for an unknown period of time, would you be interested in helping me build this?"

Sal pointed at the blueprint of the proposed sniper, and all three looked at him as though he had two heads. Upgrade was shaking her head and it looked like she was about to move into lecture mode about responsibility and managing expectations, but Martin interjected first.

"Since it's a hypothetical...I'll say yes."

Upgrade gave him a quizzical look, and Gosia put up her hand too.

"Sure, I'd help."

With a roll of her eyes, Upgrade shrugged and gestured at the blueprint. "Okay, yeah. If I could make sense of this, then I'd help you...but it's not that simple."

Sal raised his hand to stop her from speaking for a moment. Upgrade cocked an eyebrow and placed a hand on her hip as she gestured for him to continue.

"Next part of the question. Would you mind if I tried to enhance your power? You don't have to do anything, and I don't even need to touch you. It probably wouldn't even work." Sal grinned as he looked at Martin with a raised eyebrow.

Martin grinned. "Go for it!"

Upgrade narrowed her eyes at Sal. "Even if you have that Skill Master ability. There's no way for you to affect the abilities of others. Your heart is in the right place, and it's great that your ambitions for crafting are making you think outside the box ...but this ...this is insane, Sal."

Sal smiled through Upgrade's lecture as he unknotted Martin's weave. The threads reacted to Sal's touch, and it took all of a few seconds to undo the loosest of the knots.

Martin's eyes widened as he took a tentative step back. He looked off to one side, refusing to look Sal in the eye as he hastily brought his hand to his eyes to wipe away his tears.

Upgrade rushed around the table to check on him, but Martin's face was positively beaming as he breathlessly nodded.

Despite his best efforts, Martin couldn't articulate what was happening. His eyes widened further, and he stared at Sal in shock.

Sal continued to navigate Martin's weave. He had started with a few easy knots on the outside that practically melted away with his touch. It was pretty tiring, if he was honest, and the weaves were stubborn in comparison to his own.

Some knots were wound so tight that it would have taken an age to pry them loose. Sal ignored those for the moment and continued to unravel the easy ones. After the third knot was undone, he released his power and blinked a few times until he was back to reality.

Martin stared back at him with a goofy smile and red eyes. He exhaled and chuckled at the same time. "Sal, I don't care if this is temporary...this is probably the best I've felt in my life."

Gosia's hand shot up. "Me next!" She glanced at Upgrade and then back to Sal. "I mean, if that's okay!"

With a nod, Sal closed his eyes and repeated the process on Gosia. She didn't have many knots to begin with, and the few that she had were at the center of her weave. Rather than just giving up because there were no simple ones, Sal worked on one of the core knots, despite how difficult and tightly wound it was. It took longer to work out that one knot than it did to do three of Martin's. He couldn't explain it, but Sal felt more exhaustion than before...but continued regardless.

When he was done, the knot tried to reform, albeit slowly. Maybe it was because of the work he had put into it, but Sal had no intention of letting it knot itself once more, and moved the weave in such a way that it couldn't form again.

He made a mental note of what it had looked like before, just in case it had any negative effects on Gosia. When he opened his eyes, he wasn't sure what to expect, but the grin on Gosia's face was an absolute relief.

"You're both fucking with me, aren't you?" Upgrade scowled as she looked between the three of them. "You planned this when I went into the blueprint room, yeah?" With a shake of her head, she crossed her arms and stared them down. "Okay, if this is some big joke at my expense, I'll bite. Go on, Sal, make me more powerful! I can't wait to see the punch line."

Rather than activating his power immediately, Sal reached into the chest and took out a small core. He didn't want to have to rely on his own power for this one, because Upgrade's ability was the most important part of the puzzle if they were going to create the blueprint with the materials they had.

With a steady look, Sal caught Upgrade's eyes. "You need to promise me that you'll make this first, before you work on the drone. Okay?"

He said it with a smile, and Upgrade's demeanor faltered.

"You're actually serious, aren't you?"

Sal gripped the core as he activated his ability. The surge of essence washed through him, and he felt more than energized. Upgrade's weave was an absolute mess, and he was astounded at how much power she had been able to utilize with what she had available. Martin's three knots and Gosia's one tough knot were nothing in comparison to Upgrade.

If he had to estimate, there were about a dozen knots of various severity and a few flow issues where the weave just kept tangling. With the added essence, Sal got to work and untangled everything he could see. After the first five, he wondered whether he was maybe going overboard, but he reasoned that he needed her power to be potent to make the rifle.

The issue that he could see was the weave losing its strength, and he wasn't sure what to do with it. As that thought crossed his mind, his skill seemed to nudge him into guiding the weave in a different way. Sal complied, and it felt right. He listened to a few more of the nudges, which allowed him to strengthen the weave considerably. The thickness of it had grown, and Sal knew that it would be much tougher to knot or tangle it. He took one last glance and was happy with his handiwork.

When he finally opened his eyes, he felt as if he were choking. Panic set in, and Sal frantically tried to escape from whatever was trying to kill him.

"You're strangling him," Martin cautioned, but Upgrade kept up the tight embrace.

Her fists gripped his sweater as her chin buried into his shoulder. "Thank you. Thank you. Thank you."

When Gosia finally pulled Upgrade off Sal, he was able to catch his breath. The first thing he saw was her pendant, ripped off her neck and placed on the table. Her grin was wide as she breathlessly laughed at something that only she could see. Sal recalled the same expression for both Martin and Gosia, but Upgrade's transformation was that much more dramatic. When she turned to look at Sal, her expression was one of excitement.

"I can channel essence!" She closed her eyes as her body transformed into its armor. "I don't need the core!"

Sal stared in disbelief as the armor transformed into something extraordinary. What had once been Rare-grade armor, was now…Legendary?

Upgrade looked at the schematic on the table, the grin never leaving her face. "Well, we made a promise, didn't we?"

They all turned their heads to Sal, and Upgrade asked the question all of them were thinking. "How long do we have with these powers?"

Sal scratched the back of his head as he shrugged. "I think it might be permanent."

CHAPTER 39:
LEGENDARY

SAL OPENED HIS EYES TO THE SOUND OF EXCITED VOICES ALL AROUND HIM. HE blinked a few times and realized that he was laid out on the couch in Room 17.

Upgrade placed a cup of coffee on the surface beside him and gave him a wink. "You're just in time. All the components are ready for assembly."

Sal rubbed his face, and he glanced at the clock. It was nearing six in the morning. It jolted him awake as he looked at the group accusingly. "You said you'd wake me up at three!"

Upgrade's smile never left her face as she gestured across the table at Martin. "He wanted to re-make the mechanisms, and they turned out great. We also had another little project we wanted to work on while you were out for the count, so don't be too annoyed."

Sal sat up and blinked a few times before lifting the cup of coffee. He took a drink and was disappointed to find that it wasn't one of Alex's brews. Those coffees were on par with the ones from the vendors. It took a few moments for Sal to register Upgrade's words. As he got to his feet, he felt a slight twinge in his back that he tried to ignore. His eyes scanned the table, and he could scarcely believe what he was seeing.

All the components he had envisioned sat in front of him, waiting to be assembled. Each one was of a higher quality than he anticipated, and all it took was one look at the grinning Upgrade to discover who the culprit had been.

Sal was happy to see that they had respected the original components of Watcher's gun, so the barrel and stock were still the same, albeit enhanced.

Gosia sidestepped into an empty space on the other side of the table which seemed incredibly suspicious. Sal just gave her a look, and she turned away to smile at Martin.

With a laugh, Upgrade gestured for her to move. "You might as well show him. See what he thinks."

Gosia moved back to reveal what looked like folded pieces of silver fabric. When she lifted up the first part, Sal saw that it was a new uniform. His eyes had been tracking the items on the table, so they immediately got to work when they saw the fabric. Sal's breath caught in his throat as he identified the shirt as an Epic-grade item.

Upgrade pointed at both Martin and Gosia. "Just want you to know that none of this was my idea—it was all them!"

Sal was genuinely speechless as he moved closer to touch the material. It was leagues ahead of his original design but looked vaguely familiar. Where his had the silver-infused metal, this shirt had a series of live circuits, all in black, darting erratically across the shirt. Sal could see at least eight different runes, all blended together and coexisting happily.

Name	Argento Shirt
Origin	Crafted
Age	New
Grade	Epic (Middle)
Dimensions	Chest 42 inches | Neck 17.5 inches
Materials	Refined Upgrade Essence | Refined Enchanter Essence | Voidsilk | Essence Core
Attributes	**Defiant**: Shirt negates piercing and blunt damage. Chance to reflect damage. **Synergy**: Abilities are shared among set items. **Chameleon**: Shirt morphs to match the ability essence of the wearer.
Abilities	Defiant | Synergy | Chameleon
Power Source	Enhanced Core
Evolution	No
Quality	Excellent
Condition	100%
Value	Est. $45,000.00 – $70,000.00

His eyes finally landed on the collar, which was lined with what looked like a black metal. It glistened against the light, and Sal could tell that a core had been worked into it. He opened his mouth to speak, but nothing came out.

Gosia reached behind Martin and revealed a pair of matching black slacks with silver trim.

Name	Argento Slacks
Origin	Crafted
Age	New
Grade	Epic (Lower)
Dimensions	Waist 32 inches | Leg 34 inches
Materials	Refined Upgrade Essence | Refined Enchanter Essence | Polyester | Dreadwool
Attributes	**Steady:** Removes any movement penalties or abilities that would hinder the wearer. **Synergy**: Abilities are shared among set items. **Impact:** Slacks negate fall damage and incoming attacks. Chance to reflect damage.
Abilities	Steady | Synergy | Impact
Power Source	Enhanced Core (Set) | External Essence
Evolution	No
Quality	Excellent
Condition	100%
Value	Est. $35,000.00 – $50,000.00

"These work independently by themselves, but they get a good boost if you wear them with the shirt. Ideally tucked in, so the essence can connect."

Neither Gosia nor Martin were the types to make someone feel uncomfortable, so with their part said, they folded the clothes and handed them over to Sal.

Martin gave him a warm smile. "We just wanted to say thank you for what you've given us. It might not be permanent, but it's the most alive we've felt in a long time…" He looked at Upgrade with a raised eyebrow. "So, we all made something for you."

Sal looked at Upgrade incredulously, and without any pomp or ceremony, she slid a small container across the table toward him.

"I was hardly going to wear my first attempts, so you can consider them my first test run with this new power level." She smiled and nodded at the box.

Sal opened it up and saw a pair of fingerless gloves that looked like a more high-end version of the ones Upgrade wore. He looked at her in shock, and she just nodded. "Channel your essence into them and they'll turn into your toolkit, just like mine."

Just to showcase the capability, Upgrade flaunted her hand, which transformed into a series of mechanical apparatus that was all controlled by her fingers and essence. "It'll take some time to get used to it, but when you do…you won't even know yourself."

Sal looked at the gloves, and his eyes told him the exact same as the new uniform. Everything was Epic grade and way beyond anything he had ever owned. If he was to give them all his accumulated Q-Cred, it still wouldn't be enough to pay for even one of them. He couldn't even come up with the words to thank them as he just gestured numbly at the presents. The information continued to pour into his brain as he stood there awkwardly, not knowing how to express his gratitude.

Name	Argento Gloves
Origin	Crafted
Age	New
Grade	Epic (Upper)
Dimensions	Circumference 8.5 inches
Materials	Refined Upgrade Essence | Refined Enchanter Essence | Phantomweave Bolt
Attributes	**Pocket:** Gloves can summon Crafting tools from a limited interspacial pocket. **Transform:** Tools stored in the pocket can become extensions of the wearer's hands. **Overcharge:** Grade and Abilities of the gloves are enhanced for a short period of time. **Synergy:** Abilities are shared among set items.
Abilities	Pocket | Transform | Overcharge | Synergy
Power Source	Enhanced Core (Set) | External Essence
Evolution	No
Quality	Excellent
Condition	100%
Value	Est. $65,000.00 – $90,000.00

Upgrade clapped him on the back, grinning. "Don't worry, you're welcome. We used a few bits and pieces of your materials, so don't go thinking that we're completely altruistic." She turned and gestured at the rifle on the table. "Are you fully awake now? Because it's time for the fun part!"

Sal nodded and placed the uniform and gloves on the couch behind him.

Martin snorted at how careful he was being. "Sal, that shirt can take a direct hit from a Hulker. It'd probably knock a Prowler unconscious, so you don't have to treat it like it's a fucking egg."

Sal just stared at Martin, and Gosia laughed out loud.

"If you think that's cool, wait until you give it a proper Appraisal!"

A cough from the other side of the table drew their attention to Upgrade, who pointed at the assortment of materials on the table. "Come on! Am I the only one who wants to see a Legendary weapon?"

All three of them moved around the table, and Sal took up the central role in front of the items. Upgrade pointed at each of the things that needed further Upgrading from him.

"I was able to bring everything to Epic grade, but there are a few parts that need to move up to Legendary. I've calculated the likely amount of materials you'd need and essence, which you'll find stacked beside each of the parts. I added about ten percent extra so you wouldn't run out."

Upgrade placed the Epic core that he had Restored on his first day onto the table. "Call me sentimental, but I think your first Epic should be used to create your first Legendary, don't you think?"

Sal activated his eyes. Upgrade's calculations were perfect. He shouldn't need more than what she had allocated, but he was happy to stay on the safe side. Without any more waiting around, he activated the core and drew on its essence. Next, he activated his Mythcrafter ability and started to use the materials around him to Upgrade the component to the Legendary grade.

It was such a different sensation than when he had done it with the gauntlets, because this time the materials were incredibly high grade and he had a bountiful amount of essence to use. He didn't need to rush it, and was able to transform the piece gradually into what he needed it to be. It felt like he was pouring liquid gold into a cracked bowl. It moved slowly enough that it sank between the cracks, and invisible hands held it in the shape it was meant to be.

Previously, Sal wouldn't have known what to do and likely would have rushed it for fear of running out of power. But this time, he could feel that it just needed time and precision. His eyes found every crack that needed a blend of essence and molten material. The whole sensation was oddly therapeutic, and Sal got lost in the action. He was almost saddened when the process came to a stop, but a warmth spread through the item and Sal's sense of accomplishment skyrocketed as his hands opened to reveal a Legendary component.

Upgrade stared at it before a wide grin broke across her face. "Okay, twenty minutes well spent! You've another five to go, so don't stand there staring at it! Let's go, chop-chop!"

Sal laughed as he handed it over to her and moved to the next section. He didn't rush it, but it was easier and faster than the first one. He wasn't as sentimental about this process, but he did everything the same and it gave him another Legendary piece.

Martin and Gosia watched in fascination as Sal completed each upgrade using the Epic core and the laid-out materials. The excitement in the room was building. They all knew what was coming next.

Sal took a step back and finished his cold coffee in one large gulp. He was very much in the groove, and he finally felt ready to bring it all together. All of them looked at one another as Sal assembled the sniper rifle. It was going to be a blend of Epic and Legendary parts, but Sal was going to need to Upgrade it as a set to give it the evolutionary trait.

Martin and Gosia gripped the table as they watched, and Upgrade was no better on the other side. Sal didn't give them any warning as he activated his ability and threw himself into the task. It was truly an incredible weapon, and as it stood right now, it was on the cusp of becoming Legendary grade. Sal brought the schematic to the forefront of his mind and was delighted to see that some of their necessary components were of a higher quality than he had set out for. He hoped it would make the process that little bit easier.

Unlike the bowl analogy from before, the sniper rifle was a whole different beast. There were hundreds of little nooks and crannies that needed to be smoothed out with essence. Where the gun had previously been modular, and capable of being dismantled, Sal was actively pouring essence into it, turning it into a single unit. All the detachable parts were blended into each other, and Sal had to almost fight with the weapon to make the new components cooperate with each other. It took him almost an hour to refine the sniper rifle to the point that it was at Legendary grade. With a breath, he doubled down and moved to the most important part of the process.

Sal's energy carved the evolution rune into the weapon. Strands of energy connected every part of the rifle, and Sal slowly burned those strands into the very fabric of the weapon's energy signature. Before he could double-check his work, the sniper rifle vibrated on the table, causing everyone to jump back.

Everyone but Sal. He could see that the weapon was trying to absorb the Epic core and it was acting just like Blink's knife. He didn't let the setback upset him and went back to retracing the lines. He had set it, which was great, but it would actively siphon anyone who tried to use it. The schematic he had created solved the issue by tethering the energy to the bullets. Which would allow the rifle to siphon off the essence of anything it successfully shot.

Sal wound the strands of essence in tight circles around the barrel, coiling it in such a fashion that any bullet that went through it would bring a strand upon firing. It sounded stupid, but the schematic said it worked and his eyes told him that it was the best solution. With full faith being put on his Mythcrafter skill, Sal bit his lip gently as he delicately placed the weave on the barrel.

After nearly another hour of painstakingly slow progress, Sal finally stepped back from the sniper rifle and looked at it curiously. He didn't dare look away from it. "My eyes aren't seeing any more improvements to make, and it isn't absorbing even a bit of essence. Let's see how it goes!"

And with that, Sal released his ability and let the result take form. Unlike all the other projects that had a brief cooldown time, the gun continued to glow for a few minutes while everyone around it watched in suspense. Sal gratefully accepted another mug of instant coffee from Upgrade as they waited.

Martin slumped onto the couch and closed his eyes, and was soon followed by Gosia. Upgrade insisted that they should go to bed to get some rest, but both wearily refused and claimed they were just resting their eyes. Their breathing said otherwise.

Upgrade chuckled. "One of the most intense moments of my life, and it's to the tune of Martin snoring."

Sal was about to respond when the glow started to fade. Neither said a word as the sniper rifle took shape in front of their eyes. When Upgrading items, it was natural for them to change in appearance, and Sal had made sure that the engraving that said "Maslow" remained intact. Everything else was fair game for the essence to work with, and it looked like it was taking that as a challenge.

The barrel extended by a few inches, with its muzzle swelling to resemble a cylinder at the end. The once stocky and oval scope had tightened and turned into a long telescopic. The rifle transformed from a patchy assortment of parts into a technological masterpiece. As the glow disappeared, Sal whistled at the black matte finish that covered it.

He activated his eyes and was delighted to see that all their hard work had paid off. They had created a Legendary-grade weapon that had a fully functional evolutionary trait. With enough kills, it would evolve into a Mythic-grade weapon and be, quite possibly, the most powerful long-range weapon in existence. Sal knew he wouldn't be able to wipe the grin off his face for days. Upgrade surprised him with an excited hug, which was over as quickly as it had happened.

She held up an engraver to him and gestured to the sniper rifle. "You need to sign it."

Sal took it from her apprehensively, and she laughed.

"Everyone is going to be looking at this. Do you want them thinking that some guy called Maslow made it? It didn't fucking fall out of a demon's arse, Sal. Sign it!"

Martin and Gosia awoke with a start and jumped up at the sight of the completed weapon.

Upgrade turned to them and repeated her case. "He needs to sign it, right?"

"Absolutely! It's your craft; you have to take ownership of it. Who's going to complain about a name on a Legendary weapon?" Martin's voice was almost as exasperated as Upgrade's.

Gosia smiled reassuringly at Sal, who looked conflicted. "You can write it on the butt plate if you don't want people noticing it."

Upgrade shook her head. "No. This is a fucking masterpiece. His name should be sprawled over the side of it."

Martin gestured to Upgrade. "I'm with her."

Their exhausted bickering was good-natured, and Sal appreciated that all of them were close to delirious at this stage. It was hard to know how long they had been working before Sal showed up, so they were likely running on fumes.

Sal clapped and stopped them from arguing. "I'll sign it!"

He moved first to the butt plate, and heard Upgrade growling at him from the other side of the room.

"Trust me!" Sal answered the guttural noise as he carefully wrote on the metal plate. When he withdrew, he moved to a prominent area below the sights. Gesturing at the large open space, he looked around at Upgrade, who nodded in approval. With a laugh, Sal turned and carved the name "MYTH" in capital letters.

"Done! But I'm sure as shit not doing an Appraisal now. We have to get to class."

"We?"

He turned to Upgrade with a grin. "Introduction to Crafting with Upgrade! Starts in twenty minutes."

If looks could kill, Sal wouldn't have made it out of Room 17 alive.

CHAPTER 40:
CRAFTING

UPGRADE SIGHED IN SATISFACTION.

"Alex, I would kiss you if you didn't repulse every fiber of my being." She brought the Alchemical coffee to her lips and gave a relieved sigh as thanks.

Alex grinned as he poured a cup for Sal. "You joining the All-Nighter crew? If so, we'll be seeing a lot of each other, I guess." As Sal brought up his Q-Card to pay him, Alex waved him away as though he were being silly. "First few are free, to get you addicted."

He gestured to Upgrade, who was happily smiling as she clutched her treasured cup. Sal gratefully accepted the cup and glanced at the clock again, which didn't escape Upgrade's notice.

"Stop worrying. We'll take the workshop elevator. You can be teacher's pet today!"

Sal just stared at her as she patted the top of his head.

Upgrade laughed. "We're in the same building, and the workshop one actually goes straight to the classroom. If we're lifting up machinery or stuff, it's useful. We don't let students use it because it'd never stay still, and the workshop would be pandemonium."

Upgrade led the way to the elevator and lazily tapped the button as she waited for it to reach their floor. With a glance at his hands, her smile curled upward. "Going to give your new gloves a test drive?"

Sal nodded as he admired the fingerless gloves on his hands. The moment he had put them on, they felt like an extension of his skin that he had been missing all this time. He was finally able to appreciate what Hannah meant when she said that her gauntlets were a part of her. But he had so many questions for Upgrade about the pair he was wearing.

When the doors opened, Sal followed Upgrade inside and wondered whether he should wait until after class to ask her. After another sip of coffee, he knew he would end up overthinking it throughout the class, so he just asked.

"How were you able to make your suit of armor to Legendary grade, when you're only able to Upgrade to the Epic-grade level?"

Upgrade blinked. "You saw that?"

Sal nodded as he recalled the moment she had activated her suit. His eyes had definitely Appraised it correctly; it was the Legendary grade.

With a shrug, she looked at his gloves again. "It's a part of the Upgrade ability but requires a ridiculous amount of essence control. You know the way you kept the gun in that sort of stasis, limbo state? It wasn't bleeding your essence dry, and it was holding the gun in a state of Legendary? That's pretty much it." Upgrade transformed into her suit to show him.

"The actual materials aren't being transformed or fixed into this state. My essence is filling in the blanks and showing me what the result of the upgrade could be like if I had the ability to lock it in."

Sal had to do a double take. "So, you're overloading your power for short bursts? Isn't that exhausting?"

Upgrade grinned as she gestured to her neck. "It was, until someone changed how I process essence. Now I'm able to handle it much better! I don't need this core to store power for the overload anymore."

Sal didn't look convinced, and she waved her hand in front of him.

"The tools become Legendary grade when I'm in this state. I can work fast and get the use out of them before they revert to normal. If I had made those gloves without this ability, they likely wouldn't have been nearly as good." Upgrade sighed as she went back to her coffee. "You probably think it's cheating. It's not. I'll show you how to do it and then you can decide, okay?"

Both Sal and Upgrade paused at the exact same time. Upgrade looked at his gloves. "Would that make your tools…Mythic?"

Before either of them could discuss it further, the doors opened to reveal a wide corridor across from the classroom.

Upgrade turned to Sal and lowered her voice. "Don't you dare Appraise that weapon before I get back to it, okay?"

With a glance at the horde of students excitedly chattering among themselves as they entered the classroom, Upgrade visibly shuddered at the sight before downing her coffee. Sal was about to make a comment when she took his cup and repeated the process. When both were drained, she grinned at him.

"Much better. You got sleep, so you don't get to complain. Now, pay attention in class and don't be an insufferable know-it-all, okay?" Upgrade plastered a fake smile on her face and followed the students into the classroom, leaving Sal holding two empty mugs in the corridor.

"Okay, I want to get a sense-check of what we're dealing with here. Who picked Crafting because it'll keep you out of the field?" Upgrade laughed as she looked around the room. A few hands went up, and she didn't even hesitate.

"There's no judgment here. I just want to know the motivations. How about…people who want to make money?" This time a good number of people raised their hands, and Upgrade nodded with a smile.

"Who joined Crafting…because they haven't found something they're good at yet?" As if to encourage them, Upgrade raised her own hand with an awkward grin. "I had no idea what I wanted to do when I got here!"

Just like that, the whole class relaxed. She was nothing like Jez, Rust, or Sinclair, and Sal could almost hear the collective sigh of relief. Upgrade sat on her desk and planted her palms down behind her to steady herself.

"This is an introductory class, so we're not going to be doing anything too hands-on today. Instead, I thought we could find out more about you all and decide on your semester-long project! To ensure that we're all on the same page, I'll need people to be completely honest with me…so that means eyes closed, everyone."

Sal closed his eyes along with everyone else and waited for Upgrade to continue. Her voice carried across the now quiet room.

"All of you are here, not because you have abilities…it's because you want to become a Hero. In this class, we have about a hundred students, made up of different cohorts. All of you will have different goals and life experiences. Personally, I wanted to build things that would help save people. Which is very subjective! An incredible weapon could kill a demon and save countless lives. A barrier could repel demons and prevent them from slaughtering hundreds. Faster transportation, better signaling systems, enhanced targeting...or even durable shirts. What if we made protective clothing? Crafting can be whatever you want for it to be, and there is no perfect path to take with it, other than the road to self-improvement." Upgrade's voice was steady as she spoke to them.

"Each of you will learn techniques and expertise while you're here. They are the great equalizer. Your special skills or abilities won't master the basics for you. So, keep your eyes closed and think about this. All of you are on a level playing field right now and none of your ranks or powers matter. Be honest with yourself about what it is that you want and raise your hand when you hear something that works for you."

Upgrade's voice became closer as she moved toward the students. "Raise your hand if your primary focus with Crafting is to make money."

A few shuffles could be heard throughout the crowd, and Upgrade laughed.

"There are a few of you! Don't worry, it's not a negative thing. We're not all altruists here, and being able to make Q-Cred is important to your future at the academy. I just need to know which of you has it as your primary driver, so I can tailor my teaching for you."

Sal had been tempted to raise his hand, but it ultimately wasn't true for him. Money was a bonus outcome. Right now, he couldn't wait to see Watcher's reaction to the sniper rifle and to see all the different options the completed weapon held.

"What about wanting to create items that help people? Sure, it's a wonderful endeavor and all of us could likely put up our hand...but who here has that as their primary focus?" Upgrade's voice was close to Sal, and he was about to raise his hand.

As if reading his mind, Upgrade stood in front of him and asked her next question.

"Or maybe, you want to challenge yourself in making the greatest thing possible? If it makes money, great. If it saves people, even better." Sal's hand went straight up, and Upgrade's words felt as if they were aimed at him. "Thought so. You can all open your eyes now."

Upgrade was pacing in front of the assembled students with a wistful smile on her face.

"I know a lot of you were out last night in the amphitheater, and I can't for the life of me understand why you'd all do that on a Thursday rather than a Friday, but I'll take it easy on you for today. My lecturing style is a little different than the others, in that I operate with mutual respect. If you show up and do the work, then you'll do well in this class!"

At the mention of the party, most of the students shifted uncomfortably or exchanged a few looks of dissatisfaction, which didn't escape Upgrade's notice. "Ah, so it's like that then...I'm guessing it was organized by students who don't have this class? Why stall a day just to accommodate the Support class? Nice to know some things don't change, but we'll get to that."

Upgrade activated her ability and smiled when gasps rippled through the crowd. Her clothing transformed into her trademark suit of armor, with her mechanical claws draped over her hands in anticipation of something to improve.

Sal looked around the room and saw quite a few expressions of awe. He had that very same look on his face when he had seen the transformation. Some of the girls in the crowd didn't look too pleased, and Sal appreciated that Upgrade's form-fitting attire was drawing some unsavory glances. If she was conscious of it, she didn't let on as she continued speaking to the group.

"When I first came to the academy, I could only see flaws in everything I looked at. It wasn't a healthy perspective to have, knowing that everything you saw could be made better. Classmates called me elitist and bossy because I constantly strove toward making everything better than when I encountered it. So, why is this important? Why am I telling you all my awkward journey to where I am now?"

Nobody in the crowd said a word as they assumed the question was rhetorical, so Upgrade waved her hand and continued.

"It's perspective. If I had listened to all those people back then, I would never have found my calling. Crafters like us typically fall into the Support category, which has been seen as a sort of miscellaneous camp for unknown skill sets. If we don't know what they do, or understand their abilities…lump them into Support. It's easy to feel like you're secondary to the heavy hitters or those with flashy abilities, and I just want to abolish that thought right now."

Upgrade's tone took on an edge as she flexed her mechanical claw. Each mechanism whirred to life and moved independently like fingers as though it reached for something invisible.

"Who makes their weapons, their armor? The gadgetry that guides them? The analysis that informs them? Potions that keep them alive? Barriers that keep them safe at night?" Upgrade grinned at the students. "We do. Support is the backbone of the Hero industry, so never lower your head to them. Without us, they'd still be trying to shoot the demons without essence-infused weaponry…and we know how that would end."

Laughter rippled through the class of students, and Upgrade deactivated her ability, once again standing in her regular clothing.

"I told you about my personality and ability for another reason. My goal with this class is to improve each of you…not through some skill or ability, but rather, by teaching you the skills you need to make an impact on society. I will be judging you on your willingness to learn, your general progress, and your individual project, which will be due by the end of the semester. I've also alluded to a class project, which will be something I'll be working on with you all. Crafters by nature are individualists, but…they're capable of some extraordinary things when they work together. I want to show you what's possible when you all work together."

Upgrade grinned as she returned to her desk.

"Today is a write-off, so instead of getting into theory or practical lessons…let's spend the remainder of the class with two questions. What is your proposed invention for a personal project? Disregard your abilities or limitations and reach for the stars. Write down what you'd make and why. Second, I want you to pitch an invention…something incredible that could be made by a team of the greatest Crafters. Same as before, no limitations. Feel free to discuss among yourselves, but I want those two answers from each of you before you leave the room."

Sal glanced down at his desk and saw that the screen offered him two text boxes that needed to be filled in. He smiled as he picked up the stylus and started to write.

CHAPTER 41:
ORGANIC

SAL WAS PLEASANTLY SURPRISED BY THE FACT THAT HE WASN'T OVERLY TIRED when he left the Introduction to Crafting class. He wondered whether the group letting him sleep an extra few hours on the couch was the reason behind it, but he put it out of his mind.

Upgrade was surrounded by a group of students at the end, each of them asking questions or just fawning over her, so Sal decided to step out rather than wait for her. He wanted to ask her more about using his gloves with the ability but it could wait. Just as he was about to chance his arm by using the staff elevator to get back to the workshop, one of the students appeared at his side.

"Whoa, where did you get them?!"

Sal turned to look at a sandy-haired man, who aimed a tracker at his gloves. It was essentially a visor that was worn over one eye and allowed the user to activate the Appraisal or Analysis ability Sal had seen a few of them worn by customers who came into the auction house, but this one was quite bulky and outdated. Before he could stop himself, Sal's eyes activated on the device, and he saw the countless ways it could be improved.

Maybe it was the sudden activation of the power, but the newcomer raised his hands apologetically and stepped back in alarm.

"Sorry! Didn't mean to get too close. They've just made this thing go haywire!"

His awkward laugh was accompanied by a gesture at the device clipped onto his ear. A single rectangular lens covered his left eye, making it a darker shade of blue than its counterpart. Before Sal could get a word in, the newcomer extended his hand for a handshake before pulling it back instantly.

"Sorry again! I don't want to touch them. They're clearly worth more than…everything I own."

Sal extended his hand and tried his best to give him a reassuring smile. "Trust me, it's fine. I'm just a bit jumpy…too much coffee. Salvatore Argento. You are?"

With what looked like a mountain of trepidation, the newcomer accepted the handshake, his eye still aimed directly at Sal's gloves.

"Sorry. Josh. Josh Mitchell. People call me Twitch. It's because of a thing, but that doesn't matter. Sorry, eh, nice to meet you!" Josh quickly clasped hands and then withdrew. "You're like, really high up in Silver, aren't you? I saw your fight against Dom and couldn't believe you were in the Crafting class!" He shook his head with a laugh before turning quickly in a panic.

Sal had never seen him before and tried to recall whether they had ever crossed paths in the last week.

"Were you at the party last night?" Sal reluctantly walked away from the staff elevator. He walked in step with Josh and the other students as they made their way to the staircase.

"Me? Hah, no. Wasn't invited…" Josh laughed as he waved away the suggestion. "They organized it knowing that Crafters had a class this morning. Those sorts of people aren't really…my sorts of people. You know?" He gestured around at the other Crafter students.

"This is my sorta scene right here. But yeah…wait, Argento?" Josh's eyes widened as he whirled around to look at Sal. "Argento Auction? Whoa! That's awesome!" He shook his head and gave Sal an appraising look with a smile.

"Man, why are you here? You're…you could…you don't have to be a Hero!" Josh exclaimed finally.

Sal had no idea how to process this encounter. He didn't need to provide much input as Josh was happy to take the reins.

"Must be cool having such a well-known family name. Mitchell? Yeah, nobody knows us…but why would they? Mitchell Maintenance doesn't really have the same ring as the Argento Auction, does it?"

Sal smiled apologetically. "The family business isn't really down to me. My parents built it from the ground up…so I can't really take credit for it. But look, it's only week one! You heard Upgrade—we're all on a level playing field and can build our own skills." He looked at Josh as he spoke and could see the impending scoff.

Josh didn't disappoint and shook his head as though Sal were talking nonsense. "Yeah, maybe in her class…but we don't get assessed on just Crafting, do we? Fighting in Rust's class…Survival with Sinclair? Even if I ace Upgrade's class…I'm out of here in six months."

Josh turned back to Sal apologetically. "Sorry, I get too much into my own head sometimes. You going to do any of the outings this weekend?"

Shaking his head, Sal gestured over his shoulder to where he assumed the dorm tower was located through all the walls. "Nah, going to have a quiet weekend and work on some Crafting stuff, I think. Get myself ahead for next week. My parents aren't expecting any visits from me for at least a few months." He chuckled to himself before glancing back to Josh. "What about you?"

It was as if Sal had flicked a switch that read doom and gloom. Josh rolled his eyes.

"My old man would have me repairing shit the moment I stepped through the front door. No thank you. It makes no sense…it's like they're punishing us for that stupid fucking race at the start of the week."

Sal frowned, not sure what he was getting at. "You mean like the ranks and stuff? It's not permanent. We'll be reshuffled in a few weeks, I think."

Josh shook his head in exasperation. "No, the outings. They have one with the Paradox reclamation guild this weekend, but it costs like two hundred Q-Cred…which means that only the top ranked can go on it." Josh gritted his teeth in annoyance. "So the only people who can get an 'in' with the guild are the ones who did well in a stupid test. How is that fair? How do they expect us to earn that much in a damn week?"

Another male voice called out from behind them on the stairwell. "Suck it up, Twitch! The academy doesn't owe you shit…you could set up shop and start doing repairs instead of feeling sorry for yourself."

Without missing a beat, or even turning around, Josh shot back at the other voice, "Fuck off, Anders! How many sales did your little pop-up shop get you so far?"

Sal turned to look at a black-haired guy walking behind them, shooting Josh a withering look.

"Thirty Q-Cred, which is thirty more than you've managed. When things ramp up, I'd say I'll be able to afford an outing by the end of the month. What's your plan?"

The two continued to bicker as they descended the staircase. A few others watched, but Sal kept to himself and listened politely, not wanting to get drawn in any further.

When they finally got to the lobby, Sal gave them a polite wave and tried to extract himself from the group, but Josh caught his attention.

"Hey, are you heading to the workshop? Was thinking of going there…wanna join me?"

A few of the others looked to have the same idea and started to stand around, but Sal just shook his head.

"Was up late last night…gonna go and catch up on some sleep. I'll see you there another time, though?" He turned to leave, when he heard an unfamiliar voice ridicule Josh.

"Trying to suck up to the Rank #2 Silver, Twitch?"

Another voice piped up to add another layer. "Up late, ya hear that? Probably at the party too!"

Sal sighed as he made his way back to the dorms. He wasn't in the mood to confront them, nor was he in the mood to play nice and head to the workshop. Classes were over, and he felt as though he had been chasing his tail for the last few days. He'd collect his new uniform from the workshop after getting some rest, and then he'd figure out what he was going to do for the weekend. With a glance to his right, Sal saw the black-haired guy from earlier but couldn't recall what Josh had called him.

When they caught each other's glance, he smiled and offered a hand.

"Anderson Royce. Anders works fine." When Sal shook his hand, he jutted his chin backward to the group that still stood around the exit of the tower. "Don't mind them, they're just looking for someone to blame for their own shortcomings. Top of a class always looks like an easy target."

"Salvatore Argento. Everyone calls me Sal," he answered with a weary smile. It was nice to have a glimmer of positivity after the gloom of their descent in the stairwell. "Are you heading to the dorms?" Sal asked as they walked in the same direction, but Anders shook his head.

"Nah, haven't eaten since yesterday, so was on my way to the canteen."

Sal blinked as he realized that the same was true for him. "Mind if I join you?"

Anders smiled as he gestured ahead of them. "By all means. But you're going to have to tell me what you wrote down in that class. I had so many ideas and it was killing me to pick just one."

Sal laughed as he followed Anders to the canteen, now painfully aware of the growing hunger in his stomach.

*****

"A bandage…bot?" Sal repeated between mouthfuls.

Anders laughed. "She said without any limitations! I don't need to understand how it works, but…imagine if we didn't have to rely on a Healer out on the battlefield? Something that could do like, emergency first aid, but better than the drones." His arms moved around wildly as he explained.

"You could like, administer clamps over open wounds or…like, laser them shut or something. I don't know much about Healing, but maybe it could save lives." Maybe he finally heard his own pitch and realized how unfeasible it was, but Anders's expression softened. "It's stupid, but I wrote it down anyway." His sheepish grin returned as he rooted around his salad for the remaining pieces of chicken. "So come on, you heard my shit one. What did you write for the personal project?"

Sal leaned back in his chair with a laugh. "No way, I'm not following that masterpiece. I'm team bandage-bot!"

Anders gave up on finding the chicken and gave Sal a deadpan expression. "That's revolutionary bandage-bot to you."

Sal chuckled as he slid his now-empty plate off to one side. He placed his hands on the table and took a deep breath.

"My pitch…is for a battle-bot." When he caught sight of Anders getting up to leave, he laughed and called him back. "No, I'm serious. I saw some blueprints of a concept battle drone before, and well…I wanted to put my own spin on it. Imagine it had self-replenishing cores that could act as never-ending batteries? It could be equipped with the same lasers that break down essence-crafted gear—I saw them in the workshop. I'd say they could slice straight through a demon if they had enough power behind them." Sal smiled as he explained his personal project as he saw it in his head.

"Maybe a kind of magnetic device that could pull out their cores? I'd have to figure out how to do the tracking for it, but I was thinking of remotely controlling it with a headset…but ideally, it'd be awesome if it could be programmed to just go out and attack anything it recognizes as a demon!" Sal thought that his idea would sound just as outlandish as the bandage-bot, but judging from Anders's expression, he was very much off the mark.

"What's your ability?" Anders asked suddenly, catching Sal off guard.

"Appraisal for the most part, but I'm learning how to Craft. There's a lot to be said for understanding how things work and the qualities they have. What about you?" For some reason, Sal expected Anders to become defensive. There was something off about his body language, but Sal couldn't put his finger on it.

"Sorry, Sal. I was just checking. Friend of mine works in the Credit floor, which is this big fancy auction area above the workshop. He was telling me that some big shot from our year was holed up in the blueprint office for the last few days and that they're some kinda legendary Crafter. When you said you saw blueprints, and talked about that drone, I got thinking that you might be that guy." Anders laughed as he leaned back in his seat. "Just scared the crap out of me."

Sal shrugged. "Even if I was some legendary kinda Crafter, what would be an issue?" He kept his expression neutral, but he was dying to know why it had caused such a shift in Anders's behavior.

Anders snorted and looked at Sal as though he were crazy. "Imagine my first pitch to them was a fucking bandage-bot!" He burst out laughing again, his salad now shifted to one side, much like Sal's.

"Oh yeah," Anders mused, as though he had forgotten. Picking a leaf of lettuce from his salad, he held it up to show Sal. "In an age of plentiful food, nobody told my ability."

Sal frowned as he looked between the piece of salad and Anders, not connecting the dots. A few moments later, a stream of golden light blossomed from Anders's fingertips, branching across the wilted leaf. Just as Sal was about to question what was happening, the color became incredibly vibrant as the leaf started to form and grow.

Anders's expression was nonchalant as the fragment of vegetable furled and grew into a full head of lettuce, its roots entwining around his fingers. With a laugh of contempt, Anders deposited the lettuce onto the plate and untangled his fingers from the roots.

"I present to you, the most useless power in our current age!" Sal stared at the lettuce as Anders laughed. "Maybe we could get a drone to do vegetable deliveries?"

CHAPTER 42:
OUTINGS

AFTER SPENDING AN HOUR OR SO JUST CHATTING WITH ANDERS, IT WAS FINALLY time to head back to the dorm. He wasn't going to waste the entire day by sleeping but justified that a few extra hours of sleep wouldn't be a bad idea. The talk of invention had been a definite driver for him, and he wanted to jump straight into it, but it was a surefire way to burn out if he kept spending all-nighters in the workshop.

Upgrade's class had opened his eyes to how Crafting was supposed to be approached, and his method of rushing head-on into it was fine for the moment, but not sustainable. He didn't have the basics, and without the expertise of Martin, Gosia, and Upgrade, he would never have been able to finish the sniper rifle. Sal thought back to the old adage that if you only had a hammer in your toolkit, everything would eventually start to look like a nail. He didn't want to rely on flooding a component with essence to get a result. Although he was taking steps in the right direction, he had a lot to learn.

Sal exited the elevator and got off on his floor. There was nobody around, which he was grateful for, as he didn't really feel like getting drawn into another conversation. Maybe it was the effect of getting close to his room that made him all the more tired, similar to when you're in running distance of the bathroom that you suddenly wonder how you've held it at bay so long.

He had barely managed to lock his dorm room door behind him when he flopped onto the bed with a smile. The warm light from the sun washed through the windows, and it didn't bother him in the slightest. No amount of light was going to keep him awake, and just a few moments after that thought, he was out for the count.

***

He awoke with a start and panicked momentarily as his bedding wrapped around him and held his arms hostage. A few thrashes later, he was on the floor, fully awake. With a groan, he untangled himself from the blankets and got to his feet. The sun was still very much in the sky, which was a small relief.

He didn't remember the last time he was able to wake up naturally, so he intentionally hadn't set any alarms. But something had woken him abruptly. He checked his tablet and saw that he had managed to get around four hours of sleep, which put him in the late afternoon. A series of messages had come through and while Sal held the tablet, another two or three popped up on the screen.

Unread Messages: 64
- Credit Floor: Admin (41)
- Credit Floor: Vanessa (12)
- Quest Academy: Admin (3)
- Quest Academy: Upgrade (3)
- Silver Cohort: Divinity (2)
- Purple Cohort: Hannah (2)

- Green Cohort: Anders (1)

Sal had to do a double take when he looked at the screen. There hadn't been any notifications before he went to sleep, and he had no idea what was going on. Another notification rang out, bringing the Credit Floor: Admin number up by an additional one. After a few moments of just staring at the screen, he tapped open the new message and saw a slew of similar ones drop down below it.

Urgent Appraisal Request – Reavers Guild – Item 492 – Details Attached

Urgent Appraisal Request – Reavers Guild – Item 493 – Details Attached

Urgent Appraisal Request – Reavers Guild – Item 494 – Details Attached

Sal flicked through the list to see that the vast majority of them were requests for Appraisal work. He scrolled through them all to reach the first message that thankfully added some context for the barrage of mails.

Reavers Guild have successfully defeated a dungeon!

As a preferred supplier and Silver token holder, you have been given priority on the following listings. Please confirm your availability and capacity to conduct the following Appraisals, so we can facilitate in-house Appraisals and pass work onto our third-party network.

Failure to respond in the next twelve hours will result in forfeiture of the Appraisal work, which will then default back to the Credit floor.

We shall undertake the cataloguing of the 73 items looted from the Dungeon and send across details for your consideration. You can confirm via message or in person at the Credit floor.

With a shake of his head, Sal exited the chain of messages and checked on Vanessa's messages. If she was messaging him, did that mean his cover as Myth had been busted? As far as he was aware, she wouldn't know him as anything other than Myth in person, and he hadn't interacted with her as Sal. With only the slightest bit of trepidation, Sal clicked into her messages.

Quest Academy: Credit Floor

Happy Friday! My name is Vanessa, and I work on the Credit Floor. I've had personal dealings with Myth in the past, and he spoke highly of your capability as an Appraiser. We've recently gotten a large amount of goods come in, and the Credit Floor is trying to push the work to our internal vendors.

Because of how great Myth has been to work with, I thought I'd send across the most exciting listings that could earn you some serious Q-Cred! I've seen on your file that you prefer to work down in the workshop, so I'd be happy to set up the listings for you in a private room. I hope you'll forgive my direct approach like this, but I hope we can work together!

Sal clicked into the remaining messages and saw that they were all attachments, with some choice words from Vanessa about why she picked them out of the seventy-three listings. He had to give it to her—she definitely knew how to work people. A part of him didn't care if she knew that he was acting as Myth, but it was somewhat fun to be leading a double life and getting paid twice. He was willing to forgive the fact that she was lying about Myth praising Sal, because it was definitely in his best interest to have Vanessa looking out for him.

A few clicks of his fingers revealed the listings that Vanessa had put aside for him, and he agreed that the quality looked high. With each listing he looked at, Sal's smile grew wider. It was probably for the best that he had napped during the afternoon, because it looked like he was in for a busy evening. With a concerted effort, Sal exited the listings and looked at the other messages.

Quest Academy: Administration

You are required to report to the Headmaster's Office on Saturday Morning at 9:00 a.m. to follow up on the effects of the Skill Master ability on Divinity Khan.

Quest Academy: Administration

You are required to report to the Doom Society, which will gather on Sunday Evening in the Sky Lounge at 7:00 p.m.

Quest Academy: Administration

Congratulations, you have been selected by Upgrade to take part in the Crafting Fast-Track Course. Please find more details attached.

Sal exhaled. He had gone a full week of not receiving a single message, to suddenly having everything thrown at him at once. The Doom Society was the group Neuro had spoken about, the ones who predict the calamities and put in countermeasures to stop them from happening. He didn't know how much value he'd bring to the table, especially seeing as they already knew most of what he saw, but he was hopeful that he'd be able to contribute something. The follow-up about Divinity had completely slipped his mind, but he was grateful that they had at least taken it seriously. The last message about the Fast-Track course made no sense to him, so he clicked out and went into Upgrade's messages for context.

> ### Quest Academy: Upgrade
>
> *Hey Sal, just wanted to send on a message. I didn't get a proper chance to talk to you after class today, but your ability…whatever it is, it's completely changed my power. As thanks, next time you swing by the workshop, I'll show you how to transform your gear into armor!*

> ### Quest Academy: Upgrade
>
> *I can't believe you signed our names on the butt plate! You absolutely didn't need to do that, but Martin and Gosia have been practically dancing around the workshop all afternoon. It was very considerate of you, so thanks for that.*

> ### Quest Academy: Upgrade
>
> *I've put your name forward for the Fast-Track Course. It gives you one-on-one mentoring with yours truly and pairs you up with some of our seniors. Don't thank me, though, because it's going to be hell! It's designed to get you through the Foundation, Basics, Intermediate, and Advanced levels for Crafting in record time. I think that you have an extraordinary ability, and I want to give you every chance to reach the top! Okay, maybe you can thank me a little. :)*

Clicking out of it, Sal moved to the last few messages. Divinity was asking which outing he was going to enroll in and to sync up with her before making any choices so they could go together. He wondered whether she knew that he wasn't interested in the outings, and that by asking him it would change his mind?

After a few moments of going down that rabbit hole, Sal shook his head and blinked slowly. He'd drive himself insane if he started second-guessing everything Divinity said to him. She likely had much better things to do than looking at all the permutations of his decision-making on a Friday afternoon. With a chuckle at his own expense, Sal quickly messaged back that he hadn't made any decisions and that he'd be spending the rest of the day in the workshop doing Appraisals for the Reavers Guild.

Next, there were a few messages from Hannah that pretty much asked the same question about the outings and if he was going to go on them. Her second message was asking if he'd like to hang out later that evening, which made him pause. He didn't want to give her mixed signals, so rather than making an excuse, he sent her a screenshot of the seventy-three listings from the Credit floor and said he'd likely be in the workshop all night.

It took a few minutes of deliberation before he hit send, and immediately doubted he made the right choice. Q-Cred was the backbone of everything at the academy, so he wasn't going to throw such a great opportunity away…especially when it was going to be reported to Jez in the Administration class. Sal couldn't keep the grin from his face when he thought of Jez seeing his Q-Cred income. Even if he only managed to Appraise the eleven listings that Vanessa sent him, he'd be miles ahead of the others in the class.

Finally, Sal saw a message from Anders, which actually caught him by surprise. It was a simple message that thanked him for lunch earlier in the day and that he hoped they could do it again sometime to talk about bandage-bots and attack-drones. Sal sent him a quick response to say that he'd like that, and they should set something up before the next Crafting class.

He spent the last few minutes clearing the notifications from the Credit floor that continued to pour in. It was like the mythical hydra: for every message he marked as read, two more would filter in to replace it. With a sigh of defeat, Sal placed the tablet back on the bed and made his way to the shower. He was rested, and he wanted to be clean and presentable before he went to the workshop. It was likely going to be another long night, but Sal didn't care. There was a Legendary sniper rifle waiting to be Appraised, and bags of Q-Cred waiting to be earned.

CHAPTER 43:
APPRAISAL

Dressed in a simple T-shirt and jeans, Sal made his way into the workshop. He wasn't sure whether there was protocol for wearing the uniforms considering it was technically the weekend, but he didn't really want to subject himself to the boring gray attire when a newly crafted suit was waiting for him. His gloves felt like a second skin, and it had almost pained him to take them off before his shower. He wondered whether that was the same sensation that Hannah had spoken about with her gauntlets.

Upgrade had promised to teach him how to use them, and Sal couldn't wait to take her up on that offer. When he entered through the doors, he was surprised to see that the normal lull had been replaced with absolute chaos. Dozens of students were clamoring around the workbenches, shouting across to one another, with many rushing between the spaces. Sal had to crane his neck to see the regulars, who looked positively dismayed by the situation. Before he could even clear the entrance to the workshop, a familiar voice shouted out his name.

"Salvatore! Come over, there's a free bench here!"

Josh's voice pierced through the noise, and Sal saw him waving erratically from the far side of the workshop. A few heads turned at the sudden bark of his name, and more than a few of them contained looks of contempt. Sal deliberated on whether he should ignore him and continue over to his desk, but he eventually thought better of it. With a tight smile, he made his way over to Josh, who was gesturing eagerly at the space beside him.

"I knew you'd come! You missed the tour of the other floor…but you need to wait for the guy with the beard to come back. Wears a big apron, think his name was Forge," Josh nattered as he gestured toward the elevator to the side. "Upgrade sits over there! She's busy, though, so she couldn't talk to us much. But how cool is this place!"

Sal looked over to where Upgrade was sitting and saw her pained expression through the fake smile she directed right back at him. He wanted to laugh, but he strangely felt a sense of solidarity with her. The invasion of students felt like intruders on their sacred place of work.

Sal turned back to Josh and kept his smile fixed. "Thanks, Josh…I really appreciate it. I'm actually here to do a bit of Appraisal work, to earn a bit of Q-Cred on the side." With that, Sal tried to extricate himself, but Josh wasn't finished.

"Are you for real? How did you get that in only a week?"

Sal heard the accusing tone and knew that Josh was seconds away from jumping to conclusions. Leaning in close, he brought his voice down to a whisper. "First day when we were doing the rounds, I went over to the regulars and did some free Appraisals for them. Asked if they'd have any odd jobs that needed doing and they took me up on it." Sal bent the truth a little, but it was enough for Josh, who looked back at him with wide eyes.

"Just like that? Think they'd need some Restoration work done?"

Sal shrugged and gestured over to them. "You'll never know unless you ask. It would at least put you on their radar. Appraisal is a tricky skill set to find, so I was really lucky. Restoration is a great skill, though—my mother has it. You could make a fortune with this group. When they fuck up something in Crafting, you can bring it right back to how it was…for a price."

And with that, it looked like it dawned on Josh how he could commercialize his ability. A mixture of disbelief and excitement washed over his face as he looked around the room, as though seeing Q-Cred everywhere. Sal gave him a wave as he made his way over to Upgrade, but Josh seemed to barely notice his departure.

"Did you tell them to come here?" Upgrade groaned quietly as Sal approached her bench. "They don't know anything yet, and all they're doing is sitting in those benches and shouting out their hopes and dreams." With an aggravated sigh, she finally looked at Sal. "Get my messages?"

He grinned and nodded in return. "Thank you for selecting me for the Fast-Track course. I've got no idea what it's all about, but it sounds important."

Upgrade sat up and stretched her back with a tired sigh. "You're very welcome. So…I'm willing to risk all the rumors these shits will concoct when I drag you into that room over there to Appraise that beautiful sniper rifle." As her arms came down, a grin appeared on her face. "Credit floor can get their pound of flesh from you afterward."

Sal didn't need much convincing as he made his way toward the room, with Upgrade only a few steps behind him.

"Should I turn around and give them a wink?" Upgrade mused quietly to Sal as they walked. "Maybe drape my arm over your shoulder?"

She teased him with a few more suggestions until they finally reached the room. Sal held his hands up to her, and Upgrade stopped abruptly, confused. He wiggled his gloved fingers and smiled at her. "Appraisal first, then you can teach me how to use these!"

Upgrade paused for a moment in thought before countering. "Appraisal. Coffee from Alex…then I teach you?"

Sal conceded immediately, suddenly craving more of the Alchemical concoction. Alex was right when he warned that it would become an addiction.

Upgrade continued as she walked around to the other side of the table. "Some of us didn't get to have our beauty sleep last night…" Bending over, she retrieved the neatly folded shirt and slacks that had been meticulously Crafted the night before. Sal extended a hand out to take them from her, but Upgrade stopped suddenly with a grin.

"Appraisal first. Then clothes. Then coffee…and then gloves." Sal stared at her for a moment before Upgrade broke with a laugh and a shake of her head. "I've been awake far too long…I'm getting delirious."

Sal gestured to the couch. "You're more than welcome to have a nap while I work on this. The longer we're in here, the better your rumor sounds," he finished with a laugh.

Upgrade didn't so much as hesitate as she dropped the clothes onto the table and threw herself onto the couch. "I'm just closing my eyes for a little bit. Wake me when you're done. I want to know everything!"

Before Sal could even retort, Upgrade was asleep. She hadn't even used the blanket that was folded on the armrest.

He unfurled the blanket and gently draped it across her. He couldn't believe that he had known her for less than a week, and she had managed to make such a profound impact on his life. Without her Upgrade skill, he would never have created the Mythcrafter ability, and he wouldn't be standing where he was right now.

His gaze moved to the Legendary sniper rifle, and it humbled him to think that he orchestrated the creation of it. He wasn't naive; he knew that it would have been impossible without the capabilities of Martin, Gosia, and Upgrade. But it was his design and his power that brought those perfect parts together to create a masterpiece.

Activating his eyes, Sal started his Appraisal. The documents were already sitting there waiting for his feedback, so he got to work. What usually took minutes lasted closer to an hour. Appraisal was similar to reading a book, as every item had its own individual story.

For someone learning to Appraise without the ability, they would see the materials, the composition, the characteristics, quality, and craftsmanship. What Sal saw with his eyes was an innate understanding of the item's essence. Rare items gave off a blue hue, Epic would show off purple, and Legendary was an orange light. When the rifle had first been presented to him, Sal saw the different colors that weren't aligned with each other.

His eyes questioned the weapon until it revealed its secrets. He rapidly wrote down the range, impact, and damage rating of each hypothetical round. The recoil was drastically reduced from before, and the sights were capable of tracking targets by essence signatures. There were three modes of fire, which included silenced, explosive, and essence-tethered.

Surprisingly, the weapon had a trait of self-cleaning, which it had somehow picked up during its evolution. The rate of fire had increased, and every shot was guaranteed to be a critical hit. Sal tried to find some flaws, but there was nothing to be found.

Sal moved the weapon around and inspected it from every angle. His eyes found the same information again and again until they discovered an unseen element that Sal would quickly write down. It was difficult to be precise without a frame of reference, so he could only go by what the rifle was telling him. With a better understanding of firearms, Sal would be able to interpret the information much better, but for now he had to settle for what he could officially validate.

It went on like this for another twenty minutes before Sal finally conceded. He couldn't believe what he was witnessing. There were no drawbacks or downsides to the weapon at all. Sal couldn't fathom how a Mythic-grade item could possibly surpass the weapon in front of him.

He stood in silence for a few moments, looking at the rifle in awe. His Appraisal was complete, and he would need to submit it to the Credit floor and Vanessa. With that thought in mind, Sal wondered whether he should go up to meet her as Myth and ask her to send down everything to the room for Sal.

Turning around, he saw that Upgrade hadn't moved a muscle and was still fast asleep. Glancing back to the table, he caught sight of the clothes and entertained the thought of changing in the room while Upgrade slept. Every part of his brain told him it was a terrible idea and that she'd absolutely wake up and ridicule him for the rest of his life. When he picked up the shirt, he overruled his brain and decided that now was the perfect time to change. In the interest of decency, Sal moved to the other side of the table and quickly started to change.

Despite all his fears and thundering heart, Upgrade didn't so much as budge. When the shirt made contact with his skin, he gasped in surprise. It contracted around his chest and shrank to fit his physique perfectly. Sal twisted and turned and raised his arms over his head, and there was zero discomfort. It felt as if it were tailored specifically for his body. The slacks fit perfectly at the waist and leg, and Sal wondered whether it was a tailoring trait that made it fit so well. Much like the gloves, Sal felt as though the clothes were an extension of his body. There was no leap in power capability, and it didn't feel like the clothing was brimming with essence. His eyes could see that the tucked-in shirt, the slacks, and the gloves were all connected by an invisible circuitry of essence.

Just as he was about to further Appraise the new clothing, a vibration from his jeans caught his attention. He picked them up and rooted through the pockets until he found his folded tablet. Opening it up, he was greeted with another stream of messages from the Credit floor, offering him the opportunity to Appraise the new haul from the successful dungeon clearance.

He was about to take the rifle Appraisal papers and make his way up to the Credit floor, but the sight of Upgrade stopped him. He didn't want Vanessa to come down to collect the rifle and see Upgrade asleep, so he decided to leave the papers for later. She had let him sleep the night before, so Sal was happy to return the favor. She had her own card for the door, so he dimmed the lights and locked the door behind him. The noise of the students had only managed to get louder, and Sal was grateful to be on his way to a different floor.

CHAPTER 44:
HYPOTHETICALS

IF SAL THOUGHT HE WAS GOING TO BE ESCAPING THE CHAOS BY GOING UP A couple of floors, he was in for a rude awakening. The entirety of the Credit floor was absolute mayhem, with staff rushing around and transporting goods and attendants talking to frustrated-looking strangers. He almost wanted to laugh because it was a scene he was very familiar with from back home.

Whenever a dungeon clearance happened, or a new floor was beaten on a tower, the guilds would swamp the auction houses to find out if they had picked up something valuable. He could see that the attendants had been dragged into the cataloguing process, and judging by their pained expressions, it wasn't something they particularly enjoyed. A few of them glanced up at his arrival, but nobody made any effort to engage with him.

Sal couldn't blame them, as it was likely going to be just as hectic for a few more hours. There were stacks of empty stylized chests that were being carefully packed by the attendants at the different booths, all under the watchful eyes of who Sal assumed were the Reavers Guild. He didn't see any familiar faces around him, so took out his tablet and sent a quick message to Vanessa.

While he waited, he looked to his right and saw dozens of chests stacked up against the wall. The item numbers were all in the four hundreds, which matched the listings that he had been receiving throughout the day. He barely managed to blink before Vanessa appeared from the other side of the room. Her high heels clicked against the marbled floor and her smile was both radiant and genuine when she saw him. As she got closer, her head tilted ever so slightly in surprise.

"And who might you be?" Her tone was playful as she stepped around Sal, making a show of looking him up and down. "May I?" She reached forward to touch the fabric of his sleeve, and Sal gestured that it was fine. He desperately hoped she wouldn't hear his increasing heartbeat from where she stood.

Vanessa didn't go for the sleeve, and instead traced her fingers along his chest before bringing her hand up to caress the collar of his shirt. Moving closer to get a better look, Vanessa's voice turned into a whisper that washed through his ears.

"Incredible craftsmanship…might have to get you to make me something just like this."

Sal couldn't tell whether she was genuinely flirting with him or teasing, but he was okay with either of them. He was skilled at negotiation, but Vanessa was proving to be a terrifying opponent. As he opened his mouth to reply, Vanessa moved in front of his face with a smirk.

"Maybe you could measure me and see if it gives you any inspiration?" With that, Vanessa took a step back and gestured at her tight-fitting uniform. When her eyes locked back onto Sal, her sly grin was still in place.

Maybe it was because of how flustered he was, but Vanessa seemed to sense an opening to push him one step further. Having grown up with compliments about his silver eyes, Sal was used to attention from the opposite sex, but this was completely new territory.

"Whenever you're done with the sniper rifle, I'll book us a private room and we can...explore some ideas and see what pops up! How does that sound?" Vanessa's voice was borderline seductive and the playful wink she gave him before stepping back was going to stick with him for life.

Just like that, the air of professionalism returned, and Vanessa was once again the dignified attendant of the Credit floor. It just furthered his suspicion that this was just a game she was playing.

Sal composed himself as best he could. If he was honest with himself, he doubted that Vanessa wanted him for anything more than his Mythcrafter ability. He felt way out of his depth but the knowledge of the Legendary rifle down in the meeting room gave him a negotiation advantage that helped calm his nerves.

"Crafting an Epic-grade item is pretty difficult, and should take quite a bit of time...but, since we're talking about hypothetical meeting rooms, and hypothetical commissions..."

Sal chose his words carefully and watched Vanessa's reaction. Her smile was still predatory, and Sal realized that she enjoyed this back-and-forth very much. If it was a game, he'd play with her.

As if to spur him on with his current train of thought, Vanessa tilted her head slightly to one side. "Go on..."

Sal forced a laugh as he pretended to come up with an outlandish concept. "What would happen if I put an evolutionary trait on the Epic rifle? Allowing it to reach to Legendary grade over time?"

Vanessa's eyes widened, and her lips parted. He could almost see the gears turning in her head as she processed what he had just told her.

Before she answered, she raised her two hands and gave him a playful smile. "So, we've two answers here, but I've a feeling you want to know one of them more than the other." Her right hand extended her index finger as she spoke formally.

"I can tell you how the Credit floor would act as a broker with the Reavers Guild to get you compensated, and we'd give you our VIP rates going forward to ensure we keep you happy and working with us." Vanessa then raised her left hand with her index finger raised, her voice turning once again back to a sultry whisper.

"Or...I could tell you how I would keep you happy and working with me."

Sal didn't even pretend to think about it as he immediately gestured to her left hand. Vanessa lowered her right hand and brought her left to her face, where she rested her finger against her lips. She looked to be in thought, and Sal watched her lips curl into a smile.

"Since we're talking hypothetically...I'd probably push you into the VIP track anyway and become your personal broker." Her eyes locked onto Sal as she continued to think aloud. "That would put me ahead a few years in my career plan, and that would make me...very happy." Biting her lip, she moved closer again and leaned over his shoulder until her lips were almost touching his ear.

Her breath was warm against his skin, and Sal was practically frozen to the spot.

"You satisfy my needs, and I'll satisfy all of yours. That's how I'd keep my handsome Crafter happy."

Vanessa turned to look over her shoulder, but nobody was paying attention to them. When she looked back, she raised an eyebrow at Sal with a smile. "Hopefully you can read between the lines, because I'd hate to have to spell it out how I'd fuck you senseless."

Any composure that Sal had remaining left his body violently, and he practically gaped at Vanessa. Her laugh was musical as she tried to stifle it with her hand. With a slight shake of her head, she gave Sal an almost sympathetic look.

"I'm going to break you, aren't I?" Without missing a beat, she raised her left hand again. "Speaking hypothetically of course…but in all seriousness, Myth. Don't break yourself trying to achieve the impossible. You get that rifle back to me on time, and that's a good starting point for our working relationship."

Sal was genuinely surprised by the soft tone she finished with. It suddenly dawned on him that she didn't believe he could deliver on his suggestion. A part of his brain wanted to keep the suggestive tempo going and to ask how she'd feel about Legendary grade, but he had already seen her cards, and he'd be able to call her bluff soon.

He was intrigued by Vanessa's balance of self-interest and her attempts to seduce him. He respected her more for being honest with her goals, and from that conversation alone, he knew that her ambition very much outweighed her loyalty to the Credit floor. With that thought in mind, Sal came to a decision that felt right.

"Vanessa, there's something I need to tell you," Sal started apologetically, and Vanessa cocked an eyebrow in curiosity. Rather than answering immediately, he lifted the Silver token from his pocket and handed it to her.

She took it from him and looked at it in confusion before answering. "You work with Salvatore? I already knew—he messaged me that you were here." Vanessa handed back the token with a perplexed expression, but Sal laughed as she gestured at him.

"I *am* Salvatore Argento. Myth is an alias we created so I could keep the Crafting and Appraisal work separate, so I could negotiate better rates for each one, rather than lumping them together." To give her further proof, he presented his Q-Card and tablet, which were both registered to Salvatore Argento.

She accepted them and looked them over for a few moments. Vanessa finally looked back up in utter disbelief, then burst out laughing, which turned more than a few heads. She looked back at Sal with glittering eyes and a wide smile.

"Are you for real? You're the Appraiser for the Reavers Guild *and* a Mythcrafter?!" She kept her tone hushed, but excitement rippled through each of her words. Shaking her head, she placed her hands on his shoulders. "So, can I call you Sal?"

Sal nodded, and Vanessa grinned as she sighed deeply. "Your secret is safe with me…but boy, did you just make one hell of a mistake."

A sudden lurch of anxiety hit Sal, but Vanessa's next words put him at ease.

"I was interested in you before, but now…well, let's just say that I'm starting to get really invested in a future partnership with you." Just as Vanessa was about to hand back the tablet, she saw something on the screen that caught her interest. A knowing smile crossed her face as her hand paused before giving it back. "It's nice to know that you're not completely innocent!"

Sal looked at the tablet to see that Hannah had just sent a few pictures to him. He quickly closed the messages and put the tablet back into his pocket. "Sorry about that!"

Vanessa just waved her hand. "Oh, don't be. So, Sal…are there any other secrets I should know?" She crossed her arms and pretended to be stern.

Sal saw the opportunity to boast a little and gestured over his shoulder. "The sniper rifle is done, but it's Legendary grade with an evolutionary trait. Appraisal has been completed and it's perfect. I needed to enlist a few others to help with the components, but I managed to Upgrade it successfully. When it gets enough kills through essence-tethering, it'll evolve into a Mythic-grade weapon."

Vanessa stood very still for a few moments. Her eyes narrowed. "Why do I feel like I'm being played?"

***

Upgrade sat up on the bed and accepted the offered cup of coffee that Sal presented to her.

"How long was I out?" Her voice was groggy as she blinked a few times to get her bearings.

Sal glanced at the clock on the wall and made a quick estimate. "Roughly around five hours? I thought the chests would have woken you, but you were very much unconscious."

Upgrade looked toward a couple of dozen crates stacked up against the wall on the far side. The Legendary rifle still stood proudly on the table, but it was pushed to one side. Sal handed her the official Appraisal documents as he took a sip of his own coffee.

He was halfway through the catalogued items when Alex announced he was calling it quits for the evening. Sal had managed to get them an order before he closed.

"I've done a few runs up and down from the Credit floor. There was a big haul in from the Reavers Guild and Vanessa picked out the most promising ones for me to work on."

"Of course she did," Upgrade muttered as she stared at the blanket in confusion. A small smile appeared as she propped herself up on the couch and lifted up the papers. As her eyes darted across the sheet, her mouth gradually opened until she was blatantly gaping at the specifications.

Name	Maslow's Legacy Sniper Rifle
Origin	Crafted
Age	New (Reworked)
Grade	Legendary
Dimensions	62 inches | 27 lbs.
Materials	Refined Mythcraft Essence | Premium Infused Gunmetal Alloy | Ether Crystal
Attributes	**Tether**: Shots will tether the rifle to its prey, siphoning off essence over time. **Hunt**: Shots have a certain chance to home in on locked targets. **Headshot:** Shots will have a certain chance to apply critical damage when vitals are hit. **Cleanse:** Rifle uses a portion of siphoned essence to clean and repair itself. **Recharge:** Rifle uses a portion of siphoned essence to amplify shot damage. **Grounded**: Rifle negates distance penalties and gives a drastic boost to range. **Evolution:** Rifle will gather essence from kills and evolve into Mythic Grade over time.
Abilities	Tether | Hunt | Cleanse | Headshot | Recharge | Grounded
Power Source	External Essence
Evolution	Yes | 0% to Mythic Grade
Quality	Perfect
Condition	100%
Value	Est. $215,000.00 – $750,000.00

"This is accurate!" She was fully awake now and her coffee sloshed precariously in her hand as she looked between Sal and the pages in front of her.

Sal laughed and felt another swell of pride for their work. "Congratulations on creating a flawless Legendary!" He gave a theatrical bow and gestured at the pages. "It's amazing, isn't it?"

Upgrade shook her head in disbelief as she re-read the report. "This is phenomenal! We're going to have to talk to the headmaster about this. Otherwise, the guilds will cause a riot. Myth is going to be in high demand, and we'll need to protect that identity at all costs." She laughed to herself as she shuffled through the pages. "I can't even begin to think how much this would take in at open auction. That it is guaranteed to become a Mythic grade over time…what would that even look like? Like, how can this be improved?" Upgrade lifted the coffee to her lips and sighed as the essence-infused liquid clearly started to work its magic.

Sal winced slightly. "I may have told Vanessa that I'm Myth."

Upgrade snorted. "I'm going to hope that it was because you're a good judge of character, and not because she batted her eyelashes at you." She shook her head slightly. "We graduated around the same time, but from different tracks. She's one of the good ones, but I can't for the life of me understand her game." And with that, Upgrade changed the subject by gesturing at the chests against the wall. "Appraise anything fun yet?"

Sal wanted to know more about what Upgrade meant about Vanessa, but he didn't press the topic. He walked over to the row of chests and pointed at each of them individually.

"Rare helm in this one. It looked like it had a plume of some sort in the past, but it's in pretty rough shape. Damaged on one side, which destroyed whatever rune was previously etched on the inside. Best guess was that it was a warding to protect against psychic abilities. It's incredibly light, though, and the material is practically vibrating with essence. I'm recommending that they seek Restoration rather than using it as is. Too many risks of wearing an incomplete rune and an unstable core." Sal looked over to Upgrade, who nodded in agreement.

Rather than waiting for him to move onto the next one, Upgrade pointed at another chest and looked at him expectantly.

"It's a curved sword with a guard around the hilt. Embedded core in the pommel, which I thought was pretty cool. It's another Rare grade and has a special ability that creates projectiles when the sword is slashed. Having the ability to use it at range makes it much more valuable, and I'll be recommending it being Restored or going straight to auction. The blade is brittle and chipped, so likely wouldn't withstand any close-range combat. Few missing pieces on the guard but wouldn't be a nightmare to fix up." Sal thought back to the image of the sword. When he looked back at Upgrade, she was eagerly pointing at another chest with a wide smile.

"This is super fun. What's in that one?"

Sal shook his head with a sigh, only half regretting that he woke her up.

CHAPTER 45:
EARNINGS

Sal whistled softly as the elevator doors opened. Compared to the indifference he had experienced earlier in the day, he was now being watched by every single attendant on the Credit floor. He was single-handedly responsible for keeping them awake. As Sal approached the nearest guy, who he had learned was called Greg, he was met with a look of astonishment.

"Are you a machine? How many more did you get through?"

Rather than answering immediately, Sal shuffled through the requisition forms and placed them down in separate piles. "That's another sixteen completed, one Epic grade—which was a surprise—seven Rare grade, five Uncommon grade, and three Common grade. They're in the chests down in the room and ready for collection with all the Appraisals attached at the top. I'm ready for the next sixteen, so can you send them on down when you get a chance?"

Sal double-checked everything in front of him before looking up with a smile. "And no, I'm not a machine…as far as I know."

Greg glanced at one of the other attendants, who also shook his head in disbelief.

Sal watched as they moved to assemble the next load of chests, and he was happy to see that the pile had been drastically reduced.

Greg counted the pages in front of him and verified them with clinical efficiency. "They're so detailed…" As if catching himself in his own reverie, Greg blinked and shook his head. "Sorry, Mr. Argento…that brings your total to fifty-three total Appraisals. I can always cash you out now, and you could come back in the morning?" His voice was hopeful, but Sal just shook his head with a grin.

"The timer has elapsed on my exclusivity, so I'd be competing against your in-house Appraisal team tomorrow. I don't see them around right now, so I might as well keep going until the job is done. I think the Reavers Guild will be more appreciative of getting them done as soon as possible, and there's likely a bonus in there for the Credit floor for such a fast turnaround time." Sal shrugged indifferently. "At least, that's how we do business at the Argento Auction."

Greg sighed and nodded in defeat. "Should we just send down the last twenty all in one go? Save you another trip?" He looked across to the attendants, who held a couple of chests at the ready, as though waiting for Sal's verdict.

Sal gave them a thumbs-up gesture. "Sounds perfect! Thanks for all your help."

With a single glance at the clock over the counters, Sal saw that he was very much becoming a night owl. It was almost five in the morning. He wondered whether he'd manage to make it back before the Credit floor opened for business in the morning. The thought brought a smile to his face as he continued to whistle softly on his way back to the elevator.

***

Just shy of eight in the morning, Sal was back on the Credit floor with a coffee from Alex in hand. Tucked under his arm were the twenty remaining requisition documents.

Greg clapped in excitement at the sight of him. In a momentary lapse of professionalism, Greg turned to one of the attendants and laughed. "Pay up! He made it!"

Sal couldn't help but laugh at the dismayed expression on the attendant's face. Greg had certainly earned his tip, but Sal no longer felt obliged to pay the guy who bet against him. As he placed the papers on the desk, he went through them in front of Greg.

"Twenty additional Appraisals completed. No Epic grade this time, but eleven Rare grades! You've got three Uncommon grade and six Common grade. All ready for collection with the Appraisals attached at the top. So…the words you've been dying to hear all night, Greg. I'm ready to cash out!"

Greg's shoulders sagged in relief as a wry smile tugged at his lips. "I cannot wait to see management's face when they realize you did them all in one night!" He spoke in low tones as he expertly sifted through all the papers and information, tallying the numbers and generating a report on the screen in front of him. After a few more checks, just to be thorough, he finally turned the screen to Sal for him to see.

Client: Reavers Guild

Service: Appraisal (Silver Token)

Contractor: Salvatore Argento

Items Appraised: 73
- Fee: Epic Grade (x7) - 137 Q-Cred (959 Q-Cred)
- Fee: Rare Grade (x26) - 87 Q-Cred (2,262 Q-Cred)
- Fee: Uncommon Grade (x28) - 37 Q-Cred (1,036 Q-Cred)
- Fee: Common Grade (x12) - 12 Q-Cred (144 Q-Cred)

Credit Floor Costings:
- Appraisal Transaction Fee: 13 Q-Cred (Auto Deduct)
- On-Call Staff (Night Service): 125 Q-Cred (To Be Paid)
- Discretionary Tip: TBC

Total:
- 4,276 Q-Cred

Sal stared at the numbers for a few minutes, and Greg understood completely as he, too, looked just as shocked at the totals. It took a few moments before Sal finally exhaled. The numbers didn't lie, and even though the transaction fee for each item meant he was losing close to a thousand Q-Cred to the Credit floor, he didn't anticipate that he'd be walking away with over four thousand…for a single night's work. When Sal looked up to the equally shocked Greg, he saw a wide grin appearing on the attendant's face.

"Well fucking done, man." Greg glanced over his shoulder to make sure nobody heard him.

Sal returned the grin and reached for his cup of coffee, his hand shaking with nerves. It was such a surreal moment, and he had no idea how to process it all.

"In-house Appraisers earn a fifty-fifty split," Greg said quietly. "They're going to be pissed."

The concept seemed to delight Greg, and from Sal's interactions with Vanessa, he was starting to get the idea that many of the Credit floor employees were unhappy with their current management. There wasn't much he was able to do, but Sal decided on the discretionary tip while he was there.

"Greg, for the tip…I'd like to 50 Q-Cred to be split among the floor attendants who took the chests up and down." A momentary flicker of disappointment crossed Greg's face, but he kept it together as Sal continued. "I'd like to give 100 Q-Cred to Vanessa."

Greg's eyebrow lifted ever so slightly at that, but there was no judgment passed.

Sal tried to keep the smile from his face as he finished his tally. "Since I like even numbers, I'd like to give you a tip of 126 Q-Cred, for betting on me and helping me get through the night. I really appreciate it."

"Fuck off!" Greg blurted before quickly covering his mouth with his hand; he looked positively shaken and mortified.

Sal laughed as he offered his hand to give a signature.

Greg, still pale, added in the caveats for the tip and just shook his head in wonder. "Thank you so…so much, Mr. Argento."

Sal grinned as he signed the form then extended his hand to shake Greg's. "It's Sal to my friends, Greg. Thanks again for all your help."

Greg took the offered hand and continued to shake his head. "I need to apologize for the amounts of times I cursed you during the night."

Sal laughed as he watched his Q-Cred balance increase dramatically on the tablet. "You can make it up to me, Greg. Just talk me up to any guilds you're close with. Always happy to get some work!"

Greg barked a laugh. "I don't think you're going to need me to talk you up, Sal. You just Appraised seventy-three listed items in less than twenty-four hours…to a standard that makes our in-house guys look incompetent. We're going to be telling everyone what you did!"

Sal picked up the coffee and waved goodbye to the staff, who looked positively relieved to see him leave. As the doors to the elevator closed, Sal saw Greg dancing behind his desk and speaking to the other staff members, who rushed over to the screen he was showing them. It was a beautiful start to the day, and Sal regretted absolutely nothing.

When Sal made his way out of the workshop, he saw several students, in uniform, gathered in the lobby. He took another sip of his coffee and approached one of the students.

"Need something?" the student asked in a neutral tone.

Sal gestured around with his coffee cup. "Just wondering what's going on here."

Another student turned and gave Sal a curious look. "It's the outing, with the Paradox Guild?" The other student nodded before looking Sal up and down. "Even if you have the Q-Cred for the trip, you can't wear civilian clothing." As he spoke, his features softened. "But there should be another outing in the afternoon, so you have time to change for that one."

Sal waved his hand. "Thanks, but I'm not heading out this weekend. Just wasn't expecting to see the lobby so full at this time and wanted to check." With a turn to the rest of the little group, Sal smiled. "Best of luck with the outing. I hope it's a great one!"

"Thanks, man!" one of the students said and returned to their conversation.

Sal continued through the lobby, looking to see whether he recognized anyone. He didn't give the outing much thought because it seemed incredibly contrary to what he wanted to do at the academy. There were countless students who were raring to get out into the field to fight the demons, but Sal was more than happy to remain in the workshop, Crafting and Appraising items and earning Q-Cred. Just the idea of being out there on the field was terrifying.

As Sal made his way toward the elevator, a notification on his tablet caught his attention. He opened it up to see a reminder about his appointment with the headmaster in less than an hour. Sal sighed in defeat. He had completely forgotten about it.

Clicking out of the message, Sal saw the messages from Hannah. She had offered more than a few times to come visit him in the workshop to keep him company, but that likely would have evolved into sex. Sal wasn't a presumptuous guy, but even he was able to read between the lines when she'd sent those pictures earlier.

The elevator in front of Sal opened to reveal a few more students who were departing on the outing. Sal moved to one side to let them pass and realized that he had zoned out again. He turned on his heel and went over to the premium coffee area. It was a very different sensation than the coffees that Alex made, but they were effective. After throwing his now-empty cup in the trash, he bought two fresh coffees and made his way back to the elevator that was thankfully still waiting. He selected his floor and waited quietly, enjoying the heat emanating from the piping-hot coffee.

A few minutes later, Sal was outside Hannah's room and knocked on her door. He had intended on messaging her to find out what she wanted, but he defaulted to the chai latte that he remembered from the first day. He didn't remember whether Kane had ordered it or whether she did, but he could always switch with her if she hated it. Sal needed to kill some time, and if she didn't answer, he'd leave the latte in his room and head to the headmaster's office early. Just when he thought that was going to be the case, the door swung open to reveal a very flustered-looking Hannah, in a state of undress.

Sal barely had the opportunity to speak before he was pulled into the room.

CHAPTER 46:
CAUTION

As Hannah closed the door behind Sal, she turned and placed her arms around his neck, drawing him in for a quick kiss. Sal held the two coffees out wide as their lips connected, with Hannah pressing herself against him. Her hands pulled back to cup his face as she finally stepped away with a frustrated sigh.

"I'm running late! So we can't…wait, is that for me?" Her eyes lit up at the coffee and a delighted grin swept across her face as she leaned in for a more sensual kiss.

Sal was happy to oblige; her soft lips parted slightly as her tongue danced against his. As his breath caught in his throat, Hannah's right hand slid down his chest before homing in on his crotch.

Her left hand pulled his head closer as her right found its prize. With a playful squeeze, she broke the kiss and whispered in his ear. "Is this for me, too?"

Sal moaned at the pleasant sensation and wanted to throw the coffees to one side, but Hannah disengaged with a grin as she took one of the cups from him and moved around the room. Well, room might have been an overstatement. It looked like a bomb-scare of clothing and sheets. It seemed as though Hannah had spent the week throwing everything she owned across any available floor space. Sal's heart thundered as Hannah threw him a wistful smile over her shoulder.

"Sorry, I really am running late! That outing is today, and we're supposed to be heading off in like ten minutes."

She took a swig from the coffee before looking at it in confusion. Without so much as another word, she returned to Sal and gave him another kiss as she placed her coffee cup in his hand and took the other one from him. Making eye contact with him, she took a tentative sip before her face broke into a wide smile.

"You arrive at my door, looking hot as fuck, and with my favorite coffee…I think I'm going to have to keep you." With a contented sigh, Hannah looked Sal up and down slowly as she bit her lip. "While I'd love nothing more to unwrap you…"

Sal smiled as he gestured at the room. "You're late! I've got a meeting with the headmaster coming up at nine, so I was only popping by to apologize for last night."

Hannah snorted as she pulled on a simple white T-shirt that somehow managed to accentuate her physique in all the right places. "Don't apologize! It's not like we're dating, or you're obliged to come see me when I'm bored. You were busy last night, and I'm busy today…so we'll find another time that works. Eh, can you throw me the jacket?" Hannah turned and pointed to the gray uniform that was crumpled on the edge of the bed. When Sal picked it up, Hannah winced.

Sal activated his ability and focused on Restoring the uniform with his essence. It was such an automatic sensation after years of refusing to iron his clothes. In half a heartbeat, the job was done, and the jacket looked like it was freshly pressed.

"Here you go." Sal threw the jacket to Hannah, who stared at it in disbelief, then grinned.

She moved over to Sal. "Can you do the same for my pants?" She took his free hand and pulled it down behind her to rest it on her ass. "Please?"

With zero complaints from him, he repeated the process until Hannah looked as perfect as the gray uniform would allow.

She gave him another deep kiss before laughing and breaking away. "You really are full of surprises, aren't you?"

He returned the smile as his hand gave her a playful squeeze. "Let me know when you're back from the outing?"

Hannah took his hand and twirled away from him with a laugh. "Only if I get to see more of those dance moves…"

Sal held her at arm's length and tried his best to sound reluctant. "Deal."

***

Sal waited patiently outside the headmaster's office and glanced around the room to distract himself. He had made eye contact twice with the secretary and tried to look everywhere else but at her again. Hannah had done a fantastic job of sexually frustrating him, and maybe it was just the lack of sleep and the added stimulus of essence-infused coffee, but Sal was feeling more restless than ever before.

A small part of him was annoyed by the fact that he wasn't fully awake for this meeting, but the Q-Cred balance in his account was a much louder voice and it told him he made the right call. He wanted to browse through the Q-Cred store to see what he could buy with his newfound wealth, but he wasn't going to touch the money until he had his next class with Jez. Sal couldn't wait to see his reaction when he saw that he had taken in over four thousand Q-Cred in a single night. It was ten times the amount Jez had quoted as a solid weekly income for a Crafter.

"Mr. Argento? The headmaster will see you now. Please follow me." The secretary spoke as she appeared from behind the desk. With a gentle smile, she gestured to the large doors beside her desk.

Sal got to his feet and lifted his now-empty coffee cup. "Thank you. Is there anywhere I can throw this?" He looked around, but there was no bin in sight.

She took the cup from him with a smile and placed it on her desk. "Not to worry." With that, she moved to the doors and opened the left-most one, pulling it toward her and gesturing for Sal to enter.

Nodding at her gratefully and mumbling his thanks, Sal walked into the headmaster's office to see Quest seated at his desk.

"Salvatore! Please, take a seat!"

Sal barely walked a few paces before he heard the door close behind him. He couldn't pinpoint the unease he was feeling, and instead of dwelling on it, he put it down to exhaustion. Going to the headmaster's office felt like he was in for a scolding, even though he hadn't done anything wrong.

Quest tapped at the console in front of him. "Just give me a second, I need to pull up your profile…" He smiled apologetically as he tapped away at an unseen screen with his fingers.

Sal took the time to slink into one of the plush chairs, where he waited in silence.

Quest tapped a few more times before sighing in exasperation. "It takes a few seconds to get to the right screen, so just give me a…ah! Here we go!" He smiled at Sal warmly. "So, how has your first week been?"

Sal blinked as he thought about the question. "Eh…good. It's been really good so far. I've been spending a lot of time in the workshop with Upgrade. It's been great learning from her."

Quest nodded, the smile still on his face as he scrolled through the unseen information on his screen. A few moments of silence fell between them, and Sal wasn't sure if he was supposed to elaborate on his answer.

Quest suddenly frowned at something and looked at Sal in confusion. "Did the Reavers compensate you for the sniper rifle? Upgrade gave me a report on everything that happened, which is one of the reasons I was so eager for us to have this meeting."

Sal shook his head slowly. "No, I haven't given them the rifle back yet…"

Quest's frown deepened as he tapped a few times at the interface. "Well, something is off…because it's saying here that you've got over four thousand Q-Cred in your account, which seems to have gone in overnight. As a systems guy, who literally created this whole framework, you can imagine how annoying it is to see mistakes like this."

The headmaster muttered half apologetically and half lost in thought as he tried to discern the anomaly in the system.

Sal perked up. "Oh, yes…sorry. That's from the Credit floor. I did seventy-three Appraisals overnight for the Reavers Guild with my Silver token. I just finished up an hour ago."

Quest looked at Sal with what could only be described as an expression of absolute incredulity. "Seventy-three? In one night?"

Sal shifted uncomfortably as he tried to find the words to explain. "I only get exclusivity for a short period of time before they outsource the work to their in-house guys, so I wanted to earn as much as possible before my next Administration class with Professor Jez."

Quest reclined in his seat with a thoughtful look. "Remarkable. You're very much surpassing our expectations, Salvatore. Which is why we need to urge caution from this point forward. Your gift, the Skill Master ability…"

Quest placed his hands on the desk as he chose his words carefully. "Upgrade, Martin, and Gosia. You used your Skill Master ability on them, and…as you've described, you untied the knots in their abilities. We've looked at Divinity Khan's feedback, and while there is a marked improvement in capability, there has also been side effects while their bodies have acclimatized to the sudden leap in power.

"They're going to be fine! Each of them will be undertaking some time in the skill-pods to help them adjust, but I wanted to discuss it with you. Essence control is something you'll be learning about next week, and you'll likely understand all this a lot better when that happens. Your power is able to bring out the full potential of others…but their bodies might not be ready for it."

Sal's breath caught in his throat as the looming sense of dread washed over him. He hadn't considered that he might be putting his friends in danger. *Was it because he was so used to taking other powers for himself? Did he suddenly disregard the safety of others?* Sal's stomach lurched, and he had to steady himself in the chair to prevent himself from throwing up.

"Salvatore, listen to me. Your ability is groundbreaking in so many ways…which means we know very little about it. You're not in trouble, and everyone is safe. We just want to take gradual steps forward and monitor the changes in their power levels, and see if they acclimatize to their new gifts. If they have an adverse reaction to it, we can simply get you to recreate those knots, okay?"

Sal nodded numbly as he tried to come to terms with what he had done. The idea of putting his friends in danger by testing his ability on them…just to make a damn weapon. "I'm so sorry. I'll never do it again!" he promised earnestly as he fought for control of his emotions.

Quest shook his head with a gentle smile. "No, Sal, you absolutely will do it again…because your power could very much be the key in our success against the demons. We just need to be cautious in how we best utilize that power. Which brings us to the topic of…Myth."

Quest's face broke into a wide smile as he placed his palms behind his head and leaned back in the chair. "You managed to Craft a Legendary sniper rifle, with an evolutionary trait. Are you aware of the impact that will have?"

It took Sal a few moments to realize that the question wasn't rhetorical. He nodded slowly. "I think so. It'll be a lot more reliable, and it'll hopefully allow Watcher to be more effective against future outbreaks."

The headmaster laughed as he shook his head. "Myth can create Legendary-grade equipment. Although a sniper rifle is fantastic, what would happen if you outfitted the people on the frontlines? That's going to be the thought of every single Hero who hears about your work. All of them will try to monopolize you and offer you the world to have you work with them exclusively. This academy is tasked with training you to be the best Hero you can be, but we can't make the decisions for you. We're here to guide you on your path…but I'd like to give you a piece of advice."

Quest sat back up in his chair and folded his arms in front of himself. "Focus on your training and learning for now, and don't get swept up in the excitement of it all. You have a long road ahead of you at this academy, and there are some extraordinary people who will be teaching you in the months and years to come. It'll feel like you're at the top of the world, because you can master abilities and your Crafting is at such a high level…and yes, it would probably be enough for you to live a great life if you were to drop out now and join a guild."

Sal listened to Quest in disbelief, but the headmaster was smiling. "But there exists another route, that I hope you'll someday explore. Our goal with the Saviors was to create the next generation of exceptional guildmasters. You'll be deciding your goals after you've finished your introductory classes and assignments, and it'll be a great opportunity for you to decide on what direction you'd like to take your career after graduation. My advice would be for you to look at being more than just a Crafter or an Appraiser. Just something to think about."

Quest gave Sal one last smile as he got to his feet with an extended hand.

Sal stood and shook it, reeling from everything the headmaster had just said.

"In summary, Salvatore: don't alter powers, keep Crafting, be cautious, and aim high. I'll get Joanne to schedule us in for another catch-up next month. Enjoy the rest of your day, okay?"

With a click of the door, Sal saw that the secretary was back in the room and holding the door open for him.

CHAPTER 47:
INTROSPECTION

Sal lay on his bed and stared at the ceiling. He had woken up a while ago and, judging by the lack of light streaming in through the wall of glass, he was well into Saturday evening. The conversation with the headmaster was playing repeatedly in his head.

What sort of side effects had Upgrade and the guys reported? When he thought about it, it made total sense that their bodies wouldn't have had the time to acclimatize to their abilities. Upgrade suddenly being able to utilize enough essence to power her suit should have been a wake-up call for them all, but all he could see was their happiness at having their internal blockers removed.

Sal closed his eyes as he thought about the other powers he had interacted with. *If he had unknotted someone with a destructive power, would it have caused them serious injury or even death? What if he had amped up the speedster guy—would his body have been able to keep up with it?*

All those bleak thoughts culminated with another that he had pushed out of his head for too long. Healer Bitch said that there was damage to his eyes when she was healing him. *Did that mean that his body was deteriorating because of his power? What were the skill-pods the headmaster mentioned?*

With a sigh, Sal turned on his bed and sunk his face into the pillow. The high from being rich had long since waned and he was left feeling empty. It had only been a week, and he had gotten swept up in the excitement of new abilities and discoveries. Being able to Craft Legendary-grade items was of course an incredible feat, and when he put it into perspective with the Argento Auction, he knew he'd be able to make an absolute fortune if he returned to the family business.

Sal lay on the bed for a while, just thinking about that. *Was money his real motivation?* He was ambitious to a point, but not in the realm of setting up his own guild. That was for powerful people who were natural leaders…so it made sense that the Saviors would be in that track.

Groaning to himself, Sal reluctantly left the warmth of the bed and got to his feet. His eyes caught sight of the tablet on the desk, but he wasn't going to check it just yet. He still needed to get his head straight. With that thought in mind, he made his way to the shower and turned the dial to give him cold water.

"Okay, let's do this," Sal muttered as he psyched himself up.

He kicked his clothing to one side and slid under the water, gasping as the cold spray hit his skin. Placing both of his hands against the wall, he looked down at his feet and focused on his breathing. Speaking aloud, he asked himself the question that had been holding him back since he arrived at the academy.

"Do you want to be a Hero?"

Gritting his teeth to stop them from chattering, Sal tried to answer his own question. He had come to the academy with the full belief that he would learn how to use his abilities and then get recognized as a capable Appraiser or as an

Analyst, maybe open his own branch of the Argento Auction and live as comfortably as possible. With his ability now revealing itself as something that could help others…Sal had to reassess his thoughts for the future.

Would he be able to sleep at night if he became an auctioneer? Knowing that his power could help thousands of Heroes push back the demons? Even if he was content with being a Crafter, he'd be holding back his true ability. Sal turned the dial, dropping the water temperature further.

Inhaling sharply, Sal realized that he hadn't really planned his future at all. *Two weeks ago, he wouldn't have even considered the possibility of being a Crafter…but now it was going to be his career? The Mythcrafter ability hadn't existed before he created it, so why was he letting it dictate his future?*

Sal turned off the shower and took a few moments to catch his breath. He had somehow fallen prey to the expectations placed on his shoulders. His ability wasn't originally a Mythcrafter; it was Skill Master. Sal recalled Upgrade's expression when he unlocked her power.

Yes, the guilt about those side effects were still present, but the absolute joy and wonder on her face was permanently etched into his soul. It was something that he had done with his own power, that wasn't an amalgamation of stolen skills. He owned the Mythcrafter ability, and it was incredible, but his true power was Skill Master.

He pulled a towel down from the heated rack. The thought of a Support being a guildmaster was pretty funny, and Sal actually stopped drying himself as that fact occurred to him. Supports don't lead. They advise, facilitate, help…they do everything in the background.

He had been putting himself in a box labeled Support because his parents worked in that function, and his ability seemed to belong to it too. Even now, with Crafting and Skill Master, they were still very much in the Support category.

Upgrade's lecture had inspired him greatly, and he felt like there was a clear divide in the student body, or at least in the perception of the different classes. Support was lesser than the others, for the simple fact that they were plentiful. That there were all these useful roles and designations for the future of humanity, and that Support was like a miscellaneous pile where they threw people they didn't have an immediate need for. Sal gritted his teeth as the thought gained momentum.

Offense, Defensive, Controllers, Healers…they were the useful people who guild scouts would foam at the mouth for, but Support were pretty much the final picks of the draft. Sure, Myth would likely be at the top of the lists because it was an anomaly of a skill set, but where would Sal be as an Appraiser? Would they pick him or Dominic Walters from the Defensive side? What about Hannah? She was Defensive…would she be picked up by a guild before him?

Sal had spent his whole life learning how to Appraise the value of things, and now he was seeing that value in people. *Did Quest share the same thought? Was that why the Savior class was created? To give talented Supports a platform and an opportunity to showcase their capabilities? Why wasn't Upgrade in one of the top guilds? She was a Hero and incredibly capable as a Crafter…but was her talent best spent in teaching others?*

Sal's previous apathy was gradually being replaced by annoyance as he started to question the disparity between classes. With a towel wrapped around his waist, he made his way to the tablet on the desk and searched through the Guild Directory. Toggling the filters to search by function, Sal stared at the results with a grim expression.

Active Guilds: 384
Sorted by: (Function: Support) (Status: Active) (Academy Approved: Yes) (Accepting Applications: Yes)
Total Results: 13
1. Agri-Essence (Tier 4)
• Agricultural / Food & Beverage Services
2. Amplitude (Tier 4)
• Skill Assessment Services
3. Assessors (Tier 4)
• Appraisal Services
4. Bureau (Tier 3)
• Administration / Research Services
5. Conscript (Tier 4)
• Hero Recruitment / Talent Scouting Services
6. Craft Corp (Tier 3)
• Crafting / Commission Services
7. Credit Floor (Tier 3)
• Auction / Appraisal / Commission Services
8. Domaintain (Tier 3)
• Construction / Restoration Services
9. Halo Kit (Tier 4)
• Emergency Treatment Services
10. Premier Recruit (Tier 5)
• Hero Recruitment / Talent Scouting Services
11. Traversers (Tier 4)
• Courier / Transport Services
12. Utility+ (Tier 4)
• Crafting / Commission Services
13. Wreckers (Tier 3)
• Demolitions / Construction / Restoration Services

Sal stared at the list in utter disbelief. Out of the entire roster of over three hundred active guilds, there were only a dozen or so that were viable options for graduating students. Even though there were countless businesses that would hire Support staff, these were guilds that gave the Hero designation.

He played with the filters to see how much they would change, but the results continued to dishearten him. It was a truly competitive landscape for Support classes. He had no idea how long he searched through the different guilds…but it did nothing to improve his mood. When he finally put down the tablet, he returned to his bed, where he once again lay back and looked at the ceiling. Compared to before when he had been racked by guilt, this time was different.

Quest was a Support Hero who had created an entire academy to help the next generation of Heroes. He had encouraged Sal to think about the guildmaster track, and Sal finally understood why. With a shake of his head, he bit his lip as he thought about what he wanted. The question from before that he asked himself…did he really want to be a Hero in the first place?

Throwing the towel to one side, Sal pulled the covers back over his body and thought about the possibilities for the future.

***

"How the hell do you forget to eat for a full day?" Divinity asked in disbelief, but Sal could only shrug uselessly as he stacked the empty plates of his two meals.

"I had the meeting with the headmaster, and then went back to the room to sleep, then I woke up…then I just kinda went back to sleep," Sal admitted lamely, as though it made perfect sense.

Divinity shook her head as she placed her half-eaten salad on top of his plate stack. "Did you pull another all-nighter? You're going to burn yourself out if you keep those up!"

Concern was written all over her face, and Sal nodded in return. "I know. I'm going to take it a bit easier. How are we for time?"

Divinity pulled out her tablet and gave it a glance. "We should probably start moving to get to the meeting on time." She looked at him with an awkward smile. "Are you nervous? I'm kinda nervous."

Sal waggled his palm left and right as he answered. "A little. I still feel kind of numb after the chat with Quest."

Divinity smiled and gave him a playful nudge with her elbow. "You've nothing to worry about. The side effects were a few minor headaches and getting tired faster. I just need to relearn my limits, which are higher thanks to you. I also get to sit in a skill-pod and do absolutely nothing—it's going to be bliss!"

Sal smiled. "Wait! Quest mentioned them, but I've never heard of them before. What are they?"

Divinity looked at him in a mixture of amusement and confusion. "I'm not sure if this is you flexing that your power is all-natural, or if you really don't know?" At the clueless expression that covered Sal's face, Divinity laughed. "Remember the cube that we fought in during the Combat class? That removes all essence and cuts off your power?"

Sal shuddered, causing Divinity to smile.

"Well, a skill-pod is the exact opposite. It's a smaller space designed for one person, and they flood it with essence. I've been using them for years to heighten my essence control and to allow me to see further into the future. Quest is probably going to get us to use them to help our bodies catch up to our powers. Essence can be channeled to strengthen the physical body, too. It's all about finding the balance."

Sal was about to ask another question, but Divinity was speaking again. "We have Skill class tomorrow morning, so you should be able to learn more about it then. Any favorite classes so far? And why is it Crafting?" She laughed as they made their way toward the Sky Lounge.

"I love Crafting and Upgrade is fantastic…but my favorite is Administration, so far. I've high hopes for Analysis, though."

Divinity shook her head without saying anything, but Sal wasn't going to let that go.

"Come on, what is it?"

She gave him a sideways glance as if to ask if he really wanted to know, but Sal was too curious to drop it.

Divinity sighed. "Remember how you created the Mythcrafter ability? All those hypothetical meetings in the future where you'd tell me about the best ability, until we found your favorite? The Upgrade skill?"

Sal nodded slowly, wondering where she was going with this.

She pointed at him with a mock-stern expression. "Don't come blaming me when you see his ability, okay? You made your choice."

Sal had a dozen questions and the look on his face caused Divinity's facade to break. She laughed as she tried to get him to slow down, but it was no use.

"You mentioned Analysis. I don't know the name of the lecturer for that class, but he has an ability that's super similar to Appraise. In our hypothetical futures, you constantly gushed about the potential of using it alongside your own ability, but felt it was too close to your comfort zone."

Divinity raised her finger and pointed it at him accusingly. "So, when you start gushing about it, don't go blaming me, okay? Mythcrafter is way cooler! You're going to make something awesome in the future, I just know it!"

With that said, Divinity entered the elevator with a smile, with Sal following behind her, laughing. She looked at Sal with a raised eyebrow.

"I'm serious! I don't need to see the future to know you're going to use it for great things. Trust me!"

With an innocent shrug, Sal gave her a wide smile as he waited for them to reach their destination.

"Wait, why are you smiling? Did you already make something?"

Sal turned and gave Divinity a sideways glance. "Weren't you curious why I untied the knots of Upgrade, Martin, and Gosia?"

Instead of answering, Divinity pointed at his Epic-grade shirt, pants, and gloves. Sal could almost see the gears working in her head as she realized that she assumed incorrectly.

"I got a commission from the Reavers. Well…Myth did. It was to fix up a sniper rifle, but we went a bit all out after the Mythcrafter ability found a way to create an evolutionary trait."

The look of astonishment on Divinity's face was absolutely priceless, but Sal couldn't help himself from adding the cherry on top. As the doors opened to reveal the Sky Lounge, he said, "It's also Legendary grade."

CHAPTER 48:
SOCIETY

"Legendary grade!" Divinity exclaimed as the doors opened, causing a number of faces in the Sky Lounge to turn toward them.

Sal had to bite his lip to stop himself from laughing as Divinity's face went bright red. Her eyes were still wide from the revelation, mingled with a surge of embarrassment.

A friendly face appeared from the side as Neuro stepped forward to shake their hands. "Glad you could both make it! Let me introduce you to everyone." His tall frame moved elegantly as he swept his hand to show off the group of seated people, some of whom were getting to their feet.

"Everyone, this is Salvatore Argento and Divinity Khan. Both Quest and I feel that they would be excellent recruits for the Doom Society, so please treat them well."

A few acknowledging nods were directed toward them, but several people stepped forward with smiles on their faces. Neuro gestured to the nearest arrival and turned to Divinity.

"This is Scry! He's been instrumental for the Doom Society for the last number of years and shares a similar precognition ability to yours. You'll have plenty of time to talk about future events, but tonight is just a meet and greet. Okay?"

His last words were very much pointed at Scry, who looked a little crestfallen. Divinity, on the other hand, looked elated at the prospect of meeting him. Before Neuro could so much as blink, she was bombarding the scruffy-looking Hero with questions. Scry looked at Neuro as though asking for permission, and the telepath eventually conceded and waved them away.

"Just make sure she meets everyone else, okay?"

Divinity clapped happily as she shot Sal a look of excitement. Both Scry and Divinity moved toward the bar area, and judging from their hand gestures and animated expressions, they were deep in conversation already.

Neuro sighed as he shook his head. "I can't see the future, but I knew that would happen." Looking back to Sal, Neuro gestured to one of the other people standing nearby.

"Sal, I'd like to introduce you to a good friend of mine. This is Harlan Geist. He's the best demon profiler we have. Any question you could ever have about the demons, this is your man. Harlan, this is Salvatore Argento."

The two shook hands, and Harlan smiled warmly. "Neuro tells me that you've enrolled in the Analysis class? You'll likely be working on a few case studies I've designed, so I hope you won't hate me going forward!"

Sal laughed as he shook his head. "I'm looking forward to it! It's great to meet you."

Neuro let them chat for a moment before excusing them to continue the tour. Harlan nodded and returned to the group.

Neuro gave Sal a small wink. "You got major points with him for signing up to Analysis. If you get Harlan Geist in your corner, he'll invite you to one of his Masterclass events. It's an invite-only module that opens up a lot of doors, so make sure to do well in Analysis to keep his attention."

Sal nodded and continued to watch the retreating form of Harlan, who made his way across the lounge.

Neuro continued the tour, gesturing at a person who was leaning against the back of a leather armchair.

"This is Liam Payne, who you might know as Pulse. He's been consulting with us for a few years now and brings a lot of strategic insight when it comes to changes in environmental essence!"

Sal offered his hand, which Liam accepted with a grin.

"Neil doesn't like to make things simple. I can sense towers, dungeons, and portal breaks before they happen."

Neuro laughed. "Okay, well, if we're explaining like that…he can also grade their power levels, which makes him our top threat assessor."

Liam pointed across the room to where a girl sat by herself. "Don't let Dawn hear you say that! She'd probably send one of her pets to kill me."

Sal was about to turn around when a small chirping noise caught his attention. Perched on Neuro's shoulder was a small glowing bird that looked to be made of some form of otherworldly energy.

Liam's face broke into a wide grin. "Too late, Neuro. You're in for it now."

Sal wanted to ask what was happening, when the bird flared its wings and glided over to where Dawn was seated. Her eyes were locked onto Neuro, and a playful smile tugged at her lips.

Neuro sighed and gestured toward Dawn. "Perfect segue to our next introduction."

They walked over to her and she looked up at him with a smile.

"A little bird told me that you've been lying!" Her brown eyes darted over to where Sal stood awkwardly. "Ah, are you the one who can see the future? Us threat assessors need to stick together. I'm Dawn. Nice to meet you."

Sal gestured to Divinity across the room. "That's her, I'm afraid. I'm just an Appraiser!"

Neuro snorted as he looked at Sal with amusement written all over his face. "Quest already briefed them, so they know you're not just an Appraiser."

Dawn's eyes lit up as she shot to her feet. "Ooooh, so you're the Skill Master?"

Before Sal could answer, Neuro jokingly pretended to whisk him away. The telepath shot Dawn a look of feigned surprise. "Oh, did your little birdies not tell you that?"

Sal couldn't tell whether there was actual animosity between the two, but when Dawn's face broke into a grin, he felt more at ease among them. As Neuro was about to introduce him to another person, the elevator doors opened again with a chime. Everyone turned to see Quest stepping out of it, with two people behind him: a girl with jet-black hair who wore a black uniform, and a tired-looking man wearing a white lab coat. Without wasting any time, Quest gestured for everyone to take their seats as he walked purposefully around the seating area.

"Thank you, everyone, for waiting, and apologies for being a little late. I hope you've had an opportunity to meet our potential recruits, Salvatore Argento and Divinity Khan!" Quest spoke quickly as he took his place on one of the high-backed leather armchairs. When he saw that some people were still standing, he gestured at the seats around him. "Come on, don't be shy. We've a lot to get through, so you'll want to be comfortable at least."

Neuro and Sal took a seat on one of the available couches. Liam Payne sat beside Sal and gave him a brief smile. From the other side of the lounge, Divinity and Scry took a seat, both of them grinning excitedly. Sal didn't know whether that was an indicator of what was to come, or whether they were just delighted to have met each other.

Quest raised his hand and gestured at the two new arrivals who had joined him in the elevator. "This is Anna Sakura, one of our recently elected Saviors from the third-years. Many of you already know Doctor Bob, but for those who don't, he's our in-house physician and can heal pretty much anything we can throw at him. I've asked them to attend our meeting so we can best showcase the abilities of our new arrivals."

Sal looked at Divinity, who still seemed excited. *Did he miss some form of memo about what they'd be doing?* He didn't hear anything about showcasing abilities.

Neuro leaned closer to him. "No need to worry. They just want to see your power in action."

Quest was barely seated for a few moments before he was back on his feet. "Salvatore, if you don't mind, would you come up here for a moment. Divinity, if you don't mind, if you could join us too."

Sal and Divinity took their positions as Quest pointed at a person Sal had yet to meet. "Recall, I'll need you to stand over here…and Anna, if you could stand behind Sal, that would be perfect."

The arrangement looked quite odd, and Sal had a growing sense of unease at having the third-year standing directly behind him. As though she was able to sense his discomfort, she tapped him on the shoulder to get his attention. When he turned around, she smiled at him gently.

"I'm here to protect you, so feel free to go all out."

With a nod and a mumbled word of thanks, Sal turned back to Divinity, who stood in front of him with a wide smile on her face.

"It's going to be great, Sal. Don't worry."

"Doctor Bob, if you could stand on Sal's right side, and Recall, if you could take the left…then we're good to go!" Quest studied the setup before nodding and clapping.

"Salvatore, we would like you to re-create the event where you saw the future. Doctor Bob will be healing you throughout the process, so your body won't be affected. Ah, yes, the core. You probably remember this one…" Quest smiled as he withdrew an Epic-grade core, which he handed to Sal. It was the same one that he had Restored on his first visit to the workshop.

Quest gave him a reassuring smile. "Anna will be working with Doctor Bob, so if there are any signs of adverse reactions or we need to pull you out, she'll cancel your power with her Nullify ability. Our goal here is to assess the upcoming calamities as a group, with Recall using his power to project your visions for us all to see. Are there any questions?"

Sal had a thousand questions, but all the eyes in the room were on him. It felt so surreal that only a day ago the headmaster had been cautioning him against using his powers recklessly, but now he was being instructed to use those same powers in front of a group of strangers.

Doctor Bob raised a hand, and Quest nodded for him to continue.

"Can I do a quick check-up, first?"

Quest gestured for him to proceed. "Of course! While you're doing that, I'll fill in the others on the new directives from the council."

Doctor Bob offered his hand to Sal, who took it, thinking the man wanted a handshake. A surge of foreign energy shot through the connection and coursed through Sal's body. If Healer Bitch's power was a ball of essence that bounced around his system, Doctor Bob's was a wave. It wasn't unpleasant but was a shock for him to experience.

Sal did his best to keep his own power at bay, making sure that he didn't unintentionally fight against the invading energy. Doctor Bob frowned ever so slightly as the wave of energy darted toward Sal's head. Up until that point, there had been nothing other than a sense of unease with the influx of power, but Sal felt a sudden tingling sensation at the back of his eyes, which caused them to water.

Before he had a chance to wipe at them, Doctor Bob placed his other hand over Sal's eyes and sent a concentrated burst of essence into his vision. Sal gasped; warmth spread around his eyes, and it took all his willpower not to collapse to the ground.

"Check-up is complete," Doctor Bob announced, without any further commentary.

Sal wiped at his eyes and looked at him for any form of explanation, but he was met with a passive expression and nothing more. Sal was inwardly grateful that everyone had turned to look at Quest, so nobody had seen him cry. A tissue appeared over his shoulder, and Sal looked back to see Anna Sakura grinning at him.

"I always carry a few spares in case someone bursts into tears randomly."

Sal took the tissue and tried to distract himself from the lurch of embarrassment he felt. Quest's words finally found his ears and he listened along with the rest of the group.

"Which is why we've had to schedule this today. I was hoping that we'd be able to keep this light and go through introductions, but the order came in after our last report. They want us to get as much information as possible regarding the underwater dungeon located at the port, and Salvatore is the only person to have seen it. We're being instructed to utilize all our resources in learning about this particular calamity. So, as usual…the council says jump. Society says?"

"How high?"

Sal blinked in surprise at the monotonous tone that echoed throughout the members of the Doom Society.

Quest spread his hands wide and sighed. "Glad we're all on the same page!"

Divinity smiled at Sal. She extended her hands in anticipation, and Sal took one of them in his own. With the other, he held up the core, and Divinity nodded in understanding. He didn't need physical contact for the power to work, but he didn't want to leave her hanging in front of all their new peers.

Quest leaned over to Sal and shook his head regretfully. "I'm very sorry about this, Salvatore. The Doom Council is pushing for answers, and I hope you'll be able to help us get them."

Sal nodded. "I'll do my best."

The headmaster turned to Recall. "Are you synced with everyone?" When the Hero gave him a nod of affirmation, Quest clapped. "Right then, let's get started. Salvatore, whenever you're ready."

Sal looked at Divinity and took a steadying breath. There was a lot of pressure on him that he really wasn't used to. So many high-rank people were watching him intently and the expectations were beyond anything he had done before. His heart raced, and he felt incredibly out of place.

"You're going to do amazing. I've seen it."

Divinity's voice reached his ears, and he saw the warmth in her smile.

It somehow managed to settle his nerves, and Sal returned the smile as he activated his power. The core vibrated in his hand, and Sal tapped into it seamlessly. He wondered whether the boost of essence would change the ability, or just let it last longer.

He weaved Divinity's power with his own and replicated her ability. But rather than activating it immediately like he normally would…he took the time to go over it again, refining it and ensuring that it was perfect. He subconsciously understood that certain curves in the weave were inefficient, so he tightened them up. It was only a few extra seconds, but he didn't want to risk making any mistakes.

Sal used the power of the core, mixed with his own, and activated Divinity's ability. The first thing he realized was the answer to his earlier thought. The extra essence had definitely changed the ability.

CHAPTER 49:
CAUTION

ETHEREAL WINGS FLARED OUT BRILLIANTLY FROM BEHIND SAL. JUDGING FROM the startled noise that came from Sakura, the sudden angelic appearance had caught her by surprise. The wings were much larger than the previous time Sal had transformed, but there were other differences too. His silver shirt had morphed into a gleaming breastplate that shined brilliantly.

A crown of light appeared over Sal's head as he gradually opened his eyes. He looked straight at the look of hurt on Divinity's face. He was showing her a pinnacle of her power that she was unlikely to ever reach.

Around the room, everyone looked on in absolute shock. Quest and Neuro had known what to expect, but the reality was so far from the report that they, too, were rendered speechless. Harlan, Dawn, and Liam had similar reactions, with each of them gaping at the angelic form of Divinity's power in a mixture of awe and wonder.

"You're going to cut off my circulation at this rate," Sal muttered.

Divinity's shocked expression melted into a gentle smile as she loosened her grip on his hands.

"Will you guide me, Divinity?" Sal requested as he started to look into the future.

Activating her own ability, Divinity nodded. "Always."

Sal was once again in the forest of trees. He remembered the lessons that Divinity had taught him, but there were so many to consider that it was almost overwhelming to his senses. With a flicker of light, one of the trees below started to glow. Sal could feel Divinity's power tugging at his own. Just as Sal was about to investigate it, another energy source made contact with him, and he instinctively knew that it was Recall's power.

Sal didn't fight the invading energy and instead just ignored it. He was being shown the way by Divinity, and her power was checking the trees at an alarming rate, much faster than he was capable of searching. Sal wished he could put Divinity in the driving seat and let her navigate his power, but it didn't work that way. When the various pinging stopped, one tree in particular continued to glow; Divinity had found the event they were looking for.

Just like in his last vision, he started at the base of the tree and looked at where they were right now. It was a good portion of the trunk and there were a number of branches and twigs that represented the different variables. Sal started with some of the branches and saw flashes of information that made no sense to him.

Scenes of open water, a group of Heroes swimming…and then an underwater battle? There was so much content to explore, and Sal gritted his teeth as he tried to focus on the main branch. Each vision threatened to slip out of his control with the slightest lapse of concentration. They were incredibly vivid to the point that he could make out every detail, but the cost was how unwieldly the visions were.

"You're doing great, Sal!" Divinity spoke softly as she helped him through the different scenes.

Sal tried to slow down the scenes to give them time to interpret them, when Recall spoke from beside him. "Just focus on getting all the information. I can slow it down later and break it down for the group."

It was a huge relief to hear, as he felt as though he had been slowly shuffling his way through things and had now been allowed to run. His power was constantly trying to show him everything, and the slow and measured approach wasn't comfortable in the slightest. With the floodgates released, Sal inspected each branch of the tree. Every twig and stub of the calamity was looked at with lightning speed.

Sal barely saw the flashes as he moved from outcome to outcome, finding out every endpoint. It was a relief to be able to fly through the information without looking at it too closely, because it prevented him from dwelling on the sights and worrying about possible outcomes. Sal had no idea how Divinity shouldered the pressure of knowing the future. He knew he wouldn't be able to handle that responsibility even half as well as her.

In a matter of minutes, Sal was finished with the entire branch. He could have continued, but all the main events were covered with a ridiculous number of variables thrown in for good measure. Rather than waiting for their permission, he moved to the next one and repeated the process with Divinity as his trusty guide. She discounted the variables that were too unlikely, and focused on the ones that had stronger connections to current events.

With her as a co-pilot, they stormed their way through future events with clinical precision. As Sal moved through one of the last main branches of the tree, Divinity started to look for their next target. Much to Sal's surprise, the area she highlighted was in a completely different section of the forest, and Sal had to move a good distance to catch up with her.

Almost automatically, Sal started the process again from the very beginning and looked through the events. To his continued surprise, he seemed to be acclimatizing to the new power as his control over the scenes deepened, and they showed him even more information as he flitted through them. The flash of colors revealed snippets of scenes, even though he was going incredibly fast. At the sudden tightening of Divinity's hand, Sal slowed his power and looked at what Divinity was seeing.

A single scene broke through the haze, and Sal was shocked to see himself and Divinity at the center of it. *Screaming civilians, dying students…humanoid demons?* In his panicked state, the scene slipped from him and jolted forward. More death and destruction met Sal as he saw the dying form of Sinclair screaming at them to run away.

"What's this?" Sal asked as his voice cracked with emotion.

He pulled back to the events before it and saw himself standing with a group of unfamiliar students. Everyone was separated into groups of five, and Sinclair was barking instructions at them. Sal tried his best to hear the words, but the scene moved too quickly and snapped forward again. A towering inferno showed one of the academy towers completely destroyed and engulfed in flames.

"That's enough!" Quest's voice cut through the room, and Anna pressed her hands against Sal's wings.

Everything suddenly cut off, and Sal was instantly transported back to the Sky Lounge, where he stared at the Doom Society in complete disbelief. His wings were gone, his shirt had taken its original shape, and the only sign that any of it was real were the tears flowing down Divinity's face. Turning his head, he saw Recall clutching at his head and bowed on one knee.

Doctor Bob stood over the Hero, with a hand resting on his back. He gave Quest a slight shake of his head. "He pushed himself too hard with this one. It's going to be a while before he's ready to process everything."

Sal looked at Quest and realized that they had stopped for Recall's benefit and not because of the vision. Just as Sal was about to open his mouth, Divinity's hand tightened, which made him look at her again. There was an imperceptible shake of her head, warning him not to say anything. It was in that moment that Sal realized that she was still using her power.

"Absolutely spectacular, Salvatore!" Harlan beamed as he rushed forward to shake Sal's hand. "The sync was in place for the first part, but Recall needed to focus his all on just getting the information from you both. Didn't get to see a whole lot, but what we did see was extraordinary. There's a whole slew of amphibious demons in that dungeon and I cannot wait to investigate them further. As far as debuts go, this was a definite highlight. Welcome to the Doom Society! We're lucky to have such gifted students joining us this year."

Sal thanked him for the kind words and saw Neuro giving him a thumbs-up gesture in the background. When Liam and Dawn swooped in to talk to Sal, Quest intercepted them with an apologetic smile.

"Just give me a few moments, will you?"

Both of them backed off, giving Sal and Quest some space to have a chat.

"How are you feeling, Salvatore? Are you hurt, or fatigued? We can get you checked after Recall is treated." Quest's voice was filled with concern as he looked over Sal, as though looking for some visual cues regarding his well-being.

Sal was pleasantly surprised by the reaction and smiled back. "I feel perfectly fine. The core did most of the heavy lifting."

Quest let out a sigh of relief as he turned around to look at the group of Doom Society members. He gestured for Sal to move a little farther away from the crowd.

When they were out of earshot, Quest looked at Sal carefully as he chose his wording. "The Doom Society does fantastic work here, Sal. We answer to the Doom Council, who sit at the pinnacle of the food chain, and both you and Divinity are now on their radar. Membership with the society is a tricky thing, as you'll need to do some weekend work with us to build up your trust score. The higher your rank, the more information you'll be privy to." Quest's smile faded ever so slightly.

"Recall retracted everyone's sync with your vision, and he'll be omitting the last scenes that you witnessed. Both Neuro and I saw the same events that you and Divinity discovered, but I must urge you to keep that information to yourself. Scry had the same premonition and we sent it straight up to the council, so countermeasures are being put in place."

Quest's tone was still in a hushed whisper, and Sal couldn't understand why they were having this conversation in private rather than with the other members of the Doom Society.

"Shouldn't we assess the threat with everyone else?" Sal asked earnestly. The whole purpose of the society was to prevent things like this, so the idea of keeping it a secret seemed ridiculous.

Quest shook his head. "There are a few new Doom Society members, and we haven't yet built up a sufficient level of trust in them. Believe it or not, there are people who would seek to capitalize on disasters rather than preventing them." Quest winced ever so slightly as the words left his mouth, but it was soon replaced by his steady and reassuring smile.

"Both you and Divinity will be taking interviews with Scry next week, and he'll assess your motivations and goals against future events. It's nothing to worry about, and will bring you up to the next rank in the society. All I wanted to ask was that you keep those last events quiet."

Sal looked over Quest's shoulder and could see Neuro off to one side with Divinity, speaking to her in a secluded space at the edge of the Sky Lounge.

Quest placed a hand on Sal's shoulder. "Any new information that comes from Recall will be a huge help to us, but there is a process to how we create countermeasure proposals. Telling everyone what you saw would only cause panic and uncertainty. Do you understand?"

"Yes, Headmaster. I understand." Sal answered slowly, even though he was conflicted on the inside. He wanted to talk to Divinity to find out what she saw in her visions, but that would have to be later. She had looked incredibly tense when she'd warned him against speaking.

Sal shook Quest's offered hand and nodded in understanding. "I won't say anything."

Quest smiled and gave him another light clap on the shoulder. "Great! Now, come on over and meet the rest of the Doom Society."

CHAPTER 50:
ASPIRATIONS

"I graduated with one of the officers for the Paradox Guild. I'd be more than happy to make the introduction if you'd like?" Liam offered Sal, which was followed by a derisive snort from the other side of the room.

Dawn looked at Liam as though he were insane. "He's barely finished his first week and the guilds haven't even posted their quotas. What use will an introduction be if he hasn't even passed his basic training? No offense, Salvatore," she added quickly, making sure that Sal knew her condescension was aimed at Liam.

The two bickered for a bit until Alastair came to his rescue. The bearded man wore a waistcoat and a friendly smile as he sat next to Sal. Quest had introduced them earlier, but there were so many people, that Sal was having a hard time keeping up. Alastair's deep voice cut across Dawn and Liam, interrupting their conversation.

"Let the boy breathe! Rather than telling him what he should do, have you tried asking him?" And with that, Alastair turned and gestured for Sal to speak. More than a few heads turned at the sudden booming of Alastair speaking, with their attention now locked onto Sal.

Sal thought about the question, and decided to go with the answer that was at the top of his mind. "I always thought I was going to join the Argento Auction with my family, but...a few events in the last week have made me reassess that goal. I think there is a lot more I could offer the world than a few Appraisals."

A few good-natured chuckles met his words, and Sal smiled as he continued. "I haven't picked any particular track yet, but I'm looking forward to learning more about Analysis, Administration, and Crafting. It might sound unrealistic or maybe a bit of a lofty goal, but I'd love to dispel the myth that Support classes are secondary to the others."

Much to Sal's surprise, Alastair barked out, "Hear, hear!"

Practically everyone around him nodded, wide smiles on their faces. It struck Sal in that moment that most of the people in the Doom Society had Support-based classes. Sal felt an odd kinship with the group and explained his findings from the other evening.

"There are only a dozen or so active Support guilds, and none of them are higher than tier three. If I was successful in getting into the Savior class, then I'd likely consider pushing for the guildmaster track."

Sal expected some ridicule from the group, but the smiles were still in place. He understood that he was only a week into his first semester, so his words shouldn't carry any weight at all, especially with how many students ended up not making the cut.

Alastair crossed his arms and grinned over at Liam. "Well, looks like you can stuff your Paradox offer!" When the laughter settled down, Alastair turned to Anna Sakura, who sat quietly by herself off to one side. "What about you? What's your goal?"

The sudden question seemed to jolt her out of her reverie. She vaguely gestured over to Sal with a passive expression on her face. "I'll probably join his guild."

With a barking laugh, Harlan threw his own hat into the ring. "I'll need at least a director-level position, Mr. Guildmaster. Head of Demonic Behaviors? I could work with that."

Alastair raised his hand to halt Harlan as he looked at Sal in mock disbelief. "You promised me the first director role!"

Sal laughed at their banter and felt incredibly at ease. Testing the waters, he decided to poke a bit of fun at Neuro. "I'm going to need a Head of Threat Assessment, too. Who would you recommend, Neuro, as the best person for the job?"

Both Liam and Dawn looked directly at Neuro, who gave Sal a withering look in jest.

Alastair's laugh tore through the crowd as he turned over to where Divinity was seated with the headmaster. "What about our new Seer? Miss Khan, what do you see yourself doing in the future?" He grinned at his own terrible joke, but Divinity took the question seriously.

"First officer for a tier-one guild. Learn and earn everything I can, and then move over to Sal's guild and bring them up the tiers."

From across the room, Anna Sakura raised her hand. "That answer sounds way better. I'm going to do that too."

Harlan spoke up as the voice of reason in the room. "It's easy to laugh and joke about it, but if he knows what he wants to do now…it'll give him a good shot of having enough Q-Cred to set it up when the time comes."

Many of the Doom Society nodded at the logic, but Quest snorted from his seat across the room. "He has over four thousand Q-Cred in his account, and he's only been here a week. He could afford the registration already."

And with just that sentence alone, the entire room fell into a deathly silence.

Alastair chuckled, but the serious expression on Quest's face caused even him to falter. Anna Sakura, Divinity, and even Neuro stared at Sal in shock. While all eyes were trained on him, Sal tried to make light of the situation.

"Well, if I'm going to afford all of you heavy hitters…I need to be earning at least that much a week!"

Alastair's arm appeared over Sal's shoulder as he was pulled into a half bear hug. "Quest, we're keeping this one! Don't go expelling him!"

***

Over the course of the evening, Quest, Divinity, and Anna Sakura left with a few others from the Doom Society. Sal was still seated with Harlan, Alastair, and Neuro, who had produced a bottle of whiskey from behind the counter of the bar. Liam had been the most recent exit at the sight of the bottle, and Sal felt as though he was intruding on their time.

When he stood to leave, all three of the men protested and told him that he should stay. Sal felt much more at ease at that point and happily stayed to listen to them. Neuro gave each glass a healthy pour before placing it in front of each person.

"So, what did you all think of today's meeting?"

Alastair sighed and shook his head with a smile. "Why don't you just read our minds? It'll be faster on everyone."

Harlan, on the other hand, paused as he took the glass away from his lips. "Oh, that's gorgeous. Great choice, Neil."

Neuro gave a mocking half bow before he took his own seat.

Sal left his glass on the table for the moment and looked up at Neuro. "It was pretty intimidating at first, but I've become best friends with Alastair here, so it's been worth it."

The bark of laughter was followed by a playful shove to his shoulder as Alastair grinned. "Is nobody going to talk about the fact that he walked in here with two girls who suddenly want to join his guild? Support classes have changed since my day!"

With a shake of his head and a rueful smile, Harlan turned his attention toward Sal. "Have you given any consideration to what you'll use all that Q-Cred for?"

Both Neuro and Alastair looked at him expectantly, and Sal could only shrug.

"I wanted to keep it until Jez had a chance to review it for the Administration class. After that, I don't know…the outings don't really appeal to me because I don't want to be out on the field fighting demons, or consciously putting myself in danger. I might just use it for Crafting equipment or something like that?"

Leaning forward, Harlan placed his glass on the table with a thoughtful look. "Here's my counterproposal! As Quest already mentioned, you have the funds to register a guild already…which is the last step of the process. I'd suggest that you put aside a chunk of that fund for course selection."

Both Neuro and Alastair nodded in agreement as Harlan continued. "Right now, you'll be in the basic classes for Survival, Field, Combat, Analysis, Administration, and Crafting. It costs Q-Cred to transition from Basic to Intermediate, then to Advanced. Masterclasses are necessary in certain subjects, and especially if you'd like to become a guildmaster."

Alastair turned in his seat with a nod. "Whenever you see a Masterclass, you should absolutely do it. You'll get an accreditation, which will increase your value as a Hero. The guilds have a checklist of sorts, and the higher their tier, the more they expect from their recruits. The other reason to keep the money to one side is because the Masterclasses don't occur on a regular schedule. They'll pop up randomly throughout the year with the availability of the instructor. So, you could find out that in one week there will be an Assassination Masterclass and it will cost up to two thousand, five hundred Q-Cred."

"Surely it's not that expensive?" Harlan asked, but Alastair just nodded.

"It's designed so the guilds can offer contracts to students, to pay for their tuition. If Sal wants to go solo, then he'll need to pay for everything himself." Alastair turned to Sal with a grim expression. "Everything costs Q-Cred, but the highest fee I've seen so far is for work experience. That would be in your third year, and it'll cost a minimum of three thousand if you want to get in with a good guild."

Sal finally picked up the glass and took a drink. He was no stranger to whiskey as he'd had more than a few of them with his father over the years, but he wasn't expecting it to taste so good. "That's beautiful!" he remarked with an appreciative sigh before putting the glass back on the table.

Neuro gave him a playful smile. "You truly are full of surprises! Half of me expected you to throw up."

Sal laughed as he reclined in his seat, enjoying the warmth of the whiskey coursing through his body. They had given him a lot to think about, but it wasn't all doom and gloom.

"Do I get a Doom Society discount on Masterclasses?" Sal laughed as he threw the question to the room, expecting them to break into smiles.

"It wouldn't be a huge one at your current rank, but it becomes more substantial as you build on your trust rating. I think it's ten percent to begin with?" Harlan turned toward Neuro to verify the information, and the telepath shook his head slightly.

"I think it starts lower but can build up to around sixty percent. It would be pretty shit if you were stuck in here on the weekends and getting nothing for it."

Alastair's laugh cut through the din of conversation. "Thanks for saving humanity…fuck off."

Sal chuckled with the rest of them, enjoying their company. They continued to talk about a few different topics, and Sal learned that Alastair had graduated around the same time as Sinclair. Sal wasn't sure whether it was the drink talking, but if they were to be believed, Harlan and Alastair were going to enlist him in their next available Masterclass.

Neuro had waved away his protests that he was only in the Basic training at the moment. Apparently, they'd introduce him to a few guilds for work experience as they were well-connected. Sal kept it to one drink as he had classes the following evening, but he enjoyed himself a lot more than he expected. Just as the conversation was winding down, Alastair spoke about one of his recent students who had so much potential for tactical warfare.

"He can clone his body! One mind controlling a whole squad of people! It's similar to Erika…" He gestured to Neuro, who nodded quietly. "But…different! If any of the clones perish, then what of it? The main body is still safe! It was just a clone."

Alastair whirled around on the shorter man. "I swear, Harlan. Don't try to talk to me about clone ethics!" Harlan burst out laughing as Alastair continued. "Imagine it, a one-man army with no cost of life?" He finished off his glass and slid it toward the center of the table, indicating that he was done. "Now, if only I could get the fucker to sit down and learn. He'd be unstoppable."

Sal grinned as he, too, finished his glass. "Well, if he doesn't work out, let me know. I've a friend with a similar power." Sal frowned as he thought about it. "Although, there's no cost of life…but I'd imagine it carries way more ethical issues."

When he was met with silence, Sal faltered before Alastair finally broke with a laugh.

"You can't just drop that bombshell and then clam up! Come on, spill it! Who is it and what is their power? I only half promise that I won't scout them immediately."

"Her name is Melanie. She's in the Orange cohort and really low in the rankings. Right now, she believes her power is Spirit Channeling, but it will evolve into Necromancy. Divinity and I saw it in a future vision. She becomes incredibly powerful."

Alastair shot to his feet as he clapped. "Lads! Are you hearing what I'm hearing?"

Harlan face-palmed, but Neuro grinned and humored his friend.

"That there's a first-year who can actually be trained…before they get all those bad habits?"

Alastair frowned. "Okay, it's no fun when you just read my mind." With a turn to Sal, the bearded man grinned. "Sal, can you introduce me to this Melanie?"

CHAPTER 51:
CATEGORIES

"I'D LIKE TO WELCOME YOU ALL TO YOUR VERY FIRST SKILL CLASS! MY NAME IS Professor Lombardi, and I was granted the Hero name, Forte. I want to get to know each of you in this class, but before we get to that, we need to know more about your ability…or more specifically, which category of essence it belongs to." Lombardi spoke as he brought a screen up for the entire cohort to see.

"I'd ask each of you not to interact with the core on your desk yet. We'll be using them later as part of your first exercise. If you could have a look at the screen, you'll see a list of essence categories which all known skills fall into. I'll give you a few moments to find yours, but if you have any questions or need guidance, please don't hesitate to raise your hand."

Essence Categories (Skills)
Psionic
Mimicry
Influence
Invention
Movement
Body Manipulation
Body Transformation
Energy Manipulation
Augmentation / Replication

Lombardi walked in front of the screen and raised his hand to point at each of the different categories. "Just to run you through them really quickly. Psionic comes in all forms but isn't to be confused with Influence or Energy Manipulation. Psionic abilities are controlled with the mind, and can take forms like Telepathy, Mind Control, Clairvoyance, Divination, and so on."

Turning toward the students, he listed off the different options with his hands. "There are a lot that fall under this category that look like they should be in the others. Like Teleportation, for example! There are ongoing debates if it's a form of Psionics, but for the purpose of this class, we'll be keeping it in the Energy Manipulation category.

"Next on the list is Mimicry! This is a nuanced one, so pay attention if you think this one might be your category. Mimicry allows the user to take on the traits of creatures and demons, but not like a transformation or a full replication. It could be enhancing certain characteristics, like strength, speed, sight, and so on. Mimicry users are typically excellent all-rounders as they can cover their weaknesses by amplifying traits. Most Mimicry users have no idea they're even in this category, so if you're unsure, I'll be happy to help."

Sal looked around the room and saw that more than a few people were looking at the list in complete confusion. He personally felt like his belonged in the last category, but he wasn't sure about telling the professor about his secondary ability, which very much belonged in the Invention category. It got him thinking others might have two or more distinct skill categories.

Divinity sat beside him in the lecture hall and leaned back against her chair as she waited for the explanations to come to an end. Her skill was definitely in the Psionic category.

Lombardi looked at one of the raised hands in the room and pointed at the student in question. "Yes…" He glanced down at the tablet in front of him for a moment. "Victoria?"

Sal turned around to see Victoria smiling sweetly, her hand raised.

"That's me, Professor. My ability allows me to control the opposite sex by releasing essence…but I do it with my mind, so would that fall under Psionic, or would it be Influence?"

Lombardi smiled back and clapped. "Excellent question! So, to dig a little deeper here…are you making the opposite sex more suggestible or full control? Would they inflict self-harm if you were to order them to?"

Victoria blinked in surprise and stumbled a bit with her answer. "I'd never…I mean, no. I don't think they would."

Lombardi opened his hands wide. "Let's find out. Try your ability on me."

Victoria's face paled as she looked around the room to see whether she was the only one that felt this was absolutely insane. The shared looks of concern told her that she most certainly wasn't alone.

"Professor, I'm not sure if—"

Lombardi smiled. "It's fine, Victoria. My ability will kick in to protect me, so you don't need to worry about harming me. Give it a try."

Victoria raised her hand, pointed directly at the professor, and activated her ability.

A few moments of silence passed before Lombardi clapped, breaking everyone out of their suspense. "Excellent job, Victoria! Your ability is definitely in the Influence category…but you might be surprised to know that it's not actually what you think it is. But we'll get to that in just a moment!"

Sal could see Victoria's face pale as her ability was completely disregarded by the professor. Not only that, he told her that it wasn't what she thought it was. If there was a moment that the entire class started to take the lecture more seriously, that was it. A dozen hands shot straight up, but Lombardi pointed back to the screen with a laugh.

"All in due time. So, we're moving on to Influence. Persuasion and Charm are the usual suspects in this category, but in the case of Victoria, the ability is Unity. With proper training and cultivation of your essence, you'll be able to influence more than just the opposite sex. You probably find it easy to make friends? People gravitate toward you? I've no doubt you've a winning personality, but your power is also at play, so make sure you learn to harness it!"

Lombardi turned back to the screen to look at the next category, and Victoria sat there with a blank expression. In just a few minutes, her entire sense of self had been flipped on its head.

"Right, next up is Invention, which can be Upgrade, Restoration, Craft, Repair, and so on. There are, again, arguments that the last few can fall into Energy Manipulation, but creationist principles say that if you're bringing something to a new state, it falls under Invention. Probably too much information, but the main opponents to Repair being in the Invention category are the guilds that want a sweeter tax bracket." Lombardi laughed at his own joke as he pointed at the next one.

"Movement! Pretty self-explanatory unless you factor in that confusion around Teleportation. We classify Movement as an enhanced mobility, rather than a change in location. Speedsters are the most common in this category, with Haste being much more common than Reflex! Incredible combatants with the right training, or very efficient couriers for those wishing to avoid the battlefield."

Turning around to look at the class, he held both palms outward toward the class. "Now, I need a bit of maturity from you all on the next one. Body Manipulation allows the user to change their appearance, which…can mean growing or shrinking parts of the body. It can also be physically altering oneself to enhance performance."

A number of sniggers rippled through the crowd, and Sal smiled.

Lombardi didn't dwell on the implication and moved swiftly on with his explanation. "Extra strength, speed, or even enhanced senses. This isn't Mimicry because it's completely unique to the individual and not imitating another power. Body Manipulators typically have outstanding essence control, and they make for terrifying opponents."

Divinity turned in her seat, and Sal followed her gaze to see a girl grinning from ear to ear in the second row.

Lombardi noticed the sudden attention she was getting and smiled. "Oh, do we have one? Excellent! You're likely going to fly through the exercises later, but we'll see!"

Sal nudged Divinity for context, and she looked at him in confusion before it dawned on her.

"Ah, remember that Combat class with powers? You were in the infirmary after the Skill Registration. She absolutely destroyed her opponent…turned into a giant and just kicked her opponent around the room until he gave up."

Sal stared at the grinning girl. "Okay, that does sound terrifying."

"Body Transformation!" Lombardi called out before pausing for a moment. "I assume you've all met Sinclair?"

The collective shudder that rushed through the cohort was answer enough.

"Yes, he's the perfect example of Body Transformation as a skill. It can be partial or full, but isn't restricted to creatures. There are skills out there that allow the user to transform parts of their body into weaponry, or defensive equipment. Solidify, Transform, Harden, and many other buffing skills fall under Body Transformation."

Lombardi clapped and then pointed at the next one on screen. "Energy Manipulation, which used to be called Essence Manipulation…don't ask me why they changed it, because nobody knows. Skills like Teleportation, Phase, Amplify, Shield…anything you can think of that looks super flashy, usually belongs to Energy Manipulation. Which leaves us with Augmentation and Replication. It's not to be confused with Mimicry, because Replication can copy actual skills rather than characteristics. Augmentation can be an enhancement to an existing skill, but shouldn't be confused with the likes of Upgrade and Repair, which only work on objects. Just like the Body Manipulators, Replicators typically have outstanding essence control, and they can also be terrifying opponents. Do we have anyone here that thinks they fall into that category?"

Lombardi looked around with a hopeful expression.

Sal tentatively raised his hand, and Lombardi grinned widely.

"I've had this class with three of the other cohorts so far, and you're the first one I've come across. You guys have a Body Manipulator and a Replicator! I'm going to expect great things from this group!" Lombardi took a few steps back toward the desk as he looked up at the students in the stands.

"Okay, so hands up if you don't know which category you belong to. Don't be shy!"

As Lombardi pointed at different students to answer their questions, Sal glanced around and listened to the types of powers other people had. The Body Manipulator from before was staring at Sal with a curious expression on her face, and Sal broke eye contact immediately.

"Great questions, everyone. So, let's all get on the same page. Everyone in the Psionic category, raise your hand!" Lombardi instructed, and a good number of people raised their hands. "Let's count them up. Thankfully, they've limited it to one hundred people per cohort, so you've made calculating percentages easy for me."

Counting aloud as he moved around the room, he nodded and entered the figure onto his tablet. "Fourteen of you in Psionic. Next up, Mimicry? Okay, that's…eight! Influence? Just the four of you? Invention…the one that always tests my counting ability. Let's see…" Lombardi started from the left to the right and had to assign numbers to people so he could remember and not get confused.

"Thirty-four for Invention! That's going to be quite the competitive space this year. I don't envy Upgrade!"

Sal turned in his seat and couldn't believe how many people were in the same category. He didn't see them in the Crafting class, so what were they doing with their skills?

"Movement?" Lombardi called out as the hands for Invention dropped down. "Twenty-one! That's great to see. As a matter of interest…if you don't mind sharing with the group, how many of you are considering going into Combat-oriented roles?"

A few of the Movement-based students hesitated in lowering their hands for fear of it looking like cowardice.

Lombardi didn't demean any of them, though. "There's absolutely no shame in wanting to be a Support. For the five of you who are interested in Combat, I'll have a chat with you after class. There are some excellent training methods that give the best results when you start them early, and there's no better time than week two!"

Lombardi pointed to the girl in the second row. "We have our Body Manipulator. Are there any others in the class?" When he looked around and saw no hands raised, he tapped his tablet before continuing. "Body Transformation? There's usually a couple in each cohort. Ah! Nine of you? Fantastic!"

Sal noticed that each category of students smiled as they were acknowledged by Lombardi. He had given them another sense of identity outside of the ranking system, and there were a few of them in the lower ranks who looked like they really needed it. A sign that this was an intentional act was that it was easily deduced how many Energy Manipulators remained in the room, but Lombardi asked them to raise their hands regardless.

"Energy Manipulators? Eight! Excellent. That's my own category, so I might have a few tips and tricks for you to maximize your training outputs." Before Lombardi turned to Sal, he looked back at the group with their hands raised. "Actually, do we have any Amplifiers in the room? It's a skill within Energy Manipulation."

Of the eight people with their hands raised, seven of them went down, leaving one girl looking around anxiously with her hand raised.

Lombardi smiled warmly as he pointed to the student. "Everyone, meet your new best friend in the Silver cohort." With a glance down at his tablet to check the name, he laughed. "Whisper, is it?"

The girl nodded and quickly withdrew her hand, sinking into her seat as every set of eyes in the room bore down on her.

Lombardi laughed as he tried to provide context. "Your ability causes you pain, doesn't it?" Whisper's eyes shot up to stare at Lombardi, which caused his expression to soften. "Looks like we have the same ability. I'd also ask you to stay after class so we can have a chat."

"Which leaves us with…Salvatore?" Lombardi quickly checked the tablet as he looked over to where Sal was seated. "Are you in more of an Augmentation-based or Replication-based category?"

Sal didn't know how to differentiate the two of them, so pushed the question back to the professor. "It's called Skill Master. I can replicate abilities, but without the knots." As he said the words, Sal inwardly groaned, Lombardi would have no idea what he was talking about. Much to his surprise, though, Lombardi stared at him in absolute disbelief.

A moment of silence washed across the room as Lombardi moved closer to where Sal sat. "Can I check your Q-Card, please?"

A murmur of conversation broke out among the students as Lombardi inspected Sal's card. With a whistle of surprise, Lombardi handed it back with a wistful shake of his head. "Okay, this just got very interesting! We have the makings of a dream team in this class."

Lombardi was about to step away when he suddenly glanced down at the tablet in front of him. He read a name before turning his attention to Divinity. His voice was quiet, so only she and Sal could hear him.

"You're the student who's scheduled for the skill-pod, aren't you?" When she nodded, Lombardi grinned. "And was it this guy who unknotted your power?"

Divinity faltered as she cast a panicked glance toward Sal.

Rather than having her put on the spot, Sal nodded. "Yes, it was me."

Lombardi smiled as he stepped back from their row. "Let's bring up the composition, and then we can rush through all the theory, and then…we'll get to the fun part!" As he spoke, he tapped his tablet and the screen changed behind him to include the percentages of the class.

Essence Categories (Skills)
Psionic (14%)
Mimicry (8%)
Influence (4%)
Invention (34%)
Movement (21%)
Body Manipulation (1%)
Body Transformation (9%)
Energy Manipulation (8%)
Augmentation / Replication (1%)

Lombardi looked between Whisper, Sal, and the Body Manipulation girl with a wide grin on his face. "I can say this with absolute certainty. I have never been this excited to teach a group!"

CHAPTER 52:
CONTROL

LOMBARDI PROPPED HIMSELF UP ON THE DESK AS HE TURNED OFF THE SCREEN behind him to ensure they were paying attention to him and not it. "Let's get the theory out of the way first. Without this turning into a history lesson, I'm going to explain what we know about essence, and how it's relevant for your ongoing development.

"The first portals opened around sixty years ago. They came before the dungeons and the towers, but we'll focus on the portals for now. When they opened, they released essence into our atmosphere…weak at first, but as time went on and they were left unchecked…our atmosphere became enriched with it."

Lombardi waved his hand as he added in a disclaimer. "Some will say it polluted our atmosphere, but we're not here to be political. The fact is, sixty years' worth of essence has poured into our atmosphere, and has changed us in the process. Each demon we defeated added more essence, and as time went on, our lost territories began to terraform and became the first reported dungeons and towers. Havens for powerful demons. But what does this have to do with a skill class?"

Lombardi extended his arms out wide and smiled. "Absolutely everything. Our entire planet has been flooded with essence, and no matter how many portals we've closed, more and more are opening. My father's skills were weaker than mine, and yours are likely stronger than mine. Children born today will have a higher capability with essence than any of you here, just because of our rapid evolution and acclimatization to atmospheric essence. So, in the years that we've been studying this, we've learned to harness it and categorize the various manifestations we've come across. We have training methods for each category in place, but all of you here are adults now. The essence in your bodies has existed for years without any guidance, which has likely stunted your development. Some of those barriers will be permanent, but some of them can be broken down and corrected. Now, look at the core in front of you on your desk."

Sal wondered where Lombardi was going with this. *Was he going to get them to use it like a battery?* Divinity looked equally confused, which told Sal that she likely hadn't glimpsed into the future for this class.

Getting to his feet, Lombardi picked up a core from his own desk and held it up.

"Inside each of you is one of these. We were able to create artificial cores through the study of internal cores. They can operate like a battery that can amplify your capabilities, but rather than seeking external solutions…we should be training our internal core. Over the course of your first semester with me, we're going to train you to unlock the potential of your internal core. This will involve two main exercises. First, you'll need essence control, which will be second nature to our Replicator and Body Manipulator. It is the visualization of your own essence, allowing you to control its path throughout your body and externally. Second, you'll need to work on essence refinement, which will remove a number of the blockages in your system and enhance the quality of your internal core. We have a few tools that we'll use in later classes that will measure your internal core, but for now, we'll start with a basic test. Can you tap into the energy of the core in front of you?"

Sal frowned at the question and wondered whether there was something special about the core that would block him from accessing it. With a touch of his finger, he realized that there was zero resistance, and he had full access to the core's limited amount of essence.

Looking around, Sal was surprised to see that most of the class were deep in concentration as they tried to access the core. Even Divinity was struggling, which came as a shock.

Lombardi caught his expression and gave him an approving nod. A few more minutes passed, with Lombardi asking the students who successfully managed it to raise their hands. There were a few smug smiles among them, but Lombardi ignored them as he encouraged the others to try their best.

"Okay, that should be it. Now, for those of you who weren't able to visualize your energy or tap into the essence in the core, don't worry! It means that you'll likely have a lot of room for development and growth. See it as an opportunity to level up your ability to the next stage. Essence control is vital to move to the next stage, which is essence refinement. For that reason, we'll be separating the class into two categories, so that everyone will be learning. If I could ask those of you with your hands up to move over to the left side of the room, this will be for those learning essence refinement. On the right side of the room, will be everyone who is learning essence control. Sorry, my right and left is different than yours." Turning around to face the screen, Lombardi gestured with his left hand to one side of the room and then to the right and clarified where they should go.

Divinity gave Sal a resigned look as she got to her feet to move seats. "I'll catch up with you later," she muttered as she went over to the other side of the room.

Before Sal could even reply, the Body Manipulation girl sat beside him, and Sal was shocked to see that she had silver irises like his.

"Salvatore Argento." She extended her hand and introduced herself with a perfect recreation of his voice.

Sal was left baffled for a moment then burst out laughing. "Please tell me that's not what my voice sounds like."

In the blink of an eye, her eyes reverted to a vibrant green and her voice changed to a completely different pitch. "That's exactly what you sound like…and you always shake people's hands. What's with that?"

Lombardi's voice carried through the room, and everyone looked back at him. "Whisper, if you don't mind. Could you sit down here with Salvatore and…" He checked the tablet in his hand. "Lucia Hernandez?" He glanced at the Body Manipulator, who gave him a thumbs-up.

When she looked back at Sal, she shook her head. "Most basic bitch name, I know. I prefer going by Nova."

Sal glanced back to where Whisper stood awkwardly near the back row. She looked terrified, so Sal gave her a friendly wave as he replied to Nova.

"You can call me Sal. Also, I think Lucia is a nice name."

With a derisive snort, Nova shook her head again. "You probably like Sofia too, yeah?"

Sal turned to her with a confused expression. "Well, yeah. It's my mother's name."

Nova bit her lip to suppress a smile as she glanced at the now approaching form of Whisper. "You're going to shake her hand, aren't you?" Nova teased, and Sal made a concerted effort there and then to stop shaking people's hands.

"It's an auctioneer thing. It's good manners." His attempt at justifying it fed her amusement even more, so Sal let it go.

"Hi," Whisper said meekly as she slid into the chair beside Nova.

Sal was initially worried that Nova would tease the girl, but much to his surprise, she took a different route.

"I'm Nova, and he's Sal. Welcome to the dream team!" With a hike of her thumb over her shoulder to reference Sal, Nova gave Whisper a gentle smile, which resulted in the smaller girl's shoulders dropping in relief.

"Oh, can I be on the dream team, too?"

A familiar voice sounded out from directly behind Sal to reveal the grinning form of Dave. Sal stared at him as the context finally dawned on him.

"Wait, Dave? Do you have good essence control?" Sal realized that he had unconsciously ranked Dave as somewhat inept from how he gushed around higher ranks, but he was pleasantly surprised with being proved wrong. Dave frowned and Sal realized he had likely just offended him, but before he could apologize, Dave pointed to the other side of the room.

"Wait, is this not the group that can't access the core?"

Nova gave him an amused look. "Dream team application denied. You're on the wrong side, bud."

Dave didn't seem remotely upset, though, as he laughed. "No worries. Maybe get lunch later, Sal?" Before Sal had an opportunity to respond, Dave rushed to get to the correct side of the classroom, calling over his shoulder that he'd see Sal later.

Lombardi clapped, and the chattering around the room quieted down.

"Great work everyone! So, now that we have you separated, I just want to emphasize that this isn't an exclusionary exercise. Nor is it uncommon." With a tap of his tablet, a barrier of blue light appeared down the center of the classroom, separating the two groups.

"This will ensure that those of you meditating to improve your essence control aren't interrupted while I instruct the others on essence refinement. As an example, while I'm standing here, all of you can hear me, but the moment I step over here..." Lombardi's mouth continued to move on one side of the barrier, but nothing could be heard.

He stepped around the other side of the barrier to where Sal sat and repeated the process. "And just like this, the students on the other side can't hear a thing. This will allow both sides to work effectively throughout the lesson."

Lombardi stepped back so both sides of the class could hear him. "I'm going to use my Amplify ability on all of you in the essence control side of the room. This will increase your sensitivity to essence and allow you to see it. It's much easier to aim toward a goal when you know what you're looking for. Before I do that, I'd like everyone in the essence refinement side of the room to meditate. Just close your eyes and use your power to explore your body. I'll be putting up a diagram on the screen to show you the route I'd like you to channel the essence throughout the body, and we'll later discuss your progress, okay?"

Everyone on both sides nodded in understanding as Lombardi activated the screen again with his tablet.

Sal looked up and saw a humanoid figure with over a hundred points scattered across it. Each was numbered and had a small description.

Lombardi glanced up at it and pointed at the center, which was marked as number one. "Start there and move in sequence to get as high as you can, and I'll check back with you after I finish with the essence control side. Understood?"

Everyone nodded once more, and Lombardi moved to the other side of the barrier. Sal stared up at the board as he looked at the various points. This whole concept was completely new to him, but he imagined that it should be straightforward enough.

Nova turned to him with a sly smile. "Race?"

Sal shook his head. "I've no idea how to do this, so I doubt I'd be much competition."

Much to the surprise of both of them, Whisper spoke. "I'm game." She had twisted in her seat so that she was sitting on her own legs, but her eyes were locked onto the diagram in front of her.

Nova raised an eyebrow and grinned. "Excellent! Sal can keep score while he's figuring it out."

"Can you lot just shut up? We're trying to concentrate." A voice sounded out from the row behind them.

Sal turned to apologize, but Nova whirled around first. Her eyes locked onto the male student, and her face broke into a predatory grin.

"Oooh, brave man outside of the combat ring! You weren't this chatty when I was kicking you around the cube."

In a surprising diffusing of tension, Whisper said, "Just passed the fifth point."

Nova grimaced and pointed at the student she had tormented in the ring. "I'll deal with you later."

With that, all conversation evaporated as everyone started to channel their essence through the points.

Sal activated his ability and tried to visualize the points within his own body. He didn't need to keep his eyes closed for any of it, which was a nice bonus, but it was still challenging to find what he was looking for. It took a few moments for him to ignore his internal skill weaves, but when they were gone from his subconscious, he was able to proceed more comfortably.

Rather than trying to memorize all of them, Sal started with the first five points, which were all relatively close to each other. He tried to imagine them as rings that he could thread his essence through, which made it much easier to navigate. What he hadn't expected was for each threading to have a layer of resistance. This hadn't happened to him before, and Sal frowned as he struggled to pierce through the second ring.

Instead of simply threading through, it was as though he had to push past it with his essence. After a few rotations of his essence coiling around the ring, it finally gave way and allowed him to proceed. An imperceptible shift happened within his internal core. He couldn't describe the sensation, but it was as if the coil of his essence had grown by a fraction.

"Just passed the twentieth point," Whisper said quietly, followed by Nova's only a second later.

"Seventeenth."

Sal was suddenly very conscious of the fact that he had only gotten to the second point. He wasn't particularly competitive and much preferred to do things the right way, but this was supposed to be one of his key strengths.

Why was he struggling so much? With that thought in mind, Sal pushed to the third point and found that it had even more resistance than the last one. He rotated the coil rapidly around it and bathed it in his essence before attempting to punch through it. The backlash of his essence being rejected caused him to physically wince and deactivate his power.

Sal looked around the room and saw that everyone was deep in concentration, with many of them smiling as they moved through the points. *Was he the only one struggling with it?*

Nova glanced at him. She paused for a moment, as if deep in thought before leaning closer to him and speaking in a quiet voice. "Need a hand?"

CHAPTER 53:
MANIPULATION

Sal stared at Nova, but she just held out her hand and gestured for him to take it. He had no idea how to take this girl and suspected that she was likely leading him into some form of elaborate joke.

Whisper sighed as she slumped back against her chair. "Stuck at thirty-seven. How did you do?"

Nova glanced over to her with a wry grin. "Maxed out at around twenty-eight...but I've a feeling our dream team has hit a snag."

Whisper followed Nova's gaze to where Sal was sitting. "Oh, it's your first time?" she asked, and he saw an understanding in her eyes that he wished he felt himself.

Rather than just sitting there quietly and nodding, Sal tried to explain, in hushed tones, what had happened. He didn't want to distract the other students, but he desperately wanted to know what he was fucking up. A part of him was tempted to hold out for Professor Lombardi, but he was only on the second row of students on the other side.

"I tried to visualize the points as rings, and thread my essence through them, but it didn't work. I coiled the essence around the rings instead and then pushed through the first one and it was great...but the second one bounced me straight back."

Nova shook her head immediately, as though it were obvious. "There's your problem. It's not threading a needle; it's filling a pool. Imagine the points as empty buckets that need to be filled with essence before moving onto the next one."

She casually glanced at Whisper, who nodded and waved her hand side to side. "More or less. I imagine them as chunks of metal that need to be melted down with essence and then it gets added to my core to reach out to the next one. It takes a while to heat up, though, and that comes down to the strength of your own core."

Sal looked down at Nova's offered hand. "How would this help?"

Whisper gestured at Nova, as though it were obvious. "Body Manipulation. She can manipulate the bodies of others she touches..."

At the look of panic on Sal's face, Whisper quickly clarified, "But not permanently!"

Nova chuckled and threw a disappointed glance toward Whisper. "Spoilsport."

Sal still couldn't understand how it was supposed to be helpful. "How could your ability make this easier?"

Nova cocked an eyebrow and shrugged. "I'd change your senses so you can see how much essence is required to pass each point. It'd be a lot faster if you got amped up, though." She gave Whisper a meaningful look, and the smaller girl leaned across to offer her own hand.

Sal stared at the two of them and couldn't for the life of him understand why they were doing this. "Why are you offering to help me? I mean, we just met."

Nova gave an exasperated sigh as she took one of Sal's hands and pulled it over to Whisper, who took it. "We would be pretty shit Heroes if we didn't help people. Stop overthinking it. Give me the other one."

As soon as he complied, he regretted it. The contortion looked and felt absolutely comical and with a stifled laugh, Whisper suggested they move seats so that Sal sat in the middle of them. A few glares were shot their way with the reshuffle, but nobody said a word. Sal felt incredibly uncomfortable as he held the hands of the two girls. He didn't know what to expect, but Nova's voice cut across his thoughts.

"Try again and let us do the rest, okay? Then you can have your hands back."

Sal pushed his embarrassment to one side as he concentrated on the diagram in front of him. Activating his ability, he was happy to see that the first point remained under his control and his essence slid through it with ease. Just as he was about to glance up to see the next point, it instinctively appeared in his mind. Guiding his essence carefully, he thought of it like an ingot of metal that needed to be melted.

Much to his surprise, he knew exactly how much essence it needed to be bypassed. He guided his essence toward it and started to fill the point with it, enjoying the satisfaction of feeling its resistance melting away. In just a few moments of effort, the point was gone, and he was onto the third one. The fatigue he had felt before when trying this was no longer there, and Sal wondered whether this was down to Whisper's power.

Each point melted away with ease, and Sal felt a surge of relief with each point passed. After a short time, the twelfth point took pretty much all of his remaining essence, but it wasn't enough to melt it. Any thoughts he had about Whisper's involvement up until that point were immediately overruled by a surge of power that blended into his core. Sal smashed through that point and hastily guided the newfound essence through the next few points. When he hit the sixteenth, Nova interrupted his concentration.

"That's enough for now."

With his power deactivated, Sal turned to see Nova looking over at Whisper in concern. The smaller girl was sweating profusely but grinning from ear to ear.

"You did great, man. Really great." With a pained expression, Whisper untangled her legs out from under her, but the smile never left her face. "You got to sixteen! That's pretty damn impressive. How does your core feel now?"

Sal felt like her words were genuine, but their numbers were so much higher than his.

Nova withdrew her hand from his and gave him a light shove. "She's being serious. You did great for someone starting from just their core. I could already do the first twenty unconsciously, and I'm sure Whisper had something similar."

With a nod, Whisper confirmed it. "Around twenty-five for me."

Nova gave Sal a nod of approval. "Check your core! I wanna know the results of our hard work."

She gestured to herself and Whisper in quick succession, and Sal did a fast check. Without Whisper's power bolstering his own, Sal could finally appreciate the significant jump in his core's capacity. The thread fluidity was beyond anything he had before, and he felt as if he'd be able to weave skills much more effectively.

All these thoughts were purely instinctive, and he had no idea what they would be like in practice, but Sal just…inherently knew that his power had become stronger. When he surfaced out of his own skill, he saw that Whisper was much more composed than before, and Nova was still grinning at him.

The Body Manipulator laughed as she jokingly placed her hand out in front of him. "That'll be fifty Q-Cred, thank you."

Sal stared at her hand before he looked over at Whisper. "That rate work for you too?"

The smaller girl smiled. "When I tried amping up your ability, I think I went to the wrong one. Do you have two?"

Sal debated on whether he should admit to it or not, but she had essentially powered him through a huge blocker, so the least he could do was repay her with honesty. "Yeah, I created a new skill with my Replication ability. I'm not supposed to tell people about it, though, so please keep it to yourself."

Nova's hand stretched out a little farther. "Looks like the rate just went up to seventy-five Q-Cred, thank you." She laughed at her own joke before a thought struck her. "Are you the guy who exploded the Skill Registration machine?"

Whisper's eyes widened. "You imprinted the new skill, didn't you?!"

Sal raised his hands defensively as he grinned. "Okay, in my defense, I didn't know it would explode!"

Nova's burst of laughter caused more than a few people to shush her audibly. She granted them a withering look before turning back to Sal.

"So that means you didn't get to see me kicking the crap out of that guy?" When Sal shook his head with a laugh, Nova waved it away like it was nothing. "Don't worry, you'll get to see round two eventually." Her eyes locked onto the guy in the row behind him, and he did his best to keep his eyes on the diagram on screen.

***

Lombardi moved to the essence refinement side of the room with an expectant look on his face. "Good news is that we might have a few students ready to join this side of the class. As I just explained to them, we'll be using part of our weekly classes for this exercise throughout the semester. There will be more practical and individual training as we progress, but for now, we want you to reach your natural limits. I've sent the diagram to each of you, so you'll be able to work on your own progression in your downtime in the evenings. I cannot stress enough how vital this development is for your success in the future. It's either pay now or pay later! You don't want to see your friends cut down on the battlefield because you ran out of essence."

It was a sobering thought that slashed through the self-satisfied expressions that many of the students wore. Lombardi gestured at the diagram behind him. "Who couldn't get past the first ten?" He looked across the room and nodded at the large number of hands in the air.

"Don't despair. It just means that you have a longer road than the others…but it also means that your ceiling is much higher. The outputs that you have right now will drastically improve as you develop your core. Everything you know about your current skill is going to be meaningless as you progress, because with time, it will evolve into a higher form."

Lombardi pointed to another area of the diagram. "Who couldn't get past twenty? Okay, this is good. It means that you have a lot of growth potential, but that your core is accustomed to your body. This isn't a limiting factor and is the place where most new students find themselves when they enter Quest Academy. With guidance and effort, you'll be able to unlock more regions for your cores and you'll have a drastic uptick in capability."

Before continuing to the next point on the diagram, Lombardi paced in front of the group. "These points should be seen as gates that are preventing you from reaching your full potential. As you step through those doors, you're strengthening your internal core with more capacity and freedom to roam throughout your body. Those gates will act as small batteries that continue to charge and store essence for your abilities. Some of them will be much tougher to break through, and it won't always be the same number for everyone. What is important, though, is that you continue to pass through them as far as you can go, never stopping or growing complacent. Our hope for all of you is that by the end of this semester, you'll have passed the thirtieth gate."

Lombardi raised his hands before the students had time to react. Many of them had expressions of disbelief on their faces; all signs of smugness had evaporated from the room. "Your grade in this class will be individual, and on your own level of development. Those who pass the thirtieth gate will pass this class. That is the minimum expected of you, and anything lower than that will be deemed a fail. Now, what happens if you get past the fortieth and beyond? Well, that's when we start talking about your chances for the Savior class. You all undoubtedly heard about skill imprinting and skill implanting? All of that happens in this class, and there's a very special reason for that. Your core won't be able to handle a new skill unless it has passed a certain threshold. If you were to try it, you'd likely shatter your entire core and you'd need to rebuild it through painful refinement until it was ready to begin the process all over again."

Nova and Whisper turned to look at Sal, who had suddenly gone very pale.

Lombardi glanced in their direction for a moment before turning back to the class. "To be eligible for skill imprinting, you would need to be past the thirtieth gate. For skill implanting, you'd need over the sixtieth. We did have an interesting case, though, where a Replicator simulated a skill implant during an imprinting process, but the artificial core rejected it and shattered. It ensured that the internal core was safe, but the imprinting machine…not so much. I only tell you this as a cautionary tale, so our very own Replicator doesn't get any ideas, okay, Salvatore?"

Lombardi gave him a wink, and Sal wanted the ground to swallow him up as he nodded in response. It told Sal that Lombardi knew about the Skill Registration, and he was keeping the secret safe.

"So, who here got past the thirtieth gate?" Lombardi asked, but only two hands rose. Whisper was one of them, but there was another individual at the back of the room with their hand raised. Lombardi pointed at them with a surprised smile. "Could you introduce yourself and maybe tell us your category?"

"Evan McGregor. Energy Manipulation category, and I can use Teleport." It was a curt answer. Evan propped their chin up lazily with a palm.

Lombardi's smile grew wider. "Can I ask you if you intend on using your abilities for fighting demons?"

With zero hesitation, Evan shrugged. "That's why we're all here, isn't it?"

Lombardi's smile widened into a grin. "Yes, it is. I'd like to speak with you after class with the others."

CHAPTER 54:
STAKES

Lombardi kept them over time, which took a chunk out of their lunch hour, but nobody really took notice. As they poured out of the classroom, Sal could see the excited faces of students comparing their experiences. Once the barrier had come down and class had ended, the cliques and groups had reformed. Sal was rejoined by a frustrated Divinity, while Whisper and Nova disappeared to go to the canteen ahead of the crowd. It didn't take a genius to figure out why she was frustrated.

"Were you able to get a handle on essence control with Lombardi's help?" Sal asked tentatively, ready to drop the subject at a moment's notice.

A small shake of her head was answer enough, and Sal found it hard to believe that someone as capable as Divinity was struggling. That said, without the help of Nova and Whisper, he would have been at the very bottom of the group in terms of essence refinement. In an attempt to brainstorm a solution, Sal asked whether she had looked into the future to find a training that worked for her, but to his surprise, it resulted in a glare from her.

"Not everything can be solved by looking into the future, Sal. I won't learn a thing if I keep using my powers to skip ahead." Her words were barbed, and it was only a moment after they left her lips that her tone softened, and she closed her eyes. "Sorry, Sal. I'm frustrated with myself, not with you."

Sal wasn't offended in the slightest. "Well, I hit a wall the moment I tried to refine my essence. Whisper and Nova helped me push through the first few gates. Amplification and Body Manipulation—they're a real killer combination. So, I guess you could say that I'm still skipping ahead by using other people's powers?" He laughed with a shrug, but Divinity gave him a reproachful look.

"That's not what I meant, Sal. I won't learn any form of mental resilience if I'm never challenged, and I'll become complacent if I keep relying on my powers to see the future. What happens if I'm put into a situation where I can't use them, and I'm just regular Divinity? You heard Lombardi—we can either pay now with effort…or pay later on the battlefield. I don't want to risk the lives of anyone because I skipped ahead during training." Divinity's tone was firm, and Sal had no intention of arguing with her.

As they made their way to the canteen, Sal wanted to lighten the tone but didn't exactly know how. Divinity was still visibly annoyed by her own performance, and Sal knew that any attempt from him to reason with her would fail miserably. They continued in silence and separated at the queue with a slight nod.

Dave was waving at him from the other side of the canteen, and he reluctantly waved back. After a few moments, Sal had managed to shuffle halfway down the serving area where one of the attendants looked at Sal wearily.

Without saying a word, the attendant reached for the steak and put it on a plate for him with a resigned sigh. "Please try something else in the future."

Sal laughed as they went through their now daily ritual. The next serving area gave him a bowl of steamed vegetables and then he went to the drinks dispenser, where he settled for sparkling water.

By the time he had emerged from the queue, he could see that Dave had moved seats and was now sitting with a small group. Sal wondered whether this was a sign that he could sit somewhere else, when Dave turned and waved at him again, motioning for him to come over. Letting out a breath, Sal made his way over to the table. While he looked around, he saw Divinity sitting with a few others, and she was pretty absorbed in her own meal. Sal made a mental note to check in with her later.

"Sal!" Dave's voice sounded out. Despite the fact they could both see each other, and he was already heading over to him, Dave somehow felt the need to announce his arrival. Dave pointed directly across the table to one of the people across from him.

"This is Evan! Thought they were a chick, but apparently…they're a 'them.' Wait, that sounds wrong?"

Sal frowned as he tried to recall who they were when it suddenly struck him. "You can use Teleport?"

Evan nodded and continued to eat their bowl of steamed vegetables. It was abundantly clear from their body language that they had not invited Dave over for a conversation.

Dave turned to Sal with a questioning expression. "Well, what do you think? Would you have said they were a guy or a girl?"

Sal just stared at him in utter disbelief, but Evan surprisingly came to Dave's rescue.

"It's fine. I'm nonbinary. It's no big deal. Just don't want to be gendered. If you're referring to me, just use they or them." And then with a smile, Evan picked up their tray and gave them a nod. "Thanks." With that, both Evan and the tray teleported to the opposite side of the canteen.

Dave shook his head as he watched Evan leave the canteen. "Man, I think you spooked them. You need to brush up on your social skills."

***

Professor Rust waited for the red light above the door to fade before he spoke. "Looks like everyone learned their lesson from last time. We won't be doing any extra drills for latecomers today!"

A collective sigh of relief washed over the crowd, but Rust wasn't going to let them relax too much. "You've fought each other with powers, and you've fought each other without them. Other than me assessing your capabilities, the reason we did those two exercises first was so you could witness each other's strengths and weaknesses. All those reports you made will come in very handy for the next assignment, which will be taking place at the end of the month."

A virtual screen appeared on each side of the cube so that the surrounding class could see it displayed clearly. It was the list of rankings for the Silver cohort. "In the interest of fairness, we've decided that the best way to test the top rankers…is to give them a challenging scenario. On the other hand, we think that it's only fair to give the bottom ranks a chance too. You can currently see the rankings as they are."

1. Divinity Khan
2. Salvatore Argento
3. Dominic Walters
4. Lucia Hernandez
5. Christopher Gage
6. Evan McGregor
7. Victoria Chase
8. Michael Welling
9. Xander Michaels
10. Zachary Lowe

Sal noticed Nova staring at him from across the room. She held two fingers out with one hand and pointed at the screen with the other, as though asking whether he was really the number two. Her disbelief was a nice little boost to his ego, so he just smiled back and held up four fingers and did his best to look impressed. It seemed to placate Nova, who grinned back at him before turning to listen to Rust.

He was pacing around the cube as he continued to explain their reasoning behind the end-of-month event. "...As Heroes! But to do that, you need to learn how to work as part of a team. We don't send out individuals to take care of threats; we send out squads that complement each other's capabilities. For the last week, I wanted you all to see each other with and without powers. You likely have a few ideas of what synergies might work between powers, or maybe you identified a winning strategy? Don't worry if you did neither, because you're not expected to create teams until this Thursday." Rust elevated his voice to be heard over the chattering that had broken out from some of the group.

"Each of you will be part of a five-person team. You will have a team captain who will act as an impromptu Controller for this exercise. Captains will be assessed on their leadership capability as well as the performance of their team. We'll also be looking at individual contributions on each team. All the captains have been decided in advance, which will be the top ten and the bottom ten of your cohort," Rust explained slowly and Sal could see some unrest from the middle ranks, who obviously felt like they were being punished for no reason.

"Maybe this next part will cheer you up! Each captain will select four people from the cohort to join their team, but we will be starting from the bottom. Which means that Divinity Khan, as the current top ranked in the cohort…will have whatever four people remain from the selection as her team. Salvatore will have second-last pick. Dominic will have third last, and so on."

91. Trent Golde
92. Whisper Ding
93. Con LaFleur
94. Marta Virgo
95. Borja Diez
96. Sanna Sinervo
97. Jenni Stravos
98. Crypto Daniels
99. Harold Gunn
100. Gerard Kilsee

Rust gestured at the screen, which now reflected the changes. "So, to make it very clear…Gerard from the bottom of your cohort will have the first pick. After he selects his best four, then it will be Harold's turn and then onto Crypto, and then Jenni. This will go all the way until Divinity takes the remaining four people."

Just as he had predicted, the entire class looked shocked by the format of the team selection. Those in the bottom ranks looked absolutely elated, while the vast majority of the top ten looked somewhere between disgruntled and pissed off.

Waving his hand to get their attention again, Rust started to explain the best approach to the end-of-month event. "Research each of your top picks and talk to them over the coming days. This will be a test of your scouting capabilities too, as you'll need to determine who is useful for your squad. Having a team of heavy hitters sounds well and good, but what about Defense? Mobility? Healing? All factors that should be considered, so make sure to read all the Combat reports that you submitted last week!"

Sal looked over at Divinity, who stared at the list with a passive expression on her face. He didn't know how to feel about it because he intended to drop the Combat module as soon as the first semester ended. This wasn't a class he wanted to excel in, so he didn't mind having a less than incredible grade for it.

However, for people like Nova and Divinity, who wanted to get into the Savior class…this was likely a pretty horrible setback. Sal glanced across the room to where Nova stood. Her situation wasn't as bad, as she was able to pick from a pool of sixteen people. Despite that silver lining, she looked furious and stared daggers at Rust.

Almost as though he sensed the challenge, he turned and added yet another revelation. "Your performance in the end-of-month battle will directly determine your rankings in the cohort and will also affect your overall standing. We'll be having a rank reshuffle at month end, so make sure you put in your best effort!" Rust's smile didn't reach his eyes, and all but ten people in that room hated him more than anyone else.

Sal turned to see Fuck-Face, the guy from the bathrooms on his first day. Turned out his name was Gerard, and because of Sal's actions, he was put into second-last place in the entire academy. Only the attacker from the bathroom was a rank lower. Sal shook his head at the way the cards had worked in Gerard's favor. He was getting the first pick from the entire class.

The shit-eating grin on his face was a stark contrast from the looks of disdain that Sal was accustomed to getting from him. One nice thing about it, though, was that Whisper was going to be getting the ninth pick, so it wasn't too bad in Sal's opinion. His eyes flicked back to Divinity, who still stared up at the screen. He'd need to have a chat with her about it, to see if they could come up with a strategy, where she could take the best people from the final eight and he'd take the people she didn't want.

Rust winced ever so slightly as he looked back at the class. "Now, I know that some of you here aren't enthused about combat…or maybe you're only here because this module is compulsory for the first semester? There are a lot of Support class in here, and I'd like to stress the importance of this end-of-month event. You will all fight each other, and the top six teams will go head-to-head against the other cohorts. The bottom six teams will be placed into an elimination battle with the other cohorts." Rust looked at each of the students as he spoke.

"Historically, the bottom teams from this exercise failed to make it past the first semester. You all need to remember that this class is mandatory because you're learning the basics of how to work together. If you're unable to form any sense of cohesion with your group after countless fights with them, then it's likely that you're not a fit for this academy. If you learn to work together, but your composition is bad…then that's a different conversation. What I want you to focus on now are the reports from the previous week. You may discuss them among yourselves and exchange information if you wish. I'll be around to answer any questions you may have, but we'll be starting properly from Thursday, when the selections are being made."

With that, Rust finished up and gave the class permission to talk among themselves. The twenty captains were feeling a rollercoaster of emotions as some were elated beyond measure, and others were stuck feeling sorry for themselves. A few jeers were directed at the top ten from the bottom, but Sal couldn't pinpoint which voice said it.

"Q-Cred can't buy you a good team!"

A few laughs came through the crowd before another insult was thrown in. "Maybe you should have run a little slower in that race?"

This went on for a while, and Rust made no effort to stop it. Some insults were about assumed wealth, while others targeted their looks…with some crude language thrown in about how they could entice team members to join their group. Nova had to be restrained from attacking them there and then.

When Divinity appeared beside him, Sal gave her a smile. "Sorry about earlier."

Instead of answering immediately, she shook her head and stared at the bottom ten from the cohort. "No need to apologize. You didn't do anything wrong. I'm going to try my best at the Skill class, using only my mind and body. But for this class? I'm going to use everything at my disposal to destroy them." She gave the hecklers a murderous glance that just resulted in more mocking laughter. When Divinity turned to Sal, she had a serious look on her face. "I'll need your help, though."

Sal didn't even hesitate as he gave her his answer. His eyes were locked onto the sneering face of Gerard. "Absolutely. Whatever you need."

CHAPTER 55:
TEAM COMBAT

"EXCELLENT QUESTION! FOR THOSE OF YOU WHO DIDN'T HEAR IT, WE'VE JUST been asked about the ideal team composition. This will be particularly relevant to the first teams when picking as there is more opportunity to create a balanced team. First is the team captain. As we're looking for leadership qualities, it would make sense for them to act as the Controller of the team. Think of them as the shot-caller who is watching everything develop on the battlefield and adapting accordingly. Leaders need to know the strengths and weaknesses of their team to bring out their potential," Rust explained as he walked around the deactivated cube in the center of the room.

"Next, you'll need a good Offense type! This will be your attack power and the person responsible for dispatching your opponents. They need to be used strategically so they don't tire out. Make sure to use them tactically, rather than relying on them to win by themselves! You'll need a Defense type to protect your team. This could be a person who blocks the enemy attacker, or it could be someone who shields your leader. For early-stage combat, it's normal for teams to prioritize attacking and defensive capabilities, so the ideal teams right now would be a mixture of attack and defense. As your capabilities develop, it's worth having a Support-class character who can provide backup support, enhanced mobility, tactical information, or maybe even better equipment!"

Rust looked around the room with a slight smile. "We have a lot of Support-class types in this cohort, and that can be either a strength or a weakness depending on the effectiveness of the leader. We'll be taking team composition into account when we're grading your capabilities, so it could be worth extra points for your team to include one or two Supports on your team. So, you have a Controller, Offense, Defense, and Support. The last category is highly uncommon but usually vital for success, which is Healing! If you can grab a Healer for your team, you'll have a much higher success rate as your capabilities will be pushed beyond your normal limits."

Many of the students nodded in understanding, but the top ranked in the cohort still looked conflicted.

Rust smiled as he looked at where they had gathered on one side of the room. "In the interest of fairness, we'll be more lenient on team composition for the last leaders making their selections. The difficulty spike will be very real, and we want to test your strategic capabilities. Commanders out on the battlefield don't always get to choose who they're leading, so this will be a great exercise for each of you!"

Divinity raised her hand, and Rust gestured at her to continue. "Yes, Divinity?"

All eyes turned to look at her.

"You mentioned that Support class can create better equipment. Are we allowed to use armor and weapons?"

An excited murmur of conversation washed through the students, and Rust chuckled.

"Absolutely! We encourage all teams to equip themselves to the best of their ability. This is a key area where Support classes can show their value and capability as a team member. There are limitations, though, where you need to register your equipment before any fights, so we can create countermeasures for anything that would normally be fatal. Your fights will be at the end of the month, so you'll have a better understanding of your team's needs with each match. You should acquire equipment that covers your weaknesses and builds on your strengths."

Sal had a follow-up question and raised his hand, but Rust moved to a different raised hand. "Just a moment, Salvatore. Yes, Mr. Kilsee?"

Sal turned to see Fuck-Face grinning broadly on the other side of the room.

"What are the stakes? Is there a prize for coming first? Will we get some Q-Cred?"

It was a good question, and Rust laughed.

"The lecturer part of me wants to tell you that the true prize is what you learn from this, but the Hero in me knows what you want to hear. Each match will be held in an offsite location, where we will be inviting a number of guild scouts to watch. This is an incredible opportunity to showcase your abilities and get on their radar, but I'll add the caveat that most of the top-tier guilds don't attend until the later stages of the competition. There will be Q-Cred prizes for the six teams that progress to the inter-cohort part of the competition. That's when the top six teams from this cohort will fight against the top six teams from the other nine cohorts."

Rust paused as though he was deliberating on his next words. Eventually, after a few moments of silence, he continued. "We don't normally talk about relegation at the early stages, but as I mentioned…the top six teams out of the twenty will progress to the inter-cohort competition. The next eight teams will compete to stay in the safety net, which won't result in any form of penalties." Rust tried his best to look reassuring as he continued. "The last six teams will fight against relegation. Relegated teams will be deemed as a fail in the Combat class and it will be a negative mark on your final results for the semester."

Before the class could fully come to terms with what Rust had said, the lecturer turned quickly and pointed at Sal. "You had a question, Mr. Argento."

Even though Sal was still somewhat reeling, he managed to get his question out. "Are there any equipment caps? Like, can we use all grades of equipment in our team matches?" A few mocking laughs echoed out and Sal didn't need to look to know it came from the lowest-ranked students.

Before Rust had a chance to answer, Fuck-Face piped up. "Feel free to spend all your Q-Cred. It won't change the result!"

Rust threw him a disapproving glance but made no effort to interrupt the taunting. Rust sighed and shook his head before turning back to Sal.

"You can use any grade of equipment as long as it passes our registration requirements. If something is deemed too dangerous for competition, then we'll notify you in advance that it cannot be used. We haven't had an instance before where this has happened, but it's unlikely to be an issue. Most of our second-

and third-year Crafting students who take commissions specialize in creating armors and uniform upgrades. If you are intending on spending your Q-Cred, please ensure that you know what you're paying for and how long it will take. Competitions tend to fill up their order queues, so reserving a spot with them might be tricky!"

Rust continued to answer questions from students but encouraged them to use their terminals to begin researching the abilities of their peers. Divinity looked extremely conflicted, and Sal asked her whether she was okay.

With a weary sigh, she shook her head. "I want nothing more than to look into the future to get more context, but I'm too exhausted after that damn Skill class with Lombardi. I won't be able to do it until later."

Her frustration was written all over her face, and Sal wanted to reassure her that everything would be okay, but he felt the exact same tension. Divinity eventually smiled and shook her head, as though she were physically able to dispel the fogginess. Her grin was almost mocking.

"After that vision with the Doom Society, I tried to take a break from looking into the future. I didn't want to fall into a rabbit hole of potential outcomes, so I didn't look at anything we'd learn today. What a day to come in blind!"

Sal laughed and gave her a reassuring smile. "Welcome to how literally everyone else lives! Exciting and terrifying, isn't it?"

Divinity's smile was real as she nodded. "It's a genuine wonder how you've survived so long!"

"Mr. Argento?" Rust's voice called over the chatting students, which pulled everyone's attention to where he now stood at the entrance of the classroom. Vanessa stood beside him, smiling confidently as every set of eyes locked onto her. Rust gestured for him to come and join them. "You can take your things with you and finish up early today."

Divinity cast a curious look at Vanessa but smiled as she told Sal they'd catch up later.

As Sal made his way toward the door, he felt a lot of incredulous stares boring into the back of his head.

Vanessa looked at the students as Sal approached and her face broke into a knowing smile. Before Sal could react, Vanessa stepped in close to him and raised her lips to his ear.

Everyone watched as she took Sal's hand in her own and whispered something into his ear. When she stepped back a moment later, she was biting her lip. Rust cleared his throat as Vanessa pulled at Sal's hand and led him out of the class. She shot the lecturer a grateful smile and winked, and Rust just watched them leave together in disbelief.

"Lucky son of a bitch." He chuckled before clapping loudly. "Less ogling and more researching! You only have a few days before the first pick!" Rust admonished the students who stared at the place that Vanessa and Sal had just occupied.

***

Vanessa's hand gripped Sal's tighter as they left the classroom. When they were clear, she let go of his hand and rounded on him with a wide grin on her face.

"We have some good news and some bad news, so which would you like first?" She continued to walk backward as she spoke to him, the clicking of her high heels the only sound in the empty corridor.

Sal wanted to know what was so urgent that he had to be pulled out from class, but he humored her for the moment. "Let's start with the bad news."

With a nod, Vanessa turned around and slowed her pace so that she could walk beside him. "The bad news is that Villa wants a word with you. She arrived for a surprise visit and is currently being attended to in one of our private meeting rooms on the Credit floor. From what I've heard, it sounds like they've got an urgent mission, and Watcher needs his rifle back early."

Sal blinked at those words; not sure he heard them correctly. "That's the bad news?"

Vanessa winced ever so slightly. "Well, maybe it's bad news for Myth. But the good news is for Sal. She wants to thank you personally for the extraordinary Appraisal work you've done. I think the Reavers Guild might have prepared a little present for you as thanks."

Sal was pleasantly surprised and couldn't help but laugh at the situation. He was going to see Villa's expression when he showed her the Legendary sniper rifle.

With a surge of curiosity, Sal turned to Vanessa. "Did you tell her about the rifle?"

Vanessa must have confused his curiosity with panic, as she turned to him with a sympathetic expression. "Don't worry, I've told her that repairs can take a substantial amount of time and that she should lower her expectations. Even if you're able to just reassemble it back to the state it arrived in, then we'll likely be able to frame that as a win. Villa is aware that Myth is untested, and although she might be disappointed that you introduced 'Myth' to the guild, your work as an Appraiser has cemented you as one of their top performers." Vanessa placed a comforting hand on his shoulder as she spoke. "Let me do the talking when it comes to the rifle, okay?"

Sal grinned as they made their way toward the workshop.

After a few moments of silence, Vanessa's voice took on a teasing tone. "Imagine my surprise when Greg told me about the tip I got from our new favorite Appraiser? I hope you don't think you can buy my affection…"

Her playful tone, coupled with the mock indignation, caused Sal to laugh.

Vanessa lowered her voice and smiled. "It was really sweet, Sal. Thank you for that."

When he turned to look at her, he was surprised to see an earnest and grateful expression, which caused his heart to pound. With what he hoped was a nonchalant shrug, he told her not to worry about it.

They exited the tower lobby and switched to the tower that housed the workshop. There was nobody around the amphitheater, and Sal assumed that all the students were in their classes. An idea suddenly struck him, and he smiled at the thought.

"Vanessa, would you mind waiting for me up at the Credit floor? I want to pack up the sniper rifle before bringing it up. I have some of the cases from the Appraisal work down in the workshop that I can use."

With a slight frown, she turned to him. "Are you sure? I can get one of the floor staff to pick it up. I'd rather we didn't keep Villa waiting for too long. She has a bit of a…short fuse."

Sal nodded. "I'm sure. I just need a few moments to pack things up and make it presentable."

Vanessa reluctantly nodded as she spread her hands. "I'm not disappointed, so don't start doubting yourself, okay? Is it in a functional state? Would another Crafter be able to get it up and running?"

Sal pretended to consider the question before eventually nodding. "Yes, it's functional. It's just not the best it could be at the moment. I think with more time, it'll be something amazing."

Vanessa smiled and gave him a playful nudge with her elbow. "That's the spirit! You're working as Sal and Myth, and you've already done the impossible with all that Appraisal work. You should be proud of yourself, so don't let anyone take that achievement away from you. Okay?"

Sal felt a twinge of guilt for withholding the truth from her. It was going to be worth it, though, and it took all the effort he could muster to stop himself from grinning like an idiot.

"I'll leave you here and meet you up on the Credit floor!" Vanessa touched his arm.

She turned as she walked toward the elevator, and Sal stared at her swaying hips as she left.

Sal moved to the private room where the Legendary sniper rifle was waiting to be packed up. He really couldn't decide what he was more excited about. Was it Vanessa's reaction…or Villa's?

CHAPTER 56:
REVEAL

GREG WOULDN'T TAKE NO FOR AN ANSWER, AND SAL ENDED UP FOLLOWING THE Credit floor attendant, who carried the case containing the sniper rifle.

"You probably haven't seen it yet, but the private room they've set up in is like a mansion. You're going to absolutely love it!" Greg spoke over his shoulder with a grin as he led the way down the corridor.

The atmosphere on the Credit floor had pretty much changed overnight, with the air of indifference vanishing and being replaced by warm smiles everywhere Sal looked. It was the power of a generous tip, which had clearly spread through the employees like a portal break. Sal smiled back at Greg; he was looking forward to seeing it. They continued to walk for a few moments before entering a private elevator. Greg made small talk as they were lifted to the next part of the Credit floor. To say it was different from the former was quite an understatement.

Lavish. It was the only word that Sal could conjure up to describe the place. Everything screamed wealth. And the only thing that told him that he was still on the Credit floor was that the attendants all wore the same black uniforms, albeit, they had silver markings etched on their sleeves…likely denoting their higher rank within the Credit floor hierarchy. A few inquisitive looks were directed at Sal, and a few disapproving glances were aimed at Greg.

Sal finally understood Greg's eagerness to come up to the floor with him and decided to run with it. "Lead the way, Greg!"

With a grin, the attendant happily obliged as they stepped toward one of the private meeting rooms. It had an ornate black door with golden trim. A single placard was placed on the face of the door, reading "VIP." Greg repositioned the case under his arm as he dutifully knocked on the door. When it opened, Vanessa appeared and gave Greg a curt nod before moving to one side. Sal entered the room, but rather than letting Greg follow, Vanessa took the case from him and closed the door in his face with a smirk. Sal caught a glimpse of his dismayed reaction but couldn't feel too bad for the guy.

One side of the room was a fully stocked bar with an attendant on duty. There were a few ornate tables surrounded by plush leather chairs, but Villa had chosen to recline in one of the large couches on the other side of the room. A dagger fell from where it was embedded into the ceiling, and without any apparent effort, Villa caught it between her fingers and flung it back upward. The dagger sliced through the air and thudded into its previous position. With a lazy glance, she turned her head to see Sal and Vanessa approaching. A predatory grin crossed her face as she clicked her fingers, making the dagger disappear.

Before either Sal or Vanessa could say a word, Villa was on her feet and looking toward the door. "Where's the fucker who wrecked Watcher's rifle? I asked you to bring him to me."

Sal felt the intense aura that had previously drowned him in pressure and dread, but it felt different now. With a quick glance, he realized that Villa was targeting Vanessa with the ability, but Vanessa didn't falter in the slightest. A few moments passed with Villa staring down Vanessa, but she didn't back down.

In a flash, Villa's face broke into a grin. "This is why you're my favorite."

Vanessa smiled at the compliment but didn't make any further remark.

"Long time no see, Mr. Argento. You've certainly been busy!" Villa grinned at Sal, and he felt an uncontrollable need to shudder. "I warned you that I was taking a risk by giving you that Silver token, but you earned it. I hope you'll continue to prioritize our work."

Sal had to take a moment. Even though she was still imposing, Villa was complimenting him on his work. With a practiced smile, Sal bowed a little.

"Thank you for the kind words. I look forward to working with you more in the future too." Then, in a moment of boldness, Sal decided to test their relationship. "I'm hoping to expand my Appraisal service to other guilds but will always remember how you took a chance on me and helped me become established in the space."

Vanessa's back straightened ever so slightly, and Villa cocked an eyebrow as her smile widened. "Well, would you look at that? Our little cub is growing some fangs! How do you see this ruse playing out?"

Sal kept his eyes locked on Villa as he returned her smile. "I'll be sure to let you know if another guild offers me an exclusive contract. I just need to ensure I've a stable income stream while I'm enrolled here."

Villa shook her head slightly, the smile not leaving her face. "Be very careful, little Argento. You're good, but you're not yet in a position to make demands. Choose your next words carefully."

Vanessa looked over at Sal, but he didn't turn to face her. His eyes were still on Villa. "Sincere apologies if I sounded like I was making demands of the Reavers Guild. I'm just establishing my own worth. You've seen my Appraisals so far, and you know the quality and speed that I deliver. That is my value proposition right now. If another guild offered me work, how should I differentiate it from the work you give me? All item grades offer the same fees, so I'd naturally prioritize what will earn me the most money. It's nothing personal, just logic."

Villa tilted her head ever so slightly to the right as she looked at Sal. "You want preferential rates? When there are no other guilds sniffing at your doorstep? Are you willing to risk the work you have on your plate right now, for something that might not exist?" Villa countered as she took a step closer to him. "What makes you so sure that they'll want you?"

Sal didn't waver at all as he spoke. "As I said, I will work on projects that earn me the most. Yes, that could be from other guilds, or it could be working with Myth."

Vanessa coughed, which brought the attention of both Villa and Sal toward her. With a placating smile, she moved in to attempt damage control. Her eyes were telling Sal to stop what he was doing, but Villa raised her hand to stop Vanessa from interjecting.

"No. Let the little Argento dig his own grave. He wants to bet on an unknown Crafter rather than our tier-two guild. Or is it that you want to increase your rates because maybe, sometime in the future, another guild might want to work with you? Is that right?" Villa's expression was neutral, but her words were venomous.

When she cast her glance back to Sal, he felt a surge of panic and he tried to wrestle it under control. After a moment of composing himself, he continued as best as he could. "An unknown Crafter? Did Vanessa not tell you?" Sal looked over at Vanessa in confusion, and she looked to be keeping her composure despite being completely blindsided.

Villa rounded on Vanessa with crossed arms. "What is it that Vanessa…didn't tell me?"

Sal shook his head as he lifted the case up to the table. Clicking it open, he lifted the lid to reveal the gleaming Legendary sniper rifle. With no hesitation, he propped it up on the table and placed the case back on the ground. Both Villa and Vanessa gaped at it, but Sal didn't give them any time to process what was happening.

"Original state was a flawed once-Epic-grade sniper rifle with a rating of Upper Rare grade. Currently, it has been upgraded and refitted to be a Legendary-grade sniper rifle, with an evolutionary trait that will guarantee its evolution to the first known Mythic-grade crafted weapon. It can fire essence-tethered bullets in a range of firing modes, with every shot being a guaranteed critical hit and dealing massive damage. Scope allows for target tracking and homing bullets. The barrel is self-cleaning and has been elongated to increase the range to just under five thousand meters. No essence absorption required, so the user won't become fatigued through use. Everything is documented in this Appraisal, which I did for free, as a thank-you for the chance you gave me."

Sal handed over the Appraisal documents, and Villa could do nothing but accept them numbly, her eyes not budging from the sniper rifle on the table. Vanessa was clearly trying to compose herself, but she was in just as much shock as the vice-captain of the Reavers Guild.

Name	Maslow's Legacy Sniper Rifle
Origin	Crafted
Age	New (Reworked)
Grade	Legendary
Dimensions	62 inches | 27 lbs.
Materials	Refined Mythcraft Essence | Premium Infused Gunmetal Alloy | Ether Crystal

Attributes	**Tether**: Shots will tether the rifle to its prey, siphoning off essence over time. **Hunt**: Shots have a certain chance to home in on locked targets. **Headshot**: Shots will have a certain chance to apply critical damage when vitals are hit. **Cleanse**: Rifle uses a portion of siphoned essence to clean and repair itself. **Recharge**: Rifle uses a portion of siphoned essence to amplify shot damage. **Grounded**: Rifle negates distance penalties and gives a drastic boost to range. **Evolution**: Rifle will gather essence from kills and evolve into Mythic Grade over time.
Abilities	Tether | Hunt | Cleanse | Headshot | Recharge | Grounded
Power Source	External Essence
Evolution	Yes | 0% to Mythic Grade
Quality	Perfect
Condition	100%
Value	Est. $215,000.00 – $750,000.00

"Fuck." Vanessa finally breathed as she looked at Sal in complete disbelief.

Sal stared at Villa, who gaped at the Appraisal document. The first rule of negotiation was to never accept the first offer, so Sal kept his mouth shut. He wanted to say more, but he had more power by remaining silent. Villa would need to come to him for this one, and without Myth in the room…she could only negotiate through Sal and Vanessa. With a passing glance at Vanessa, Sal felt his heartbeat elevate erratically as he decided to add in one more thing. Just to make his stance clear.

"Vanessa told Myth to try his best, and he's apparently smitten with her…so you have her to thank for him going all out on this." Sal gestured at the Legendary sniper rifle with a smile.

Villa's eyes snapped up to regard Vanessa. "Bring him here. I need to speak with him immediately."

For the first time, Sal saw uncertainty on Villa's face. The cogs were clearly turning in her head as she realized how incredible this item was, and how pivotal Myth was going to be in the future.

Vanessa, now fully in the loop, pressed Villa. "Unfortunately, I can't do that, on orders of the headmaster. As you can likely appreciate, we can't endanger a student with such an incredible skill. I'm not sure if you're conscious of it, with how powerful you are, but your threatening aura would likely hurt him gravely. We can't take that risk, so he's not going to be meeting with any of the guilds." Vanessa smiled sweetly and Villa, instead of answering, turned her head back to the Appraisal sheet with a frown.

Without glancing up, she spoke. "And you Appraised this? A Legendary grade?"

Sal nodded as he gestured to a few points on the rifle. "You can see here that Myth credited some of the Crafters who helped him in the process. He also signed his name but left the engraving of Watcher's father. Those details are listed on the next page. I thought it worth mentioning because Myth is still learning his craft. He wasn't happy with the final product, but…you didn't give him a lot of time. Who knows what he could make with enough time and resources?"

Vanessa gestured to Sal to slow down, and he nodded in understanding. Silence enveloped the room, but Vanessa's smile kept Sal from panicking. It was one of the most stressful and exciting moments in his life, and he just wanted to know what was going to happen next.

He couldn't fathom how Vanessa maintained her composure in such a stressful situation, but she was as steady as a rock. Her smile should have been gloating, but it was still a picture of politeness. She was a professional at this.

Eventually, after what was a torturous silence, Villa threw down the Appraisal sheet and placed her hands on the edges of the table, staring intently at the Legendary-grade rifle. "I can't verify any of this…and I can't think of a single Appraiser who can tell me if you're bullshitting me. The only one I have is related to you, so that's off the table." Villa sighed as she twisted her neck to one side, eliciting a series of cracking noises.

With another moment or two of thought, she reached into her pocket and withdrew a small earpiece, which she tapped twice before placing it into her ear. Villa looked off to one side as she started to speak. "No…shut up. Just listen. Get Blink to bring Watcher to the VIP room at the academy. Stop asking questions and just do it."

Taking the device out of her ear, Villa threw it onto the table with a grimace. When she looked up at both Sal and Vanessa, she had a conflicted expression on her face. "Watcher is going to test this rifle. If it verifies even half of this shit…" She gestured at the Appraisal document in front of her. "Then we can talk about your partnership with the Reavers Guild and how we can best work with Myth going forward."

Vanessa gave Sal a meaningful look, but he just nodded. He knew that the rifle would perform exactly as specified. That was enough for Vanessa, who turned back to Villa with a smile. "This is exciting, isn't it? A Legendary Appraiser and a Mythcrafter who love working together. Sounds like a perfect package, doesn't it?" Her silky-smooth voice held a hint of teasing that didn't escape Villa.

"Don't fucking push it."

CHAPTER 57:
VERDICT

"HOW LONG DOES IT FUCKING TAKE TO FIRE A FEW BULLETS?" VILLA COMPLAINED through gritted teeth as she flung the dagger into the various fissures in the ceiling, all of which were likely created over the course of her repeat visits to the academy.

Blink and Watcher had left a while ago, and Sal wished he could have seen more of Watcher's reaction to the weapon. But Villa's mood didn't allow for any small talk. Vanessa seemed to be the only person in the room at complete ease as she lounged on one of the seats across from Sal. For the sake of their cover, she had to pretend that she knew everything about the rifle…and she played off the fact that Myth wanted it to be a surprise for her. Villa readily accepted that Myth was wrapped around Vanessa's little finger and made a few comments about how they'd be able to use that to their advantage if the rifle turned out to be as good as they thought.

"That wasn't a rhetorical question!" Villa warned threateningly, and both Sal and Vanessa looked over at her in surprise. Much to their collective relief, she was holding her earpiece and likely talking to one of the Reavers Guild members.

"You can't be serious?" Villa sat up abruptly. "From how far?" Villa's jaw practically dropped in astonishment as she stared at Sal. It was the most uncharacteristic thing he had ever seen, and he absolutely loved it. "Tell them to come back here now!"

Villa took the earpiece out and got to her feet with a sigh. A bright smile lingered on her lips, and she walked over to the table. Both Sal and Vanessa followed her example and got to their feet too. Villa grinned at them.

"It's actually real! Watcher is currently at the top of our guild tower, firing into the closest Red Zone over three kilometers away. He's killing everything with a single shot!" She shook her head in disbelief. "The essence-tethering thing, he's able to shoot through the barrier without damaging it! How is that even possible?"

Sal shrugged as he gestured at the Appraisal document. "I just see what it can do. I can't make sense of how it works, though. I'll make sure to ask Myth in our next class together!"

Villa nodded. "Please do."

Sal was surprised at the sudden change of tone. He didn't think Villa was capable of using polite words, yet here they were. In almost a complete role reversal, Vanessa became the predator in the room.

"I wonder how long it would take for the Reavers Guild to rank up to Tier One with such an amazing weapon."

Villa sighed as she placed her face in her hands. "You're not going to let me off easy, are you? Well, we might as well start off by sweetening the deal." Turning her head, Villa gestured at a case that was propped up on one of the couches.

"This is a gift from the Reavers Guild, Sal. Out of all the items you Appraised for us, this was one we didn't need and were going to sell. Maybe Myth can fix it up into something even better." Villa then turned toward Vanessa with a meaningful look, as if to say, *I can be nice.*

Sal wondered whether it was the damaged helm that he had Appraised, but he wasn't expecting anything of that level. It was likely going to be one of the more basic pieces. His head started to go into overdrive because a lot of the stuff he had looked at was really interesting.

When he clicked open the lid, he saw the Rare-grade sword that could create long-ranged attacks. He couldn't keep the smile off his face as he thought back to what Rust had said about them being allowed weapons in the team battles. This would definitely give him a better shot at avoiding relegation. Villa's voice brought him right back to reality.

"It's just a token of our appreciation for the Appraisal work that you completed for us…"

"I'm very grateful. Thank you," Sal answered as he closed the case and returned to the table.

With a sudden burst of essence, Blink appeared in the room with Watcher's arm around her waist. In his other arm, cradled against his body, was the sniper rifle.

Villa sighed. "Finally! What's your verdict? I got some information from Blink while you were shooting, but what's your take?"

Everyone looked expectantly at Watcher, who continued to hold the rifle as if it were his child.

"It's by far the most incredible thing I've ever used. Even the stories my father told me about when it was in its prime…this weapon is beyond that. It's…beyond everything."

Villa looked at Watcher as if he were a simpleton. "Very useful. What sort of stats?"

Watcher blinked as he looked at Villa. It was as if he sobered up in an instant and had suddenly realized who he was talking to.

"Apologies, Vice-captain. Forty shots, thirty-four confirmed kills. An extra three were for range markers, and I managed to get an accurate hit at five thousand, two hundred meters. Multiple moving targets, took down mostly Leechers and a few Prowlers, all with one hit. Three shots to take down the first Hulker, and then two shots to take down the second one. It was like the gun was learning how to kill them! Before, it would take at least a dozen bullets to take one down!"

Everyone in the room stared at Watcher in complete disbelief.

Villa exhaled loudly and said what everyone was thinking. "Prowlers are a one-hit kill—that's impressive, yes…but a Hulker? In just two shots? How the fuck did you see that many? They don't just stand out in broad daylight!"

Watcher pointed to the scope at the top of the rifle. "Essence tracking! Literally can see them through walls, and the bullets rip through to hit them. Had to stop using my actual visor, as it was impeding the scope. It was showing a huge collection of them underground, which I think is probably an undiscovered dungeon." The entire time he spoke, he beamed at the rifle like a proud father gushing about their child.

Sal stared at the rifle in a whole new light, finally understanding how much of a difference it made. It was an exhilarating and terrifying thought all at the same time. The next thought that came to his mind, he said openly into the room, causing everyone to fall silent.

"What will it be like when it evolves into the Mythic-grade version?" Both Blink and Watcher looked at Sal with dumbfounded expressions. "The knife that Blink showed me, with the evolutionary trait. I told Myth about it, and he put it on the sniper rifle. With enough kills, it will evolve." Sal turned to Vanessa.

"So, technically…it's not as amazing as it could be." She smirked before turning to Villa. "So, how would you like to proceed?"

Villa waved at both Blink and Watcher, as if telling them they could leave. They nodded before waving at Sal.

Blink pointed at him meaningfully. "We're going to get loads of shit for you to Appraise, Sal!"

Watcher raised the sniper rifle in his hands. "I'll kill 'em, and she'll loot 'em!" And with that, Blink teleported, and they were gone.

Sal smiled and was happy that he got to see them again.

Villa, on the other hand, had her arms crossed as she looked directly at Vanessa. "So, which one of you is going to be playing with me? Which one gets me an in with Myth?"

Sal raised a single hand and pointed at Vanessa. "She pretty much says jump, and he's already in the air."

Vanessa smirked and gave Sal a sideways glance. "Jealousy doesn't suit you, Sal."

Looking back to Villa, she gave her a curt nod. "But it's true. Myth will do what I ask him to do…and I'm seriously considering branching out from the Credit floor to represent him full-time."

Sal gave Vanessa a surprised glance, but it was Villa who made it even more surprising.

"Makes total sense. The broker fee for a weapon like that would probably pay more than a year's wage on the Credit floor." The vice-captain of the Reavers Guild looked at Vanessa closely before continuing. "I can only imagine that you're telling me those plans so I can incorporate it into my proposal, is that right?"

Vanessa spread her hands and shrugged but didn't say a word.

Villa groaned. "Cloak-and-dagger bullshit is exhausting. Can you not just put your cards on the table? What do you want? Guild backing? Set yourself up as an affiliate with preferential rates?"

Vanessa pretended to consider the option before she gestured across at Sal. "I'm trying to think of an outcome that will give me a full-time job, while also setting up this guy and Myth for the future. Affiliate sounds good, but what if I pushed Myth into creating his own guild? Maybe a partnership would solve all our issues, and allow Myth to work independently for the highest bidder?"

Villa snorted. "He's a Crafter, and Sal is an Appraiser—you'll be stuck in Tier Five for years!" In the same moment that she dismissed the thought, a sudden realization hit her.

Vanessa finished it for her. "But if we could guarantee high-grade weapons and armor, that would attract the top Heroes. It's the long game, Villa. Right now, you can't have exclusivity on Myth. Nobody knows about him, and only the people in this room know the full extent of his Crafting capability. You can either continue as you were, sending in stuff for Appraisals and Sal will look after them…or, you can make us an offer that benefits everyone. You help them get to graduation and set them up for the future. All it would take is a bit of investment and preferential treatment from you."

As Villa bit her lip, she turned to look at Sal. "What does the little Argento think of all of this?" She crossed her arms again and looked at him expectantly.

Vanessa resumed her polite smile and waited for him to speak.

Sal shrugged. "I agree with Vanessa. I'm good at Appraisals, but I'm being assessed on my Combat abilities, survival, and field work. Getting to graduation isn't going to be easy for someone with my skills, so I need to align with powerful people who can help me along the way."

Sal tried a little bit of charm mixed with self-deprecation in the hopes that it would soften Villa's opinion of him. "You already helped me by giving me that Silver token, and all the Q-Cred I've earned is likely going to be pumped into making it through this first semester. That's why I want to work with as many people as possible to earn more. I hope I didn't come across as ungrateful, because I really appreciate all the help you've given me so far."

Sal looked at the empty space on the table where the rifle had previously rested. He felt the need to manage expectations so Villa wouldn't expect the same sort of output on a weekly basis. At the risk of lowering their leverage, he decided to address one of the biggest obstacles in their way.

"When I first Appraised the rifle, it had a few Epic-grade components already. Myth enlisted a few of the senior Crafters in the workshop to help him. There's no doubt that he has incredible potential and capability, but he's only been in the academy for a week. Whatever investment you make in him will need to come with the understanding that he's still learning his craft. I've been Appraising items since I was a kid, so I'm fine, but Myth only discovered his ability last week."

Villa stared at Sal with a dumbfounded expression. Whatever fears Sal had about lowering their leverage went out the window as Villa shook her head in disbelief.

Vanessa slid into the conversation with a smile. "Even if it was a collaborative effort, it was Myth who made the weapon. To think that he managed that with so little experience, it really does make you wonder how his skills and expertise will develop. My guess is that he'll be able to customize the traits of each individual piece, which is much more common at the earlier Crafting grades."

Vanessa changed her tone from wonder to practicality in a heartbeat. "With the right investment and guidance, Myth will undoubtedly become one of the major players in the Crafting scene. How do you see the Reavers Guild supporting him?"

Villa crossed her arms and looked down at the table before answering. When she started to speak, she looked at Sal directly. "Quest has made it very clear that the guilds can't interfere with new students or start scouting them until after the first semester. We can't give you access to any of our resources yet, but that doesn't mean we're completely useless."

With a glance at Vanessa, Villa continued. "We were offered a few slots for outings but rejected them. We're not babysitters and didn't think there would be any value in it, but now that I'm thinking…what if we were to take Sal and Myth on an outing later in the semester? Nothing too dangerous, just an opportunity to train them up a bit? Maybe take a few other top-ranked kids to make it look natural. It would boost their chances of getting through the Survival, Field, and Combat classes, and we could give them a few pieces of kit to help fast-track them?"

Vanessa shook her head. "I don't want to risk Myth in an outing, so we could probably keep him exempt from anything that might hurt him. Sal, on the other hand, would probably benefit quite a bit from that support. It only covers them for the next six months, though, so what are your intentions for beyond that?" Her practiced tone and reassuring smile would likely have worked on any other person, but Villa wasn't like everyone else.

"You can just admit that you don't want me meeting Myth, but it's going to happen eventually, Vanessa. You worried I'll lure him away from you?" Villa laughed as she stared intently at Vanessa, as if daring her to contest it. In the moments of silence that passed, Villa finally sighed and looked back to where Sal stood.

"As I said, our hands are tied until the first semester is over. We can put things in place to set up a trainee guild, and I'll act as mentor for it…but I'll need to get approval from the guild master." Villa's face didn't mask her disdain in the slightest.

With a placating smile, Vanessa nodded. "That's a great start, and we can work out the details once you have approval. Once we have your offer, we'll review it against any other potential ones that come through in the meantime. I'll be setting up conversations with the Tier Ones in the coming weeks, so we'll hopefully have a verdict before the end of the semester."

Sal looked over at Vanessa in surprise, but she didn't react in the slightest.

Villa gritted her teeth. "Is there a way for us to conduct this exclusively? Without involving the other guilds?"

Vanessa slowly shook her head. "Your offer would need to be extraordinary for Myth, Sal, and myself…So, I guess only you know the answer to that. As a show of good faith, I won't reach out to anyone else until the end of the month. That should be plenty of time for you to test the sniper rifle more thoroughly and come to a decision." Vanessa's smile widened into a grin as Villa's shoulders slumped in defeat.

CHAPTER 58:
SETBACK

Vanessa closed the door behind her and leaned heavily against the wood. Her eyes practically sparkled with excitement as she looked across the room to where Sal stood patiently. Villa had just left, and the air of tension in the room had finally evaporated. There was no small talk after Vanessa laid down their conditions, and Villa had excused herself shortly afterward.

Sal raised his hands and clapped a few times before gesturing to Vanessa, who gave a graceful bow. He still couldn't believe how well the conversation went. "I'm glad you were here for that. I'd have been eaten alive if I had to face her alone!"

With a grin, Vanessa made her way to one of the chairs and allowed herself to fall back into it. "Villa is a piece of work, but she's fair. You did great today! But don't go thinking that you're off the hook…a little warning about that gun would have been nice!" Her smile was still playful as she pointed across the room at him.

"You crafted a Legendary grade! Do you have any idea what this means? It's an absolute game-changer, Sal!" With a slight shake of her head, she leaned her head back against the leather of the chair. "Everything I said in that meeting was just coaxing out the best possible offer from the Reavers, but there's no pressure on you to accept anything you don't like the sound of, okay?"

Sal nodded as he took a seat in the chair opposite her. "I appreciate that, but I trust you when it comes to these sorts of things. You'd probably be able to give my father a run for his money in a negotiation, and that's no easy feat." He chuckled at the thought of the two of them squaring off against each other.

Vanessa raised her head and returned the smile. "I appreciate that trust, but we need to make a few things clear before we work together." She sat up in her seat and looked at him carefully. "Right now, you're the most valuable Crafter in this entire academy. You've proved that you can make unique weaponry of incredible quality, and there are going to be people who will want to capitalize on that. I'm one of them."

She crossed her arms as she watched his reaction. "I've teased you relentlessly, and although there's a fun chemistry here…that can't transition into a healthy business partnership. There's too much of an imbalance right now, and if I was to act on that chemistry, it would quite literally be me taking advantage of you. You really don't understand what you're worth yet, but I do."

Vanessa gave Sal a reassuring smile and placed her hand on his knee. Her eyes stared into his. "So, you need to make a choice for your future, and I'm sorry to put this on you now. If you want me to work with you, then we'll be moving forward with a professional relationship. I don't mix business with pleasure, as it puts a strain on everything."

Sal laughed and shrugged. "Well, to be honest, I never expected anything to happen anyway, so it's no problem. I'd absolutely love to work with you, so I'm fine with a professional relationship."

Vanessa paused at that, before laughing. "I'm not trying to twist the knife or anything, but something absolutely could've happened…which is why I'm saying this now." With a wistful shake of her head, she gave Sal a dazzling smile.

"You're one of the good ones, Sal. My job will be ensuring that nobody takes advantage of you." With a slight pause, she added the caveat and tapped her hand on his knee. "Except me, of course. I'm the only one allowed to take advantage!"

Sal smiled. "Don't suppose you're going to stop the relentless flirting?"

Vanessa pointed at herself in mock surprise. "This is my default, but I can tone it down, if it makes you feel safer?"

Sal laughed and got to his feet. "So, just to be clear…nothing will happen between us because you feel like you're taking advantage of me?"

Vanessa smiled.

Sal continued. "But if I become a guild master and have you working with me in the future, is that not me taking advantage of you? You'd be giving up your career just to bet on my success?"

Vanessa's smile turned into a grin as she also got to her feet. "Career? The Credit floor is just a job, Sal. Working with you and building up the next best guild? That's a career! When I make you the most successful guild master in the city, then we can revisit some of that chemistry. How about that?"

Sal grinned and countered, "You think I'll still be single at that point?"

Vanessa didn't even blink, nor did the grin leave her face. "Absolutely! You won't be able to meet anyone if I have you locked in a workshop all the time."

***

Sal glanced up to see Divinity place her meal tray down on the canteen table.

"Was starting to think you stood me up. Everything okay?" His smile was met with a look of exasperation, and Sal immediately regretted his joking tone.

Whatever it was about today, his conversations with Divinity seemed to be on edge. Just when he thought she was about to explode at him, she took a steadying breath and sat down at the table. She pushed her trademark salad to one side and composed herself. She brought her hands to her face and rubbed her eyes, before finally sighing and looking at Sal.

"Today has been a pretty shit day. Sorry for being late, and sorry for being snippy with you earlier."

Sal shook his head. "It's totally okay. What made everything so shit? The team picks for the Combat class?"

Divinity gave him a level stare before shaking her head. "I'm starting to think that you're living on a different planet half of the time. You missed most of that class…and it's starting to feel like that original vision might be coming true. Where Sal disappears regularly."

Her words were barbed, and Sal knew better than to argue with her. There was no point in being hurt or offended by something that hadn't happened yet. She was clearly in a bad mood, so he tried to change gears.

"Tell me what made today so shit."

Divinity closed her eyes and placed her face in her palms. "I'm sorry, Sal. I'm just…it's just not a good day today." When she removed her hands, there was an annoyed expression on her face as she bit her lip. "That Skill class pretty much told me I'm shit at using essence. That was one hell of a start. Then, being moved into a remedial section because I lack control? Okay, that's fine…but then to have the last pick in the Combat class? Do you know how much of a setback this is? I'm going to be assessed on the contributions of students who don't even want to be here!"

Sal just listened quietly as Divinity continued her rant. "I was late meeting you because Lombardi kept me in a skill-pod to see if your unknotting did any damage—which it didn't, by the way—but I was stuck in a tank of essence that I could barely channel or interact with. If I hear him tell me to relax and breathe one more time…"

Her teeth gritted as she looked across at him. "I checked the future, to see what our chances are in the class battles. Spoiler alert! We lose…badly. Your first eight matches are all losses. My first ten are all losses. I didn't have the willpower to watch another one, so I just stopped. As it stands, right now…we are completely fucked."

Divinity violently pulled her salad toward her, which caused a tomato to leap from the dish and roll across the table. She pointed a fork at Sal. "That's why my day has been shit. How about yours? How was your mystery rendezvous with the girl in the uniform? Have fun?"

Sal watched as Divinity angrily attacked her salad and decided to stay quiet for a bit. He fought the urge to talk about solutions. Divinity likely just needed to vent her annoyances, and he was happy to be her sounding board for that. She had done so much for him in the last week, that listening to her was the least he could do.

The fork fell to one side as Divinity took out her tablet. "When you left the class, we spent the rest of the time asking Rust questions about the battles and researching the students. I looked into the future and saw the lineup that I get, which is pretty abysmal. Who do we have…"

Divinity's eyes scanned the tablet as she gestured with her hand. "Three Supports and a weak Defense person. They all lost in both of their fights, with powers and without. Apparently, the only reason that I don't have four Crafters is because you picked all of them to leave me at least one Defender. Thank you, by the way, but it doesn't change the fact that we're fucked."

Sal nodded politely but saw that Divinity wasn't continuing; she stared at him as though waiting for an answer.

Swallowing his urge to problem solve once again, Sal just sighed. "That does sound absolutely shit."

Divinity stared at him before she picked her fork back up and started to eat while she sulked.

Sal kept quiet for the next few minutes and started thinking about how they'd be able to get out of their current predicament. "On the upside, we should be able to help Melanie pick her team. She should have like first or second pick because of her current ranking."

Divinity glanced up, a smile finally tugged at her lips. "That's a good upside. We should help her with the selections so she can stand out in a good way."

Figuring that he had bought himself a bit of momentum, Sal tried to make another suggestion. "What if we coordinate with the other top rankers? Like, predetermine who we pick so all of us have a better chance?"

Divinity didn't look up from her salad. "Nova and Victoria go along with the plan, but Dominic fucks us over because of self-interest. Sees it as an opportunity to move up the rankings and takes it."

Sal sighed as he rocked back in his chair, balancing on the back two legs as he looked up at the ceiling. "So, we're stuck with the current team compositions. I can make equipment for us, which might tip the odds in our favor?"

Divinity looked up from her salad and shook her head. "It's good, but not enough. Our teams are terrified of combat, and they freeze up at any sign of danger. Even if you were to equip them with the best technology, it's no use if they faint on the spot."

Sal laughed. "Surely nobody faints?"

But Divinity gave him a somber look. "Three of your team faints in the first match-up. They've never been so much as punched before, so how do you expect them to take on Offense class students?"

Sal brought his chair forward and leaned against the table. "So…why don't we punch them a few times before the matches? They'll be acclimatized to it then." He laughed, hoping that it would break the tension in their discussion, but Divinity stared at him.

"That's it!" Divinity clapped excitedly, and Sal desperately wanted to figure out where her current train of thought was.

"You're not seriously going to punch them?" Sal inquired carefully, but Divinity waved his suggestion away.

"No, no. We're going to train them! You said it yourself earlier about the Skill class…that I should come up with the optimal training method with my Foresight ability. But what if we created the perfect training program for them? It won't be anything amazing with the little time that we have, but if I could get them to a point where they're not terrified…we might get a couple of wins out of them!"

Sal was eager to keep this level of optimism going, so he quickly jumped in with another suggestion. "I could make some equipment to boost our chances, too! Maybe defensive equipment or something that gives them range? If my team are all Crafters, we might be able to make enough for our two teams?"

Divinity nodded thoughtfully as she leaned back in her chair. She appeared to finally be distracted from every setback the day had thrown at her. Putting her half-ravaged salad to one side, she looked at Sal intently as her eyes turned milky white.

"Okay then, time to get to work!"

CHAPTER 59:
SELECTION

Sal and Divinity spent the next few evenings around classes trying to concoct the best plan of action for their teams. Tuesday and Wednesday had been straightforward, with mostly theory being thrown at them for Survival and Skill classes. Having sat between Whisper and Nova, Sal had managed to get another boost through the zones in his body, bringing his total up to the eighteenth gate. It was only an improvement of two, and Sal felt like it was getting much harder to progress with his essence refinement, but it was still better than before.

When Thursday eventually arrived, it was the moment of truth. Divinity had predicted how the teams would be divided, so Sal wasn't too worried about the outcome. If any variables did pop up that changed the vision, that could only be a benefit to them.

Rust stood at the center of the room and requested that Gerard come forward. Everyone watched as the lowest ranked in the Silver cohort sauntered over to the lecturer like he owned the place. A shit-eating grin was plastered across his face as he looked around at all his peers.

"So, you've had a few days to ruminate over the various options. Who are you going to pick to create your team?" Rust asked as he gestured for Gerard to speak.

Rather than just naming the students he wanted, Gerard took it upon himself to gloat. "Since I'm going first, I'd likely be able to make a cohesive team…but then I was thinking to myself, why not take all the top Offense people? I'd have the best attacking strength, and it would remove the available attackers from the other teams." He grinned as he started to look around the room, making it feel more like he was choosing his victims than assembling a team to work with him.

Rust sighed as he gestured for Gerard to continue, but not before making his opinion known. "You're not going to earn any additional points for composition, and it's a strategy that will leave you vulnerable against Defense-heavy teams. Are you sure you don't want to reconsider?"

Gerard shook his head and pointed into the crowd. "Bolt! You're my first pick."

Sal watched as a student suddenly appeared beside Gerard, looking somewhat disgruntled at being selected by the lower rank. It took Sal a moment to realize that he was the incredibly fast guy who could wield lightning. Divinity had spoken about him on the first day, and they had met briefly at the party. A few of the other low ranks looked dismayed at Bolt being taken by Gerard. It looked like he was a top pick for a lot of the team captains.

"Rogue is my next pick," Gerard declared as he pointed to another area in the crowd.

Rust sighed and looked at Gerard with barely contained distaste. "Use their real names." He looked out toward the group of students. "That goes for all of you. Hero names are earned through hard work and perseverance. You may all be aspiring toward that, but you're not there yet."

With a roll of his eyes, Gerard pointed again at the same location. "Michael, you're my pick."

A slender student walked toward the center of the room with his hands in his pockets. He didn't look particularly pleased with his team captain but shared a knowing look with Bolt.

Sal turned around to Divinity with a confused expression, and she filled him in immediately.

"Rogue. Has a stealth skill and he's trained in martial arts. He's really good."

Nodding, Sal turned in time to see the third member being picked.

"Archer!" Gerard practically shouted before turning to look at Rust. "No, it's his surname. It's real."

Rust rotated his hand, urging Gerard to get on with his final selection, which turned out to be another male student.

"Rodrigo," Gerard finished with a grin as he looked at his assembled team.

He had two high-mobility and high-damage attackers with Bolt and Rogue. Archer was great for ranged attacks, and Rodrigo could burn pretty much anything to a crisp. It was the perfect team composition in his eyes, and judging from the smug expression on his face, he felt incredibly confident in his choices.

"Stand over there to one side. Next up, Harold Gunn. Do you have your selections ready?" Rust gestured for the student to move to the center of the ring. His approach was a stark contrast to Gerard who seemed to be terrified of all the eyes that were resting on him. It became apparent very quickly why he was so nervous as he glanced over to Gerard's assembled team.

Rust had to lean over to hear the student's whispers and an aggravated sigh escaped the lecturer's lips as he turned to the rest of the room. "I thought it would have been obvious to you all, that your first picks might be taken by someone else...please ensure that you have a few backups in mind, so you're not standing up here with me without a clue of who to pick!"

Harold looked as though he wanted the ground to swallow him up, and Sal felt bad for the guy. After a few moments of deliberation, and being informed by Rust that Gerard had taken the 11th, 14th, 18th and 23rd Ranks from the cohort, he made his decision. Without any context of who they were, Harold picked the 12th, 13th, 15th, and 16th ranked. Rust stared at him in disbelief as Harold welcomed each of his new team members. The simplistic nature of his selection was oddly endearing, and Sal couldn't help but hope he did well.

He looked at Divinity; she just shook her head. "Relegated."

The next hour passed quickly as all the teams were created, leaving a smaller pool available. With every new team created, the selection process took a little longer as each team captain tried to work with the remaining options. By all accounts, the last good options were taken by Victoria as the fourteenth team was assembled.

There was an Energy Manipulator left in the pool of students, and she snapped her up gratefully. It caused a ripple of anguish through the remaining team captains, with Nova cursing audibly from the other side of the room.

Her other pick was a Defense type, which almost caused Nova to scream. What made the entire experience that much worse was Gerard laughing with a few of the other low-rank captains. Despite Rust's warnings for them to be respectful, they continued jeering at any signs of dismay.

When Sal's turn finally arrived, he could see the almost apologetic expressions on the remaining student faces. It was like they knew they were deadweight, and they didn't want to drag someone else down with them. Despite that, he was familiar with all their faces and profiles.

With a wide smile, he pointed out the first girl. "Blathnaid."

Rust raised an eyebrow at the fact that Sal knew the student's name, but nobody was more shocked than Blathnaid herself. She actually pointed at herself in surprise, and Sal had to nod at her before she awkwardly shuffled toward him. Sal turned around and pointed at a guy who was idly scratching his beard and staring at a piece of the floor in front of him.

"Anthony."

With a startled glance, Anthony looked up and just laughed as he walked to the center of the room. With a turn to the other side of the room, Sal pointed at another figure who was grinning at him.

"Jack."

The shorter man pulled his long red hair back in a ponytail as he moved to the center of the room.

Sal turned around almost in a full circle, and wondered why the remaining students didn't just huddle together to make it easier to spot them. He almost missed his last guy because he was practically reclining on his terminal out of boredom.

"Barry! He's my last pick. Blathnaid, Anthony, Jack, and Barry."

Rust watched him curiously. "Did you memorize all the student's names?"

Sal was tempted to tell the truth, but instead just lied. "Of course. That was the assignment you gave us. Learn about everyone in the class."

With a wide grin, Rust shook his head as he turned to Divinity. "By process of elimination, you have your team. We'll be taking into consideration how the teams were formed, so please don't let this process get under your skin." Raising his voice for everyone to hear, Rust clapped. "That's it for today. Next class, we'll be going through basic formations, and if we've got time, weapon selection! You're all dismissed."

Sal looked over at Divinity, who was greeting all of her team members. Their surprise was evident on their faces, and Sal almost felt bad for them knowing what sort of hellish training they were going to be subjected to.

***

"So, let's hear the excuses!" Jez laughed as he looked at the assembled crowd of students. "Who here has yet to earn a single Q-Cred since you were last here? Hands up." He waited expectantly and seemed no way surprised when more than half of the students raised a hand. With a brief nod, he raised his palms. "Stand up and stay standing. Since you're only getting your bearings, and there's so much happening right now…I'll give you all the benefit of the doubt.

Maybe one of you will be exemplary in the future? I hope to be proved wrong about each and every one of you."

Jez's smile was wide as he watched them get to their feet. "We're going to have a little reshuffle of the class. Each of you who is standing, I want you to move to the sides of the class. Stand alongside the walls and pay attention. You'll be standing for the rest of the lesson, and you're going to listen to your peers who actually went out and did their assignment." A few uncertain glances passed between the students as they looked back at Jez in disbelief. With a hearty laugh, he looked at them with a smile that didn't reach his eyes. "Did I stutter?"

As they were moving, Jez addressed the seated students. "Now, as much as I'd love to hear all their inventive excuses...none of that will benefit you. Each of you has earned Q-Cred since our last conversation...except Jeremy." Jez's eyes snapped up to one of the seated students, who balked at the sudden call-out. "I don't know why Jeremy is still sitting, when both he and I know that he hasn't earned a single thing. Maybe he got confused or hoped that I don't keep an eye on all of your progress. What do you think, Jeremy?"

With a start, Jeremy got to his feet and slid into a gap at the wall, keeping his head down low as he pulled out his tablet, as if it would shield him from Jez's glare.

With a groan, Jez turned and pointed to the door. "Jeremy, I can stomach failure. It's a part of every worthwhile endeavor, but I cannot stomach liars...so, was it an error of judgment, or did you just try to pull a fast one? Because I'm very much inclined to kick you out of this class right now."

Sal watched everything play out in shock. The tempo had completely changed from their first lesson. Jeremy launched into an explanation of how he had managed to buy and sell off the Credit Store, and that the transaction only went through that afternoon. He produced his Q-Card for Jez to verify and explained that he thought he had successfully completed the assignment. After a gesture from Jez to throw the Q-card, Jeremy complied and Jez caught the haphazard throw with ease.

Jez looked at the Q-Card before going through his own ledger on the desk. A smile crept onto his face as he looked back at Jeremy. With a flick of his wrist, he threw the Q-Card back to Jeremy with pinpoint accuracy.

"Take your seat, Jeremy. I can admit when I'm wrong."

Sal raised an eyebrow.

There was no apology from Jez as he turned back to the class. "Who raised more than one hundred Q-Cred?" A few hands went up and Jez smiled as he gestured to the front row. "This class will be assigned seating from now on. Front row is for top performers in the class. I'll be allocating spot prizes for class participation and for exemplary work...which leads me to my next question. Did anyone get over a thousand Q-Cred?" Jez asked with a grin.

The disbelief on the faces in the class showed that they didn't think it was possible. Sal wasn't sure how he felt about drawing this sort of attention to himself, but he felt Jez's eyes locked onto him.

"You know how I feel about liars, Mr. Argento."

Sal reluctantly raised his hand, and Jez looked around the room. "You see that? There's one among you who went above and beyond and reached a thousand Q-Cred…isn't that incredible?" His grin widened even further. "What about…two thousand Q-Cred?"

Sal kept his hand in the air and didn't dare look around for fear of looking arrogant. He didn't want to face a lynch mob after this, and looking anything but humble would likely paint a target on his back.

"Three thousand Q-Cred? Would you look at that, Mr. Argento still has his hand in the air. I'll put them all out of their misery now, the final tally…and the record-breaking first year result in the history of this Administration class…is four thousand Q-Cred, earned solely by Mr. Salvatore Argento here." Jez beamed at Sal and gestured for him to look around the room.

When Sal turned, he expected looks of jealousy and hatred, but was met with expressions of amazement and wonder.

Jez laughed at the surprise on Sal's face. "The reason for this exercise is not to name and shame…it's to show you your peers, and for them to see what's possible! I'd like to personally compliment you on nearly bankrupting the Credit floor. I've heard from some reliable sources that their in-house Appraisal team have put a bounty on your head." Jez grinned as he clapped, and Sal was shocked when the students joined in with the round of applause. The only ones who didn't join in were standing along the sides of the room.

Jez clicked his fingers and raised a single hand. "I didn't think I'd be handing out a milestone prize so early, but…you've absolutely earned it!"

CHAPTER 60:
FORMATION

JEZ PRESENTED SAL WITH AN ORNATE METAL BOX THAT HE PLACED GENTLY ON the desk. The grin never left his face as he waited for Sal to open it. Feeling pretty much all the eyes in the room resting on him in that very moment, Sal obliged and lifted the lid carefully. Inside was an intricate crest made of cloth, resting on a bed of purple fabric. None of the symbols looked familiar to Sal, and he was grateful that Jez chose that moment to explain the prize to both him, and the rest of the class.

"Challenge crests! They're earned for extraordinary achievements and are worn on your uniform for everyone to see. They are a mark of honor and acknowledgment that will set you apart from your peers. This is the first time I've ever acknowledged a student this early, but it's deserved! I'll be expecting great things from you in the future, Mr. Argento."

Jez rapped his knuckles against the desk before moving back toward the center of the room. He picked up his ledger from his desk and read through it for a few moments before looking back up at the assembled students. His eyes moved to the sides of the room as he tapped the ledger in his hands. "It's very easy to make excuses, or to point fingers at others. Salvatore has the Appraisal skill, so obviously it's going to be so much easier for him, right?"

When a few of the heads at the side nodded, Jez snapped the ledger shut. "Wrong. There is a chasm between drive and ambition. All of you in this room may want to succeed, and you may have a burning ambition to be wealthy beyond measure. None of that will come to fruition without the drive to realize those goals. Mr. Argento negotiated terms with the Reavers Guild to become a preferred Appraiser, which was a relationship he didn't have before stepping into this academy. He stayed up throughout the night and completed seventy-three, back-to-back Appraisals."

Jez paused as he let that information sink into the crowd. Many of the seated students looked at Sal in a whole new light, but Jez wasn't done. "I'm not standing here singing his praises just to make you all feel bad. He made a connection, negotiated terms, did the work, and has now positioned himself as an Appraiser who gets shit done. People talk, and three separate employees on the Credit floor were eager to tell me about the overnight Appraiser. That's how you build a reputation, which leads us back to our first point of business. Reputation. What do you want to be known for?"

Jez gestured to each side of the room. "You're standing at the sides right now because you didn't complete your assignment. You have two avenues available to you now. Either you can let this moment steel your resolve, or you can let it break you. If you resent Mr. Argento's success, then I'm afraid there won't be much for you in this class. On the other hand, if you feel the heat of competition…and you want to surpass him? Then this is absolutely the place for you." Jez laughed as he leaned against his desk.

"We're going to be putting in thresholds from this point forward. By next week, anyone who has earned less than fifty Q-Cred will be asked to stand at the sides. Above fifty, you're allowed to sit. Anyone who arrives with no Q-Cred earned will be asked to leave the class. Each week, the threshold will rise." A few gasps came from the sides of the room, but Jez paid them no mind. His eyes were locked on the center of the room.

"Those who make it to the end of month one will accompany me to a private auction, where you will have the opportunity to purchase items that don't appear in the Credit Store. If you make it to the end of the first semester, you'll have access to a private marketplace used by the top guilds…but that's a conversation for another day."

Jez opened the ledger again and looked through the crowd. "So, let's go through the rest of our rankings, shall we? Who was it that earned over a hundred Q-Cred?" The rest of the class consisted of Jez going through each earning, offering advice with snippets of praise sprinkled throughout.

Sal listened intently and found that there were quite a few enterprising individuals in the class, with one of them going so far as to sell a dating service, where they would use their ability to match-make people with similar essence types. The ones at the bottom of the list were all low tier Crafting types who tried to sell their services traditionally on the Credit Store, which Jez strongly advised against.

"We're running out of time today but let me just finish on this note." Jez placed his ledger back on the desk and looked around the room. "Reputation is what it all comes back to. We have an Appraiser who has positioned himself as an expert in his field and backed it up with evidence. How would he have fared as an unknown Appraiser selling his services on the Credit Store? Each of you are more than your ability, and you need to create your own personal brand. Create individual experiences with your customers so they'll remember you and recommend you to others. Create your own market segment instead of trying to conform to what is already established! What is your value proposition? The identity behind your brand? What can you offer people that your peers cannot? Those are the questions you need to answer before you can become successful. Simply being willing to do the work isn't enough—you need to chase down opportunities or create them for yourself!"

Jez clapped and gestured to the door. "Remember. Thresholds are now in place. Come to me next week with results, not excuses! I want to see more people sitting in this class."

***

"I'm sorry!" Blathnaid exclaimed as she accidentally broke formation again.

Anxiety swept across her features, but Sal just raised his hands to indicate that it was completely fine. With a gesture to the others on the team that it was time for a break, Sal moved over to the side of the training area and retrieved the next batch of refreshments.

"These ones boost cohesion, so make sure to drink it all and then we'll try again." Sal read the label on them before handing them out to each member of his team.

Blathnaid accepted the drink gratefully and gave him an awkward smile, while Barry's face was a picture of reluctance. Divinity had warned Sal that Barry was likely to be an issue for the team, and if the grumbling between sessions was anything to go by, he was nearing his breaking point. Jack and Anthony took their drinks without any complaint, much to Sal's relief.

Divinity had given Sal the instructions for the first evening of training, which was just going to be light drills of formations and switching through different stances. Even though they were basic commands that involved moving to set locations, the team was struggling.

"Are we ready to start again?" Sal asked as he placed the empty cup off to one side. Barry nodded as he drained his cup and tossed it to where Sal's was. Blathnaid, Anthony, and Jack rushed through the rest of theirs before nodding. Sal smiled and gestured for them to retake their positions in the training area. Divinity had drawn a series of chalk shapes on the ground that showed the movements they needed to learn.

"So, that last drink was for cohesion. We're all going to be very aware of our surroundings, the locations of one another and any sudden movements. When we familiarize ourselves with one another's movements, we'll be able to better predict them in the future. Well, that's the plan at least. Any questions?"

Sal looked straight at Barry, who raised a single hand. Without missing a beat, Sal withdrew a folded piece of paper from his pocket and handed it to Barry.

"Divinity took the liberty of answering all your questions and wrote them down, so we'd save time on arguing."

"What makes you think I was going to argue?" Barry countered as he took the piece of folded paper. He unfurled the page and his eyes darted through Divinity's handwriting, but his facial expression didn't give away anything. A moment later, he refolded the page and pocketed it with a sigh.

"No questions from me."

Everyone else on the team was looking at Barry's pocket with eager curiosity, but it was clear he had no intention of explaining the contents of the note.

Sal clapped to draw their attention back to him. "Excellent. Let's get back to work! Vendor drinks don't last forever and the less Q-Cred we need to spend on getting this right, the better."

All five of them took their positions, with Sal at the very back of the group in the center. To his left and right, wide on the wings, stood Jack and Blathnaid. In front of them, tighter at the front, stood Barry and Anthony.

"Shield!" Sal shouted as he stepped forward.

Everyone moved as one, congregating together in the center with their backs facing each other. Their bodies took on a defensive stance that they didn't fully understand, but it was how Divinity had told them to stand. A few seconds passed before Sal shouted out the next command. "Spear!" All of them blended into a line, with Barry at the very front, assuming a lazy attacking stance.

Sal stood at the very rear of the formation and looked over their progress. Divinity had only given them a few formations to start off with and wanted Sal to run them through the different options to build up their symmetry and cohesion as a team. She had her own hands full with her own team on the opposite side of the room.

"I have a question that isn't on the note!" Barry called out from the front of the formation, causing more than a few of the others to groan in resignation.

Sal ignored him and moved through the formations another few times, and Barry thankfully followed the instructions. Sal reviewed their progression and was delighted to see that a lot of the awkward shuffling had been replaced with fluid movements. What had started with nervous laughs and a constant stream of apologies had morphed into a somewhat competent group of beginners. Even Blathnaid, who looked terrified of the team, was sliding into place gracefully with a smile on her face.

Barry's hand waved in the air again, and Sal finally relented. "Okay, what's the question, Barry?"

Turning around to look at Sal, Barry withdrew the note and held it up. "My original question was about the viability of our team. No offense to all of you, but we're shit. No amount of formations and practiced movements will save us from a bolt of lightning launched at our faces."

Barry flicked the note in his hand. "Divinity claims that if we work together and follow your schedule, we can potentially survive relegation. My question, that isn't answered here, is how? We have zero attacking power, no defensive capability, no healing, and an overabundance of useless Supports. No offense, again." Barry's eyes narrowed as he looked at Sal carefully. "What happens in the future that gives us a chance?"

Sal pointed at the team that were still standing awkwardly in their last formation. "We're going to use equipment, that's how. I have a Rare-grade weapon that can shoot projectiles…which gives us a long-range attack. But what use will that be if one of you runs in front of it in the heat of battle and gets taken out? I'm going to work on getting the best gear for us, but anything I can't buy or acquire, we're going to make ourselves. That's our competitive advantage."

Sal had wanted to sound inspiring, but it looked like they only focused on the mention of him having a long-range weapon. Jack raised his hand for a follow-up question, but Sal continued.

"You asked what gives us a chance in the future? What saves us from a bolt of lightning? All our opponents are going to be using their essence, likely for the first time in a prolonged combat scenario. They won't know how to pace themselves throughout group battles, so they're likely to run out of essence very quickly. When they're burned out and exhausted, we'll be able to take them out if we work together as a team and seize the opportunities as they arise."

All of them were looking at him with surprised expressions, and Jack had lowered his hand.

Sal smiled and shrugged. "The high-rank captains will likely try to solo the fights, so our countermeasures will be against a single person. The strategy for those will be to pick off the captain as soon as possible. The lower-rank captains will likely have poor leadership capabilities, or not have the respect of their team. Those fights will likely be chaotic and explosive to start, so we'll need to really focus on defense for them. All the formations that we are going to learn in the Combat class have been dissected by Divinity. She's created a crash course that will put us ahead of the others, and from what she's seen in the future, it gives us a fighting chance of survival."

Sal gestured to Jack to see whether he still wanted to ask his question, but he grinned and shook his head. Blathnaid and Anthony were the same, which left Barry. Sal turned to him to see whether he had any other questions, but instead of answering or arguing further, Barry just laughed and resumed his place in the formation.

"Those drinks aren't going to last forever, right?"

CHAPTER 61:
SECRETS

SAL COULD ONLY WATCH IN HORROR AS DIVINITY DISPATCHED ONE TEAMMATE after another. Each of them was tasked with defending against a random attack from a sequence, using basic stances and martial arts moves, but nothing could have prepared them for her wrath. Each attack started the same, with a slow and signaled trajectory that gave them time to prepare the correct counter. Divinity would then slightly increase her speed and reduce the amount of telegraphing.

Sal had managed to block her first four attacks, but the fifth had knocked him down. Before he could get to his feet, she had moved onto her next opponent, which was Barry. Surprisingly, he had lasted through the first seven attacks before being thrown over Divinity's shoulder. Jack moved forward and was put down in two moves; Blathnaid barely made it past the first counter. Anthony got to the third counter and then Sal's team had a momentary reprieve while Divinity fought everyone from her own team.

Their formations training had been separated, so they could learn how to work as teams. Divinity wanted to give everyone a taste of real combat before the next Combat class, so she insisted on running an extra evening training. There was a lot of reluctance, a bit of screaming and a lot of panicking from the Support members of the team, but Divinity managed to convince them that it was the best chance they had to get through the class.

With each hour that passed, Sal dreaded the attacks less and less. The anxiety and rush of adrenaline had calmed down, and he was suddenly focusing on each attack as it came, rather than moving out of panic. What genuinely surprised Sal was the sense of rivalry that was forming with Barry, who seemed to naturally adapt to everything better than Sal. Despite all his complaining, he managed to fend off Divinity for longer than anyone else, and Sal pushed harder against his limits to beat him.

Between one of the sets, Barry turned to Sal. "Professor Lombardi said that you were a Replicator? And that it was up there with Body Manipulation in terms of capability. So, why are you so weak?" Just to add salt to the wound, Barry's face split into a grin as he gestured at the approaching form of Divinity. "Oh, looks like you're up!"

With that said, he stepped back to give them space.

Up until this point, Divinity hadn't exchanged much conversation with Sal, other than correcting his movements. However, on this approach, she wore a smile. "You're thinking of using Rust's ability?"

Sal sighed and was about to apologize when Divinity interrupted him. "I think it's a good idea! It'll test my own abilities, and it'll show them that you have a few tricks of your own up your sleeve."

He grinned as he replicated the ability, he had memorized the week before. He had been so terrified of fighting Dominic that he had weaved Rust's Absolute Counter ability a dozen times to the point that it was practically etched into his memory. When the pattern was complete, he didn't hesitate in activating it and felt a rush of power course through his veins.

It was a similar sensation as when he had taken the speedster's ability, but this time was different. Sal knew instinctively that the progress he had been making with his gates had opened a whole new reserve of capability for him, and he felt more in control of the power, despite it being the first time he had ever activated it properly.

Divinity gave him a look as if to ask if he was ready, and Sal could see at least a dozen openings in her stance. He pulled back on the new power to ensure that he wasn't adding essence into the attacks, but even with that, he felt unstoppable. At his nod, Divinity launched forward at a dizzying speed, causing everyone to gasp in shock. Her knee launched straight at Sal's chin but met only air.

Barry's jaw practically dropped as Sal weaved seamlessly around each of Divinity's attacks. A single hand slapped away each incoming punch, while his foot negated any attacks that launched from below the waist. Divinity's eyes turned a milky white and the tempo of attacks surged to the point that Sal had to activate more of the power just to keep up. His lazy defense was discarded as he started to take the fight against Divinity seriously. She moved away from his punches and kicks, and he slid out from her grapples and clinches.

Divinity saw his attacks coming and did her best to counter them, but Sal's ability allowed him to flawlessly forestall any attack that came his way. The result was an incredible stalemate of capability, at high speed, with each of them negating the attacks of their opponent and seeking to find an opening.

Sal pulled deeper on his ability but made sure that it didn't make his attacks stronger. He just needed them to be faster. Divinity's laugh almost broke him out of his concentration and with that minor lapse, his body reacted, cartwheeling him backward to create space between them.

"Draw?" Divinity called out as she deactivated her power.

Sal nodded as he deactivated Rust's ability. He closed his eyes and grit his teeth to withstand the pain that coursed through his body. The ability had allowed him to use his body to its maximum potential, but Sal lacked a lot of the mobility that it used. Each of his muscles and joints were screaming at him to curl up into a ball and die. Sal desperately wanted to listen to them, but when he opened his eyes, Divinity was handing him a cup.

"Restoration Juice. Perfect for muscle pain. You can thank me later!"

Sal very nearly chugged the entire contents of the cup in one go and enjoyed the immediate numbing of his existential pain.

"I think you've earned yourself a few fans," Divinity teased as she gestured to where the two teams gaped at them in shock.

Barry shook his head with a wistful smile as he approached them. "Nice to know that our team captain isn't a complete pushover. Maybe we do have a chance at avoiding relegation?"

Divinity cocked an eyebrow at Barry. "What's that? You want more sparring?" Barry's face paled as he started to back away, but Divinity was faster as she moved into an attacking stance. "Better start defending!"

Barry cursed as he defaulted into the correct pose and defended against a flurry of Divinity's attacks.

Sal couldn't help but appreciate how quickly he was adapting to the training, and he wasn't the only one. The rest of the team watched the sparring intently, and when Barry got past the twelfth consecutive attack, Sal cheered for Barry, along with the others.

Maybe Divinity took that as a cue to ramp up the tempo, or maybe she was annoyed at the previous stalemate, but whatever the reason…Barry was unceremoniously flung over her shoulder, to land heavily on the ground beside Sal.

Sal extended his hand to pick Barry up, who begrudgingly accepted it. By the time he had gotten to his feet, Divinity was addressing the two teams directly.

"This was a great first night of training. You've learned basic formations with your own teams, led by your captain. You've also had individual sparring practice that was tailored for your level of capability, and then pushed outside of that comfort zone. As of right now, you're all three weeks ahead of the Combat class in terms of theory, but you're about a month and a half ahead in terms of combat capability. If we keep this pace up, and meet here each evening, you'll be formidable foes for anyone who steps up against you."

Divinity looked over at Sal and gestured for him to take the reins.

Still feeling a series of dull aches and pains, Sal gritted his teeth and straightened his back. "Could everyone send me over their uniform sizes? I'll be working on getting us some good defensive gear."

Much to everyone's surprise, Blathnaid raised her hand excitedly. "Can I help with that?"

Jack glanced at Blathnaid and then at Sal before he also raised his hand. "I'd like to help too, actually. If that's okay?"

Sal was about to tell them that it was fine when Jack persisted and gestured at the two of them. "She makes great stuff, and I'm pretty handy with runes, engraving, and enchantment."

Blathnaid grinned as she gestured at Jack. "We'd like to contribute and not be deadweight."

With a smile, Sal conceded. "Okay, that's fine. You can both help with the equipment side of things. We might just end up purchasing what we need from the Credit Store. If that happens, it'll be out of my own pocket, don't worry."

A collective sigh of relief came from both Jack and Blathnaid before Anthony's hand shot into the air. Sal looked at him, and he was once again scratching at his beard.

"I can make items better, but only temporarily…and I need to be holding them the whole time. So, that Rare-grade sword would probably be an Upper Rare grade in my hands. Not sure if that's useful or not, and I've never used a long-range sword before, but thought I'd mention it."

Sal nodded slowly. It sounded like the ability Upgrade used to transform her gloves into those mechanical arms. "Thanks for letting me know. Barry, do you want to share your ability with the group?"

Barry gave Sal a thumbs-up. "As soon as I figure out what it is, I'll let you know."

Every head turned in his direction in absolute disbelief, but Sal went one step further and activated his eyes.

"Are you fucking kidding me?" Sal said as he looked at the perfect weave in Barry's core, existing without a single knot.

Whatever it was, it looked untouched, as though it hadn't been used before.

He stared at Barry. "Are you able to use essence control and refinement? Or do you not know how to use them either?"

Barry grinned. "Nah, they're easy. I'm at the sixtieth gate or something."

Sal looked over to Divinity for some semblance of support, but she was doubled over and laughing.

"Sal, your face is priceless!"

Anthony turned around to face Barry. "What about the Skill Registration? It should have given you a name of your ability. Do you know that at least?"

Barry shook his head with the same smile. "Nope. You need to activate your ability during the registration…which I didn't know how to do, so I got a blank card."

Barry fielded a few more questions before slumping his shoulders in defeat. Everyone was thoroughly confused as to how he managed to get into the academy without knowing his own ability, and even more confused as to how nonchalant he was about it. It was an excellent note to end their first night of training, and Divinity slid into step beside Sal as they made their way to the exit.

She looked back to where Barry was walking with the others. In low tones, she spoke to Sal. "He's lying, by the way…about his ability. He knows exactly what it is and how to use it." Sal turned to look at her sharply, but Divinity shook her head slightly. "I'm only telling you, so you don't try to replicate it."

Sal nodded. The thought had crossed his mind. It was reckless trying to replicate established powers, but to take on unknown ones was just asking for trouble. Sal wondered when he stopped being cautious about using his ability. It had only been a few weeks, but he had probably replicated more than a dozen powers by this stage. If his mother knew, he'd likely be dead.

Sal gave her a reassuring smile. "I promise I won't try to replicate it. Do you know what it is?"

Divinity glanced at Barry, who smiled right back at her. Turning back to Sal, she shook her head. "I've only seen him use his powers once, but it made no sense. It's the future that the Doom Society is taking care of. You know, with Sinclair." Her facial expression darkened.

Sal suppressed a shudder as the image of Sinclair dying pierced his mind. Trying to change the topic, Sal shook his head. "Like, how far did you look? That can't be the only time he's used them."

Divinity looked at Sal with a humorless smile. "You're underestimating him. In the entire three years at Quest Academy, he doesn't reveal his power at all. It literally takes a life-or-death scenario for him to do it, which is kinda cool if you think about it."

Sal glanced back at the grinning form of Barry. With a reluctant sigh, he agreed with Divinity. "It is kinda cool."

CHAPTER 62:
COMPETENCE

UPGRADE SWIVELED AROUND IN HER CHAIR AT THE FRONT OF THE CLASS. SHE had a resigned expression on her face, and her arms were folded.

"You know, I'm starting to think that I'm getting the short end of the stick here! My job is to teach you how to be the best Crafters you can possibly be, not to lift your spirits up every time you get knocked down. Sure, the other classes having a party probably sucked…and yeah, finding out about the Combat class assessment is an absolute bummer, but you need to be resilient! So, give me a show of hands. Who wants me to throw out my intricately detailed lesson plan…and teach you how to make battle equipment?"

Upgrade's feigned disappointment turned into a grin as a huge majority of the class shot their hands into the air. Throwing her arms up in fake exasperation, Upgrade gestured to the far wall, where several cylindrical containers were stacked.

"Probably a good thing that I prepared for this, isn't it? You're all going to learn blueprints today! They're the basis of every design, and you should build the habit early of designing by hand before jumping into the creation part! Everyone pick up a cylinder and bring it back to your workstations. They're all the same, so don't go fighting each other over them."

Upgrade grinned as she saw the looks of relief cross their faces. "Don't open them until everyone has theirs. I don't want to have to repeat myself, so we're all going to start this at the same time. We're going to create a pattern for a new uniform, which will be of great use to you in the upcoming battles. You've probably noticed that some people have already begun customizing their equipment in the last few days. Don't be shy, Sal—give us a twirl."

Upgrade's grin widened as she gestured across the room at Sal, who stood awkwardly. Every eye was drawn to him, and he felt like the entire faculty was conspiring against him. First there was Jez pointing him out to everyone, and now Upgrade.

"You'll all notice that Sal is no longer wearing a gray uniform. His equipment has been upgraded extensively over the past few days, and he could likely withstand a Prowler attack with just his shirt alone. For what it's worth, I don't recommend trying out that theory."

Upgrade hopped off her chair and walked toward Sal at his workstation. She gestured at his shirt as she spoke to the class. "For those of you in the Administration class, you can probably piece together how Sal was able to afford it, but for those not in that class, you'll just have to ask him yourself. I personally oversaw the creation of that equipment, and the blueprint you all have in front of you is a reverse-engineered variant of his new uniform. You won't be able to afford the materials or commission costs, but you can absolutely make a lower-grade version of it. By the end of this class, each of you will have at minimum…a new uniform of Common grade. By the end of our next class, it will be Uncommon grade. That alone will put you two tiers above your peers in the upcoming fights. Sound good?"

A resounding *yes* echoed throughout the classroom, and Upgrade smiled as she gestured for everyone to open their cylinders. "Then we best get to work! Sal has graciously offered to help assist with his Appraisal ability throughout this class, as he doesn't need to work on his own equipment. All together now— 'Thank you, Sal!'"

Upgrade led the entire class in a chorus of thanking Sal, and he just stood there, staring daggers at the obviously delighted Upgrade. When she moved over to his bench, she leaned in close and gave a few parameters for the help he should offer. "Just monitor their blueprints and keep them from getting too adventurous. Offer suggestions rather than corrections. We want everyone to learn as much as possible with this exercise. Sound good?"

Even though she phrased it like a question, Sal knew it wasn't one. He shook his head with a smile as he looked around the class to see who looked the most lost. Josh was waving from the far corner, and Sal pretended not to see him immediately. Instead, he moved to where Blathnaid and Jack were stationed together. Both looked at him in a mixture of disbelief and awe.

Jack shot Upgrade a quick glance before whispering to Sal. "Man, how did you manage to get Upgrade to work on your equipment? That's fucking awesome!" He smiled and looked to Blathnaid for backup, who just nodded in agreement.

Sal saw the beginnings of nerves appearing on her face as she rolled out her blueprint. Before he could calm her nerves, though, she surprised him with a short laugh.

"Wow, this is super basic."

Jack rolled out his own and had a slightly different reaction. "What's super basic? Oh, the runes?"

Sal looked between them as they pointed at different parts of the blueprint.

Blathnaid gestured at the pattern. "I was expecting something complex because Sal is wearing Epic grade equipment, but I could probably tailor this in an hour or so."

Sal blinked at the sudden confidence in her voice.

Jack frowned at his own blueprint. "Any chance you could make mine too? I could knock out those runes in half the time."

Blathnaid nodded and looked up at Sal. "I think we're good here for now. You don't need to babysit us."

Sal couldn't help but laugh at the sudden turnaround in demeanor from the two of them. Rather than moving on to the next bench, he went to his own workstation and retrieved the blueprint that was assigned to him. Taking it over to Jack and Blathnaid, he laid it down on the edge of Jack's table and borrowed one of the styluses.

"Since it's too easy for you at the minute, why don't you aim for the Uncommon grade from the start? It's only a few changes here and here...do you see what I'm doing?"

Sal looked up to see whether Blathnaid was following his suggestions, and to his surprise, she was sketching the changes on her own blueprint at the exact same time as him. Where Sal's lines were guided by the Mythcrafter ability, Blathnaid's was down to pure talent.

She instinctively made corrections as her face broke into a wide smile. "Okay, this is fun!"

Jack, on the other hand, just shook his head. "It's like a whole different language. Don't suppose you've got any idea what the Uncommon Runes look like?"

Sal nodded as he completed the amendments to the blueprint. "I do, but the material cost and cores might be an issue. I'll need to buy us stuff to work with, because the base materials probably won't cut it. Same goes for the fabric. They probably only have rolls of cloth available today."

He glanced behind him to a locked storage container, which he assumed held all the materials they'd be using in the class.

Jack snorted and puffed out his chest. "Clearly, you've never met an Enchanter! I can imbue materials with essence to boost their quality. Basic cloth can become sturdy leather and so on. It's just a bitch to Enchant things that have already been Crafted, but raw materials should be easy!"

Blathnaid turned to Jack excitedly. "Does it still feel like cloth, though? It's so much easier to Tailor with!"

Jack nodded as he gestured to Sal's shirt. "Same as that. It'll feel like silk but can take a ridiculous amount of punishment. Well, similar to that. Epic grade is way beyond my abilities for now."

Sal chatted with the two of them as he completed the blueprint for the Uncommon-grade variant of the pattern. Just as he was about to leave them to move onto another bench, Blathnaid stopped him.

"Should we make some for Anthony and Barry?"

Sal could almost see the gears working in her head as she calculated the workload she was putting on them, and Sal shook his head. "Focus on making your own for now, and we can worry about them in the future."

Jack glanced over his shoulder and looked into the sea of workstations. "I think Anthony is actually here somewhere. Yes, there he is!"

Sal followed Jack's pointed finger and saw Anthony holding the pattern up to the light and turning it in the air, as though he were trying to make sense of it. With a laugh, Sal wished them the best of luck and made his way up the steps to where Anthony was. He didn't make it more than a few paces before someone gestured to get his attention.

Sal didn't recognize the guy, and before any introductions were made, he launched into a series of questions about what they were supposed to be doing. Sal smiled and turned on the backlight of the workstation to illuminate the blueprint. "You don't need to use the stylus to make amendments to it. It's already a complete pattern."

The student nodded and placed the pen back into the slot on the workstation as they looked at the design cautiously.

Sal gestured to the different segments and did his best to simplify it. "It all looks like shapes and numbers, but they're measurements that you can adapt for your own body. You can use your own uniform as a guideline for sizes, but don't be intimidated. It's like a puzzle, where you need to cut out the parts and assemble them."

A few of the students around them were listening in to his explanation and nodding as they referenced the images in front of them.

"Using quality materials as well as good craftsmanship will increase the overall grade of the finished product. You don't need to worry about screwing up anything at this stage, because it's just going to be cutting fabrics to make all the pieces of the puzzle. You only need to ensure that the cuts will fit you when they're assembled later."

A collective sigh of relief came from the surrounding students, but another raised their hand and gestured for Sal to come help them.

He bounced between workstations for the next hour, and answered questions as best he could. He felt like such a fraud because he wouldn't have known any of the answers without the Mythcrafter ability. All he was doing was reverse engineering what his eyes were instinctively telling him was the right way to proceed.

There were moments where people asked about technique and although Sal knew how to get to the end product, he wasn't able to answer them. In those instances, he called over Upgrade, who solved their queries instantly. Sal contented himself with helping people with the basics, and he was warmed by their reactions to his assistance. He never really fancied himself a teacher, but he was enjoying the experience, which didn't escape Upgrade's notice.

"Sal!" Upgrade was back at the front of the classroom when she called out his name.

With a gesture for him to join her, he made his way over. The excited chatter of students talking between workstations was a definite improvement on their mood from when the class had started.

"What's next?" Sal asked as he finally neared her.

Upgrade shook her head. "They have enough to keep them occupied for the next while, so I thought you might want to use the remainder of the class to start prototyping some Combat-oriented designs. I brought a few blueprints for you to have a look at to see what you think." Upgrade opened half a dozen cylinders and withdrew a series of rolled-up blueprints.

"They're all basic enough that you'll be able to manufacture them yourself, and they'll push you to learn techniques that will be vital for your future as a Crafter. I've included some that aid mobility, offense, and defense. They might spark some inspiration, but I'd caution you to use this as an exercise to master the basics before rushing ahead to make another Legendary grade. You get me?" Upgrade raised an eyebrow at him as she held the blueprints away from him.

Only when Sal agreed to pace himself did she hand them over to him. "You can use the workstation at the front of the class to go through them, but none of the materials that you'll need will be in the lockup. You'll have to wait until you're back in the workshop to get started. As much as I want to help you with these and see what you come up with, it's unfair for the faculty to interfere with the class Combat assessment. You're on your own for this one, okay?"

Sal nodded eagerly. He rolled out the first design and his eyes lit up when he saw it. "This almost makes up for making me twirl."

CHAPTER 63:
PRACTICALITY

UPGRADE CUPPED HER FACE IN HER PALMS AS SHE GROANED. "WHAT PART OF this is basic? Help me understand, because I'm pretty sure I told you yesterday that this was an opportunity for you to master the basics!"

Pulling her hands away, she stared again at the modified blueprint before looking back to Sal. "You did another all-nighter, didn't you? I'm not even going to ask about the other designs." With a sigh of exasperation, she stared at Sal before finally conceding to her curiosity. "Fine! Show me the others."

Sal shook his head and made a poor attempt to block the other blueprints from her grasp, but Upgrade snatched one of them and unfurled it onto the workstation. When it was revealed, she shook her head again.

"You're insane."

Sal moved around the table to see which one she had opened.

Upgrade gestured at the blueprints. "Come on then, at least explain them."

Sal laughed at that and shrugged. "I genuinely didn't intend for it to get so out of hand, and I made sure that any improvements I made to them were possible for my skill level...well, mostly. The grappling hook kinda got away from me a bit, and it's definitely outside of my skill set."

Upgrade shook her head and moved around the table to look at the other designs. "I didn't put in a grappling hook! Why the hell did you create a grappling hook?"

Sal's laughter only grew as he held up his palms defensively. "It started out as that arm guard. The defensive shield one, but it was placed over the mobility design and then my eyes just kinda...combined them a bit, and it created this awesome design. I had to sketch it out!"

Upgrade unwrapped one of the other blueprints and stared at it for a few moments before pulling out the next one. She didn't even give Sal a passing glance as she went through them, until she found the grappling hook. When her eyes flitted over the design, she sighed again in exasperation and looked at the ceiling in defeat. "Why are you like this?"

Despite her words, a smile had crept onto her face as she went through the designs. With a pointed finger, she looked directly at Sal and shook her head. "You're not getting help from me or the others with creating this stuff, okay? I'm going to have to supervise literally every step of it, though, because we don't want you killing yourself prematurely."

Upgrade continued to shake her head as she opened the last one. Her face went from exasperation to curiosity as she tilted her head and studied the design in more detail.

"What is this?" When she looked up, all annoyance, both feigned and real, had evaporated. All that was left was genuine curiosity.

Sal didn't need to look to find out which one she had opened. It had started as a back brace that increased defensive capability and strength, but Sal had played with it to turn it into a form of Healing apparatus, using the ability weave of Healer Bitch.

"I tried to come up with defensive equipment that would heal the user. It evolved into an exoskeleton suit. I'll admit that one is definitely outside of my skill set, but it looked really cool. It would probably turn out Legendary if we made it properly." With a shrug, Sal pointed at one of the first blueprints. "In my defense, though, the boots are achievable! Enhanced speed and jumping capability…but yeah, imagine them with the grappling hook!"

Upgrade slumped her shoulders again. "Sal, do you understand what scope-creep is? This is the perfect example of it! None of these are achievable with the time you have before the fights. Hell, one of these pieces would constitute a semester-long project."

With a shake of her head, Upgrade sighed. "I think the sniper rifle has skewed your judgment on what is possible versus what is practical. If you continue Crafting things like this, you'll never appreciate or learn the basics. I'm not trying to place barriers in front of you or trying to limit your potential in any way. I love your designs, but you need to approach this practically." Upgrade lifted the design for the boots and placed it on top of the other blueprints. "I'll supervise you if you decide to Craft these items, but I'd ask you to reconsider them."

Sal smiled, nodding; judging from Upgrade's surprise, she had anticipated a drawn-out argument. He activated his workstation and loaded the designs to show on the screen. Flicking through the iterations, he eventually got to the most recent ones, which were much more basic in scope.

Upgrade stared at them quietly before turning her head to glare at Sal. "You let me rant on for ages and you never intended on making them!"

Sal mimicked Upgrade's voice. "We need to approach this practically."

Upgrade circled around the workstation, and Sal hopped out of her way.

"Okay, I'm sorry. I just wanted to see your reaction! I thought you'd realize it was a joke when you saw the grappling hook!"

Despite her grumbling, Upgrade's face broke into a wry smile as she looked through Sal's proposed designs. Relief softened her scowl as she moved through the concept blueprints. "Okay, these are great. I'm guessing they all fall under Rare grade?"

Sal nodded as he pointed out a few features. "Boots have a minor speed enhancement and leap capability, nothing like the other design that would have you clearing buildings. It'll be good for traversal around the arena."

Upgrade nodded as she pulled up the design for the arm guard. "And this one?"

Sal pointed at the weave design he inscribed at the side. "This one is like the gauntlets I made for Hannah. It uses her shield ability and creates a mobile barrier that's attached to the arm. Should be able to fend off projectile attacks, but I'm playing with the idea of getting it to reflect attacks back. It's probably scope-creep, but if I have the time, that's what I'd like to build toward."

Upgrade nodded again. "Might be a bit ambitious, but it's good to have as a stretch goal for it. What about your exoskeleton?"

Sal grimaced as he flicked across to the next design. "I tried combining it with the arm guard, but it conflicted too much with the shield. It's a separate chest piece that fits over the uniform, and I'm debating on having it use a single charge of restorative essence. I'll admit, though, I've no idea how it would work and the Mythcrafter ability couldn't create anything lower than Epic grade for the functionality I was looking for. Might need to bench that one."

Upgrade nodded again. "Wise choice. I'd suggest going without it for now and focusing on the other pieces. Do you have anything for offense?" Without waiting for him, Upgrade moved to the next blueprint to see a gauntlet design. When she looked up at Sal, he mimicked Hannah's signature pistol gesture.

"Got the idea to shoot bursts of essence by pointing like this. The advanced function is that an open-palm attack creates a pulse that should push people away." Sal raised his right and left arms and demonstrated. "Shield with the left. Shoot with the right. Push back anyone who gets too close." He gestured down at his feet. "Boots help for repositioning and escaping from danger. If I can make sets of these for the team, then we should be in with a fighting chance of avoiding relegation."

Upgrade's eyes widened. "Whoa, slow down for a second! You want to make five sets of these? Sal, it's going to be ambitious just to create a single set! You need to manage your expectations. Why are you smiling?"

Sal withdrew his Q-Card and held it up. "You said that you won't be able to help me, but what if I commission help from the workshop? I've got a lot of Q-Cred that's practically burning a hole in my pocket!"

Upgrade's mouth hung open for a moment before a laugh escaped her lips. "You absolutely knew all of this before meeting me, didn't you? Thank you for the completely unnecessary emotional rollercoaster. Is there anything you actually need from me, or can I get back to work?"

Sal moved the workstation to the last blueprint and grinned at Upgrade. "That Rare-grade sword that I got from the Reavers Guild. I'm going to try to Upgrade it! Was wondering if you had any advice?"

Upgrade just looked between Sal and the blueprint before she grumbled with a lighthearted smile. "Next time, lead with this!"

***

"Ah, Mr. Argento! Thank you for coming to see me at such short notice!" Quest said as he got up from his seat and gestured for Sal to take one of the chairs in front of his desk.

The summons had pulled him from the workshop, but if it ran long enough, it might save him from the grueling training with Divinity and their teams. For that, Sal was inwardly grateful. He took a seat opposite the headmaster and waited expectantly to find out why he had been called in the first place.

Quest wasted no time and jumped straight in.

"So, again…sorry about how last minute this was, but I had an opening in the calendar and wanted to put your mind at ease. We got the reports back from Professor Lombardi regarding Divinity, Martin, Upgrade, and Gosia. There were no negative effects in the last week, but we'll be monitoring their progress as they continue using the skill-pods. In Professor Lombardi's opinion, he doesn't foresee any problems with the unknotting that you performed on them."

Quest's relief was apparent as he ran through the details, and Sal felt a pang of guilt that he had practically forgotten about it with everything that had been going on over the last number of days.

Quest slid a tablet across the table for Sal to look at as he continued. "In such a short space of time, you've made a considerable impact at the academy, and I wanted to offer you a few reassurances. Your value as a Skill Master and Mythcrafter won't be overlooked when tallying the final results at the end of the semester. It's a stressful time for Crafters and those in the Support classes as we enter the Combat-oriented cycle, and although we want you to try your best and to learn as much as possible…there are multiple avenues at Quest Academy for people like yourself to succeed. Which brings me to a sensitive topic."

He paused for a moment and framed his next words carefully, watching Sal's reaction. "You are the first student we've had who was able to create an entirely new skill. When I debriefed Professor Lombardi on it, he made a proposal that we'd like to explore over the coming months. On that tablet is a shortlist of skills that we believe could have a strong cohesion. The proposal that was made was to see if you could combine those skills to create something new that would benefit everyone."

Sal stared at the headmaster, wondering whether he was hearing this pitch correctly.

Quest put up his hands and laughed. "Don't worry, we're not asking you to do this, and everything is hypothetical at this stage…but I wanted to ask you if it was something you'd consider in the future? It would be a great help to the academy and the Doom Council. I can appreciate that this is likely an overwhelming proposal at this point, and we'd obviously consult with your parents to ensure they were comfortable with any sort of arrangement we were to come up with. Even if you refused, your value as a Mythcrafter and your ability to permanently unlock latent capability in others…well, it goes without saying how vital those skills will be for us in the future. Our ask is that you consider what your next ability would be and to consult us before deciding."

Quest smiled warmly. "Maybe it's my own hubris speaking, but I'd love it if you incorporated my ability in the future as it would allow you to see the world completely differently and ensure the legacy of the Quest Academy. Maybe having a system in your brain would drive you insane, though." With a laugh, he looked at Sal expectantly, who didn't share the same jovial energy.

Sal wanted to clarify what was being asked of him, because even though words like "hypothetical" were being thrown around, it sounded like a genuine request.

"First of all, I'm happy to hear that everyone is safe after the unknotting of their skills." He started off slowly, choosing his own words carefully.

Quest nodded appreciatively and waved his hand with a smile. "Come on, you can say what's really on your mind. You don't have to be worried. I'm asking a lot of you here, and I'd rather know your true feelings instead of platitudes."

Sal relaxed at that, and he spread his hands in exasperation.

"Honestly, I never thought I'd be qualified to be a Hero. I was going to come here, try my best and then likely go back to work with my parents at the auction. Unlocking the potential of others was a wonderful feeling, and I felt horrible when I thought I might have caused them harm." Sal started rambling through his own thoughts, and Quest just smiled reassuringly as he sat quietly on the other side of the desk.

"Getting the Mythcrafter ability was incredible, and I finally feel like I have my own ability…that I can make things with my own power. I had no idea how amazing the sniper rifle was until Watcher explained it to me. It made me realize that I'm naive and that I've got a lot to learn. I didn't know that I was risking my internal core by creating the Mythcrafter ability, and I'm worried that my lack of understanding is going to either hurt me or someone else."

Sal grimaced as he spoke. He couldn't believe he was pouring out his feelings to the headmaster of all people, but he needed to get it off his chest. "It feels like everyone has really high expectations of me, and I'm worried I'll end up letting them down. Does that make sense?"

Quest nodded. "It absolutely makes sense. You should have seen me when I pitched the concept of an academy. I was a quivering mess and second-guessed every decision I made. I was surrounded by capable people, and we all wanted the same thing—to take back our home and push the demons out. The solidarity of a shared vision is a powerful thing, Salvatore. You're creating strong bonds with your classmates and the members of faculty, and you've only been here a few weeks. Things will make more sense as time goes on, and you familiarize yourself with your own limits and capabilities. We want to support you and nurture your gifts as much as possible, but not at the expense of your sanity. It probably feels like the weight of the world is on your shoulders, which is why I wanted to show you that list of abilities."

Quest tapped the tablet again. "It's more than just a collection of abilities. It's a reminder that you're not the only exceptional person in this academy. There are people here who can bend time, nullify essence, summon ethereal dragons! We've got people who can project a barrier that could cover the entire campus! All of them are your peers, so don't worry that the fate of humanity is depending on you…it's all about solidarity and us working together. Everyone is here to learn, develop, and grow. We're just trying to guide you as best we can, that's all it is."

Sal sighed in relief and an enormous weight lifted off his shoulders. "Ethereal dragons? Really?" The question came out before he could stop himself, and Quest laughed.

"Yes, it's pretty impressive. It's a third-year who's being scouted by pretty much all the Tier One guilds at the moment. But to bring you back to the question at hand…take the tablet with you and have a think about those compositions. There's no urgency on our side. We'd rather you had as much information as possible if it results in unlocking a new skill that helps humanity. Sound good?"

Sal nodded with a smile. "Sounds good."

Quest clapped and then got to his feet. "Excellent! I won't keep you any longer as I know you've got another commitment down in the training rooms."

Sal laughed. "I'm not even going to ask how you know about that."

Quest opened the door and held it for him. "Spies everywhere, Mr. Argento. They tell me all the students' secrets. From divined training regimens to unorthodox grappling hooks…I hear it all."

CHAPTER 64:
ROUTINE

Sal slipped into a routine over the following week, with most of his time out of classes being spent on training with the teams or in the workshop. Even though he trusted in Divinity's training, it was still surreal for him to attend Rust's class, where they learned basic formations. It was an absolute shit-show, with most of the teams breaking down and shouting at one another.

As each evening passed, their training got tougher, and their team synergy increased. The aches and pains persisted throughout, with Divinity finding a new way to inflict pain when she got past someone's defenses. Skill class had resulted in three new gates being achieved, which brought Sal's total up to twenty-one. He had intended to spend some time during the evenings on meditation, but the sparring left him exhausted beyond anything he had ever felt before.

When he did have energy, he poured it into Crafting in the workshop and improving on the components that he commissioned from the staff and students there. All in all, it was a busy week and on the night he had specifically taken off to hang out with Hannah, he ended up falling asleep on her bed within minutes. He got a few teasing messages after that particular episode, but she was understanding when she found out how much work he was doing outside of class.

Jack and Blathnaid had successfully Crafted their Uncommon-grade uniforms, which they wore proudly to each class. Anthony eventually caved and asked for help with the construction of it, which they happily obliged with. Barry hadn't uttered a word about the uniforms and just threw himself into the training. His backhanded comments and remarks had faded over the evenings and turned into a strong resolve to improve.

Their formation work improved drastically, and the teams followed instructions without any hesitation. With the help of the vendor drinks, their progress was fast, and Divinity visibly relaxed with each successful training meet-up. Every time Sal asked her for an update on their chances, she refused to answer and told him that they needed to focus instead of becoming complacent.

When the following Monday finally arrived, Sal was a sleep-deprived husk of a man. He sat in the canteen like a zombie, clutching a coffee with both hands, knowing that the moment he moved it to his face, the sharp pains from the previous night's training would kick in. The vendor coffee would bring relief, but to get that relief, he needed to endure pain. It was the vicious cycle of his morning routine.

"Is someone feeling a little delicate this morning?" Divinity teased as she gingerly took her seat across from him.

"Oh! I think he is!" Barry's answered the question aimed at Sal, as he took a seat beside them.

Sal gave them both a withering look, which only amused them more.

Barry hiked a thumb over his shoulder to gesture at the remainder of their teams queuing at the vendor stall. "They're going to take a couple of minutes. You might want to down that drink so they don't think you're on the verge of death."

His shit-eating grin made Sal want to punch him, and Divinity's musical laugh didn't help in the slightest. When the coffee took effect, Sal sighed as the pain evaporated from his body.

"Only a few more days of this hell and then we can stop the training, right?" Sal pleaded, and Divinity nodded.

"I was starting to think you were enjoying it. What happened last night?"

Instead of answering, Sal pointed at Barry, who turned to Divinity and held his hands up innocently. "Sal made the executive decision to try out the new gauntlets he commissioned. Let's just say that the pulse attack is much stronger than the shield defense."

Divinity's eyes widened. "They're done? How did they go?"

Sal closed his eyes for a moment and bit back the retort that came to his lips. With a slight shake of his head, he finally muttered an answer. "Effective. They're...super effective."

Barry laughed. "He was knocked back like ten feet. His shirt didn't even register it as an attack, so he took the full force of it. You should have seen it—it was hilarious!"

Divinity burst out laughing, which she quickly tried to stifle. "I'm sorry, Sal. But it does sound funny. Try to imagine Gerard on the receiving end of it?"

Sal finally conceded and let out a reluctant laugh, which caused a shooting pain in his midsection. With a groan, he drank more of the coffee and shot Barry another dark look. A moment later, the rest of the teams were seated around them, and Divinity called for their attention.

"So, we're on the final stretch now! We're going to continue training for the next three evenings and leave Thursday and Friday for recovery. On those days, we'll familiarize ourselves with the new equipment, courtesy of Sal. The first fights will start on Saturday, and we'll be swapping out equipment between our teams. As discussed, if we're matched up against each other, the team with the highest number of victories will forfeit the match convincingly to the other team, and we can ensure there are no injuries. Over to Sal, who is a little delicate at the moment."

Divinity gestured across the table to Sal, who shook his head.

"Shield gauntlets and pistol gauntlets are completed, but after a bit of testing yesterday...I'd like to give them a few tweaks. Jack, if you could help look over the runes on the shield gauntlets, that'd be great because I think I've missed something."

Jack nodded eagerly and gave him a quick thumbs-up.

Sal thanked him and moved on. "Leaper boots are still being worked on because of the different sizes, and they might not work well for switching between teams, but we'll try our best in the time we have left. I'll bring everything to the training room tonight, but I need a few people to help me carry them all. We can test everything then and see what you think. Altogether, we've poured in just over a thousand Q-Cred into this plan...and I'm convinced the vendors have seen the majority of it! For what it's worth, I think it's an absolute bargain for what we've accomplished so far, and it's putting us on the right track."

Barry nearly choked on his coffee at the mention of the cost, and he looked at Sal in disbelief. His reaction was mirrored by several of the faces around the table.

Sal grinned and shrugged. "Honestly, with the effort everyone has put in, I don't regret a single transaction. The luck of the draw and the way these teams were created, we were pretty much set up to fail. They just want to see how we adapt to adversity, and that's exactly what we're doing. Just try your best when it comes to the fights—that's all we can ask for."

Barry raised his coffee cup up high. "I propose a toast. To the most desperate team captains in the Silver cohort! Thanks for picking us…even if you didn't really have a choice."

Everyone broke into smiles as they raised their own cups in a silent salute. Divinity and Sal glanced at each other and laughter overtook them.

***

Upgrade grinned as she inspected each of the completed pieces on the table. "Gotta be honest with you, Sal. I've never watched the first-year student battles." She glanced up at Sal, who was hunched over the Rare-grade sword. He was completely absorbed in his Appraisal and didn't even look up. Upgrade would know that he was listening, though, as she'd gotten used to his work style over the last few weeks.

"I always hated seeing the crafting students getting punished for not having combat-oriented abilities. With it taking place so soon in the semester, they never had a real opportunity to showcase their potential." Upgrade looked up from the sets of arm guards, boots, and gauntlets with a smile. "Everyone in the workshop wants to go and watch this year! I never thought I'd see the day that we'd all be excited to watch a crafting team compete! Are you nervous?"

Sal blinked as he took a step back from the sword. With a slight shake of his head and a pinch to the inner edges of his eyes, he turned to Upgrade with a wry smile. "Maybe apprehensive more than nervous. I think we've prepared enough to represent ourselves well, even if it's not enough to be competitive. The aim is to avoid relegation rank and put all of this behind us."

He looked at the equipment on the table with a proud smile. Information about each piece popped up in front of him, pulling his smile wider. "I know that you said you wouldn't help, but I really appreciate you getting the other Crafters onboard. I'd still be queuing in their backlogs if it wasn't for you."

Name	Pulse Gauntlets
Origin	Crafted
Age	New
Grade	Uncommon (Higher)
Dimensions	Circumference 8.5 inches
Materials	Refined Mythcrafter Essence | Faux Bovine Leather | Iron
Attributes	**Repel**: Creates a pushback effect in targeted area. **Essence Bullet**: Creates low impact projectiles at high speed.
Abilities	Repel | Essence Bullet
Power Source	Basic Core
Evolution	No
Quality	Excellent
Condition	100%
Value	Est. $2,200.00 – $3,500.00

Name	Tactical Boots
Origin	Crafted
Age	New
Grade	Uncommon (Lower)
Dimensions	Size 11
Materials	Refined Mythcrafter Essence | Faux Bovine Leather | Infused Rubber
Attributes	**Feather**: Weight of wearer is reduced, increasing jump height and movement speed.
Abilities	Feather
Power Source	External Essence
Evolution	No
Quality	Excellent
Condition	100%
Value	Est. $1,000.00 – $2,000.00

Name	Shield Guard
Origin	Crafted
Age	New
Grade	Uncommon (Upper)
Dimensions	Length 8 inches | Circumference 9 inches (Adjustable)
Materials	Refined Mythcrafter Essence | Infused Iron
Attributes	**Barrier:** Creates a protective shield in front of the wearer. **Impact:** Negates incoming attacks with chance to reflect damage.
Abilities	Barrier | Impact
Power Source	Basic Core | External Essence
Evolution	No
Quality	Excellent
Condition	100%
Value	Est. $3,000.00 – $4,500.00

Upgrade shook her head. "Nothing to do with me. I just told them that we might have a competitive team in the Combat class this year…and they decided to prioritize those commissions themselves. I know a lot of them are curious about how you assembled them and what they look like now. Sure you don't want to invite them in for a peek?" Upgrade gestured over her shoulder, but Sal shook his head.

"The less people know about them, the better. I don't want the other teams creating countermeasures before we even get started."

Upgrade snorted then brought her hand to her face with a laugh. "Sorry! It's just adorable how you think the other teams are that tactical."

When Sal frowned, Upgrade looked at him in disbelief.

"You do know that it's going to be a complete shit-show, right? They start this thing off in the first month so you can all learn how shit you are, so you throw yourself into your training earnestly. The big stakes aren't going to happen until the inter-cohort segments, which won't be until later in the semester."

Sal shook his head at that. "Divinity looked into the future and saw that we get relegated unless we took it seriously, and I trust her judgment."

Upgrade shrugged. "Well, if she was able to see into the past, she'd know that historically…there's not much to expect of the first few fights. I didn't mean to discourage you or make you complacent. Just remember that this is all about learning, and that trying your best will be noticed by Rust. That's all that matters, really."

When Sal didn't answer immediately, Upgrade's expression softened. With a feigned sigh of exasperation, she moved over to the sword and gestured for him to move out of the way. "Come on, let me have a look at your latest masterpiece. Walk me through it."

Sal's face broke into a smile as he moved to the side. "I was going to use Restoration on the blade, but I took your advice to get it reforged completely. It's even better than the original state, but it meant we had to redo all the runes on it. I got Jack to trace them out, but I channeled the essence into them because his ability isn't strong enough yet. He was able to enchant the blade, though, which is something the original sword didn't have."

Sal gestured at the intricate hilt at the base of the sword. "This was cracked before, so we recast it with the help of Forge. I switched out the core for one with more essence storage capacity, and it adapted well to it. The weave of metal that acted as a guard was broken, so I tried to design them as little tentacles, but I don't think it really worked."

Upgrade raised an eyebrow as she inspected it and burst out laughing when she saw the little face at the bottom of the sword. "Did you create a little octopus?"

Sal laughed as he shrugged. "I'm pretty sure I was delirious at this point, but I thought it might add a little bit of character to it. All the components are in place. I just need to flood it with essence, and it'll be complete. I've got the Skill class with Professor Lombardi later, so I'll probably have to wait until tomorrow. Need my essence at full strength to push through more gates."

Upgrade tilted her head as she looked at the sword. "I kinda want to see it now, though…" When she looked at Sal, she held up the key to the core storage room. "What if you didn't have to use your own essence?"

Sal grinned. "I won't tell if you don't."

CHAPTER 65:
OVERCHARGE

"Aren't you forgetting something?" Upgrade chided as she shot a meaningful look at Sal's hands. Sal gave her a pleading look, but she shook her head. "You're not going to get better at it unless you practice. Even if your Mythcrafter ability allows you to manage everything with your essence, you need to learn how to do it with your hands too. Control the tools with your essence, and I'll be here to guide you."

Sal sighed in defeat as he started to channel his essence through the Epic-grade gloves that Upgrade had Crafted for him. In the last few weeks, he had tried a handful of times to use them like Upgrade did, but it was incredibly difficult to maintain and slowed his pace dramatically. After a few false starts, Sal's heartbeat started to race. He didn't want to jeopardize the sword by using a technique he couldn't control.

When that panic blended with the pressure of Upgrade's expectations, Sal's gloves continually failed to activate.

Before he could say a word, Upgrade spoke to him calmly. "It's actually a relief that you're not perfect at everything. Really warms my heart as an educator that you've still got shit to learn."

Upgrade stood beside him and raised her own hands. "You're overthinking it. Essence is something that you need to carefully negotiate with, and when it comes to Crafting, it can be particular. It needs to be smoothed out with precision."

Sal nodded, as he felt the exact same way about it.

Upgrade pointed at his gloves. "Those are tools that are made to withstand ridiculous amounts of punishment. Overloading, or supercharging…whatever you want to call it…is all about aggression. You need to flood the gloves with your essence and control them. Tentatively asking them if they want to comply with you isn't going to work. Drown the fuckers in essence and make them work for you. When they activate, pull the leash and control your flow of essence. Understand?"

Sal just stared at Upgrade. It was by far the most outlandish instruction he had ever heard, but it strangely made sense to him.

Upgrade looked at the gloves and pointed at the sword on the table. "Show me if you understand."

Sal nodded as he raised his hands. He had a core set aside for essence, so he didn't really have anything to lose from trying it Upgrade's way. He threw his essence at the gloves aggressively and felt an immediate resistance from them. Rather than backing off like his instincts told him, he pushed the essence through them as he was told.

Just when he was sure the gloves had hit a breaking point, they activated fully and synergized with his uniform. A warm sensation in Sal's collar told him that the core in his uniform had activated, and the black circuitry from his shirt shot straight to the gloves.

Upgrade's voice sounded out beside him. "Push more for the transformation and then yank on the leash."

Sal didn't acknowledge her words as he was desperately trying to get control of the gloves. All his instincts told him that he needed to back off, but he trusted in Upgrade and flooded the gloves with even more essence. The result was immediate, and his entire torso transformed into a mechanized suit of armor. Both of his arms were plated, but the most impressive thing by far was that his fingers had turned into mechanical claws.

"Leash it!"

Upgrade's warning snapped him out of his stupor, and he yanked at his essence to control the flow, leaving just enough to keep the transformation active. When he did it, he felt a sense of harmony, as if he were cloaked in a reassuring blanket of essence. His hands practically itched to get to work on the sword, and Sal instinctively knew that he could control every component of his armor. Raising his left hand, Sal imagined it as a sword, and was shocked to see a blade slide out from where his knuckles would have been. Upgrade's laugh brought Sal back to reality, and he deactivated the sword attachment.

When he looked over to where she stood, Upgrade was happily admiring his new appearance. "Now, isn't that just gorgeous?"

Sal didn't know how much longer he'd be able to use the setup, so rather than talking it out with Upgrade, he focused on the sword. The first thing he did was tether himself to the essence core on the table, which gave him more breathing room for maintaining the mechanical arms as well as full rein with the Mythcrafter ability.

For some reason, Sal wanted to try redesigning the little tentacles on the guard. They were clunky, which he put down to his own lack of design experience. Now that he had the mechanical arms, Sal had a growing sense of competence and he wanted to fix them a bit. It was only an aesthetic modification but would be a good test for the new arms.

Upgrade raised an eyebrow as she moved around to watch him work.

Each of Sal's fingers were imbued with essence and were like fine needles as they scratched away at the metal. Sal couldn't explain how it was happening, but the vision in his head was being translated perfectly through his fingertips.

What had once been a crude attempt at a creature turned into a lifelike replica of a tiny octopus. Intricate little suction cups were being carved into the tentacles, and Sal's eyes started to make minor suggestions on how they could be improved. Before he could debate on including the rune suggestions, his fingers had masterfully etched them onto it. Complete runes the size of Sal's fingernail now lined the tentacles of the octopus and made it look even more lifelike.

After about ten minutes of refining the tentacles, Sal moved to the small head, which he shaped even further. He knew that it was the core and he needed to be careful, but the Mythcrafter ability and his fingers knew what needed to be done. He didn't have any time to think about his actions as they were completed almost automatically.

Sal was exhilarated by how efficient everything felt. There was no second-guessing, just action. When the guard and hilt pieces were done, Sal started to notice other little aesthetic elements that could be improved with his newfound precision. He didn't feel any guilt in tweaking the sword at this stage, because it was just about making it look better. There were some runes that were tightened, and the Mythcrafter ability made suggestions that Sal had previously ignored as he lacked the necessary expertise.

With more space on the blade, Sal instinctively added additional runes that popped into his head. This went on for another thirty minutes, where Sal's fingers moved rapidly across the sword, all under the watchful eyes of Upgrade, who smiled in approval.

Just when Sal was about to move back to the guard of the sword, Upgrade coughed. "I know you're having fun, but it's time to put it all together with your essence."

Sal smiled ruefully at that. He was running the risk of reworking it constantly, so he heeded Upgrade's caution and lifted his hands away from the sword. With a quick check on the core's essence, he was surprised to see that more than a quarter of it had been used already.

With a flex of his now-mechanical fingers, Sal channeled his essence into the sword. It was nothing like the experience with the sniper rifle. As most of the components were extensively worked on by Sal, he was already heavily attuned to it. The sword happily drank the essence, and Sal was able to meticulously guide it with his needle-like fingers. Areas where the essence didn't smooth out, he was able to manually massage it into the blade. Pommel, guard, hilt, and blade all took the essence without issue. The area that was most greedy for it was the little octopus, which ultimately brought the essence core down to about ten percent.

Sal continued pouring essence into it and was happy when it reached a point where it couldn't take any more. The sword started to glow vibrantly, which was similar to the sensation he felt with the sniper rifle. Sal's eyes looked for any sort of issue, but the Mythcrafter skill was telling him that it was done. With that in mind, Sal took a step back and deactivated his suit transformation, as well as cutting off the Mythcrafter ability.

"That's it?" Upgrade asked as she moved around the table to wait for the completed result.

Sal nodded. "That's it!"

Both watched in silence as the glowing sword pulsated with essence for a few moments, continuing to vibrate slightly on the table. When the glow finally disappeared, Upgrade whistled.

"That doesn't look like the sword from the blueprint."

Sal laughed awkwardly as he moved forward to have a closer look at the result. "Yeah, I made a few changes when I had the gloves activated…and I think I probably went off script in the heat of the moment. The Mythcrafter ability kinda put me into autopilot, and I think I ended up adding more stuff than was necessary."

Upgrade frowned. "Build quality is very important, but don't over-engineer it. Otherwise, it'll end up being a conflicted mess of runes and fail to activate. Are you going to Appraise it now or later? It still looks like a Rare grade to me."

Sal debated whether he should leave early to get to the next class or just get the Appraisal done. In the back of his head, he was disappointed that it turned out so lackluster with all the effort that he had put into it. After a moment of deliberation, Sal reached out and picked up the sword. "Might as well check out the—"

Upgrade gasped as the tentacles started to move around Sal's fist. The dull blade that looked the exact same as before suddenly transformed into a vibrant silver. Without wasting any time, Sal activated his eyes and started to Appraise the sword. His eyes widened as he saw its secrets.

Name	Voracious Rapier
Origin	Portal Artifact (Reworked)
Age	New (Reworked)
Grade	Rare (Upper)
Dimensions	45 inches | Blade length 36 inches | Blade width 1 inch | Blade thickness 1/4 inch
Materials	Refined Mythcraft Essence | Enhanced Core | Reforged Hellfire Titanium
Attributes	**Absolute Counter:** Sword will successfully counter all short-ranged attacks. **Overcharge:** Grade and Abilities of the Sword are enhanced for a short period of time. **Arc Strike:** Mid to Long-Range projectile attack. **Attune:** Wielder can change trajectory of attacks at will.
Abilities	Absolute Counter | Overcharge | Arc Strike | Attune
Power Source	Enhanced Core
Evolution	No
Quality	Excellent
Condition	100%
Value	Est. $50,000.00 – $85,000.00

"What is it?" Upgrade asked as she took a slight step back from him, her eyes watching the moving octopus warily.

Sal had never seen anything like it before, and tried to explain as best as he could.

"It has a trait called Overcharge, so it doesn't show its true skills unless it's being given a stream of essence." Sal glanced down at the tentacles that had made their way up his forearm. The sword felt powerful in his hand, and the essence it siphoned wasn't that demanding. "It still has the long-range projectile attack, but…everything is dependent on how much essence the user puts into it. I think it's just like the gloves!"

Sal looked through it in more detail and laughed sheepishly. "I thought I had added the shield rune to it, but apparently I created a different one from a skill weave I've been using every night." Upgrade looked at him quizzically, and Sal turned the blade to show off the glowing white runes. "It now has Rust's ability. Absolute Counter."

Upgrade frowned and looked at the blade carefully. "Overcharge, long-range essence attack…and Absolute Counter? Yeah, I'm changing my verdict. There's no way that's a Rare grade anymore."

Sal nodded in agreement. "It's a Low Epic grade at this point, but it really depends."

"What do you mean?"

Rather than answering immediately, Sal pumped his essence into the blade and watched the silver metal transform into a shiny black. The tentacles swept farther up Sal's arms to grasp onto his shoulder, giving him an entire sleeve of protective metal. He bent his elbow and was happy it retained all flexibility. On the blade itself, the white runes transformed into an electric yellow.

"It's now an Upper Epic grade…and the abilities are much stronger."

Upgrade stared at the transformation of the sword.

When Sal deactivated his essence completely, the sword regressed back to its dull form, with the tentacles retracting and solidifying around the guard.

Upgrade held up the engraver and handed it to him. "Sign it, right now."

Sal laughed as he took it from her and wrote "MYTH" on a free space along the blade.

Upgrade watched over his shoulder to make sure that he did it, and when he was completed, she clapped him on the back. "I'm taking full credit for this because I taught you how to use those gloves." With a wide grin, she turned to him. "You're welcome."

CHAPTER 66:
WILDCARD

"Excellent work, Blathnaid!" Divinity shouted out from across the training hall.

Rather than acknowledging the praise, Blathnaid continued to use the leaper boots to dodge and weave through her opponents. When she was finally faced with Barry, who launched at her head-on, Blathnaid jumped over him, flipping her body and landing on her feet on the other side. All that was left was the energy attacks, and she was already running toward the finish line.

Sal whipped his sword in a slashing motion, which sent a wave of white light straight at Blathnaid, but she managed to block most of it with her shield. The force of the blow almost knocked her off her feet, but with a quick pivot, she was back to a full sprint. The next two attacks missed her completely, and she practically flung herself across the finish line to rounds of applause from the two teams.

Divinity tapped on her tablet and grinned. "You're in third place after me and Barry! Well done!"

She looked around to see who was next. With only a few days left before the first fights, Divinity had proposed a gauntlet-style training plan. Each person would face off against eight others and must run from one point of the training area to the other. They would have a shield, pistol gauntlet, and leaper boots, but the aim of the run was evasion rather than defeating opponents. It proved to be a fun exercise that allowed Sal to train with the long-ranged attacks, too.

Blathnaid grinned as she lay on her back on the ground, pulling off the gauntlet and arm guard lazily. Her breathing was heavy, but she was delighted with her performance. "Where is Jack on the list?" Her eyes sparkled.

Sal had never expected her to be the competitive type.

Divinity glanced at her tablet for a second. "He's currently second from the bottom, with only Anthony below him."

Sal turned to look at Anthony, who stood awkwardly in the center of the training area.

"Give me a second, Divinity." Sal gestured at Anthony.

Divinity grinned as she motioned to the sword in Sal's hand. "Even though I know what happens, it's still one of my all-time favorite visions."

Barry looked between them. "What am I missing here?"

Much to the surprise of everyone, it was Blathnaid, still panting on the ground, who answered.

"Anthony's ability is Supercharge. Sal's sword gets better when it's pumped up with essence, so…my guess is they're going to trade and see what happens?"

Divinity smiled as she turned to Barry. "It's worth watching, trust me." Barry grinned as he started to move to where Anthony stood, but Divinity pulled him back. "You'll want to stay back here, though. It's about to get chaotic."

When Sal approached Anthony, he turned around with a grimace. "Divinity wants me to do another run, I take it?" When Sal shook his head, Anthony's shoulders slumped in relief. "I'm getting better at the formations and stuff, but this is just…I'm not made for it. Know what I mean?"

His earnest expression showed Sal just how uncomfortable he was with everything that was happening. In the weeks that they'd been training together, Anthony had put in the effort but wasn't seeing the same progress as the others. Sal offered Anthony the sword, but the bearded man didn't make any moves to take it. Instead, he looked at Sal as though he were crazy.

"No, man. The highest chance we have of winning is if you have that sword. I don't want to jeopardize your chances by being useless."

Sal laughed and reached out with the sword farther. "*Our* chances. You're a part of the team, and we want to see what happens when you Supercharge the sword. Divinity says it's a good call, and I trust her."

Anthony reluctantly took the sword and almost dropped it. "Oh! It's a bit heavier…than it looks." He finally got a good grasp on it and shot Sal an awkward smile. "How does it work?"

Sal walked him through the main functions of the sword, and Anthony's eyes widened in surprise. He was even more eager to hand it back after the explanation, but Sal wouldn't allow it.

"Just activate your ability with it, and we'll see what happens. A few of us will come up with shields and the pistol gauntlets after you're a bit more comfortable with it."

Anthony's face drained of color. "Wait, like a sparring session?"

Sal waved his hand around. "Something like that. But only when you're more comfortable with it. Anyway, wait until I'm a bit away from you before you activate it, okay? And don't worry when the tentacles start moving around your arm—it's just an effect of the sword."

Anthony laughed as he looked down at the little octopus. "Okay, but don't hold your breath. I'll probably fuck this up, too."

When Sal got back to where the group stood, Divinity handed him one of the arm guards with a meaningful look. Sal took it without complaint and activated it the moment it clasped around his forearm. A bright blue shield appeared in front of it, and he kept it raised.

"We're ready when you are, Anthony!" Sal shouted across to him, and all they got in return was a thumbs-up gesture.

Divinity and Barry had their own shields raised, with Blathnaid, Jack, and the others huddled behind them, peeking over shoulders to see what would happen. It was an incredible anti-climax to start, where Anthony activated his ability and panicked when the tentacles coiled around his wrist. A brief apology sounded out before he tried again. Sal knew that the blade turned silver before turning black, and he hoped that Anthony would be able to achieve a level close to that to maximize their potential as a team. The reality, however, was not what Sal had expected.

"Fuck!" Anthony shouted as the tentacles wrapped around his torso, coating him in a writhing suit of red armor.

A pure-white blade glowed brilliantly, to the point that Anthony had to shield his eyes from the sudden exposure to it. Sal's eyes activated, and he tried to see how the blade had evolved in Anthony's hands, but he was too far to see it properly. Anthony grimaced and tentatively swung his arm in a wide arc, creating a thunderous crackling noise that sounded out across the entire training area.

Sal's jaw dropped when the projectile whipped forward at lightning speed, and suddenly halted in mid-air. Anthony twisted the blade in his hand and the projectile reacted, moving to a different trajectory and slamming into the protective walls. The training room shuddered ever so slightly, and everyone gaped at Anthony in absolute shock. The most terrified of all was Anthony, who stared at the wall he had just hit in horror.

"I'm not fucking attacking him while he has that," Barry whispered harshly to the others, but Divinity shot forward toward Anthony.

"Get ready to attack!" she warned him with a laugh, and Anthony whirled around to look at her as though she were crazy.

Sal could see the conflict on Anthony's face, so he made it much easier of a decision. "If you don't hit her, she's going to hit you!"

Maybe it was the trauma of the last couple of weeks, but that threat was enough to get Anthony back to his senses. He moved into a protective stance and brought the blade around to slash directly at Divinity's location. It was only when the projectile launched viciously at her that Divinity reacted, planting her leaper boots firmly on the ground and launching herself above the swordsman. Rather than redirecting the projectile, Anthony whipped the sword around and launched another at her. The first attack sailed straight to Sal and Barry, who looked at each other nervously.

"You better have fixed these shields," Barry warned, just as the attack hit the barriers.

Sal laughed at the destructive power of the attack, as Barry was flung mercilessly backward. Sal's uniform deflected the blow completely this time, as it was perceived as a threat. When he looked back, he saw Divinity leaping around, shooting at Anthony with her pistol gauntlet, but the blade intercepted every single shot and launched them right back at her.

Despite his better judgment, Sal rushed forward with his equipment and entered the fray, shouting behind him for the others to join him. Anthony's face was absolutely priceless as he watched his arm move by itself, the sword utilizing the Absolute Counter ability, and his projectile attacks being incredibly destructive.

"How much longer can you last?" Sal shouted to Anthony, who glanced over at the noise. Without him even looking at the incoming attack, the sword snapped over and blocked a sneak attack from Divinity's pistol gauntlet.

Anthony thought about the question and then looked back at Sal with a perplexed expression. "I could probably keep this up for about another hour. Is that bad?"

Divinity's laugh was his only answer as she moved in close to launch a kick at his knees. The sword pulled Anthony's body in a different direction, and the kick bounced uselessly off his armored torso. Blathnaid and Jack appeared with their pistol gauntlets, and the tempo increased dramatically. Bullets of essence were being fired at Anthony, but the sword deflected all of them with ease. In between attacks, when they got too close to him, he sent a projectile wave at the ground in front of them, knocking them back farther. The other members of Divinity's team watched from the sidelines as they didn't have any means to attack or defend, and Barry lay in a heap, probably unconscious.

The sparring match lasted only a few more minutes before everyone was pretty much taken out. Although the shields were decent at deflecting the pistol gauntlet bullets, they weren't capable of withstanding attacks from the supercharged sword. After a few attacks, Jack and Blathnaid bowed out, and Sal wasn't far behind them. There was no real way to get past the sword's defense, and even with Divinity's knowledge of the future, it was a war of attrition that Anthony was much likelier to win. When Divinity put her hand in the air and called it, Anthony deactivated the sword.

He looked at it in complete disbelief and continued to shake his head as he moved to give it back to Sal. "Where did you even get something like this? Who is Myth?"

Sal wearily got to his feet and stretched his back, hoping that he wouldn't be in agony the next morning. He gestured to Anthony to hold onto the sword.

"After all the Appraisal work I did for the Reavers Guild, they gave me a Rare-grade sword for the upcoming battles. Myth is a guy who does work with them, and he added a few improvements to it. He clearly doesn't understand his own worth yet." Sal laughed as he looked at the sword in a whole new light.

Anthony could only nod in appreciation as he cradled the sword in his hands.

When Divinity approached them, she was smiling. "Amazing, wasn't it?"

Sal nodded as he looked at Anthony. "No pressure, but you're likely going to be the deciding factor in the fights to come."

Just when it looked like the color had finally returned to Anthony's face, that comment brought him right back to a state of anxiety. But rather than denying it, Anthony gripped the sword and smiled. "I'll try my best."

Sal clapped him on the back. "That's all we can ask for!"

Barry got to his feet when they were packing up the equipment. The entire time he was helping, he glared daggers at Anthony, who actively tried to avoid meeting his eyes.

Sal laughed. "Is something feeling a little delicate, Barry?"

Divinity chuckled at that, too, as they left the training rooms together. When they were coming out of the tower, Sal turned to her.

"Don't suppose you'll give us an update on how we're pacing? Or are you still worried we'll get complacent if we know?"

Divinity shook her head. With a glance over her shoulder to see whether anyone was listening, she lowered her tone. "I've been looking into the future, and I can't trust what I'm seeing at the minute. So, we're going to have to go into this competition blind."

Sal frowned. "What do you mean you can't trust it?"

Divinity looked at him meaningfully and checked behind again. "The vision we had at the Doom Society meeting…with Sinclair. It's supposed to happen this weekend."

Sal stared at her in complete shock but before he could say a word, Divinity put her finger to her lips. "Quest assured me that it's being taken care of. I've met with him every few days to keep him in the loop, but there hasn't been a change. It's apparently only one potential outcome, and he's saying that because I'm worried about it, I'm predicting it out of fear…rather than out of likelihood."

Sal couldn't believe what he was hearing. "If it is the future, and they're not listening to you…what should we do?"

Divinity gestured at their teams behind them. "We've done all we can to prepare for it, and now all we can do is hope that I'm wrong."

CHAPTER 67:
OMENS

"Look, I'm sorry I mentioned it! I don't want to distract you with this when it's being taken care of." Divinity apologized earnestly, but Sal just shook his head.

"You've been holding this in for the last few weeks? You should have told me! Sorry, I mean…I'm not annoyed—I just can't believe you've been carrying this on your shoulders the whole time." He turned in his seat to look at her properly. After their teams went to bed, Sal and Divinity decided to have a proper chat in the amphitheater where there was nobody around to listen to them.

Sal exhaled slowly as he tried to find the right words. "Like, how are you supposed to sleep at night when this is still a possibility?"

Divinity straightened her back and slapped her knees. "That's just it! I might be the crazy one here. They have Scry on their team, and they already know the future. We saw how capable they all are, and Recall saw pretty much everything we saw that night. They have the full report and should know about the breach."

Her voice was desperate as she clearly tried to convince herself that everything was fine. "I've been doing this since I was a kid, Sal. I know what the future looks like, and it hasn't changed at all, yet. That's what's scaring me more than anything…that not only is this thing potentially going to happen, but that we're being told it's being taken care of!"

Sal didn't want to even consider that train of thought. *If the faculty were lying to them about taking care of it, did it mean that they didn't believe Divinity…or were they just willing to let it happen?* Divinity should have earned enough credibility from their weekend evenings with the Doom Society, so that shouldn't be it, which left one other conclusion—which was much worse.

Divinity cupped her head in her hands. "The only thing I could think of doing was to prepare for it. I convinced myself I was going crazy, but if…if it did happen? We would need to be strong enough to survive it. Then we might be able to save Sinclair and the others."

Placing a hand on her shoulder, Sal tried to prevent her from spiraling. "Let's assume the worst, and it does happen. We've learned some formations and we're ready to fight other students…but the closest these guys have been to a demon is likely the Sinclair demonstration. If it's going to happen, the preparation we have in place isn't going to cut it. We need a better plan than just hoping for the best."

Divinity clenched her fists and let out a groan. "None of this would be a fucking issue if they had listened to us! We've been in this stupid academy for all of twenty minutes and we're supposed to be the ones to prevent a demon attack? How the fuck is that fair?"

She looked at Sal with tears in her eyes, and he shook his head. "Nothing has happened yet, so we still have time. We can figure this out, but we need a lot more information…"

Divinity shook her head. "I don't want to see it again, Sal. It's…people die. You saw what happens to Sinclair!"

Removing his hand from her back, Sal took a deep breath. "This whole situation is fucked, I get that. What if I look at it instead? I can look into the future with your ability, and I can see everything that we need to find out?"

When Divinity didn't react, Sal continued to throw out ideas. "I can invite the Reavers Guild to watch the fight. I'll tell them that Myth created a new weapon that they should see in action. Maybe tip off Watcher and Blink too? We have options, Divinity. We could make decisions now that would stop it from happening, where nobody gets hurt."

Divinity finally straightened her back and looked toward the night sky. "I'm being forced to either trust in the people looking after us, or trust in my own power. I haven't been wrong before, but I've misinterpreted events. Neuro's daughter is in the Gold cohort! He was the one who calmed me down at the Doom Society meeting and told me that it was being taken care of. What kind of person would throw their own daughter into harm's way? That's what has me so conflicted! I'm a good judge of people, Sal. Quest and Neuro are good people, and they're telling me that it's taken care of…so I've just spent the last few weeks smiling through it and trusting in them."

She brought a hand up to wipe away her tears. "I'll look again, and see if it's changed…"

Divinity's eyes clouded over until they were completely white. After just a few moments, her brow furrowed as she fidgeted slightly in her seat. "It's different this time, but…" She continued to frown at whatever vision she was seeing.

Sal waited patiently beside her, wishing that he could be of more help to her.

Divinity's eyes widened ever so slightly. "They've changed the venue! Looks like we're going to be competing in some abandoned stadium. Maybe in a newly reclaimed zone? Students are in the stands…watching the competing teams on the field, four teams at a time…" Divinity's voice filled with emotion as she let out a sigh of relief.

"There are huge barriers around the stadium, and they've got loads of guilds in the stands." A wide smile appeared on her face as she turned her head in Sal's direction. "I think it might actually be different now!"

Before Sal could celebrate with her, Divinity's face paled. "No, no, no! Fuck. No!" She clenched her eyes shut and returned her face to her cupped hands. She sat there for a moment before an aggravated groan left her lips. "Yeah, we're still fucked." With a shake of her head, she looked at Sal helplessly, her eyes back to their normal blue. "I think we've actually made it worse."

She pulled out her tablet and tapped at it furiously, shaking her head. "I'm messaging Quest about this. I don't care if I have to camp outside his office all night—we can't allow everyone to walk straight into a trap."

Sal had to do a double take. "A trap? Wasn't it just a demon outbreak?" He wanted to slow Divinity down and get her to explain, but she was too absorbed in her own thoughts.

With only a slight turn of her head, she responded, her full attention still on the tablet. "It can't be a coincidence that the event has been targeted twice. I was wrong before about the outbreak. It had nothing to do with a barrier being breached. The demons came from below ground!" Divinity turned to look at Sal, anger written all over her face. "It's a coordinated attack on the students!"

***

Neuro grimaced as he finished reading Divinity's mind. He tried to give her a reassuring smile, but she knew better than anyone how horrific the scene was. When he turned back to the assembled group of people, Quest looked at him expectantly, with his hands interlocked and elbows resting on his desk.

"How bad is it?"

Neuro took a seat with a slight shake of the head. "It's worse than we could have imagined. There's a humanoid variant leading the attack this time, with what looks like a premeditated dungeon break. Right from under the stadium!"

Quest's eyes widened as he looked sharply to where Harlan sat. Their emergency Doom Society meeting had been called at the last minute, with Divinity and Sal sitting uncomfortably around the small group of people.

Harlan leaned forward and looked at Neuro directly. "Are you positive? Commander grades don't reveal themselves lightly, so for them to lead a charge is incredibly uncharacteristic from everything we know about them!"

Neuro spread his hands wide. "It's a Commander. Demons were all coordinated and moved in packs, and it was looking for someone. I'm certain of it."

Quest waved off Harlan, who had another question. Instead, he looked straight back at Neuro with an incredulous expression. "It was looking for someone. Like…hunting them?"

Neuro nodded. "I can scarcely believe it myself, but there's no question about it. Hulkers were literally picking up students and returning with them to the dungeon. Voiders and Prowlers went straight for our defenses and swarmed the stationed guild officers. Leechers hung above to attack any student who got brave. It was a concentrated attack, and the demons knew what they were looking for."

Quest was positively dumbfounded as he looked back at Harlan, who didn't fare much better.

Their demonic behavior specialist was visibly disturbed by everything he was hearing. Harlan knew more than anyone else in the room how dangerous a Commander variant was and tried to explain why it was such a terrifying proposition.

"Commander types control essence the same way we do, but at a native level. The essence exposure we've had over the years has only given us a taste of their inherent capability." Harlan twisted in his seat as he gestured at Divinity. "If this attack has changed alongside our own preparations, it's not naive to presume that this Commander shares Divinity's abilities. We know from facing off against other Commander-level variants in the past that they can hold multiple skills, which makes this one even more of a threat."

Neuro looked directly at Quest with a somber expression. "We need to cancel the event this weekend. There's no way we can send the students out, knowing that this is a possible outcome."

Quest frowned as he looked over at Divinity. "The best way for us to determine if this Commander can alter their behavior based on knowledge of the future…is by testing it. I'm making the decision now that we'll be hosting the event in-house, here at the academy. Divinity, can you look into the future one more time?"

Sal turned to Divinity to see her reaction, but her eyes were already a milky white. The apprehension she had about looking into the future had melted away, and her expression was determined. Neuro got to his feet and placed his hands near Divinity's head as he closed his own eyes in concentration.

A few moments of silence passed while everyone held their breath. Divinity winced ever so slightly before her eyes widened and her mouth hung open. It wasn't her voice that alerted everyone, though, as Neuro broke off the mental connection with a curse. With a few blinks to get his bearings, he placed a reassuring hand on Divinity's shoulder, cupped her face in her palms.

Neuro looked over at Quest. "Well, do you want the good news or the bad news?"

Quest just stared at him, and Neuro chuckled humorlessly. "Jez manages to take off one of its arms, which is the only good news." The telepath walked back to his seat, which he slumped into. "The bad news is that it massacres hundreds of students, and we lose a couple of towers. Multiple portals open inside the buildings and…yeah."

Neuro shook his head. "The collective power of over a thousand students, the stationed guilds, and all the protective measures we can muster…it all goes to shit. Protecting the students stops our people from going all out, which creates a window for the demons. That Commander can definitely see into the future, as every attack is essentially negated immediately. It's a complete clusterfuck."

Sal stared at Neuro in disbelief. "What about the turrets on top of each tower? Are there not countermeasures for things like this? How did they get past the barriers?" When he looked around the room, nobody jumped in with an answer.

Quest pinched the edges of his eyes as he waved his hand. "Barriers are only effective in keeping things out. If they find their way in through portals, that's a different story. Turrets won't attack areas with civilians or students. Our countermeasures are our staff, which are apparently ineffective in this case."

With a resigned sigh, he looked back at Divinity. "I'm sorry to put you through this. Scry is on his way, which will hopefully alleviate the workload…but we're going to have to test a series of outcomes to find one that allows us to counter this situation."

Harlan looked at Quest apprehensively. "Shouldn't we report this to the Doom Council first?"

The snort of derision escaped Quest before he could stop himself, which then developed into a dark laugh. "Honestly, they'd just slow us down. We only have a couple of days to get this right, and I don't want to put any lives in danger by sitting around and waiting for their verdict."

Neuro's voice sounded out from across the room, and everyone looked at him, but he was staring at Divinity. "Don't suppose you could check to see if it still happens if we call off the contest completely?"

Just as Divinity was about to activate her ability, Sal raised his hand.

"Why don't I do it? We can check every outcome, and Divinity can guide me?"

CHAPTER 68:

ENLISTMENT

When Upgrade caught sight of Sal, she made a beeline across the room to where he stood. She looked tired, as usual, but her eyes were filled with concern. "Hey, why are you here? Do you know what all of this is about?"

Behind her, the members of the faculty streamed into the room, all of them wearing the same look of confusion as Upgrade. Jez gave Sal a quizzical look before his face broke into a grin. The Administration lecturer made his way to the back of the room, where Sinclair was sitting lazily with another bald man Sal didn't recognize.

Glancing back to Upgrade, Sal nodded. "Quest is debriefing everyone on the event this weekend. It's not good."

Upgrade turned to look at Quest, who stood at the front of the classroom with Divinity; they were engrossed in conversation. When she turned back, her expression was torn between concern and confusion. "I'll save you a seat. Forge is on his way too."

Sal tried to smile, but he couldn't even pretend. He had spent hours trawling through hypothetical scenarios, and he had watched his new friends die repeatedly. It was taking everything in his power just to remain standing and not to throw up.

With a turn of his head, he spotted Alastair, Harlan, Lombardi, Rust, and a few of the other lecturers he recognized. There were many more who he didn't know, all chatting to one another without a care in the world. It was odd seeing them in the seats that were typically reserved for students, and Sal wondered whether they'd be able to retain that jovial energy when Quest delivered the news to them.

When the stream of people finally stopped, Sal reckoned that there were nearly fifty people seated in the room. Quest gestured for Sal to join both him and Divinity on the podium, and he complied quietly. Divinity looked in his direction. She harbored the same feelings of anxiety and dread. Both took a seat, and Sal felt everyone's eyes on him.

Why were two first-year students accompanying Quest at the front of the classroom? Why was everyone being summoned in the middle of the day for a surprise meeting? Their questions were clear in their expressions as they waited for Quest to enlighten them. He didn't waste any time.

"I'd like to apologize to all of you for what I'm about to ask. It's come to our attention that a demonic attack is imminent." The atmosphere changed immediately, with several smiles disappearing in an instant. Quest continued, his voice strong with resolve as he laid out the facts.

"This weekend, at the Combat class event, our students are going to be attacked. We've identified a Commander variant as the one leading the attack. We've also established that this Commander has the ability to foresee events in the future, which makes them a deadly threat to us."

At the mere mention of a Commander, the faculty members, with a few notable exceptions, exchanged worried looks. Sinclair and Jez looked excited.

Quest gestured to both Divinity and Sal. "Divinity Khan and Salvatore Argento were the ones to predict this attack and have been working with us to create potential countermeasures. Our issue is that we're fighting a demon that can adapt instantly to our plans. We've run through dozens of simulations, some of which result in the death of hundreds of students. Others result in the deaths of many of you in this room right now."

He gripped the sides of the lectern as he spoke. "Through the countless visions we've done of future events, we're certain that the attack will happen regardless of our choices. Doing nothing results in the academy being attacked, which has the highest number of casualties. Going to our first offsite location that was locked in until a few days ago? That results in a higher number of abductions as well as the death of key faculty members. The stadium event that is currently scheduled has the lowest number of casualties, but the highest number of abductions. We've gone through a series of hypothetical situations, and all of them put us at a disadvantage and endanger the students. All of this is because of the Commander variant. It wants to kill or abduct certain individuals in our first-year group, namely in the Gold and Silver cohorts. Something is pushing them to act on this now, but we can't ascertain what that reason is. What we do know is that until this demon is taken down, our students are at imminent risk."

Quest gestured at the door. "I wanted to explain the stakes to you first. It would be unforgivable if we carried out any of these plans, that hold your lives in the balance, without warning you of the risks. For that reason, anyone who would like to be excluded from this discussion and leave the academy for a few days is welcome to do so. There is no judgment and no expectation on you to put your life in danger."

Not a single person moved.

Jez's voice cut through the eerie silence that followed.

"We're Heroes, mate. What do you need us to do?"

A few chuckles followed, lightening the mood and causing Quest to smile.

"My proposal is to create a series of strike teams that will hunt down the Commander variant. We've narrowed down its current location to a few key areas and will be bringing in the guilds to assist us. Although it's capable of opening portals at will, Harlan Geist, our demonic behavior expert, believes that it's lurking somewhere local. We've seen evidence of this from surprise underground attacks in several of the visions, which points to a dungeon that is being tunneled underneath our protective barriers."

Quest looked at Divinity and Sal with a grim expression, before turning back to the crowd. "Should the strike teams fail, we'll need to proceed with the Combat class competition to draw the Commander out."

Sinclair snorted and folded his arms. "So that's it, yeah? We either kill the Commander or we use the kids as bait? What sort of fucking arseways plan is that?"

Jez nodded, and the bald guy beside them put up his hand. When Quest gestured at him, he spoke with a heavy accent.

"Can't you send the kids home? We'll sort this out and avoid putting them in danger."

Quest shook his head. "To give you a better understanding of how we determined these actions, I should explain the abilities of the two students here." He gestured over to where Sal and Divinity were seated.

"Salvatore Argento possesses a Replication ability called Skill Master, which allows him to use abilities to their fullest potential. We had him replicate Divinity's ability, which is a more advanced version of Scry's Foresight. With their help, and Neuro watching their progress, we analyzed hundreds of variations of the events over the coming days. To answer your question, Lars," Quest gestured up at the accented man who sat between Sinclair and Jez, "if we evacuate the academy and send the students home, the demonic attack will happen in civilian areas and the casualties will be much higher. Which furthers our belief that this is a calculated attack, aimed at dispatching or abducting certain students."

Lars brought his hand down with a frustrated sigh and his voice was laced with anger. "There has to be a way for us to do this without endangering them. What are the best solutions you've come up with?"

Quest turned to Harlan and gestured for him to come up to the lectern. With that, he stepped to one side to allow the demonic behavior expert to take the stand.

Harlan leaned forward and rested his arms on the lectern. "Countermeasures are difficult to plan when you're facing an enemy that can see the future. We've determined that the best course of action is to overwhelm by launching a series of different plans, selected at random, just before the event. It will force the Commander variant to fight us with the same information, at the same time. Our potential advantage is that we've seen countless futures' worth of attacks from this Commander, which has allowed us to study their strategies and attack styles. We know what they're looking for, their points of attack, their demonic forces, and who they bring with them. It allows us to make calculated approaches in how we deal with each scenario."

Harlan paused as he looked over at Divinity. "Miss Khan here, along with Mr. Argento and Scry, are our secret weapons, as they'll be able to use the Foresight ability to keep our teams up to date on every development. Our primary proposal is to integrate them on each of the strike teams."

Upgrade jumped to her feet. "Absolutely not!"

Several people glanced over at her, mixed with a few annoyed faces.

"Are you listening to yourself? They've never seen a demon before and you're going to throw them into the battlefield? Sal is a Mythcrafter! You all heard about the Legendary sniper rifle—he's the one who made it! You absolutely cannot risk his life on a plan that you've pulled straight out of your arse!"

Beside Upgrade, Forge's rumbling voice added to the sentiment. "Hear, hear!"

More than half of the group nodded in agreement, with the others looking at Sal in a whole new light.

Upgrade didn't give Harlan or Quest any time to respond as she launched into a counterproposal. "How much time do we have? We can mobilize the entire workshop and Sal can build something to take this Commander down. You said yourself, you know a shit ton about it now! We can literally build a countermeasure...we just need a bit of time." Her tone was pleading as she looked over at Sal.

When Quest shook his head, Upgrade tried again in a strained voice. "Mobilize the third-years! He can't be the only Replicator in the academy, but he is the only Mythcrafter. It's ridiculous to believe that this is the only option available to us."

If Sal had only heard her argument, he would have thought she valued his Mythcrafter ability above all else. But the distraught expression on her face, filled with the pleading tone in her voice, almost broke his heart.

Upgrade remained standing as she stared Quest down. After a moment of hesitation, she resolved herself and pointed directly at the headmaster. "I won't let you take him onto the battlefield."

Quest's expression tightened. "I don't want any of our students to be placed in harm's way." He looked around the room. "And I don't want any of you to be put into danger, even if you're vastly more qualified to handle it. This entire situation places us as victims of circumstance, and we're being forced to adapt with the information that we have available to us." Quest clenched his fists and closed his eyes for a moment.

"We've put out an emergency call to all the guilds and we'll be discussing strategies tomorrow morning when their representatives arrive. The Doom Council has been briefed and they're currently deliberating on the best course of action, but we can't wait for them to reach a verdict. If the guilds have suitable people who can replace Salvatore and Divinity, then we will absolutely exclude them both from this operation. Please understand that everything we've calculated so far has been with the limited resources that we have available to us. We want to save as many people as possible."

Forge rose to his feet and placed a hand on Upgrade's shoulder. "Anger isn't going to get us very far. Sit down and hear him out first."

She was still staring daggers at Quest as she retook her seat beside Forge.

Quest gave Forge an appreciative nod, but the burly man didn't acknowledge it. Quest gestured to Alastair in the audience and moved to the next stage of the meeting. "Alastair is going to explain our tactical approach and detail the different strike teams we've proposed. Please give him your full attention, and we'll open the floor for discussions afterward."

With that, the room darkened and the screen behind the podium illuminated to show a detailed map of the stadium grounds where Divinity had foreseen the dungeon break.

Alastair tugged at the bottom of his waistcoat as he addressed the group. "Let's jump straight into it."

CHAPTER 69:
CONFRONTATION

DIVINITY CUPPED HER FACE WITH HER PALMS AS SHE GROANED EVER SO slightly in her seat. The other students in the canteen didn't spare her a passing glance, with most assuming that she was just dreading the upcoming cohort fights. When she finally pulled her hands away, she wore an expression of frustration, which she aimed directly at Sal, who sat across from her.

"Why are they keeping us out of the conversation with the guilds? We were there for the briefing with the professors—why not the guilds? What if Quest isn't convincing enough? They might not help us!" Divinity grasped both sides of her coffee cup and drew it close, staring at the wisps of steam that plumed upward from the hole in the lid.

Sal gave her a level stare. "Of course they're going to help us. It's just a question of what resources they'll give us, and what the plan of action is going to be." Sal thought of Upgrade's expression when she'd pleaded with Quest to remove Sal from their plans. With a slight shake of his head to put the thought away. "We'll hopefully find out soon if we're going to be part of the strike teams or not."

Divinity sighed. "I feel like such a hypocrite. I've been talking about how much I want to be a Hero…but I find myself wanting to stay behind on this mission. I don't know if it's fear, or if I'm worried I'll make a mistake. I don't want to have so much pressure resting on our shoulders."

Turning her head to look around the canteen, similar expressions of dread reflected on a number of faces. She placed her chin on her upturned wrist and leaned her elbow against the table as she looked at the other cohorts. "Kinda wish we could just go back to worrying about the rankings for a while."

Sal followed her gaze and watched the other students for a few moments. When he turned back to Divinity, he found that he didn't share her sentiment.

"You're the least hypocritical person I've met, Divinity. We went through those visions together. You know more than anyone how many lives you've saved, regardless of which course of action they choose." Sal laughed humorlessly as he gestured at the students in the canteen.

"How many of them would have died needlessly if you didn't use your power? You've already proved yourself as a Hero, and you've done your part. There's no point in agonizing over your effectiveness in the strike teams, because we're going to be sitting in the background while they go out and save the day."

Divinity smiled as she continued to look at her coffee, but it only lasted a few seconds before her frown returned. "I wish I could see it the same way, but all I can think about are those outcomes where everything goes to shit."

Before Sal had a chance to respond, Barry appeared beside them with his own coffee. "What's going to shit? You looking at Sal's performance in the fights to come?" Without any sign of reading the atmosphere, he sat down beside them and looked between them expectantly.

Sal shook his head with an easygoing smile and waved his hand. "It's nothing to worry about."

Divinity, on the other hand, turned to Barry with a deadpan expression on her face. "I predicted the future and saw that a demonic outbreak happens during the class battles. We went to the headmaster, and he's currently briefing the guilds on the fact that students are likely to die this weekend. How's your day going?"

Barry burst out laughing before taking a swig of his coffee. "And here I was thinking you didn't have a sense of humor! What about you, Sal—have you been thwarting any demonic conspiracies, or have you been playing around in the workshop?"

When Barry saw the somewhat horrified look on Sal's face, he turned back to Divinity with a frown. "Okay…is Sal spacing out? What's going on?"

Divinity shrugged. "It's a Commander-level variant that can predict the future, and all our countermeasures are known to them. We're just discussing how everything is likely fucked, and even if all the guilds work together and the Doom Society and faculty help, it's probably not going to be enough."

Sal's hand came down on the table with a resounding crack. "Divinity!"

Divinity blinked before chuckling. With a slight smile, she turned her head to Barry and shook her head. "Sorry…bad joke."

Barry took one look at Sal. "You're not fucking around, are you?"

Sal reached across the table and grasped Barry's forearm, giving him an almost pleading look. "She's been through a lot in the last few days, man. Everything is being taken care of."

Barry stared at Divinity, his voice suddenly becoming very low. "Do I die in the vision?"

Sal closed his eyes and sighed, shaking his head. "No, Barry, you're fine. You don't appear in the visions and pop up a few days later."

Divinity laughed darkly as she glared at Barry. "You use whatever secret power you have and escape every single time. So don't worry."

Sal stared incredulously at Divinity, not understanding where the venom in her voice was coming from. When he looked back at Barry, he tried to apologize on her behalf, but Barry just shook his head. Clearly he was still reeling from the fact that there was going to be a demonic attack.

"In the countless visions I've seen," Divinity continued, "everyone fights or tries to protect one another…except you. You're nowhere to be found at any point, and you're the only one to appear unscathed at the end of the day. I'm not angry with the current you, but it's hard for me not to be angry with the future version of you. So, if it's all the same, I'd prefer if you'd let us discuss this in private as you're unlikely to be of any help going forward."

Sal was absolutely dumbfounded by Divinity's sudden shift in character.

Barry gripped his coffee tightly as he got to his feet. His face showed how hurt and confused he was, and without so much as another word, he left the canteen.

Divinity cupped her face in her hands and started to cry. Sal knew it was a stressful situation, but it was no excuse for what she had just done. Barry hadn't done anything wrong and didn't know what was coming, so to blame him for self-preservation during a time of panic was ridiculous. Sal didn't choose his words carefully; he was too shocked to even consider Divinity's feelings.

"What the actual fuck, Divinity? Why would you talk to him like that? He didn't do anything wrong!"

Divinity shook her head as she sobbed uncontrollably. Her voice cracked as she tried to get the words out. "I'm sorry, Sal! I didn't want to do it, but I had to!"

Sal threw a napkin in her direction. It was so uncharacteristic of her to be mean like that, and he wanted to trust in her, but there was no excusing her behavior just now. She had dismantled Barry in just a few sentences. The poor guy was likely wracked with guilt for something he had no control over.

Divinity took the napkin and pressed it against her eyes, with an aggravated sigh. She opened her eyes, and Sal was surprised to see they were milky white.

"What are you doing, Divinity?"

She was searching for something in the future, and a wide smile finally appeared on her face. With a wipe of her eyes again with the napkin, her eyes returned to their normal icy blue, and she smiled happily at Sal.

"I'm so sorry, Sal. I needed you to be good cop for that one, and you did great!" She tapped the table with both her palms excitedly. "When we were looking at potential outcomes, I was tasked with looking at the different students who feature in each vision."

Divinity gestured to where Barry had just been seated. "Barry used his powers in about eight percent of the visions I looked at, because of fear, indecision? It's hard to know. Quest suggested that we tell him about the upcoming attack, but that reduced the number of times he used his powers."

Sal just shook his head. "You're playing with his emotions to game for a better outcome? That's horrible, Divinity."

Her excited tapping ceased, and she looked at Sal carefully. "It was what he needed to hear, and I feel horrible about it…really. But, from the looks of it, he's going to use his powers now." She gestured at the canteen full of people. "If it saves even one more person, is that not worth it?"

Sal clenched his jaw. "Wouldn't it have worked if you just explained things to him rationally? Asked him to use his powers to help people instead of guilting him into it?"

Divinity looked at Sal as if he were naive. "Not everyone works like that, Sal. Barry needed to hear that he wasn't helpful, which will make him change his future decisions." She pointed a finger at him, almost accusingly. "So don't go to him now and apologize, otherwise it'll undo the changes."

Sal crossed his arms. "This isn't right, and you know it."

Divinity threw her hands into the air. "What do you want us to do, Sal? Everyone here is training to be a Hero, to fight against demons and protect civilians. You might have come here with completely different expectations, but the rest of us knew what we were signing up for. It's not about happiness, belonging, fairness…or whatever ideals suit you. It's about fighting demons and saving lives."

Her eyes were wide as she stared at him. The anger in her voice was clear, and Sal wondered how long she had kept all this bottled up. With his arms still crossed, he looked up at the ceiling of the canteen and took a steadying breath.

"We've only been here a month, Divinity. Are you expecting us to be soldiers, ready to march into war at the drop of a hat? Everyone might be here to become a Hero, but we're not Heroes yet. Asking someone with a few weeks of training to risk their life is insane! Your words could end up putting him in a situation that he hasn't been trained to face. How will you feel if he dies because he tried to prove you wrong?"

"That's not fair!" Divinity shot back.

"You just said it's not about fairness. Fighting demons and saving lives, remember? You're manipulating others in whatever this fight turns out to be, and you'll have to live with those outcomes. If we lose Barry because he tried to be brave, is that because the demons got him, or because of what you just said to him?"

Sal's heart broke when he saw the dismayed expression on Divinity's face, but he pushed onward. "You told me my future, and I changed for the better. Why can't we do the same with Barry? Sure, he might be competitive, and your approach might have the best outcome, but what if we present him with the facts so he can make an actual decision…rather than being treated like a tool."

Sal winced when Divinity's eyes welled up with tears again. "I know you're doing what's best for everyone, but I don't want you living with guilt over your decisions. That shouldn't be on you. We have guilds and faculty that know about our abilities and visions. It's up to them to find the solution that works best…not us."

Divinity got to her feet, and Sal felt a pang of dread that he'd pushed her too far. He was about to apologize, even though he stood by everything he said, but Divinity let out an aggravated sigh. "I'll find Barry and apologize to him, okay?" Her eyes were still welling, and Sal just nodded.

"Thank you, Divinity."

She left the table, walking off to where Barry had gone.

Sal drained the remainder of his coffee and got to his feet, wondering whether the guild meeting had concluded yet. He picked up Divinity's discarded cup and his own, depositing them in the trash can before leaving the canteen and heading off to Quest's office.

CHAPTER 70:
COUNTERMEASURE

"WE'RE GOING TO CHANGE THE PARAMETERS OF YOUR VISIONS WITH THE NEW information we have," Quest explained to both Sal and Divinity, who were seated on the same couch in the Sky Lounge.

They were joined by a range of new faces they didn't recognize, but Quest had assured them that it was okay. In addition to that, there was a familiar face in the room that had caught both of them by surprise. Barry sat beside Alastair, deep in conversation, while Harlan and Neuro stood behind them. Most of the other unfamiliar faces watched Sal and Divinity carefully.

Quest drew their attention back to him as he took a seat on the coffee table across from their couch. "Your friend came to us and asked how he could be of help, which hopefully hasn't changed his contribution in the fights to come?" He looked at Divinity meaningfully, but she shook her head.

Quest looked visibly relieved as he turned to Sal. "Desperate times call for desperate measures, and I hope you won't misinterpret Divinity's actions. I asked her to ensure the best outcomes from the students, which led her to bringing Barry and Anna Sakura along. Both Barry and Divinity explained the events to me, and I fully appreciate your misgivings about how she approached the situation. Not everyone is going to agree with our plan of attack, and if we need to ruffle a few feathers to ensure the safety of everyone, then I'll most certainly start ruffling."

Sal nodded but didn't share the headmaster's sentiment. Divinity's conflicted expression showed that she was still debating her actions from earlier. When Quest's eyes landed on her, she gave him a slight smile, and he continued with his explanation.

"We're going to run the series of simulations again this time, with the added context of having guild support." Quest hesitated before continuing. "I don't want either of you to look at the success of the strike teams that are going out tonight. We devised a theory that if we keep the Commander countering our future actions for the cohort fights, then they'll be distracted from the attack launching tonight. Both of you are going to keep it busy by creating new future events and strategies, which will give our teams the time they need to launch a pre-emptive strike on the Commander."

Divinity's eyes widened as she stared at Quest. "That can't possibly work! All the futures need to have a reference point, and you can't just fabricate those."

Quest gestured behind the couch, for people to approach. His smile was tired, but he looked somewhat hopeful.

Sal didn't understand what Divinity was talking about, but it made sense. From the visions he looked at in the past, they were always rooted in facts.

Divinity looked over at Sal. "He's asking us to look at visions on branches that aren't attached to tree trunks."

Sal's eyes widened. "Yeah, that's impossible for me."

Barry and Neuro arrived at the same time and stood on either side of the couch. Quest gestured at Barry. "Meet our fabricator. Barry here will sync up with Neuro and create a false future for you to use."

Divinity laughed as though he were crazy. "Even if this worked, and we're able to create a completely different vision, it's of no use to us when the Commander is predicting the real future. We'll be creating meaningless visions that won't impact their plans!"

Neuro looked at Divinity with a concerned expression before anger flashed across his features. When he glanced at Quest, his voice was strained. "You didn't tell her." It wasn't a question.

Quest pinched the bridge of his nose before waving a hand away. "Could you let me protect the sanity of just one student, Neil?"

Neuro stared at Quest until the headmaster finally relented. Turning back to Divinity, he grimaced and chose his next words carefully. "We believe the Commander variant is able to track your visions. Just like how you were able to jump in and help Sal navigate your power during our Doom Society meeting, we've concluded that this Commander is able to watch what *you* see."

Quest watched Divinity's reaction cautiously, but when she merely stared in stunned silence, he continued. "Harlan is at the top of his field with demonic behaviors, and it's his opinion that no demon should be able to counter visions at that speed. We're not underestimating it by any measure—it's just very unlikely that it can create countermeasures against everything we come up with."

Quest raised another hand. "We already know they have a form of Psionic capability to control the horde of demons. Harlan's hypothesis is that the Commander is waging psychic warfare on your visions, which is why they're so one-sided in its favor." Quest looked at Divinity and Sal intently as he placed his hands on his knees.

"This is only a hypothesis and might not be the case, but it does make a lot of sense. We have the might of the entire academy and the guilds, yet in every encounter we look at...we lose dramatically? After a lot of discussion and cooperation with the guild masters, we've concluded that we need to launch a Psionic-based counterattack—fabricated visions to throw the Commander off guard."

Divinity slumped back on the couch. "You think they've been using my power to trick us all this time?"

Neuro shook his head as he sat on the armrest beside Divinity. He placed a hand on her shoulder and gave her a reassuring smile. "We don't think the Commander is able to see the future at all and is just an incredibly powerful Psionic user. Your contributions to all of this so far have been invaluable for us to come up with this counterattack proposal. Otherwise, we'd have been ambushed this weekend. We don't want to even consider how many lives would have been lost if you hadn't intervened."

Divinity's shoulders sagged as the weight of guilt was finally lifted.

It was clear she was still confused, but Quest raised a hand to Neuro to prevent him from continuing. "We're on a tight schedule, so we need to move this along. As part of our counterattack, we're going to have Professor Lombardi amplify the capability of Neuro to trace the Commander when they start looking at your visions. Once we have a location, it'll be sent to the strike teams that are currently in the air and awaiting orders."

Barry held up his hand, and Quest added with a roll of his hand. "Yes, yes, of course. Barry...could you sit beside Salvatore there? For these visions, I'd like Salvatore to activate the power with Divinity guiding and Barry projecting the future we discussed earlier." Quest got to his feet and looked around the room, gesturing at a few individuals to take their places.

Sal turned to Barry, who shook his head in confusion.

When they locked eyes, Barry chuckled. "Really doesn't fill you with confidence when you see them like headless chickens, does it?"

Sal laughed, feeling the atmosphere alleviate ever so slightly. "You should have seen us when we first came to him with the visions—this is a drastic improvement. You finally going to show off your super-secret power then?" Sal teased him, but Barry grinned.

"I was hoping for a lot more spectacle, to be honest, but if I'm able to help out and save people...then I guess it's worth the compromise." With that said, Barry raised his right hand and channeled his power.

A series of green rings swirled around his arm, complemented by small runes that shifted into a series of patterns. Each of the rings contracted to create a sleeve of pulsating symbols, rotating gradually around it. Barry glanced back to Sal, who watched it curiously.

"Whatever you do, Sal, don't try and replicate this ability...okay?"

Sal smiled but was surprised to see a serious expression on Barry's face. Curiosity got the better of him, and he had to ask. "Why? What is it?"

Rather than answering, Barry waved his right hand in front of him, causing everything around Sal to disappear. The room, people—everything was replaced by complete darkness. All of Sal's senses were completely useless, and he started to panic. It felt like a void of nothingness, and Sal's body started to reject it instantly. His heart thundered, but he couldn't hear it or feel it. There was just...nothing, other than a growing sense of dread. A moment later, he was back on the couch, and Barry held his arm reassuringly. Sal focused on the sensation of touch as his heartbeat started to calm.

"Breathe slowly. It was just an illusion." Barry's voice was unnaturally gentle, and Sal stared at him in bewilderment. Barry held up his arm and pointed to it with his left hand.

"That vision you just saw is what the first few years of my power looked like. It's bleak and it's hard to train, so I avoided using it as much as possible. Trust me when I tell you, it's not one you ever want to replicate."

Sal nodded, curious to know how Barry had managed to both overcome and control it. His lack of knots suddenly made sense and he saw Barry in a whole new light. "How will that be useful in the vision?"

Barry grinned as the patterns on his hand shifted ever so slightly. "I've only shown you Purgatory, but I can do so much more than that!"

Behind them, Neuro coughed lightly to get their attention. They turned to look at him. "We're going to start, so could I ask you to lean back, Sal, and clear your mind before activating Divinity's ability? Barry, take his right hand in your left. Divinity, take his left in your right."

All three of them followed his instructions as they leaned back onto the couch, closing their eyes.

"Professor Lombardi, whenever you're ready," Neuro continued, addressing the shorter professor, who stood behind him.

Lombardi didn't waste any time and placed both his palms on Neuro's back, activating his power and amplifying the capabilities of the telepath. Neuro created a link with all three of the students and tapped Sal on the shoulder as a signal. Sal activated his power and hoped the wings wouldn't cause any issues on the couch. When he opened his eyes, he saw a forest of trees…with countless futures just waiting to be seen.

Divinity's presence was beside him, but she didn't guide him immediately like usual. Instead, they waited silently as another presence joined them in the forest. Sal could scarcely believe his eyes when the forest rippled and changed, revealing a small copse of trees that hadn't existed before. There was a slight green hue to them, which faded to blend in with the dense white of the forest.

Divinity navigated Sal to the trees, and he got to work with reading the future. When he investigated the trunk of a newly created tree, he could see that it was a vision of the cohort battles, with their team fighting against Divinity's. It looked familiar to the scenes that Sal had witnessed countless times over the last few days, but it didn't include the dungeon break. The battle continued slowly, and Sal started to doubt they had gone to the right one as it was a perfect representation of the stadium and the students.

Sal trusted in her judgment and Divinity's guidance continued. The scene shifted, which caused a slight ripple in Sal's vision. It became clear that Barry's illusion was being altered forcibly, and Sal watched in grim satisfaction as the illusion twisted and contorted to reveal a dungeon break, similar to one of the first visions that Divinity witnessed. It was proof that Quest's theory was correct, and the Commander was actively shifting the visions to create a completely different narrative.

Neuro's thoughts transmitted to each of them, telling them that he needed more time…but there was nothing that Divinity or Sal could do to prolong the vision other than watching it play out. However, their secret weapon took the challenge wholeheartedly.

"Oh, it's on." Barry's said out in the room as the illusion once again shifted.

The destruction of the grounds resulted in demons pouring out and launching themselves at the students. Screams of terror and dismay sounded out from every angle, and Divinity's guidance faltered. Sal couldn't blame her in the slightest. It was tough to watch, but both were left speechless as the scene shifted to reveal Divinity standing in a glowing suit of armor, holding the sword that Sal had Crafted.

Each sweep of the blade threw the hordes of demons back, and Divinity within the vision sprouted wide angelic wings that she used to rise into the sky, her sword held aloft while the sun beamed strongly from behind her. As quick as Divinity's character had appeared, the Commander's side pulled forth Voiders and Hulkers from the breach in the ground. Sal and Divinity were reduced to spectators in the ensuing battle between the Commander and Barry. For every reinforcement that was pulled from the breach, Divinity produced a counterattack.

Sal noted that, off to one side, his own avatar was mercilessly defeated by a lowly Leecher, which would have made him laugh under any other circumstances. Neuro's thoughts once again came to the forefront of their minds, telling them that they needed to keep it going as long as possible. Barry was very much in the driver's seat for this operation, and he masterfully created a scenario that looked like the future was bright before allowing the Heroic Divinity to be defeated.

It moved in phases, where a new Hero would rise to fight, picking up the discarded sword and launching another elaborate counterattack. The Commander learned from that and twisted the vision to break the sword, which Barry replaced with the pistol gauntlets that were ridiculously overpowered in his illusion. It went on like this for the next hour as Barry pulled up new scenarios that the Commander tried to counter. Barry allowed the Commander to win barely before moving to the next one.

Finally, Neuro's hands rested on Sal's shoulder again. "You can stop now."

CHAPTER 71:
STRIKE TEAM

When Sal opened his eyes, he saw that Quest was once again sitting on the coffee table in front of them.

He wore a wide smile as he spoke, with Neuro behind them. "You did great, all of you. It looks like we were right about that Commander not having the ability of Foresight! Neuro was able to track them down and the strike teams successfully scouted the area and confirmed the target. Anna Sakura has been teleported to the scene and will nullify the area, preventing them from using any abilities in retaliation."

At the looks of shock on their faces, Quest laughed. "Oh, don't be fooled by her appearance. She's in the Savior class and is top ranked in the Assassination module. She's well-trained for these kinds of operations. With Jez, Sinclair, and Lars on the team...it's pretty overkill if I'm honest. The scout guild, Source, is formally in charge of the mission, but our strike team will likely handle it easily."

Sal sat up on the couch and looked around at the smiling faces in the room. He couldn't help but feel a huge sense of unease. "Aren't we being a bit too complacent? We've seen countless attempts being foiled by the Commander. Are you sure this is enough to take it down?"

Much to Sal's surprise, Neuro chuckled.

"I can appreciate how it might feel from your perspective, Sal. You've only seen us reacting until this point. All our countermeasures were reactions to the bad information that we had. Sorry, that's a poor choice of words." Neuro shot an apologetic smile in Divinity's direction.

"We were playing to the Commander's tune and acting with the information that we had. All our capabilities were tied down to ensure the safety of the students. When we don't have our hands tied behind our back, for lack of a better term, we're pretty capable. Why don't you show them, Quest?"

The headmaster smiled as he lifted a tablet from the coffee table. "Source is streaming live to our Analyst team, but I doubt they'd have much issue with us seeing your handiwork in action." With that, he tapped on the tablet, and an entire portion of the Sky Lounge's wall turned into a screen.

Neuro gestured to the glass walls on the other side of the lounge. "You'd probably be able to see it from there. It's Jez we're talking about."

Quest smiled ruefully as he glanced at the screen in anticipation. "Why that man became a lecturer is beyond me."

Most of the people in the room moved around the couch to get a better look at the screen, many of them exchanging smiles of relief.

Sal turned to Divinity, who shared his expression of unease.

Barry nudged Sal's shoulder with a grin. "Did you see the Leecher fight? I almost thought you had it…"

Sal couldn't help but laugh, which earned him a look of confusion from Divinity. She looked past Sal to see the grinning Barry, and a small smile appeared on her lips.

"That was a flattering version of me you had in that illusion. Is that how you see me normally?"

Barry's laughter faded as color rushed to his cheeks. With a shake of his head, he turned his attention back to the screen. "I was thinking of something cool, and you just happened to pop into my head. Just a coincidence."

"So, I pop into your head regularly, is that it?"

Sal leaned back and enjoyed the back-and-forth, with Barry becoming increasingly defensive as Divinity teased him.

"Nothing like that! I had to work with the people I know, and you were there…so it just happened that way. I didn't have enough time to plan it out."

Divinity nodded slowly as she leaned closer to Barry, making him move away slightly in his seat. "Well, for what it's worth, I thought it looked incredible."

Barry glanced back at the screen, his face showing his clear embarrassment. "Thanks."

The screen came into focus, causing everyone in the room to fall quiet. It followed a Prowler that was running purposefully through a dimly lit cave. The only sources of light were coming from embedded rocks in the walls of the cave, pulsating silently as they moved. A set of hands appeared on screen, moving in quick succession as they created a series of patterns.

Quest enlightened the students to their meaning. "Dungeon entrance discovered. Sinclair leading. No enemy contact."

Sal and the others nodded in appreciation as they continued to watch. A fully armored knight appeared to the side of the person recording as they set off silently after the Prowler. The tunnel skewed off a few times, but the Prowler didn't hesitate and guided them with ease. When the camera turned sharply, Sal gasped at the sudden sight of a Voider within striking distance. Its clawed arm was drawn back to launch a surprise attack; the remainder of its body was nowhere to be seen as the Voider's torso materialized out of the wall. Before the attack landed, a slender figure dressed completely in black flashed forward, resulting in the now dismembered torso falling to the cave floor.

Quest turned around to Sal with a grin. "Told you she was good."

Sal stared in shock as he realized the slender figure that dispatched the Voider was Anna Sakura.

The screen flickered a few more times, with the camera pointing to each combat encounter. None of them could really be called combat, though, as it looked like Anna Sakura killed every opponent with a single touch. Her ability to nullify essence allowed her to cancel the Voider's ability to open portals, which usually resulted in them getting cleaved in half when the portals were abruptly closed.

Sal lost count of how many she had killed as she moved silently from wall to wall, flashing in front of the camera every so often.

Barry pointed out pieces of loot that they were walking straight past. His cries of anguish made more than a few of the veterans in the room chuckle. The excursion into the dungeon continued, with the whole strike team moving at a fast pace.

Sinclair, in his Prowler form, guided them continuously and ran past opponents, knowing that the strike team would dispatch them. Messages were relayed through the camera to explain location information, and highlighting observations from the team, all of which were explained by Quest. The tunnels had managed to reach far beyond the protective barriers, and they were laid out to have access points to all the venues for the Combat class event. When that message was relayed, it was a sobering moment for Sal and Divinity as they realized that the attack was pretty much guaranteed.

There was a blackout for a few moments before clearing, and it became obvious that they had climbed down to a lower area of the dungeon. The tunnels were much wider and the hand gestures on camera indicated that there was evidence that it had been carved out by Hulkers.

Rather than move onward, the team stopped and adjusted their equipment in preparation of the potential fights to come. Sal and the group watched as the armored knight lifted his helmet to take a drink from what looked like a hip flask and saw that it was Jez. Each of them communicated with hand gestures before Jez finished it off with a series of crude gestures, including a pelvic thrust.

The camera operator tried to cover the screen, but everyone had already seen it. Sal laughed, and he was relieved to see that Divinity was enjoying the lighter atmosphere.

Quest smiled as he looked back at Neuro and gestured at the screen. "Sure you don't want to join our faculty? It's not a very high bar."

Neuro shook his head, a slight smile forming. "My daughter would kill me, so no."

When the strike team continued their advance, they moved more cautiously but maintained a good pace. The few Voiders that appeared were taken out by Anna Sakura, but when an entire flock of Leechers detached from the ceiling to ambush them, a burst of light blinded the camera, causing everyone to look away or shield their eyes.

When it returned to darkness, all that remained were dozens of Leecher corpses on the ground, with Jez kicking one down the tunnel and receiving what everyone imagined was a glare from the camera operator. The only clue they had was the apologetic shrug from the armored knight as he continued on his way. Sinclair was only barely visible in the distance as he determined their route, and there were a few occasions where he had stopped ahead to wait for them.

Eventually, after what felt like an age of nothing happening, Sinclair bounded back to the group at lightning speed and transformed his body fully into a Hulker. With a turn of his body, he leaned toward the darkness ahead and braced his body for impact. The camera bounced erratically and judging from the others on screen, the entire dungeon was shaking.

Sal, Divinity, and Barry leaned forward in their seats, their anxiety spiking at the sudden danger. Sinclair's enormous body was covered in scales that looked like black rock. His muscles underneath were a dark purple and when he turned his head to check on his team's location, Sal saw blood-red eyes shining out from a slab of darkness. A small gap to the side of Sinclair showed at least four Hulkers rushing toward him.

Jez stepped up beside Sinclair and raised his right arm into the air. A burst of light appeared in Jez's palm and took the form of a long polearm that illuminated the entire tunnel. With zero hesitation, he planted his left foot in front of him and arced his back, before throwing the polearm viciously down the tunnel. The camera operator twisted their body to try to see between Sinclair and Jez, but all that was visible was the same blinding light from before.

Sal blinked a few times and looked away from the screen. Barry's gasp indicated that the sight was worth it, and Sal persevered through the stinging of his eyes to refocus on the screen. The remains of the Hulkers were dramatic, with a perfect semi-circle created over their bodies. Fragments of light remained on the perfectly carved husks. It looked as though Jez's attack had burned straight through them.

Whole chunks of their bodies had been vaporized and their glowing remains suddenly felt ominous at the end of the tunnel. Jez merely patted the Hulker form of Sinclair as he gestured for him to lead the way. In an instant, Sinclair was back in Prowler form and padding carefully around the Hulker remains.

Sal and the group watched as they carefully made their way through the rest of the dungeon, with the team going two levels deeper. The hand gestures on camera continued to relay information to the group, and Quest explained that they were closing in on the target. It had already been a couple of hours since the stream had started, and Sal couldn't believe how quickly the time had passed.

Sinclair suddenly came to a halt and returned to his human shape, creating hand gestures as he pointed farther down the tunnel. His expression was resolute and professional, and Sal couldn't believe this was the same man who had traumatized the entirety of the first-years. When the gestures came through on the camera, Quest sighed in relief as he turned toward their sofa.

"The other strike teams are up ahead...no casualties by the sounds of it." Sal almost had to do a double take, which didn't escape Quest's notice. "We're thorough when it comes to the safety of our students. We sent in all the teams as soon as we had a lock on the target location. Didn't want them escaping!"

Sal watched as Forge came into view, dressed in a full plate of armor and wielding an incredible hammer that was almost as tall as him. It looked like there was an engine of some description attached to the head of a hammer, powered by a glowing ball of fire. Behind him was Upgrade in her suit of Epic-grade armor; each of her mechanical hands had been morphed into what looked like hand cannons. Her whole body shimmered, and Sal knew instinctively that she was covered in a protective shield. He was absolutely speechless when he caught sight of her on camera.

Neuro's voice sounded out quietly from behind him. "You've made quite the friend in Upgrade, Sal. I never thought I'd see her back in the field, but there she is…and she somehow managed to get that old tyrant to come with her. All to ensure your safety, apparently."

When Sal turned around to look at Neuro, the telepath had returned to looking at the screen with a small smile on his face. More people joined the primary strike team, all communicating with one another briefly with sign language. Forge and Jez clasped hands, and Sal saw a rare smile cross the workshop master's face. It was surreal seeing the people he knew in a dungeon, working together as Heroes. Just the thought of being there with them was enough to send a chill down Sal's spine.

Quest grinned. "Looks like it's time for the main event!"

CHAPTER 72:
HEROES

WHEN THE CAMERA OPERATOR MOVED INTO THE OPEN SPACE, SAL AND EVERYONE in the Sky Lounge finally got a look at the inner chamber of the dungeon. It looked like the passage that the strike team had come through had been just one of the many routes available. A huge crater filled the area, with a series of holes in the walls that made it look more like a catacomb than anything else.

When the camera panned around, it showed several Heroes standing by and waiting for the attack to launch. They were too far to make out properly, but each of the strike teams looked menacing and ready. Shuffling darkness rested at the center of the crater, but brief flashes of light from the far end of the cavern highlighted the hordes of demons that lay in wait.

The camera panned to the origin point of the light, and it revealed a large glowing rock that seemed to flicker in time with the screams of a demon latched to it. Behind the rock, at the very edge of the dungeon, a portal was gradually opening, getting larger in size with each agonized cry. A series of hand gestures appeared on the camera, reporting on the scene.

Quest exhaled sharply as he turned to Harlan. "Looks like we've found our Psionic Commander."

Rather than answering immediately, Harlan stared at the screen in disbelief. When he finally turned to Quest, he shook his head. "We've seen those dungeon hearts before, but at a dramatically reduced size. They're similar to cores that the demons use to amplify their capabilities in our low-essence environments, and they've clearly used this one to hasten the terraforming of the dungeon. I've never seen a demon being latched to one, though, so I can only hypothesize that it's being used as a tool. Which then opens the possibility of a stronger entity that's able to enslave a Commander-level threat."

Harlan's expression was a mixture of confusion and excitement as he watched the scene carefully. He pointed at the portal in the background and looked back to Quest. "I think I've figured out what's going on!" Without waiting for anyone to inquire further, Harlan looked around at the Heroes in the room.

"That dungeon heart is flashing because it's near breaking point. The Commander is having difficulty using it, and my guess is that the huge number of tunnels that were created were all done as potential countermeasures for Divinity's visions! All the locations that we moved the Combat class event to, all of them have tunnels! They now lack the capability to open the portal for reinforcements or escape."

Neuro tilted his head as he looked over to Quest. "Maybe that's why they were targeting that student in the Gold cohort? The one who can open portals?"

Harlan nodded excitedly as he gestured back to the harnessed demon. "My guess is that the Commander wanted a replacement! Self-interest makes a lot more sense from a demonic behavior standpoint."

A burst of light on the screen caused the conversation to end abruptly and everyone winced. When the camera refocused, it was in time for them to see a spear of light shooting straight at the Commander. Jez's body was twisted at the waist, revealing himself as the main culprit of the surprise attack.

As the light-based attack soared over the crater, it pierced through the shuffling darkness to reveal hundreds of demons hunkered down in wait. Before the attack could find its target, a humanoid demon appeared out of nowhere and brushed the attack off to one side, causing a massive explosion in the wall behind it. Thanks to the light, everyone in the dungeon was able to see the demon in all its glory: Black armor that moved like smoke. Two glowing yellow eyes flickering from beneath its plumed helm. A shield had materialized on its right arm to deflect the attack, but it dissipated a moment later, replaced with a menacing blade.

What made the scenario all the more terrifying was that the whole area fell into darkness after Jez's light-based attack disappeared. When the next spear of light was thrown, the illuminated dungeon showed a very different landscape. The pit of demons had mobilized; the black-armored Commander was gone, and none of the Heroes were in their original locations. Halfway through the spear's journey across the pit, it was deflected. It revealed the black-armored demon running across the air with its shield visible once again.

Sal gaped at the screen in horror at how quickly the newly revealed Commander moved. Fighting in pitch darkness looked terrifying beyond belief, and he held his breath. Flickers of light on the screen showed countless horrors as the Heroes were swarmed by the army of demons. If there was any doubt in Sal's mind about his suitability for the battlefield, this encounter quashed it. There was no way he'd be able to survive in that battle, and he knew that for a fact. Sinclair's demonstration was just a single Prowler and that had caused him to freeze up…having an army of demons to contend with was incomprehensible.

A burst of light appeared on the screen again, but rather than the blinding light of Jez's attacks, it was a widespread inferno. The camera operator caught sight of Forge in the center of the pit, with his hammer resting on the ground. Waves of fire swept out in circles around him, igniting countless demons in the vicinity. In half a heartbeat, the hammer swung around in a wide arc, impacting heavily against the chest of an approaching Hulker. The Hulker was thrown backward dramatically, with a crumpled midsection. Forge didn't falter as he continued to swing the hammer, billowing out flames with each attack and destroying any demon the weapon connected with.

When he had made a clearing in the demon pit, he launched himself into a densely packed area to repeat the process, causing another towering inferno of flames as the hammer slammed into the ground. Upgrade appeared in the first clearing he made, her hand cannons firing with pinpoint accuracy at the wounded demons. She moved fluidly and in time with Forge, following his widespread attacks to finish off the survivors.

The camera moved sharply as the operator retreated hastily, his vision catching sight of a surprise Voider attack that almost took him out. A shadow moved quickly past him, and the Voider dropped dead to the dungeon floor, alongside dozens of other Voider corpses. When the camera stabilized, it revealed the guild master of the Delvers Guild, Shade. He winked at the screen before his body melted into smoke and disappeared.

Bursts of light drew the camera operator's attention, and the screen turned to watch a glowing Jez duking it out with the black-armored Commander. The plate armor Jez wore glowed vibrantly as he swung a bladed polearm in a series of vicious attacks. The Commander was clearly under pressure as it held a shield with both arms, and the camera revealed a series of daggers embedded into various parts of the demon. Each time the Commander defended against an attack from Jez, another dagger would find an opening.

Sal assumed that it was Blink, but his jaw practically dropped when Villa appeared in a flash, her hands ripping the daggers free from the demon before she disappeared again. Sinclair was transformed into a Hulker and clearing the pit with Forge and Upgrade. Behind him was a slender man, with a wide grin on his face, using martial arts. He looked incredibly out of place among the Heroes, but when his fist connected with a Prowler, Sal saw the head of the demon explode with what looked like a regular punch. The martial artist moved a bit faster with each attack, and his techniques became more powerful. It looked as if he had some form of momentum-based ability, but Sal had never heard of anything like that before.

A sudden explosion caused the black-armored Commander to turn with an agonized scream. Its yellow eyes locked onto the shattered remains of the dungeon heart. The camera panned to show Anna Sakura standing over the dead Psionic Commander and the shattered heart. With just that move alone, their ability to open portals and meddle with visions of the future was gone.

Before Jez could restrain it, the demon launched viciously across the pit, fully visible with the illumination of Forge's fire. It was terrifying in its approach, and the screams of rage cut through the dungeon as it launched itself at Anna Sakura. In a split second before its sword reached her, Villa appeared and slammed her dagger into the visor, bursting the enraged yellow eyes of the demon. It should have been enough to kill it, but the demon had a high regenerative ability and swung mercilessly at the space Anna Sakura had occupied.

A guttural roar sang out over the battlefield as it swung indiscriminately around the corpse of the fallen Commander. Villa waited for an opening to attack while keeping her distance, but surprisingly, Anna Sakura dove straight in and activated her ability to negate essence. The black sword disappeared instantly, along with the smoke-like armor, leaving the blind Commander confused as it struggled to survive without essence. Her pale hand appeared and gripped the demon's neck as she delivered the killing blow, cutting off the remainder of its essence. What had previously been a powerful guttural roar had reduced to panicked screams as she ended its life. Villa stared at her in disbelief, but Anna Sakura had already disappeared back into the fight.

A round of applause rang out in the Sky Lounge, which snapped Sal out of the fight. Everyone in the room looked as though it was the only logical outcome and none of them looked surprised by the results.

Alastair seemed to notice his mood and approached their couch. "Say, isn't that the girl who said she'd join your guild?" The look of horror on Sal's face caused Alastair to burst out laughing. "Honestly, Sal...this will look like an insurmountable step for you right now, but you must appreciate that you're only just in the door. Everyone you're watching right now has been training extensively, night and day, for years! That goes for you both, too."

Divinity managed to look a little less ruffled by the events on the screen, but Barry was very much in the same situation as Sal.

Neuro glanced over at them and gave a warm smile as he joined Alastair. "It's a good lesson, though. At least you know that you're being trained by the best there is!"

Sal nodded numbly but he didn't feel the wave of reassurance they were trying to give him. *Even if he had years to train, would he ever be able to step into a dungeon like that?* Sure, Upgrade was a Support class like he was, but she had thrown herself into the deep end with the other Heroes, and she was killing everything around her with ease. He couldn't wrap his head around the fact that Anna Sakura was still a student at the academy. She had essentially killed two Commanders at the upper levels of the demon hierarchy, and it looked effortless for her.

Neuro laughed, and it drew Sal's attention. The telepath put up his hands and apologized.

"I'm sorry, but with the look on your face, I needed to see what was racing through your mind. It's somewhat healthy to compare yourself to others, but not to the extent of what you're doing right now. You all have your own strengths, which will be a force to be reckoned with in the future." Neuro laughed as he glanced at Divinity. "Which you should know better than anyone!"

Quest clapped to get their attention. "It's wrapping up…let's see them through this and then we can have a debrief."

Neuro and Alastair nodded and shot apologetic glances at the students on the sofa.

The screen was showing absolute pandemonium as the Heroes cleared up the remaining hordes of demons. Without their Commanders, they defaulted to individualistic mindsets, except for the Prowlers that still hunted in packs. At the center of the pit, Sinclair was ferocious as he throttled demons as a Hulker, transformed into a Voider to relocate to another area, then shifted into a Prowler to rip out the throat of another enemy. His human form wasn't seen at any point as he killed everything around him by exploiting weaknesses. Speed, strength, and mobility showed Sinclair's true potential as a massacre on the battlefield.

The slender martial artist who was picking up momentum earlier was now drenched in demon blood. He whirled around with deadly spinning kicks and an explosive battery of jabs and punches. Anything he hit was sent flying or died instantly on impact.

Throughout the fight, none of the demons attempted any form of retreat, and continued to swarm around the Heroes. Explosions rang out in every direction as the guilds worked cohesively together. There were Heroes who were literally flying into the air above the pit before plummeting to inflict a devastating slam attack that sent shock waves throughout the area.

Forge and Upgrade were in perfect sync as they killed everyone within their fiery circle of death. Shields surrounded Heroes in the moments they revealed an opening, and exhausted forces were healed and restored by Supports standing at the wings. Villa and her strike team of Reavers were dispatching forces with ease, none of them looking the least bit tired as they launched coordinated attacks. Trench, one of their Heroes who Sal had met on the Credit floor, was creating walls of stone to funnel the demons to their deaths. Most magnificent of all, though, was the glowing form of Jez as he launched spear after spear of light, devastating anything that got in their way.

Pandemonium was an understatement as the Heroes flexed their capabilities to their fullest extent. In less than twenty minutes, hundreds of demonic corpses were all that remained of the once terrifying dungeon. The camera operator surveyed the battlefield as everything came to a close. It was a bleak sight, except for the grinning faces of the triumphant Heroes.

CHAPTER 73:
DEBRIEF

SAL WAS GLAD TO FIND OUT THAT THE LECTURERS AND MEMBERS OF THE DOOM Society were happy to include them in the debriefing of the event. Harlan had gotten them underway with a few observations after the screen switched off.

"I think we can all agree that those Commanders were in very weak states. It's just a guess for now, but my thought is that they overextended that dungeon heart by expanding their domain aggressively. It was clear from the manifesting armor that one of the Commanders is reliant on atmospheric essence, which was likely very limited in the area. Without a portal to their native, essence-rich environment, they were essentially trapped in that dungeon, with the dungeon heart not having enough essence to do more than sustain them," Harlan hypothesized freely, with a few hand gestures as he gathered his thoughts on the subject.

"It's really easy to throw around scenarios, but the fact remains that those Commanders were not at the same level as the ones we've studied in the past. It's a foreign behavior to see a demon latched onto a device like that, and it suggests that there was likely a more intelligent demon at play here. From the rash attacks of the armored Commander, my guess is that it wasn't the Controller in this scenario. What do you think, Alastair?"

Alastair shrugged as he looked around the room with a wry smile. "Can't fault any of those observations, to be honest. We all saw the marked change in their behavior when the Commanders were taken out, which means that our Psionic attacker was likely leading them with its mind. I can't talk too much on the behavioral aspect as it's not really my domain, but from a tactical perspective, it doesn't make sense for two Commanders to be in that level of dungeon. I'd have personally expected there to be around a thousand demons with that sort of leadership capability. Maybe those two were runts of the litter? Cast out from their own ranks? It's hard to judge, really, and I almost felt bad for the demons…those strike teams really went all out!"

Alastair finished with a laugh that was shared by several of the surrounding Heroes. The conversation between them went back and forth, with a few other voices offering opinions or suggestions, but the overall sentiment remained that it felt too easy for what was threatened in the various visions.

After a few more minutes of everyone saying their piece, Quest approached Divinity, Sal, and Barry and sat on the coffee table. He had a tired smile as he looked at them. "Thank you. All three of you went above and beyond to help us with this matter, and we're almost ready to put it all behind us. You probably know what I'm going to ask you to do."

Divinity nodded but waited for Quest to give her the actual instruction.

He obliged a half second later as he interlocked his fingers tightly. "Would you be able to look into the future for us, and see if the Combat class has any more surprises lined up?"

The jovial attitude of the lecturers calmed down as they looked over at Divinity. Without any more prompting, she activated her power and looked into the future.

Sal subconsciously held his breath as he waited for her verdict, and the air left him explosively as her face broke into a relieved smile.

"There are no attacks! Just the terrible matchups where we try not to get relegated!"

Her tone was playful but held a slight edge that told everyone how she felt about how the team selections were orchestrated. Neuro got a good laugh out of that, and the atmosphere turned into one of relaxation.

Quest looked as though a visible weight had been lifted from his shoulders as he cupped his face in his hands and let out a sigh of relief. "Wonderful. Just...wonderful. Thank you, Divinity." He pulled his hands away and smiled gratefully at her. With a slight turn of his head, he nodded again to Barry and Sal. "Thank you all for everything you've done. We'll absolutely be factoring in your contributions to the next shift in rankings, and we'll throw in some Q-Cred for good measure. It's just a token of thanks from me."

Divinity, Sal, and Barry sat uncomfortably as a series of lecturers and visiting guild officials gave them thanks.

Quest's tone lightened as he gestured at the guild officials. "You're not allowed to scout them until after the first semester, but you're welcome to chat with them!"

Just like that, the trio were swarmed with guild members who launched into questions about their abilities and their proposed developmental tracks over the course of their studies. Barry was pretty much cornered by Alastair but didn't seem concerned by it in the slightest. Divinity had a few scouts talking to her, while Sal had the vast majority of interest by far. He could barely remember the names of the people who spoke to him, but he did his best to maintain a polite front while answering their questions.

Inwardly, he was still reeling from everything that had just happened. They had successfully thwarted the threat of the demons attacking during the contest, but it still felt incredibly surreal. People were telling him that they'd be in the stands and watching his fights this weekend, and Sal smiled and nodded. Divinity seemed to be in the same boat as she gave short and noncommittal answers to their questions. Barry, on the other hand, was in his element, talking to everyone who came near him, with Alastair happily making introductions. As the evening dragged on, the guilds made their exit from the Sky Lounge, which finally gave them some breathing room.

Barry collapsed back on the couch with an exasperated sigh, a smile on his lips. "Do you think they're actually going to come and watch our fights? I'd say they were just being polite."

Divinity shook her head and pointed at her eyes. "Saw them in the vision. They're definitely going to be there. I also saw something else that has changed in the future." She gave Barry a knowing look, and his smile widened as he shrugged nonchalantly.

"They already know about my ability, so I might as well give them a bit of a show. Can't hurt our chances if I help a bit, right?"

Sal looked over at Barry in surprise. "Are you actually going to use your powers in the competition?"

Barry laughed and gave Sal a slight shove. "Hey, I'm pretty useful without them, thank you very much." Placing a hand on his chest, he gave Sal a reproachful look. "So, I've told you my secret ability…are you going to finally admit that you're Myth?" Barry's eyes locked on Sal as he waited for his suspicions to be confirmed.

Sal laughed. "What the hell makes you think that?"

Instead of answering immediately, Barry's eyes narrowed as he looked over at Divinity for support. "There's no way that some random guy would outfit both of our teams with equipment, no matter how much Q-Cred you're throwing at him. We've only been here a few weeks, and nobody has seen or heard of this guy before until now. Which means he's probably a first-year, too. I asked around the Crafting class to see who was the most impressive person, and would you believe what name they came back with? Salvatore Argento. Administration class? Same answer. Upgrade apparently spends all her free time in the workshop hiding away in a private room with, guess who?"

Barry pointed at Sal. "So, it's either a lot of coincidences happening in quick succession…or you're secretly smuggling in weapons from the Argento Auction. I know that you're a Replicator from our Skill class, and you're able to use other people's abilities without limits. Maybe you just copied a Crafting ability?" Rather than looking straight at Sal for an answer, he looked at Divinity to see whether she was on his side for this.

"Deduction capabilities, too?" Alastair chuckled as he sat down heavily in one of the armchairs. He placed his bearded chin on his palm and waited for Sal's reaction.

Sal gave Alastair a mock withering look before turning back to Barry. "Before I answer, I've got a question for you. Why did you go searching for Myth? I'm pretty sure we've kept you busy with the training, so it's not like you'd have been bored."

Divinity perked up at that and leaned in with a grin. "We can always go for more training if you'd like? If you've got time to daydream, you've absolutely got more time for sparring!"

Barry barely managed to suppress the involuntary shudder that crept over his body. He raised his right arm that held the glowing green runes on it and pointed at the symbols with his left hand. "I need to create these symbols manually to use my power. They're kinda like a safeguard so I don't get lost in that purgatory I showed you earlier. Just wanted to see if Myth was able to make something like the ones he made for Hannah, that helped her with control. How is she, by the way? I heard you two were pretty close." Barry's grin grew even wider.

Alastair didn't help things by gasping loudly. "Hannah! The plot thickens! Have you been holding out on us, Sal?"

Sal sighed and closed his eyes as he turned to Alastair with a wry smile. "You stay out of it." When he looked back at Barry, he could only shrug in defeat. "Okay…let's say that it's me. I'm Myth. You're aware that the price of whatever you're asking for is going to skyrocket because you're a dick, right?"

Barry sighed contentedly. "I knew it. I don't actually need anything made…I just thought your overwhelming sense of empathy would kick in and you'd admit it."

Divinity laughed out loud, and Alastair shook his head in surprise.

"That's it? I was hoping for at least a bit of drama."

Sal turned to the Tactics lecturer and pointed to the area where the screen had been. "That was enough drama for a lifetime!"

Alastair brushed the comment off with ease as he turned back to Barry. "So, we have Mr. Argento here. He's going to create his own guild in the future, and Miss Khan will join him sooner or later, if I'm recalling that correctly." He waved them away as though their aspirations were boring. "I'm betting on them being my retirement plan, fighting over directorship seats with Harlan." Alastair grinned as Harlan turned away from a conversation with Neuro, his expression one of confusion as he only heard his name.

Alastair pointed at Barry. "But what lies in store for Mr. Francis here? Have you considered what path you'd like to take?"

Barry looked at Sal in disbelief. "You're really going to create your own guild?"

Sal shrugged and shook his head. "Honestly, I've got no idea what I'm doing with my life, but that's the goal that I've set for the moment."

A few moments of silence passed between them as Barry thought of his answer. Finally, he grinned as he jutted his left thumb in Sal's direction. "I'll make a guild that's even better than his."

Alastair cupped his face in his palms and shook his head with a groan. "Could you aim just a little lower than that? Can't you see the olive branch I'm trying to give you?" Alastair gripped his chest and looked at Barry with feigned anguish. "If you had said you wanted to become a Master Tactician, I would have happily put you on the fast-track…but it seems you're set on being a thorn in Salvatore's side."

Barry tried to interject in a panic, but Alastair was on a roll now. He looked up toward the glass ceiling of the Sky Lounge and spoke to nobody in particular in his dramatically deep voice. "Imagine it! An Illusionist Controller, orchestrating the tides of war with just their mind! I guess I'll have to hold out for that Melanie girl the others mentioned. It's a shame, really." To finish his speech, he looked back down at the coffee table with a pained expression and slowly got to his feet.

Barry reached forward and gripped Alastair's arm with a laugh. "I was just playing around with Sal. I'm definitely interested in exploring other opportunities. Tactics does sound fun!"

Alastair grinned as he sat back down. "Well then, consider the upcoming Combat contest as your opportunity to get invited into my class. I'll need to see something truly incredible, but if you manage it, you'll have a free ticket into my class." His eyes darted over to Divinity and Sal. "That goes for the two of you, also."

With that said, Alastair got to his feet with a groan. "All this sitting and standing is killing my knees. It's getting late and we've got a few more things to discuss here, so it's probably a good time for you lot to duck out and get some rest. You've got a big debut coming up, and you'll need to be ready!"

CHAPTER 74:
RELIEF

As Sal walked through the lobby of the apartment tower, he looked around and saw a few students chatting excitedly. All of them were talking about the competition that was taking place tomorrow, and not even one of them looked as if they had a care in the world. Sal was somewhat jealous of them. None of them had gone through the anxiety that he'd shared with Divinity and Barry.

Just a few hours ago, Sal was certain that some students were going to die because of a dungeon break. With a shake of his head, he tried to put those thoughts out of his head and made his way to the elevators. It wasn't long before one opened in front of him, and he was inwardly grateful that it was empty. He couldn't hold a conversation with anyone at this point and just wanted to get back to his bed. Not even the lure of the workshop was enough to distract him.

A small part of his brain wanted him to double-check the equipment before the competition, but it was just obsessing at this point. Everything had been registered and verified for use in the fights, so there was nothing to worry about there.

Sal leaned against the wall of the elevator as it moved to his floor. His hopes of it being an easy journey were dashed when the doors opened after just a few floors. A group of happily chatting students flooded the elevator and pushed nearly half a dozen buttons for different floors between Sal and his destination. He tried to zone them out, but it was impossible in such an enclosed space. Sal closed his eyes and sighed quietly.

"So, wait, which floor is the party on? Kaycee, you said it was on the fortieth, right?" One girl's voice drowned out the others in a momentary panic as another button was pressed.

"Yeah, but I have to get changed! I'm not rocking up in my uniform!"

The conversation was from the opposite side of the elevator, and everyone in the center was speaking all at once, so Sal was quite literally bombarded with their shouts and concerns. He couldn't believe that some of the students were going to be drinking and partying on the night before the contest. *Was it overconfidence, or did they just not care?* Sal opened his eyes and saw that most of them were absorbed in their own affairs, but one set of eyes looked at him curiously. Before Sal could avert his gaze, the guy who was looking at him took a step closer.

"Hey, you're that Admin guy! The one who earned all the Q-Cred?" He smiled as he spoke, but it didn't reach his eyes.

Sal looked at him warily as he nodded slowly. With a quick glance, he saw that he was still about five stops before he got to his floor.

The guy turned to the group that had quieted a little. "We should invite him along to the party. The more the merrier!"

With a shake of his head, Sal tried to give the guy a placating smile. "Sorry, I'm exhausted, so I'm going to call it a night. Thanks for the invite, though."

The guy didn't react, almost as though he didn't listen to Sal's response. He placed a hand on Sal's shoulder and grinned at him. "What cohort are you in?"

Sal's smile tightened as he looked at the hand on his shoulder. With a slight twist of his body, he stood upright and moved out of the grip. "Silver."

Rather than taking the hint, the guy moved in closer to Sal's personal space. "Yeah? What rank are you?"

Behind him, the conversation had died down and one of the girls, who Sal guessed was Kaycee, stepped in. Just as Sal thought he was being ambushed; Kaycee jabbed the other guy in the shoulder with an annoyed expression.

"Stop it!" She turned to Sal with an apologetic look. "Don't mind him— he's a competitive idiot."

A flicker of annoyance crossed the guy's face before the fake smile returned. He backed off slightly, his hands raised. "Hey, we were just talking, isn't that right?"

Sal's eyes glanced over to see that it was only another three stops to his floor. When he didn't say anything, the imposing guy laughed humorlessly.

"Hey, Silver…why don't we make a bet? You win, I'll introduce you to some of my friends back here. I win, I get some of that Q-Cred you've been stockpiling. What do you say?" He gestured back at the group of girls who were looking at Sal curiously.

Only Kaycee was looking at the guy in disgust.

Maybe it was exhaustion, but Sal didn't have his usual composure and burst out laughing. Without any hesitation, Sal looked over the guy's shoulder to the girls and smiled. "Hey, I'm Salvatore. Nice to meet you."

He turned his attention back to the imposing figure and gave him a grin. "Introduction done. Guess I don't need that bet, now. Have a nice evening." Sal shook his head as he moved toward the doors of the elevator and waited for the next floor.

Kaycee's sharp intake of breath was the only indicator Sal had that something was wrong. With a sharp sidestep, Sal watched as a fist punched straight into the elevator door where his head had been. Sal was about to move into a fighting stance, his heart thundering, when the guy dropped to the ground, unconscious. Behind him was Kaycee, her hand outstretched and glowing from where she had hit him. All the girls laughed as Kaycee eventually deactivated her power. Sal looked at her in surprise, and she shook her head with a grimace.

"Apologies about Sleeping Beauty here. He's our team captain for tomorrow." Her tone was one of annoyance as she gave the collapsed body a sharp kick in the side. When Kaycee looked at the other girls, she raised an eyebrow. "Vote on leaving him here?"

Sal laughed at the unanimous show of hands. When the door opened, a wave of relief washed over Sal as he saw his corridor. He thanked Kaycee before the door closed but didn't catch her response.

With his Q-Card clutched in his right hand, Sal made his way toward his door, counting down the seconds that he'd be able to collapse onto his bed and sleep. Just as he opened his door, a vibration in his pocket signaled that he was getting a call. Every part of him wanted to ignore it, but he rarely got calls and was curious about who it was. Taking out the tablet, he looked at the screen and saw that it was his parents.

Sal didn't hesitate to answer the call. "Hey, is everything okay?"

The words were met with laughter from the other end of the phone as Petro's voice came through crisply. "Just checking in on our favorite son! Is now a bad time? We can call you back if you'd like?"

Sal smiled as he entered his room. Closing the door behind him and kicking off his shoes, he took a seat at his desk. "It's a good time, don't worry. I just got back to the room and was about to head to sleep, but I can stay up for a little while. How are you both doing, and how is the auction?"

"Ah, the auction house is doing fine, nothing out of the ordinary happening there. Your mother and I are doing great, which is a surprise. We've just got off a call with the headmaster, who told us about everything that's been going on."

Whatever Sal was about to say died in his throat. *Quest had spoken to his parents.* Sal was terrified of them knowing how recklessly he'd been using his power, because it would just worry them. His mind raced with how he should approach the conversation, but his father made it very easy for him.

"Now, before you start overthinking everything, let me put you out of your misery. Quest told us that you were instrumental in helping the academy foil a demonic attack. Ugh, wait…sorry, your mother has a question. Okay, I'll tell him. Right, sorry, Sal. You need to tell your mother all about this Divinity girl we heard about, okay? Your mother wants to know if we'll get to meet her in the future."

Sal laughed at their reaction. He could just imagine his mother in the background, telling Petro exactly what to ask. The anxiety and dread that he had been feeling about everything dissipating at hearing his parents' voices. "Can you tell her that Divinity is just a friend? I'm not going to be bringing anyone home to meet you, at least not anytime soon, okay?"

"She says that you should make sure that you're careful, and that we don't need to know what you get up to at the academy. So, the reason we wanted to call was because of something the headmaster said. Your ability of Skill Master…he said that you managed to create an ability that uses Restoration, Appraisal, and Upgrade? He called it Mythcrafter and said you're top of your class already in Crafting and Administration. You probably know what I'm going to ask, but before you start worrying, your mother and I are incredibly proud of what you've achieved so far there. Administration was something we knew you'd excel in, but Crafting? Why didn't you tell us about this new ability?"

Sal bit his lip as he thought about the question. He could just see his mother's disappointed face in his mind and decided to tell the truth. He told them about the Skill Registration, and Divinity's ability to look into the future. Sal went through the events of the last few weeks, and his time in the workshop and all the interactions with the Credit floor and the Reavers Guild. What had started as a panicked explanation turned into an impressive story of his achievements. Sal was encouraged by the delighted gasps from his parents at all the right parts, and he felt relieved at their reactions.

"Salvatore. This is your mother speaking. You know how I feel about you using the powers of others, and how reckless it can be…but you've managed to use that power to help others, and we couldn't be any prouder of you. You're in that academy to learn how to use this Skill Master ability, so learn as much as you can. Just be careful and be safe, okay? That Mythcrafter ability sounds like our retirement plan, so should I start looking up holiday homes now, or wait until later? I'm giving it back to your father now."

Sal heard her laugh as she handed the phone back to Petro. He couldn't describe how much pressure had been lifted from his shoulders. The worry that he carried of them disapproving of his actions was huge, and having their support was an incredible feeling. All his noncommittal calls with them, of explaining that things were fine or that they were okay…all those conversations had continued to pile on the pressure that he was lying to them. Now, he felt completely at ease and was excited to tell them what was happening.

"So, that Legendary-grade sniper rifle that you made for the Reavers Guild. It has an evolutionary trait on it? I'd love to see it sometime! What else have you made? When you're home next, I'll make sure to have everything you need to do some Crafting. I want to see your skills in action! But Sal, before we let you get some sleep, your mother and I had a chat before we called you. We've always known that you've been special, and we're so happy that you're finding your own path. Please don't limit yourself to thinking that you need to work at the Argento Auction, okay? Aim for whatever makes you happiest, because we're always going to be proud of you, no matter what you decide."

Sal's throat tightened, and he blinked back the tears that welled. He laughed at himself for getting so emotional and shook his head. "It's only been a month, so I've got no idea what my future will hold…but the current aim is to become a guild master, so we'll see how long that ambition lasts!"

"If you want to do it, you'll make it happen! Now, we'll check in on you later in the week. Good luck in the Combat class, and don't be disheartened if things don't work out. That was from your mother. I say, give them hell! Sleep well, Sal. We love you."

"Love you too." Sal smiled as he ended the call.

When he placed the tablet back on his desk, he turned to the glass windows that covered the entire wall. He stood there for a few moments in silence as he gathered his thoughts. A smile crept onto his face as he thought about his parents' words. He didn't have any secrets from them now, and he had their support. There was no longer going to be a demonic break this weekend, and now, his only concern was doing well in the Combat class.

CHAPTER 75:
BRACKETS

THE AMPHITHEATER WAS PACKED WITH ALL THE FIRST-YEAR STUDENTS. EACH of the ten cohorts were seated in anticipation, all of them separated into their teams of five. It was ridiculously early, but nobody was stupid enough to arrive late. Maybe it was just from the conditioning of Rust's alarm bell that punished latecomers?

Sal didn't think about it too much as he waited patiently. He and Divinity had bought coffees for their team, and it looked as though they were the most relaxed out of everyone there. A few people shivered with the morning chill, while others were halfway back to sleep. Sal didn't pay them much attention as he focused his gaze on the stage below, where Rust and Quest stood at the ready. They spoke to each other quietly for a few moments, but the sign that they were ready to begin was when the holographic screen burst into life, abruptly waking a few dozing students.

Quest smiled as he tapped at the device in his ear.

Good morning, students!

Today is going to be one of the most challenging moments in your academic calendar. You're going to be pitted against each other, in a round robin tournament, to determine who among you is the best. It will be a test of your endurance and capability as you fight against the other nineteen teams in your cohort. We will be watching you and grading all of you as individuals and as teams. We will look at your efficiency, teamwork, leadership, ability, and so much more!

Your grades will be tallied at the end of the day, and tomorrow you will receive your new ranking. We will then begin the shortlisting of the inter-cohort battles, which will be scheduled in the coming weeks.

Know that all of this will be taken into consideration when we're selecting the candidates for the Savior class.

We're going to be joined by a series of guild representatives today who will be watching each of your fights. Normally, we wouldn't have them here at such an early point in your academic journey, but they insisted that they wanted to see you perform. In addition to the guilds, our lecturers and professors will be watching your performance. They will be looking for talented individuals who they can invite into their Advanced classes and modules.

All of you here should know that this competition is your opportunity to showcase your capabilities to the people who could drastically influence your future. Don't hold back, don't be afraid. Try your best and show us that you want to be a Hero!

Quest's smile transformed into a grin as the entire amphitheater burst into applause. There were obviously a few surprises in there, but his rousing speech had done wonders and created an excited atmosphere across all the students. Even the lower-grade teams that didn't have much of a shot in the competition looked hopeful. Excited chattering started between the teams as they discussed all the new information they had when Rust's voice cut across them.

Listen up!

I want all of you to look up at the screens.

A copy of the tournament brackets will be sent to each of you after this presentation, so don't worry about taking notes.

You all heard the headmaster. You're going to be competing nineteen times today, with minimal time for rest and recuperation between fights.

It will absolutely be a test of your endurance and your strategic capability. If you expend all your essence in the first fights, you will be vulnerable throughout the rest of them.

We will be offering basic first aid between fights, as each of you should have made your own preparations for the tournament. Anyone who is unable to compete will withdraw from the remainder of the contest and receive full treatment.

Each cohort will have a dedicated break area that will have refreshments, but you'll need to manage your time effectively as there are no scheduled break times throughout the tournament.

This is also a test of your efficiency.

Rust gestured over to the train stop where Sal had arrived just a month ago. Literally every head turned in unison to see where he was gesturing, but Sal was focused on the screen in the air. It flashed through the different cohorts, showing all the fights that would be happening. Sal waited patiently for the Silver cohort to appear, and a wry smile tugged at his lips.

Divinity didn't miss his expression and followed his gaze, before laughing and giving him a shove. "It was bound to happen sooner or later. It's probably a good thing that we're fighting each other in the first round. Take it easy on us, okay?" Divinity teased, and Sal chuckled.

He was delighted to see Divinity back to her cheerful self, and all it took was thwarting a couple of demon Commanders and an entire dungeon filled with a demonic army.

He gave her a sideways glance. "You sure you're not tricking me? How do I know you're not going to kick our asses?"

Before Divinity could answer, Barry leaned over from the other side of Sal. "Could you two stop flirting for two minutes? I'm trying to listen here."

Divinity narrowed her eyes at Barry, but remained silent as she turned back to Rust. Barry celebrated his minor victory by shooting Sal a satisfied smirk.

Sal turned to look at Rust, who was continuing to explain the format of the tournament. Divinity had already briefed Sal on the important details, but it didn't hurt to hear it live.

…train station. We've separated the twenty carriages by team rank, which will allow you to strategize on the journey without fear of being overheard by someone from your cohort.

All of Rank #1 teams will be in the first carriage, with Rank #2 teams in the second carriage, and so forth.

There will be a complimentary breakfast on the journey, and we encourage you to eat as it might be the last meal you have before the end of the tournament. That will be up to how well you manage your time.

In an ideal world, we'll be able to complete this entire tournament within fifteen hours, but we'll be here until the last fights are complete…no matter how long it takes.

The headmaster explained that you'll be graded individually and as a team. Pay heed! You're not a one-person army, and you're not deadweight in a team.

Each of you are being monitored in this tournament, so make sure to show us everything you've got! We're looking for opportunities to give you high scores. Mistakes happen, and if a few fights don't go your way? So be it!

We're going to be calculating your top ten results out of the nineteen fights, so make sure to try your best and not get discouraged.

Quest gave Rust a quick nod and tapped his wrist, indicating something to do with timing. Rust acknowledged the gesture and called out to the students with a clap.

Rather than have a thousand of you leaving here all at once, we're going to go in phases.

Ranks #1 and #2, can you make your way to the train station, please? When they're on their way, we'll invite Ranks #3 and #4 to follow them.

Come on, you can chat on the train!

Let's go!

***

Whatever Sal had expected with the train, the reality was far from it. He had traveled to the academy in first class when he arrived, and it had been quite lavish. The train he entered now was nowhere near that standard and looked to be a regular commuter train that prioritized seats over space. There was a stairway that led up to a second level of the carriage, which resulted in incredibly low ceilings for both compartments.

All the seats were worn down and had a ragged appearance, with the tables having years' worth of carvings and graffiti etched onto them. Some of the windows looked to be cracked, and Sal hoped that it was the result of occupants, and not from traveling through the Red Zones.

When he turned around to see the other teams following through, he noticed that none of them paid much attention to the state of the place. With a shake of his head, he ignored his silly sense of unease and slid into one of the available seats. Barry sat across from him, with Jack, Blathnaid, and Anthony joining as they found their way to the carriage.

Sal didn't bother wasting any time and got the team up to speed with what was happening. "You might have noticed that our first fight is against Divinity and her team. It doesn't make sense for us to exhaust ourselves and fight against each other, so we've determined that the best solution is for Divinity's team to forfeit the match."

Sal smiled at the shocked expressions on Jack and Blathnaid's face. He elaborated to help them understand. "We need as much of an advantage as possible over the other teams, so being fully rested and having to fight one less time will give us a slight competitive edge over the others, especially when we go into the second fight. Since Anthony has the sword and I have my armor, we're going to give Divinity two sets of equipment—power gauntlets, shield guard and leaper boots. Jack, Blathnaid, and Barry will wear the equipment for our team."

Sal paused to look at their faces, curious whether they had any pressing questions. Blathnaid was the one to raise a hand, a conflicted expression on her face. When Sal gestured for her to speak, she started with a frown.

"Won't it look bad for Divinity's team if they just give up? I know they're only really calculating the best ten results out of nineteen, but…it'll make them look unmotivated or weak, I think."

Barry waved from the other side of the table. "Don't worry about that. I'll be taking care of it. As far as the spectators are concerned, they're going to see an incredible battle between our two teams. Think of it like a highlight reel of all the best moments from our training the last few weeks!"

Blathnaid looked at Barry and then at Sal in confusion, but it was the Illusionist who enlightened her. With a twist of his arm, the entire table became crystal-clear and tiny figures appeared in a mock battle. Sal raised an eyebrow at the incredible detail of each fighter, but Blathnaid went a step further by poking one of them with her finger, only to be dismayed when the digit passed straight through the illusion.

With a wave of his hand, Sal gestured for Barry to dispel the illusion, which he did without complaint. Blathnaid looked a little disappointed that it had disappeared but refocused her attention on the schedule that Sal placed at the center of the table.

"We're starting our fight with Divinity. Next after that will be Lucia and Team #4. I'm expecting it'll be a difficult one, as she's a powerful opponent and a Body Manipulator. You all have your notes on our future predictions, so you'll know some of her attacks already. After Lucia will be Evan and Team #6. They're able to teleport and likely have a weak team, so if we're able to trap them with some illusionary distractions, we can take them out."

Sal went through the list of fights and consulted the notes that he and Divinity had prepared over the previous weeks. It was a mixture of the Combat assessment reports that Rust instructed them to complete, and some of the visions that Divinity had about the tournament. Although Divinity had kept the results of the tournament a secret, she still gave him an in-depth analysis of how the teams could be beaten. A lot of the data was old because they had been distracted by the demonic threat, but it was still somewhat useful, and better than nothing.

Sal looked through the list and smiled. "After those is Michael Welling and Zachary Lowe. Teams #8 and #10. From what Divinity saw in the future, we should be in a good position to come out of them on top if we go all out. That'll be our first five fights…why do I get the feeling that they're going to leave that slimy bastard until last?"

Sal scanned through the fights to find out where Gerard Kilsee was on the list. "Oh, he's our tenth fight…and Victoria is fifteenth. Both are going to be tough, but at least we have our secret weapon for one of them."

Everyone turned to Blathnaid, who went bright red at their sudden attention.

Sal laughed and spread his hands wide. "It's a fight that rests completely on your shoulders. No pressure!"

CHAPTER 76:
STRATEGY

A FEW MINUTES AFTER ALL THE COHORTS WERE ABOARD THE TRAIN, IT DEPARTED the campus station and moved toward the first tournament site. Trolleys were pushed through the carriages by white uniformed members of the academy. Their breakfast wasn't remotely gourmet, but it was serviceable and soon after departure, everyone was busy eating and chatting about the upcoming fights.

Sal had scanned the room and seen a lot of unfamiliar faces. It wasn't particularly difficult to spot the team captains in each team, as they were typically the only well-equipped one out of the five. Because all the team captains had the second-to-last pick in each cohort, there were a lot of insecure and awkward people sitting on the train. Only Sal's team looked composed and confident, which was a fact that didn't escape the notice of a few teams.

One went so far as to ask whether they were in the right carriage, which entertained the group to no end. Sal was delighted to see how much confidence the team had developed over the last couple of weeks, with Anthony being the most drastic change in only a few days. He was typically silent, but ever since he had taken the sword from Sal, he had become much more assured in his own capability. When they spoke about strategy, he even offered suggestions rather than sitting and waiting for instructions.

Barry exhaled loudly as he pushed his breakfast carton to one side. His eyes were locked onto the brackets that were displayed on the tablet in the center of the table. "Dominic is probably going to be an issue with his defense. Think Anthony could overwhelm him with the sword while we take out the others? Then just blitz from there?" He looked over to Anthony, who shook his head slightly.

Sal looked at him curiously, wondering what he was thinking, and it didn't take long for him to speak his mind.

"By the time we're facing Dominic, he'll know our fighting style from the other battles. Since I can direct the onslaught of the essence attacks, why don't we feint instead? We can pretend to aim for him, but then at the last moment, take out one of his team? He'll shield himself and won't be able to protect them in time."

Barry's eyes lit up at that suggestion and immediately countered it with his own idea. "What if we create multiple essence attacks? I can create duplicates with illusions, so he'll never know which one is real, which should allow us to isolate him."

Sal smiled as he watched them devise their own counterattacks. Even though he had the final say as their leader, he was happy that they were thinking independently about everything. One of the keys to success for them was going to be in how they adapted to change on the battlefield.

The other students on the train had only had a handful of lessons from Rust on how to fight, whereas they had been fighting every day for two weeks. Blathnaid, a Crafter who specialized in tailoring, was actually one of their strongest combatants because of her quick thinking and agility. Sal wondered whether she would have been one of the students to be sent home after the first semester.

The team continued to make suggestions to one another, incorporating the strengths of each individual and covering blind spots. It went on like this for the next twenty minutes as they moved from each combatant to the next, until they had a firm grasp on what strategies they'd likely go with for all nineteen fights. In comparison, the other teams were still bickering over their first fight, with many of the team captains struggling to control their groups.

We're now arriving at our third destination.

Purple and Blue cohorts, please exit the train and follow the attendants to the combat area.

Thank you.

Sal watched as two more teams left the carriage, one of which was in a heated discussion with the team captain, complaining that he was being an idiot. It caused a few laughs from the remaining teams, but Sal was just curious about how unprepared the other teams seemed to be. Upgrade had told him that the tournament was going to be a complete shit-show, filled with students who had no idea what they were doing.

Sal thought she was being facetious, but the more he looked at the people around him, the more he started to think that maybe she was telling the truth. When the departing teams had finally disappeared, Sal wondered when the Silver cohort was going to be called. The first to leave had been Red and Orange. Second was Green and Yellow. Third, which were now leaving, were Purple and Blue. That left Gold, Silver, Bronze, and Black. Sal decided that whatever time they had left, they wouldn't waste it. There was no point in being complacent because the other teams were having issues.

"Okay, we might be off on the next stop, so let's make sure to go through the first five fights again! Barry, can you bring up the mock battles, please?" Sal asked as he moved the tablet and cartons off to one side.

With a flick of his wrist, an illusion flooded the table and created two teams squaring off against each other. All of them huddled around the table and listened intently as Sal walked them through the proposed strategy, taking all their suggestions into account and finalizing their plan. They continued this until the next announcement signaled their arrival at the tournament grounds.

We're now arriving at our fourth destination.

Silver and Gold cohorts, please exit the train and follow the attendants to the combat area.

Thank you.

With wide smiles, Silver Team #2 packed up their equipment and moved to leave the train. They didn't even spare a passing glance at the other teams, who were looking at the packed equipment in disbelief.

Sal smiled at his team as he stepped off the carriage and looked at the stadium in the distance. "Let's do this!"

***

The stadium was previously a football field, with an audience capacity of around fifty thousand people. The number of people who had showed up to the fights wasn't even a single percentage of that, as only a few dozen people sat in the crowd. It was ridiculously early in the morning, on a Saturday, so Sal could understand why so few people had shown up to watch. There were going to be nineteen fights throughout the day, so it was much likelier that the main groups would arrive later in the day. At least, that's what he told himself as he looked at the sparse group of people that looked lazily at the arena grounds.

The field itself had been paved at some point in the past, and there were now markings going down the middle of the pitch, separating it into four equal rectangles. Similar to the Combat classroom, gigantic rectangular prisms were erected in all four quadrants of the pitch, creating separate battlefields for the upcoming fights. Sal wasn't surprised by the sight, as he had seen it in his visions for the last few days. He realized in that moment why he had been anticipating a crowd. They appeared in the visions he had seen in the past.

**Team Captain, Divinity Khan of Silver Team #1,
will be fighting Team Captain, Salvatore Argento of Silver Team #2.**

**Team Captain, Dominic Walters of Silver Team #3,
will be fighting Team Captain, Gerard Kilsee of Silver Team #20.**

**Team Captain, Lucia Hernandez of Silver Team #4,
will be fighting Team Captain, Harold Gunn of Silver Team #19.**

**Team Captain, Christopher Gage of Silver Team #5,
will be fighting Team Captain, Crypto Daniels of Silver Team #18.**

Fights will commence in five minutes.

Prepare yourselves accordingly and good luck!

"Where are the others fighting?" Barry asked as he looked around to see the other teams waiting in the stands.

Sal shrugged, as he had no idea whether it was just going to be four fights at a time. When he looked at the team, he gestured for them to start suiting up.

"Blathnaid and Jack, get your equipment on. Barry, can you help me bring these over to Divinity's team?" Sal picked up the bags that contained the gear he had Crafted.

Anthony stood off to one side, holding the case that contained the sword. Sal couldn't wait to see people's reactions when Anthony started using it.

Barry picked up the other bag and grinned. "It's not like Divinity's going to need this, but hopefully it gives their team a shot at climbing up the ranks." They quickly brought the gear over to Divinity, who gave them a warm smile.

As she took the bag from Barry and handed it off to one of her team, she gave him a pointed look. "Can you at least make us look cool? I don't want this forfeit looking like you crushed us!"

Barry winked at her. "I'm starting to think you don't trust me, Divinity!" He laughed before his expression turned a bit more serious. "For real, though, don't worry. I'll make you all look incredible. Think of it more like a highlight reel of your best performances in training. I have it all stored up here!" Barry tapped the side of his head with a smile.

Before Divinity could respond, a one-minute warning echoed throughout the stadium, telling participants that they needed to get into their respective battle areas.

Barry shook his head in surprise. "They're being quite militant about this! We better head in, I guess."

Sal gestured for Anthony, Jack, and Blathnaid to join them as they made their way into the prism.

It had a similar amount of space to their training room, which was perfect, and the sudden familiarity of facing off against opponents they knew made everyone smile. Even though it was a farce and there wouldn't be a fight between them, they wished each other well in the fights to come. Sal stood at the back of his team and watched Divinity on the opposite side, speaking to her own team. A countdown timer began and the few people in the crowd started to cheer politely.

Battles will commence in...

3...

2...

1...

Fight!

Neither team made a move as they waited in silence. Both teams turned to look at the other fights that were taking place, studying the movements of their competitors, and seeing how they worked together. A noise in the stands drew Sal's attention, and he was shocked to see at least a dozen people on their feet, cheering and staring at their prism.

With a glance back to Barry, Sal saw that his entire torso was covered in green runes as he gave the audience a show. Judging from the excited disbelief on the viewers' faces, it was something extraordinary.

In the next prism, Sal watched as Dominic Walters was bombarded by explosive attacks. Lightning skewered through the air and slammed into his protective shield, causing him to falter ever so slightly. A blur of shadows to Dominic's right signaled the arrival of Rogue, who lashed out at Dominic's teammate, knocking him unconscious with a single strike. Bolt continued to launch lightning at Dominic, which prevented him from moving from his position. Rogue took out another member of the team, and Archer picked off another.

The last member ran to Dominic for protection, but Gerard had already moved in, launching an attack at his midsection, which caused another explosion of essence and knocked them out. In just a few seconds, Dominic was completely by himself and surrounded.

Sal watched in shock as Gerard's team continued to launch attacks at him, attacking his barrier from all sides until it finally broke. Gerard landed the final blow, punching the exhausted Dominic in the face and bringing him down.

With a turn to his left, Sal saw the last moments of Lucia's fight, where she had grown to massive proportions and towered over her competitors. She was facing the ragtag group that Harold Gunn had assembled in a panic, and the lack of cohesion and leadership was evident a mile away.

Lucia kicked one of the team squarely in the chest, and the victim flew backward dramatically, crashing into the top corner of the prism before falling uselessly to the ground in a heap. Three others were unconscious, likely dispatched as Sal watched Dominic's defeat. All that remained was poor Harold, who was on his knees, staring up at Lucia in horror. If Nova had any sympathy for him, she didn't show it as she flicked his torso powerfully with her finger, knocking him out in an instant.

The last fight was dragging on as both teams seemed incredibly unsure how to attack each other. Neither Crypto Daniels nor Christopher Gage were particularly noteworthy, and their teams seemed apprehensive of launching any attacks. There was a lot of chasing around, very few abilities being used, and a lot of chaotic shouting at each other as they tried to gain control of the situation.

Sal watched it for a few more moments before Barry's voice caught his attention. "Let's shake hands for a well-fought victory. Well done, everyone!"

Sal laughed as he turned around to shake Divinity's hand. Both teams shook hands and laughed at the ridiculous situation: Dominic was exhausted. Gerard's team had likely expended more than half of their total essence. Nova had soloed her entire fight…it was all a lot more chaotic than they had expected. And it was only going to get more exciting.

CHAPTER 77:
TOURNAMENT

"Don't expect me to go easy on you, Sal," Nova warned him as they shook hands before the fight.

The stress of the tournament was evident on her face and judging from the looks of scorn that she shot at her team, they weren't much help in the previous fights. Her gaze moved to the equipment that Sal's team wore, and she looked a little confused as she stepped back to group up with her team.

The announcer signaled the countdown, and Sal did his best to calm the surge of adrenaline that coursed through him. He needed to be rational if they were going to pull this one off.

Nova was one of the most powerful students in their cohort, so they needed to be careful and stick to the strategy they created to counter her. From the old data they had, Nova didn't turn into a giant in this match…but instead, manipulated her body into becoming faster and stronger. Sal didn't know whether it was to conserve essence for the later fights, or whether she underestimated their team of Support-class students.

As the countdown reached the end, Nova was the first off the mark, launching forward at an incredible speed as she whipped her arm around in a devastating punch aimed at Sal.

"Defend!" Sal shouted, and both Blathnaid and Jack appeared in front of him with their barrier shields raised.

Nova's eyes widened as her fist connected with the impenetrable barrier. The shield vibrated slightly as Nova was deflected backward, and both Jack and Blathnaid had to steady themselves against the momentum of the attack.

A shout of surprise from behind Nova caused her to turn around in shock. An arc of essence slammed into her team, sending two of them flying backward into the prism wall. Another arc launched from Anthony's sword, aimed directly at the remaining two team members, and Nova launched herself toward him in a panicked fury.

"Flank!" Sal shouted, and Nova barely had any time to react as Barry appeared out of thin air, his power gauntlet aimed directly at her side.

His open palm emitted a powerful pulse of essence that threw her off to one side with a startled gasp. Nova rolled to her feet and started to heal herself as she took a tentative step backward. With a panicked glance behind her, she could see that another arc of essence sliced toward her group. In an act of desperation, she roared at them to get out of the way, but they were frozen to the spot as they watched their demise fly straight at them.

Anthony's aim was true, and the arc of essence collided with the remainder of Nova's team, knocking them backward in a dramatic fashion. Nova could only grit her teeth as she backed away from Sal's team.

Sal saw the sudden halt to her movements and guessed what was happening. "Blitz! Don't let her grow!"

As soon as the order left his lips, the entire team sprang into action.

Nova could only gasp as Blathnaid and Jack leapt high into the air. Their gauntlets were aimed at her like guns, and a sudden barrage of essence bullets rained down on her. Nova tried to retreat and get her bearings, but a vicious slice of a blade closed in on her position. Her eyes widened as Anthony moved into a close-range attack, and despite her confidence in her hand-to-hand martial arts, the sword managed to find every one of her openings.

Nova modified her hands to be as hard as metal. It was enough to parry the sword a few times, but she was vulnerable against the attacks of the others. The overwhelming display of power caught her by surprise, evident by her stricken expression, and Nova cursed aloud for taking it lightly.

Sal watched as Nova desperately tried to defend herself, but it had turned into a war of attrition. He knew that he'd be able to get Barry to put her in purgatory, which would allow them to win the fight with ease, but this wasn't just about quick wins. Sal needed to showcase the capabilities of his entire team, so having a drawn-out fight with them attacking and listening to his commands…it would obviously result in a higher score for them.

"Flank!" Sal shouted again, and this time Nova was prepared.

She whirled around to her blind spot in a defensive stance, but nobody was there. She gritted her teeth at the clear deception play. Anthony leaped back and launched another arc of essence directly at Nova, who wasn't in a position to shield herself. Barry, Blathnaid, and Jack held their shields up to block off Nova's escape, which left her to face the essence attack head-on.

Nova laughed as she took the direct hit; her body flew backward and bounced against their raised shields. Her body crumpled to the ground with an aggravated sigh, but she made no effort to get back up. With that, the fight was decided, and Sal's team got to enjoy their first real victory.

All of them moved to help their opponents, with Sal approaching Nova personally. "Hey, are you okay?" He touched her shoulder, and Nova groaned as she rolled onto her back. The look of disdain on her face was almost enough to make Sal laugh, but he fought the temptation.

With a slight shake of her head, she looked at him accusingly. "What the fuck just happened? Our teams were supposed to be shit…how did you do it?"

Sal offered her a hand, which she took.

When he pulled her to her feet, she accidentally fell against him with a grunt. "Ugh…" She groaned with another shake of her head. Looking back to her team, she sighed. "Hopefully they're not too injured for the next one…I've no idea how the fuck we're supposed to do nineteen of these fights!"

With that, Nova steadied herself and removed Sal's arm. She exhaled slowly and extended her hand for him to take. "You fought well, Sal. Well done."

Even though her tone was jaded, Sal could see that he had earned her respect.

In the prism next to theirs, Sal saw Divinity launching a series of vicious kicks at Dominic Walters. Her team had managed to dispatch the majority of his team, with some of them still engaged in hand-to-hand combat. But the real highlight of the fight was the battle between the team captains.

Momentary bursts of blue light signaled Dominic's attempts to erect his shield, but Divinity slid into the gaps of his defense and littered him with a series of punches and kicks. With each attempt to block, Divinity got two or three attacks through. It wasn't even a war of attrition and looked more like the strong bullying the weak.

When Divinity's team activated their power gauntlets and started to fire essence bullets, it practically acted as the final nail in the coffin. Dominic's chances were completely dashed, and after a few more attacks, he fell once again in defeat.

Sal grinned as Divinity joined her team in celebration, all their faces showing their surprise at the outcome. He paid special attention to Dominic, who punched the ground in front of him in frustration.

***

Sal had anticipated a much more difficult fight with the Team #6 captain, Evan McGregor. Their ability to teleport around the battlefield was a huge variable, and Sal wondered whether he'd need to rely on Barry to get them through the fight.

However, Evan made a poor choice in aiming for Anthony as their first target. He had barely supercharged the sword when Evan appeared beside him with a raised fist, and the sword acknowledged the threat immediately. Sal watched as Evan was countered ruthlessly. The flat of the blade smacked the side of their head, knocking them to the ground, unconscious.

Blathnaid and Jack played their roles masterfully and closed in on the now leaderless team, launching each member backward with pulse attacks from their gauntlets. Sal had barely managed to shout out an order before the fight was decided.

With three victories under their belt, Sal started to get a bit more attention from the other teams. A few choice remarks were made about the outfits that Blathnaid and Jack had Crafted for the team, but all eyes were on the sword that Anthony used. Sal smiled when he heard the low-rankers complaining about him buying weapons, when that was their mocking suggestion for him, back when the teams were decided.

The atmosphere was anything but calm, with some captains shouting aggressively at their team members. Tension crept in for the other teams as they started to realize how much effort the tournament was going to be, and how their management of essence was going to be vital. Communication had broken down on a number of teams and weak leadership became very apparent. Some teams were just outright terrible. Poor Harold Gunn, the Team #19 captain, had become the butt of nearly every joke after losing each fight in a dramatic fashion, and Sal could only feel sorry for him.

"Michael Welling is next?" Barry asked as he looked at his own tablet for a few moments, not taking a seat beside the rest of the team. Sal nodded, but it was Anthony who replied to the question.

"Yes, pretty straightforward fight. His team hasn't been doing well so far. Same with Zachary Lowe, who is the fight afterward."

Barry nodded in thanks as he put away his tablet. With a glance at Sal, he grinned. "We're pretty lucky, to be honest. We're matching up against the strong high-rankers first with weak teams. In the later fights, the strong teams with weak leaders will be exhausted!" Barry turned and pointed at the different teams sitting in another stand, waiting for their turn in the prism.

"If we beat Michael and Zachary, we'll have taken out five of the top ten, which just leaves ourselves and four others. Michael is Rank #8, and Zachary is Rank #10."

Sal laughed with a shake of his head. "Let's not get ahead of ourselves. We'll focus on the fight with Michael and take it one step at a time. How is everyone doing in terms of essence? Is the equipment holding up okay?"

Each of them closed their eyes to inspect their own internal essence reserves, with Barry and Anthony being the fastest to check.

Barry gave him a thumbs-up and a grin. "Don't worry, I've still got plenty left in the tank. You don't get to the eightieth gate by being shit at managing essence."

Sal turned to Anthony, who gave him a small nod and a smile.

"All good on my side. The core in the sword is doing most of the work, and it still has a ridiculous amount of charge left."

A few more minutes of silence passed before Blathnaid and Jack opened their eyes and answered. They were a little embarrassed with how long it took them to check, and they offered apologetic smiles. Apparently, both had plenty of essence left and their equipment was practically all at full charge. Sal had considered breaking open the supplies that they had bought from the vendors, but nobody was even close to exhaustion yet.

When he looked around at the other teams, he saw Lucia hunched over in pain as she controlled her breathing. *There had only been three fights so far, and she was already that exhausted?* Sal debated on whether he should give her one of the drinks to help her recover, but he eventually decided against it. It had only been three fights, and he had no idea how much his own team might need those resources in the fights to come.

Sal steeled his heart as he focused on the task at hand. Almost as soon as he resolved himself, the announcement came to signal the next round of the tournament. Sal and his team got to their feet and made their way to their assigned prism.

It was a completely one-sided slaughter, with Anthony devastating Michael's whole team with just three swings of the sword. Blathnaid had deflected a weak projectile attack with her shield, and Jack picked off a fleeing student with a shot of his pulse gauntlet. It was one of the most anti-climactic fights that Sal had ever witnessed, and he was practically speechless when the fight was decided in less than thirty seconds.

When he turned to look at the other fights, he saw Divinity in the distance fighting against a team of guys. She looked to be winning.

Barry followed his line of vision and added context. "Christopher Gage, Rank #5. He's useless—she'll be fine. That one over there is the one you should be watching." He pointed at the prism to their left, and Sal turned to see an incredible sight that didn't belong in a student competition.

A series of explosions erupted out of thin air, creating plumes of smoke across the battlefield. The student responsible was a woman standing defiantly, with two hands raised. Each click of her fingers created a new explosion in the area she was pointing, but the attacks weren't going through as her opponent continued to throw up temporary shields.

The pace was dizzying, with both teams looking incredibly competent. A laser attack sliced across the crowd and knocked down one of the combatants, while another on the opposing side was nearly crushed by a shard of pavement that was flung viciously.

Sal could only stare in disbelief at the sight of it, and his eyes only widened when he realized that one of the captains was none other than Whisper. The girl who sat beside him in their Skill class! Her face was a mask of concentration as she darted between the attacks from every direction. Her right hand was glowing white, while her left was covered in darkness. Sal could see she was in a great deal of pain, but it didn't stop her from amplifying the abilities of her team.

Each of them moved in harmony, with their Defender managing to shield Whisper from all incoming attacks. Their offense continued to use the laser attack as he hid within the cover of smoke. One of their Supports was using an ability to create a smokescreen across the battlefield. Sal watched the high-octane fight and wondered whether their team would be up to that sort of battle.

Barry whistled as another explosion erupted at the center of the smokescreen, lighting up the darkness and briefly displaying the silhouettes of Whisper's team. "That's Jenni Stravos…she's Rank #17 and someone we should definitely be wary of."

Sal agreed as he watched the blonde woman continue to snap her fingers viciously. It looked like his team weren't the only ones taking this thing seriously.

Barry laughed as he clapped Sal on the shoulder. "Oh, and we're fighting Whisper after Zachary, so make sure you're paying attention."

CHAPTER 78:
STREAK

Sal had been right about the atmosphere getting louder as the day progressed. More and more people had started to arrive at the stadium, and they brought with them a whole new level of tension. It hit home that they were being watched by the guilds, and that pressure made some of them self-destruct during their battles. Simple mistakes, like shouting out the wrong orders or missing attacks, started to happen as the stadium filled with people. When the fifth round concluded, the organizers put up a screen on each crowd-facing side of the rectangular prisms. It showcased the current standings and caught everyone up on what was happening.

Position	Team Captain	Rank	Team Classes	Wins / Losses
1st	Salvatore Argento	#2	S/S/S/S/S	5-0
2nd	Whisper Ding	#12	C/D/O/S/S	5-0
3rd	Victoria Chase	#7	C/S/S/S/D	5-0
4th	Lucia Hernandez	#4	O/S/S/S/S	4-1
5th	Gerard Kilsee	#20	O/O/O/O/O	4-1
6th	Crypto Daniels	#18	O/D/D/C/S	4-1
7th	Divinity Khan	#1	C/S/S/S/D	3-2
8th	Jenni Stravos	#17	C/O/D/D/S	3-2

With the fight against Zachary being incredibly straightforward, Sal's team retained the top spot with a clean streak. It was only when the scores went up that he realized it was a shared podium, with Whisper and Victoria having the same flawless record. The thing that seemed to get the audience's attention was the class composition, and the fact that a team of Support classes was currently in joint first position.

Sal looked at the scores for a few more moments and frowned. It was clearly saying that his team was first, and that Whisper and Victoria were second and third. *Did that mean that there were other calculations at play other than just the wins and losses?* He didn't dwell on it too much because the next round was going to be against Whisper, and one of them was going to experience a break in their perfect run.

Sal wasn't getting used to the addition of applause before the fights, but he did his best to zone it out as they entered their assigned prism. Whisper was all business on the other side of the arena, and Sal steeled himself for the fight to come. They had a better team composition, with a Controller, Offense type, Defense type, and two Supports. Just from seeing the snippets of Whisper's fight with Jenni, Sal knew that he was in for a bit of a challenge.

"Blitz!" He shouted the order as he ran forward with the rest of his team.

It was the first time in all their fights that Sal had moved from his position of their impromptu Controller. He activated his power and sent a supercharge of essence toward his gloves and uniform. The result was dramatic as the mechanical arms burst to life from his fingertips, and his entire torso became plated in glistening black armor.

Sal saw Whisper's shocked expression at the sudden transformation, and he used that to draw their attention further. Maybe it was inspiration from watching the demonic Commander, or maybe it was just his desire to have a sword…but Sal willed his mechanical arms to shift and morph into a weapon he could use. On his left arm, a shield blossomed, and on his right, a long black sword slid out from above his knuckles.

Jack and Blathnaid leapt high into the air, shooting suppressing fire from their pulse gauntlets before they landed. With Whisper's Defender shielding upward, he wasn't prepared for the slice attack that was fired at a low angle by Anthony. The projectile of essence slipped under the barrier and knocked the Defender off-balance. Whisper hastily extended a hand toward him, and his shield grew dramatically. Her amplification ability was now in effect, and it was going to take more than a surprise attack to take them out.

When her Offense teammate started to scream, Whisper whirled around to see him firing lasers erratically in their own area. The two Supports were taken out in an instant, and the best Whisper could do was minimize the attack power of her Offense teammate until he came to his senses. Confusion was written all over her face as she gritted her teeth.

Sal didn't even need to look to know that Barry was responsible for the laser guy's horrifying visions. With just a single illusion, he had managed to disable their main attacker and take out two of their Support teammates.

Rather than falling to pieces at the sudden shift in momentum, Whisper reacted by shouting out concise commands to her team. With a stifled gasp, she managed to get one of her Supports back by jacking up their power. The Offense type closed their eyes and listened to her instructions as he tried to fire his attacks without seeing Barry's illusions.

It might have worked if they weren't against a trained team that had studied their abilities. Anthony launched three consecutive attacks at Whisper, and predictably, her Defender jumped forward with his barrier to protect her. At the last possible moment, each projectile skewed off in a different direction, with two of them hitting the Offense guy, and the last one taking out the struggling Support. Whisper leapt behind the barrier and looked around at Sal's team apprehensively. It was clear that she was trying to come up with a counterattack, but Sal had no intention of giving her that time.

"Overwhelm!" Sal shouted as he launched forward in attack.

With them having no counterattack potential, the best solution was for them to overwhelm Whisper with attacks that didn't sap too much essence. Sal's blade connected with the barrier and, to the shock of everyone, it sliced through the protective bubble as though it were paper.

Sal kept his shield raised for anything that Whisper might attempt, but the opening was all Anthony needed to launch the final projectile at the Defender. His own bubble had turned into a death trap as he had nowhere to escape, and when the essence hit, it was explosive. Sal was grateful for his shield and armor as it protected him perfectly. Whisper, on the other hand, was coughing on her back as she groaned in defeat.

Everyone was down, and Sal breathed a sigh of relief as he deactivated his power and let his uniform and gloves return to normal. The applause that welcomed their victory was practically deafening, but Sal didn't pay it any heed as he went to lift Whisper to her feet. They were barely a third of the way through the competition, and there was no way that he was going to lose his cool. He was going to be facing off against Gerard soon, and it was almost worrying Sal how much he was excited about it.

***

Blathnaid stared at the scoreboard in absolute disbelief. Everyone else was seated in the stands as they had some lunch, but she was still standing and gaping at the scores in shock.

Sal laughed and offered her a sandwich, but she didn't react immediately.

Barry shook his head and snapped his fingers to get her attention. "What has you spacing out all of a sudden?"

Blathnaid turned and gave them an incredulous look, as though they were the ones who were weird for how they weren't reacting. She pointed at the screen. "We have eight straight wins! Statistically, even if we lose every single other match…we're still going to avoid relegation! We're not going to get expelled!" Her smile was one of wonder as she looked back at the screen again.

This time, Jack followed her line of sight with a dumbfounded expression. "Are you serious?" He turned back to Barry and Sal, his voice lined with emotional incredulity. "Are we definitely out of the relegation zone?"

Barry tilted his head and looked at the two of them as if they were idiots. "Of course we're not getting relegated. Have you seen these teams? Half of them don't even know each other's names, let alone how to work together. We've been training for weeks, we have great equipment, and we're a lot more strategic than all of them. Don't aim so low. We're going for the top!"

Sal chuckled, which turned into full-blown laughter when he saw the expressions of disbelief on Blathnaid and Jack's faces.

Anthony seemed to be somewhere in between the two standpoints as he smiled from his seat. "Honestly, I didn't expect it to be this easy. We still have the stronger teams to face off against, though. All we can do is try our best."

Barry nodded and raised his cup as though he were making a toast. "To trying our best…and winning."

That got a few laughs from the team, and Sal smiled at how well everyone was working together. It was bizarre to think that he was terrified of their performance a couple of weeks ago, and now they were in the lead of the whole cohort!

When Sal turned around to look at the other teams, he could see Lucia hunched over in pain. Her arms shook and her entire team tried to help her, but there was nothing they could do. The essence exhaustion was likely setting in for her, and it was astounding that she was single-handedly carrying her team through the competition.

Sal couldn't help but admire her. After another quick glance at the scoreboard, and he justified that it couldn't hurt to give her one of the recovery drinks from the vendors. He had already fought against her, and the excuse he gave himself was that her performing well against his competitors would only help his overall score.

He accepted that internal logic as he got to his feet and made his way across the stands to where she was sitting. Her team instinctively made way for Sal, and he wasn't sure whether it was because of the previous battles, or whether they knew that he was friends with Nova.

Lucia could barely turn her head without wincing, but she managed to give him a wink. "Don't worry, Sal. I just need a breather, and I'll be fine."

"Drink this," Sal instructed as he handed her the metal hip flask. "All of it. It'll make you feel better."

His tone was firm, and Lucia didn't question his motives as she brought it to her lips and took a tentative swig. Her eyes widened, and she practically chugged the remainder of the liquid in one go. Sal was about to tell her that it would take a few minutes for the effects to properly work, but he was stunned to silence as her body started to emit steam.

Lucia cracked her neck and flexed her shoulders as a grin spread across her lips. She stretched her body out before she locked Sal in a grateful embrace.

He was surprised at the sudden show of affection and wasn't exactly sure how to react.

"I appreciate that, thank you. I'm still going to get even with you for the beating you gave me…so you can look forward to that."

Her smile was sweet, even if her words weren't. Sal had no regrets in giving her the recovery tonic and returned to his team in the stands.

They were looking at him as though he were crazy, but Barry nodded appreciatively. "Didn't think she was your type, but I can see it." He tilted his head as he appraised Lucia, and Sal just laughed with a shake of his head.

"Just helping a friend. I'm not sure I want to date someone who can literally change their appearance to look like anyone…" Sal thought about that statement before he turned back to Barry with a laugh. "Actually, scratch that. I think I'd be okay with it!"

Blathnaid rolled her eyes, but Jack turned around with a serious expression.

"Don't forget, Sal—she can turn into a giant too!"

Everyone got a smile out of that, which turned into uncontrollable laughter when Barry created a mock illusion of a giant Lucia flattening a normal-sized Sal.

When everything settled down, Sal turned and looked at the upcoming fights that would be happening in a few minutes. The first one was against Crypto Daniels, the Rank #18. He apparently had a rough start but found his groove throughout the next few fights. He was definitely in contention for the top spots, but Sal saw him as a speed bump on the way to his true destination.

The tenth fight, which would be after Crypto, was with Gerard Kilsee, the Rank #20. Fuck-Face, from the bathrooms on Sal's first day, and the ringleader of all the taunts from the Combat class. Sal wasn't a particularly competitive person, but Gerard had managed to rub him the wrong way too many times. He was looking forward to their fight—five Support classes against five Offense classes. All the odds should have been against them, but Sal didn't care in the slightest. He just wanted to see the look on Gerard's face when he was defeated.

CHAPTER 79:
SHOWTIME

ALASTAIR GRIMACED AS HE LOOKED DOWN AT THE SCHEDULE IN FRONT OF HIM and then at the time. "We spent a bit too long with the Gold cohort, so we can't hang around here for too long."

He turned around to the group of guild officials, who were still chatting excitedly to one another. Alastair couldn't blame them in the slightest because he had witnessed it too. Neuro's daughter, Erika—the first-year who held the #1 rank in the whole academy—was effortlessly dismantling the Gold cohort teams, one by one. She was, without question, the top prospect for pretty much anyone who watched her. Quest had to intervene and force the scouts to attend other tournament grounds, and Alastair counted himself among the disappointed people. He wanted to stay and watch the rest of her fights.

"Is the next one the Black cohort?" Alastair asked as he entered the stadium with a frown, looking around to see if there was a visual clue.

"Silver."

The answer came from Anna Sakura, who walked beside their group quietly.

Alastair nearly flinched at the sudden sight of her. He hadn't noticed her presence. "What are you doing here?" He couldn't fathom why she was watching a first-year tournament, especially considering that she had been in a dungeon raid just the previous night.

Anna Sakura sighed as she gestured toward the prisms in the center of the stadium ahead. "There's a guy here I'm supposed to scout for the Assassination module. He's on Team #20 and has a stealth ability."

Alastair chuckled as he shrugged. "I thought you'd be here to cheer on our new recruits in the Doom Society."

For the first time, Anna Sakura's passive expression changed. She looked at Alastair in confusion, and he pointed at the schedule in front of him.

"Sal and Divinity are in the Silver cohort. Team #20, you said?" Alastair double-checked as he pointed at the groupings with a grin. "Oh, that's rough! Sal is scheduled to fight them next. Make sure you cheer for him, okay?"

Anna Sakura leaned over and looked at the teams with a raised eyebrow. When she saw the team compositions, she let out an involuntary sigh. "Five Support classes against five Offense classes? I'll probably have to hang around to see Team #20 fight against other Offensive and Defensive people to get a good read on their skills. This one won't be much of a fight."

Her voice carried a note of finality, and Alastair smiled at her as they finally arrived at the prisms. Just as he was about to move toward the nearest seating area, he noticed that Anna Sakura stared at one of the prisms in shock. Turning to see what she was looking at, Alastair's jaw dropped in disbelief.

Position	Team Captain	Rank	Team Classes	Wins / Losses
1st	Salvatore Argento	#2	S/S/S/S/S	9-0
2nd	Lucia Hernandez	#4	O/S/S/S/S	8-1
3rd	Jenni Stravos	#17	C/O/D/D/S	7-2
4th	Gerard Kilsee	#20	O/O/O/O/O	7-2
5th	Divinity Khan	#1	C/S/S/S/D	7-2
6th	Whisper Ding	#12	C/D/O/S/S	6-3
7th	Crypto Daniels	#18	O/D/D/C/S	6-3
8th	Victoria Chase	#7	C/S/S/S/D	6-3

Alastair had to do a double take when he looked down at the schedule. "What the hell happened here?" The answer came from behind him.

"Welcome to the party." Jez grinned from the stands as he raised a hip flask in Alastair's direction in greeting.

Anna Sakura was still staring at the results. "How is it possible for a Support team to be leading the group?" She tucked a strand of jet-black hair behind her ear as she turned around to Jez with a frown. "Are all the other teams terrible or something?"

Instead of answering, Jez gestured at the row of available seats in front of him. "You need to see it for yourself. Alastair, you should keep an eye on that Whisper girl. She's something else!"

Anna Sakura didn't hesitate in the slightest as she moved to take a seat, her dark eyes trained on the prism the entire time, as though she might miss something if she looked away. Alastair exhaled heavily as he moved into a seat beside Jez. The Administration lecturer handed the hip flask to Alastair, but the Tactics lecturer declined with a wave of his hand.

"It's too early for that."

Jez chuckled as Sal's team entered the prism in front of them. "Don't get your hopes up too much, though. They've got solid teamwork and good equipment, which is pretty much the only reason they've gotten this far. If that Offense team gets their shit together, they should be able to break the winning streak," Jez muttered as he leaned forward in his seat in anticipation.

With a passing glance at Anna Sakura, he grinned. "Well done yesterday, by the way. You did great!"

Anna Sakura gave Jez a respectful nod but didn't say a word.

Alastair frowned as he looked at Sal's team closely. "Have you seen anything…out of the ordinary? Illusions perhaps?" He watched Barry with curiosity.

Jez laughed. "Nope, they just jump around and the guy with the sword takes people out. Pretty straightforward stuff."

Alastair laughed, which surprised Jez considerably.

When he looked at Alastair, the Tactics lecturer took the hip flask from him. "Sounds like they're not using their trump cards yet. This could be interesting!"

Anna Sakura looked over at Alastair but didn't ask anything. She turned back to watch the two teams, a small smile appearing on her face.

***

Sal turned around to look at his team in the moments before the fight began. Everyone seemed focused and determined. It wasn't enough to just win this fight; it needed to be an overwhelming victory, and the whole team was on board with the plan. Rather than conserving energy, they were going to go all out from the very beginning.

Because their top ten fights would be counted out of the nineteen, a positive result here would give them ten straight wins. For that reason, Sal had instructed them to disregard their essence conservation. Jack and Blathnaid weren't going to have much of a marked change in performance, but Anthony and Barry had the potential to create a major impact. Barry gave Sal a knowing wink as he got into a combat stance. On the other side, Anthony was breathing slowly as he stared at the blade in his grip. It was surreal to see him so determined, but oddly reassuring.

On the opposite side of the prism, Gerard spent his time shouting taunts at Sal. His whole team looked at him distastefully, but Gerard didn't care in the slightest. In his eyes, this was the perfect opportunity to get back at Sal for their first day at the academy. Bolt, Rodrigo, and Archer all looked to be tired from their previous fights, but Gerard was still in relatively good condition.

As the countdown to the fight started, Barry activated his ability, coating both of his arms in glowing green runes. Anthony threw all his power into the Supercharge ability, making the sword burst into a bright light. Sal activated his ability and channeled his essence into the gloves, creating the suit of black armor from before.

When Sal turned to look at Anthony, he saw that the sword tentacles had covered his entire torso, creating a writhing suit of red armor. The blade itself was glowing a vicious red, and sparks of black energy seemed to course through the metal in anticipation of a fight. Sal knew that it was being pushed to its absolute limits as the color was different from when they had trained, and he desperately wanted to Appraise it. There was no time for that, though. The fight had begun.

"Overwhelm!" Sal shouted, causing each of his team to jump into action.

Jack and Blathnaid used the speed of their leaper boots to burst forward with their shields raised protectively. They needed to keep it up to avoid any sudden attacks as they closed the distance. Bolt and Archer were both ranged, with Rodrigo lacking a lot of mobility. Rogue was one they needed to keep an eye on with his stealth-based ability, as he'd likely ambush someone during the fight.

For that reason, Sal ideally wanted Rogue to be taken out first.

Barry weaved his hands around in an intricate pattern and his face was a picture of concentration and effort. He gritted his teeth and brought his ability under control before unleashing it on their opponents.

"How much do you want to bet that they'll shit themselves?" Barry whispered as he summoned all the illusions from his mind, into the prism. For theatric effect, he roared out, "My summoned minions! Go forth and crush our opponents!"

Gerard and his team were completely stunned at the sudden appearance of an armored angel.

Sal recognized the features immediately and knew that this was a variant of Divinity from the illusions Barry had created the night before. Rather than showing her face this time, Barry had created a fully concealed battle-angel in a suit of metal armor. In her hand was a similar sword to the one Anthony was wielding.

As if that wasn't enough, the next figure to materialize was a black-armored silhouette that caused Sal to inhale sharply. Seeing the Commander variant on screen had been scary enough, but to have one materialize in front of them was all the more terrifying. Just like the footage they had seen, the black armor was physically smoking as the Commander raised a sword and shield in a threatening manner.

Barry's grin grew wider as he launched his hands forward, causing absolute mayhem to unfold. The attack pattern from Jenni Stravos, that used explosions with the click of a finger, started to appear around the battlefield.

Gerard stood frozen in fear as he watched the arena light up in a series of explosions. The flying angel was swooping toward him while the Commander rushed toward Bolt. His team looked at him for a moment, waiting for the instructions that never came. A close explosion obscured their vision of the battlefield but was quickly dissipated by a vicious kick that connected with the side of Rodrigo's head.

Blathnaid landed gracefully and leaped forward again, launching her knee directly at Archer, who only barely managed to evade. Blathnaid's hand swung backward to the crumpled form of Rodrigo, where she activated her pulse gauntlet. The blast knocked him unconscious and propelled her out of harm's way. A bolt of lightning shot past the area she had just occupied in the air.

Gerard whirled around to Bolt and screamed at him to focus his attacks on the Commander in black armor. He looked around in a panic, raising his hands to give more orders, but faltering each time. He backed away from his team while he pointed to where Barry stood at the back of the group. "Rogue, take that one out!"

With a burst of smoke, Rogue appeared behind Barry and launched a vicious attack at his neck…attempting to take him down in a single hit. Before his hand could get close, a blue barrier appeared and nullified the attack completely. Barry smirked as his right hand whipped around with a snap of his fingers. An explosion of light caused Rogue to stumble backward in shock; when his eyes readjusted, Barry was nowhere to be seen. Instead, he was faced with a red knight, who pointed a red blade directly at Rogue's head.

Anthony's voice sounded out from the helm. "I'm your opponent."

Rogue grinned at the sudden turn of events as he activated his ability. In a burst of smoke, Rogue was behind the suit of armor and launching an attack at every exposed area he could find. The red sword flashed out menacingly and slapped his hand away. Without thinking, Rogue pulled two daggers from his boots and threw himself into the rhythm. A flurry of attacks was deflected instantaneously and rather than being discouraged, Rogue burst out laughing. He used his Shadow Step ability to move around the red knight, but no matter what he tried, his attacks were countered.

Rogue grinned as he slid backward and spat at the ground. "There has to be a limit to your power! I'll find it!" With that, he burst forward into an even faster set of attacks that would put Divinity to shame.

The red blade countered everything with ease, even going so far as to let off a blast of energy when Rogue got too close. Anthony looked like he was on autopilot, with the sword doing most of the work for him. He had to keep the bloodlust of the sword at bay at all costs, causing him to pull back on some of the more vicious swings that it attempted.

Sal inspected the battlefield and was delighted to see that Blathnaid had managed to take out Rodrigo with a flying kick, and she was holding her own against Archer. Jack was struggling to hit Bolt, but the lightning user was fully preoccupied with the Commander illusion and hadn't yet noticed that it wasn't real. Rogue was in a one-on-one battle with Anthony that looked insane.

All that remained was Gerard, who stood with his back to the prism wall. He looked like he was in complete shock with the turn of events.

Sal threw even more power into his gear as he stared at Gerard with a grin on his face. "Finish them off!" Sal roared out, causing Bolt, Rogue, and Archer to whirl around in a panic to survey their teammates.

That opening was all Blathnaid needed to activate her leaper boots. She cartwheeled backward in an arc, with her right foot connecting with the underside of Archer's chin, knocking him unconscious instantly. As though he was able to predict what was about to happen, Bolt burst toward Archer to try and prevent the attack, but out of nowhere, Barry materialized with his pulse gauntlet aimed directly at Bolt's face.

"Checkmate," Barry said with a grin as he shot Bolt with a full blast attack.

Bolt's momentum into the attack made it all the more devastating, and the speedster buckled to the ground in a dramatic fashion. Barry didn't spare him a glance as he threw the pulse gauntlet back to Jack, who caught it gracefully.

Blathnaid sped back to where Anthony and Rogue were fighting. Jack circled the area and ran to the other side. Both started to fire their pulse gauntlets at Rogue, who was incapable of blocking the attacks on all sides. A moment later, he left himself open and the red blade slapped his ribs under his right arm.

Rogue's smile finally vanished as he crumpled to the ground, gasping for air. When it looked like he was about to get up and try again, Anthony sliced the ground in front of him with the sword...creating an explosion of rock and dust. Rogue fell backward in shock as he stared at the crater the attack had created.

Rogue dropped his blades and raised his hands in surrender. He turned to look at the panicking Gerard and shook his head with a wistful smile. "Looks like he was holding back this whole time!"

Sal walked toward Gerard slowly. Behind him was the red knight, the black Commander, and the armored angel. Barry, Blathnaid, and Jack stood off to the sides with their hands crossed, watching the scene play out.

Gerard lashed out with an attack, his fist glowing as it sent a shock wave toward Sal.

Rather than evading it, Sal let it bounce off his armor. His gear was on a whole new level, and he wanted Gerard to understand the difference in their capabilities. Gerard launched attack after attack in his direction, but all of them were nullified by the armor. With each step that Sal took, Gerard's attacks got more erratic and started to miss Sal's body completely.

When Sal finally stood in front of Gerard, he gave him a withering look. "Your loss, Fuck-Face."

Gerard looked up at Sal with burning anger, and before he could lash out, Sal launched a solid right hook across his face. The impact was heightened by Sal's Epic gear and the result was dramatic. Gerard's eyes rolled into the back of his head as he fell to the ground with a loud thud.

CHAPTER 80:
REVELATIONS

"How the fuck did he do that?" Jez gaped in shock at the prism in front of him.

He looked around to see Anna Sakura sitting rigidly in front of them, along with the guild officials, with only Alastair beside him looking composed. Jez pointed to the space where the illusions had just disappeared at the conclusion of the fight. With an accusing look at Alastair, he pointed at him meaningfully with his other hand. "Were they really illusions? It was beyond any of the deception style powers I've seen before."

Alastair handed the hip flask back to Jez and shrugged. "Barry Francis. He was the one who kept the Psionic Commander busy while Neuro got the location for the raid. I had high hopes, but this was very much beyond my expectations. He's able to craft illusions, but somehow is still able to retain mobility around the battlefield? Having a tactical sense in such a high-pressure environment is extraordinary at such a young age."

Jez looked back to the prism, which was now empty, and shook his head with a wry grin. "I watched like five of their matches before this one…they were holding back their true power all this time? What made this one different?" He looked at Alastair for more insight, but the larger man just shrugged and waved his hand.

"No idea. Maybe they wanted to crush the Offense team to show the power of a Support team?"

Anna Sakura turned in her seat and looked up at Jez and Alastair. "The candidate on Team #20, Rogue. He's made no secret that he dislikes his team captain, Gerard Kilsee. Apparently, Gerard has it in for Salvatore Argento because of something that happened on the first day." Sakura tucked a strand of black hair behind her ear and gave them a conflicted look. "I think this was a grudge match, but it was painfully one-sided."

Jez's smile broke into a grin as he clapped his hands together. "I'm sticking around to see the next few fights, just to see if there are any more surprises. What about you, Alastair?"

Alastair frowned before getting to his feet. "I spent too long over at the Gold cohort, so I'll have to cut this one short…I've seen everything I need here, and I'll be inviting Sal and Barry into the Tactics class. I would have liked to watch Divinity's match-up, but I'll watch the footage later. What about you, kid? Anyone you need to see from the Black or Purple cohort?" Alastair looked at Sakura with a raised eyebrow, but she shook her head.

"I'm going to stay here and watch the next few fights, because I didn't get enough information from that one."

Alastair nodded as he turned to Jez. "You sure you don't want to come? I got a tip that there's another diamond in the rough hiding among the first-years."

Jez shook his head as he pointed to where Sal was seated with his team in the stands. "Gonna keep an eye on my star pupil. Skill Master and Mythcrafter…but also a decent team captain? I'm going to watch until I find his limit."

Alastair chuckled. "Just be gentle with him—he's my retirement plan!"

Jez snorted. "When have I ever been gentle?"

As Alastair left the stands, Jez watched him wade through a large group of guild scouts chatting to one another excitedly. It was a dramatic shift from the earlier fights where the stadium had been practically deserted.

Jez looked down to where Sakura was seated. "I'm not going to talk to the back of your head for the next few fights, so why don't you sit up here?" He waved his hip flask at her as though it were the perfect incentive to join him.

Sakura got to her feet and moved up the stands to sit a seat away from Jez. Much to his surprise, she extended a hand and took the flask from him, taking a healthy swig before handing it back.

Jez laughed as he screwed the cap back onto it, looking at Sakura in a different light. "Had you pegged as one of the serious and studious types…happy to be wrong on that front!"

Sakura smiled as she returned to look at the prism. "You said that Salvatore was a Mythcrafter? What did you mean by that?" Her face turned slightly to look at Jez, waiting for his answer.

With a guilty laugh, he shook his head. "Ah, you weren't supposed to hear that part. It can be our little secret."

"After you tell me everything about it…right?"

Jez sighed as he looked at Sakura with a glint in his eye. "I'm not getting anything out of this deal, so I'll have to pass."

Sakura gestured over to where Sal was sitting. "One of the guilds has enlisted me to check out Sal. I could tell you which one…"

Jez laughed in genuine surprise. "Villa isn't making any secrets of her approach, so it's not really big news."

Sakura shook her head. "It's not the Reavers."

"Okay then, I'll bite."

Sakura just gave him a sweet smile as she held out her palm. "Mythcrafter information first."

Jez's grin widened. "Are you sure you don't want to drop Assassination and come over to Administration?"

Sakura laughed and shook her head. "No chance…unless you're offering me a place in one of your Masterclasses? I suppose I could fit it in my schedule."

A mock grimace covered Jez's features as he pretended to think about it. "Having a third-year Savior in my Masterclass? I guess I could stomach that, but let's put it down to your performance in that dungeon. Don't want people thinking I'm going soft or sentimental."

Instead of answering, Sakura smiled at Jez, who eventually sighed and waved his hand at the prism.

"Mythcrafter is exactly what it sounds like. Sal can craft Mythic-grade items. He created the skill himself at the registration at the start of the semester, and it looks like he's already made a Legendary sniper rifle for the Reavers, which has Villa's knickers tied up in knots. She wants him bad…or rather, she wants Myth. That's Sal's alias for the crafting stuff. I'd bet that he created all the equipment they're using in those fights."

Jez looked over to the stands to see Sal getting to his feet with the remainder of his team. "It really goes to show what a few pieces of well-crafted equipment can do with a solid formation."

Sakura turned to look in Sal's direction with a surprised expression on her face. "Okay, that definitely changes things.".

"It's Shade, isn't it? From the Delvers Guild?"

Jez clearly caught her off-guard by guessing the answer immediately. Sakura just gave him a nod in response, which made Jez chuckle.

"Should have guessed that slimy bastard would want to get him. I guarantee that it's down to the Appraisal fiasco on the Credit floor."

When Sakura gave Jez a blank look, he filled her in on the details. "He Appraised over seventy items in one night for the Reavers Guild. Shade's guild has a massive chokehold when it comes to Appraisals, and they have the Argento Auction on retainer for high-profile dungeon loot. They're notoriously stingy with paying out fees on low-grade items, which is why most Appraisal outfits refuse to work with them. If they were able to get Sal on their team, it would solve a lot of headaches for them. I do have to wonder what they're thinking of offering him…maybe it would be worth teasing Villa, stoke the fires on Sal's worth a bit."

Jez was almost talking to himself at this point, while Sakura looked conflicted. She drummed her fingertips against the back of the chair in front of her as she looked at Sal's team in the prism. After a few minutes of silence, she turned back to Jez with a raised eyebrow.

"The drops I got from the Commanders…do you think Sal would be able to Craft something from them?"

Jez smiled. "Over fifty members of faculty heard that Sal is a Mythcrafter, so my guess is that his order queue is going to fill up dramatically from this point onward. If you're hoping to get in before he understands his own value, now is the time."

Before Sakura could respond, the countdown for the next fight began, drawing her attention back to the prism.

Jez chuckled and raised the hip flask to his lips. He eyed Sal and his team thoughtfully, wondering whether they were in for any more surprises.

***

After the fight with Gerard and the all-Offense team, it was like every other team had a permanent de-buff to morale.

Dominic Walters stood apprehensively at the other end of the prism. He watched Sal carefully in the moments before the fight, and Sal couldn't blame him. The winning streak had somehow become a wall to them that nobody had been able to scale.

In the other prisms, Sal could see that Divinity was about to square off against Whisper, while Nova was up against Gerard's very shaken team. The fourth prism held Jenni Stravos pitted against Victoria. Sal wanted to watch all those fights personally, which made him all the more eager to end the fight with Dominic as soon as possible. It was an alien thought for Sal, who had feared his one-on-one fight with Dominic, to now be in a scenario where he was confident that it would end almost immediately in their team match-up. With a glance around him, Sal saw his confidence mirrored across his teammates.

As the countdown ended, Sal shouted his command. "Blitz!"

Barry had been instructed to keep his illusions ready for any surprise encounters in the later fights, so this one was an opportunity for him to flex his combat capability. He was taking it seriously, and Sal watched him leap high into the air with his pulse gauntlet aimed directly at Dominic. The shield that came up to protect the team captain was incredibly thin, and Sal could only imagine how exhausted Dominic was.

Despite it, Barry's attacks were successfully blocked, but it left the remainder of the team wide open to attack. Anthony's sword had already started its third wave of projectile attack, with each of them sailing over Dominic before redirecting to flank his team. Shouts of confusion echoed throughout the prism before deteriorating into cries of panic and alarm. As his team struggled to evade the waves of attack, Blathnaid and Jack closed the distance to intercept them.

In less than ten seconds, Dominic stood alone on his side of the battlefield, his entire team knocked out with barely any resistance. Even for the eleventh fight, it was a poor showing for him, and Dominic looked like a broken man as he surveyed the immediate destruction around him.

Suppressing fire came from three directions as Barry, Blathnaid, and Jack continued to fire their gauntlets at him. Anthony's attacks battered against the shield, and Sal watched with a grim satisfaction as the shield cracked under their relentless onslaught.

Dominic staggered back. He lifted his hands to attempt another shield, but rather than activating it…he fell to his knees in defeat.

Sal raised his voice. "Hold!"

Thankfully, the team felt the same as him and immediately cut off their attacks. Anthony redirected an attack that was aimed at Dominic. The thunderous crack that rang out as it hit the wall of the prism almost drowned out Dominic's voice as he forfeited the match. Sal walked over to Dominic and offered his hand.

Dominic looked at Sal with a resigned expression before accepting the handshake. "Well done."

His voice was devoid of emotion, and Sal could only imagine how crushing this experience was for him.

Sal didn't try to make him feel better or offer any form of consolation. Instead, he steeled his resolve and turned with his team to watch the remainder of the fights.

Divinity was in a heated battle with Whisper, and it was a hell of a sight to behold. With her eyes white, Divinity was shooting her pulse gauntlets into areas she knew the enemy team would soon occupy. It was perfect hit after perfect hit, while her team worked in formation to overwhelm Whisper and her Defender.

Sal glanced to see Jenni Stravos destroying Victoria's team. In an interesting move, Jenni's team wore face coverings that blocked Victoria's ability from influencing them. Best of all was in the second prism, where Lucia was absolutely tearing through Gerard's team. Maybe it was the exhaustion from their previous fight, or just the fear of Lucia in her giant form…but they were stomped on relentlessly by the towering giantess of destruction. Bolt's attacks did nothing against her, so he was practically ignored while she kicked Gerard from one side of the prism to the other. Sal laughed and wondered whether Gerard's team was intentionally letting their captain get beaten up.

CHAPTER 81:
SURPRISE

His words were muffled as he spoke under the protective layer of fabric. Looking around at his team, Sal inspected them to see whether they had successfully plugged their ears and covered the lower parts of their faces. All of them had followed his instructions, leaving only Blathnaid without the apparatus. Judging from the scowl on Victoria's face, Sal's team had been right to take precautions against her influence ability. Blathnaid was their secret weapon for the simple fact that she was a woman. Victoria didn't yet know how to influence women, so they'd use it to their advantage.

It was going to be a lot more complex in delivering commands while his mouth was covered, but he was confident that they would win. With a signal to Barry, Sal gestured for him to start his counterattack. Green runes lined his arms and chest as he activated his illusion ability. Victoria crouched low and started to charm her own team, but nothing happened. Whirling around to look at them, Victoria was shocked to see that all of them were wide-eyed and frantically searching for something in front of them. Screams came next as they floundered around in Barry's summoned purgatory. He took away each of their senses, removing Victoria's ability to control them.

Gritting her teeth, Victoria turned back toward Sal, ready to scream at him, when a boot connected with the side of her face. Victoria barely had time to register the flying form of Blathnaid, who had closed the distance in a heartbeat. The impact of the kick wasn't anything dramatic, but for a non-Combat-oriented role like Victoria, it was enough to send her flying to the ground. She gasped in shock and scrambled to her feet, clutching at her face in fright.

Maybe it was through fear or desperation, but she flooded her influence ability into Blathnaid, who only hesitated for a moment. Victoria's eyes widened at the prospect of influencing her, but Blathnaid's arm snaked out and gripped Victoria's wrist. Sal laughed as he saw one of Divinity's moves being used.

The entire team shared the same reaction and all of them pitied Victoria for what was about to happen next. Blathnaid's face was resolute as she hooked her shoulder into Victoria's armpit and pulled on her arm viciously as she turned with the momentum. Victoria's face was priceless as she was thrown onto her back. All the air in her chest exploded out violently, and she lay, struggling to breathe.

"Sorry." Blathnaid sighed as she raised her pulse gauntlet to each of the panicking team members.

All of them were still trapped in Barry's illusion, and the point-blank blast from the pulse gauntlet was more than enough to knock them out cold. Blathnaid repeated the action four times before moving over to the struggling Victoria.

"Forfeit?" Blathnaid asked hopefully, but Victoria gritted her teeth as she struggled to get to her feet. Blathnaid sighed again as she raised her gauntlet. "Suit yourself, then."

With a powerful blast of essence, Victoria was slammed back against the ground, with her eyes rolling to the back of her head. Blathnaid shook her head as she looked at her handiwork. Her hands shook, and she turned back to her team with the brightest smile on her face.

"Fifteen wins! Just four more to go!"

A deafening roar caused Blathnaid to flinch as she turned toward the standing ovation from the crowd. She looked at the other prisms to see what was going on, but all of them were still mid-battle. Everyone in the stands was watching her team, but judging from the confusion on her face, she couldn't for the life of her understand why they were cheering.

"Are you only just noticing it now? They've been doing that for every fight." Barry's voice sounded out from behind her, causing her to turn around in surprise. "Maybe it's because you single-handedly took out the second-top Controller?" Barry suggested as he turned to Sal. "What do you think?"

Rather than answering immediately, Sal pointed at the wall of the prism. "There must have been questions about Victoria's ability with all of us wearing masks, so they showed the nature of her ability to the viewers."

Blathnaid was still reeling from the applause directed at them but managed to turn to Sal with an incredulous expression. "That doesn't really warrant this sort of reaction, though. Does it?"

Sal moved his finger to point at the other end of the prism. "It does when they showed your ability, too. Looks like everyone just watched a top-ranked Controller getting destroyed by a Tailor."

Barry's laugh reached new heights as Blathnaid's face went white in shock. Jack clapping her on the back didn't help in the slightest. Blathnaid practically mumbled the entire way out of the prism, much to the delight of her entire team.

Sal couldn't wait to see her individual performance score and really hoped that the fight would lift her overall rank in the academy. Even though they could happily forfeit the remaining fights, Sal wanted to showcase the individual strengths of the team as much as possible. Any chance they had of climbing up the ranks and improving their future, Sal was going to take it.

***

With the last of their energy drinks depleted, Sal looked around at his team and was happy to see them all looking composed. Anthony had pretty much reached his limit with the sword, so rather than having him going into the last fight with it, Sal decided that he'd use it himself. Anthony was a little apprehensive about using the gauntlet and shield, but he was reminded that it was literally the last fight of the evening.

Their team had managed to maintain the winning streak through all eighteen fights, and they were finally up against a challenging opponent who was tearing up through the ranks. Jenni Stravos, the #17 team captain, could create explosions with a click of her fingers. Each of her team were from the early picks, and she had three Defense on her team, with a Support for backup. With sixteen wins out of eighteen, she was currently in joint second place with Lucia, who had somehow managed to drag her team to the top of the board.

"How are you faring, Barry?" Sal asked quietly so the others wouldn't hear.

Barry closed his eyes and checked his essence levels. After a moment of silence, he opened them and gave Sal a wry grin. "Not enough in the tank for flashy moves, but enough to see us through to the end. Yourself?"

Sal didn't need to check his essence as he was completely fine in that department. "Few aches and pains, but nothing compared to Divinity's sparring sessions."

Barry snorted and looked around at the other teams, who were slumped in the stands. "A few of this lot could have done with some training beforehand. Half of them are just flopping in defeat as soon as the buzzer sounds."

Sal smiled and looked around to see Blathnaid staring at the prism with a determined expression. Jack was beside her, tightening the clasp of his gauntlet. It was remarkable how a few fights had changed them. The awkward anxiety from the start of the day had grown into unshakable confidence and determination. Sal couldn't really say for sure, but from a growth perspective, both were head and shoulders above their peers.

People like Dominic had lost their spirit in the earliest rounds and were going through the motions to get it all over with. Sal checked the scoreboard and wasn't remotely surprised to see that Dominic was firmly in the relegation zone. A few of the top teams were down there, and Sal could only feel sorry for them.

"Why is the crowd not dispersing?" Anthony asked as he looked around the stands. Throughout the afternoon and evening, the stands had gradually become fuller. It was beyond what the visions had predicted, and Sal could only guess the reasons.

"Maybe they want to see us through to the end? See if we get that perfect score?"

Barry snorted and looked at Sal as if he were crazy. "What's this 'if' shit? We're taking that team down, and then we're going to roll around in a pile of Q-Cred!"

Blathnaid and Jack turned around in unison to stare at Barry.

"There's a Q-Cred reward for top performance! Didn't you listen to Rust's explanation when we were getting briefed? Or were you too busy worrying about coming dead last?"

Sal smiled. It was an incredible turn of events, and it had brought them much closer as a group. Having Q-Cred as a reward was certainly going to be a cherry on the top for them. Although it wouldn't make much difference for him and Barry, who were promised a reward for their help with the dungeon…it would be a dramatic improvement for Blathnaid, Jack, and Anthony, who hadn't yet earned a single Q-Cred.

"Looks like we're up!" Barry exclaimed as he got to his feet with a groan.

The night sky was oddly calming, and the quick turnaround between fights ensured that they never sat still long enough to become cold. Sal also guessed that their equipment was doing a great job of keeping them warm and protected from the elements. He looked down at the sword in his hand and smiled at the little octopus that was facing upward.

It was the last fight, so he wanted to try to activate the sword like he did with the gloves, just to see whether it would transform with the uniform he wore. It was going to be demanding of his essence, but he had barely used his own power and instead focused on ordering the team during their battles. With a firm grip on the sword, Sal followed his team into the prism and couldn't help but overhear the encouraging cheers from the stands.

When he turned to look at the crowd, his eyes locked onto the familiar form of Anna Sakura. She gave him a radiant smile and he genuinely wondered whether she was confusing him for someone else. Despite that, he smiled back and gave her a friendly wave.

"Cheating on Lucia already?" Barry mocked as he shuffled past Sal and entered the prism. "What is it with you and dangerous women?"

His smile was friendly, and Sal chuckled as they got into position. When both teams were in place, Barry turned to Sal with a smirk. "Don't suppose you're into Explosions Girl, too?"

It caused a few of the team to laugh, and Sal tried to rein them in before the fight.

"Firstly, fuck off, Barry. Secondly, focus…this may be our last fight, but there's nothing to be gained by being complacent. Remember formations and use your heads! They're going to be just as exhausted as you are, so be prepared for a scrappy fight."

The change in demeanor was instantaneous as the team readied themselves in formation. It didn't escape Sal's notice that Barry gritted his teeth as he activated the runes on his arm. Ideally, they wouldn't need to rely on his abilities for the fight. The sword would hopefully be enough for them to get through it.

Before the countdown started, Sal gave them another note of caution, knowing that he had their full attention. "This team was the only one that prepared a countermeasure against Victoria. Assume they know our strengths and weaknesses, so don't be reckless."

When the buzzer sounded, Sal activated his power and threw it into the sword and the gauntlets. At the exact same time, an explosion erupted inches from his face, knocking him backward onto the ground. Smoke filled his nostrils, or they would have if it wasn't for the blood that freely flowed from them. His ears were ringing, and his eyes fought for focus.

Lifting the sword in front of him to parry any incoming attack, Sal tried to focus his power again, but it was impossible to maintain any sort of composure through the pain and ragged breaths. The next explosion flared up in front of him, and Sal flinched back instinctively.

CHAPTER 82:
RESULTS

"Sal!" Jack shouted as he slid into position in front of him.

The blue shield burst into light a fraction of a second before the explosion erupted. The blast swept around Jack, who gritted his teeth but stood his ground.

Before Sal could so much as blink, two new explosions materialized on either side of him, but Jack flung one arm out to block and raised his pulse gauntlet to repel the other one. It was a dramatic display, and Sal watched in horror as Jack's shield arm buckled from the recoil at an awkward angle.

Despite the pain of what had to be a broken arm, he held the shield in place and looked back to Sal with an agonized face. "Are you hurt?"

Sal gritted his teeth and shook his head. "Thanks, Jack. Keep it up!"

He had been bought some time at the expense of Jack's arm, and he sure as shit wasn't going to waste it by feeling sorry for himself. In a fury he didn't realize existed, Sal pumped the sword and armor with every bit of essence that he had. Just like Upgrade had taught him, he gave it everything beyond its breaking point and then yanked back the leash to maintain control.

When he turned to Jack to thank him again, all he could see was a picture of astonishment. It felt weird to have him react like that when he had seen the suit of armor before, but Sal didn't have time to think about that. He needed to help his team and change the tempo of the fight. When Sal sidestepped to the right, to move out of the protection of the shield, he felt as though time around him slowed down. Without questioning it, he used the time to look across the battlefield to see what was happening.

Barry was pushing against his limits. The clear proof of that was the winged angel that swooped down between the Defense members of Jenni's team. They were preoccupied with defending against the illusion, and Barry was visibly sweating as he held his shield up to block the barrage of explosions sent in his direction. Jenni Stravos was controlling the battlefield with her two arms raised and pointed at both sides of the prism. Blathnaid and Anthony were being pushed back relentlessly, with Anthony looking like his beard was charred and smoldering from a too-close explosion. Sal didn't waste any time in coming up with a countermeasure as he launched a slice attack straight at Jenni.

An arc of black essence flickered into existence, accompanied by trickles of yellow static electricity. With a scream from Jenni, time came back to its normal flow, and Sal got to watch as two Defenders leapt up with their shields, sacrificing themselves to the illusion that swooped down on them. When the angel moved through them, Barry cursed audibly from the sidelines and let it disappear.

Jenni's eyes were wide as she realized that it had been an illusion all along, and a smile flashed across her face.

That smile didn't last long. The wave of essence smashed into her Defense team and broke through the barriers. Both of her hands snapped around to point at the running form of Sal, and all color left her face at the sight of him. Her fingers clicked faster than she had done before, fueled by the fear written all over her face.

Each explosion erupted uselessly against the armor as Sal swung his sword again and again, each arc creating a vicious ethereal blade of energy that threatened to kill her. Jenni whirled around to see that her Support had been knocked unconscious; Blathnaid stood over him with her shield still raised protectively. One of her Defenders was down on his knees as he fought to erect another barrier. The two remaining Defenders launched at Sal and threw their bodies against the black armor.

Sal didn't know whether it was a Solidify or Harden ability, but one of them was like steel. The other had an abundance of strength that he used to punch Sal square in the chest. With a flicker of activation, Sal's equipment recognized the attacks as a threat and repelled them…dramatically.

Jenni could only stare in bewilderment as her two strongest Defenders were sent flying by the armor. One flew over her head, while the other slammed forcibly into her remaining Defender, who was still on his knees.

Sal arrived in front of Jenni and kicked the kneeling Defender, who had finally created a protective barrier. The armored boot shattered the bubble of protection and continued through to hit the Defender squarely in the chest. All breath left his body as he crumpled on the spot, gasping for air.

None of her team were on their feet as Sal squared up against her. She stared defiantly at Sal, as though asking him to end it…even though her body was shaking. But much to everyone's surprise, the final attack came from her left. Jenni clearly hadn't anticipated it as a powerful force of essence smacked into her violently, sending her into a heap beside her downed Support.

"That's for my fucking arm, you bitch," Jack snarled as he lowered his gauntlet.

Sal released his leash on the essence and allowed the sword and armor to return to its natural state. He hadn't anticipated such a drain on his essence and was happy that he left that until the final fight.

Jack turned to him. "You should really look in the mirror the next time you transform like that. It looks insane!"

Sal looked at Jack's twisted arm. "Let's get that checked out first before we do anything else. Okay?"

Jack nodded as Sal turned to look at the rest of the team. Each of them looked haggard and broken from the fight, but they had survived to the end of it. It was like the facade had finally slipped and they were allowed to show their true exhaustion. Sal looked at their injuries and felt a sense of shame that his fuck-up at the beginning had led them into a painful fight.

Barry's grin lit up as he gestured to where Jenni lay on the ground. "So, you're not shaking her hand like everyone else because your favorite Assassin is watching?"

Sal gave him a withering look, but he couldn't help but smile at the joke. He walked over to Jenni and offered her his hand, but she was very much unconscious. He stood there awkwardly, and his entire team laughed even more.

With a shake of his head, he looked at them in exasperation. "How the fuck did we manage to win first place?"

***

Place	Captain Results	Cohort Rank	Team Classes	Wins / Losses
1st	Salvatore Argento	#2	S/S/S/S/S	19-0
2nd	Lucia Hernandez	#4	O/S/S/S/S	17-2
3rd	Jenni Stravos	#17	C/D/D/D/S	16-3
4th	Divinity Khan	#1	C/S/S/S/D	16-3
5th	Evan McGregor	#6	O/S/D/S/S	15-4
6th	Gerard Kilsee	#20	O/O/O/O/O	14-5
Safe Zone				
7th	Whisper Ding	#12	C/D/O/S/S	13-6
8th	Victoria Chase	#7	C/S/S/S/D	13-6
9th	Crypto Daniels	#18	O/D/D/C/S	11-8
10th	Sanna Sinervo	#16	O/O/S/D/C	10-9
11th	Marta Virgo	#14	O/S/D/D/S	9-10
12th	Borja Diez	#15	O/S/D/D/C	8-11
13th	Con LaFleur	#13	S/D/D/O/S	6-13
14th	Trent Golde	#11	S/D/S/S/S	6-13
Relegation Zone				
15th	Zachary Lowe	#10	S/C/D/S/S	5-14
16th	Dominic Walters	#3	D/D/S/S/S	4-15
17th	Xander Michaels	#9	S/D/C/S/S	3-16
18th	Michael Welling	#8	S/D/O/S/D	2-17
19th	Christopher Gage	#5	S/S/S/D/C	2-17
20th	Harold Gunn	#19	S/O/C/C/S	1-18

"You know, you can look away from the screen. It's not going to change," Sal chided Blathnaid with a smile, but it did nothing to sway her.

She continued to stare at the scoreboard in complete disbelief.

Barry gave Sal a shake of the head, as if to tell him he was going about it wrong. Moving up to Blathnaid, he pointed over to where Jack was being treated. "Looks like Jack isn't going to make it back with us."

Blathnaid whirled around, concern crossing her features as she searched for Jack.

Barry smirked at Sal and gave him a thumbs-up. Sal laughed when Blathnaid continually smacked Barry with her hands.

"That's not funny—don't joke about stuff like that!"

Even though she looked flustered, she smiled as Jack waved erratically with his good hand from the healing bay.

The moon was high, and nobody had the energy to pack their gear up, but they tried their best. The train wasn't due to arrive for another while, so the atmosphere was chilled out in the stadium. Apparently, the Gold cohort had finished much earlier, so the train was taking them back to the academy first, rather than having them wait around the tournament grounds needlessly.

Anthony frowned as he scratched at his beard; a few tufts of hair come away in his hand. "Looks like I'm going to have to shave this off. Thanks, Jenni," he muttered darkly to himself before he noticed that Sal was looking at him. "Ah, sorry! Was just talking to myself."

Sal placed the sword back into its case. "We wouldn't have been able to do all this without you, Anthony. Thanks for the hard work!"

In a completely uncharacteristic moment, Anthony burst out laughing.

"Are you kidding me, Sal? I saw you in that armor! It was incredible and terrifying all at the same time. I thought you were going to kill her when you transformed!"

Sal stared at Anthony. "Wasn't it the same as the knight transformation?"

Anthony shook his head. "Not even close! I think your outfit and the sword worked together, because it just looked like a complete set! Mine had all those tentacles, but yours looked like a death knight had walked straight out of hell."

Sal frowned as he tried to think about what was different from when he activated the sword in the training area and in the workshop. He didn't get much time to dwell on his thoughts as Barry appeared in front of him, with two bags slung over his shoulder.

He dropped one in front of Sal and gestured at it with his free hand. "Since you took an explosion to the face and put us through hell, you can carry more equipment."

Blathnaid whirled around again. This time, her face was red. "Barry!"

His chuckles accompanied him as he walked toward the train, ignoring Blathnaid's outburst.

Anthony shook his head as he leaned over and picked up the discarded equipment case. "I'll take it, don't worry."

Sal didn't even have time to complain as Anthony set off after Barry.

Blathnaid looked at him with a resigned sigh and a shrug. "You can go with them. I'll wait for Jack."

Sal shook his head and gestured over to where Jack was getting to his feet. "I'd be a pretty terrible team captain if I just left him to fend for himself. Besides, who knows? Maybe some disgruntled students will jump us on the way to the train as revenge," Sal joked.

Blathnaid raised her fist threateningly. "They can try, and we'll beat them all over again."

Sal laughed more at that, and Blathnaid joined in with him.

Jack eventually arrived at their side, wondering what was going on, but Sal just gestured for them to move toward the train.

"Am I the only one desperate to know how our ranks have changed? What Q-Cred we're getting? How the other cohorts did?" Sal gave them a meaningful look as he pointed toward the train stop. Both nodded eagerly and set off ahead of him, laughing and joking as they went. Sal picked up the sword case and slung it over his shoulder. With another look at the moon, he smiled contentedly as he followed his team.

CHAPTER 83:
REWARDS

WHEN SAL LOOKED AROUND THE AMPHITHEATER, HE WAS SURPRISED TO SEE that it was only the Silver cohort in attendance. He wondered whether they had really taken that long to complete their fights in comparison to the other groups, but Quest appeared on stage to answer that very question. He looked quite energized as he tapped the earpiece on the side of his head, a wide smile on his face.

Welcome back, everyone!

You might be wondering why you're the only ones here, and that was an intentional decision on our part.

We've been debriefing individual groups as they've arrived back at the academy. There are still four cohorts out in the tournament grounds due to unexpected delays in their schedules, but we expect everyone to return safely in the coming hours.

You've all done an incredible job in your brackets, working together and persevering through your natural limits. We wanted this event to show you the areas you need to improve on, at an early stage of your academic journey.

I'd like to offer congratulations to the top six teams that went above and beyond in this exercise! At the same time, I'd like to encourage those in the lower ranks to not lose heart.

Our staff have been going through your results on a team level and individual level. We'll be sharing how those results will impact you all tomorrow morning at assembly, here in the amphitheater.

To give you a bit more insight into how we'll be making our assessment, here is the breakdown of criteria.

Individual Assessment: 50%
- Endurance - Stamina / Perseverance (10%)
- Effectiveness - Initiative / Impact (10%)
- Order - Cohesion / Leadership / Following (10%)
- Ability - Skills / Equipment (10%)
- Wildcard - Exemplary Effort (10%)

Team Assessment: 50%
- Composition - Team Structure (10%)
- Leadership - Team Captain (10%)
- Teamwork - Formation / Assists / Following Orders (10%)
- Efficiency - Stamina / Win Time (10%)
- Eliminations - Total Takedowns (10%)

Quest pointed up at the screen that had suddenly appeared. Most students had to shield their eyes from the bright lighting, which led to more than a few curses emanating from the crowd. The headmaster didn't pay any heed as he went through each of the stages and explained how they were calculated.

Sal was going through a mental checklist in his head, assigning cynical scores for how he believed his team performed, just to see what sort of result they'd be coming away with. If he was being harsh, he thought that his own leadership was lacking and that their composition was a mess. When he compared his team to the others, it felt like they had a distinct advantage over them, but Sal didn't want to become complacent. Looking around, he could see that more than a few faces were frowning at the assessment criteria.

Assessments will be done on your top ten fights from throughout the day.

Your individual contribution on the team will be specific to you, but your team assessment will be fixed for each team. We will be allocating Q-Credit rewards for those who finished in the top six, and we'll respect the efforts that they've put in today.

However, this leaderboard is not final. We will be taking the results of the individual and team assessments, which will shake things up a bit.

The passing grade for the Combat class is sixty percent.

Sal guessed that the percentage requirement for a passing grade was put in place for the lower performing teams. It was actually much fairer than he had thought it would be, and it gave a few of the lowest-ranked teams a shot at passing the class. He couldn't help but wonder whether it would punish Gerard for being a weak leader as well as his horrible team composition.

Sal's gaze caught the wildcard factor on the individual assessments and wondered whether the staff put that in to be a deciding factor for promising students. Maybe it would allow them to discreetly ramp up a student's score to get them over the passing line. It wasn't a pleasant thought, as it made Sal question the fairness of how they assessed students just one month into the semester. It felt like the only people who were rewarded by the curriculum setup were the fast people and the ones who could fight. Supports were just being punished by the semester so far.

You might be wondering why you've been gathered here when the rankings won't change until tomorrow? Well, even though we know there's going to be a reshuffle, the results of the fight today need to be respected, so we'll be allocating some prizes before you're all sent off to bed. Some inquiries have been made from the visiting guilds, which isn't unheard of…but very uncommon. We've also had a few professors express interest in sponsoring students from the Silver cohort to attend their Masterclasses in the coming months, which is an incredible opportunity that could heavily influence your future career prospects.

So, it's getting late, and we have the next train arriving shortly. Let's wrap this up with what you've been waiting for. Here is the breakdown of prizes for the top teams today.

Combat Class Results (Silver Cohort)

1. Team #2: 7,500 Q-Cred (1,500 each)
2. Team #4: 6,000 Q-Cred (1,250 each)
3. Team #17: 5,000 Q-Cred (1,000 each)
4. Team #1: 3,000 Q-Cred (600 each)
5. Team #6: 2,000 Q-Cred (400 each)
6. Team #20: 1,000 Q-Cred (200 each)

Congratulations to our top six!

As I've said, there will be a more in-depth discussion tomorrow and a few more prizes to be allocated when you're joined by the other cohorts.

For tonight, though, get some rest!

We know that your bodies are going to be in agony tomorrow, so we've set the assembly at a later hour in the morning.

No need to thank me.

Quest grinned at the crowd as he gestured for them to head off toward their dorms. Sal couldn't help but laugh at the stupefied faces of his team. Even Barry was having a hard time of retaining his composure at the prospect of having that much Q-Cred hitting his account. Blathnaid just covered her eyes and huddled in her seat, and Jack put his hand on her back while staring at the screen in a daze.

Anthony pointed at the bottom of the list and turned to Sal. "I don't think Gerard is going to like that very much."

Sal followed his gesture and saw the ridiculously reduced prize that Gerard got, and it positively warmed his heart. He would have preferred Gerard had been knocked down to the lower ranks, but he was happy that Gerard's team didn't leave empty-handed after everything they had to put up with. Sal smiled to himself as he made his way back to the dorm. He didn't know whether his rank would change much, but he couldn't wait to see what happened for his team.

***

Sal could barely believe his eyes when he looked at the breakdown of his report card. The assessments must have been completed throughout the night, and all his predictions were way off the mark. Maybe it was because of the veiled challenges and secret assessments that Quest loved pulling, but Sal was convinced that they'd be marked down on everything, rather than up! His hands shook as he went through it line by line, not sure whether he should feel relieved or anxious at what was to come.

Salvatore Argento: Combat Assessment Report - 96% Overall Grade

Individual Assessment: 49% / 50%
- Endurance - (10%)
- Effectiveness - (9%)
- Order - (10%)
- Ability - Skills / Equipment (10%)
- Wildcard - Exemplary Effort (10%)

Team Assessment: 47% / 50%
- Composition - (9%)
- Leadership - (10%)
- Teamwork - (10%)
- Efficiency - (8%)
- Eliminations - (10%)

The report went through a series of notes that listed areas for improvement. It was incredibly in-depth and educational rather than hyper-critical. One of the main points was that the team had only started using their trump cards during the tenth fight. That resulted in a loss of effectiveness as they could have ended previous fights sooner with a full display of their capabilities.

It noted that Anthony had too much reliance on the sword and didn't showcase any mobility capability until the last fight. Blathnaid was praised in practically every report, only losing minor points for endurance and ability sections. Jack's protective shielding in the final battle gave him the wildcard bonus, which negated his loss of points in the effectiveness category. Apparently, he had the least number of takedowns on the team. Despite all the notes, which seemed to paint a bleak picture, the overall result was still shocking for all of them. No matter how many times Sal read through it, he couldn't understand how their scores were so high.

Team #2: Combat Assessment Result - 93.2%
- Salvatore Argento - 96% Overall Grade
- Barry Francis - 95% Overall Grade
- Blathnaid Clean - 94% Overall Grade
- Anthony McGuinn - 91% Overall Grade
- Jack Allen - 90% Overall Grade

Sal brought the vendor coffee to his lips and took a sip as he tore his eyes away from the report on his tablet. He had gotten there early with his team because most of them couldn't sleep. Blathnaid admitted that she spent about two hours going through the Credit Store on her terminal before going to bed. She wanted to see what she could buy with her newly acquired Q-Cred.

It wasn't an insubstantial number, and it literally gave them access to so much more that the academy had to offer.

Sal had to admit that he wasn't putting his own funds to good use yet, but now that the stress and worry of the Combat class was over, he'd be able to start mapping out his future by picking smart modules and classes to attend. When he looked around, Barry was staring right back at him. It seemed as though they were both on the same wavelength when he asked a question.

"Do you think the headmaster was talking about us when he said that stuff about the Masterclass? If Alastair took me on and I got a Tactics Accreditation, then I'd probably get assigned a Controller class!" His voice had an uncharacteristic edge to it that Sal realized was a hint of hope.

Sal nodded. "I don't think he was bullshitting us, but it could be a great move for you! If you get it before the inter-cohort competition, I'd happily hand you the reins of leadership!" Sal expected him to laugh, but Barry was looking at him seriously.

"You're joking, right?" When Sal shook his head, Barry offered his hand to him. "Shake on it then. Auctioneer promise?"

Sal laughed as he clasped Barry's hand. "You're making it sound like I wanted to be a team captain. I'd be happy if we got knocked out of the competition and didn't have to set foot in one of those prisms again!"

Barry looked at Sal as though he had two heads. "How do you expect us to get ready to clear dungeons and towers with that attitude? Don't worry, I'll ace the Controller class and we'll be unstoppable. You'll all be my little chess pieces, and I'll bring us to certain victory!"

Sal snorted, but Barry turned to Jack with a sympathetic grimace. "Some pawns will need to be sacrificed, though. So, be prepared!"

At that, Blathnaid gave Barry a friendly shove while Jack just pointed at himself in confusion. Anthony chuckled from his seat behind them.

Sal wanted to respond, but Quest was already on the stage and tapping at his ear to address them.

Barry shot Sal a grin as he turned toward the stage excitedly. Sal couldn't for the life of him understand what caused the sudden change in Barry. *Was it the Q-Cred? The potential to become a lead on the team?* He couldn't figure it out.

Okay, welcome back, everyone!

We've had one of the most compelling Combat class events in the history of the academy, and you are all responsible for that. We set a high bar, and many of you went above and beyond our expectations!

We had two teams with a flawless record! Nineteen straight wins out of nineteen fights. Most impressively was that our first winner, in record time…had the last pick of the roster! Gold Cohort Team #1, led by Erika Clifton, with an average team score of 92%! It's one of our highest average ratings on record!

Can I get a round of applause for Erika and her team?

Searching through the crowd of a thousand for just five people was made a lot simpler by watching the Gold cohort all turn in unison to look at a girl seated in the front row. She had her arms crossed in front of her while the rest of her team sat sullenly beside her. For a team that had just placed first with a flawless record, they looked miserable.

To Sal's absolute shock, Erika's face turned sharply and locked onto him. Even though they were on opposite sides of the amphitheater, he knew that she was glaring directly at him. A sense of uneasiness washed over Sal as he saw not even a flicker of friendliness in her stare.

"Well, that's foreboding as shit," Barry muttered as he looked at Erika and then at Sal. "Seriously Sal, for your own health…you need to stop catching the attention of the crazy women."

A moment of awkward silence passed before Barry laughed. "Can you imagine if you went home with her to meet the parents? Trying to hide your intentions from Neuro? Good luck with that!"

Sal's attention snapped back to Barry. "That's Neuro's daughter?"

Barry gave him a slow nod, as though he were an idiot. "Top ranked in the whole academy. What rock have you been living under?"

Sal sighed as he shook his head and looked back at Erika, who still stared at him. "I've been hiding in the workshop."

So, one of our highest results!

Only broken by our next group. A flawless record of nineteen straight wins, as well as an average team score of 93.2%! Silver Cohort's Team #2, led by Salvatore Argento.

To have two teams with the last picks of the roster, achieving results like this? It calls for an acknowledgment.

Your rewards have been allocated based on cohort, but now, we'd like to allocate some spot prizes for exemplary performance across the whole group of first-years.

Who better to start with than our flawless teams?

Both will be exempt from outing costs for the remainder of the semester, to give them more experience out in the field. In addition to that, we'll be giving them Challenge crests to showcase their incredible achievement. This will be worn on their uniform and accredited on their Q-Cards, for all the guilds to see.

Now, before we move on to the rankings, which I know you're all desperately interested in…we need to shuffle the cohort leaderboards to reflect your overall grades in the class.

Sal looked up at the screen and was pleasantly surprised to see that a whole screen was dedicated to the Gold and Silver cohorts. His eyes locked onto Erika's name first, before flitting over to the Silver column to see his name. It was showing their current standings, as it had been before. And then the shuffle began.

1. Salvatore Argento - Team #2 - 93%
2. Jenni Stravos - Team #17 - 89%
3. Divinity Khan - Team #1 - 87%
4. Lucia Hernandez - Team #4 - 83%
5. Whisper Ding - Team #12 - 82%
6. Victoria Chase - Team #7 - 79%
7. Evan McGregor - Team #6 - 72%
8. Crypto Daniels - Team #18 - 71%
9. Gerard Kilsee - Team #20 - 68%
10. Sanna Sinervo - Team #16 - 65%
11. Marta Virgo - Team #14 - 64%
12. Borja Diez - Team #15 - 63%
13. Con LaFleur - Team #13 - 61%
14. Trent Golde - Team #11 - 60%
15. Dominic Walters - Team #3 - *Fail*
16. Xander Michaels - Team #9 - *Fail*
17. Zachary Lowe - Team #10 - *Fail*
18. Michael Welling - Team #8 - *Fail*
19. Christopher Gage - Team #5 - *Fail*
20. Harold Gunn - Team #19 - *Fail*

Sal couldn't believe there was such a small margin between the teams. The average scores were crippling a lot of the teams that had a strong captain and a weak team. He was delighted to see that Divinity had gone up a place, but sad for Lucia going down two. It made sense to him, though, considering Lucia was very much the strongest on her team, which likely didn't give them much opportunity to shine. Gerard dropping down the list was a beautiful thing to see, too.

Okay, you should have had ample time to see your new position on the board.

Every team that achieved over 80% is an example to the rest of you. As a reward, all that got over 80% as an average will be eligible to fast-track into the Intermediate Combat class from this point forward.

The top six you see on each board right now will be moving into the inter-cohort competition. We've rewarded the previous listings with Q-Cred prizes, but the competition will be for those who heeded our teachings and achieved cohesion and synergy on their team.

Now, I think it's time for us to show the new rankings!

Sal's stomach was tied in knots. Not only were his rewards terrible, but now he was potentially going to be fast-tracked into the next tier of Combat class? Outings sounded like the last thing he wanted to do in the first place, so having an exemption for those was somewhat useless. The only thing that kept his smile intact was the look on Gerard's face at hearing that he was out of the competition.

CHAPTER 84:
RANKINGS

As this day marks the end of your first month at the academy, I'd like to remind you all that the rankings will be determined by more than just the results of this competition. Your behavior, performance, and willingness to take that extra step…all of those factors were taken into consideration. Some of the students in this amphitheater helped save countless lives by using their abilities to prevent a horrific outcome.

We had a group of Controllers come together to stamp out bullying and anti-social behavior, making the campus safer for first-years than ever before. Community outreach programs were established by some of you, volunteering your time and abilities to helping those in need. We've had students spending sleepless nights working for the guilds to build their reputation and personal brand.

We even have a secret Healer who has been submitting anonymous diagnostic reports to faculty, which resulted in helping a lot of people who didn't even know they were sick.

I tell you all of this so you know that just attending your classes and doing the bare minimum required of you? It's not going to help you in the rankings, because we see everything. This shift in rankings will not affect your cohorts. From this point onward, it's very possible that one of the cohorts with the highest increase in rank will become substantially stronger than the others. But that's something that's not relevant just yet.

So, you can stop holding your breath!

Here are the new overall listings!

Sal's eyes shot upward and started to look for his name but was dismayed to find that it was starting in reverse order. He knew it was to build suspense for the finale, and the look on Quest's face confirmed that very suspicion. What was more troublesome was the fact that these were the new rankings. Every name that appeared, starting from one thousandth, was likely going to fail at the end of the semester and lose their place in the academy. If the estimates were to be believed, the first two hundred and fifty names out of the thousand that appeared, in reverse order, would be going home in a few months.

Blathnaid's knuckles were white as she gripped her knees tightly. Her eyes watched the screen as it flicked through a new name every second.

Sal leaned across Barry and placed a reassuring hand on hers. "You're going to be fine! We did great."

Her quick look to Sal had a half smile, but the lack of color in her cheeks told Sal that he wasn't going to convince her any time soon. Jack was playing it nonchalant while he reclined in his seat, but his eyes were also locked onto it.

The first familiar name that appeared on the screen made Sal's stomach lurch, because it suddenly became real. Kane was in the nine hundreds and had somehow lost places from his original rank. Sal hadn't seen him at all really since they had those coffees together in the first week, apart from that awkward encounter at Administration class. He knew that Kane had been injured, but with everything going on with Combat class and the workshop, Sal had completely forgotten about him.

Harold Gunn was the next familiar name to appear on the list, still in the nine hundreds and likely another decrease in rank. When it entered the eight hundreds, Sal realized that Melanie's name hadn't yet appeared. If he recalled correctly, her original rank was somewhere in the high nine hundreds. He and Divinity had managed to give her a list of instructions with Divinity's premonitions of who to pick for the battle, but he hadn't even thought to check her results. He couldn't believe that he had left a potential calamity to chance like this.

"You know, you could always just ask?" Divinity laughed from behind him, causing Sal to whirl around to see her seated beside Anthony, with her team to her left.

Sal smiled sheepishly as he scratched the back of his head. "Was I that obvious in my concern?"

Instead of answering, Divinity gestured to where Melanie sat. "While you were busy making toys for the team, I saved the world. Don't worry about it."

Sal exhaled in relief as he sank back into his chair. "This way of revealing the rankings is torturous. Are you sure you don't want to just tell us all where we end up?" Sal gave Divinity a pleading look, but she shook her head with a small smile.

"I wanted it to be a surprise, so I didn't bother looking today. Other than for Melanie, and that worked out rather well, so no need to fret."

With that, she gave Sal a wink, and he was left to wait with everyone else in a state of constant dread.

When the ranks counted down from seven hundred and fifty, a collective sigh of relief coursed through three-quarters of the amphitheater. It was insensitive to the bottom two hundred and fifty, but it was at least a sign that they weren't at risk of being expelled. Smiles started to appear on the mid-rank faces in the crowd, but all the top rankers were tense. There was likely going to be a hectic shuffle in the last few hundred, and everyone wanted to know where they stood.

As if to reinforce the relief of the rankings, cheers and celebration started to pop out from the stands as names were revealed. It looked like many of the teams had managed to elevate some of their lower ranks through the tournament. Sal watched for names that were familiar, but he hadn't networked all that much with the others in the class. It was a reminder of what Divinity had warned him against, of not getting to know his classmates.

Sal stopped looking at the new updates and scanned the lower ranks again to see whether there were any he missed. His eyes eventually landed on Joshua Mitchell, who was down at #846, but he wasn't really sure where he had started. Anderson Royce was another name that Sal spotted in the early seven hundreds, which was a small relief.

"Well done, Stephen!" Divinity's voice sounded out from behind him, and Sal looked around to see her congratulating one of the Supports on her team.

Jack and Blathnaid turned around with smiles, and Sal wondered whether being in the six hundreds was really something to celebrate at this stage. Going by Stephen's bright grin, it was worthy of celebration to him. This happened a few more times with Divinity's team, and that's when the first shock happened.

Sal almost missed it, but Barry was watching the names closely. "Dominic is down in the six hundreds!"

Everyone in their row looked at the board in shock at the sudden upset, with none more horrified than Dominic himself, who let out an aggravated roar of denial. It was drowned out by the sporadic cheers from everywhere in the audience, and there didn't look to be a single person who empathized with the Defender. For someone as promising and as strong as him, to drop from the top thirty…it had to be a crushing blow to his self-confidence. Some of the lower team captains from the Silver cohort started seeing their names, with Gerard Kilsee having found his way into the five hundreds.

"You can't be serious…" Jack said when he saw his name appear on the screen. He must have thought that his name had got lost among the others in the lower tiers, but it shone proudly at the top of the board, indicating that his new rank was #473.

Blathnaid screamed as she slapped his shoulder in excitement, and she whipped her head around to see whether her name came up close to it. But the names kept coming and hers was nowhere to be found. Anthony appeared next, with his new rank of #412. And judging by his gaping mouth, he hadn't been expecting such a dramatic shift up the ranks either. When Blathnaid's name did finally appear, it was beside the #391 rank, and Jack held her as she started to cry into her hands. The next surprise for Sal was Melanie's name, who popped up after Blathnaid, taking the #365 spot.

Barry shook his head as he looked over at Sal. "This is killing me. Should we just go and take a walk and then come back when it's done?"

Sal wanted to agree, but Divinity gave them both a playful slap at the back of their heads.

"Nope! You're staying until we're all accounted for…besides, you'll look smug if you leave before your name is called!"

Barry slumped into his seat and continued to shake his head as he watched the names. He sat in silence before a wry smile crossed his lips. "Looks like your girlfriend is doing well."

Sal grinned at the sight of Hannah's name on the screen. She had managed to snag the #272 spot for herself, which was a definite leap up the table for her. He couldn't wait to find out how she had done in the tournament and how much of an impact the gauntlets had made for her team.

"Is it bad that I only know the names of the team captains?" Sal laughed nervously, but Barry snorted.

"You're doing better than me. I barely remember Jacob's name."

He gestured over at Jack without looking at him. Blathnaid brought her hands away from her face long enough to slap Barry's shoulder with a laugh. "You're the worst."

Sal looked at the names and noticed that Barry's hadn't appeared yet, which was a great sign for his progress. It suddenly dawned on him that he had no idea about Barry's starting rank. "What was your rank when we started?"

Barry shrugged as he continued to look at the screen. "Somewhere in the low nine hundreds. I had a nap when I got to the dorms and didn't see the message about the race or the mixer. Trust me, I'm just as perplexed as you about all of this."

Sal burst out laughing and looked at Barry with tears growing in his eyes. "Are you serious—you had a nap?"

Barry waved his hands like it was no big deal. "I was tired." Eventually, Barry's face cracked into a smile as he shook his head. "Most expensive fucking nap of my life when you think about it. Looks like I'm being boosted up the ranks, though…so I guess I should thank Divinity for guilt-tripping me into using my powers?" With a turn, he gave Divinity a wide smile and in the most uncharacteristic moment of Sal knowing her, Divinity just raised her middle finger.

He laughed at Sal. "Couldn't resist."

In one of the most dramatic jumps, Whisper managed to break into the top two hundred. Her original spot as one of the lowest team captains had her down in the nine hundreds. Sal looked over to see her being hugged tightly by Lucia, and it looked like she was moments from being squeezed to death. It warmed his heart to see her being rewarded for her performance in the tournament, as she had definitely been one of the hardest opponents Sal faced.

With that thought in mind, his eyes wandered across the Silver cohort to see Jenni Stravos looking anxiously up at the scoreboard. Since she was the seventeenth captain, her starting rank was #969. For her name to not appear yet meant that she probably had one of the most dramatic jumps out of everyone in the amphitheater.

Sal was waiting to see the top one hundred ranks, as that would reflect the top ten original team captains of each cohort. Barry raised his hand into the air, and Sal saw the green runes activated on his arm. Before he could ask what he was doing, an explosion of fireworks appeared over the audience, catching everyone in a delighted surprise. Sal looked at him as though he were crazy, but the reasoning behind it was on the scoreboard above them.

Barry Francis - Overall Rank #98

"They're hardly going to knock me down a few places for celebrating!" Barry chuckled as he quickly deactivated his ability.

Sal clapped his knee and laughed. "Well done, man. You deserve it!"

Rather than his usual default of deflecting away from anything serious, Barry nodded. "Thanks, Captain." There was no hint of mockery in his tone.

Divinity, on the other hand, frowned at Barry. "You're happy with that? You should be higher. It only puts you at #9 in our cohort if you use the original rank system."

Barry turned around and was surprised to see that Divinity wasn't joking. He gave her a grin and shrugged. "It's only month one…plenty of time to get into the Savior roster!"

Sal tapped Barry on the knee to catch his attention. "Looks like things are heating up. Michael, Xander, and Zachary have dropped out of the top ten with Christopher. With Dominic gone too, that means there's likely going to be five new people in the top ten. Four, actually, since we know you're there."

Divinity sighed as she shook her head. "That's not how it works. You heard Quest…some cohorts might have more top-ranked people with this reshuffle."

Sal nodded as he kept his eyes locked on the scoreboard. He was obviously waiting on his own name to appear on the board, but he was curious about where Lucia would land on the list. Familiar names started to pop up, and Sal was surprised to see that many of the Silver captains had stayed relatively high.

Divinity's voice sounded out from behind Sal. "Oh, Victoria isn't going to like that. Looks like she dropped around twenty places?"

Barry pointed at Blathnaid as if to say that it was her fault for Victoria's demise, which only earned him another shove.

Divinity continued as she watched the names. "Evan dropped too…looks like they've had a similar shift. What was Lucia before the tournament?"

Sal glanced over his shoulder. "She was #39, so in fourth place in the cohort. Looks like she won't have too much of a drop, though."

Divinity sighed as she looked at the scoreboard. "If you think about it, for the Savior class and our cohort system, the top three out of each cohort are the ones eligible for a spot. Really puts it into perspective how competitive it's going to be."

The smiles on everyone's faces faded a bit at that, but Barry just shook his head.

"It's only the first month. We've got another five to get our scores up, and we're all in the inter-cohort competition! That's another chance to show off our skills! Just imagine what sort of equipment we could get with all this money and all that time…" Barry gave Sal a meaningful look before he returned his attention to the screen.

When Sal looked up to the scoreboard, he grimaced at the sight of Lucia's name. She had been pushed down to #46 in the rankings, and he doubted she'd be delighted with that. When he glanced over at her, he was surprised to see her smiling back at him with a thumbs-up gesture. Lucia pointed at Sal and then at the scoreboard before holding out a single finger. She wanted him to take the top spot, but he could only shake his head and flash both of his hands at her twice, as if she'd be able to understand that he'd be happy to stay in the top twenty.

"You look like a failed mime." Barry mocked Sal without moving his eyes from the board. "She has a point, though. There's no reason you couldn't take the top spot."

Sal shook his head as though he were being ridiculous. Without looking, Sal knew that Erika was likely still staring at him from the other side of the amphitheater. He had no ambitions to take the top spot and would happily yield it to her.

"There are people with far more capability than me who deserve the top spot," Sal said as he turned around and gestured at Divinity for reference.

Rather than being dismissive, she gave him a small smile and pointed back at the board, as if telling him that he should be paying attention.

"Jenni hit the top thirty?!" Barry suddenly blurted, causing Sal to look up in shock.

It was a lurching sensation in his stomach, which was a mixture of relief and anxiety. If they were in the top thirty now, it meant that he was still very much in contention for the Saviors class.

Divinity's hand squeezed his shoulder reassuringly. "Stop overthinking. They're just numbers."

The top thirty transformed the entire amphitheater. Nine hundred and seventy people already knew their ranking, and they now had something new to cheer for. Their own cohorts. Each person who was listed in the thirty was met with a huge cheer from their own cohort. It was a blend of camaraderie and belonging as each group tried to out-cheer their opponents. Unknown names appeared, and Sal only knew who they belonged to from the section of the crowd roaring their approval.

As each name ticked down, Sal's heart started to thunder. Despite how many times he told himself that he didn't care what rank he got, the atmosphere had created a surge of tension and anticipation…and Sal wondered whether he really was going to get a higher rank. Each name ticked down, and they hit the twentieth rank. The cheers were getting louder and louder, and when the nineteenth name was revealed and it wasn't Salvatore, Sal's chest tightened and his breathing elevated.

"Welcome to the party." Barry spoke quietly as he clapped Sal on the shoulder excitedly, now seeing that he was getting a higher rank.

Blathnaid, Anthony, and Jack were all staring at him and twisting their necks to look at the board, not wanting to miss his reaction. Divinity's hands started to clap on each of his shoulders as the names continued to fly onto the board. When they hit the top ten, Sal felt as though he couldn't breathe, and Divinity's hands tightened on his shoulders. Their names were nowhere to be seen as the countdown continued. Cheers and roars erupted around the amphitheater as cohorts started to scream their fan favorites for the top spot. When the names reached the fifth rank, the countdown slowed to what could only be described as a crawl.

Sal wanted to turn and face Divinity, but he was rooted to the spot. He needed to know where he was placed on the board. The fourth name was revealed to deafening applause, and Sal finally realized that the cohort causing the most noise was his own. All around him, the Silvers were screaming and on their feet. They knew that two of their very own captains had yet to be revealed! The next few seconds, time felt like it had slowed down, until the third name was revealed.

Salvatore Argento - Overall Rank #3

The weight of the world lifted from Sal's shoulders as he was finally able to breathe. A relieved laugh escaped his lips as everyone in the Silver cohort jumped up and down in celebration and started to chant his name. Never in Sal's wildest dreams did he anticipate a scene like this—a hundred people all singing and cheering his name. He finally found it in himself to turn to Divinity with a wide smile.

He had to shout over the noise, but he knew that she'd hear him. "Worst-case scenario! You've kept your spot!"

Just as she opened her mouth to respond, her eyes widened as she stared dumbly at the screen. The only roars in the crowd were from Silver, which made Sal think that Divinity had kept her rank…but he was in for a shock.

Erika Clifton - Overall Rank #2

None of the Gold cohort made any noise for her drop into second place, but even if they did, there was no way they were going to outdo the thunderous cheers from the Silvers. Everyone knew what was coming, and Barry already had his runes activated.

Sal turned back to Divinity and knew, in that moment, that she definitely hadn't looked into the future. It was the first time he had ever seen her truly shocked.

"Well done, Divinity!" he shouted, but it didn't hit home until she saw the proof on the board.

Divinity Khan - Overall Rank #1

CHAPTER 85:
RESPITE

IT TOOK A FEW MINUTES OF QUEST CALLING FOR EVERYONE'S ATTENTION BEFORE the cheers died down. Barry's fireworks were cut off the moment Quest's eyes locked onto him, and the Illusionist thrust his hands into his pockets to look as innocent as possible. The electric energy coursing through the audience finally dispersed, but there were a lot of smiles and excited chatters of which cohort was currently the strongest with the new rankings. Some were even remarking about how the Gold cohort seemed to treat Erika as some kind of pariah, as nobody interacted with her, not even the team she competed with. Quest's hands continued to rise and lower as he gestured for people to take their seats and quiet down.

Well, that certainly got very heated toward the end!

I'd like to offer congratulations to all of you who increased your ranking today.

As I've said before we revealed the results, our decisions were based on your continued performance across all classes in the last month. If you've found yourself dropping down the list, don't fret.

You'll have more chances to move up the roster, by working hard and embodying what it means to be a Hero. That is what we're striving toward, to make the world a better place and to finally end the war against the demonic threat that's plagued us for decades.

One year from now, many of you will be returning from your first offsite expedition. Our second-year students have been off campus for the last three weeks, integrated with specialist groups and learning firsthand how the real world operates on the other side of the barriers.

Don't forget why you're all here.

We're training you to be ready for the outside world. This tournament was designed to highlight your weaknesses and strengths. It was to show you how teams work, and how much stronger we can be when we work together. We wanted to show you how strong teams can crumble with weak leadership, and how capable individuals can carry the weak with them.

Many of the Silver cohort will have seen the power of great equipment. The Gold cohort saw the terrifying power of a perfect strategy. Purple saw the overwhelming destructive power that can be held by a single person. Orange witnessed how a single Healer on the battlefield can turn the odds drastically.

All of these are valuable lessons for you to learn from, and I would encourage all of you here to attend the inter-cohort competition that will take place in the coming months. We'll also be having a showcase from the third-years when they return from their guild work placement program.

All of you have worked incredibly hard in the lead-up to this event, and we'd like to reward your efforts.

Classes will be postponed tomorrow to ensure that you're all sufficiently recovered…from whatever you get up to tonight. We'll be having a mixer later in the afternoon for all of you to mingle with the guild scouts and some of our visiting professors. It's a good opportunity for you to learn from them and start planning your academic trajectory. Find the classes that blend with your ambitions and introduce yourself to people who can help you on your journey.

For our top-ranked people who are in the running for the Savior class, we'll be inviting you to a private gathering in the Sky Lounge.

On behalf of myself and the rest of the Quest Academy faculty, congratulations on a great tournament and enjoy yourselves!

The students gave another round of applause as they started to shuffle away from their teams to find their friends. It was pandemonium as everyone started moving all at once, and Sal could only sit there in disbelief. He turned around to see that Divinity's eyes were white. Sal couldn't help but think it was a bit late for her to be looking into the future, as they already had their rankings, but he didn't make any effort to get her attention. Both teams were talking to each other excitedly, comparing how shocked they were at the results but how well deserved everything was.

Blathnaid turned over to look at Sal with a smile. "How are you feeling? Is it sinking in yet? You're top three!"

Barry nodded in agreement as he leaned back in his seat so Sal could see Blathnaid better. "They better give you some Q-Cred for the new rank, though," was his only contribution to the conversation.

"Incoming." Divinity's voice held a sliver of amusement, but the tone was warning.

Sal glanced at her for a moment and saw that she was looking at the staircase to their right. When he looked around, he saw Erika a few steps away from them, her arms once again folded in front of her. She was tall for a girl, but that was where the similarity to Neuro ended. Piercing blue eyes and brown hair tied back in a ponytail were the only definable features other than the default gray uniform that nearly everyone wore.

When Sal was about to speak, she raised a hand to halt him. Her eyes were locked onto Divinity. "How did you do it?"

Rather than answering, Divinity just sighed, which didn't dissipate any of the growing tension. More than a few students in the area had stopped to watch the interaction, but there wasn't going to be a show.

Erika took another step forward and tilted her head ever so slightly to the right as she considered Divinity. "You placed fourth in the tournament, which should have resulted in you losing rank. Disregarding any composition bonuses for having the last pick, there was nothing in your performance that warranted an increase in rank. So I repeat, how did you do it?"

Barry nudged Sal in the ribs. "And I thought you had shit social skills." He laughed at his own joke.

Sal wanted to smile, but he couldn't help but feel a growing sense of unease.

Divinity gave Erika a calm look as she gestured to the stage. "You heard the headmaster. People who embodied the values of Heroes were rewarded. Me, Sal, and Barry here…all of us worked on preventing a calamity, which saved lives. We've been working with the Doom Society and your father. We also set up a training group for our teams, preparing them for the tournament. But, Erika, what did you do?"

Sal's eyes widened at the accusing tone in Divinity's voice. He had no idea what she saw in the future, but it wasn't like her to be this blunt with a person they had just met. Even Barry, who was always the one to take serious situations down the lighthearted route, kept his mouth shut.

Erika's arms unfolded as she glared at Divinity. "I was the perfect student. Top of my classes. Top of the cohort. Top of the tournament…unless we go by average score, where he only edged past me because of equipment." Erika gestured at Sal without so much as giving him a glance. Her entire focus was on Divinity. "You're not top of any of your classes, so you don't deserve the top rank."

Divinity got to her feet and took a step toward Erika, a smile fixed on her face. "If you have a problem with it, take it up with Quest."

Erika didn't back down. "Admit it. You don't deserve the top rank."

Divinity scoffed and gave Erika a withering look that bordered on pity. "The only way you're going to get that validation that you so desperately seek is if you use your ability to make me say it. I imagine that's how you get most things you want?" Divinity was not holding back in the slightest as she gestured over to the Gold cohort. "Didn't look like you had a lot of support. Is it because you use them like stepping stones toward your goals? I saw how you won that race on the first day, Erika. You've no right in telling anyone what they deserve."

Sal was sure that Erika was going to explode or attack Divinity, but contrary to everything he was seeing, she tilted her head again and studied Divinity with a calm expression.

"Your attempts to goad me into an argument won't work. I excelled in every assessment criteria we were given. You capitalized on an opportunity that came from your ability. It doesn't matter if it prevented a calamity; the question is academic merit. You are not the top rank in my eyes."

Divinity's eyes turned white, and she pointed at them. "Well, in my eyes…you don't become a Savior. How's that for goading?"

Erika's eyes narrowed. After a moment of silence, she uncrossed her arms and turned away from Divinity. All of them watched her ascend the steps out of the stands, none of them knowing how to react to that encounter.

Divinity gritted her teeth as she looked over her shoulder at the retreating form of Erika. "She really is a fucking piece of work."

***

When Sal ascended the stairs to the Sky Lounge, he wondered whether they should have taken the elevator. Divinity had told him that it was busy taking all the other students up to the floor, so they'd be faster using the stairs. It was also an opportune time for him to find out more about the slight altercation with Erika.

Barry and the others made them promise to ditch the Sky Lounge and come back for the party with the other students, and they readily agreed. They'd show their faces for a little bit, listen to whatever Quest and the others had to say, and then they'd rejoin the students.

Sal looked over to Divinity, trying to figure out whether she was tense, but her expression was unreadable.

She caught his glance and shot him a smile. "You want to talk about Erika, don't you?" Divinity sighed and waved her hand as though it were nothing. "Don't worry, she's not a big calamity or anything like that. Just a stubborn girl who's always gotten her way."

Sal continued up the steps, and his eyes fell on the vacant area that previously held the Skill Registration machines. It was hard to believe that it was a month ago because so much had happened in those few weeks.

With a wry smile, Sal nodded. "Still, I didn't think you'd talk back to her like that."

When Divinity cocked an eyebrow, Sal sensed he had entered dangerous territory and decided to make his stance very clear.

"Oh no, I'm not saying that you were in the wrong. I'm just not sure I've seen you push back. Usually, you'd kill them with kindness." The eyebrow lowered, and Sal knew he was safe again.

Divinity gestured up to the floors above at the top of the staircase. "She's up there right now, standing with her back to a wall and watching everyone. She doesn't respect a single person in our year and has a crippling superiority complex. The only way she's going to break out of that shell is when she finally acknowledges her peers and the value they bring. Like, if she controlled your mind and made you create a piece of equipment…would it be as good as the piece you poured your heart and soul into?"

The question was rhetorical, but he shook his head anyway as Divinity continued.

"No! She doesn't understand people at all! And the rest of this semester is going to be absolute hell with her and every other asshole up here gunning for us."

Sal exhaled loudly as he followed Divinity's gaze to the top floor. "But at least she doesn't become a Savior! You said it yourself."

Divinity snorted and shook her head. "I was just trying to get under her skin. She's pretty much guaranteed a spot on the Saviors, but I'm not going to tell her that or make it easy on her."

Sal laughed, which eventually cracked a smile on Divinity's lips.

As if to explain her reasoning, she added, "I wanted to see a sliver of uncertainty on her face, so I'll settle for the minor glare it got me."

With another glance upward, Sal wondered whether they could streamline the process. "Any chance you could give me the highlights of what's to come?"

Divinity shrugged as she raised a hand. "Yeah, mostly boring stuff, to be honest. We get a few glares from the top-ranked students, a few jabs at you relying on equipment and me relying on the visions." She started counting through the different events on her hand.

"There's a long talk from Quest about responsibility, and how we need to lead our teams and cohorts to success in the future. Oh, and Neuro apologizes to me about Erika, and jokes that she takes after her mother. We stand around chatting to students for a while, and Alastair saves you and Scry saves me. Overall, it's pretty lackluster."

Sal slowed his pace as he looked up again. "Should we just bail on it and head back to the others?"

With a laugh, Divinity shook her head as she continued walking. "I only told you about the boring parts. You won't want to miss the good stuff!"

Sal's grin reappeared as he took the steps two at a time to catch up with Divinity, who laughed and increased her own pace as she called for him to slow down.

"Hey, hey! They're not going anywhere!"

Sal continued on, enjoying the panicked laughter of Divinity behind him as she tried to match his pace. He could hear people talking and light music being played in the background. With another set of stairs to go, he considered slowing down, but could see that Divinity was actively racing him.

It wasn't much of a competition, and Divinity was gloating a few seconds later as she stood at the entrance to the Sky Lounge with her arms raised over her head. Sal joined her a moment later and was surprised to see a smattering of applause welcoming them. Alastair, Harlan, Dawn, Liam, Scry...all the members of the Doom Council were talking to indistinguishable gray uniforms, but looked up at Divinity's arrival and started to clap.

Her gloating quickly turned to mortification, and Sal knew for a fact that she hadn't foreseen that particular moment.

"Ah, Divinity! There's the woman of the hour! Congratulations on your first place!" Quest beamed as he moved to shake her hand. His smile was warm and genuine as he turned and placed his palm on her back. When he disengaged his hand from her surprised grip, he pointed to an area across the bar, where a series of tables were stacked with equipment. "We can start now that you're here!"

As Sal reached the top of the steps, his eyes went into overdrive at the sight of so much equipment and weaponry.

Quest caught his surprise and grinned. "Our staff brought back a lot of loot from a recent dungeon clearance, and we thought it best to reward our top students by letting them pick out an item of their choosing."

There was a sparkle in his eye, and Sal realized that their prize was from the dungeon that the strike teams had cleared.

Quest raised a single finger. "One item per student, and we'll be giving the first pick to Divinity, second to Erika...and so on."

Some of the students were eyeing certain pieces of equipment, despite not having a clue about them. Sal smiled at seeing a group of guys standing around a black breastplate protectively, as though trying to guard it from Divinity's sight.

Divinity looked over at Quest. "Can I consult with Sal before picking?"

The headmaster grinned and gestured to where Sal stood. "By all means! But I want to steal him away for a moment."

Divinity's smile grew wider, and Sal guessed that she knew what was coming next.

Quest moved over to Sal and pointed across the room to where an elderly man was watching him. "I'd like to introduce you to someone, Salvatore. You'll be meeting them regularly in the next few weeks when they start teaching the Analysis module."

Sal nodded as he approached the elderly man and extended his hand. "Salvatore Argento. It's a pleasure to meet you, sir."

With a wry grin, the Analysis professor shook Sal's hand. "You can call me Beck. I couldn't help but admire that incredible weave. Quest tells me that you Crafted it yourself? Mythcrafter?"

Sal faltered and realized that Beck was looking at his chest, rather than at his eyes. Sal suddenly remembered that Divinity mentioned something about the Analysis lecturer having an incredible ability. Before he activated his eyes for a look, he was thrown by Beck's next comment.

"Could you replicate my ability, Mr. Argento?"

CHAPTER 86:
ANALYSIS

SAL BLINKED IN SURPRISE AS HE HEARD THE QUESTION. WITH A TENTATIVE LOOK at Quest, Sal got a nod of approval from him. "Apologies, Mr. Beck. I usually need to understand the ability before I can replicate it, otherwise it might harm my body…I've already gotten an earful from my mother about creating the Mythcrafter one."

Sal wanted more context from him and an explanation, but Beck shook his head with a smile. "Trust me. My ability doesn't need explaining, and it won't hurt you in the slightest. Give it a try and tell me what you see!"

At the urging of both Beck and Quest, Sal activated his eyes and saw an incredibly intricate weave within the lecturer. It was coiled around his eyes, which made Sal even more curious about it. Although it didn't look incredibly powerful from first glance, the threads were quite thin, with many tight knots. Sal had to take his time in reconstructing the weave, and he triple-checked it for fear of screwing it up under their watchful gaze.

Beck, on the other hand, grinned from ear to ear. "Truly remarkable! I can see it changing!"

Sal's eyes snapped up in surprise. *Beck was able to see what he was doing with his threads?* Curiosity got the better of him, and he decided to trust in the weave he constructed. With a surge of internal essence, Sal activated the unknown ability and saw a blinding light appear in front of his eyes. He clenched his eyelids shut for a moment, waiting for them to adjust when he heard Beck's voice again.

"He even managed to get a higher proficiency than me! I can't believe it!"

Sal wanted to ask what Beck was talking about, and when he opened his eyes to look at the lecturer, he was rendered speechless. A screen of information, more detailed than any Appraisal he'd ever conducted, appeared in front of him. There was so much data being thrown at him that it was impossible for him to keep up with it.

"What is…this power?"

Beck grinned as he looked over to Quest delightedly. "You've just replicated my Analysis ability. It's similar to Appraisal, but rather than seeing everything about items, now, you can see everything about people! I can make this a little easier for you…" Beck pulled out his Q-Card and held it in front of Sal.

It was too far for Sal to make out the words, but the new ability locked onto the essence signature on the card. The data was still too much to comprehend, though, and Sal couldn't make sense of all the words and numbers.

Quest pulled an object from his pocket and stood behind Sal for a moment.

Sal barely noticed as he tried to keep up with the waves of information being thrown at him from every direction. Suddenly, a tracker was placed over Sal's right eye and the information began to condense and sort itself into understandable chunks.

"It's not a perfect solution, but this device has a part of my skill essence in it. I normally use it when I've overworked my ability, so maybe it'll help you adjust to Beck's power."

Sal was rooted to the spot as he stared at Beck in wonder. He couldn't believe that this was actually a real skill.

Name	Beck Syme
Alias	Specs
Profession	Quest Academy Lecturer: Analysis
Class	Support
Rank (Hero)	Guild Association: 2,139th
Ability	Analysis (Rating: Advanced) (Category: Psionics)
Essence	**Essence Control** - 100% **Essence Refinement** - 53% **Essence Calibration** - 97%
Reputation	**Quest Academy**: Esteemed **Guild Association**: Esteemed **Hunter Bureau**: Well-Regarded
Threat Level	[*Unknown*]
Wealth	Confidential
System Notes	Confidential

Quest laughed at the stupefied expression on Sal's face as he pointed at the tracker. "It's not great quality, but it suits my day-to-day administrative needs. I'm sure you'd be able to harness much more of Beck's ability with an upgraded device."

Beck cleared his throat and waved his hand with a smile. "Excuse me, we're not here to teach shortcuts! He can learn how to control it in my class, without the constraints or context of your System ability! Isn't that right, Salvatore?"

Quest laughed and patted Sal on the shoulder. "You can keep that tracker for a while and test it out."

Beck pretended to grumble, but the wide smile was still on his face while he looked at Sal. "What are you seeing right now?"

Sal read out all the information that was being presented to him, which seemed to disappoint Beck in some way.

With a shake of his head, he turned back to Quest and pointed at the tracker. "That's holding him back…he should be able to see a full rundown of my capabilities. Analysis can work on physical and emotional behaviors. You're not receiving any information on my combat prowess? It's not analyzing my speech or movement at all?"

When Sal shook his head and confirmed that he couldn't see anything, Beck reached for the tracker on his head, but Quest intercepted him. "He's only had it on for two minutes, and we're already holding him back from our other guests. We can have a sit-down with Salvatore later in the week and see if he'd like to learn how to use the ability. Sound good?"

Beck chuckled as he brought his hand away from the tracker. "Fine…we can wait until later." With a wink in Sal's direction, the lecturer raised a single finger in front of him. "Just promise you'll give it a fair chance, okay? It's intimidating at first, but once you learn how to use it…you'll be unstoppable!"

Sal managed to stammer out a few words of thanks as his mind reeled with the constant barrage of stat boxes. With a gesture from Quest that he could rejoin Divinity, Sal did just that. He tried to close his left eye to only see the information coming in through the tracker, but it was really disorienting.

Divinity gave him an odd look as she saw the tracker clipped on one side of his face, but she didn't say anything about it. Instead, she pointed at the table. "I think that headpiece is probably the best fit for me. While you were talking to the headmaster, I decided to have a peek into the future to see what would be the best choice."

Sal nodded as he turned to look at the arsenal of weaponry and equipment laid out on the table. He didn't want to keep everyone waiting on them, so he activated his Appraisal ability out of reflex. When the Mythcrafter ability activated alongside Analysis, Sal was dumbfounded to see a completely different type of Appraisal window pop up. The black crown was adorned with jagged spikes, some of which had been snapped off at some point. It looked like more of a tiara that had been charred to pieces after being stripped of anything valuable.

Sal stared at it as prompt after prompt appeared in front of his eye. Unlike the blueprints in Mythcrafter that allowed him to see how things could be evolved and improved, the Analysis ability was breaking down each component and adding more context of why they were important. Attributes and traits were possible to generate based on the materials and crafting method.

Name	Shattered Crown
Origin	Portal Artifact
Age	[*Unknown*]
Current Grade	Rare (Lower)
Restored Grade	Epic (Upper)
Potential Grade	Legendary (Upper)
Dimensions	4 inches tall | 22.5 inches circumference
Materials	**Shattered Lord Crystal**: Certain chance to create Psionic and Influence type abilities. (Restoration Possible) **Hellfire Titanium**: Premium material. Increases Quality and Grade of equipment. (Reforge Possible) **Remnant Essence**: Slight increase in Essence Control for Psionic and Influence type users. (Reforge Impossible)

Runes	**Broken Amplification Rune**: Slight increase in Essence Control. **Broken Self-Replenishment Rune**: Slight increase in Essence Absorption.
Attributes	**Control**: When wearing the crown, the user will have a higher base proficiency with their essence ability. **Untouchable**: Attempts by others to remove the crown will cause Repel to activate.
Abilities	Siphon | Vital Thrust | Jagged | Cleave
Power Source	External Essence
Absorption Rate	35% Passive | 65% Active
Evolution	No
Quality	Terrible: Missing key components for functionality.
Condition	13%: Missing key components for functionality.
Value	Est. $68,000.00 – $92,000.00

"Are you okay? You look like you've seen a demon!" Divinity's voice could be heard at his shoulder, which caused Sal to jump. The prompts disappeared as he lost hold of the Analysis ability for a moment. When he turned to her, he saw a gentle smile on her face.

Name	Divinity Khan
Alias	[*Unknown*]
Profession	Student
Class	Controller
Rank (Student)	First-Years - 1st
Ability	Divination (Rating: Intermediate) (Category: Psionics)
Essence	**Essence Control** - 12% **Essence Refinement** - 42% **Essence Calibration** - 82%
Reputation	**Quest Academy**: Known **Guild Association**: Known **Hunter Bureau**: Known
Threat Level	[*Unknown*]
Wealth	Confidential
System Notes	Confidential

Before Sal could lift the tracker from his eyes, the ability snapped back into place and showed him all of Divinity's stats. It finally gave him context in comparison to Beck's profile, and he was curious about how they were calculated. He wanted more time to think about everything, but the sounds of grumbling students caught his attention.

With another glance at the black tiara, Sal nodded. "It's an amplification tool for Psionic ability types. It's perfect for either yourself or…" Sal paused as he looked at Divinity. "Are you just taking this so Erika can't have it?"

Divinity burst out laughing and waved her hand in front of her like he was being ridiculous. "Of course not. That would be incredibly petty of me. Wouldn't it?" Her smile told a different story, and Sal shrugged as he looked at the other options while talking to her.

"It's Rare grade at the moment and will need a bit of work, but I think it'll suit you."

Divinity didn't need anything more than that, and carefully picked up the black crown.

"Erika, whenever you're ready!" Quest called out from one side of the room.

The #2 Rank turned around from her conversation and moved over to the table to where the crown had been. She stared at the empty space in confusion before looking back to where Divinity was standing with the crown. Erika looked absolutely lost. It was a strange thing to see the most confident person in the entire year looking so uncertain.

Sal decided to put her out of her misery and moved up beside her.

Erika took a step back and looked at Sal warily, but he raised his hand to point at the different pieces of equipment.

"There are four pieces of equipment that have minor buffs for Psionic users. That bracelet over there, the necklace beside the breastplate, and the two rings over there and there." Sal looked back to Erika's shocked face and smiled. "If you want something even better than that black crown, go to the workshop and ask for Myth. He's able to Craft Epic and Legendary equipment for the right price."

Erika didn't so much as blink. When he was done talking to her, she nodded and moved away from him, picking up the necklace on her way.

Divinity joined Sal with a frown. "But you'll make my crown better than whatever hers is, right?"

Sal winked. "Of course…as long as you're prepared to pay full price."

Quest looked at Sal and gestured for him to take the next piece from the tables. After so many Appraisals for the Reavers Guild, Sal was underwhelmed with what he saw in front of him. Rare seemed to be the top quality on the table and none of the designs interested him in the slightest. Maybe it was arrogance, but Sal knew he could make better objects than anything on the table. It was such a bizarre confidence, and Sal smiled at how far he had come in such a short space of time.

After a few moments of glancing through each piece of equipment, his eyes landed on a large chunk of rock that he recognized immediately. It was a large shard of the dungeon heart that had been destroyed. His Analysis ability was going haywire, and the tracker couldn't tell him anything about it. Sal remembered how Joshua described his tracker going crazy when they saw the Epic-grade gloves on Sal's hands.

Sal looked at the rock carefully, but the Mythcrafter ability needed some kind of blueprint or basis to activate. *Did it mean that the dungeon heart was of a higher level than the equipment could handle?* Sal didn't hesitate. Even if it turned out to be a dud, he needed to investigate it back in the workshop.

"I'd like to select this one!" Sal pointed at the large shard with a grin.

Quest nodded and called for the fourth person to choose their prize.

As the procession continued, and students picked items from the tables, Quest explained to all of them the importance of guiding their teams and representing their cohorts. It went on for a while before the students, now excited with their new gear, started to actively chat to one another. Sal's head couldn't take it anymore with the Analysis ability, so he purposefully shut it off and removed the tracker.

Some of the students started to joke about Sal's equipment being the primary reason for his success and then proceeded to pepper him with questions about commissioning from the workshop. Divinity was met with multiple requests for glimpsing into the future. Some wanted to know who they'd be dating later in the semester; others asked what the best guild would be to join. It was all straightforward conversation, but not enough to hold their attention. Alastair and Scry came over to whisk them away, and Sal realized that the evening was now playing out all the boring moments of Divinity's vision.

"Is it time to go back to the others?" Sal asked as he touched her shoulder.

Scry grinned from across Divinity as he gestured at Sal. "There's hope for him yet." Sal wasn't sure what he was talking about but Scry continued as he turned to Sal. "She's been waiting here for a while, wondering when you'd come to save her."

Divinity laughed as she waved Scry off. "Don't listen to him. We were chatting about calamities and all that fun stuff. I'm ready to go!"

***

Barry cleared his throat as he raised his glass up high. "I propose a toast!"

Judging from his swaying hands and merry smile, Sal would have guessed that he had made quite a few toasts in the last few hours. Blathnaid snorted and shook her head but raised her glass into the air. Jack followed suit, with Anthony just raising a hand. Sal offered to get him a drink, but Anthony politely declined, simply saying he didn't like the taste.

Barry stared daggers at Divinity's team that stood to one side. "I said…I propose a toast."

Catching the hint, or just hoping to humor Barry, they all raised their drinks.

"To the best two captains all of us bottom-rankers could have asked for! None of us are in the relegation zones…none of us are at risk of getting chucked out at the end of the semester…we have good equipment, and we work great together. All of that is down to these two desperate people!" Barry grinned as he pointed his glass at Sal and Divinity, who both felt more sober than ever before.

"Who would have known?" Barry continued. "That we would make it this far? Other than Divinity, I mean. She knows everything. She's so great, isn't she?" He smiled dreamily as he raised his glass again to celebrate.

Sal bit his lip as he watched the travesty unfold. "Think he'll remember this when he sobers up?"

Divinity grinned as she stared at him. "If he doesn't, I'll keep reminding him."

Sal turned to place his empty glass on a table when a pair of hands were placed over his eyes.

"Guess who!"

With a warm smile and a pause, Sal pretended to think. "Erika?"

Before Hannah could hit him, he turned around and brought her in for a hug. She wasn't content with just that, and he found himself getting kissed in front of all the other cohorts. "Well done on your performance! You really moved up the ranks!" Sal congratulated her, and Hannah wiggled her gauntleted fingers.

"All thanks to my Crafting savior!"

With a hand on Hannah's back, he turned around to introduce her to his friends. That was when it suddenly struck Sal. He was surrounded by people he considered friends. Just four weeks ago, he was a nervous wreck coming in on the train with his parents, and now he was introducing the girl he was kinda seeing to his group of friends. He had studied, trained, Crafted, and even helped thwart a demonic threat. None of those things seemed remotely real and possible of the old Salvatore Argento. As he watched Hannah and Divinity laugh at Barry's next speech, he smiled. He was only at the start of his journey. There were so many things he didn't know, but one thing was for certain in Sal's mind.

He knew he belonged at Quest Academy.

SALVATORE'S CHARACTER SHEET

Name	Salvatore Argento
Alias	Myth
Profession	Student
Starting Role	Support
Rank (Student)	First-Years - 3rd Silver Cohort - 2nd
Ability	**Skill Master** (Rating: Advanced) (Category: Replication) **Mythcrafter** (Rating: Master) (Category: Invention)
Essence	**Essence Control** - 79% **Essence Refinement** - 22% **Essence Calibration** - 26%
Academic Reports	Core Modules: (M = Mandatory) • (M) Skills: Pacing Well • (M) Survival: No Grade • (M) Combat: Exemplary • (M) Crafting: Exemplary Elective Modules: • Analysis: No Grade • Administration: Exemplary
Reputation	**Quest Academy**: Well-Known **Doom Society**: Approved **Guild Association**: Known **Hunter Bureau**: [*Unknown*]
Affiliations	**Argento Auction** (Sponsorship: Tier 3) **Reavers Guild** (Sponsorship: Tier 2) **Quest Academy**: Credit Floor (Sponsorship: Tier 3)
Scout Status	**Reavers Guild**: Interested **Delvers Guild**: Interested
Accreditations	**Jez's Challenge Crest**: "Work Horse" **Quest's Challenge Crest**: "Semester 1 Tournament Champion"
Threat Level	[*Unknown*]
Wealth	5,825 Q-Credit
System Notes	Savior Class: On Track

AUTHORS NOTE:

First of all, I want to thank you for giving Quest Academy: Silvers a chance. I really hope you've enjoyed it and that you'll stick around for Quest Academy: Scavengers. There are so many people that were instrumental in getting Quest Academy to where it is right now, and I just wanted to highlight a few of them.

Jez, Chrissy and Geneva over at Legion Publishers have managed to turn my story into something that I'm truly proud of. Michelle taught me that my first drafts are not in fact, clean. I've thrown in some likenesses to author friends in the genre, all with their permission, as my own way of saying thanks for all the guidance and support they've given me on my journey so far. From Chatfield, Head, Jez, Kev, Lars... to Erika, who harassed me for chapters on a daily basis.

In my own personal life, my family has supported me throughout it all and they've never seen me as happy. I would have likely given up a long time ago without their encouragement, so it's been wonderful to have them cheering me on from the side-lines. My circle of friends, who have famously told me that they'd read it when it's done... well, here it is! The first of many books!

In all seriousness, a huge thank you to my friends that have pushed me to follow my dreams. It's been one hell of a ride so far, and I'm genuinely so excited to find out where it takes me. Growing up in a small town in Ireland, I never thought I'd get to write an author's note for a published book, but here we are.

Thank you for being on this journey with me.

Brian

REVIEWS!

So, how did I do? Did you enjoy reading Quest Academy? If so, it would be a massive help to me if you left a review for the story. With millions of books being published on Amazon, it's very hard to get any sort of traction and discoverability. If you share the book with people that you think might enjoy it, that would be incredible. I'd love for as many people as possible to have the chance to read the story, and for that, I need your help.

If the story does well enough, I'll be able to spend more time writing, which will cut down the time between releases...and fuel my coffee addiction.

If leaving reviews isn't something you can do, then I'd really appreciate you helping to share the story to people that might enjoy it. No matter what though, you've read my story and that's the most important thing to me.

Thank you!

FACEBOOK AND SOCIAL MEDIA

If you want to reach out to talk about Quest Academy or just get to know me a little bit, you can find me on my swanky new author page on Facebook. There's a very high chance that you'll be one of the very first people to like it that wasn't involved in getting me published:

www.facebook.com/BrianJNordon

Alternatively, we've a new Facebook group to spread the word about cool LitRPG books, called LitRPG Legion. It's a fun space to share old and new books, and to discover great titles you might have missed along the way.

Only rules for joining are to spread the word about great new books, and not being a dick! As a bonus, if you join…you'll have access to dozens of author interviews conducted by me or Jez.

www.facebook.com/groups/litrpglegion

If you'd prefer to catch me over on Discord, here's a link:

https://discord.gg/GAN5RgNJGn

I created the Discord for my first ever series that I started over on Royal Road, called Wildcards: The Dread Captain. It's a fun story that I absolutely loved writing and will get back to after Quest Academy is established. I'm not the fastest at replying, but I do always reply!

PATREON!

Okay then, now for those of you that don't know about Patreon, its essentially a way to support your favorite authors, you can sign up for a day or a month or a year, and you get various benefits for it, ranging from my heartfelt thanks, to advance access to the books, to me sending them books, naming characters and more.

My Patreon was very focused on my time writing Wildcards, and I'll be incorporating new tiers in the future for advanced chapters of Quest Academy. I'm talking with Legion Publishers to find out what we could offer fans outside of more chapters, so it might be worth keeping an eye on. If not now, maybe in the future when there's more on offer!

All support is appreciated, but not compulsory. Honestly, a review or just recommending my story to others is more than I have any right to ask.

www.patreon.com/BrianJNordon

WANDERING WARRIOR

By Michael Head

A divine quest to deliver justice. One year to accomplish his mission. After nineteen planets, there's something different about this one.

James Holden has reached the maximum level there is for a human. That's perfect, since he's the only one of his kind. A wandering warrior, without control of his destination, tossed between universes by gods who've failed to tell him why. James is the lone Judge on a new world in need of someone to balance the scales. He isn't afraid to do so with extreme prejudice. As the Chief Justice, he has to right the wrongs the innocent can't fix themselves.

As James quickly discovers, the roots of corruption run deep. Guilds choose to protect themselves rather than the people. Monsters roam the wilderness unchecked. Judgment is usually a decision between right and wrong, but nothing is ever that simple. This time, being the strongest human won't be enough to punish the guilty. James might have to recruit some new blood, even if he prefers to work alone.

On his twentieth world, he is going to win, no matter the cost. James will have to find a way to break past the limits of the system if he's going to have a chance at making a difference.

Buy on Amazon!

ARISE ALPHA

By Jez Cajiao

Stolen money. Greek Islands. Werewolves and Enforcers...
What could possibly go wrong?

When you steal a hundred grand from some very bad people, the best way to survive is to stay small and quiet...

Possibly its not to save a pair of drowning girls, not go 'viral' on social media and certainly not to let the local police take your passport, trapping you on a small 'party' island in the middle of the Mediterranean Sea.

But Steve isn't the average guy, he's ex-military, ex-enforcer and ex-human. He's a one man nanite fueled nightmare for those that cross the line, and he's decided that its time to clean up his act. He's going to make up for the things he's done, and save 'the little guys'.

It's a nice fantasy, but even he has to admit, it's really just a justification, because he's a very bad man, with horrifying abilities, and he's only just learning what he's capable of. He needs a reason to not go to the dark, and if that's hunting down the creatures of the night and beating them to death with their own femurs?

Well, he's just the man for the job.

Buy on Amazon!

RECOMMENDATIONS

I'm not sure if they'll be your thing, but if you like reading my stories, then you might be interested in these books too. This is only from my own personal enjoyment though, so take my words with a pinch of salt.

Artem: The Rise of Oshbob by Kevin Sinclair

Artem: Underdog by Lars Machmuller

RE: Trailer Trash by FortySixtyFour

Castle Kingside by Gennon Asche (Royal Road)

Dressed to Kill: A Seamstress LitRPG by Crownfall (Royal Road)

Cowboy Necromancer: Infinite Dusk by Harmon Cooper

Builders Legacy: Connection Unknown by Michael Chatfield

Wandering Warrior by Michael Head

First Fist: Seventh Bridge to the Heavens by TJ Reynolds

The Good Guys/Bad Guys by Eric Ugland

LITRPG!

To learn more about LitRPG, talk to other authors including myself, and to just have an awesome time, please join the LitRPG Group

www.facebook.com/groups/LitRPGGroup

FACEBOOK

There's also a few really active Facebook groups I'd recommend you join, as you'll get to hear about great new books, new releases and interact with all your (new) favorite authors! (I may also be there, skulking at the back and enjoying the memes…)

www.facebook.com/groups/LitRPGsociety/

www.facebook.com/groups/LitRPG.books/

www.facebook.com/groups/LitRPGforum/

www.facebook.com/groups/gamelitsociety/

www.facebook.com/groups/litrpglegion